THE HUNTERS OF SHADOWS

A Portal Fantasy (The Chosen, Books 1-4)

AMY PROEBSTEL
BETHANY HALL

Cavaliers Publishing

ISBN-13: 978-1-946292-64-3

ISBN-10: 1-946292-54-8

Printed in the United States of America

Cover art by Wynter Designs

First Printing, 2018

Second Printing, 2018

Third Printing, 2022

Website: https://geni.us/LOA-Home

BookBub: https://geni.us/BBFollow

Goodreads: www.goodreads.com/aproebstel

Facebook: https://geni.us/FB-LOA

Twitter: https://geni.us/Amy-T

Instagram: www.instagram.com/amyproebstel

BOOKS IN THIS SERIES

Chosen Origins Trilogy
Book One: The Keeper of Secrets
Book Two: The Secrets of Magic
Book Three: The Magic of Time

The Chosen Series
Book One: The Time of Shadows
Book Two: The Shadows of Destiny
Book Three: The Destiny of Hunters
Book Four: The Hunters of Souls
Book Five: The Souls of Children
Book Six: The Children of Fire
Book Seven: The Fire of War
Book Eight: The War of Realms
Book Nine: The Realms of Rising
Book Ten: The Rising of Dragons

DEDICATION

This book is dedicated to my friends and family. You all have been so supportive in helping me carve out time in our busy lives to write and encouraging me to keep going. I've been so inspired by all of your thoughtfulness and I hope it shows in my writing.
To the readers of this series, I greatly appreciate all of your kind words, amazing reviews, and support along the way. None of this would be possible without your enthusiasm for the world of Tuala.

THE TIME OF SHADOWS
BOOK ONE OF THE CHOSEN

CHAPTER 1

Amanda stared in disbelief at the daughter she had not seen for almost two years. How her mother came to have her was something she was definitely going to find out as soon as possible. She could restrain herself no longer as she leaped forward, hugging her mother with some restraint since Jena remained sandwiched between them. She pulled back and spoke softly to the blonde-haired, blue-eyed, little girl clinging to her own mother's side. "You probably don't remember me, Jena, but I'm your mother."

Diane recovered sufficiently to yell over her shoulder, "Chris, come quick! You won't believe who's at the front door!"

Shuffling noises sounded from the adjacent room followed by footsteps hurrying forward. He rounded the partition wall, spotted his youngest daughter, and ran the rest of the way. "Amanda? Is it really you?" Chris stepped onto the porch to embrace Amanda tightly in his arms to know he was not dreaming. His daughter had been gone for so long, he and Diane determined she had planned on remaining in Tuala. He released her from his hug to hold her at arm's length to see for himself that she was truly alright.

Amanda grinned at her father's exuberance and answered, "It's really me, Dad. I came home when I found out Shemalla had found a safe home for Jena on Earth. We stopped first in Roswell, but couldn't find her, so we came here hoping you would know something. Imagine my surprise when Mom answered the door holding Jena!"

"I told you she was our granddaughter, Chris!" Diane had a smug expression on her face as she gently hugged Jena closer to her side. "Come inside, come inside!" She ushered everyone into the house to swiftly shut the front door. The last thing they needed was for the neighbors to witness the strange reunion.

They all filed into the living room where everyone could be seen in the light. Amanda took the lead by starting introductions, gesturing to each individual in turn. "This is my friend and boss, Riccan, and he is holding Juila. Riccan, this is my father, Chris, my mother, Diane, and she is holding Jena."

Chris moved to the side of the couch to reveal a dark-haired boy who was around the age of five, to make one more introduction, "And this is Willian who is supposedly Jena's brother. Can anyone explain to us how that's possible?"

Amanda nodded toward the young boy in acknowledgement even as her brain tried to come up with a plausible explanation for her parents. She definitely did not want to tell her parents how the little boy they had been fostering was actually betrothed to Jena. They did not understand Tualan culture, and she knew unequivocally they would not approve of an arranged marriage at so young an age. She swallowed and replied with only a partial truth. "Elder Debbon and his wife, Chelesa, adopted Jena into their family when she was six months old. They already had Willian, so they became brother and sister."

Chris nodded slowly and Diane smiled at Amanda's simple explanation. Chris stepped forward and held out his hand to his daughter's new friend. "Riccan, I'm pleased to meet you. I assume you are responsible for making sure Amanda arrived here safely?"

"I did have the honor, sir. It's nice to meet both of you as well; your daughter has often spoken fondly of you."

Diane looked admiringly at the handsome, dark-haired, dark-eyed, man standing in her living room who held the identical twin to the little girl she carried. "I think we should put Jena and Juila down on the floor together to play and get reacquainted. They've been apart for so long I doubt they remember one another."

Amanda was pleased her mother wanted them to play together;

however, she had to say, "Actually, Mom, I believe they've probably talked just about every day through their twin connection. They really know one another quite well."

Chris raised his eyebrows in surprise at Amanda's statement even as he gestured for everyone to take a seat. The twins sat facing each other on the floor, clearly communicating, yet not with anything spoken aloud.

Amanda could just imagine the stories they were sharing with one another using their unique mental way since it was the only method they remembered ever doing with each other.

Diane played the hostess and asked, "Can I get anyone anything to eat or drink?"

"We're fine, Mom. Sit down and let me tell you both what's been going on."

Diane was pleased to know she would not miss a single thing which was going to be shared. She would have gratefully prepared food and drinks for everyone; however, she desperately wanted to know what had happened to keep Amanda away for so long. Just the idea of Jena being adopted into another family certainly raised quite a few questions in her mind.

"Let me start from the beginning. Shemalla took me to the Gate in Campeche, and it worked perfectly. I was really glad I had everybody's notes with me to help me remember why I was there in the first place since I lost my memory again in the transfer. Oh! That reminded me of something!"

She turned to Riccan and added, "When I was resting after my transfer into Tuala I had the weirdest dream about a swarm of beetlesnatch attacking me before you came to my rescue, Riccan."

Riccan wore the oddest expression on his face as he stammered to reply, "Amanda, you won't believe this, but I had the exact same dream! I knew I'd seen you before you came to the job interview, I just didn't remember about it until just now as you described it."

"How strange. Another coincidence we'll have to think about later." She reluctantly turned away from Riccan to continue her story. "Anyway, I made it to Bryon and Alena's house before it got dark that night and they were just as shocked to see me on their doorstep as you were tonight." She smiled at her recollection of her host family in Tuala.

"I found out immediately Jena had been kidnapped just a couple of days before I returned and they were in the process of trying to locate her. The three of us took turns attempting to use the link with Jena's birth crystal until one day Jena had her adoption ceremony with Debbon and Chelesa which dissolved our connection with her. We spent almost the next two years following up on leads for locating Petre MacVeen, who was the person responsible for abducting her, and all of the wise-women who could possibly perform the ritual. Am I going too fast?"

She took a deep breath and looked from her mother to her father. They shook their heads, and her mother gestured impatiently for her to continue. "Okay, well we finally got a lead from Captain Ahn. Mom, you remember he's the husband of your sister. Oh! I have a letter from Barla." She stood up, removed the tattered letter from her pants pocket, and handed it to her mother.

Amanda resumed her seat next to Riccan to continue her summation of events. "Bryon and I ended up going over to Ahn and Barla's house the next day. However, when they saw Juila with me, they were stunned at how much she looked like their daughter, Rasa, at the same age.

"When I told Barla about her being my aunt and gave her the letter you had written for her, she was so happy to finally have her family again. I don't know if you remember me telling you how their daughter had been selected to train with Jehoban, but Barla had the brilliant idea that Rasa might be able to help me track down Jena.

"Since we had exhausted all of our other leads, I ended up moving to Durseni where Rasa was training with Elder Debbon to become a wise-woman. Since I had Juila with me, I needed to have a house and a job to support myself until Jena was located. Captain Ahn sent a letter of recommendation with Bryon when he helped me move to the island which allowed me to get a job working for Riccan at the Telepod Engineering Company." Amanda turned and grinned at Riccan before she continued.

"Rasa confirmed our idea about the connection between Juila and Jena. She also attempted to get a message to you through Shemalla. Did you ever get it?"

"We did, and I knew something was wrong when you only talked about yourself and not your daughters. Now I know I was right about that as well since Jena ended up here with us." Once again, Diane felt vindicated since her instincts had been accurate.

"Rasa will be very pleased to hear the message got through. She'd never tried to use the technique across the veil into Earth before so she wasn't entirely sure it had worked. She also determined, because of the messaging experiment, that Jena had been sent to Earth. The link between the twins felt like the same distance as the letter she had sent for both of you.

"When we saw Petre on Durseni, after he had been missing for two years, I called Bryon. He and Alena came over to the island immediately where Bryon located Petre and turned him into the authorities on the same night. Petre admitted to having taken Jena, and he bragged to Bryon about selling Jena to Elder Debbon.

"Alena made arrangements for me to meet with the Elder since he had been her teacher while I was pregnant with the twins. It was while we were talking everything over with him that we discovered Jena and Willian had been sent to Earth. Elder Vargen was unable to tell Elder Debbon where the children had ended up since Shemalla had failed to report back to work at the museum.

"Do either of you know where she is? She wasn't at home. Should we be concerned?"

Diane showed a puzzled expression as she replied, "I tried calling her the next day after she dropped off the children, but she never answered. She hasn't returned my call even though I left her a message. I figured she was busy with work, but now you're saying something may have happened to her. What can we do?"

Amanda was now officially worried since Shemalla was a good friend and an ally on Earth. She certainly did not want to report her missing to the police. Shemalla was a person from Tuala who did not want to be brought to the attention of any governmental entity. She looked anxiously over at Riccan and asked, "Is there anything we can do to locate her? I've used her birth crystal before, so maybe I've made a link with Shemalla. What do you think?"

"We can certainly try. Even though she may work for Elder Vargen, she's your friend, and she deserves our help after everything she's risked to help you."

Everyone nodded in agreement at Riccan's statement. The room remained silent as everybody absorbed all of the events Amanda had described. Turning to face her on the couch, Riccan held Amanda's hands, and linked his mind to hers to feel if any connection still existed with

Shemalla. After several minutes of exhausting every known avenue, Riccan withdrew his energy and had to admit defeat.

"I'm sorry, Amanda, there's just nothing to be found. We'll have to discover another way to locate her. I'll hire some people to check out her financial trail."

Seeing Amanda remained quite upset, Chris wanted to change the subject and finally asked, "So what kind of a job did you end up getting?"

Diane rolled her eyes at her husband's absurd inquiry. She always knew she could count on him to ask a trivial question during a stressful moment.

Amanda smiled at her parents' interaction and answered, "I'm an Engineering Resources Analyst."

Riccan placed his hand on her shoulder with pride as he added, "She's very good at her job. I'm glad I was able to give her the opportunity."

Diane wondered if that were the only reason Riccan had in mind where her daughter was concerned. *What boss would put himself at such risk for a new employee?*

Chris thought of another detail which had not been covered. "How did the three of you get here? You said you first went to Roswell. How long have you been back on Earth?"

"We came in Riccan's telepod." Amanda knew this announcement would derail any other conversations since her father was intensely curious about any new technology.

"Really? Where is it? Can we go see it right now?"

"Chris, for Pete's sake, they just got here. Don't you think they're probably tired? For goodness sake, there'll be plenty of time for that nonsense later."

"It's not nonsense, Diane. Riccan may have to leave immediately for all I know. I don't want to miss a chance to see a real telepod. The replica at the Roswell museum was interesting, but this telepod is real!"

"It's okay, Diane," Riccan interrupted before the argument could get any more heated. "We don't have any plans on leaving soon, but I'd be more than happy to show anyone in the family who wants to see my telepod."

Now it was Amanda's turn to interject, "Dad, Riccan designed the telepod himself, even using some of Earth's technology to make it better than anything anyone in Tuala has ever seen before."

"Really, Riccan? You designed it yourself? That's fascinating. I'd love to hear all about it."

"We could go right now if you want."

Chris was truly torn between being reunited with his daughter and granddaughter and getting the rarest opportunity of a lifetime to see an alien aircraft. His expression was comical, and both Amanda and Diane began laughing out loud since they knew exactly what he had been thinking.

"Go ahead, Dad. Mom and I can catch up while you go satisfy your insatiable curiosity!"

Chris' smile beamed at his daughter as he jumped up from the couch to find his car keys. With a sudden thought, he realized he had no idea where they had landed. He turned and asked, "Where did you park it?"

"Just outside of town down by the water."

With a satisfied nod, he rushed out of the room. A few moments later Chris returned with his keys and announced, "I'm ready if you are."

Amanda stepped forward, kissed her father's cheek, and said, "I love you, Dad. Go have fun with Riccan."

Riccan had the unexpected desire for Amanda to give him the same farewell. He had not told her about his wish for them to start dating, so until then, he could hardly expect anything other than friendship from her. He grinned at both of the women in the room as Chris led the way toward the front entrance.

CHAPTER 2

As soon as the door slammed shut, Diane noticed how late it had gotten and realized the children should have gone to bed almost an hour before. "Help me put the children to bed and then we can talk more."

She went over to where Jena sat on the floor, picking her up at the same time as Amanda lifting Juila. Diane held out her hand for Willian, waiting patiently for him to scoot himself off of the couch. She worried about how quiet Willian had been during the entire reunion. He was such a serious child who had deep thoughts.

They walked down the hall, planning to put the girls down together in the same bed. Both Willian and Jena had already been in their pajamas, so they were ready to go. Diane took Willian across the hall to his room to tuck him in while Amanda changed Juila into night clothes borrowed from Jena.

Diane returned to the girls' room in time to pull up the sheets to cover the little girls. She thought the twins were adorable with how close they were lying next to one another. It really did seem as if they knew one another intimately without any insecurities about meeting.

They left the bedroom, automatically turning toward the kitchen to continue talking. Diane spoke quietly to Amanda, "I believe you're right about how close the two of them are, it's like they've never been apart."

"Well, they haven't been apart mentally, except the night Jena was sent to Earth. Juila's connection became so weak she thought Jena had been lost. She was very upset until Rasa re-established the link. This whole journey has been incredible, Mom."

"I'm glad you all made it home safely. When did you begin your trip home? Your father asked the question, but then got so sidetracked with the telepod you never had the chance to answer."

"We left Tuala only a couple of hours ago. We would have been here sooner, but we had to walk for about a mile to get into Roswell. Riccan wanted to make sure nobody saw the telepod, so we had to land pretty far away."

"How long did it take you to get to Earth from Tuala?"

"I'd say it was about six seconds."

"That's it?"

Amanda chuckled as she answered, "Believe me, it feels like a lifetime when all of your senses are gone. Plus it was twice as long as it normally takes for transit on Tuala, so it was starting to become alarming. Something else happened which is amazing."

"What's that?"

Amanda pulled up the ornate chain from under her shirt and held a clear diamond, tree-of-life pendant in her hand for her mother to inspect.

"You have a birth crystal? How did you manage to get it?" After having examined both Jena and Willian's birth crystals, Diane was quite familiar with the significance of the necklace.

Both of the foster children were able to use the elemental energy naturally found in the earth to make things happen. Willian had caused water to boil instantly, and Jena had levitated toys as they played. The birth crystals were given to the children of Tuala shortly after being born and could not be taken off of their necks until after they turned eighteen.

"To make a long story short, Alena heard I didn't have a birth crystal. I had to lie and tell her I lost it when I escaped from Petre. She performed a crystal ceremony immediately where Jehoban Himself made this pendant appear on Alena's ceremonial chest after the original sapphire pendant she handed me turned to dust in my palm.

"Also, I found out another benefit of having received this talisman. I kept my memory while transferring from Tuala to Earth with Riccan. He seems to think Jehoban has made me an honorary Tualan citizen with this gift. Riccan also said I was now able to access all of the benefits of the Tualan people."

"Do you think it's true?" Diane could hardly imagine her daughter being able to do the same amazing tricks the two little ones had already demonstrated upon arriving several weeks before.

"I know it is. I began training with Alena on how to access the elemy, that's short for elemental energy in case you didn't remember. I was able to master the first ten skill levels before I moved to Durseni to be available to meet with Rasa whenever she had a break from school."

Diane shook her head in amazement. Amanda had changed and matured in the two years she had been away in Tuala; there was so much more about her daughter she still needed to learn. She could not believe the girl she had raised for eighteen years was now telling her she was able to do almost magical things with only her mind and the silly pendant around her neck. Eventually she would ask for a demonstration; however, tonight she just wanted to hear Amanda's voice to be reassured she was alright.

"Tell me more about your friend, Riccan. He seems very nice."

Amanda blushed at her mother's obvious implication and replied, "He's my boss, Mom."

"I believe he wants to be more than just your boss, Amanda."

"Really, Mom, you watch too many soap operas!" She tried to convince herself her mother was reading too much into Riccan's reason for bringing her home, yet she had to admit it was a tremendous risk for Riccan to take for just any employee. "Okay, maybe you're right, but we haven't discussed anything beyond work."

"What's not to like, Amanda? He's tall and handsome. He has a good job. He's good with Juila..."

"And he lives in a different world."

"Well, there's that!" Diane chuckled at the minor complication. "When's he going back to Tuala?"

"He said we could stay for a while because he'd be able to time our return to Tuala so we'd only be gone for one night."

"Wait, are you saying you're going to go back to Tuala with him? But you just came home, Amanda. You've recovered both of your daughters, so why would you go back?"

"Well, for starters, Elder Debbon doesn't know where his son is on

Earth. I know the feeling of having a child lost in a strange place and I wouldn't wish that experience on anyone. His wife, Chelesa, is just beside herself with worry."

"Riccan could tell them where their son is, you don't have to go, Amanda." Diane was trying to find any angle to keep her daughter earthbound.

"Mom, it's okay. I do have to go back to tie up loose ends. I started a job several weeks ago, and I can't leave Riccan in the lurch like that, it wouldn't be fair. Also, Alena and Bryon were going to spend the night at my house tonight, and they're expecting me to give them an update in the morning. I need to say goodbye to my cousin, Rasa, and Aunt Barla and her husband, Ahn. I can't just disappear from Tuala, Mom. I have to go back."

"But it's too risky. What if you get lost in the transfer? Shemalla had told us the Gates were dangerous."

"Riccan has a sanctioned portable Gate built into his telepod since his father's an Elder. We could come and go from Earth every day, and it'd be perfectly safe."

"So what you're saying is you plan on commuting from Earth to Tuala every day just to go to work?"

"Not exactly, Mom. More like I'd be coming home for the weekends."

"No, Amanda! I feel as though I'm losing you all over again."

"It's called growing up, Mom, and I had to do it sometime." Amanda gave her mother a hug and rubbed her back. "I'll always be your little girl, but I have responsibilities of my own now. I found a job I really love, and I want to see where things go with Riccan. I think I might be falling for him, but I don't know how he feels about me."

"How come your announcement about growing up makes me want to cry?" Diane held her daughter tighter in her arms. "Let me mother you for a little longer. I'm sure you haven't been eating well since I can feel all of your ribs. Let me make you something."

"Okay, but first I want to show you something." Amanda concentrated for a moment before a glass of water appeared on the counter beside her mother.

With a small jump of surprise, Diane looked at the newly materialized glass and then at her daughter. "Did you just make that appear from nowhere?"

"It's one of the things I learned, but far from everything. It's amazing how fast I got used to using it for cooking and cleaning. The more I practice, the less I can understand how people function without it."

"Well it seems to be handy, but, honestly Amanda, it's kind of creepy!"

"No it's not, you're just not used to seeing it." She picked up the glass of water and took a drink. "What do you have to eat?"

PETRE MAY HAVE BEEN CAUGHT, but he was not about to give up the location of the stolen goods. Without proof he had taken the shipment, he would not willingly give them another reason to keep him longer by admitting his guilt. After being surprised by Bryon boarding his watercraft, being kicked in the face and knocked unconscious, he was in no mood to be congenial.

He expected to be taken back to Kirma where he had abducted Jena, so it came as no surprise when the authorities told him he had a visitor. After leaving his cell and being taken to the interrogation room he sat quietly for another official to come get him to be transferred. The door opened and his jaw tightened as he discovered who entered the room.

"Elder Debbon, I'm surprised to see you here."

"I don't know why you would be after what you've done."

"I've done nothing wrong, Elder Debbon; however, you are the one keeping me from seeing my daughter."

Trying to maintain patience with this insufferable man, Elder Debbon took a deep breath and exhaled before he continued. "You stole Jena from her adoptive family, Petre. Surely you didn't think you would get away with it, even you aren't that stupid."

"I can't exactly steal somebody who already belongs to me, now can I, Elder Debbon?"

"And just what makes you think she's your daughter, Petre. You told me your wife died and left the child with you. That wasn't true, so why should I believe you now?"

"I learned my wife died while she was living with that family and left our daughter without a parent. I seriously doubt it was legal for Bryon and his wife to adopt Jena without ever trying to get in touch with me. I know he knew I was the father because he had talked to acquaintances of mine trying to look for me."

"So you admit he tried to find you, yet you remained elusive?"

"Are you not hearing what I'm saying? The man stole my daughter out from under me. I'm seriously thinking about pressing charges against him for that and for assaulting me tonight!"

"Give it up, Petre. Bryon had every right to make sure you were arrested after what you've put his family through for the past two anons."

"And what about you, Elder Debbon? What do *you* deserve for what you've put *me* through for the past two anons?"

"I've done nothing to you, Petre. You used my money to outfit your water craft for all this time. I offered you an honest agreement for your daughter to be betrothed to my son and you freely signed the contract and took the money. How am I responsible for you not trying to see Jena for all this time?"

"You purposely tricked me into signing that agreement knowing full well I wouldn't see the abandonment clause until it was too late."

"I can't believe that you, a master deceptor, would concede to someone getting something over on you. Are you really admitting I outsmarted you?"

"So you don't deny you tried to keep it from me?"

"I admit to nothing of the sort, Petre. I gave you the same contract I kept for myself. I had no reason to believe you wouldn't read it completely the night you returned to your water craft."

Petre's face began changing to a darker shade of red as his frustration mounted. He wanted to strangle the smug expression off the Elder's face. Before he could think it through he warned, "You'll be sorry you messed with me, Elder Debbon."

"I'm surprised I need to remind you it's against the law to threaten an Elder. If you insist on holding this matter against me, I'll be forced to wipe your mind. Is that what you need, Petre?"

Petre shivered at the thought and immediately wished he had kept his mouth shut. It was uncharacteristic of him to play his hand before it was ready. "Why did you come here, Elder Debbon?"

"I wanted to see you one last time before you were taken to the Elder's Council for sentencing."

Petre's eyes widened perceptibly with the Elder's announcement. He figured he would be sentenced locally like he had always been in the past. This was turning more serious than he ever imagined. There must be something he could do to get his case moved to the local jurisdiction. He recovered his voice and asked, "Maybe we can come to an agreement to avoid the inconvenience?"

"Not even I can help you this time, Petre. Your actions have gone too far and you will pay the price for it." Elder Debbon turned on his heel and strode from the room. He had gotten what he came for anyway. While Petre was trying to figure out a way out of his mess he had let down the mental guard he usually held tightly. Elder Debbon knew what had happened and now he just had to locate Petre's accomplices.

LILLIA BOARDED Petre's impounded water craft without being seen, walked across the deck, and down the stairs to the main cabin. Right where the power drew strongest, Lillia lifted down the brown, cloth-wrapped bundle and felt the familiar tingle enter into her fingers. She shivered with remembered pleasure the feel of the crystal on her bare hands. The intoxicating power pulled at her, but she had not come here to feel the power, she had come to remove it from Petre.

Petre had turned out to be such a disappointment to Lucinden. Every task he had been assigned had been bungled by the unpredictable petty criminal. She could almost feel sorry for the man, had he just been a little smarter with his life choices. Lillia had tried to convince Lucinden to give the crystal to an Elder rather than to Petre, but he had insisted his course was better. Now she had been proven correct and Lucinden had sent her to retrieve the crystal to be reassigned.

Without even attempting to leave the cabin, Lillia translated herself from the vessel. With the added power of the crystal skull she could easily transport herself anywhere she wished. She had so much power coursing through her she could have sent herself to Earth without the benefit of a Gate had she been so inclined.

Walking across the darkened room toward the chair positioned on the raised dais, she smiled inwardly at Lucinden's attempt to create his own reception chamber reminiscent of Jehoban's. Lillia wondered if Lucinden could see the similarity or if he truly thought it original.

"I feel the success of your mission by the power spike in the room."

"Yes, Master, you are correct." She placed the bundle at his feet and stepped away while continuing to bow.

"Master now, is it? I can feel your impertinence even in this darkness. Remove yourself at once and leave me."

Lillia slowly smiled while turning to leave the room. Lucinden refused to admit his error and the terse dismissal came as close to an admission as she would ever expect to get. She closed the massive black doors to the throne room and returned to the guest quarters for the evening.

Once inside the private room, she leaned on the door as she watched the woman sleep on the bed. They had not planned on taking her so soon, but events had transpired to create the perfect scenario for her to be removed from Earth. A couple of anons earlier, this woman had come to their attention when she translated herself to Earth. If it had not been for that particular occasion, she might never have been discovered living among Earth's people.

Lillia was not exactly sure what Lucinden had in mind for this middle-aged woman, but she could well imagine it was not going to be something pleasant. Her task had been set to keep the prisoner well drugged with resh, maintaining the delicate balance to keep her sedated without addicting her to the nasty herb. This was not her favorite duty, but she was willing to do almost anything for her lover. She had learned over the declans how her cooperation merited many benefits with the powerful Master.

CHELESA REFUSED to speak with her husband unless the conversation related to her wise-woman training with him. At his behest, she had risked her children's lives and now they were both missing somewhere on Earth. No word had been received from Elder Vargen regarding his contact which meant they still had no clue who retained care of them.

The threats to their family which had precipitated her journey to Durseni had also given her a rare opportunity to learn a skill she had believed forever out of her reach. Her position in society as the wife of an Elder kept her busy with all the requests of the people, so much so, she never felt as though she should abandon their needs to meet her own.

Also, her children were a top priority and she wanted to be a hands-on mother to both Willian and Jena.

Her thoughts returned to her husband, causing her anger to rise yet again. She pushed away the book she had been pretending to study and slammed her fists onto the tabletop. It was time she spoke to her husband.

"Debbon!" Chelesa yelled over her shoulder through the apartment. She expected her husband to be sitting in the next room, yet no answering call sounded. Their living quarters were not so large that he would have a hard time hearing her calling for him. She pushed away from the table to go into the bedroom to confront him when the front door behind her opened.

"What's wrong, Chelesa?" Debbon inquired as he swiftly entered the room. He could instantly tell something had upset his wife and he hoped she had not received another threat from the street thugs.

"Where were you? I thought you were in the other room," she accused angrily.

"I went to see Petre before he was transported to Kirma."

Clearly she had not expected his answer and rocked back on her heels before having to sit back down in the chair she had just vacated. "Why?"

"You were busy studying, so I thought I should try to get some answers about our trouble back home."

"You think Petre had something to do with it?"

"I know he did. He threatened me at the station and I took the opportunity to read his mind."

"Debbon, that's not ethical. Why would you take the risk? Especially with him."

"There was no risk really. He is in serious trouble for this new succession of crimes. He's been scheduled to appear before the Council of Elders."

"Wow, that's bad!"

"Yes, I was thinking the same thing. If he's sentenced, as I believe he will be, then his mind will be wiped clean before he'd be allowed back in society. I knew tonight would be my only opportunity to get any answers regarding his part with Jena as well as the trouble he started for you at home. My guess was correct; he orchestrated the whole thing. Now I just have to find the people he used to harass you."

"It would be nice to know the situation has been taken care of before we're done with this class. Then we could focus our attention on finding out where our kids went and then getting them back."

"One thing at a time, Chelesa. I'm only one person and I have a few other obligations on my time right now."

"Our children should be your first priority."

"They are! That's why I need to take care of these thugs before I bring the children back home. Elder Vargen assured me his employee was placing our kids with a very good foster family."

"If only we were sure they made it to their final destination…"

"We don't need to borrow trouble. Jehoban will watch over the children, we can be assured with that regard."

"Thank you, Debbon. You're so wise and always know just the right thing to say."

"It's probably why Jehoban made me into an Elder."

"And also why you were voted First by the Council of Elders. I love you, Debbon."

"I love you, too, honey." He looked down and saw the text she was reading and knew she had not gotten far on the day's lesson. "It looks as though you still have quite a bit of reading to finish, so I'm going to take a shower and give you some quiet time." He walked into the bedroom and continued on to the bathroom without looking back.

Chelesa agreed with her husband about the studying, however her mind still raced with his newest revelations. How big was Petre's operation against her family? Could they be in danger on Durseni? Petre was found here on the island, could he have been planning something against them? Her unproductive thoughts definitely showed a lack of faith in Jehoban. With a final shake of her head, she decided to leave it up to the Creator and pulled the textbook forward so she could resume her studies.

CHAPTER 3

Riccan smiled at Chris' enthusiasm for seeing his telepod. He was used to people clamoring to see his racing telepod, however those people were from Tuala and had most likely ridden in a telepod before. Being from Earth, Chris did not have any other experience with this form of transportation other than hearing what Amanda had described.

As Chris drove, Riccan used his telepod's homing beacon to give directions. The drive took about ten minutes and Riccan recognized the surroundings when he finally told Chris to park the car. They soon began walking the considerable distance to get to where he had landed near the water. He could understand Chris' nervousness, however there was nothing he could do about it until they reached the vehicle.

"How much further?" Chris asked, as they continued to walk away from the car through the brush and marshy footing.

"I landed just on the edge of the open water. I figured nobody would be around during this time of night so it would be relatively safe." He looked down to the hand-held locator and added, "Another ten feet and we should be there."

"I don't see anything, Riccan. Are you sure this is where you landed?"

Riccan smiled as he continued forward with confidence. He reached out and rapped his knuckles on the side of his telepod. From Chris' view, he knew it would look as though he were knocking on nothing but air. Riccan ran his hand along the side of the craft until his fingers felt the button to open the side door.

Chris stepped back as he heard something opening, yet he still could see nothing in front of him. He looked questioningly at Riccan for any indication of what they should do.

"Come inside, Chris. Once I shut the door behind us, you'll be able to see everything clearly."

Had Chris not been so intensely curious he would have found the whole scenario quite creepy. Later he would probably feel as though he had his own alien abduction story, but right now he followed Riccan's directions. He took three steps and felt the door close behind him and all he could do was stare in wonder around himself.

"This is way better than the display at the museum in Roswell!"

Riccan laughed out loud since there was absolutely no comparison between the two vehicles.

Inspecting the cabin around him, Chris saw several rows of seats covered in a soft, smooth leather. All of the interior was covered in either fabric or plasfilm so none of the metal framework showed, even on the floor.

Without waiting for permission Chris continued into the craft until he got to the control panel. It came as no surprise none of the panel looked even remotely familiar. He sat down in one of the control seats and stared at the construction and design of the cockpit. "Is this what you do at your company?"

"Yep, she's my pride and joy. She has all of the latest technology, most of which has yet to be seen by anyone outside of our company."

"This is amazing, Riccan." He ran his fingertips lightly along the sleek dashboard and wondered what it would look like during flight. "How fast does she fly?"

Riccan smiled because Chris asked the same question his daughter had not too long before. He answered, "Faster than anything else in Tuala. I haven't had the opportunity to really test her paces, but I imagine she'd surprise everyone. I discovered a new way to align the power crystal so it's more responsive even when a lesser crystal is used. The control panel is mostly handled the same way as the conventional telepods, but the displays are all located within the plascreen.

"On other telepods, each function has its own light on the board, this one integrates them all to one screen so there's less chance of missing something vital. There's even a built-in safeguard against pilot error which is almost equivalent to an auto-pilot."

"Amazing! Can I see the power system?"

"Certainly, it's at the rear of the cabin." He backed out of the cockpit and walked the few steps to the aft section of the craft. He turned a few knobs and pushed aside a panel to reveal the intricate design of the main crystal and the brackets suspending it. The bracketing had wires attached to them to power the various components throughout the vessel.

"It's such a simple and clean design." Chris kneeled on the floor and wished he had a schematic of the ship to see how it really worked. The whole idea of powering a vehicle with a crystal seemed such a novel concept and he wanted to know more. The biggest problem he ran into now was he just did not know what questions to ask since he knew nothing about this technology.

"Would you like to go for a ride?"

"Do you really have to ask? I'd never turn down the opportunity!"

"Let's go get buckled in and I'll take you up." He took the lead, returned to the cockpit, and sat down in the left-hand seat.

Chris managed to figure out the fastening system of the right-hand seat before grinning eagerly at Riccan to indicate his readiness. He watched intently as Riccan began the start-up procedures.

Riccan touched the plascreen to turn it on before activating the telepod's crystal drive. The vessel rose several inches above the ground soundlessly and hovered in place while Riccan verified each green light on the screen. If this were a standard flight he would then switch to mental steering, but he wanted to show Chris how the craft performed before teleporting to a secondary location. He would save the best for last by ending the trip with a teleportation home.

"I'm going to take us further into the wetlands to keep out of the public's sight. It'd be hard for me to explain my presence on Earth if the press made a big deal of a new UFO sighting. The Elders frown on any publicity and I tend to agree with them." He skimmed across the water until he came to more trees. The telepod rose in the air giving them an amazing view outside the panoramic windows. Except for telepod racing Riccan hardly ever took the time to joyride and appreciate the scenery.

"The ride's so smooth it doesn't even feel as though we're moving." Chris stared out the windows with a boyish grin plastered on his face.

"What do you think, should we see how fast she can travel in manual mode?"

"Absolutely!"

"Okay, hold on, I'm going to ascend fast to an altitude where we won't be bothered by prying eyes." He touched the screen and typed in an altitude of four gania. He could feel the pressure in the cabin begin to normalize as they climbed rapidly. Within a minute they were at the designated elevation.

Chris could hardly believe how far they had gone in such a short amount of time and asked, "How far up are we?"

"Roughly ten miles from the surface. Okay, now let's see what she can do!"

"Let's go. Whoa!" Chris' breath burst from his mouth as the scenery below became a blur and nothing could be identified as they raced to the east. At this rate, he was certain they were traveling as fast as a space shuttle. Never in his life did he imagine he would fly at such a rate of speed. He also wondered why he was not feeling any G-forces. "I can see we're moving right along, so how come we don't feel it as well?"

"Because I activated the anti-gravity force before we began. If I hadn't done so, we would have passed out well before now. I think we might've found her top speed."

"What is it?"

"Just under 20,000 miles per hour. At this rate we will circle the Earth in just over a hour. Did you ever imagine you would travel the world tonight?"

"Not in my wildest dreams!" He leaned forward to see if anything could be recognized below, but everything remained a blur until Riccan suddenly stopped the telepod. Concerned, Chris looked over at Riccan before asking, "What's wrong? Where are we?"

"We're a couple of miles off of the Pacific coast. I'm pretty sure you'd like a demonstration of how we normally travel. Are you ready?"

"Absolutely."

"Okay, I'll warn you that during the transfer you won't have any sensory input. Some people have a hard time with that even when they know what to expect. My best advice is to keep track of your breathing and remain calm."

"Deep breathing and remain calm…I got it. Let's go!"

Riccan reprogrammed the plascreen to take them back to the same location from where they started. He pressed the button to switch from manual to mental control and took his hand from the controller. With one more movement he clicked on the final destination and everything turned black and all feeling ceased.

Three seconds later they appeared back at the waterfront mere inches above the ground. Riccan issued all of the shutdown procedures and reactivated the cloaking shield. Since they were landed Riccan was able to finally check on his passenger. "Are you okay, Chris?"

"I'm sure I'll never be the same, Riccan. That was the most amazing adventure I've ever been on. Amanda tried to explain this type of travel, but words do *nothing* to describe the reality. I wish Diane had been here, too. Although I don't think she would've enjoyed it nearly as much as I did."

"We should probably get back to your house; Diane's probably wanting to go to bed sometime soon. I doubt she'd rest easy until you got home."

"It sounds as though you already know my wife."

"I know my own mother. Diane is a lot like her in some ways."

They exited the vehicle where Riccan paused to palm the door shut. As they drove back to the house, Chris kept shaking his head in disbelief at his latest adventure. It was possibly the most thrilling thing ever to happen in his life and yet he would be unable to share the excitement with anyone other than his wife. However unfortunate the circumstance, he would do it all again in a heartbeat. He pulled into his driveway and waited for the garage door to lift.

"Thank you for taking me, Riccan. I know you risked a lot just to satisfy my curiosity."

"No thanks needed. I was just as ready to test her paces. I've been so busy at work I haven't had the time to really try her out since I finished building her."

"That's your build?" Chris could hardly believe Riccan designed the telepod, let alone built it as well.

"Yep, she's my pride and joy. I've loved telepods ever since I could remember and I learned everything I could about them. When it came time for me to pick my major in post-study it was an easy choice to decide on becoming a telepod engineer."

"It's too bad I can't have one here on Earth. It sure would be a blast to play with on the weekends."

"No offense, Chris, but people from Earth don't have the ability to operate a telepod. We use the link between our birth crystal and the crystal drive to navigate."

"That's unfortunate. Amanda had once told me she'd like to learn to fly one."

"Amanda could learn."

"But you just said…"

"Amanda received her own birth crystal from Jehoban."

"Seriously? I can't wait to hear that story!"

"You'll have time."

Chris pulled the car into the garage and shut off the engine. "Will you all be staying for a while?"

"Yes, but we'll have to go back soon. We can discuss it tomorrow."

"Okay, let's get back inside so I can tell Diane about the ride."

CHAPTER 4

Amanda looked around as she sat at the breakfast table with her parents, her twins, Riccan, and Willian, feeling relieved to finally be reunited with everyone. It had all worked out so well it almost did not feel real. Her parents had gotten to know Jena over the past few weeks of her and Willian living in the house even though they did not know she was their granddaughter.

Diane insisted she knew Jena was her grandchild the moment Jena's eyes opened the morning after they were dropped off. She had kept it to herself so Chris would not become more upset with what he would have termed as her 'irrational' idea.

Now Amanda had some decisions to make and her time was running out. Riccan had said they could spend a few days on Earth before they had to go back. There was no reason for her to return except to continue with her job and get to know Riccan better. Did she really want to risk her future on Earth to possibly have a relationship with someone from a different world? The idea was so crazy, but she was seriously considering doing just that.

Her eyes shifted over to the little boy sitting beside Jena. Willian was only about five years old with dark hair, eyes, and complexion. His presence was the only thing stopping her from having the perfect reunion. She had yet to tell her parents about the boy being betrothed to her daughter. Alena had informed her the betrothal was irrevocable except by the children themselves since the ceremony had been completed which meant the union was blessed by Jehoban. Amanda knew Jehoban had been instrumental in so many of the coincidences surrounding her journey in Tuala, she did not want to anger Him with breaking the betrothal.

Willian would eventually have to be returned to Elder Debbon and Chelesa. Only Amanda and Riccan knew where their son was being cared for on Earth. Amanda hoped she could come to some arrangement with the Elder to be able to retain custody of Jena, but still honor the agreement. She hoped to speak privately with Riccan, but the opportunity had not yet arisen.

Her mother was in such a great mood to have her whole family back on Earth and in her house. She had gotten up early to make a special breakfast for everyone to enjoy before her father had to go off to work. Chris had offered to call in to get the day off, but Amanda assured him they would still be around when he got home. If he had not had a new account to work on, he probably would have called in anyway.

Amanda picked up her beef bacon and ate a piece. She had not seen any beef bacon in years and wondered why her mother had bought it. When she had asked, her mother told her the children were used to eating fried foxl and this was as close as she thought she could get. Amanda smiled at her mother's effort even though the taste was nothing alike, but her mother could not know that.

Looking at the daughter she had not seen grow up, Amanda wondered what Jena wanted to do. She obviously loved being back together with her sister, but she was not as happy at being reunited with her mother. Amanda could hardly blame her since she had been raised by Chelesa and not herself.

She was not exactly angry over what had transpired, more sorry for the loss of the relationship. Obviously, Jena had been well-cared for since she seemed a very happy toddler. She did not want to take her away from the mother who had raised her, yet she wanted to have a part in her life as well. Amanda was, however, a little bit hurt because Jena was more excited to see Juila than herself.

Then there was Juila to consider; with her sister back in her life she flourished with more animation than Amanda had ever seen in her. They were inseparable, which was where Amanda ran into the heart of the problem. She wanted them to stay together.

If nothing else, Amanda needed to go back to Tuala to talk about this situation with Alena and Bryon. She trusted them to have the best understanding of the entire convoluted situation. Maybe she would sit down with Bryon, Alena, Barla, Rasa, and Riccan where together they could figure out how to work out an arrangement where everyone could be satisfied. She was not exactly sure how she would get the group gathered with everyone's busy schedules, but she had to at least give it a try.

"Wasn't that fortunate, Amanda?" Diane asked.

"I'm sorry, I wasn't paying attention. What were you talking about?"

"I told Riccan we were on the verge of moving to New Mexico several months ago. Chris finally agreed to quit his job and sell the house so we could be closer to Shemalla and any news from you. One thing after another cropped up to delay our move. Now I'm so thankful we didn't go, because then you wouldn't have known where to locate us. Weren't we all so fortunate for it to work out so well?"

Amanda smiled at her mother's story. She had known her mother would be anxious to get word from her and she was grateful her note had made it to her parents through Rasa. "Yes, Mom, I can't imagine you two living anywhere but here. This is where we all grew up. Do you think you'll stay put since we've returned?"

"Oh, most definitely. It did make me sad to think about leaving, but I worried so much about how you were doing in Tuala and I wanted to be as close as possible to the only link we had in Roswell."

"I understand, Mom, but now we need to figure out where Shemalla went. It's not like her to abandon her post at the museum. She respects Elder Vargen too much to let him down, so something must have occurred which was out of her control. What happened during the last contact you had with her?"

"She was only here for a few minutes while she and Chris put the sleeping children into their beds. Her cab was waiting for her in the driveway to take her back to the airport. She got in the cab and drove away and we haven't seen or heard from her since."

Amanda contemplated her mother's statement, feeling to her core something seemed wrong. Suddenly she realized the glaringly obvious problem, Amanda could understand Shemalla needing to fly to Florida with the two children, but not the return flight. "Why would Shemalla fly back to New Mexico when she could just translate herself in an instant?"

"Oh, I don't know. I never thought about that since it's what we'd normally do to go home. I forgot about her ability to travel on her own. It's possible she decided to take a vacation. Did you check with her work?"

"No, but I think I will today." Amanda did not like the ominous ideas which swirled around in her brain. What if Elder Vargen found out about Shemalla's dealings with herself and her parents? Could she have been taken back to Tuala to be interrogated by the Elder? She had been afraid of the possibility, yet thought it unlikely when she had helped Amanda before. Maybe her fears had been realized.

Chris scraped his chair back from the table and stood up. "I've got to head out for work. I wish I could stay home and visit. Save some stories for me to hear when I get back."

"Oh, Dad, I'd tell them all over again just for you. I love you."

"I know, sweetie." He gave his youngest daughter a hug, kissing the top of her head where she sat in her chair before he repeated the farewell with Diane. Chris gathered his keys and waved to everyone at the table. "I'll see everybody in nine hours."

Diane wished her husband could stay and visit, however she was also thankful for her time alone with Amanda and Riccan. She could see the chemistry between them even if they had not acknowledged it yet. She liked how Riccan handled the children as though it were a natural thing.

The children all appeared to be done eating and were just playing with their plates and silverware waiting to be excused from the table. Diane eagerly stated, "Okay, children, you may be excused to go play now." All three kids hopped down from their chairs and raced back into the living room to begin a game of building cabins with Lincoln Logs, something they had never seen before.

Diane had hoped to speak privately with Riccan and began, "Amanda tells me your father's an Elder. What does he think about you coming here with Amanda?"

"My situation is a little different than that of the other Elders' children."

"Really? How so?"

Riccan wondered how much detail Diane might be looking for so he opted to go with the short version of the story. "My grandfather's from Earth. He moved to Tuala after meeting my grandmother. They had my father, Daven, and then moved to live with Jehoban when he was asked to become a student.

"Because they lived with Jehoban they had access to a Gate where they traveled to and from Earth regularly to visit with my grandfather's family. When my dad grew up, Jehoban made him into an Elder who had access to his own Gate in Boca Raton. When I was growing up we came here to vacation and also visit the few relatives still living. I've grown up knowing both worlds and I even lived here for a few years."

"How amazing!"

"Now I use the things I've learned from Earth and apply my knowledge of flying to my telepod. I've also integrated the training from my father into the telepod as well."

"What training would your father have given you? I thought he was an Elder. Aren't you an engineer?"

"I am for now. When my father's ready to step down, it's expected for me to follow in his footsteps as an Elder. From the time I was a small boy, my father has been training me in all of the aspects of being an Elder."

Diane still looked confused.

Amanda took pity and simply said, "Riccan created a portable Gate in his telepod. Only Elders have access to portable Gates."

"Oh! I guess that would make your telepod a one-of-a-kind then, wouldn't it?"

"Absolutely. It also allows me to travel with impunity."

"Also very convenient. So what does your father do as an Elder?"

"He works with petitioners, patrons, and citizens by handling all of the disputes from his District. He also takes care of adoptions, crystal ceremonies, healing, teaching, and weddings."

"It sounds like he is kept pretty busy."

"For sure. He has several people who assist him, but the needs of the people never seem to end."

"How long does a person stay an Elder?"

"It depends on the person, but usually between thirty to fifty years.

"What about your mother? What does she do?"

"Her name's Nena and she's a teacher."

"What age group?"

"First and second year students. She loves to teach them how to access their birth crystals and see how they grow in confidence as they achieve success."

"Do you have any siblings?"

"No, I'm an only child."

"What do you two plan to do?"

"I'm up for whatever Amanda wants." Riccan looked over to Amanda to hear how she would answer her mother.

"Like I said before, Mom, there're some things I need to take care of back in Tuala. I think we should go back tomorrow or maybe the day after. Since Willian needs to stay here until the trouble at home is taken care of, I was thinking of leaving Juila with Jena here so they can have more bonding time. Would that be okay with you?"

"I would love it, but when will you be coming back?"

"I'm not sure. It could take me a week or two to get everything accomplished. Do you want to write a letter for Aunt Barla?"

"Oh! I forgot to read the letter you gave me last night!" She jumped up from her chair and rushed into the living room to get the letter from the coffee table. She returned a few moments later with a pleased expression on her face. Diane opened the envelope and rapidly read the three pages and sighed as she set it down. "I miss her."

"What did she write about this time?"

"She told me stories of her children growing up and a few things about her husband. You can read it if you want. I figured you had already seen it when Barla gave it to you." Diane pushed the pages over to Amanda and thought about what she would write back.

Amanda looked through the pages and smiled at the stories Barla had written to her sister. They were similar to the ones she had been told when catching up with her aunt a few weeks before. She wished there were a way to get the two sisters reunited at some point, but the crossing through the gate blocked a person's memory so that would make it complicated.

"Are you going to write back?"

"Absolutely. This is kind of fun sending letters back and forth. I never dreamed a time would come when I'd be able to speak with my sister again and now this..."

"What is it, Mom?" She could see her mother was trying to hold back tears.

"I'm just being silly. So much time has been lost, but at least I know she's been happy and healthy. This outcome is so much better than what we believed for longer than you've been alive."

"Have you talked to Grandma about her yet?"

"No. What would I say? Your daughter didn't drown decades ago and she's alive, but you can't see her because she lives in a different world. She would think I'd lost my mind."

"There has to be some way. Grandma has to know her daughter's still alive. Wouldn't you want to know?"

"Yes. I already know how it feels to live with the thought you were gone. I wouldn't wish that scenario on anyone. I'll have to come up with something to tell her. Maybe Barbara, I mean Barla, could write a letter for Mom. It's so hard to think of her living with a different name. Did she ever tell you why she changed it?"

"No, but then again, I never thought to ask either. I'll have her write a letter for Grandma."

"Do that, and see if she has any ideas about telling Mom about her situation. I'm sure she's had time to ponder it all these years."

Riccan captured their attention and motioned toward the children and whispered, "Look at what they're doing."

Both women turned to peer into the living room. The children had constructed a log cabin from the play set and now they were making the blocks float above the house. The children were not using their hands to play, just their minds linked with the elemy through their birth crystals.

"What're they doing?" Diane asked with her brows furrowed in confusion.

"It looks like they're pretending to fly telepods," Riccan answered.

"Is that normal?" Diane had not seen any displays like this while they had played before.

"Not at their age," Riccan replied as he watched in fascination.

"I told you the children were learning fast. Alena was testing Juila's limits before we moved to Durseni. She was amazed at how many levels she was able to achieve."

"Where did she learn it from?" Riccan asked. He knew the levels could be difficult to learn as they were not a natural instinct. Someone had to have taught her.

"Jena taught her."

Both her mother and Riccan stared incredulously at her. Riccan asked, "But Jena hasn't been anywhere near her. Who taught Jena?"

"Elder Debbon must've since Jena taught Juila through their twin link. Alena once told me that Juila had made blocks fly across the living room while she chased them. I've seen her do it myself when we were at home in Durseni. When I asked her about it she told me 'her other self' showed her. That was how she described Jena since she didn't remember actually having a sister. They looked just alike so she believed Jena to be herself somewhere else."

"That's amazing. I wonder if it happens with all twins."

Diane remained silent as Riccan and Amanda spoke. Memories of her past dreams plagued her as they discussed her grandchildren learning to do amazing things with their minds and yet they both did not seem to think it odd at all. The journey to Tuala had changed Amanda more than she had originally believed.

Amanda saw her mother's expression and laughed out loud. "We sound insane, don't we?"

"I'm glad to hear you agree!"

"Things are definitely different on Tuala. You could tell the children were different the first time you heard them talk, right?"

"Yes, thankfully you had told us they were advanced for their age when you came home the last time. It was hard to imagine it as you described, but since these kids have been here, I understand what you described before. Their motor and language skills are much further along than Earth children their ages. How do they do it?"

Riccan attempted to explain, "The connection to the elemental energy through their birth crystal helps mature their minds. They're able to talk and move at a much earlier age so they're able to learn about the association between Tuala and Jehoban. Spirituality is an important part of our society."

"Why would Elder Debbon be teaching Jena if she's too young?"

"I'm not sure, but I'll be finding out. Elders are supposed to teach the children, but there are guidelines for when to start. Elder Debbon is the First Elder so he may have had a reason to begin which I don't know about."

"Will Alena get in trouble for testing Juila?" Amanda was concerned her friend would be reprimanded for her part in educating the children.

"No, testing is different than teaching. A test can be administered at any age; only the teaching is restricted to begin at the age of three. Willian should have started his training and it's possible Jena sat in on his lessons."

Amanda shook her head as she remembered a conversation she had had with Juila. "That's not what happened. Juila told me Willian was jealous of Jena's time with his father. She was learning how to use her skills and Willian was not included."

"Interesting," Riccan mused as he wondered what Elder Debbon had been thinking. This was a curious development.

"Let's go in the living room to watch the children play," Amanda offered. With the idea of leaving on her mind, she wanted to spend as much time as she could with her daughters. She hoped she was making the right decision with leaving them with her mother while she returned to Tuala. She did not actually have any real reason for going back except she wanted to say goodbye to her friends and family.

They spent the day in idle conversation and with being entertained by the children. They had lunch and moved to play outside. Amanda relished the time she had with her family as much as she appreciated hearing Riccan talk about his life on both Tuala and Earth. It sounded as though he had enjoyed an eventful childhood.

After Chris got home they continued to visit and finally put the children to bed. Diane had been thinking about Amanda returning to Tuala and she could not come up with any real reason for her to return. She decided to ask, "Amanda, why don't you stay home and let Riccan handle informing Elder Debbon of his son's whereabouts?"

Amanda had been anticipating this question and had already decided to tell her the truth. She knew her mother would not appreciate the implications of the actual predicament, but thankfully her father's influence and wisdom would keep her reasonable. "It's complicated, Mom. Do you remember when I first came home and told you about Bryon and Alena's children?"

"Yes. What's that got to do with this?"

Ignoring her mother's question she continued, "Do you remember how I told you their oldest son was betrothed to Andera? Andera was living with their family as their first-daughter. Well, it appears we have the same situation between Willian and Jena."

"Are you trying to tell me that Jena is betrothed to Willian?" She stood up, angrily pointing her finger toward the bedrooms, and continued, "You're saying those two children are supposed to get married?"

"Calm down, Mom. You're going to wake them up." She had known this reaction would come; her mother had been upset about the whole betrothal idea even without knowing the children involved. Having her granddaughter involved brought her mother to a new level of anger.

"What are you planning on doing, Amanda?" Chris asked calmly.

"I spoke to Alena about this before we came home. I was just as upset to think my daughter's future had been set without my knowledge or consent. Alena told me the contract was irrevocable unless I wanted to offend Jehoban. He has already helped me so much it would seem truly ungrateful to break the agreement."

Her mother looked at her in horror as she realized what her daughter was saying and asked, "Are you going to let this travesty happen?"

"The simple answer: yes. The complication comes with where Jena'll live. It would be unfair of me to take her away from the only family she's known, but it would also be cruel to keep her away from her sister. I'm going to have to figure something out with Elder Debbon and his wife to see what we can do."

"Amanda you're not making any sense. You have your daughter back; simply return Elder Debbon's son and call it even!"

Amanda sighed at her mother's obstinacy. "I think the sooner we get this ordeal sorted out the better off everyone'll be." She turned to Riccan and stated, "We should probably go back first thing in the morning, okay?"

"I'm ready whenever you are. Tomorrow works for me." Riccan felt distinctly uncomfortable in the face of Diane's anger. He knew her fury was not directed at himself, however he could not help but feel she was being unreasonable. "I'm going to head to bed now. Have a good night."

Amanda watched Riccan leave the living room and felt as though he had abandoned her to deal with her mother's anger alone. She could not blame him for wanting to get away. She had done the same thing by declaring the need to leave in the morning.

CHAPTER 5

Riccan had thought they would go back to Tuala as soon as they left the Covington residence, but Amanda surprised him by asking for something else. She wanted to see where he lived in Florida. Without missing a beat, Riccan teleported them directly into the garage of his suburban house. One of the considerations for purchasing the house with the three-car garage was that it was a large enough space to accommodate his telepod.

After setting the telepod down and powering off the controls, he turned and smiled at Amanda. "This is it. Home, sweet home!"

Amanda returned his smile and gestured for him to lead the way out of the telepod.

Riccan palmed open the passenger door and walked down the ramp into his garage. He turned in time to see Amanda's expression as she realized they were in a modern garage. He wondered if she had expected something more exotic given his actual origins.

"It's just an ordinary garage, but wait until you see the rest of the house!" He eagerly led the way across the concrete expanse to a massive wooden door. Riccan turned the knob and walked through the opening, turning so he could see Amanda's reaction to the home's interior.

Amanda could not help but drop her jaw at the beautifully decorated home which she could see from the garage entry. The dark colored hardwood floors appeared to be hand scraped. The walls had beautiful works of art as did the tables scattered throughout the rooms. They came to the kitchen which contained the highest end appliances, a huge island with an exotic granite top, the cherry cabinets extended up to the ceiling though even a tall person would have trouble gaining access to the highest shelves.

They continued through to the living room which had a gigantic flat screen television and a state-of-the-art surround sound system. The furniture was all oversized and luxurious. Amanda turned in a circle to take it all in and then saw the view to the backyard through the wall of windows. Of course there was an Olympic-sized swimming pool as well as palm trees and a perfectly manicured lawn and sculpted shrubs. She could not see any other houses nearby and wondered how much property came with the house to allow that much privacy.

Amanda kept whispering, "It's so beautiful," as they walked through the guest bedrooms, bathrooms, and the master suite. Somehow she had thought Riccan would have more rustic taste, but this house proved that idea to be completely inaccurate. Since they had arrived directly into the garage Amanda had a burning desire to see the house from the front exterior. She enthusiastically asked, "Can we go out front?"

"Sure, the entrance is this way." He led the way through a couple of rooms until they came to a gigantic foyer with a curving staircase. Amanda was not sure how they had missed that spectacle on the initial tour until Riccan said, "We took the back stairs when we went upstairs the first time." He unbolted the massive double-door entry and pulled the elaborate door handle toward him. The door swung as though it weighed nothing which spoke well of the balance of the hinges.

They walked side-by-side through the entry onto a massive front porch. Several chairs lined each side and looked out over a circular drive with a fountain with a jumping dolphin sculpture in the center. Amanda looked to see where the property ended at the front, yet failed to see that border either. Finally, curiosity got the better of her and she asked, "How much land do you own?"

"Fifteen acres. I wanted to have privacy above anything else. It didn't hurt that the house was perfect for my needs as well." He smiled as they continued walking down the porch steps and out into the sunshine. He was seeing the house through Amanda's eyes and could appreciate all over again the elegance and beauty of the property. They walked across the cobbled driveway until they were a sufficient distance from the house to get an accurate view of the entire residence.

Amanda turned around and mouthed the word 'wow' as she saw the elegant structure standing proudly before her. Everything was symmetrical including the three-car garage on each side. Massive white columns extended up from the entry porch through the second story to support another balcony. It almost looked like a colonial, yet it had a more modern flare. No words could adequately describe how utterly perfect and picturesque the house appeared. "Where is this place? Are we still in Florida?"

Riccan threw his head back and laughed before answering, "Yes, we're still in Florida. Not even that far from your parents' house actually. I'd say it's probably a thirty-minute drive south down the interstate. If you've seen enough out here then we should get back inside out of the heat and get something to eat. I have a fully stocked pantry."

At the mere mention of food, Amanda found she was ravenously hungry. They had left her parents' house rather abruptly after waking up. For some reason her mother could not be rational about Jena being betrothed and Amanda was done with the conversation. It was her decision, after all. She was grateful Riccan understood the customs of Tuala and did not have a problem with the arrangement. He seemed to think Elder Debbon's family was a good match for Jena.

"Do you think we could stay here for a couple of days without causing any trouble with getting back to Tuala 'in time?'" Amanda suddenly felt exhausted from all of the adventures which had been driving her for the past two years.

Riccan considered her question and looked over at Amanda. She did seem to be wilting into the couch now that they did not have any pressing concerns for finding her daughter. She must have been under more strain than she had been letting on. "Sure, I can make it work. What would you like for breakfast?"

"I don't care. I'll have whatever you're having. Thanks."

Riccan walked into the kitchen and stood facing the massive island. He concentrated for a few seconds before two plates appeared on the granite. He opened a drawer on the side of the island and grabbed silverware before picking up the full plates and returning to the living room. "Do you want to eat in here or in the dining room?"

"Right here, if you don't mind."

"No problem." He handed the plate down to her and took a seat beside her. "I hope you like fried foxl and scrambled eggs."

"They're my favorite, actually. Thank you." She leaned over the plate and inhaled deeply of the richly scented food. She started to salivate as she closed her eyes to give thanks for her food. "Amen," she said aloud as she set the plate on her knees and picked up the fork.

She was just about to dig in to her meal when she realized part of this dish would not normally be found on Earth so she asked, "How is it that you come to have foxl here?"

Riccan smiled shyly and replied simply, "As long as I own the food somewhere, I have access to it. The fact that it's stored on Tuala is no barrier to the power of the crystal. It takes a little more concentration to achieve, but once you learn how, it gets easier."

"Can you do the same with things other than food?" Amanda recalled Rasa's challenge in getting her message to Shemalla on Earth.

"Sure, but it does take practice. It helps that I come to Earth often. Are you going to keep asking questions while your food gets cold?" Riccan smiled to take any sting out of his words.

"Sorry," Amanda mumbled as she turned her attention back to her plate of food. Practically inhaling the meal, she discovered the taste rivaled the delicious aroma. "Thank you, Riccan, it was wonderful. Who taught you how to cook?"

"My grandmother, actually. She had a knack for seasonings. I'm glad you liked it. Let me take your dishes." He took her plate along with his own and imagined them clean and put away.

"That never gets old!" Amanda stared at his empty hands. "Do you think I'll ever be that proficient at using my crystal?"

"I don't see why not, after all, motivation is the best teacher."

"Tell me about your grandparents. What were they like?"

"Okay, well you already know my grandmother was sent over to the Roswell museum right after it opened. Murisa was a very social woman who loved to be around people, so it was no wonder she excelled at her job. She didn't believe there were any differences between the people from Tuala versus the ones from Earth; she treated everyone equally. Of course, she had to keep these opinions from Elder Vargen since he has always harbored a resentment for Earth's people ever since his son created the Roswell mess.

"Anyway, after only a few months she fell in love with her co-worker, Edwin. He was a talented engineer who was also a very skilled business-man. The first difficulty in their relationship came when she had to tell him about where she was really from. He, at first, thought she was kidding since they worked at the alien-inspired museum after all. After demonstrating her skills with her crystal she finally had him believing.

"Grandad Ed eventually decided her nationality didn't matter as much as his love for her did. He was naturally curious about her world and they decided to return to Tuala to be married. After several more months had passed they eventually discovered a way to get him to Tuala, but then they had to deal with the second difficulty in their relationship: Edwin lost his memory when he crossed the veil. Grandma Murisa took the challenge head on and made him fall in love with her all over again. Over time, Grandad Ed regained his memory and they were married."

"How did she get out of her contract with Elder Vargen?"

"That was a bit tricky since she had contracted to be at the museum for five years and only ended up being there for just over one. She began by telling Elder Vargen she wasn't suited for the position and she missed her family in Tuala. He ignored her pleas to go home and reminded her of their binding contract.

"Murisa was not someone who could easily be sidetracked from some-thing she had set her mind to do, so she did some research of her own. Eventually she discovered Elder Vargen's involvement in the trafficking of Earth's people into his research facility in Tuala. The program was in its infancy at that time and Murisa threatened to share her knowledge with the other Elders unless she were allowed to vacate her contract and go home.

"Elder Vargen was less than pleased to be cornered and he never forgave my grandmother for what he considered a gross betrayal. She was released from her service at the museum and told she could find her own way home as Elder Vargen denied the use of his Ascension Gate for her return.

"Luckily, Grandma Murisa still had access to her patil so she sent several petitions for help to her family and her local Elder. Her District's

Elder refused his Gate for her passage since he was afraid of retribution from Elder Vargen, but her family let her know of the cavern Gate located outside of Roswell. They gave her specific instructions for the passage, but nothing was mentioned about Earth people losing their memories if they went through an unsanctioned Gate.

"But, like I said before, they worked through that hurdle. Her family never knew Edwin was from Earth, but they sometimes mentioned some of the odd things he would say. Eventually, Grandad Ed set up a business supplying construction companies and my Grandma Murisa worked as his assistant.

"Within a year of being married they had my father and were very content with their busy lives until they sent my dad to school. Daven's test scores caught the attention of Jehoban's representatives and they all moved to Acaim so he could begin his extraordinary education as Jehoban's special student.

"My grandparents sold their supply business and started a consulting business once they settled into living on Acaim. Most transactions were accomplished using the patil with very little travel needed off the island. They lived a contented life. My Grandma Murisa spent many hours with her herb garden and invented new dishes to serve for meals."

"I assume she grew everything aquaponically?"

"You'd assume correctly. They enjoyed a very pastoral life on Acaim."

"You had said before you would visit family on Earth. How did Jehoban make it so Edwin would keep his memory through the transfer?"

"He gave him his own crystal."

"That must've been quite the ceremony!"

"Actually, no. My grandparents had been discussing the problem about travel in their home when a crystal appeared next to my Grandad Ed. As soon as my Grandad touched the necklace, he knew it was meant for him. He put it on that very moment and never took it off. He knew he had received a special blessing and he never took it for granted."

"Wow! I guess Jehoban really does listen to His people!" Amanda reached up and touched the warm crystal hanging from her neck. She felt blessed to have received her own talisman from Jehoban directly as well.

"Well, of course He does." Riccan looked slightly annoyed at Amanda's statement.

"That came out wrong, Riccan. I meant they didn't even have to ask for it in prayer or during a ceremony. Jehoban must have been very impressed with your family."

"He was. He also gave my grandparents access to His personal Ascension Gate so they could travel at their leisure. My dad got to experience both worlds as he was growing up which pleased Jehoban greatly. Like I told you before, my dad was eventually promoted to an Elder. My grandparents chose to stay living on Acaim until they both died about ten years ago."

"How come you say 'years' instead of 'anons?'"

Riccan smiled and replied, "It's a trick I learned as I was growing up. Whenever I'm on Earth I only use Earth terms and vice versa when I'm on Tuala. There's less chance of getting in trouble that way."

"That makes sense." Amanda stifled a yawn and turned her head to look out the window. She did not want Riccan to think his story had bored her, but she was feeling exhausted.

"It's been a long few days, Amanda, why don't you pick a bedroom upstairs and take a nap? There're a few things I'd like to take care of while I'm here."

"Okay, I think I'll take you up on the offer. I didn't sleep well after the argument with my mother last night. Thanks for everything, Riccan." She stood and headed toward the main staircase. She felt a little like Goldilocks as she tried to decide in which bed she would be sleeping. Eventually she opted for the room with the four-poster bed and the balcony facing out over the back yard. She climbed on top of the comforter, fully dressed, to try out the feel of the mattress and pillow. She did not remember falling asleep.

RICCAN SPENT some time going over the mechanicals of his telepod, making sure every fitting was secure and the parts did not have any wear. He had been so busy for the past few days he neglected the regular maintenance schedule. He thought he knew more than a small amount of paranoia played a role in his obsessive routine, he would rather err on the side of caution rather than have a mid-air incident.

With the inspection complete, he decided to walk the grounds of his estate while he waited for Amanda to finish her nap. Because of his frequent absences from the residence, he had hired professional land-scapers to care for his yard. His busy schedule prevented him from spending much time actually enjoying his property, so it seemed a good time to take a stroll.

He exited the rear door of the garage to walk down the stamped concrete path toward the pool. The drastic difference in temperature from the shade to the sun caused Riccan to reevaluate his original plan; instead of remaining on the path, Riccan veered across the lawn to intersect the garden trail. He breathed a sigh of relief as soon as he entered the forested area of the grounds, luxuriating in the tropical coolness and the fresh scents of nature.

As he walked along the shell-laden path, Riccan pondered Amanda's unique situation. The more time he spent with the woman, the more he realized she might be the one for him. His wanderings brought him to a bench where he opted to relax and contemplate his intentions regarding this complicated woman. Did he want to get involved in her drama? He felt he was already complicit in bringing her to Earth. He understood her dilemma, yet he still wanted to be with her. Obviously, she had received approval from Jehoban by getting her own birth crystal so he doubted many issues would arise should he decide to pursue a relationship with her.

Uncertain of how long he had sat in contemplative silence, Riccan realized he should probably head back to the house to check on Amanda. As his mother's example of hospitality had always dictated, Riccan's hosting skills required his attentiveness to his guest's needs. Although he had not really come to any life-altering conclusions regarding Amanda, he did want to spend more time with her, so he hurried back to the house.

"I STILL DON'T KNOW why we couldn't have stayed over at Amanda's house one night," Alena complained for the second time since arriving home in Kirma. She puttered through her kitchen, not really doing anything important.

"Look, Alena, there wasn't any reason for us to remain in Durseni. It just didn't make sense for us to sit around waiting for an indefinite amount of time to hear what happened. Amanda still knows how to use the patil when she's ready to give us an update. Besides, we have plenty of other things to keep us busy here at home with the kids, my job, and your patients," Bryon explained, holding up his fingers as he ticked off each item.

Pursing her lips in consternation at his mention of their kids, Alena recalled going to Tana's house the day before to retrieve the children and seeing their enthusiastic greeting when they spotted her. Overpowering guilt had her feeling as though she had neglected them over the course of the last few weeks in particular. The search for Amanda's daughter had consumed almost all of the family's time, even more so than it had for the previous two anons.

Without warning, Alena was suddenly left to carry on with her life as though nothing had happened. Amanda no longer needed her help; it felt as though a major piece of her life had been taken away. Alena's ruminations were interrupted when she heard a shuffling noise behind her.

"I'm headed off to work, hon," Bryon whispered as he came up behind his wife and put his arms around her tiny waist. He pulled her close to him, bending down over her shoulder to kiss her cheek. Unsurprisingly, she twisted around until she faced him, causing Bryon to smile down at her upturned face.

"I'm going to miss you." She reached up to pull his face down to her own and planted a resounding kiss on his lips. "Please don't stay late tonight. I just know we're going to hear something from Amanda very soon and I want us together to hear her news."

"I'll do my best, but please don't change your plans in anticipation of hearing from Amanda."

Rolling her eyes at his admonition, Alena nodded and decided on the spot how she would fill her day. "I'm going to continue the kids' crystal lessons. It'll give all of us something to keep occupied and they need the instruction and practice anyway. Will that please your sense of priorities?"

As if the announcement had prompted action, the kids in question came running into the kitchen, ready to eat breakfast and begin the day's adventures. The absence of Juila's toddling feet seemed to stab a fresh wound in her heart which Alena tried to keep from her expression as she leaned around her husband to smile at their children. "Who's up for crystal lessons today?" she asked cheerfully.

"I am!" the three chorused in unison.

"Then let's get breakfast going so we can get started, shall we?"

Bryon squeezed her arm tenderly and whispered, "I think this is the perfect idea." He gave her another kiss before releasing her and turning around to kneel down and hold out his arms to his children.

As if they had practiced a million times before, the trio rushed forward allowing their momentum to be stopped by their father's body. Rocking back on his heels with the combined weight of the kids, Bryon reached around to pull them close to his chest, dropping a kiss on each of their heads.

"Be sure to mind your mother," he admonished as he let go of them and stood up to take his leave. "If your hands are washed, then go sit at the table to be ready for your meal." Bryon had to smile as Kyelon rushed out of the room to wash up while both Andera and Justan took their places at the table. Giving Alena a quick kiss on the cheek, Bryon left the kitchen, hurrying slightly to keep from having to time his transfer to work in his telepod.

Only having to use a portion of her concentration, Alena instantly created four plates of scrambled eggs and fried foxl which appeared on the table. She sat down across from Justan, folding her hands as they waited for Kyelon to return. She would normally have spent this time getting Juila settled in her high-chair, yet the space remained empty beside her as another reminder of the missing pieces to her family.

The morning sped by as Alena instructed the kids, even relenting in her admonition against Kyelon learning the skills as well. Not only did she not have the desire to create more discord, she did not have the heart to tell him no when he looked at her so eagerly. Technically still too young, Kyelon should have waited at least another anon before learning the school's basic entrance exams.

As the children's skills began to get sloppy, Alena glanced at her time-piece only to discover several hours had passed and the children's nap time had arrived. "I think we've done enough crystal practice for today. Why don't we end our lesson with the basic song you'll be needing to sing on your fist day before you all go down for your nap."

The children groaned in unison.

Chuckling at their reaction she said, "I know you were hoping I forgot about naps." She stood up from the table at the same time as the kids.

They lined up and began singing. When they finished the short song, Alena smiled and clapped softly, "That was just perfect. You are the smartest little students ever! Okay, Justan you take the lead and we'll march down to your rooms." Alena's surprise compounded when none of the children put up any argument to laying down, which meant they really had exhausted themselves.

As soon as the tucking in ritual had been satisfactorily completed, Alena once again found herself at a loss for how to fill her time. Her mind returned to the song, hearing it as if it were new from the different inflections the children had used when singing it. The simple, catchy tunes were created to teach the children to remember their role in society. Sometimes she wondered if the songs were more of an indoctrination into maintaining peace, but then she decided it was not a bad thing in which to conform.

Wandering aimlessly down the hallway, she found herself standing in Bryon's office. Obviously, her mind had decided it wanted to know if Amanda had attempted contact. Alena smiled at herself, taking the few remaining steps to sit at the desk and turn on the patil. Seconds passed by before the machine hummed to life displaying several pop-ups, causing adrenaline to shoot through her system as she leaned forward intently, scanning each item for news. Unfortunately none of the waiting messages had anything to do with Alena's interest.

Sinking back into the chair, she sighed with disappointment. Surely Amanda meant to return to Tuala, if only to let them know what she had discovered. Alena was surprised it had taken so long, even though it had only been a day and a half.

Knowing she had another good two hours while the children napped, Alena decided to go over her patient records and determine who would need to be visited in the afternoon. Several clients were pregnant for the first time, so they were naturally more nervous about the whole process. Alena wanted to spend more time with them easing their fears and making them more comfortable with the pregnancy symptoms.

Alena preferred to use these checkups to familiarize herself with the woman's life-line so she would be better prepared when her delivery time arrived. Delving completely into her favorite subject, Alena soon lost track of time as well as her worries.

CHAPTER 6

Amanda came down the stairs to see if she could find Riccan. She had not expected to find him watching television on the enormous big screen in the living room. As she came around the corner she heard the roar of the funny car engines as they sped down the quarter-mile track.

Riccan spotted her out of the corner of his eye and immediately turned the television off. "I'm sorry, did the TV wake you up?"

"No, not at all. You can keep watching the races, don't let me interrupt."

"Are you sure? I was just watching John Force win another one. I think he's going to win the championship this year."

"Absolutely. I enjoy the races, too. Turn it back on." Amanda settled on the couch next to Riccan and pulled her feet up under her as she curled up.

Riccan aimed the remote at the screen and clicked the power button. The sounds of the engines immediately filled the room again.

Amanda had never experienced surround sound quite like Riccan's as the reverberations seemed to come from every direction, almost as good as being at the races themselves. After several rounds of cars went down the track, Amanda found herself no longer resting back on the couch, but rather leaning forward and cheering her favorites to the finish line.

Riccan smiled at Amanda's enthusiasm, soon involving himself equally in the viewing. He had never found a woman who actually wanted to watch the races. Certainly there had been plenty of women who had tolerated the sport to humor him, but he could tell Amanda was actually enjoying the races for herself and not for him.

When the racing ended, Riccan asked Amanda if she wanted to eat dinner. She had not realized her hunger during the excitement, but now the idea of eating sounded marvelous. She nodded her head enthusiastically and wondered what wonderful creation Riccan planned to concoct.

"I have an idea. How about we go out for dinner? I know of a nice restaurant not too far from here. I think you'd enjoy it."

"Sure, but I hope it's not too fancy. I don't have anything to change into if that's the case."

"Nothing fancy, you look perfect. Let's get going." Since Riccan had a plan, he was like a freight train in motion. Nothing could keep him from his forward progress until he had achieved his goal.

Amanda grinned at Riccan's enthusiasm, temporarily distracted from her own stress. Not knowing any better, she began turning toward the kitchen to go back out to the garage when Riccan grabbed her elbow and steered her in the opposite direction.

"The vehicles are parked in the other garage." He led the way with a foolish grin of anticipation on his face.

"Vehicles? As in plural?" Amanda asked quietly to herself, not really expecting an answer. Surprised Riccan would need to have a car, she then chided herself for her stupidity. Of course, Riccan would need to have acceptable transportation on Earth, since he could not very well travel around in his alien telepod and expect to remain unnoticed. Now she wondered just what types of cars Riccan would want to own; his taste in the telepod left her thinking they would probably be exotic models of sports cars.

Riccan opened the garage door and led the way across the concrete to the first bay.

Amanda almost laughed when Riccan opened the passenger door of a white 4-Runner; definitely not exotic or showy at all. Her estimation of Riccan's sense of decorum went up a notch. He did not feel the need to show off how rich he was in everything. Amanda sat in the vehicle and watched as Riccan walked confidently around the front of the truck and got into the driver's seat.

He reached up to pull the visor down, causing the key to drop into his outstretched hand. He pushed the garage door opener at the same time as he put the key into the ignition. The engine started immediately and soon they were driving up the tree-lined, cobbled driveway. They paused for a second as the gate registered their approach and started slowly swinging open toward them.

Riccan turned left out of the driveway, navigating the roads toward the secret destination, keeping Amanda in the dark until they arrived. Just as he had described, the pizzeria was only a few minutes away. He pulled over in front of the quaint building, pleased to see the smile of approval on Amanda's face.

A dress code definitely did not come into play with the informal setting and the casual waitstaff. The place had a down-home feel and the smells emanating from the kitchen left her mouth watering. Amanda sat in the booth, looking over the two-sided menu. She wondered how big the servings would be and whether to get a pizza for herself or if they were going to share.

As if reading Amanda's mind Riccan said, "Go ahead and order whatever sounds good. We can always take any leftovers back to the house."

The waitress came to their table and asked if they were ready. Both nodded and placed their orders. She told them it would take approximately ten minutes for the pizzas to come out of the ovens and then she turned and left them alone in their booth.

Amanda looked around and noticed there were very few people actually in the restaurant. "Why's nobody else eating? I thought you said this place was really good?"

"Oh, it is. We're just early for dinner and late for lunch. I expect by the time we're done eating the place'll be pretty full."

Unaware of the actual time, she decided she really did not care. It was enough simply to enjoy her time with Riccan. Amanda leaned her chest forward against the table and said, "Tell me more about your parents."

He smiled and leaned back against the booth seat as he considered what more to share. "Let's see, they met in school. My dad's sister actually introduced them."

"Wait, I thought your dad was an only child!"

"No, he has five brothers and sisters. My dad was just their first child, they had Sanda the next year, Stina the year after, then came Phen, Zuna, and finally Rucen. Rucen died in a telepod accident when he was just twenty-two which was really hard on the whole family. Since they lived on Acaim, they were all very close. None of the other siblings showed the same skill with their birth crystal so only my dad was part of the special teaching program with Jehoban."

"So you're saying they also have regular schools on Acaim? It's not just a school for gifted students?"

"Right, the families usually come with the gifted student, so they have other children who need their standard education. All of the children go to the regular school, whereas the gifted children have additional schooling tacked on to their schedule every day, sometimes including the weekends."

Amanda nodded although she still found the whole idea slightly confusing.

"Let's see...where was I? Oh yeah, I was telling you how Aunt Sanda introduced Mom to Dad. My mom thought he was nice enough for an older boy, but they didn't hit it off immediately. At the end of that year my dad graduated from what you'd call high school and decided he wanted to continue on to post-study. Once Dad wasn't around all of the time, then Mom realized she had feelings for him, so she attended the same post-study school as he did. They've been together ever since, but they didn't get married until after they both finished school, so Mom hurried up with her education so she could get done a year earlier."

"Did they have you right away then?"

"No. Mom wanted to have lots of children, but it was not part of Jehoban's plan. They tried for years, and eventually she did end up getting pregnant, but she lost that child long before her due date. The wise-women all told her it'd be dangerous to try again, but she had a dream in her heart to have a child, so they kept trying. A couple of years later they had me, but she never got pregnant again. She was very thankful to have even one. Dad used to say 'we don't have quantity, but we have quality.' Mom'd always wholeheartedly agree."

"That's so sad. Do you think that's why she decided to become a teacher?"

"I imagine so. She wanted to surround herself with children, even if they weren't her own. Her heart didn't know the difference and the children she taught all loved her the same as she loved them. She was the best teacher, her classes always received the highest marks on all of the tests. The District always shipped the worst students to her class to try to bring her scores down, but she was so loved by the students that she soon won over even the most difficult pupil and they learned well from her. She always created new games and songs to help them learn."

"It sounds like she really loved her job."

"Absolutely! She definitely found her life's calling. I think that was Jehoban's plan for her all along."

"Have you ever met Jehoban?"

"Yes, lots of times actually. Why?"

"What does He look like?"

Riccan cocked his head in consideration before starting to frown as he replied, "I don't really know. I'm sure I would know Him if I saw Him..."

"But I thought you said you'd met Him many times. How can you not know what He looks like? Rasa had the same reaction as you when I asked her what He looked like."

"It must just be His way. Maybe He doesn't feel it's important for us to know what He looks like, only that He is."

"I guess, but I still think it's awfully strange."

They dropped the subject because the waitress chose that moment to bring them their pizzas. Conversation ceased as they began devouring the hot and melty slices. Amanda sighed in delight as she tasted her first bite of the beef and pineapple pizza. True to Riccan's description, it was the best she had ever eaten. She wondered if they made their own cheese as it seemed so fresh and stringy. All thoughts except pleasure stopped until they were both full and resting with their backs against the booth seat.

Amanda was embarrassed by how much food she had actually consumed, but she was not sorry since it had been just as good as Riccan had promised. She was going to miss eating here when they went back to Tuala. She wondered if she would be able to come back anytime soon. She turned to ask Riccan about it, but then hastily shut her mouth as the waitress came back to their table to see if they wanted any dessert.

Riccan declined the offer after raising his eyebrows in question at Amanda and receiving an emphatic shake of her head.

With a chuckle at the response, she asked, "Would you like a to-go box?"

"Yes, please," Riccan responded.

She immediately returned with the boxes and their check.

On the drive back to Riccan's house Amanda paid more attention to the streets and other houses along the way. Counting only four houses between the restaurant and their final destination, Amanda noticed the fact each residence boasted many acres of land to maintain privacy. Each home, when she could actually see the building, was large and stately. Sometimes all she could see was an ornate gate at the end of the driveway and nothing else.

Riccan turned into the driveway and waited for the gate to swing in before he continued to drive slowly up the cobbled drive. Amanda marveled at the beauty of the landscape and asked, "Did you design all of this?"

Riccan laughed before he replied, "Yes, if you can agree that paying the best landscape designers to do their magic and oversee all of the workers! I don't exactly have what you'd call a green thumb, but I can really appreciate a beautifully landscaped space."

Amanda chuckled as well as she nodded her approval of the designer's choices of trees and flowers. She had always been interested in botany, but she had never had a yard of her own to decorate. This landscape would sure be an inspiration for a future project, if she ever got the chance.

They parked in the same spot where they had originally begun and went back into the house. Riccan put the leftovers in the refrigerator while Amanda made herself comfortable on the couch. Within a few moments, Riccan joined her and they began to talk again about the past.

"Tell me about yourself growing up in both places." Amanda wondered if his life would be similar to her own children's lives as they had family and ties on both Earth and Tuala. She hoped to hear from Riccan that it was an easy transition to ease her fears for her own small family.

"I'm sure the transition was easier for me since my father's an Elder and he had access to his own Gate. It would've been infinitely harder without that luxury, since I seemed to spend half my time in each place. You can imagine it'd be equivalent to learning another language as a baby, it comes easily and seems normal. To any other person from either

Earth or Tuala it would've seemed very strange indeed, maybe even scary."

"Were you ever scared?"

"No, I never thought about it. From the time I was very young my parents wanted me to visit with my great aunts and uncles and all of my cousins. They never knew where I was really from, but they were told we moved around a lot on mission trips. My family did travel on Tuala for Dad's duties with the District, but not as much as we made it out to be for the relatives' sake."

"Where would you stay when you came to Earth?"

"Sometimes with the family, but mostly we would rent a furnished house nearby and stay there for the month or so we'd be visiting."

"It sounds kind of lonely for a young kid. What'd you do for fun?"

"I usually found children my age to play with. Kids don't ask too many questions, they just want someone to play with them."

"What would you play?"

"We'd ride bikes, make forts, cut up the landscaping, and get into general mischief. Pretty standard boy stuff, I imagine."

"Did you ever get into trouble?"

"Oh, yeah. One time the next-door-neighbor boy, Andy Brun, came over and we didn't really have anything to do. I had this bright idea we should throw rocks into the road and see how close we could come to the cars driving by without hitting them. You can imagine how coordinated a five-year-old boy would be with throwing. I threw too late and nailed the side of a truck speeding by. The driver locked off the tires and immediately backed up to yell out his window at us.

"Andy looked at me with huge eyes, immediately turning to run back to his house, leaving me to get yelled at all by myself. Mom heard the commotion from inside the house and came out the front door to ask what was going on. I knew I didn't have any choice but to fess up, so I told the truth. Mom sent me into the house to wait in my room until Dad got home to punish me. She turned to the stranger and offered to pay for any damages. The man said he was glad I told the truth and not to worry about it since he was going to get the truck painted anyway.

"I remember staying in my room for hours and hours. I cried my little heart out because I was sure Dad was going to kill me. When he did get home, he could tell I had spent a miserable day punishing myself. He just sat down and told me he was proud of me for telling the truth and not just running away like Andy had done. He gave me a hug and told me not to throw rocks at cars anymore. I never did."

Amanda smiled at the idea of a little Riccan thinking his father would actually kill him for throwing rocks. "What other stories do you remember?"

"Let's see…when I was about ten I decided I wanted to try smoking. My uncle smoked and I thought it'd make me seem older and more mature. I stole one of his cigarettes and went and hid in the backyard behind the honeysuckle bush. I took only about two drags before I was coughing and sputtering. I decided it wasn't worth finishing, so I quickly dug a hole in the bark dust at the base of the bush and buried the nasty thing.

"I went back into the house and didn't think anything more about it until my aunt came racing in the house to tell my uncle the honeysuckle was on fire. They ran to put the fire out with the garden hose. They had no idea how it got started, eventually blaming an ember blowing over from the neighbor's burn pile. That was one time I never fessed up!"

"Oh, Riccan! That's terrible!" Amanda could not help but giggle at the near-disaster.

"As an older teenager, I spent more time here on Earth. I attended high school in Washington while I stayed with my great-aunt and uncle. By the end of my senior year, my buddies and I got a great idea to do a senior prank at the school. We drove out to old Farmer Joe's asparagus field and loaded up the decrepit outhouse into the back of my pick-up. The outhouse was well-built and must've weighed at least three hundred and fifty pounds. We took it back to the school and I backed up to the breezeway and together we hoisted it up onto the roof into a standing position. The seniors all laughed and talked about it until we graduated a couple of months later."

"How did they get it down?"

"I have no idea. The school never said a thing about it and we never saw it be taken down. Later on, during that summer after high school, my girlfriend and I went driving on the old country roads. I had borrowed her father's truck and, naturally, I felt the need to show off because she was in the vehicle. I drove too fast over a set of railroad tracks and swerved to avoid a car which pulled out in front of me when we landed on the other side. I lost control of the truck and ended up rolling it.

"When it was done rolling, it came to rest on the driver's side and slid down the pavement for a good fifty feet. Unfortunately, my hand was holding onto the window frame and my middle finger was ground down on the pavement to the first joint. Needless to say, my hand was trapped between the ground and the truck and I was stuck. My girlfriend panicked and ran away. I thought she was going to get help, but as it turned out she didn't.

"Luckily, another person drove up and stopped a few minutes later and he helped me get free. He saw all of the blood on my hand and said we should get to the hospital immediately. Knowing what I did about healing on Earth, as opposed to how it's done on Tuala, I convinced him just to take me home. I covered my hand with my shirt and told him it was just a scrape. Reluctantly, he drove me home.

"Dad knew something bad had happened…I'm still not sure how…and he was at the house when I arrived. He tied into my life-line and used the power of our combined crystals to regrow the bone, skin, nerves, and nail back to perfectly normal." Riccan held out his left hand to demonstrate how it had healed.

Amanda leaned forward and closely inspected the middle digit. She had no idea the healing could bring back missing pieces, but she was grateful that they had. She also smiled inwardly at Riccan's lack of under-standing about how his dad had known he was in trouble. As a mother, herself, she was able to see and hear what her children were doing through their crystals. Children and childless adults were never told about the power unless they became parents themselves. Only then would they be taught that aspect of the power of the crystal necklaces.

"Did you go back home to Tuala then?"

"No, I decided to go to college on Earth. I'd made a lot of really good friends and wanted to continue as I had been. I went home on weekends when I didn't have too many other things going on."

"Did you ever have any slip-ups where people looked at you strangely?"

"Not that I can think of. Why?"

"I made so many mistakes when I found myself on Tuala. They all looked at me as though I were an alien." Amanda started to laugh as she realized what she had said and then added, "Probably because I was an alien!"

Riccan chuckled as well as he could see where it would be confusing if you were not expecting to be in a new world and he said as much.

"I guess. I just hope it'll be easier for my children." Amanda sighed and thought about their futures.

Riccan remained silent, but he was thinking they would definitely have an easier time if he were a part of their lives. He surprised himself with his line of thinking because he had become convinced he would stay a bachelor after all this time of searching for the perfect woman. Amanda had landed in his life and had turned everything upside down, but he still felt at peace.

He realized it was so much easier being with someone who already knew about both parts of his life. With Amanda, there would never be a need for an awkward conversation and possible rejection. He had even more respect for his grandmother for daring to tell his grandfather. He had greater respect for his grandfather for sticking with her even with the truth known.

They shared more stories until it became so dark in the room they had to turn on the lamps. Together their evening was spent in perfect harmony and much laughter. Each person grew to find new things about the other which endeared them more to one another. Finally Riccan looked at his watch and was surprised to see it was after two in the morning.

Amanda stifled a yawn just as Riccan said, "I think we should probably think about heading to bed now." He smiled at her yawn and said, "And that just proved me right!"

"Ok, but this has been really fun. We should do it again!" Amanda stood stiffly from her curled up position on the couch and discovered her foot had fallen asleep. She stumbled into Riccan's arms as she fell forward with her first step on the numb foot.

"Do you need me to carry you?" Riccan was just teasing, but he would not have minded having her in his arms. He felt as though electricity were pulsing through him just at touching her this closely. He imagined it would be even more intense if there were more contact between them.

Amanda laughed nervously and said, "No, I just need to wait a few seconds for my foot to get some blood circulation." She sat back down on the couch and leaned forward to rub her foot to increase the blood flow. After stomping the offending appendage on the floor a couple of times experimentally, she decided it was probably safe enough to make a second attempt at walking.

They made it up the stairs without incident where Riccan gave her a quick kiss on the cheek and told her good-night before he turned and headed toward the master bedroom. Amanda had been surprised by the first display of affection and held her hand up to her cheek as she stood still and watched him go. After a few seconds she shook herself out of the stupor, whispered good-night to the now-empty hall, and turned to walk toward the room she had slept in earlier. She felt sure she would be dreaming about where that kiss could have gone had they been closer.

The morning came fast and Amanda was curious to see what they would be doing that day. She rushed out of bed and took care of her personal business in the bathroom, including a quick shower. She was pleased to see every amenity needed already stocked the luxurious bathroom. Within half an hour she had finished with her morning ritual and left her bedroom suite to see if Riccan were up and about yet.

Riccan spotted her coming down the stairs and rapidly prepared their morning meal. Since discovering she liked fried foxl, he made sure to prepare it in the extra special way in which his grandmother had taught him to bring out the subtle flavors of the tender meat. He concentrated on creating one more surprise which appeared on the counter next to the plates of food. "Good morning, Amanda! I hope you're hungry!"

Amanda looked up in surprise and noticed Riccan had already been busy in the kitchen. She would never get over her wonder at how easily the food could be created to order with just a thought combined with the power of the crystals they wore. "Good morning to you, Riccan. What have you made this morning?" She finished descending the stairs and headed across the foyer to get to the kitchen.

"I made your favorite again." He gestured to the plate of food before smirking mischievously. He pointed to the cup next to the plate and announced, "Plus a little surprise! I hope you like it."

With her curiosity now piqued, Amanda hurried the few steps remaining to step up to the island. She leaned over the counter far enough to peer inside the 'surprise' cup. She picked it up and smelled it before exclaiming, "This is steena tea!" She blew across the surface of the liquid before bringing her mouth to the edge of the cup to sip the hot liquid. The minty flavors burst across her tongue as she closed her eyes in pleasure while savoring the taste. "Oh, it's just perfect! Thank you, Riccan. This is just lovely."

"We don't have to stand, sit down on the barstool to eat, if you'd like?" Riccan pulled out a chair next to where Amanda had remained standing and pushed it back in as Amanda situated herself on the cushion. He pulled out the chair next to her and sat down, pleased to see his surprise had been met with enthusiasm and genuine delight. Getting to know Amanda quite well, he loved seeing her smile, which seemed more frequent with the reunion of her family.

They ate in relative silence with the exception of the forks clattering on the plates; it was the sound of a meal being thoroughly enjoyed. Before long all of the food had been consumed, including the tea, and Riccan used his crystal power to clean the dishes. After completing the simple task, he turned to Amanda and asked, "What would you like to do today?"

Amanda had actually been thinking the same question to ask Riccan so she smiled and replied, "I'd like a day of rest and relaxation, preferably out beside that pool." She pointed out the side window at the huge body of water sparkling in the sun as if it were inviting them to come out and play.

Riccan shifted his gaze toward the outside, agreeing it looked very tempting. "We only have one problem with that idea."

"And what would that be?"

"I don't believe you have a swimming suit."

Amanda's expression changed as she realized he was quite right. "Oh, I don't. I guess we'll have to figure something else out."

Riccan hated to see her crestfallen expression so he decided to make a slight deviation on her plan for the day and suggested, "Why don't we make a quick trip to the store, buy you a suit, and then come right back and pick up where we left off?"

"Really? You'd want to go to all that trouble?" Amanda asked hopefully.

"It's no trouble, really. Let's get going. I can already feel the day heating up without us!" Riccan slid off of the barstool and pushed it back in under the counter.

Amanda was quick to follow his example and soon they were heading off the property in the 4-Runner. She paid attention to the street names and the buildings they passed as they wound their way through the small city on the way to the store.

Riccan pulled into a parking lot of a small strip-mall. He had seen a boutique shop for women's swim suits, but he had never had an occasion to stop there before. He smiled inwardly at how much his life had changed since Amanda had come to be a part of it. He turned off the engine and said, "Are you ready to shop?"

Amanda rolled her eyes and said, "I don't actually enjoy shopping so let's get this over with, okay!"

Riccan barely contained his surprise since he mistakenly believed shopping became every woman's pastime. Thankful to learn this would be a quick trip, he anticipated spending most of the morning watching her alone at the poolside rather than pouring over the huge selection of suits with the 'helpful' sales clerk. Of course, he would not have minded seeing her demonstrate several dozen bikinis as she tried them on and asked his opinion of the cut or color. His interest would have been more inclined to see what was revealed rather than what the suit looked like.

With the precision of a seasoned shopper who hated to shop, Amanda hurriedly picked three suits in her size and asked to be let into a dressing room. She tried them on without needing any second opinion and finally decided on the suit she would purchase. She was slightly alarmed at the price of the tiny piece of fabric, but then mentally shrugged it off. *How often was she going to get this opportunity?* she thought to herself.

Amanda carefully put the two suits back which she had rejected and then took the remaining one up to the counter to purchase. She started to pull out her wallet to get her credit card when she felt Riccan pushing her to the side. She looked up at him with a startled expression.

"This was my idea, so I'm going to buy it." He already had his credit card ready to hand over to the amused clerk. Once the receipt was signed, Riccan accepted the bag from the lady and asked Amanda, "Are you ready to go?"

Amanda chuckled. "Absolutely. Let's get out of here before you decide I need something else for you to buy!"

Which always seemed to be the case, the drive home felt shorter. They parked inside the garage and walked into the house. Amanda carried the small bag as she took the stairs back up to her room to change into the suit. "I'll meet you out by the pool," she called down the stairs as Riccan continued on into the kitchen. She briefly wondered what he was up to, but then decided it did not really matter.

Once she was changed and ready to go downstairs, she wondered what she was going to use for a beach towel. She went into the bathroom and opened the linen closet. She was pleased to see there were many selections of colorful, plush towels from which to choose. Amanda picked the purple towel off of the shelf and furled it out in front of her. It was perfect. Wrapping it around her torso, she walked confidently out of the bathroom, through the bedroom, into the hall, down the stairs, across the living room, and out the doors to the pool.

She looked around to see if Riccan were already outside only to discover she had beat him. She looked up at the angle of the sun and picked the best pool-side chair to maximize her exposure. After unwrapping the towel from herself she draped it over the chair, sighing as she lowered herself onto the chair, and closed her eyes. She loved to sunbathe.

CHAPTER 7

Amanda must have dozed off because the splashing of several drops of icy water against her hot skin startled her awake. She instantly opened her eyes to look around for the cause. Unable to see anything amiss, she did notice suspicious ripples in the pool. A moment later, Riccan's head surfaced in the pool before he began making broad strokes with his arms to swim strongly through the water. Amanda enjoyed watching his muscles ripple effortlessly as he moved, recognizing he must spend a lot of time exercising in the gigantic pool.

Once he reached the far side he held onto the edge and looked back toward Amanda. He waved and yelled, "Come in, the water's great!"

Amanda, encouraged by his enthusiasm, got up out of her chair to take the few steps to the edge of the pool, and dove in head-first. She glided underwater as far as she could before coming to the surface and swimming across the top. Riccan's assessment of the refreshing temperature created the perfect way to keep cool while sunbathing. It took her longer than she expected, but she eventually reached the far side of the pool only to discover Riccan had dove underwater to head back the other direction. She pushed off from the edge to get as much momentum as possible while following him.

By the time she reached the side from which she had begun, she was exhausted and ready to get out. She pulled herself up to sit on the edge of the pool while she tried to catch her breath. She looked over to see Riccan taking another lap and she shook her head in wonder. While she enjoyed swimming, she was by no means a great swimmer. She slowly stood up, returned to her towel, and gratefully reclined back onto her deck chair.

"Are you done already?" Riccan called from the far side again.

"Absolutely! Keep going if you want, but I'm going to be soaking up some rays from the comfort of this chair!"

Amanda watched in amazement as Riccan proceeded to swim several more laps without taking a break. She could hardly believe the stamina it would have taken to go that far. She wondered if this were a normal workout or if Riccan were trying to show off for her. If it were the latter then Riccan would pay the price later with sore muscles. If not, then Amanda would be even more impressed. She could already feel several obscure muscles beginning to tighten up from her own minimal exertions.

Finally, Riccan pulled himself out of the pool and seated himself in the chair next to Amanda. He shook his head like a wet dog and sprayed droplets of water in all directions, including onto Amanda.

"Hey!" she cried as she shied away from the liquid onslaught. "That water's cold!"

"Sorry." His reply, accompanied with an impish grin, belied his apology.

Amanda narrowed her eyes suspiciously as she could tell just how 'sorry' he was and started to laugh. She closed her eyes and began to relax back in the chair when she asked, "Tell me about learning to be an Elder from your dad. What does that entail?"

"A lot of studying, really." He never knew what to expect when it came to Amanda. One moment she would be relaxed then the next moment she was intensely curious about one matter or another. The quickness of her mind kept him intrigued.

"What kind of studying? Do you have books on the subjects?" She had actually been teasing about the books. She was sure the lessons were handed down orally or on the patil.

"Absolutely! I have dozens of books, some of them are even here at the house."

"What? You're kidding!" She turned her head and squinted over in his direction since the sun angled just behind him above his shoulder.

"I'm not kidding at all. I keep them in a secret room behind the library. When we go back inside, I'll show them to you."

Amanda wondered if she were more intrigued by the idea of a secret room or by the contents of the books themselves. She could no longer relax in the sun and immediately sat up. "Don't keep me in suspense! Let's go look at them right now!"

Riccan chuckled at her enthusiasm and stood up. He extended a hand to help her up which she took. Really he just wanted a reason to look at her as she got out of the chair. She was slimly built and the bathing suit complemented all of her curves.

Seeing his gaze fall upon her body and feeling slightly exposed, Amanda hurried to get the towel wrapped back around her. She led the way back into the house. "I'll be back in a minute." She raced across the living room, up the stairs, and into the relative sanctuary of her room.

Earlier, Riccan had changed in the downstairs bathroom where he kept his bathing suit for convenience. He returned to the room and put his house clothes back on. He returned to the living room before Amanda had finished.

He had never shown the secret room to anyone, but then again, he had never met a person on Earth who knew about Tuala. Amanda seemed the perfect person in which to confide his secrets. If anything ever happened to him, at least there would be another person on Earth who could retrieve the valuable items and return them to Tuala.

Returning to Tuala would be another matter which he would have to discuss with his guest. They would have to go back today so the time difference would not become too burdensome. He was thankful they had spent just over a day resting, relaxing, and getting to know one another since he knew many time constraints would return as soon as they resumed their jobs.

Also, Riccan wanted to renew his offer to teach Amanda how to operate a telepod. It would be a comfort to him if she were able to navigate between the two worlds as he did. Naturally, it would take quite a few lessons before she became proficient in piloting, but the idea of spending more time with her pleased him immensely.

As if just the thought of her could make her materialize in the room, Riccan jumped unexpectedly as Amanda touched his arm and asked,

"What are you thinking about so intently? Oh, I'm sorry, did I startle you?"

"Why, yes you did, but that's okay. I was just thinking about a couple of important things we needed to get done."

"Like what?" Amanda was curious to see where Riccan's thoughts had taken him.

"Well, for starters, I really do want to teach you to operate the telepod. I think it'll be important for you to learn."

Amanda crossed her arms and looked at him warily before asking, "And what else are you planning?"

"I could give you a flying lesson today before we head back to Tuala?"

"When do we need to go?"

"I'm thinking we should head out no later than this evening. If we wait too much longer, the shift between both time and place will be really hard on our equilibriums; think of it as a severe form of jet lag."

"So soon, huh?" she asked, disappointment evident in her tone. "I guess I can't ask you to play hooky just because I'm having too much fun. Are you sure about wanting to teach me how to fly? I might be really terrible at it."

"Everybody is really terrible when they first begin, I'm not worried about your ability to learn. I've seen how easily you pick up new ideas at work, and I feel confident you'll excel the same way with flying."

"I'm glad you have confidence because I sure don't!" Amanda chucked and shook her head in amazement over the thought of actually operating the marvel of engineering. She hoped she would not disappoint Riccan's expectations. "What else do you have on your mind?"

"I want to show you the secret room where I keep all of my prized possessions from Tuala." He gestured for her to follow him into the library. "You'll be the first person to ever see it besides myself."

Amanda seemed startled to learn the last fact, causing equal parts of honor and alarm. Having only seen the library in passing the day before on her tour of the whole house, the room itself was impressive with its floor-to-ceiling bookshelves covered in classic, as well as modern, novels. Amanda wondered if there were an order to the books and also if Riccan had actually read them all or just liked to collect them for their appearance. The overall look seemed to support the latter idea, so Amanda inquired with a grand gesture including the whole room, "Have you read all of these?"

"Almost, but not quite all. I inherited quite a few books from my grandparents, aunts, and uncles, but I had already read through them when I lived at their respective houses while growing up."

Amanda nodded as she recalled his unconventional upbringing. There must have been quite a bit of time spent reading as he did not really know too many people other than his family each time he moved. She imagined it probably did not take Riccan long to make friends given his outgoing nature.

She stepped closer to the shelves to try to read the spines. She craned her head back to see all the way to the top shelf where the oldest books seemed to be stored. As an avid reader herself, she had collected quite a few books from the nineteenth century. Amanda's curiosity got the better of her and she had to ask, "How old is the oldest book here?"

"The oldest one I've discovered is from 1798. I attempted to read it, but the pages were so brittle and the binding was falling apart so I decided not to tempt fate and put it back on the shelf. As near as I could tell, the book was a naturalist's guide to herbal remedies."

Amanda itched to actually see a book as old as that one, but she refrained from asking him to show it to her. Instead she said playfully, "So where is this 'secret' room of yours?"

"I was just getting to that, it's over this way." He walked to the far side of the room, adjacent to the windows showing the view of the pool, and stepped right in front of the shelves. "Come closer and I'll show you how to operate the lever."

Intrigued, Amanda immediately stood close beside him. She smiled at the adventure of finding a secret place in the house, never had she imagined Riccan would have such a playful side as to create a space unknown to others. The more she thought about it, though, the more it actually made sense. She took a quick breath and asked, "What do I need to do?"

"Give me your hand." He put his own hand out, palm facing up.

Amanda placed her hand on top of his, also palm up. She was unaccountably nervous even though she knew Riccan would not cause her any harm. He pulled her hand forward under a shelf and she felt his fingers pressing up between hers as he sought to find the release mechanism.

He used his other hand to point to a book with a vibrant red spine and he said, "This book is the reference point for where to locate the lever; it should be just below it on the shelf. Now just a little further back…"

Amanda gasped as the lever shifted up until it was flush with the wood of the shelf. She had not realized the entire wall of shelving was actually the door. She stepped back and admired the efficiency of the setup. The 'door' moved effortlessly even though it must have weighed several hundred pounds or more with all of the woodwork and books.

Riccan watched her expression and finally said, "It's spring-loaded so it takes almost no effort to open it once the latch has been released. Come on, let me show you the inside." He pushed it a couple more feet inward and walked through the opening.

Amanda rushed to stay right behind him. The first thing she noticed was the air in the room was fresh, which would indicate a well-ventilated space. She should have expected no less given the opulence of the entire house. Riccan would not want to jeopardize the integrity of any of his special items with poor air circulation, which could cause mold or mildew.

She held her hands clasped in front of her to try to contain her excitement and curiosity. Given free reign, she would have been touching everything she could along the way. Textures seemed to thrill her senses, but she was making a conscious effort to contain herself as they walked into a room approximately twenty feet long and eight feet deep. Amanda noted the length of the room naturally matched the length of the library. The far wall also contained shelving, but this time it housed artifacts as well as books. She wished they had as much time as it would take to go through everything in the room, but Amanda realized it was not her place to even ask to see any of it. Just being in this room was reward enough.

Riccan walked over to the bookcase and kneeled in front of a cupboard. He opened the left door and pulled out an ancient-looking text. He stood up, turned, and walked over to a small desk where he gently placed the book. Riccan looked up at Amanda and smiled, "This is the most important item in this room. If anything were to happen to me, I'd like to ask for you to return this to my father."

"What is it, Riccan?" Amanda's fingers brushed her lips as she moved close enough to see the title on the cover.

"This is the Elder's Instructional Guide written by Jehoban Himself."

Amanda was impressed, but could not help but ask, "When was it written? It's surely older than 1798!"

Riccan laughed out loud, a hearty belly laugh, as he realized she was correct in her assumption. "Very much older, I'd say. There's no date in the book, but when Jehoban presented this book to my father He told him He had written it at the beginning of time."

"How long ago was that?"

"It's not for us to know, but I can safely assume this book is several thousand years old. The amazing fact is that the binding is still perfect and the text inside is impeccably legible. It may just be my imagination, but I think the text changes with the times. I've never had any difficulty in understanding the meanings of the lessons."

"Very interesting. Is it something I would ever be able to read, or is it reserved for Elders and their heirs?"

"I'm not exactly sure," Riccan answered slowly. "This was given to me when I was old enough to begin my training, but I'd never had anyone ask to look at it. I'll ask my father when I see him next and then I'll let you know the answer."

Amanda understood the reason for his answer, but it could not keep her from feeling slightly disappointed since she would be unable to peek in it today. She would have to practice being more patient. She could not help, but lean forward over the ancient text and wonder about its contents. Without her knowledge, her hand had reached toward the book and her finger touched the cover. She felt a strange tingle run up her finger and spread through her hand; this text was very special, indeed.

"Let me show you some of the other things I brought from Tuala." He turned away from the table and gestured for her to follow.

With more than a little trouble, Amanda managed to drag herself away from the text. She could still feel the tingle in her hand. The fact the text had most likely been in the hands of Jehoban was more than a little amazing. If just the cover could give her the reaction she had felt, she could only imagine how much more powerful the contents would be.

In a moment she had walked around the table and joined Riccan at the bookshelf. Her attention was immediately distracted from the book behind her as Riccan pulled a crystal skull from a niche in the bookcase. The object was not the type of item she would have thought would be of interest to Riccan as it was on the macabre side. "What is that?"

He held the skull up so the light from the ceiling height window could shine through it and answered, "This was given to my grandfather from his own grandmother from Earth. It has been in the family for at least seven generations."

"So it's not a Tualan treasure?" Amanda's interest waned.

"The family story says this skull has more power than any of us can know. My great-great-grandfather was told this is one of thirteen matching skulls. When all of them are brought together again then a power unlike any other will be activated. We're not sure if the legend is true, but we have been searching for other skulls on the off-chance it could be accurate." He gently set the skull back into the niche.

Amanda continued to stare at the object with renewed interest as the story Bryon had relayed to her came to mind. "I've heard about another skull, Riccan!"

"You have? Where?" Riccan felt a rush of adrenaline as he turned to face her.

"Bryon Kesh told me about when he was a teenager and he encountered one on his journey to Earth. He and another boy traveled through a gate in a cave outside of their town. When they got to Earth a Mayan woman gave them a skull to take back to Tuala. They freaked out and put the skull in a hole in the cave wall when they returned to Tuala."

"That's great! Now we know where another skull is located!" Riccan was already planning on how he could teleport over to the cave and retrieve the skull.

"Not exactly, Riccan. I used the same cave to return to Tuala and I know for a fact the skull is no longer in there," Amanda replied.

"Well that's unfortunate," Riccan felt a stab of disappointment at the missed opportunity. "At least we know another one actually exists, it is one step closer than we were before."

Amanda felt sorry for dashing Riccan's hope in finding another skull, but she could not let him have false hope. Her eyes traveled back to the ancient text on the table. She really wanted to see what was written inside. Finally she asked, "I know you're not sure if I should see the writings inside of that book, but do you think I could at least see what the writing inside looks like? Maybe just the cover page or something?"

Riccan smiled at her persistence and said, "I think the cover page would be safe." He took the two steps back to the table and gently picked up the old leather cover of the book to reveal the cover page, which he knew would be blank except for the name of the book. To his surprise, and Amanda's delight, there was more on the page than had been there before. He leaned forward with incredulity and read the new passage out loud:

"From a far-away land
There will come in time
Intuition is in hand
Strange details known.
With ties to the people
From one of my own
There will be a sign.
Those born to this one
Will transform all.
Lucinden will pursue
Elders will fall
Then all made new."

He looked up at Amanda in amazement.

"I wonder what it means," Amanda mused aloud as she read the passage for a second time. She felt a quiver pass through her. She looked back up at Riccan and noticed his odd expression. "What's wrong, Riccan?"

"I've looked at this book at least a hundred times and this passage was never there before!" He felt a shiver of excitement race throughout his body and he continued to stare at Amanda as though she were the key to the change.

"How strange! You did say you thought the book kept up with the times. I guess you were right!"

"I suppose so," Riccan mused. He had never experienced an actual change in the book, only that the dialect seemed to keep up with current trends.

"Why do you think it has shown up now? Has something changed since the last time you looked at it?" Amanda was intrigued with the mystery. She wished more than ever to be able to keep turning the pages to see what other marvels the book could contain.

"I don't know," he mused as he considered what he should do next. "I think we should write this down and take it back to my father to see what he thinks."

"That's a great idea." Amanda looked around to find paper or a pencil.

"I'll be right back! Don't take your eyes off of that page!" Riccan ordered as he rushed out of the hidden room only to return seconds later with the writing materials in hand.

Amanda watched as Riccan transcribed the odd poem into a small notebook. This was the kind of mystery her father would love to help solve. She watched as Riccan compared the two writings and then he finally closed the notebook and shoved it into his back pants pocket. "When are you going to see your father?" she asked even as she knew Riccan was planning the trip in his head for as soon as possible.

"I'm thinking we should probably stop in to see him before we make our appearance at work. I don't think you understand how important this could be, Amanda. Any change in this book is very significant."

Amanda nodded solemnly. The poem had sounded rather ominous considering it said the Elders would fall and Riccan's father was an Elder. She hoped nothing bad would happen to his dad. Then another thought struck her and she asked, "If the Elders fall, what would happen to Tuala?"

"I don't know, Amanda, and that's what scares me!" Riccan felt slightly sick. He needed to get out of the room and back to Tuala immediately.

"I know we had talked about going back to Tuala later this evening, but do you think maybe we should head out right now?" Amanda put the idea out there even though she really wished they could spend a few more days in seclusion at his home. She realized this was a selfish wish on her part and she needed to do something to repay Riccan for how supportive he had been in helping her find Jena.

"Yes, I think you're right. We need to go see my father as soon as we possibly can. Are you able to get ready to go in the next ten minutes or so?" Riccan's mind was already racing ahead to all of the things he would need to get done before he would be ready to travel. He could not get the sense of dread out of his mind as though he were having a premonition of something bad on its way.

"Sure," Amanda replied as she began moving toward the open book-case to head back to her room to pack the few things she had brought with her. She left Riccan to his own troubled thoughts as she went upstairs.

In her room she looked at the wet bathing suit and wondered what she should do with it. She hated to leave it behind, but she worried about it getting smelly if she packed it while it was still damp. Finally, she took it into the bathroom and left it on the edge of the bathtub to dry. If nothing else, it would give her a valid excuse to come back to Riccan's house to pick it up.

She scanned the room and looked under the bed to see if she had accidentally left anything behind. Amanda always had a feeling she was forgetting something and had to go over every surface at least three times before she felt she must have packed all of her things. With her small bag slung over her shoulder she left her bedroom with a sense of regret for having the retreat cut short because of her insane curiosity about the book. This really was all her fault.

Riccan was already waiting for her in the living room. He seemed quite anxious to be on his way so Amanda hurried her steps and smiled brightly as she announced, "I'm all packed and ready to make haste back to Tuala."

"Good! I've gotten everything situated here at the house. Let's get going!" He led the way back through the kitchen and out to the garage which contained the telepod.

When Amanda stepped through the doorway she looked around the garage in alarm. The telepod was missing! "Riccan, where did the telepod go?"

"What?" he asked with alarm and then realized Amanda did not know he had set the invisibility cloak around the telepod while it was on Earth. "Oh, that. I shield it when it's parked in the garage so the groundskeepers or housemaids won't accidentally wander through here and start asking unwanted questions." He walked confidently to the second bay and put his hand up to where he knew the palm pad was located to open the bay door.

Amanda was relieved to see the interior of the telepod even though the outside remained hidden. She had not really thought about needing to keep the aircraft a secret while it was in Riccan's private residence. There were a lot of things she would have to keep in mind if she planned on spending her time on both Earth and Tuala. She walked forward, entered the craft, moved through it until she was seated in the right-hand seat in the cockpit.

Even though Riccan was anxious to see his father he still could not pass up the opportunity to instruct Amanda in the procedures to activate the telepod for flight. He patted his back pocket to make sure the notebook was still there before he sat down in his seat, fastened his seat belt, and looked over at Amanda and said, "Pay attention, I'm going to teach you your first lesson on telepod operation."

Amanda looked startled that Riccan even wanted to do this right now. She thought to argue, but closed her mouth when she saw the look of resolve on Riccan's face. She merely nodded and watched attentively.

"Press this button right here," he pointed to a plastic circle on the dash.

Amanda pressed it and saw the panels light up in front of both her and Riccan. "Okay, now what?"

"When the display screens clear of all of their test messages, then you'll press the activate button on the touchscreen." He waited a few seconds and then pointed at the screen. "Right there."

"Can I do it from either screen?" she asked as she reached toward the screen in front of her and hesitated.

"Yes, they are both identically connected to the main system. Good! Do you feel us levitating?"

"Yes. Do I have to worry about us hitting the ceiling?" She anxiously looked up out of the windshield in front of her.

Riccan chuckled at her reaction and then answered seriously, "No, it's programmed to stay a few inches from the ground. However, if you are operating an older telepod then you would have to pay attention to the altitude from the moment you activated the flight switch. Good question. Now, using the touchscreen, tap on the navigate button and enter Florida Middle Ground. From that initial location we will then enter a secondary location to go to Pantano, Tuala, where my parents live."

"Where is Florida Middle Ground?" she asked even as she was typing it in.

"It's off of the west coast of Florida, it's just a point of reference really since it's just water below you. The actual coordinates are stored in the memory of the telepod. Here, let me show you really quick so you'll have a visual in mind while we travel."

He pulled up an aerial map and pointed to the spot. He had picked that location since it was far enough away from land to keep them from being seen. He wanted Amanda to get used to the idea of traveling here on Earth where she was already comfortable before he had her move across the veil to Tuala where she would be less familiar with landmarks.

Amanda leaned closer and could see the topography on the ocean floor was slightly different, otherwise, it just looked like water. She nodded her head and asked, "Now what?"

"Look over the entire dash and make sure you don't see anything lit up in red. Red is bad. If you did happen to see anything red, then you would immediately shut down the telepod and begin again. Never take off if there is any sign of trouble."

Amanda once again nodded, looked over the dash, and replied, "It all looks good."

"I agree. Now concentrate on the location we are heading to and, at the same time, press the activate travel button." Riccan did the same thing from his seat just to make sure they actually ended up where they intended.

Everything went black as they teleported between locations. With equal suddenness they appeared over the ocean in the brightness of the morning sun. Riccan's pleasure with the transfer immediately turned to alarm as he looked out the windshield and saw a small Cessna only a few yards out and heading straight for them.

There was no time to react before the two aircraft collided. All was confusion with the sound of screeching metal and breaking glass surrounding them. Riccan put his hands in front of his face to shield himself. He looked over and saw Amanda had done the same.

Never had he imagined this was how he would die, but he was glad the last thing he would see was Amanda. Both aircraft were now falling uncontrollably to the ocean below them as an explosion of gas surrounded both structures in a ball of flame.

CHAPTER 8

D r. Jasmine Medin did not like the look on Dr. Gascon's face as he read through her latest notes from Amanda's hypnosis session. She had been alarmed when Amanda had started screaming and saying all was lost at the end of her session. Jasmine had not thought the session would end on such a morbid note.

"Well it looks as though we can look at this one of two ways," Dr. Stephen Gascon declared. "One, she's finally come to terms with the delusion she's been having and put an end to it herself." He tapped the end of his pencil on the notepad before he continued, "Or two, she has finally decided she doesn't want to share with us and is declaring she would rather die than help us locate Neal Taivas."

Jasmine hastily sat forward and began shaking her head adamantly in denial of both assumptions. "Dr. Gascon, I think there's a third possibility."

"And just what would that be, Dr. Medin?" Dr. Gascon asked almost sarcastically. He did not like her always contradicting his diagnoses. As the Cannon Memorial Asylum Director of Psychiatry, he made the decision right at that moment that it was time to let Dr. Medin go. She obviously was not going to get a confession out of Amanda and he needed to move to more drastic measures if he were to get answers by the deadline imposed by the Taivas family.

"I think she is telling us that Neal can be found in the Florida Middle Ground!" she announced triumphantly.

"Hmph," he replied as he turned to his computer. He typed in Florida Middle Ground to see where exactly it was located and then shook his head. "That's nowhere near where they were sailing. This is just another false lead on Amanda's part."

"I don't think so. Please call the Taivas family and give them the location so they can check it out," Jasmine pleaded with her superior. She needed to buy more time to treat Amanda. She could feel her position slipping with every failed session.

"I'd like to thank you for your efforts with Amanda, Dr. Medin," Dr. Gascon began.

Jasmine could feel her heart racing as she listened to Dr. Gascon. She began to shake her head in denial at what she knew would be his next words.

"I've had a few matters come to my attention which concern me greatly," he continued.

Jasmine cocked her head and raised her eyebrows at this sudden departure from what she had imagined he would say next.

"I've asked a few questions of my own and have come to the realization that you have not been following my orders." He stopped talking to see if Jasmine were ready to admit anything to him.

"What are you talking about?" she asked with genuine confusion.

Understanding she was not going to admit anything he moved on and said, "The nurse's station has told me about you picking up Amanda's afternoon medication before her sessions with you. I also have proof you did not administer said medication, but rather you discarded it in the trash bin in your office. Do you deny this?"

Jasmine could feel the heat rushing up her neck and into her face. She had tried to convince Dr. Gascon that the medication was interfering with her ability to conduct hypnosis sessions with Amanda. He was the one who insisted on keeping her almost comatose with the dosages he had prescribed for her. She shook her head slowly and finally admitted, "It's true. I have been withholding the medication from Amanda."

An unpleasant sneer crossed Dr. Gascon's face and he went on with his accusations. "I've also been informed you met with Amanda in her room without authorization. You are familiar with the asylum policy to only meet with patients in your office, are you not?"

"Yes, Dr. Gascon, I'm aware of that policy as well. I just wanted to talk with her before her medication was administered. I only wanted to get you the answers you need. I never meant to cause any harm, I promise!"

"Your intentions are of no concern in this matter, Dr. Medin. You have willfully violated several policies and you have put a patient in danger. I have no choice, but to let you go. Please gather your personal items from your office. I'll have security escort you from the building in ten minutes."

"Please, sir, reconsider. I have built a trusting relationship with Amanda. If you take me away, then I'm afraid you might never get the answer for the Taivas family," Jasmine pleaded again. She felt her heart sink as Dr. Gascon continued to shake his head as she spoke.

"I'm sorry, my hands are tied. You are done here at this facility, Dr. Medin, you are fired," he said without any emotion.

Knowing it was impossible to argue with him any further she walked out of the office door and shut it behind her. She leaned against it with a sense of dread. Her mind was racing as she heard Dr. Gascon speaking on the phone behind her. She could not believe the next round of treatment he was suggesting for Amanda as he talked with another doctor about her case.

Without waiting to hear any more she raced to her office and gathered her file on Amanda and shoved it in her briefcase. She pulled each of her desk drawers out and grabbed everything personal and shoved them into a copy paper box she had below her printer. Next, she took the Rolodex off of her desk and threw it into the box and looked around the office for anything else which might be of help in getting Amanda free from this madhouse.

She opened her computer and inserted the flash drive into the side. She waited anxiously while she copied all of her case notes regarding Amanda onto the portable drive. At any moment she expected a security guard to show up and escort her from her office.

Jasmine was just picking up the box and her briefcase when the guard showed up in her office doorway and gestured for her to leave her office. She took one last look over her shoulder as she began taking a few steps to leave this unfulfilling job. There was more than a little relief because she would no longer have to work with Dr. Gascon, but then there was equal dread that she would no longer be able to protect Amanda from his plans for her future. Each step she took away from her office felt as though it were another accusation of failure.

As soon as she were able she was going to call the Taivas family and give them the update since she was sure Dr. Gascon had no intention of letting them know about the clue. Next she would be contacting Amanda's parents and letting them know their daughter needed them immediately. Finally, she was going to be contacting the Psychiatric Board to get an investigation started on Dr. Gascon's questionable tactics with the patients. She hoped it would be enough to save Amanda.

AMANDA SAT on the bed in her room and wondered why Dr. Medin had missed their afternoon session. It worried her to have anything change in her schedule. The only time where she felt safe was when she was sitting in Dr. Medin's office. As she leaned against the headboard she lifted her hand and held the crystal in her palm. She did not remember having the necklace even a few days before, nor did she recall anyone giving it to her. What she did remember was what she had told Dr. Jasmine about Alena giving it to her in a crystal ceremony.

All of those memories were beginning to feel like a long-lost fantasy as she stared around her almost empty room. The only things of interest were the comic strips a previous patient had taped to the wall beside the door. She had never enjoyed comic strips, but she did appreciate the irony of them being here in her room.

On impulse she decided to review all of the crystal lessons she remembered learning from Alena. The first lesson taught her how to pull the energy out of the crystal. She remembered how that was supposed to feel and she concentrated on the crystal inside her hand. It may only have been her imagination, but she could swear she could feel the crystal growing warmer.

Suddenly a ball of energy appeared in front of her. She smiled at her success and then moved onto the second lesson of moving the energy to a secondary location. Once again she focused her thoughts on moving the energy and was rewarded when it moved to the foot of the bed. Amanda completed the third lesson when she brought the sphere of energy back into her crystal. Either she truly had gone crazy or she had just completed the most amazing feat.

Not wanting to think negatively, she moved on to the fourth lesson by creating a breeze across her room. She chuckled when the comics fluttered against the far wall. To perform the next lesson she needed to have water. She crawled across her bed and jumped down to walk over to the small side table where the pitcher and cup was located. She poured a small amount of water into the cup and stared down on the contents until she could see small bubbles forming at the bottom which swiftly rose until the surface was bubbling with heat as the water boiled. She picked up the cup and poured the hot water back into the pitcher.

She poured a fresh cup and again stared at it attentively. Within moments she could see the edges starting to form crystals as the water began to freeze. Another minute went by and Amanda was pleased to see the water was completely frozen.

She startled out of her joy when she realized the door to her room was opening. The attendant came in just as she was settling back on her bed. Without trying to act as though she were up to something other than just sitting on her bed, she smiled a simpering smile at the big man.

"It's time for your afternoon meds," he announced as he went over to the side table. He picked up the pitcher and poured water into the cup on the table and looked down with surprise when he saw the ice cube lift from the bottom of the cup. He did not know what to make of it so he just shrugged his shoulders and turned to hand the cup and meds to the patient.

Amanda had a moment of panic thinking she would be questioned about the ice. She remained tense until the attendant turned as if nothing were out of the ordinary and handed her the two items. She reached out and tried to keep the shaking from being too obvious as she hurriedly took the medication and water. "Thank you," she said as she finished and handed the empty med cup back to the attendant, but kept holding the ice water. "When will I be leaving to see Dr. Medin?" she could not help but ask.

"Dr. Medin no longer works here. I'll let you know when you have another appointment," he replied without feeling.

She could not breathe until he finally walked out of her room and closed the door. *What had happened with Dr. Medin? Had she been responsible for getting the good doctor fired? What was she going to do to get out of here now that she didn't have anyone on her side?* Amanda felt nauseous. All of the accomplishments with her crystal would mean nothing if she did not have someone on the inside to help her.

She must have fallen asleep since she was startled awake when the attendant returned and shook her shoulder. Everything around her seemed fuzzy as the medication had fully taken effect. She wanted to roll over and continue her nap, but the man kept shaking her and telling her to get up.

Amanda sat up at the edge of the bed and waited a moment for the dizziness to pass before she stood up. She reached for her cup of water to ease the dryness in her mouth. After swishing the water through her mouth and swallowing, she asked, "Where am I going?"

"I was instructed by Dr. Gascon to take you to the exam room in the basement, now hurry up. We need to get moving," he tried to lift her from the bed by her elbow.

"The basement? Why would there be an exam room in the basement?" she asked in confusion.

"Don't ask questions, just stand up so we can go." He pulled harder on her arm until she was finally on her feet. "Can you walk or should I get you a wheelchair?" he asked as he worried they might not get to the room before the doctor and then he'd get into trouble for delaying.

Amanda thought the wheelchair would be a good idea, but she hoped the exercise would help clear her head for her upcoming meeting. She did not like the thought of going to an exam room, especially one in the basement. There was something off about this next meeting and she wanted to be able to think as straight as possible. She finally shook her head and said, "I can manage, just keep your hand on my elbow in case I start to sway."

They made their way down the hallway and waited for the elevators to open. Amanda continued to worry about the location of her appointment, but realized there was nothing she could do but go. The attendant would make sure she made it whether he had to drug her or drag her and she opted to keep her wits about her and create as little fuss as possible.

The elevator doors opened and they stepped in and turned around. Amanda watched the man press the button and the doors shut with a solid thud. The elevator dropped four floors and then opened into a poorly lit hallway. They exited and turned to the left. Amanda's throat grew dry as they walked toward the only room where the light was cascading into the hall. Just as she had feared, they turned into the room with the light on and Amanda started to turn back to the hall when she saw the empty chair in the middle of the room. She did not want to be in that room.

The attendant blocked her escape and started to push her into the room further. She had no choice but to move closer to the ominous chair. Her adrenaline kicked up a notch and the fogginess from her brain vanished instantly. This was a fight or flight situation and she needed to fly. She immediately looked around the room to see if there were any other means of escape, but only saw they were not alone in the room. Dr. Gascon was waiting in the corner with a smile on his face along with a female nurse she did not recognize.

"You may leave us now," the doctor said to the attendant. "Please shut the door on your way out."

"What kind of treatment are you planning for me, Dr. Gascon?" Amanda asked hurriedly. She hoped she could stall for time to figure out a solution to this problem.

"Amanda, I've given you plenty of time to tell me what I need to know about what happened to Nealand Taivas. You have been less than helpful during your treatment sessions with Dr. Medin. Now that she no longer works for me, it's my turn to get you to talk." He turned to the nurse and instructed her, "Please settle Amanda in the chair. Be sure to use the restraints."

Amanda felt herself stepping back as far from the chair as she could get. She would not be strapped to the chair and at the doctor's mercy. There was something wrong with the man and she had to get out before it was too late.

"Amanda, if you don't cooperate, you'll leave me no other choice than to sedate you. If we end up going that route then this will take twice as long. Please be reasonable and sit in the chair."

"No, no, no," Amanda said softly out loud as she shook her head. She could not be sedated, it would only make this twice as bad. Against all of her will she forced herself to step closer to the chair. Her heart was racing along with her mind. She had to buy time. "Can you tell me what you have planned?"

"My plan is for you to sit in this chair, Amanda. Let me worry about what happens next," he said calmly. Seeing she was not going to move unless he gave her something more he added, "I promise this will be quick if you cooperate."

She took a step forward still thinking as fast as possible. She had hoped Dr. Medin would find a way to help her, but now she knew she would have to help herself. Making her final decision, she warily sat in the oversized wood and leather chair.

"You've made a good decision, Amanda, I'm proud of you." He motioned for the nurse to fasten the restraints at her feet and hands. He did not move from his position in the room until after the first wrist restraint was fastened.

The nurse moved to Amanda's foot and hastily pulled the leather strap around the patient's ankle and buckled it tightly. She moved to the other foot and repeated the process. She walked to the other side of the chair and finished with the restraint on her right wrist. When she was done she stepped back to wait for the doctor's next instruction.

"Do you have anything you want to share, Amanda, before we begin?"

"I've told Dr. Medin everything I remember. There is nothing more to share about Neal. He's at home with his parents. His girlfriend is Angie. Why don't you go and talk to them?" Amanda's eyes widened as she started to panic.

"Please get the cart out of the storage cabinet and put the electrodes on the patient's temples," Dr. Medin instructed. He watched as the nurse turned and opened the cabinet door and rolled a cart with a lot of electrical equipment on it along with a mass of wires and electrodes.

The nurse advanced toward Amanda rolling the cart in front of her. She selected an electrode and pulled the paper backing from it and then stuck it to Amanda's right temple. She picked up the other one and leaned over Amanda to place it on her other temple. As she was straightening back up she noticed Amanda's necklace and turned to the doctor to ask, "Should she be wearing jewelry during this procedure, Dr. Gascon?"

"No, absolutely not. She hasn't had access to any jewelry since her intake. Why do you ask?" He moved forward to look at the patient. He saw the necklace and ordered, "Rip it off of her neck, we need to get started."

The nurse made to remove the necklace and yet she could not seem to touch it. She tried again and still she was unable. Finally she admitted failure and said, "I can't seem to get it off, doctor."

"Never mind, it's not like it will make any difference to the outcome of this procedure." He turned to the machine on the cart and started turning a dial on the machine until it would not turn any further.

"Whatever you're planning, please don't do this, Dr. Gascon." Amanda was near tears. She had never felt so helpless. She needed a distraction and she thanked the nurse for reminding her she had the power to do just that with the crystal around her neck.

"You leave me no choice, Amanda. You've already said you are not willing to tell me more, so I've decided to help you remember."

He fiddled with the controls of the machine for a few more seconds. He started to feel a rush of adrenaline at seeing how this patient would react to the treatment he was prescribing. The human brain was amazing and resilient and he was going to find out just how resilient Amanda's mind actually was.

"Put the leather strap in the patient's mouth. I'm ready to begin the procedure." He flipped the switch to turn on the machine and waited for it to spool up before he could press the activation button.

Amanda's heart was racing in her chest. She tried to resist the nurse's attempts to put the nasty leather in her mouth. Finally she felt her lips being pried apart, either she would open her mouth or her lips would get ripped off. She opened her mouth. In silence and stillness Amanda gathered power from her birth crystal. She would only have one chance.

"Step away from the chair," Dr. Gascon instructed the nurse. He was so excited to see how Amanda would react to the bilateral electroconvulsive therapy he could hardly stand it. He smiled sickly at his patient and said, "I'll speak with you in a couple of minutes." He pressed the button to begin.

Amanda felt the tingle begin on her temples and focused her energy on her last option. She had never attempted this before, but she remembered desperation was the best teacher. In only an instant Amanda teleported herself out of harm's way.

CHAPTER 9

Amanda heard voices around her, but she could not be certain of her location. Luckily, she was no longer strapped to a chair since she was lying on a soft mattress flat on her back. Her body seemed abnormally still so she concentrated on what she could do best: hear. She listened to the beeping noises around her and then the excited voice of a woman.

The more she concentrated, the more convinced she became of the woman's identity. Just a few more seconds and she was absolutely sure it was her mother. Finally, she had someone by her side who would make sure nothing bad happened to her again. She listened to her mother speak and her interest piqued.

"I'm telling you, we need to get the doctor in here right away. Check her machines! Her heart rate jumped as did the brain wave activity on the monitor!" she declared, immediately losing patience with the nurse's obtuseness.

"Mrs. Covington, we've seen this before and nothing ever came of it. Please don't get your hopes up. I'll look at the tapes, but I think it's another false alarm." Papers began to shuffle and the nurse quietly said, "Oh, my!"

"I'm right, aren't I?" Diane accused.

"This does look different. I'll call her doctor and ask if she will stop in to see her," she replied offhandedly before she checked the IV and the catheter bag. "I'll be back."

The nurse must have bumped into someone in the doorway since Amanda could hear the door open and the nurse had said 'Excuse me' as the door shut again.

"Oh, Chris, thank goodness you're back. Something happened with Amanda! I think she might wake up this time!"

"Diane, we've been through this several times in the past seven years. There's nothing to say she'll wake up from her coma. I think you should start thinking about taking her off of life support."

"Chris, how can you even suggest such a thing? She's only twenty-five years old. The doctors have all told us she's young and resilient. Any moment now she could wake up!"

"I would have believed you if she'd only been comatose for six months, heck even a year, but it's been *seven years.* It's too long, Diane, she's not coming back. We need to think about what's best for Amanda. We need to let her go," he said reasonably.

Seven years, Amanda thought to herself, *what are they talking about? I've only been here for a couple of minutes.* She tried to move her hand, but could only manage to twitch her finger. Fear started to overtake her as she tried and failed to move other parts of her body. A tear of frustration leaked out of the corner of her eye.

"There, Chris, did you see her finger move? Amanda, honey, can you hear me? It's your mother. Please wake up, honey. Wake up and prove to your father that you're coming back to us," Diane pled as she stroked her daughter's hair. "Amanda, honey, please don't cry. I know you're trying. I won't give up on you!" She stared accusingly at her husband until he sighed and sat down with resignation in one of the two guest chairs.

"Did I hear the nurse say she was going to call Dr. Medin?" Chris asked quietly. He knew when he was fighting a losing battle. Diane had spent almost every day for the last seven years at Amanda's bedside. He felt like he lost his wife and his daughter all in the same day. He wanted this whole nightmare to end so they could finally have some closure and move on with their lives. He did not think of it as being cruel, quite the contrary, he felt he was being merciful in letting their daughter have her final rest instead of keeping her alive artificially.

Dr. Medin is here? Amanda thought with renewed hope, *I know she'll help me!* She tried to take a deep breath, but realized her lungs were being filled with the assistance of a machine. All she had to do now was wait for the good doctor to come in and tell everyone what was really going on, Amanda did not have to worry anymore. The room was unaccountably warm and she was able to relax finally into a restful sleep.

Sometime later Amanda woke up to another voice speaking in her room. She listened in.

"I'm quite encouraged by this change in Amanda's readouts. With your permission, I'd like to give her a dose of epinephrine to see if we can induce her to wake up," Dr. Medin spoke to Diane.

"What's epinephrine?" Will it cause any side effects?" Diane asked. She was growing excited by the doctor's positive reaction to Amanda's latest records.

"In layman's terms, it's simply adrenaline. I'm hoping to excite her system to make her wake up," she explained patiently.

"Sure, let's do it," Diane spoke with renewed hope.

"I'll go get the dose myself instead of waiting for the nurses to get it. I'd like to see this happen right away as it's already been longer than I would have like to see from her recent activity."

"I tried to get the nurses to call you sooner, but nobody took me seriously!" Diane explained with exacerbation.

"I'm here now. Just one moment and I'll be back with the injection."

Amanda heard shuffling, a door opening and closing, her mother sigh, a chair scraping across the floor, and then silence. She wondered how long Dr. Medin would take to return. She had so many questions for the doctor, but she had no choice but to wait. A few minutes later she heard the door open and close, soft-soled shoes squeaking across the floor, and then the doctor started to talk.

"I'm going to start with a small dose and see how that goes," she said as she put words to actions and syringed a couple of mils from the vial in her hand. She reached for the IV valve and inserted the needle. She pressed the syringe plunger and removed the needle. Only time would tell now if the dosage were strong enough.

Minutes slipped by in silence. The two women split their stares between Amanda's face and the monitors to which she was hooked up. A spike in Amanda's heart rate was the first indication of the drug taking effect.

"If anything is going to happen, I expect it'll be in the next few minutes," Dr. Medin spoke excitedly. She had so much hope for this patient. More than anything, she wanted her to wake up so her family could finally go home. She had seen so many marriages end when the parents of comatose patients could not agree on the patient's outcome. This family was definitely special since they had remained together even after so long. "Come on, Amanda! It's time to come back to us. Open your eyes, Amanda."

As if she had been waiting for an invitation, Amanda finally opened her eyes.

Both women were stunned into silence, but only for a fraction of a second before Diane started crying for joy and Dr. Medin began racing through medical scenarios which needed to be completed. The doctor checked the monitors to make sure all of the patients vital records remained within safe levels.

Everything checked out so she spoke to the patient. "Amanda, please don't try to speak since you have a breathing tube in your throat, but if you can understand me, blink your eyes once slowly." She watched intently as Amanda closed her eyes and then opened them again. "Thank you, Amanda. Welcome back. Do you think you're able to breathe on your own?"

Once again Amanda closed her eyes and opened them again.

Dr. Medin picked up the nurse assistance button and pressed it. Once the nurse on duty came into the room she gave the order to have the breathing tube disconnected and the machine turned off. She kept watch over Amanda's vitals as the nurse followed her instructions. If her oxygen levels remained steady without the machine then they would be able to remove the tube entirely.

The machine was flipped off and everyone waited to see if Amanda would be able to take a breath on her own. Her chest lifted and fell once, twice, a third time and then the doctor was more confident in Amanda's ability to maintain her own breathing. "Go ahead and remove the tube," Dr. Medin instructed the nurse.

Amanda felt the need to cough as the tube slipped up and out of her throat. She was relieved to have the irritating thing gone. Now she would be able to ask questions of her own. She wanted to sit up, but discovered she was unable to move anything but her eyelids. "Why," she spoke uneasily with a scratchy voice, "can't I move?"

"You'll be able to very soon. There's nothing wrong with your body other than your muscles have grown very weak since your accident. We'll continue with your physical therapy and you'll be up and about in no time." Dr. Medin smiled at Amanda and patted her hand to reassure her.

"What happens now, Dr. Medin?" Diane asked with tears streaming down her cheeks. She wished Chris had been here to witness the miracle of their daughter waking up from her coma. He had gone to work for a last-minute project, Diane suspected it was just an excuse to get his mind off of this whole terrible situation. She dug through her purse and retrieved her cell phone. She flipped it open and dialed Chris' work number.

"Hi, Diane. Are you on your way home now?" Chris asked the same question he had asked every night.

"Chris, Amanda's awake!" Diane announced excitedly.

"What do you mean awake? Are you sure?" Chris tried to contain his excitement. He did not want to get false hope.

"Yes, I'm sure. They've taken her breathing tube out and she started talking. This is the moment we've been waiting for, Chris. Are you on your way over?" Diane never took her eyes off of Amanda and was impatient to get off the phone.

"Give me twenty minutes and I'll be there. I love you, Diane. I'm leaving right now!"

"Okay, bye," she said as she hung up the phone and dropped it back into her purse. She leaned forward and spoke to Amanda for the first time, "Amanda, honey, do you hurt anywhere?"

"No," she croaked. "Except my throat. Can I have some water?"

Dr. Medin turned to the nurse and said, "Can you get Amanda some ice chips?"

"Did you hear the doctor? She's sending for some ice chips to help soothe your throat. It'll just be a few minutes. Don't try to talk until then. Your dad will be here in twenty minutes. He can't wait to see you." She held Amanda's hand in her own and was pleased beyond measure when she felt Amanda's slight squeeze of her fingers. Once again the tears spilled from her eyes. Every day she had hoped for this outcome, but Chris' negative ideas had started to take root in her mind. She was so thankful she had stuck to her own convictions to keep Amanda's life-support going.

Amanda turned her eyes to watch her mother. She could feel a tear dripping from the corner of her eye. Never in her life had she been so glad to see her mother than at that moment. She had been so scared and alone in the asylum. She still did not understand why her parents had allowed her to stay in that crazy place and never even came to visit. Feeling tired, Amanda closed her eyes to rest. She felt her mother squeeze her hand. She opened her eyes again and tried to blow her a kiss to reassure her. Her lips did not cooperate and she just smacked them together.

The doctor could understand Diane's concern if Amanda shut her eyes, but she had to say, "Amanda is going to be extremely tired for quite some time. She's going to take frequent naps and you're going to have to let her so she can recover fully. I believe the worst is over, Diane."

"I hear what you're saying, but I'm just so scared she'll fall asleep again and stay that way."

"The vitals monitor will keep track of everything important. A buzzer will sound if anything goes below normal. Please let her rest." Dr. Medin once again reviewed all of the readouts including the oxygenation saturation to be sure the patient was getting enough oxygen. All was well. She wished she could stay, but she had to make her rounds. She spoke softly to Diane since Amanda's eyes had closed again, "I have to check on my other patients. I'll be back in about an hour."

Diane simply nodded, never taking her eyes off of her daughter's face.

The nurse returned with the cup of ice chips. Since Amanda was asleep, she set it down on the rolling tray and left the mother and daughter alone once again.

Chris walked into the room a few minutes later and felt an instant sense of anger and betrayal. He thought his wife had lied to him about Amanda's state. Before he spoke his mind he noticed a difference in Amanda, she no longer was hooked up to the ventilator. Just then Diane heard his intake of breath and looked up with the most beautiful smile. Chris had not seen such a look of peace on his wife's face since before their daughter had gone sailing with Nealand.

"She's resting right now," Diane whispered.

Chris walked over and sat down in the chair next to Diane and asked, "What happened?"

"The spike in activity I saw before you went back to work was different. The doctor gave her a shot of adrenaline and she woke up. Once they removed the breathing tube Amanda asked why she couldn't move and then asked for water to soothe her throat. She fell asleep before the ice chips arrived."

"Is she going to wake up again soon?" Chris worried they were in for a roller coaster ride if she decided to slip away again.

"The doctor said she would need a lot of rest as part of her recovery. She wasn't concerned about the nap. I've been holding her hand ever since."

"How long has she been asleep?"

"About twenty minutes."

Chris knew his daughter's condition had improved, but until he saw her eyes open and heard her voice for himself, he had a hard time convincing his brain her condition had changed. Chris reached over and took Diane's hand in his own. They sat in silence and watched their daughter's chest rise and fall on its own.

"When will the doctor be back?" Chris asked quietly.

Diane looked at her wrist watch and replied, "Probably in about forty minutes."

Amanda took a deeper breath and turned her head slightly to the side facing her parents. Her eyes flickered open and she saw her father next to her mother. She smiled weakly and whispered, "Hi, Dad."

Chris felt tears in his eyes as he stood up and leaned over his daughter and smiled with a trembling grin as he replied, "Hi, welcome back."

"Ice," she whispered.

Chris looked frantically around and spotted the cup on the tray. He picked it up and fished out a small chip of ice and put it into her mouth. "Do you want more?"

"Yes," her voice sounded slightly less hoarse.

They repeated this process until all that was left was water in the cup. Chris was frantic, he stood up and said, "I'm going to go get more ice. I'll be right back." He stepped around the bed and raced across the room and out the door."

"I think your dad is excited to see you awake," Diane smiled at her husband's enthusiasm.

"Me, too," Amanda whispered. She was not sure she could stay awake long enough to wait for his return. She was so tired, she felt her eyelids closing without her permission.

"It's okay to sleep, honey. We'll be here when you wake up again." Diane squeezed her hand lightly and rested her forehead on the edge of Amanda's hospital bed. She was so exhausted, she knew if she shut her eyes she would fall asleep and that was not an option right now.

Chris burst through the door with the new ice chips only to realize he was too late. He was immediately contrite for not thinking ahead that she might fall back asleep. "Oh," he said as he looked at Amanda and then took his seat again in the empty chair. He set the cup down on the tray so his hands would not melt the ice.

The next several days followed the same pattern of sleep, ice, whispered phrases, and the added sessions of physical therapy. These sessions were hard to watch as Amanda's muscles were severely atrophied and her limbs were so skinny. Amanda hissed as the therapist repeatedly asked her to resist her movement to help build the muscle back up. The added activity tired Amanda making her sleep for longer periods of time.

Amanda had sent her parents home so she could rest. When she woke up she was still alone, but she was ravenously hungry. She pressed the nurse assist button and waited.

The door to her room opened and the nurse asked kindly, "What do you need, Amanda?"

"Am I allowed food? I'm hungry," she replied with a smile.

"Let me check with your doctor. If she says yes then I can get you broth, jello, or pudding. Which sounds good?"

All of them sounded fantastic, but she decided on the first choice. "I'd like some warm broth."

The nurse smiled and nodded then left the room.

Amanda fell asleep before she had her answer.

Weeks went by and Amanda improved on a daily basis. She was getting stronger and she was able to sit up on her own and stay awake for a couple of hours at a time. Amanda had repeatedly asked about her time in the mental hospital, but her parents had looked alarmed at the outset, but then told her not to worry about it right now.

She was so sick of people not answering her questions. They always said, 'Don't worry about that just now. Put all of your energy into getting better so we can take you home.' At first the idea of going home was enough to make her leave it alone, but now she had more time to think and she wanted answers. When Dr. Medin came in one afternoon, Amanda decided she would confront her one last time.

"Hi, Dr. Medin. Do you have a few minutes?" Amanda asked diplomatically.

"Sure, Amanda. What's on your mind?" Dr. Medin settled her hip on the end of Amanda's bed.

"Why did you leave me alone at the asylum? I thought we were friends," Amanda asked matter-of-factly.

The doctor took a deep breath and waited a moment before answering, "We don't know a lot about what goes on in the mind when a person is comatose for so long. I do know you and I have never spoken before the day you first woke up and we removed your breathing tube. Do you want to tell me about what you remember of me before that time?"

"No, I guess not. Can you tell me what you know of how I ended up here?" Amanda changed the subject.

"I wasn't here when you first were admitted, but your chart said you were found by a local man in Cancun, Mexico. You were found face-down in the water on the edge of the beach and revived by the medical techs who picked you up. They didn't know who you were or where you were from so you remained in Mexico for almost three months before your parents were contacted by the local authorities. They had you brought back to this facility where you've been on life support ever since," she replied.

"How long have I been in a coma?" Amanda had a bad feeling about this answer.

"Seven years."

"Seven years? How old am I? The last birthday I remember was my eighteenth," she felt slightly sick.

"You're twenty-five now, but you still look eighteen. You don't age much when you're sleeping," she tried to reassure her patient.

"Can you get me a mirror?" Amanda had to see for herself.

"Sure, I'll be right back." Dr. Medin left the room. A minute later she returned with a pink hand mirror which she passed to Amanda's outstretched hand.

Amanda discovered her hand was shaking as she turned it around and saw her reflection for the first time. She closed her eyes for a moment in relief, she looked just the same as she remembered. There was a moment of panic thinking her reflection would show her an old woman, but that turned out to be unfounded. She let her hand with the mirror drop into her lap as she sighed, "Thank goodness!"

Dr. Medin laughed and said, "I told you you still looked the same. What else do you want to know?"

"I did go sailing with Nealand, didn't I?" Amanda was trying to determine if anything from her memories were true.

"Yes. They think a storm must have come upon you suddenly and the yacht capsized. You washed up on shore at least a week after the ship went down."

"What about Nealand? Is he okay?"

"I'm sorry, Amanda. His body was never recovered." Dr. Medin watched Amanda closely to see if she were going to have a bad reaction to the news.

"Never recovered? The ship went down? How long were we out sailing before the storm?" Amanda tried to get a time-line straight in her head.

"They think you sailed for a week before the storm."

"One week, another week, and then three months in Mexico. That's not enough time," she said to herself.

"Not enough time for what, Amanda?" Dr. Medin was concerned.

"What about my children?" Amanda suddenly asked.

Dr. Medin looked alarmed and replied reasonably, "There's never been any mention of you having children. I didn't see anything in your medical file to show you'd ever been pregnant. That must have been part of your brain activity while you were in a coma."

Amanda shook her head, something was not right. She knew she had been pregnant and delivered twins. There had to be some type of medical proof. "Can you tell if a woman has had a child before?"

"Sometimes," Dr. Medin began and then added, "Some women get stretch marks, their hips widen, and, if they had an episiotomy, then they'd have a scar. Would you like me to check you?"

"Please," Amanda agreed readily. She needed medical proof if she were to convince anyone to help her in her quest to find her lost children.

"Let me ask a nurse to step in," Dr. Medin said as she left the room once again. She returned with the nurse on duty and stepped beside Amanda's bed. "If you don't mind I'd like to examine your breasts first. They experience a change if you ever nursed."

Amanda nodded and felt slightly self-conscious as the doctor pulled her hospital gown down from her shoulders. She was already lying on the bed so she did not have to change position. She felt the doctor's fingers as she palpated the sides of her breasts and worked her way to the areola.

"Well?" Amanda asked.

"Your breasts are high and full which is not consistent. But if you didn't nurse them, then that might be inconclusive. Let me check your abdomen next," she said as she pulled up Amanda's gown to cover her chest. She lifted the gown from the bottom hem and examined her stomach. She did have slight marks showing near her pubic area, but not enough to be conclusive. "I'm not seeing anything to say you've been pregnant. Would you like me to give you a pelvic exam?"

Amanda nodded, feeling slightly embarrassed at the idea.

Dr. Medin dropped the bottom half of the bed and brought up the foot stirrups. She had Amanda move down to the edge and place her heels in the metal stirrups. While Amanda was getting adjusted, Dr. Medin opened a side drawer and brought out a speculum. She sat in the low, rolling chair and visually examined Amanda's genital region to see if any scarring were present.

She inserted the speculum and spread it open. She used the side lamp to light the area for her to visually inspect her cervix. Again, nothing presented to indicate a prior pregnancy. She closed the speculum and retracted it. She pulled Amanda's gown down to cover her up and said, "I don't see anything to suggest you've ever been pregnant, Amanda. I'm sorry, but I think you must have imagined it during your time in the coma."

With the exam over Dr. Medin thanked the nurse for her assistance and told her she would no longer be needed. She did not like the nurses to hear Amanda talk about her time in the coma. She had already created quite a stir among the staff just by waking up. She did not need any further comments to be made which might question her sanity.

Amanda trusted Dr. Medin, but she also knew she had carried twins and given birth to them. She wondered if the methods used to deliver children in Tuala repaired the effects of the birth as part of their treatment. She had never thought to ask Alena about it when she was living with them. She clarified, "You said you didn't see anything definitive, but it's still possible. Right?"

"Yes, it's possible, but given the time you were gone you didn't have time to carry any children to term. Please consider the possibility that it was part of your dream and not a reality, okay?" Dr. Medin wondered if she should have Amanda talk with a counselor just to get things straight in her head.

"I'll consider it because you asked, Dr. Medin," Amanda spoke quietly as she moved back up on the mattress so she was sitting up. She rearranged her clothing while the doctor lowered the stirrups and lifted the foot section of the bed. She watched the doctor rearrange the sheet and blanket back into place. "Thank you for checking," she said as she looked down on her folded hands.

"I've got some other patients to check on so I'm going to go. I think your parents will be back shortly. Will you be okay by yourself?" she asked. She hated to leave Amanda while she was in this delicate state, but she really did need to do her rounds.

"I'm fine, I promise. I have a lot of thinking to do, is all." She looked at the time and saw it was almost three o'clock. "One of my favorite shows comes on in a couple minutes. I'll probably watch that until my parents get here." At least she hoped the programming schedule had not changed much during the time she had been hospitalized. If not the show she had in mind, she would pick something else to occupy her befuddled brain.

"That sounds like a good idea. If you keep progressing this fast, I imagine we'll be letting you go home sometime next week. Would you like that?" Dr. Medin wanted to leave on a positive note. She knew Amanda wanted nothing so much as to go home.

"It sounds so good, I can hardly even imagine it will actually come true. Thank you for everything, Dr. Medin," she replied with feeling. She reached over and picked up the television remote and set it in her lap.

"You're welcome, Amanda. I'll check in on you before my shift ends tonight. Take care." She opened the door quietly and left the room.

Amanda did not want to think about what might be true and what might be fantasy. She aimed the remote at the television and turned it on. She flipped through the channels until something caught her attention. Staring absently at the show did not keep her mind from wandering back to the idea she was missing two daughters. There had to be another way to find out the truth to the matter. She would give her memories careful consideration, but she would not bring it up to Dr. Medin again.

Chris and Diane came together to her room. They were both smiling when they saw Amanda was awake and alone. "Hi," they both said in unison. They took their usual chairs.

Diane asked, "How was therapy today?"

"Fine," she answered and then brightened with her remembered news, "Dr. Medin said I might be released next week if my progress keeps up."

Diane grabbed her hand and gushed, "That's the best news ever! I just washed your bed sheets in anticipation of the day you'd finally come home. Isn't this wonderful, Chris?"

"Absolutely," her dad agreed. He could not wait to never step foot inside a hospital again.

They spent the afternoon talking about family and what had happened in the time Amanda had been sleeping. She was surprised to hear both of her sisters had been married and had children of their own. This, of course, reminded her of her possible loss. She changed the subject to ask about her father's work and any projects on which he was currently working.

The visit finally accomplished the goal Amanda had been hoping, she was too tired to keep talking. Her parents noticed her extended silences and her drooping eyelids. They told her they'd be back the next afternoon and left her to herself. She rolled over onto her side and fell asleep.

The next morning she met again with Dr. Medin. "Good morning, Amanda. How are you today?"

"Feeling stronger. I'm looking forward to going home soon."

"Yes, about that…I was wondering if you wanted to talk with a therapist before you go home."

"What kind of a therapist?" Amanda did not know what to think of this twist.

"A psychiatrist actually. I was approached yesterday by a preeminent psychiatrist who heard about your case. He would love to have the opportunity to interview you," she answered offhandedly. She really wanted Amanda to speak with someone, but she was not sure this doctor would be the right fit for her.

"What's his name?" Amanda asked.

"Dr. Stephen Gascon, he's the Director of Psychiatry at…"

"Cannon Memorial Asylum," Amanda finished for her.

"So you have heard of him!" She was actually surprised, but then saw the look on Amanda's face. "Are you okay?"

Amanda shook her head several times and then stated firmly, "Keep that man away from me. I want nothing to do with him. Promise me he won't ever set foot in this room!"

"Okay, Amanda, I promise. Would you like to tell me why you are so opposed to him?" Dr. Medin was very confused. She had expected Amanda to refuse, but her reaction was more like she was actually scared of him in particular. She was sure they had never met so she wanted to know Amanda's thoughts. An idea occurred to her and she suggested,

"You might want to make a journal of everything you remember from both before and after your accident. Just the act of writing stuff down can help clear your mind of any confusion."

Immediately reviewing everything she remembered, she realized she would have to keep all of her memories to herself. She did not want to find herself locked up again and put on so many drugs she could not put two thoughts together. "The journal I can handle, but I don't want to be interviewed by anyone. I just want to go home and get on with my life. I've already missed so many years and I don't want to waste another minute talking about my fantasies while I was sleeping."

"I fully understand," she agreed hastily and then added, "I'll let him know you refused."

"Thank you," Amanda sighed with relief. She had a nagging feeling this was not the last she would hear of this conversation, but she had to focus on her recovery and not the past.

"One more thing," Dr. Medin said carefully now that she had seen Amanda's reaction to the psychiatrist, "the hospital has been asked to provide some media coverage about you. Everyone is talking about 'the girl who slept for seven years' and they'd love to see who you are. Am I to assume you'd want to skip that as well?"

"You'd assume correctly." Amanda shuddered at the thought. She did not want to be on public display ever!

"We'll have to plan your discharge carefully otherwise the staff will most definitely leak your release to the media. Avoiding a circus outside the hospital doors would be in everyone's best interest," she mused as she worked out the best plan for Amanda to escape unnoticed. With how long the discharge paperwork process actually was she would have to get creative to protect Amanda's privacy. She would handle as much of the process as she could to keep the number of people 'in the know' as low as possible.

With an idea in mind, Dr. Medin smiled and said to her patient, "I know I told you there'd be a possibility of you going home next week. The staff know about it as well so I was thinking...we should probably do something unexpected!"

Amanda's eyebrows furrowed at the funny look the doctor suddenly had and she asked, "What are you thinking?"

"You've progressed better than I ever hoped and there's no reason why you can't continue your physical therapy somewhere closer to home. I think we should discharge you today, as soon as I can get the paperwork together. Nobody would expect it and you could get out of here without anyone gathering outside to try to get your picture. What do you think? Do you feel strong enough?"

"Are you kidding? Right now I feel as though I could run down that hall and not look back. Get me out of here!" Amanda could feel adrenaline coursing through her body just at the thought of being able to go home. Ever since she had woken up, heck even while she was dreaming, all she had wanted was to go home; now it could be a reality. She was overjoyed and nervous all at the same time. She would never admit the nervous part to anyone in case they would change their mind, but she had to get out of here.

"Okay, give me a couple of hours; the paperwork is a nightmare. I'll call your mom from my office and let her know what's going on so she can be the one to take you home. I'll be back before you leave," she said as she walked swiftly to leave the room and get things rolling.

Dr. Jasmine Medin was convinced the great Dr. Gascon would not take 'no' for an answer. She was sure he had connections with the hospital board who would force her to approve of the interview with Amanda. If Amanda were no longer a patient of the hospital then they would have no grounds to approve the request. For some reason she felt terribly protective of Amanda and wanted to see her safely out of the hands of the medical profession. Something about Amanda's questions about things which had happened while she was sleeping still haunted her. Amanda definitely needed to leave. She would make sure it happened today.

As soon as the doctor had left Amanda clapped her hands together a couple of times and sat on the bed with a huge smile. She could not believe this was happening so fast and yet she was so grateful the doctor was willing to help spring her secretly. She had not realized people had been talking about her even though she had seen so many people walk by her door and stare in her window. The thought of her being a medical curiosity never even crossed her mind.

Now that she was going to be leaving, she worried how much had changed 'on the outside' during the last seven years. Her mother had told her about a thing called 'the internet' which still sounded rather fantastical. She was curious to see if it were anything like what the Tualans did on their patils. Maybe she could do some research on her own to see if anybody else knew anything about Tuala.

There were so many things Amanda wanted to do once she was released. She started to feel overwhelmed with how much needed to get done. Her breathing started to come faster and she had to consciously take deep breaths and slow her heart rate so she would not jeopardize her discharge from the hospital.

"One thing at a time," Amanda said out loud to herself. "I just need to focus on leaving here right now. Maybe tomorrow, I can plan something, but today is all about going home! Going Home! Yes!" She smiled to herself and grabbed the remote and turned on the television to help pass the time until the doctor returned.

Amanda had watched a couple of morning game shows before her mother came breezing into her room. She could see her mom was excited, but trying to hide it until the door closed behind her then she squealed with delight and ran to her daughter's bedside to hug her immediately. "It's unbelievable, Amanda! You get to come home." Her voice started to rise in her enthusiasm and she put her hands over her mouth. "I know it's supposed to stay a secret, but I'm so excited."

"Sit down, Mom, you're tiring me out!" she halfheartedly joked. She felt bad when a look of concern crossed her mother's face. "I'm kidding, Mom. We need to act as normal as possible so why don't you sit down like you always do. We can talk about my sisters while we wait."

"Okay, you scared me there for a moment, but I understand." She grinned again and said, "You will never know how thrilled I was to get that phone call from Dr. Medin. I think I might have hurt her ear when I screamed for joy."

"I know the feeling! I will only admit this to you, Mom, I'm kind of scared to leave here. I'm sure there are so many things which have changed. You lived through it all so you won't have even noticed it, but it will all be new to me."

"Don't worry, Amanda. We'll go straight home where nothing has changed. We can take it slow from there, I promise." Diane patted her daughter's shoulder to comfort her. She had not really considered the changes over the years since her main focus had been keeping a vigil at Amanda's bedside. "We can discover the changes together."

Amanda smiled tremulously and changed the subject, "I can't wait to sleep on my own bed; this one is rather lumpy!"

Her mom chuckled and sat back in her chair. Her daughter had come back from the brink of death and she seemed no worse for her trouble. She never could have imagined an outcome this fantastic. She felt truly blessed and closed her eyes for a short prayer of thanks. When she opened her eyes again, Amanda was back to watching a game show. She turned her attention to the television and they passed the time, perfectly content, in silence.

CHAPTER 11

Dr. Jasmine Medin spent the morning going through all of Amanda's discharge paperwork. She usually had the nurses handle most of the documentation so she was surprised at exactly how many forms needed to be filled out and signed before a patient could leave the hospital. It made her have more appreciation for the nurses in how rapidly they handled all of the minute details. She tapped the stack of paperwork on her desk and sighed with relief at finally getting through it all.

Jasmine stood up and got an empty folder from the far corner of her desk. She put all of the forms into the folder so nobody would accidentally see the patient's name and alert the press. Trying to maintain her composure she left her office and walked down the hall to go to Amanda's room. A nurse stopped and asked her a question which she answered as fast as possible. She hoped she had not seemed rushed or blunt with the nurse. For some reason she was having a hard time acting normally even though she was not technically doing anything wrong.

She opened the patient's door and entered as she was saying, "Good morning, Amanda and Diane." She scanned the room to be sure they were alone and then held up the folder of paperwork with a triumphant shake.

"Is that Amanda's discharge papers?" Diane asked as she leaned forward in anticipation.

"Yes. I'm going to have you sign the forms, Diane, even though Amanda is of legal age. If I can demonstrate she will be in the care of her parents then there will be less questions as to her readiness for leaving." She stepped forward and placed the open folder on the rolling table. She moved it so it was between both Amanda and her mother. "As you can see, I have noted Amanda will be in your care, Diane, and that she will continue her therapy at an outpatient facility. I have a list of clinics who are currently taking patients, look through them and let me know which one you choose. I'll fax over Amanda's treatment plan thus far to whichever clinic you tell me you picked."

Diane nodded and looked up from the papers to the doctor's face.

"Okay, if I can get you to sign this form saying you will assume responsibility for the patient's care…good," she watched Diane sign with the pen she had handed her, "now you need to initial on each of the indicated sections for the next three pages."

Diane's hand was shaking as she initialed the pages. She did not even bother to read any of the items she was signing since she could not wait to get going. She turned each page and kept signing. She found another flag and turned to the page and then looked up at Dr. Medin, "Do you want me to just keep turning and signing everywhere you have marked?"

"Sure, I'll tell you what each one means as you go. That one is the discharge form. Next you'll find a release for mental health therapy should you decide she needs someone to talk to in the future. This one is for Amanda's medication should she continue to have headaches or any other side effects from lying down for so long. The rest are standard forms releasing the hospital from any and all liability during her treatment." Jasmine gathered the signed papers and put them back into the folder. "I'll go make a copy of these for you and be right back. Get dressed, I'll bring a wheel chair back with me so we can move you out right away."

Amanda suddenly realized she did not have anything to change into and said, "Get dressed in what?"

Jasmine stopped at the door, slightly flustered before answering, "I knew I forgot something. I need to get you your personal effects from the patient lockers. It's been there so long it completely slipped my mind. I'm afraid if the nurses see me bringing that bag to you then they'll know you're leaving. Let me get the copies first and then I'll bring the bag to you. Your mother can help you get dressed while I get the wheelchair."

As the door shut Diane said to her daughter, "I'm sorry, I should have thought to bring you some clothes. I was just so eager to leave the house to come and get you it must have slipped my mind."

"It's not your fault, Mom. Don't worry about it. Where did you park?"

"In the parking garage across the street. I should move the car to the emergency room parking so we won't have as far to go."

"Hurry, Mom."

Diane stood up and grabbed her purse from the floor beside her chair. She rushed to the door and then took a calming breath before leaving the room. She smiled over her shoulder, opened the door, and walked out.

Amanda could not believe how fast this was all happening. She looked around the room to see if there were anything in the room she would need to take. There was nothing personal which, in itself, was depressing. She scooted over to the edge of the bed and dangled her legs as she waited impatiently.

Dr. Medin and her mother both came back into the room at the same time. Diane had the personal effects bag in her hand and she was opening the drawstring top as she walked toward the bed. She dumped out the contents and picked up the strange clothing. These were not the items she had packed to go sailing with Neal, these must have come from the hospital in Mexico. With no other option she held out the shirt and pants for Amanda to put on.

Amanda reached out and had a moment of recognition: this was one of the outfit gifts from Barla. She hesitated, but then realized time was of the essence so she grabbed the clothing and stood up from the bed. She pulled the pants on under her gown, turned around and pulled the strings holding her gown on and pulled it from her front and dropped it on the bed. She arranged the shirt, stuck her arms in the sleeves and brought it over her head.

In a matter of moments Amanda was dressed and looking at both her mother and her doctor. "I'm ready."

"Take a seat in the wheelchair and I'll escort you out," she said as she held the handles on the wheelchair. She looked over at the bed and something shiny caught her eye. Jasmine leaned over and plucked a necklace up off of the bed next to the discarded garment bag. "Don't forget your necklace. Do you want me to put it on you?" she asked as she showed Amanda an ornate pendant crystal on a beautiful chain over to Amanda.

Amanda's eyes got big as she recognized her birth crystal. "Yes, please," she spoke breathlessly while she pulled her hair aside to assist the doctor. Once the chain was securely fastened around her neck she cradled the treasured item to her chest as her doctor began wheeling her out of her room for the last time. Her mother followed them both as she stuffed the discharge papers into her oversized purse.

They briskly went down the hall. Several nurses stopped their work to watch them pass by. Amanda wondered which one of them would be the first to call an outsider to come and take pictures of them leaving. She hoped they would be fast enough to avoid any scene at all.

Jasmine leaned toward Diane and whispered, "Where are you parked?"

"I just moved my car to the emergency room parking."

"Good, there's usually enough commotion going on down there where we might not be noticed."

They stopped at the elevator doors and waited for them to open. It felt like an eternity before the doors finally parted and they were able to enter. Likewise, the ride down to the first floor took equally long as they ended up stopping on nearly every floor along the way. Finally, they reached the emergency room and they walked swiftly through the crowded room.

As if by a miracle they did not encounter anyone as they walked through the double doors to the sidewalk outside. Diane walked ahead of them both as she wanted to get the passenger door open for Amanda to be able to get in out of the cold as fast as possible.

Dr. Medin stopped the wheelchair at the open door and stood ready to assist should Amanda have any trouble getting out of the chair. Amanda felt energized by the whole covert operation and she stood up and turned with her hand on the top of her mother's car and said, "Thank you, Dr. Medin, for never giving up on me. I know I can trust you. You've been amazing and I am just so grateful." She felt a tear coming to her eyes now that she was on the verge of leaving.

"I'm just doing my job, Amanda. I'm going to miss you. Feel free to come back and see me sometime." She looked across the car to Amanda's mother and said, "Diane, please call me if you have any questions or concerns."

"I will. Thank you."

Amanda sat in the passenger seat and put her seatbelt on. It was funny how just the act of putting on a seatbelt felt like freedom after being cooped up in her hospital room for so long. She wondered how often she would keep feeling a sense of euphoria each time she got to do something new. She smiled up at Dr. Medin through the car window as the doctor shut the passenger door and moved the wheelchair back up to the sidewalk.

Jasmine waved to the family and then walked back toward the emergency room entrance. She was thinking about the phone call she would have to make to Dr. Gascon and then all of the questions she would likely get from the Chief of Staff for allowing Amanda's unorthodox release. No matter what the consequences, she knew she had done what was best for her patient. She would have to keep that firmly in mind for the next few days or possibly even weeks.

Amanda could not help but stare out the window at all of the buildings, trees, people, and cars as they traveled. Everything looked different than she remembered. The cars were the most changed since so many models of cars had been released in the time she was sleeping. She had thought she would ask her mother what the cars were, but realized her mother was not very good with that sort of thing on the best of days; it would be a conversation her father would love to have with her.

The ride took about twenty-five minutes and Amanda was starting to feel the effects of all of her adventures catching up with her. The thought of the bed in her bedroom sounded like ambrosia. Finally they pulled into the driveway of their house. Just as her mother had said, the house looked exactly the same. Amanda was relieved to have at least one constant in her life. Her mother pulled the car into the garage and waited for the garage door to close behind them before she got out of the car.

"Wait right there in your seat, Amanda. I'm going to come around and help you out of the car. The last thing we need is for you to hurt yourself getting out and then we'd be right back at the hospital." She unfastened her seatbelt and got out of the car. She walked around the front and opened the passenger door. She leaned in and offered her arm for Amanda to use to lever herself up out of the seat.

Amanda was weaker than she had thought she would be. She was glad her mother had decided to help. She leaned heavily on her mother's arm all the way to her bedroom. Within moments she was spread out on top of her bed. She did not even care about the covers at that time, she was asleep within seconds.

CHAPTER 12

Amanda convalesced on the living room couch in front of the television. She had a view of the window out front so she could see people coming and going, but mostly she spent her time watching the news. Her parents had not let her use the computer yet, they said they wanted her stronger before she found new ways to exhaust herself.

She kept her journal on the coffee table so whenever she thought of something new to put into it, she would have it handy. Her mother had asked her what she had been writing and Amanda had answered her. She had also requested it remain private so she would not have to worry about what she wrote. Her mother had honored her request, but Amanda could tell she was terribly curious. Amanda was not ready to share for fear of being thought crazy and, therefore, being sent to a therapist like Dr. Gascon. She would not put herself in that position again.

There she was, thinking it had all been real. She did not know what had been real, if any, and what had been fantasy. She included it all in the journal so she could review the facts at a later date. At the moment she was afraid to go back over what she had already written, but she had a nagging feeling she would need to know everything.

She had been home for almost two months and she spent every

weekday afternoon in physical therapy sessions. Knowing the only way she would regain her privileges as an independent adult would be to be able to take care of herself again, she pushed herself at every appointment. Her physical strength had improved immensely, but her endurance still needed more help. Every day was an improvement.

On one of her outings to therapy she happened to see someone walking down the sidewalk who looked eerily familiar. She could not be positive, since it had only been a glimpse as they drove down the road, but she thought he looked an awful lot like Riccan. She did not know how that would be possible since she had only met him in her dreams. She had also met Dr. Medin in her dream, but she rationalized that by the fact she was treating her while she was comatose. Riccan was a different story. She needed to do some research and, for that, she would need to use the internet.

Today she would insist on using her father's laptop computer. She flipped through the channels bored with the usual choices of Maury, Judge Judy, or public broadcasting. With disgust she switched the television off and sat on the edge of the couch. She contemplated writing in her journal, but instantly dismissed the idea. Her mind was consumed with accessing the internet she had yet to see.

With her mother busy in the kitchen, Amanda went into her father's office and picked up the laptop from off his desk. She returned to her spot on the couch, plugged in the computer, flipped open the screen, turned it on, and waited for it to boot up. She startled badly when her mother appeared in the doorway.

"What are you doing, Amanda?" her mother accused.

"I'm definitely strong enough to do some research on the computer. You have to admit I've been getting along rather well, even the physical therapist told you I could stop coming every day." Amanda watched the computer screen rather than look at her mother. She did not feel nearly as confident as she sounded to her mother.

"I guess it can't hurt. It's not as if you're exerting yourself sitting on the couch," she admitted. Diane was going to speak to her husband about leaving his computer out in the open. She was not convinced Amanda could emotionally handle the things she was sure to be researching. "I came in to tell you that lunch was ready. Do you want to eat it in here or at the dining room table?"

"Here, please," Amanda decided immediately. She did not want to give her mother any opportunity to take the computer away now that she had it in her lap. Finally, the main screen came up and Amanda stared at the dozens of icons on the screen. She had no idea what to do now that the computer was ready since the operating system had changed so drastically.

She used the mouse to hover over every icon until she came to one named 'Internet Explorer.' Thinking that was the most likely one, she clicked on it and another blank screen which simply said 'Yahoo' appeared. She wondered what she was supposed to do with it when she finally noticed the box beneath the one word. She clicked on the box and typed in the one word which had plagued her mind most: Tuala. She hit the enter button and waited to see what search results came up.

Disappointed she scrolled through the screen and saw textiles and athletes with the name, but nothing about another world. She did not know why she thought it would be common knowledge since nobody seemed to know what she was talking about. That lead was obviously a dead end so she put in the next item she was intensely interested in finding out more about: Riccan Stel.

She entered the name and clicked enter. Her heart began to race as she saw several entries bearing his name. One of them contained a small picture and she clicked on it to get a bigger view. Once it loaded, she gasped as she stared at Riccan's face, the same face she knew from her 'dream.' She studied the picture and saw Riccan standing in front of an airplane. She tore her gaze away from the picture to read the caption below: 'Riccan Stel generously donates his time and his Cessna 182S Skylane to locate missing teens.'

Amanda had her first truth to her dream, Riccan was real. She was certain she had never met him on Earth before so there was no way she could incorporate him into her supposed dream. Uncertain how the internet actually worked she tried to locate any personal information such as an address or phone number, to no avail.

Diane returned from the kitchen with a sandwich and chips on a plate. She set it down on the table and sat down on the couch next to her daughter. She looked over at the screen and asked, "What are you looking up?"

"Someone I thought I knew. I saw him walking down the street on the way to therapy," Amanda replied as she leaned forward and picked up the plate. She was hungry, as always.

"Who is he? Have I met him?" she asked since she'd seen the picture of a man displayed.

"Maybe," she said offhandedly. Her memory had him staying in this very house, but that obviously had not been true since her mother did not recognize him. She bit into the sandwich and set it back down on the plate she had placed on the couch cushion on her other side.

She hit the back button and scrolled down through the other entries with Riccan's name attached. He seemed to be associated with NHRA Drag Racing and had even won a Wally which she could see a picture of him holding it proudly above his head while still wearing the racing gear. She smiled as she took note of the happy expression on his face. She missed the time they had spent together. If she could just find him again, she might get some answers to her millions of questions.

Because she had discovered Riccan was a real person and not just a figment of her imagination, she started to formulate a plan. The first course of action would be to regain her independence. To accomplish that she would need to go to the DMV and renew her driver's license. She missed the freedom of being able to get into her car and travel wherever sounded like fun.

She reviewed the last couple of entries in her journal which were about Riccan. The best plan of action seemed to be locating Riccan Stel. He was her last point of contact with Tuala so it made a certain sense to have him be her first point of contact to get back. If that did not work out then she would have to think of some other way to go back to Tuala. She had done it before when her family had traveled to Roswell, except for the fact it had only happened in her mind apparently. She could not worry about trivial details such as that right now.

If she had talked to a therapist about her latest obsession she was sure she would be locked up in Cannon Memorial Asylum. Instead she kept every detail of her plans in her head only. She could not even risk writing it in her journal for fear her mother actually did read it. Amanda was not normally a paranoid person, but her experiences, whether real or not, had made her extra cautious.

Amanda thought about what other clues she had readily available which would aid her search to find Tuala. Suddenly she raised her hand and touched the crystal around her neck. The warmth of the crystal was always present and she knew it contained a power all of its own. She was sure if she had it tested it would come back as a carbon-based stone such as that found on Earth, so that particular avenue was a dead end. The power the crystal harnessed would be something to look into when her mother was busy somewhere else.

She looked over at her mother and discovered she had been watching her closely. There was a look of deep concern on her mother's face. Feeling embarrassed at being caught daydreaming, Amanda swiftly looked away, picked up her sandwich and took a bite.

"Amanda, I wish you'd talk with me. You could tell me anything and I would support you. You know that, right?" Diane put her hand on her daughter's knee with the hope of getting her to open up about her thoughts.

With her mouth full, she just nodded and stared down at the sandwich in her hands. There were some things she just could not share; not yet anyway. She hated the idea her mother thought she was being secretive or withdrawn, but she could not take the risk in sharing until she had concrete evidence to support her story.

"I'll let you eat then. I have to go run some errands. Do you need anything from the store?" Diane asked as she stood up from the couch. She wished Amanda were still the outgoing and spontaneous girl she remembered instead of being so quiet and remote. Diane scolded herself for even being ungrateful for anything with regard to Amanda since she had practically returned from the dead.

"No thanks, Mom. I'm good," she replied as she tipped her sandwich to show she was going to continue eating. "I'm going to check out this internet thing a little more while I eat and then I'll probably go take a nap. There's no need for you to rush. You'll know where I'll be when you get back." She smiled at her mom to try to ease her worries.

Diane wanted to believe everything would be fine so she simply nodded and left the room. She had so much more time in her day now that it was not spent sitting vigil at the hospital. There was so much she had let slide over the years because of her worry for Amanda, now she was making up for lost time. Diane had even thought about returning to work now that things were finally getting back to normal. She would wait a few months before making a decision as drastic as that.

Amanda could hardly believe she had just thought about her mother finding something to do outside of the house and in the next breath her mother was actually leaving. She wanted to see if her necklace actually did have the power she remembered from before. It was as though the memory of her time in the asylum was designed to remind her of the crystal's power. Bursting with curiosity, she had to give it a try.

After a few more minutes of listening to her mother gathering her personal items, closing the door to the garage, hearing the car back down the driveway, and watching as her mother drove away, Amanda was anxious to test her necklace. She considered whether to leave the chain around her neck or to take it off, she settled on cradling the crystal in her hand. She concentrated and nothing happened. With more than a little frustration she recalled how simple of a matter it had seemed in the asylum. She wondered if her doubt played any part in her lack of success.

She finally gave up on her necklace and returned her attention to the computer. The screen had gone blank and she had to take a moment to renew her internet session. With the Yahoo screen back up she typed in the words 'Shemalla and Roswell.' She knew it was a long-shot, but Shemalla was the only other person she knew of who had any connection with Tuala. Amanda was not terribly surprised when the search results came back with nothing.

Amanda tried not to get frustrated with her lack of progress. She would just have to spend a little more time thinking through all of her clues. After about a half hour more time spent searching for random clues on the internet she finally decided to give it a break. She shut down the computer and returned it to her father's office. She took her empty lunch plate into the kitchen and put it into the dishwasher before she walked to her bedroom to lie down for a bit.

At the entrance to her bedroom she spotted the outfit which had been given to her from Barla. She raced over to the chair where the clothes were folded and picked them up. This was it; this was the clue she needed to prove Tuala was real. Barla had told her the clothing was made from foxl fur which was not a fiber which would be found on Earth. If she could have the fibers tested, she would have concrete evidence to back up her story. Amanda knew it would not prove everything she remembered, but it was definitely a good start.

"Thank you, Barla," she whispered to herself as she hugged the shirt to her chest. She refolded the clothing and set it back on the chair. With renewed hope she climbed into her bed, curled up, and fell asleep.

CHAPTER 13

Amanda bided her time and planned for her future while she waited for the doctor to finally sign off on her request to obtain her driver's license. Apparently, coma victims are not allowed to have driving privileges until they can go six months without any type of relapse. That time frame had come and gone and Amanda was chomping at the bit to regain her freedom.

At first she had only wanted to stay at home and feel safe, but slowly she had regained her confidence in herself and her surroundings. After the initial shock of seeing all of the things which had changed over the years, she was now used to the differences and was ready to begin exploring on her own. She was slightly disgusted by her mom's lack of confidence in her ability to take care of herself, but she understood how scared her mother had been for years.

Today was the day when she was meeting with Dr. Medin for her final check-up. She felt strong and healthy. There was nothing she could think of which would interfere with her getting her life back on track. She sat in the passenger seat of her mother's car as they drove to the hospital.

They parked in the visitor garage and walked across the street to enter the hospital. This was the first time she had been back to the hospital since she had first made her escape with Dr. Medin's help. She still smiled at the memory of that day. It had been both exciting and nerve-wracking, much like today was starting to feel.

After getting directions to the doctor's office, Amanda and her mother trekked through the hospital. Amanda was not quite sure what would be taking place with the doctor, but she imagined there would be a physical exam. She was prepared.

Finally, after a couple of wrong turns and questioning several nurses, they found themselves facing Dr. Medin's closed office door. Amanda knocked and waited for an answer. She heard a faint 'come in' and opened the door to reveal her worst nightmare.

Dr. Stephen Gascon stood up and faced Amanda with his hand outstretched in greeting, "Amanda, my name is Dr. Gascon. It's so good to finally meet you. I've read so much on your case I feel as though I already know you."

Amanda stood frozen with her hand on the doorknob. She did not move forward or even acknowledge that the doctor had spoken. The thing which startled her the most was that Dr. Gascon looked exactly as she remembered from her dream. She knew she had never met him before so there would be no way for her to know his steely gaze and over-confident, pompous attitude. Her eyes hastily shifted to Dr. Medin who was still seated behind her desk. The look on her face told Amanda she was sorry for the ambush.

Diane walked past Amanda and took Dr. Gascon's hand. "Hello, Dr. Gascon, I'm Amanda's mother, Diane Covington." She looked over at Dr. Medin and asked, "I was brought to believe we were meeting with just you today. Was I mistaken?"

"No, Diane. It was going to be just a follow-up, but..." she looked toward the Director of Psychiatry and finally finished, "Dr. Gascon insisted he needed to meet Amanda. He wanted to be a part of her follow-up evaluation."

Amanda had still not left the doorway so Dr. Medin walked across her office and whispered for Amanda alone to hear, "I'll be with you the whole time. Don't worry. Please come in so we can get this over with."

The trusted doctor's reassurance seemed to thaw Amanda's feet from the threshold and she finally stepped into the office. She was loathe to even touch Dr. Gascon's hand, but she forced herself to complete the introduction. When she let go of his hand she did not hide the fact that she wiped her palm on her pant leg.

Amanda picked the furthest chair from Dr. Gascon, glad her mother had chosen the one in between them. She could feel her heart racing just being in the same room as him. The confidence she had felt on the ride over had disappeared entirely and she sat in her chair, sullen, and withdrawn.

Diane saw the change in Amanda and wondered what could possibly have happened to create such a drastic difference. She had been hopeful that this would be their last appointment, but now she was not so sure. As soon as she had Amanda alone again, she was going to find out what was going on, until then, she could only sit quietly and wait.

"We're going to let Dr. Gascon ask his questions first so he can get to his next meeting," Dr. Medin spoke into the strained silence. "Dr. Gascon, if you would please begin."

"Certainly," he spoke toward Dr. Medin and then turned to face Amanda, "Can you please tell me what you remember during the time you were in your coma?"

Amanda paused as though she were considering the question and then finally answered, "I'm sorry, Dr. Gascon, but I don't recall anything from that time."

Diane's head whipped around to face her daughter. She knew she was lying since she had seen her daughter writing continually in her journal as Dr. Medin had suggested.

Amanda shifted her gaze to her mother and gave her a small smile. She hoped she would not say anything to contradict her last statement. If there were nothing to talk about then Dr. Gascon would leave sooner.

"Surely there are some memories. Please try to concentrate, Amanda. This is vitally important to my ongoing research."

Amanda pursed her lips and then thought of something to say, "I do remember Dr. Medin from my dreams, even though we'd never met before."

Dr. Gascon's expression lit up and he pounced on her statement, "You said dreams, so there were more. Please share."

Amanda could kick herself for slipping up and temporized with, "They were nothing, really, just memories from childhood and school. It felt like I was reliving the past in my dreams and Dr. Medin showed up at the end. The very day I woke up, actually. That's all I remember."

"Amanda, you are being very vague. Can you please elucidate on the exact dreams?" Dr. Gascon pressed.

"Look, Dr. Gascon, I don't know who you are and I don't really care, but I've already told you what I remember. I don't care about your research on multi-dimensional disorders and I don't want to be involved in it in any way. You are not my primary care doctor and you are not my therapist. You've had your chance to meet me, but now I'd like you to leave." She had to restrain herself from crossing her arms in front of herself as she believed that could be construed as a sign of weakness. She stared at him until he looked away.

Diane simply stared at her daughter, appalled at how rudely she had just spoken to this stranger. She could not understand the change which had come over Amanda. She was more than a little scared.

"Who told you I was researching multi-dimensional disorders? I just began my documentation on it earlier this week." He looked accusingly toward Dr. Medin who shook her head in denial.

"Call it a lucky guess, or intuition, or psychic for all I care, Dr. Gascon, I'm not interested in participating," she stated flatly and twisted her body to look out the window.

Dr. Gascon turned his attention to Dr. Medin and said, "Your patient reports failed to mention anything about the patient being defensive and aggressive. I would suggest she would benefit from meeting with a therapist to resolve these issues."

"No, it did not, possibly because she has never displayed those traits before. I think it might be because of this ambush-style interview on which you insisted. I've offered therapy as on option, though your concern is noted," Dr. Medin spoke carefully. "I believe the patient has made it clear your interview is over, Dr. Gascon. Thank you for coming." She stood up and offered her hand to the other doctor.

Dr. Gascon shook her hand and turned to Amanda and spoke quietly, "I'm sorry if I offended you, Amanda. It was nice making your acquaintance, Amanda, Mrs. Covington. Have a nice day." He made eye contact with both daughter and mother before he gathered his briefcase and notes and made his way out of the office. His movements were jerky in his controlled anger.

Amanda had made an enemy and she could not find the desire to even care. She felt euphoric when Dr. Gascon actually left the room. She exhaled loudly when the door shut loudly behind her and she smiled half-heartedly at the remaining doctor.

"I wish you hadn't done that, Amanda," Dr. Medin said softly. "Dr. Gascon has some friends in high places and he can be very persistent."

"Why was he even here?" Diane asked snippily.

"He had requested an interview with Amanda before she was discharged. I had asked Amanda if she wanted to meet with him and she refused. To avoid any delays in her release from the hospital because of Dr. Gascon's authority, I let Amanda go home a week before I had originally planned. When I let Dr. Gascon know she had been released he had been livid. He had actually called for me to be fired because of negligence. Luckily the board did not see the situation as he had described it so I was allowed to stay on with the caveat that when you returned for your follow-up then Dr. Gascon would be allowed to interview you.

"We would normally have had several follow-up sessions before now, but I wanted to give Amanda plenty of time to recover before being subjected to his line of questions. I'm sorry for the deception on my part, but I was sworn to secrecy until Dr. Gascon met with you."

Amanda had the sense to feel sorry for how she had acted. There were much better ways to have handled the interview with the shrink, but she had been flustered. "I'm sorry, too, Dr. Medin. I just do not like that man. I don't trust him and I didn't ever want to be in the same room with him again."

Jasmine heard the change in tense when Amanda had spoken about meeting Dr. Gascon, it was almost as if she believed she had met him before. She knew this was not the case since she had inquired of Stephen his level of interest in her patient. He had simply said he was researching long-term coma recovery methods and wanted to meet with her fascinating patient. If he had known her before she felt certain he would have mentioned it at that time.

"Okay, I think we should get going on my final evaluation of your progress, if you don't mind," Dr. Medin said in a lighter tone. She wanted to forget all of the unpleasantness Dr. Gascon had caused. Amanda seemed to be relaxing now that he had left the room. She was pleased to see she seemed to have a better air of confidence than she had shown upon her discharge. Naturally, it was to be expected since she had had time to reacquaint herself with life again.

"Sure, what do I need to do?" Amanda asked pleasantly.

"I'd like to check your vitals first," she said as she took the stethoscope from around her neck as she approached Amanda's seat. She put the stems in her ears and she positioned the other end over Amanda's heart on her chest. She then checked her lungs and marked the findings on her chart. Dr. Medin then took her blood pressure. Everything checked out normally.

She asked Amanda to sit on her desk, since she didn't have a patient table, and checked her reflexes in her legs as well as her arms. She also looked at her eyes to make sure there were no abnormalities. "How are your physical therapy sessions going? Do you feel they are still of benefit?"

"They're fine, I guess. I don't get sore anymore from the exercises. I'd probably get the same benefit if I joined a gym."

"So your strength is good, how about your stamina? Do you still need to take frequent naps?"

"Not as often, usually only once or twice a day now instead of five or six."

"Good, it sounds as though you are progressing normally. I don't think you need to continue with the physical therapy. Do you have any questions or concerns?"

"No, or yes, I mean. After today's meeting, will you sign off on my form for applying for a driver's license?"

"Have you had any episodes of dizziness or confusion?"

"None. I feel perfect! I'm ready to get back out into the world."

"Okay, I'll sign the form, but, Amanda," she paused to make sure her patient took her seriously, "I do think it would be in your best interest to talk with a therapist. I've told you that in the past as well, but I haven't seen anything to indicate you have used that option."

"I don't want to see a shrink. No offense, Dr. Medin. I did take your advice and I've been writing a journal of everything I can recall."

Diane was relieved to hear her daughter telling the truth to Dr. Medin.

"That's great. Have you found it to be helpful in sorting out your memories?"

"Very. It was a great idea. Some things have grown fuzzy in my memory since coming home, so I'm glad to have an accounting of the memories while they were still fresh."

"So you did have more dreams than you let on with Dr. Gascon?" Dr. Medin was genuinely interested in what had transpired during Amanda's coma, but she was not willing to go to the extremes Dr. Gascon had shown to get them.

"Very vivid dreams which felt quite real at the time."

"More than just childhood memories?"

Amanda paused before continuing, "You won't note this conversation in your file, will you?"

"Not if you don't want me to. I'm just curious for myself, not as a doctor," she answered honestly.

"Then, yes. Way more than any childhood memory. I lived a whole other life while I was sleeping. It's made me interested in the idea of life-after-death and possibly past-life regression. I don't know which idea fits better, but I lived through something I can't explain."

"Very interesting," Dr. Medin mused. She wished she had known about this before so she could have done some research to help Amanda transition better.

"So is there anything else you need from me?" Amanda asked anxiously.

"No, I think we're done. It has been my pleasure to know you, Amanda, and I wish you the best success in life. If you ever just want to come visit, I'd be more than happy to talk. We could do lunch or something."

Amanda shook Dr. Medin's hand and replied, "I look forward to it. Thank you!"

Dr. Medin sat down at her desk and finished filling out the last of Amanda's paperwork releasing her back to a full life. She signed the final form and handed the stack over to her patient. If it had not been for the edict from the hospital she would have had several more meetings with Amanda and she would have enjoyed the conversations. She felt disgusted with the politics which had kept her from being of better assistance to her patient. "This is it! Take care, Amanda."

"Thanks, Dr. Medin. I really appreciate this," she waved the paper-work. "I can't wait to get on with my life. My mom won't have to continue to be my chauffer any more either."

"I haven't minded, honey," Diane interjected.

"I know, it's just not fair for you to have to put your life on hold for so long. These papers release you as well as myself."

They walked out of the office and back to their car. The first stop was at the Department of Motor Vehicles. They had planned for everything to go as Amanda had anticipated and had already scheduled a driving appointment. Aside from the minor slip with Dr. Gascon, Amanda felt as though her life were finally back on track.

CHAPTER 14

Amanda left the windows rolled down as she drove the open roads. It was way too hot to be comfortable so Amanda also turned on the air conditioner full blast, but refused to roll up her windows. The feel of the air blowing through her hair was exhilarating and made her feel free.

Once she had gotten her driver's license back her parents had gone to their storage unit and liberated her beloved car from its incarceration. As if to pay her back for the neglect, the starter immediately went out which delayed Amanda's bid for freedom. The one week delay for the part to be ordered and installed had felt like a personal attack which she immediately forgave when she began driving again.

She was driving south on the interstate with no destination in mind. The palm trees and lush vegetation brought joy to her heart. She could drive forever. She checked her gas gauge and amended her last thought, her fuel light was on, and she needed to get gas. Reluctantly she took the next exit and slowed down for the light.

The sign said there was a station within a quarter mile to the right. She turned and drove down the quaint town road. Another light turned red and she stopped to wait. Just as the signal turned green she started to accelerate when she saw a man coming out of a corner pizza restaurant on the next block up. She did a double-take and realized the man was Riccan from her dream.

She could not believe her luck, she pressed on the accelerator to get to him before he left. The car shuddered and then died completely. "NO!" she screamed at her car. "Don't do this to me, car. Start!" She turned the key a couple of times and only heard the clicking of the starter. Without any fuel the car was not going to start. A car behind her honked. She waved her arm out the open window letting them know to pass her.

She waited until the traffic had cleared and she opened her door and got out. She could see the gas station up the street so she started to roll her car, steering through the open window while she pushed. After a few minutes, Amanda reached the gas station and pushed her sweaty hair away from her face. She grabbed her purse from the passenger seat and dug out her credit card. She activated the pump and started filling her tank.

Only at that point did she realize Riccan was nowhere in sight. Her plight had made her forget to look for him and he had gotten away. She closed her eyes at her own stupidity. She should have ditched her car and run after Riccan. It did not matter that she would have looked like a crazy person to anyone else, but Riccan knew who she was, he would not mind.

She looked around and discovered the pizza shop had been the same one he had taken her to not that long ago. The more she looked around, the more everything came back to her. There was the bathing suit store in the strip mall, there was the leaning palm tree on the corner where they turned to go back home.

"That's it! I remember how to get to his house!" she said out loud to herself. The pump could not go any slower as it glugged fuel into her tank. "Hurry up! Hurry up!" she chanted as she watched several more gallons click on the meter. Finally the pump clicked off and Amanda ripped the nozzle from her tank. She replaced the nozzle and put her cap back on. She raced around her car and got into the driver's seat.

She sped out of the gas station parking lot and turned right immediately at the leaning tree. She accelerated with excitement and kept looking for other landmarks she recognized. Amanda was so intent on her search she had not noticed the police car behind her with its lights blinking red and blue. It was not until the police car blipped its siren that Amanda's attention was pulled from her avid search.

Immediately, she pulled to the side of the road thinking the cop would just pass her to get to their emergency and then she could be on her way. Unfortunately, Amanda discovered she was their emergency. She grabbed the steering wheel and waited anxiously for the cop to come to her window.

"Good afternoon, miss. Do you have any idea how fast you were traveling?" the officer leaned close to the open window.

"I'm sorry, officer, I don't know. I wasn't paying attention."

"You were doing forty in a twenty-five. Where are you off to in such a hurry?" he asked kindly.

"Well," Amanda began and took a breath to clear her thoughts, "this is going to sound like quite a story, but, I promise, it's all true. I turned off the interstate to get gas and when I was just coming through a light back there," she waved over her shoulder, "I saw someone I knew from a long time ago. I tried to accelerate to catch up to him, but then I ran out of gas. I had to push my car to the gas station and then wait forever to fill up with gas. When the car was full I realized I recognized a couple of landmarks to get me back to his house so I was looking at the scenery more than my speedometer."

"I see," the officer replied. "Why didn't you just drive to his house if you remembered where it was?"

"I was hoping to catch him before his gate closed. It's been a while since I've seen him. You see, I was in a coma for seven years. I met him…a long time ago." She had almost said she had met him in Tuala, but realized that part of the story could not be told.

"A coma? For seven years? Driver's license and registration, please." The officer had heard a lot of tall tales in his years as an officer, but this one took the cake. "If your story checks out, then I'll let you off with a warning." He turned and walked back to his vehicle.

Amanda waited anxiously in her car. She kept her eyes glued to her rear-view mirror so she could see when the policeman would be returning. He seemed to be taking his sweet time.

After about ten minutes the officer came back to her window shaking his head in disbelief. "Your story checked out. Who were you trying to catch up with anyway? I may know him."

"His name's Riccan Stel," she replied rapidly, but then added, "He probably doesn't remember me."

"I know of Riccan," he said as he thought that Riccan was another individual who had a bazaar past. "If I see him around, I'll let him know you were looking for him. Have a nice day."

"Thank you, Officer. I'll pay more attention to my speed. You have a nice day, too." She turned on her engine, checked her mirror, and carefully pulled back onto the roadway. There was no chance of catching up with Riccan now, but she could still try to locate the driveway to his house. This felt like a step in the right direction toward getting back to Tuala.

The houses along the road began to look unfamiliar so she guessed she had missed the turn she was supposed to take to the left. After flipping her car around in the closest driveway she paid closer attention to each street along her right for any signs of familiarity. Finally one seemed to stand out more than the others so she decided to take a chance it could be correct. She began counting the houses as she remembered there were only a few estates between Riccan's home and the end of the street.

This task proved harder than she remembered from her dream. There were subtle changes to the plantings as though they had grown up since she had seen them. Most likely that was exactly what had happened since she was not sure how long ago her dream had taken place. It only felt like a few months, but it could just as easily been a few years. She turned her head just in time to see the gate she had been looking for tucked back from the road.

If she had traveled just a few more feet along the road she would have missed it. She pulled into the driveway and then had to laugh at herself. *Now what?* she thought, *If I announce myself he probably won't have any idea who I am. I need to come up with a way to meet him which would feel more organic and less contrived.* She backed out of the driveway, confident she could find it again now that she had seen it in real life.

On the interstate heading back home she was not thinking about the freedom of the drive. She rolled up the window to prevent being distracted by the wind and any bugs which happened to fly in her open window. Her thoughts were focused on how to get to know Riccan again.

She knew he was involved with the NHRA, but she had a hard time thinking she would be able to get close enough to him to make any difference. Besides, he would most likely be one-track minded on winning the competition rather than trying to meet a girl. She wracked her brain to think of any other details she had read about while she had researched him online.

Suddenly an idea struck her, he was involved in search and rescue missions. If she were to find out about any cases nearby she could volunteer to assist as well. It seemed like a long-shot, but it also seemed like the most likely to succeed.

Before long she took the exit to her home town and navigated the streets to her home. She never lost her thrill of excitement to think about going home. As she pulled into the driveway she saw her mom weeding the front yard. It was such a familiar and comforting thing to have everybody back to doing their ordinary tasks.

Then it hit her that it was probably still not back to normal for the Taivas family. She had wondered if they would come to visit her now that she was back at home to ask her questions about what she last remembered about their son. The fact was that she did not remember much of anything except them sailing on calm seas until the unexpected storm blew in. Everything after that became a confused blur of two distinctly different memory time-lines.

Maybe she would spend the rest of the afternoon trying to think of any details she might have missed with regard to Neal. She owed it to his family to at least try to remember. Her day had started on such a positive note and now she felt downright depressed as she thought about another family suffering even more than her own had while she was in the hospital.

She waved at her mom as she got out of her car and walked up the front sidewalk to go in the front door. She could see her mother still had a way to go with her weeding so she was eager to get into her room to try a few things she had been thinking about for a while.

Amanda sat down in the middle of her bed with her legs crossed in front of her. She carefully removed the necklace from around her neck and held the crystal in front of her so she could more easily focus. Assuming the crystal had power of its own she had to have enough belief in herself to make that power manifest. She stared without blinking at the crystal and willed the energy to come out of the stone. She took several deep breaths as she maintained her concentration.

As if the energy could no longer resist her onslaught it appeared to leap out of the crystal. Amanda was so surprised to see it actually work she almost dropped the necklace from her grasp and she did lose her focus on the energy. The sphere immediately popped back into the crystal.

Because she had proven to herself there was actual power in the crystal she had renewed faith in her dream and her conviction became stronger to master the other levels of using the stone. If everything from her dream were actually true then she knew children mastered the next few levels with relative ease.

She concentrated on the crystal and this time the sphere moved out swiftly. Without waiting to congratulate herself she moved on to moving the energy and then returning it to the crystal. She did not have time to mess around with the steps she now knew she could do. With her eyes closed she tried to remember Alena's directions for finding her children. She wanted to use an altered version to try to find Neal.

Her heart contracted as she thought about the possibility of her children. She had been so convinced they were real, but Dr. Medin's medical examination had put serious doubt to that part of her dream actually being factual. Instead she tried to refocus her energy to the person she might be able to find. Neal did not have his own crystal, but maybe her need to find him would give her enough power to succeed. She had heard before that motivation was a key ingredient to learning to use the crystals in unique ways.

Amanda imagined how she had last seen Neal and kept his image clear in her mind. She attempted to put Neal's image inside her crystal and then expand what she saw around him. Without any training on this technique she was just making it up as she went along. Unfortunately the improvised method did not produce any results, but it did manage to give Amanda a migraine headache.

She sighed in failure and put the necklace back on her neck with shaking hands. She had to close her eyes since the light pouring through her bedroom window was making her slightly sick. Amanda crawled off of the bed and pulled her window blinds shut.

Amanda wandered miserably into the kitchen to get medicine for her head from out of the cupboard. Every movement she made was starting to make her feel nauseas and she imagined how nice it would be to already have a glass of water so she could go back to her room when suddenly one appeared next to her hand. "Oh," she said with surprise. "I guess that works, too," she whispered as she picked up the glass and returned to her darkened room to recover.

CHAPTER 15

The next few days were spent either with research or journaling. Her failed attempt to locate Neal with her crystal did not deter her from searching her memories for any clues. One idea kept resurfacing which did not make her feel good at all: what if an Elder had found him?

Amanda had finally decided to believe that everything she remembered was actually true even if it did not seem possible. There were too many things which had happened since waking up to try to think they were just dreams. She listed off her reasons:

1. The clothing from Barla.

2. The birth crystal necklace (which actually worked).

3. Seeing both Drs. Medin and Gascon and knowing who they were without any introductions.

4. Knowing about Riccan Stel, as well as being able to find his house even though it was not published anywhere.

There were just too many things she knew to be able to convince herself it might only be coincidence anymore. Once she actually came to the realization she believed her own truth an unaccountable peace seemed to descend upon her.

Grabbing the laptop her parents had gotten for her off of the nightstand, Amanda lifted the screen and pressed the power button. As she waited for it to boot up she set it on the bed beside her so she could go across the room and pick up the shirt which Barla had given to her. She wanted to see if there were any identifying marks in it for where it was made or who had been the maker. When she had been wearing the clothes in Tuala she had never thought to look for anything of the sort. Now she needed more proof of her adventure.

After thoroughly searching the normal locations for a tag, Amanda was about to give up hope when her eye caught sight of something inside the sleeve. With a rush of hope she turned the bottom of the sleeve inside out to get a better look; sure enough, there was a small tag with a circular emblem, but no words. It was not much, but at least it was something to start with in her search.

She refolded the shirt, replaced it on the chair, and then picked up the pair of pants. Further investigation did not reveal anything on the pants. She tried not to feel too discouraged since she had actually found something on the shirt, she refolded the pants and put them next to the shirt.

Amanda returned to the bed and rested her back on the headboard. She pulled the laptop onto her legs and clicked on the internet button. Over the past month she had become quite adept at searching for everything on the internet. She was still in awe of the technology which had been created during her time 'away,' which was how she had started to think of her last seven years. She could not really say she had been comatose since she believed she had lived another life, or possibly two lives, during that time. 'Away' seemed to be the best description which also made her feel less pathetic for having lost so much time.

She clicked on the image search button and typed in 'clothing designers with circular emblem' to see if she could find anything which looked like what she had seen on her shirt. After scrolling through at least ten pages of random circular images she decided it was not to be found.

With a sigh of disgust she switched gears and went back to the regular search page and typed in 'police scanner news, Miami-Dade area' thinking she might find a live feed of police activity. There were several links to places like the Miami-Dade Police Department, but she was more interested in smaller websites dedicated to only scanner news. She kept scrolling down the page, clicked on page two, scrolled down some more until she finally found something which looked promising. She clicked on the link and waited for it to load. After checking to make sure her sound was turned on she clicked on the 'live feed' button and clapped her hands with joy as she began to hear live police action.

After several minutes of listening to sirens and police/dispatch chatter she realized her parents would probably ask questions about her newest obsession. She dug through her nightstand drawer and located a pair of earbuds. She plugged the cord into the computer and put the buds in her ears. Now she would be able to hear the scanners without alarming her parents or making them suspicious of her activities.

She left the page running and clicked to create a new tab so she could continue to listen while she searched the internet for other things: namely Riccan Stel. She had probably already seen every post on the internet which pertained to him, but she could not help but keep looking. He had seemed so real in her memories, but now she was not so sure he knew her at all. She clicked on a picture of him standing in front of his airplane, he looked so happy. She wanted to have him be that happy with her again.

They had only spent a few wonderful days together, but Amanda was sure if they had been together longer then a relationship would have formed. She felt a connection with him which was stronger than anything she had ever known, including her engagement with Neal. She felt a stab of betrayal for even thinking such a thought, but she could hardly lie to herself.

What she had experienced with Neal had paled in comparison to the relationship she had been forming with Riccan. It was almost as if Riccan had been the second half of herself, she could talk to him about anything and everything. Riccan had been thrilled with her children whereas Neal had told her repeatedly he had no interest in having children. Amanda, herself, had not been sure about children until she had her twins and now she wanted desperately to have them back.

Everything she had been thinking led her straight back to Riccan. He was the key to her finding a way back to Tuala. If she could convince him of her knowledge of the other world then he would surely take her where she needed to go to look for her children…again.

She shook her head at how pathetic she seemed, she always needed other people to help her find her loved ones. She really needed to work on being more self-reliant if she were going to go anywhere. She needed to become more resourceful. There seemed to be a reoccurring theme of losing those she loved. She understood everything happened for a reason and that, until you learned the lesson, then you would continue to be tested in the same area. She needed to figure out how to keep a hold of those she loved. First she would start with Riccan.

Her thoughts were interrupted by a news bulletin on the police scanner. She listened intently: 'missing ten year old autistic boy, last seen walking along the canal southeast of Kendall at six a.m. Search volunteers requested to report to the Kendall District Station.'

Amanda ripped the earbuds from her head and instantly closed the laptop. She jumped off of her bed and crammed her feet into her shoes. Within moments of hearing the report she was running out the front door and over to her car. The town of Kendall was only about ten minutes from her home and she drove as fast as she dared.

This felt like the opportunity for which she had been waiting. She did not like to think of the family worrying for their son, but she hoped her plan would work. Right at the ten minute mark Amanda was circling the District Station in Kendall searching for a place to park. Finally someone pulled out of a space and she immediately pulled in. She probably looked like a madwoman, but she desperately needed to find a way to approach Riccan.

Amanda crossed the street and walked into the Kendall District Station. She checked in at the front desk and was directed to a conference room which, she was told, was the first room on the left down the hall. She followed the receptionist's directions which were hardly required since the noise from the crowd made it pretty obvious where everyone was congregating.

Amanda pushed her way through the crowd as she scanned the room for any sign of Riccan. She had almost given up hope when she spotted him at the front of the room speaking with one of the officers. She was thrilled to see him and she continued to work her way through the crowd until she was standing just a few feet from the two men.

After a moment of listening to their conversation and trying to tune out the buzz from the people all around her, she heard Riccan say he would use his airplane for an aerial search. He was asking the officer to ask for a volunteer to go with him to be the 'eyes' while he flew.

Amanda pushed herself forward and said, "Excuse me. Did I hear you ask for an assistant in an aerial search?"

"Yes," Riccan replied as he looked her straight in the eyes without any recognition. "Are you volunteering?"

"Absolutely. Let's go!" Amanda enthusiastically agreed.

Riccan smiled at her eagerness and turned to the officer and said, "I guess I have my volunteer. We'll leave immediately. Thank you for the advance report. We should be airborne by the time you are finished with your briefing. I'll keep my radio tuned to your search frequency and let you know if we spot the boy."

"Thank you for your assistance, Riccan," the officer replied.

"Okay, ma'am let's go," Riccan said as he grabbed her elbow and towed her through the crowd and down the hallway the opposite way Amanda had entered.

She wondered where they were going until she saw the exit door ahead. They must be leaving out a back door, she thought to herself. She could hardly believe she was about to be alone with Riccan just as she had planned. It almost seemed to be working out too well. Surely something would happen which would ruin her opportunity. The nagging idea persisted all the way to Riccan's vehicle.

"I hope you don't mind riding with a stranger," Riccan said with a grin as he opened the passenger door to none other than his white 4-Runner. Amanda shook her head as she realized it was the same vehicle as she remembered, it could not be a coincidence.

"It's for a good cause," Amanda stated as she hoisted herself up into the passenger seat. She watched Riccan run around the front of the truck and get into the driver's side.

"My name's Riccan Stel," he stated as he started the engine. "What's yours?"

"Amanda Covington," she replied with a thrill of excitement. *This is actually happening!*

"Have you ever been flying in a small airplane?" he asked as he kept his eyes on the road.

"Yes, my father is a private pilot."

"Good! We'll do just fine then. The airport is only a few minutes from here."

Amanda watched as they headed west to SW 117th Avenue and turned onto the Ronald Reagan Turnpike where they drove for about five minutes before reaching SW 120th Street. She realized this was a perfect time for them to start talking so she asked, "Do you fly much?" As soon as it came out of her mouth she could have kicked herself for such an inane question. More important questions came to mind such as: *When are you heading back to Tuala? and Can you take me with you?*

Riccan did not seem to mind as he answered, "As much as I can around my work schedule. How about you?"

"I haven't been flying with my dad for years, but it's only been a few months since I went flying with a friend of mine," she replied as she looked at her 'friend' driving the truck.

Riccan nodded as he saw his exit coming and he changed over to the far right lane of the highway. "Only a few minutes more and we'll be in the air."

They turned right onto SW 120th Street, left onto SW 122nd Avenue, right onto SW 128th Street Avenue where they slowed down for some traffic. Amanda was thankful Riccan was driving since she was not very familiar with this area. He seemed confident in his directions so she did not worry about it. After waiting through the light, they were finally on their way again. Riccan eventually turned left on SW 146th Avenue and less than a minute later the Miami Executive Airport was straight ahead.

He parked the truck and got out. He opened the door behind the driver's seat and pulled out a large duffel-type bag and watched as Amanda got out her side of the truck. He locked the vehicle with his remote as they hurried away toward the entrance gate to the airport. He waved at a few people he knew in the FBO and they continued walking to the row of golf carts. He put his bag in the back and got into the driver's seat and gestured for her to get in also. They sped across the apron of the airport until they reached a rather large hangar. Leaving the cart outside by the door, he entered a code into the door lock and then they were in the hangar.

"This is my plane," Riccan said as he opened the pilot's door. "Go ahead and get yourself situated in the co-pilot's seat while I do the exterior preflight." He grabbed a tube to check the fuel levels and a checklist from behind the pilot's seat, flipped a couple of switches on the panel and then started to walk around the plane.

Amanda instantly followed instructions and opened the passenger side door since the flap by her head was lowering. She hoisted herself up into the plane and adjusted the seat so she would be able to reach the rudder pedals in case of an emergency. *It really would be an emergency if I had to end up flying the plane,* she thought to herself with a smile. She trusted Riccan to bring them back to the ground safely. The only time they had experienced a flight problem was when she was in control in the telepod, which had ended rather catastrophically.

She reached up and pulled down the shoulder harness portion of the seat belt from the storage compartment above the door. She fastened the lap belt and then attached the shoulder harness to it. She looked over the panel and was not surprised to see the controls had been converted to a glass panel system. *Nothing but the best for Riccan,* she said to herself.

Riccan suddenly appeared at the pilot's door and said, "Get your headset on while I pull the plane out of the hangar." He threw the duffel bag into the back seat and then walked up to the front of the plane.

Amanda noticed then that the hangar door had been opened and then she and the plane were rolling out into the open. She wondered if Riccan would take time to shut the hangar door when he came back and put the pull bar under the back seat and then he got up into the pilot's seat. *I guess not,* she thought with a smile. She grabbed the headset from the dash in front of her noticing they were Bose brand, *nothing but the best,* she repeated to herself as she put them on and adjusted the mic in front of her mouth.

Riccan sat with the checklist in his lap. He fastened his seatbelt, shut the door, moved his seat forward, and inserted the key. With an air of confidence Riccan went through the interior pre-flight check and then flipped the master switch to the on position. He primed the engine a couple of times and then yelled out the window, "Clear prop." He started the engine and the propeller began turning until it was a blur. Riccan adjusted the throttle until the engine idled at eight hundred RPM. He turned on the control panel and radio as he checked the oil pressure, oil temperature, and fuel levels. Everything looked okay so he put on his headphones, tuned the radio to 121.7, and then performed a brake check.

He turned to her and spoke through the mic as he asked, "Are you ready?"

"Whenever you are," she replied as her heart started to race.

They rolled away from the hangar until they were on the apron in view of the tower. Riccan pressed the radio call button and said, "Tamiami Ground this is Cessna 86 Sierra Tango Echo Lima at south hangar with information Delta requesting taxi for a southeast VFR departure."

The reply came back as, "Cessna 86 Sierra Tango Echo Lima, proceed to gate one two, to Charlie two, Charlie, Delta, Alpha for runway one three."

Amazingly Riccan repeated it back and began to roll the airplane along the yellow line on the ground in front of them. Amanda was amazed he remembered all of the steps as it seemed rather complicated. In a few minutes they reached Alpha and turned out to do a run-up. Once everything checked out, Riccan rolled the airplane up to the hold line for runway thirteen.

He switched frequencies on the radio to 118.9 and pressed the call button and said, "Tamiami Tower, Cessna 86 Sierra Tango Echo Lima at one three requesting a southeast VFR departure."

"Cessna 86 Sierra Tango Echo Lima cleared for takeoff on one three with immediate southeast departure," the tower said.

"Cessna 86 Sierra Tango Echo Lima cleared for takeoff on one three," Riccan repeated back and then began to roll onto the active runway. He checked over all of the controls one last time, shook his seat to make sure it was securely latched, and then pressed the throttle full in. They began rolling faster and faster on the runway until they reached fifty-nine knots and then they were suddenly airborne. A slight crosswind pushed their aircraft which Riccan immediately countered and they continued to fly straight up the runway until they were at seven hundred feet in elevation.

Riccan veered the airplane to the right, away from the airport, as he continued to ascend. He leveled off at one thousand five hundred feet and continued on the heading of 120 degrees until they were almost to the ocean and then he changed his heading to 040 degrees until they were near the town of Kendall. Riccan decreased his altitude to right at one thousand feet and said, "Do you see the canal below on your side?"

Amanda looked out her window and said, "Yes."

"I'm going to follow the canal out as far as Pinecrest and then we'll turn around and head back toward Kendall. Let me know if you see anyone along the waterway wearing a yellow jacket." He continued to fly as he gave her directions.

Amanda was silent for a few minutes as she watched out the window intently. She realized she was quite able to talk while also maintaining a vigil on the ground. "Do you fly out to the Florida Middle Ground a lot?"

Riccan's focus on flying was momentarily interrupted as he considered Amanda's question. The area she asked about was not very well known, but he was intimately familiar with it and said, "I go there occasionally. Why?"

"It's just a place I went not very long ago. I've heard it's not too far from Pantano. Have you ever been there?" Amanda asked casually as she continued to stare out the window.

"I…" he stammered and then continued uncertainly, "I'm not sure." He looked over at his passenger and wondered who she might be. She had seemed like a concerned citizen when she had offered to help on this search, but now he was not so sure. There seemed to be a story here he should probably investigate.

"Riccan, I see something! Circle around so I can be sure!" she kept her eye trained on a yellow spot which was moving along the shore of the canal. "Can we go lower?"

"I really shouldn't, but I can tip over onto your side to give you a clearer view," he said as he banked to the right in a sharp forty-five degree angled turn.

Amanda forgot her fear of steep banked turns as she focused all of her attention on the yellow spot. "Definitely someone in yellow! They look rather small, too. It's got to be our missing boy!" Amanda's voice rose as she realized they had probably found the missing child.

Riccan switched the radio to the secondary station and hit the call button to report. "Air report on the missing child: location approximately one mile northeast of Pinecrest spotted yellow jacket on child next to the west side of the canal."

"We'll send a patrol over immediately. Keep circling so we can know approximate location. ETA three minutes."

Riccan continued a tight circle and maintained his altitude. He asked Amanda to keep him posted if the child moved or if she could see any flashing lights to indicate the police were getting near.

"I see flashing lights," Amanda declared as she pointed out the window. "They're too far south. Tell them to go north three blocks and then head toward the canal."

Riccan relayed her instructions and then waited for the 'found' call.

Amanda watched as the police cars parked and the officers poured out of the vehicles and fanned out toward the canal. One officer approached the yellow coated person and looked up toward the airplane. He gave a thumbs up signal and then talked on his radio.

"Missing child has been found. Thank you air search for your assistance."

Riccan smiled and then straightened the wings of the airplane and added more throttle to gain altitude. "That just never gets old!" he said as he smiled over at Amanda.

She returned his smile with her own and then she wondered how she could extend this time together. "Now that the boy has been found, can we fly out over the water?"

"That's exactly what I was thinking, too!" he replied as they continued heading southeast at fifteen hundred feet. "That was probably one of the quickest searches I've participated in. No doubt it's because of you."

"Thanks, Riccan. I'm just glad I was able to be of some assistance. This is my first time volunteering for a rescue."

"Ah, beginner's luck, I see!" Riccan chuckled. "Do you live around here?"

"I live in Pinecrest. How about yourself?"

"Oh, just a little further south of Pinecrest," he answered elusively and then changed the subject. "What do you do for a living?"

"Well," Amanda began. This was a sensitive subject. She was old enough to be established in a career and yet she still lived at home. "It's a bit complicated…"

"You don't have to answer, I was just making small talk."

"I want to answer, I'm just not sure how to without sounding pathetic."

Riccan smiled at her and said, "I promise I won't think you're pathetic."

Amanda chuckled and said, "I've never had a job, here at least, and I still live with my parents. You see, about eight months ago I woke up from a seven-year coma. The last thing I remember was when I was eighteen years old."

Riccan had begun to think she was kind of pathetic for still living with her parents until she got to the part about the coma. Naturally she would still live with them while she was getting herself back on her feet. He could not imagine how terrible the whole ordeal had been for everyone in her family. Then he wondered about her knowledge of Pantano and decided to ask, "Who do you know in Pantano?"

Amanda had hoped the conversation would turn toward discussing Tuala so she answered, "A friend of mine has parents who live there. I've never been there myself."

"What's your friend's name? I may know them."

"At the risk of sounding crazy, my friend's name is Riccan Stel." She watched him carefully to see how he would react.

"But that's my name!"

"I know. It's not a coincidence, Riccan. You were my friend for months a long time ago."

"I don't understand what you're saying. You and I have never met as far as I know."

"Maybe not, but I know a lot of things about you, Riccan, things I have no way of knowing unless you told me."

"So you think we knew each other before your coma?" Riccan was trying to figure out a time-line to start with.

Amanda shook her head as she said, "It's hard to explain, but the easiest way for me to think of it is we met *while* I was in my coma."

"Wow, that's different," he said as he tried to wrap his mind around the odd woman's last statement. If this were a new pick-up line, she had definitely caught his attention. Before he could talk himself out of it he asked, "Would you like to have dinner with me tonight? I think maybe we should talk about what you remember and I don't."

"I think that would be perfect. I know of the perfect place, it's a little corner pizza restaurant south of Pinecrest..." she gave him a mischievous grin.

"I might just know the place you're talking about," he smiled back at her. He looked at his watch and suggested, "Do you want to meet there at four o'clock? We could talk before the rush hour begins."

"Sounds good. If we both show up at the same place then you'll have to admit I might just be right about our prior friendship," she said with a wink. She blushed at being so forward and turned her face to look out the window at the blue water which turned white as it churned over in small waves at the shoreline.

After a few minutes of silence Riccan turned the airplane left, away from the shore. They flew in silence as Riccan spoke with the Tamiami tower to receive clearance to land. Their altitude decreased to one thousand feet as Riccan maneuvered the plane into the traffic pattern for runway one three. They turned for their final approach and continued to descend. Riccan landed the plane smoothly onto the runway and followed the ground control directions on the taxiways back to the hangar.

When they were back in the 4-Runner Riccan could no longer contain his curiosity and asked, "So what else do you know about me?"

"I know your parent's names are Daven and Nena. Your mother is a teacher and your father is an Elder," she added the last part while she was staring at Riccan. She noticed his eyes widen a touch and then return to normal.

He cleared his throat and said, "What else?"

"You lived with many of your relatives as you grew up and went to high school in Washington."

Other than the part where she knew her father's title as an Elder, everything else could have been looked up on the internet. He decided to let her continue and said, "Keep going."

"Let's see…" she thought about what to say next, "Your house has two three-car garages. Your vehicles are in the left side garages while the right side is reserved for your telepod." Again she noticed his eyes widening as he stared straight out the window. "Should I continue?"

"Yes," he replied with less certainty.

"I think we should wait until we meet for dinner," Amanda decided suddenly. She wanted to make sure she had his full attention before she said any more. She almost felt as though she had said too much already and she did not want to scare him away before she could convince him of her true motives.

Riccan drove back to the Kendall District Station and asked Amanda, "Where did you park your car?"

Instead of having him wait in the street she said, "Just pull in here and I'll walk to my car."

He parallel parked along the street and said, "I guess I'll see you at the pizza place at four o'clock. I'm looking forward to talking with you."

Amanda smiled and said, "Thanks for the flight. See you at four!" She opened the passenger door and waited on the sidewalk until he pulled away from the curb and drove up the street. She looked both ways and proceeded to cross the street and down a few paces until she reached her car. Her heart was racing with anticipation and excitement. She could not screw up this perfect opportunity. She had three hours to get herself together and to plan what she would tell him.

CHAPTER 16

As she drove home she realized she would have to tell her parents she was going out on a date. She was sure they would be uncomfortable with her meeting who they would feel to be a perfect stranger. How could she tell them she had known him for months when they would obviously know this was untrue? She decided to bend the truth a little and tell them she would be meeting with an old friend for an early dinner.

As suspected, her mother was less than pleased. Her father, on the other hand, seemed to think it was a good idea for her to get out and socialize. Diane gave her husband a look to kill when he gave his approval. How was she to be able to protect her daughter from harm if she were not in their house to be monitored?

Amanda decided it was time to leave while her mother was still not completely opposed. She rushed back into her room and picked up her journal, which she stuffed into her purse. Taking one last look at herself in the mirror she left her room and rushed out the front door. She thought she had made a clean getaway until her mother ran out the same door and waved her hands to get Amanda's attention. With a sigh Amanda rolled down the passenger window and leaned over to ask her mother, "Did I forget something?"

Her mother thrust her cell phone into Amanda's hand and said, "Call us if you need anything. Oh, and call to let us know when you'll be heading home."

Amanda smiled at her mother lovingly and said, "Thanks, Mom. I'll be sure to do that. I love you."

"We love you, too, honey. Please be careful!" She backed away from the car and watched with a worried expression as Amanda pulled out of the driveway and drove away.

It was a full forty-five minutes before she was to meet with Riccan so she drove slowly along the interstate. She had been surprised when her mother had given her the phone, but the longer she thought about it, the more it made sense. Amanda was comforted to know she would have easy access to help should anything happen with her car.

Exiting the interstate, Amanda drove down the road to the pizza shop. She parked on a side street and got out of her car. With a glance at her watch she saw there were still fifteen minutes until the scheduled meeting time. She was glad she was early so she could be seated in the restaurant and calm her nerves before he arrived.

Once inside the pizzeria the hostess asked her, "How many will be dining this afternoon?"

"Two, please," Amanda replied and then added, "Could I please have that booth?" She pointed to the corner booth on the left.

"Sure, right this way," she said as she grabbed two menus and led the way to the booth. "Can I start you out with a drink?"

"Could I get two ice waters for now?"

"Sure, I'll be right back." She walked away to get the waters ready.

Amanda scooted into the center of the booth bench and set her purse on the inside edge. She checked once again for the journal and saw it was exactly where she had left it in the side pocket. When the waitress returned with the water she thanked her and then looked away nervously. She checked her watch again and saw there were twelve minutes to go. After sipping her water she wiped her moist palms on her jeans again. It was crazy how nervous she was for this meeting to go well. Everything she had planned hinged on the success of her conversation with Riccan.

As if her thoughts had conjured him, he walked through the front door to be greeted by the hostess. "Good afternoon, Riccan. I'm sorry, your usual booth was just taken. Can I seat you in the next one over?"

Riccan looked over at his 'usual booth' and saw Amanda sitting and replied, "No, I'll still take my usual since that girl is the person I was meeting here. I just thought I'd get here first."

"Oh, well, go ahead then…you know the way," she replied slightly shaken by this unusual turn of events. Riccan always ate alone.

Riccan slid into the empty side of the booth and said, "I thought to get here before you, but I guess you had the same idea!"

"Yes and I asked for this booth in particular because this was where we ate before," Amanda replied.

Riccan raised his eyebrows and asked, "So what's the plan for tonight? Do we talk first or eat?"

Amanda's stomach was tied up in knots, but she needed a distraction so she said, "Definitely eat. We can talk while we wait for the pizza to be baked."

"Do you know what you want already?"

"Sure."

He flagged down the waitress and said, "I think we're ready to order. Amanda?" He looked to her to place the first order.

"I'd like the personal pizza with hamburger and pineapple please."

When the waitress looked at Riccan she asked, "Will you be having your usual?"

"Absolutely!" he answered with a broad smile as he watched the waitress head back to place their order in the kitchen. "Where do you want to start?" He thought he should just get right down to the point. If Amanda were some schemer it would be better to find out sooner rather than later.

"I'd been contemplating that myself. Let's see, I could start with your parents. Your father's sister, Sanda, introduced your father to your mother in high school. They didn't date until post-study. When your father graduated, your mother sped up her graduation date so they could get married. You are an only child, but your mother had a miscarriage before you were born."

Riccan simply kept nodding as she had all of her facts perfect so far. He wondered how she had done her research since these things were not a part of his public profile. He motioned for her to continue.

"Your father has five brothers and sisters, but your mother is an only child. You stayed with relatives of your grandfather when you were attending school in the states. During your early childhood you and a neighbor friend…what was his name?" She stopped to try to remember the particular detail and then snapped her finger as she remembered, "His name was Andy Brun…" and then she proceeded to tell him the rest of the rock-throwing story.

Riccan was really impressed now. He had not thought about that incident from his youth in decades. He was also certain he had never shared it with anyone. He nodded for her to keep talking.

Amanda told him about setting the bush on fire with his cigarette and the outhouse prank at the high school. She started to say more, but was interrupted by their dinner arriving.

They ate in silence. Riccan was too busy trying to figure out if Amanda were really telling the truth about having known him from a dream or if she had been very busy gathering data from various sources. He really had no idea how she could have amassed so many small details, but he meant to find out. In that moment he decided to ask her back to his house after dinner. After all, she had already told him about his house, she must have already seen it. There were some things even she would not know about when it came to his private residence.

"Do you want to come over to my house when we're done eating?"

Amanda's mouth was full, but she nodded her head. As soon as she swallowed she added, "There is so much more of Tuala I want to talk to you about, but it would be better spoken in private."

"I'm sure," he replied noncommittally.

They boxed up their leftovers and stood up to leave. Riccan left a wad of cash on the table. There was the matter how they would get to his house to decide: one car or two.

Amanda solved the dilemma by saying, "I'll follow you. If we get separated, I still know where you live so just make sure the gate is open."

Riccan was slightly creeped out by her admitting she already knew where he lived. He had a privately listed address and his home was under an LLC name and not his own. Maybe she had been following him for some time. This might be a very bad idea, but he had already committed himself so he would follow it through to the end.

They parted ways at the entrance to the pizza shop and Amanda rushed to her car. She had to try twice to get her keys into the ignition since her hands were shaking so badly. Finally she pulled into the road and made a U-turn so she could head back toward the main road. She turned left and ended up just behind Riccan's 4-Runner. Without trying to be too close to him she followed him through the two turns until they got to his street. She turned her blinker on before he did to turn into his driveway.

After pausing at the entrance to the driveway for the gate to open Amanda looked ahead and could see Riccan's reflection in the side mirror. He was looking back at her so she smiled uncertainly. He did not smile back, but drove ahead since the gate had fully opened. Now she was really getting nervous.

Riccan did not bother pulling into the garage, but rather parked outside of the entrance. He waited for Amanda to get out of her car before they walked to the front door together. The door was not locked so he just opened it and walked in. He shut the door behind Amanda.

"Am I also to assume you've been inside the house before?" Riccan asked almost sarcastically.

"Sure, you gave me the tour yourself. Do you want me to demonstrate?" she asked with equal sarcasm.

He gestured for her to lead the way and said, "As you wish."

Amanda felt her face blush as she started to get angry. She accepted the challenge and marched through the foyer to the living room. Before she entered she listed off where each room was located and then walked in. Standing in the middle of the living room she pointed first one direction and then the other and said, "The garages are through each of those doors. The one past the kitchen is where you keep your telepod."

"So, let's say, for argument's sake, I really am from Tuala, how come all of the stories you've told me thus far have all been here on Earth?" he demanded.

"Because we were in a public place! Why do you think I said some things were better discussed in private?"

"Okay, don't get mad. I am a very private person and it's a little hard for me to believe we've met when I clearly don't remember ever knowing you. Why don't we sit down and you can tell me what else you remember?"

Slightly mollified, Amanda marched over to the leather couch and plunked herself down. Looking out the window, she remembered sunbathing by the pool and how relaxed and contented they both were. She wished they could get back to that level of comfort somehow. Taking a deep breath, Amanda began to speak again, "You are the Engineering Manager at Telepod Engineering Company on Durseni. The telepod you currently own is one you designed yourself using some technology from your experiences with flying here on Earth. You installed an auto-pilot feature similar to those found here. How am I doing so far?"

"Everything you've said so far has been spot on. I still don't know how you know it all, however."

Amanda smiled a small knowing smirk and then continued, "Your grandmother met your grandfather in Roswell when she was on assignment at the museum under the direction of Elder Vargen. Edwin was from Earth, but he followed her home and they made a life together. Your father's talent caught the eye of Jehoban's representatives and the whole family moved to Acaim and remained there." She started to say more, but was interrupted by Riccan's question.

"So you know all of these things, what do you get out of convincing me we were once friends?" Riccan believed they could easily be friends even without her knowing his true identity.

"We were more than just casual acquaintances, Riccan. Much more," she said as she blushed again and looked away. Now that he had asked the question she was not really sure what she wanted from Riccan other than a way to get back to Tuala.

"Are you saying we were lovers?" Riccan was truly curious now.

"No, not lovers, but not far from it. We were rapidly becoming best friends. When we stayed a couple of days here, we became even closer and you kissed me at the top of the stairs before we went to bed." She looked up at him and saw the look on his face and hastily added, "In separate bedrooms!"

Riccan laughed out loud at the look on Amanda's face. "I'm sorry to laugh, but you're expression was priceless."

Amanda liked hearing him laugh again, a real laugh. She accepted his apology with grace and then said what she had been thinking all along, "I worked for you at the Engineering Company as your Engineering Resources Analyst. You had told my parents I was very good at my job. I'd like to go back to the life I remember."

Riccan was surprised to hear he had met her parents, it must have been more serious than he had originally believed. He'd never been to meet any girl's parents, much to his own mother's dismay. There had never been anyone he felt he could settle down with because of his mixed heritage.

"So what exactly are you asking of me?" Riccan was curious to find out what Amanda was actually thinking. Did she want a life in Tuala or a life with him?

"I'm looking for answers. I have so many things I remember, but some of them seem to be an impossibility, but then I saw you and now I'm not so sure anymore." Amanda knew she was rambling, but she could not seem to help herself.

"Why don't you start from the beginning and then we can try and figure it out together?" he suggested. The more time he spent with Amanda, the more he felt he should try to help her. There was something about her which made him feel protective toward her.

"When I woke up from my coma, my doctor told me to write a journal of my memories to help me sort through them." She dug in her purse and pulled out the worn little book. "I think I captured everything pretty accurately these past months since I awoke."

Riccan felt like grabbing the book and reading it at that instant, but restrained himself as he could see Amanda was struggling with some inner conflict. "What would you like to do with your journal?"

"I think maybe I should read it to you and then you could tell me if it could all be true or purely a figment of my imagination," she answered hopefully as she looked up at Riccan with her big brown eyes full of trust in his ability to help her through this situation.

"I'll do my best. Would you like a drink before you start?" he asked politely.

"A water would be great," she replied as she opened her journal and looked at the first entry. At first glance she remembered it was about her time on the yacht with Neal, and maybe this was not such a good idea after all. She shook her head and thought everybody had a past and she should not be ashamed to share it. Amanda needed closure with regard to Neal as well so she had to include his story with hers.

Riccan came back into the living room carrying two glasses of water. He handed one to Amanda and set his on the coffee table in front of the couch. He sat down facing Amanda with his leg cocked on the couch cushion.

Amanda took a nervous sip from the glass, most likely to stall for a moment, as she was not actually thirsty. She leaned forward and put the glass down before she began to read from the pages of her journal.

Over an hour had passed as Amanda continued to read. Riccan had held his tongue from asking the hundreds of questions he had thought of while she was reading. He could tell this was a hard experience for her and he wanted her to get through it at her own pace. There were so many people, places, and events from her adventure he, too, had a hard time believing it had not happened.

Almost from the beginning, he realized Amanda was a powerful story-teller. Her writing was so expressive he could almost see himself beside her during her adventures. He was surprised to hear she had actually participated in two different lives while she had been in her coma. This was a very unique situation, of that he was certain.

When she got to the part of getting her own birth crystal he could not contain his expression of disbelief. His grandfather was the only Earth person he knew of to have received a Tualan birth crystal. "Do you actually have the birth crystal you wrote about?"

She pulled on the chain around her neck and the crystal popped out above her shirt. Riccan leaned forward to look closer at the stone and verified it was a legitimate birth crystal and not somebody's attempt to create a copy. Their intricate designs were impossible to duplicate. He was convinced.

"I'm sorry to interrupt, please continue," he apologized as he sat back and resumed his listening pose.

Amanda took a sip of water before she kept reading. She kept seeing the scenes unfold in her mind as she read out loud the events for Riccan to hear. She took courage from him accepting her birth crystal as legiti-mate. It was actually therapeutic to read her journal to another person and have them actually believe her and not judge her for her memories. Another hour went by unnoticed and it was now dark outside.

Amanda turned the page to her journal and discovered there were very few pages left to read. She had gotten to the part where she was spending time with Riccan here in his house. They had already gone to eat pizza and she looked up and smiled at Riccan at the 'coincidence' of their outing that night.

"Please continue, Amanda," Riccan requested with genuine interest. Her story was incredible to believe, but he found he really did believe she had experienced something truly remarkable. He knew some of the people she had said she had encountered, but he had never heard of Amanda being a part of any of their lives. This was truly a mystery to try to solve.

"There's not much left," she said as she reached over to pick up her glass of water. She had no idea reading could be such a taxing experience. She set the glass down and ran her finger down the page to find where she had left off. She began reading again.

Riccan managed to barely contain his gasp of incredulity when Amanda spoke of his hidden room with the treasures from Tuala. He had never told anybody about the room or its contents. If he had had any doubts before, they were effectively demolished by Amanda's revelation.

Amanda turned to the last page and finished with a flourish. She was thankful she had not included any of her research about Riccan or her practically stalking him since she had woken up from the coma. He probably thought she was strange enough without adding 'stalker' to her list of descriptions.

She waited a few moments for Riccan to say something, but he was still silent and looking down at his lap. Amanda was becoming worried with his continued silence and finally asked, "What do you think? Could it really have happened?"

"I think we have a way of proving at least part of it. Are you game?" Riccan said as he got up slowly from the couch, stretching each of his joints as he stood.

"How? What are you thinking, Riccan?" Amanda also stood with an increasing level of excitement.

"Let's go look in the ancient text to see if the new passage is actually there. I know that book like the back of my hand and it has never had anything written on the title page. Do you want to look?" he asked even as he was walking out of the room toward the library.

"I can't believe you'd even have to ask me!" she replied as she raced to stay by his side.

Riccan paused at the library door and gestured for Amanda to precede him into the room. "You can do the honors, since you seem to know so much about my house already!" he half teased.

Amanda smiled and marched over to the far bookcase. She looked for the book with the red spine and put her hand under the shelf below it until she felt the release mechanism. The wall of books opened sound-lessly and she looked back at Riccan with a pleased expression on her face.

Riccan shook his head in amazement and walked over to open the door enough for them to enter. He took out the ancient text from the cupboard and placed it carefully on the table. He opened the cover and gasped when he saw the new passage just as Amanda had read it to him just minutes ago. He needed to talk with his father as soon as possible.

Amanda felt an odd sense of déjà vu. She did not want what had happened before to repeat itself. They had died in the telepod when it collided with the small aircraft. She grabbed Riccan's arm and said, "If you want to show this to your father, we need to teleport directly to his residence. Remember what I said happened before?"

"Right," he replied solemnly. "I need to write this down." He started to look for a piece of paper.

Amanda waved her journal at him and chuckled as she said, "I've already got that covered. Let's go."

"I'd like to compare your version to the one written in the text. We need to make sure it's perfectly accurate."

"Good thinking," she said as she opened her journal to nearly the last page and then put it down next to the original.

"You do have perfect recall," Riccan praised. He was thoroughly convinced of Amanda's sincerity. He was done with testing or ques-tioning her since she was proved correct with the ancient text. It was as though Jehoban were telling him to believe Amanda and help her. He was ready.

CHAPTER 17

"We can't just take off without telling your parents," Riccan pointed out. "They'd send out an all-points-bulletin for me and say I'd kidnapped you. We'll have to take a few days to figure out the best course of action."

Amanda crossed her arms and tapped her foot on the ground impatiently. "I'm a grown woman, and I can make my own decisions," she countered.

"Yes, a grown woman who only recently recovered from a coma being taken advantage of by an older man she seemingly just met. It doesn't look good, even though we both know differently. I promise I won't go to Tuala without you if that's what got you so worked up."

"Do you really promise?" Amanda asked, seeking reassurance.

"Yes, I promise," he said solemnly, and then he looked at his wristwatch. He had no idea it had gotten so late, and he said, "You should probably think about going home. If you give me your phone number, and I'll give you mine, then we can figure out what our next steps will be. I can guarantee it will be the only thing on my mind until I see my father!"

Amanda grinned and said, "It's been the only thing on my mind since I woke up. I'm glad to have someone else similarly afflicted; it makes me feel a little less crazy!"

They laughed together as they left the secret room. Riccan closed it up, so it appeared simply to be a wall of bookshelves. They exchanged numbers before walking to the vehicles out front where Riccan felt the overwhelming need to hug Amanda. Without even pausing to consider it, he pulled her close and kissed the top of her head.

Amanda burst into tears of joy at finally being back on track in her life. She mumbled into his shirt, "I'm sorry. These are tears of joy, I promise."

"It's okay to feel your emotions, Amanda. Never apologize for that," he said as he continued to hold her close in his arms. Finally, he pulled her away and looked down into her trusting eyes as he said, "I'll call you tomorrow. We can plan something from there. Drive carefully. Most likely, I'll see you soon."

"Okay," she said as she wiped the tears from the corners of her eyes with the backs of both her hands. "Thanks for believing me, Riccan. You have no idea how much this means to me."

"I'm pretty sure I do after all you've told me tonight. We'll figure out what really happened and then we'll take it from there. Now, it's time for you to go home before your Mom calls the police on me!"

Amanda laughed as she got into her car. She thought Riccan might not be too far from the truth when it came to her mother's worrying nature. She started the car and waved as she drove down the driveway and away from the only other person on Earth who truly understood what she had gone through.

TRUE TO HIS WORD, Riccan called her the next day. When Amanda had woken up the next day, she had a hard time believing the events from the previous day had actually been real. It seemed she was just trying to plan a way to meet Riccan when events practically unfolded for her, as if on cue. Maybe she was just playing a part in some grander scheme, but she sure wished someone would clue her in to what she should actually be doing.

Riccan admitted he had not come up with a good plan yet for Amanda leaving the country, which is how he described it even though it would be a bit more drastic than that. He had learned to use Earth terms when he was on Earth to avoid any unwanted questions.

Amanda also had to admit she was at a loss. They made arrangements to meet later in the afternoon at his house. She was glad he had picked the location since it would make it infinitely easier to openly discuss their situation. When she hung up the phone with a smile on her face, she noticed her mother had been watching her from the kitchen. She stood up and went in to talk with her.

"That was my friend on the phone," she stated simply.

"So I gathered from the smile on your face," her mother said without much enthusiasm. "I think you should take your time before you jump into a relationship. You've only barely recovered from your ordeal."

"Are you sure you aren't suggesting that you have only just started to recover from my ordeal?" Amanda asked with a teasing gleam in her eyes.

"I think it's a mixture of both if you want to know the truth. It scares me to think about you being away from the house. What if something bad happens to you again? I don't think I could live through it twice!" Her mother turned away and grabbed on to the edge of the sink as she stared out the window into the backyard to control her emotions.

Amanda took the two steps separating them and hugged her mother from behind and said, "I'm sorry I scared you, Mom. You know I didn't do it on purpose, but you're going to have to let me grow up and experience life again. I can't do that if I never leave this house. It's not fair to you or to me if that's your expectation." She could feel her mother tense underneath her arms and knew she was still unconvinced. "You have grown to accept both of my sisters moving on with their lives. It's time you did the same for me."

"It's different with your sisters, I've never had to watch them die a little every day right before my eyes. I'm sorry, Amanda, I just can't let you go yet. Give me some time, and I might be able to come to terms with it better."

Amanda was thankful her mother was facing away from her since she rolled her eyes in exasperation at her mother's dramatic speech. This was going to be harder than she had originally hoped. She decided to change the subject with an inspired thought, "Riccan said he knows of a job I might be interested in taking a look at. I think I might take him up on his offer."

"What kind of job could you get with your history, Amanda? I don't mean to be critical, but you've never had a job before." Her mom pulled Amanda's hands away and then turned around to face her daughter.

"It's an analyst position where Riccan works. He said he would be my boss so I could learn at my own pace. He has faith in my ability to learn the ropes. I had thought you would have the same faith in me, but I guess not." Amanda did not like to put a guilt trip on her mother, but she had to get her to the point where it would be okay to be out of the house for extended periods of time. This was the only option she had come up with thus far.

As if she were forcing herself to come to terms with her daughter's desire for independence, she asked, "When will you find out about the job?"

"Riccan wants to meet in a couple of hours to go over the details. I'm not sure how long I'll be, but, if I can take your phone again, I'll call to let you know when I'm on my way home," Amanda reasoned.

"I have a better idea," her mother suddenly spoke up, "let's go to the phone store to get you your own. I like the idea of you having one no matter where you go, even if I'm not around."

"Okay, do you want to leave in about ten minutes? I'm almost ready."

"Sure, that sounds perfect."

WITH HER NEW phone in her purse, Amanda drove with confidence to Riccan's house. When she entered the driveway, she pressed the call button on the intercom outside of the gate. Without any words of acknowledgment, the gate began to swing open. Amanda was pleased to know Riccan seemed just as anxious to see her as she was to be with him again.

She parked in the circular drive and walked up to the front door. Even as she reached up to knock Riccan opened the door with a smile and said, "Come in. For future reference, you don't need to knock, just come on in, okay?"

"If you say so," she replied with a grin of pleasure. Things were definitely looking up in the relationship department.

"So have you come up with any ideas since we talked this morning?" Riccan got right to the point.

"Well…in a way, I guess. I told my mom you had a job for me to look into." She gave him the rest of the details, noticing he seemed pleased with the idea. "I hope it was okay for me to presume upon your generosity."

"No presumption necessary, it's a perfect plan. You can be away from your parents' house for nine or more hours a day. I think we can make this work. With that idea, you've given me an idea of my own."

"What's that?" Amanda was curious to see what he had just thought of.

"Why don't we quit standing in the foyer and get more comfortable in the living room?" he suggested as he started to lead the way down the hall.

Amanda wracked her brain for whatever solution Riccan might have come up with, and just as she was sitting on the couch she snapped her fingers and declared, "You're going to time travel with me, aren't you?"

"You're quicker than I imagined," Riccan praised. "I think we can make it work, for a little while at least. It takes a toll over time, but I think we can manage it until we come up with a better solution. How much time do we have today?"

"I told my mom I might be rather late tonight. Oh! That reminds me, I got my own phone today!" she announced as she dug into her purse and triumphantly displayed her brand new phone.

Riccan laughed at her enthusiasm and said, "Perfect! What's your phone number? At least this way we won't have to worry about your parents accidentally listening in to our phone conversations."

"I don't think they'd do that," she defended them even as she began to wonder if her mother would actually eavesdrop and rationalize it with protecting her baby from a predatory stranger. She gave Riccan her new number, and he immediately entered it into the contact information on his phone.

"Okay," Riccan announced as he stood up from the couch, "we should get going."

"What? Where are we going?" Amanda stared up at Riccan as though he had just lost his mind.

"We are going to meet with my parents. I don't think we should wait any longer for this news. Besides, my father may be able to help with your unique situation," Riccan reasoned even as he was itching to get moving.

"If you say so," Amanda agreed reluctantly. She had desperately wanted to meet Elder Daven before, but now that it was an actual reality on her immediate horizon the idea rather intimidated her.

"Do you still have your journal in your purse?" Riccan suddenly remembered they would need that important piece of information.

Amanda patted her bag and said, "I don't leave home without it."

Riccan nodded approval with a broad smile on his face. "You sound like an endorsement for American Express," he teased.

Amanda cocked her head in confusion.

Riccan realized she had probably slept through the entire ad campaign and told her about it as they walked through the kitchen and out the side door to the garage. Just as Amanda remembered, the space looked unoccupied, but she knew differently. Riccan led the way and opened the side door to the telepod in the same way he had on their last ill-fated trip.

She walked up the short ramp and sat down in her seat on the right. Riccan immediately followed and sat on the left.

"Do you want to practice the start-up procedure you talked about in your journal?" Riccan asked innocently.

Amanda violently shook her head and said, "Not a chance! The last time I operated this machine we crashed, burned, and most likely died. I do not want a repeat performance! You just do what you normally do. I take that back; you should skip the jump over to the Florida Middle Ground this time since I have a bad feeling about it."

"Good idea." Riccan shuddered at Amanda's recounting of her final memory with him. He definitely did not want that truth to become a reality. He shut the side door from the control panel and then performed all of the procedures to get them on their way. With Amanda's premonition in mind, he opted to teleport directly to his parents' house in Tuala without another Earth stop along the way. It would take a little longer, perhaps another second, but it would give him some peace of mind. Tualan telepods were built with anti-collision equipment so he would not have to worry about their safety in Tuala.

Within minutes of taking their seats in the telepod, everything went utterly dark and soundless as they teleported between locations. The transfer took the extra second as they moved across the veil out of Earth and into Tuala. They reappeared approximately fifty feet off of the ground at a well-manicured estate even grander than Riccan's had been on Earth.

Amanda was impressed as she avidly searched the grounds to familiarize herself with Tuala once more. Naturally, she had never been to this part of Tuala, but it still had the same otherworldly feel she remembered from before. It almost felt as though she were moving through a dream as Riccan set the craft down on the landing pad on the lawn. She could see several people coming out of the back door and lining up on the grand patio to see who had arrived.

Riccan led the way out of the telepod and across the broad expanse of lawn. He never forgot how good it felt to come home and this time was no different. He saw his father waiting for him next to the railing of the courtyard. Riccan waved as he got close enough. His father returned the wave enthusiastically and turned to someone standing on his right to tell them something. That person swiftly turned and went back into the house.

Excitement lengthened Riccan's steps, and he bounded up the stairs three at a time to greet his father in a bear hug. Both men thumped one another on the back, and each stated how good it was to see the other.

Amanda took her time ascending the steps to allow the father and son to reunite in relative privacy. She had just reached the top step when they parted. His father looked beyond his son and said to Riccan, "Have you finally decided to grant your mother's dearest wish? Who is this lovely woman you have brought home to meet us?"

Riccan had the grace to blush as he realized he could probably easily have those types of feelings for Amanda, but he promptly answered with, "Don't presume too much, Father. Amanda Covington, may I present my father, Elder Daven."

The two people put out their hands to shake in greeting. Both said, "Pleased to meet you," at the same time and laughed at the coincidence.

"Dad, we have an unusual matter to present to you. Do you have time to meet with us? I'm sorry I didn't consider your busy schedule when I showed up here so rudely."

"Unannounced or not, you are always welcome in this house, Riccan. Your mother will be thrilled. I'm surprised we haven't heard her squeal with delight upon hearing of your arrival. I sent one of the staff to get her when I saw it was you walking across the lawn. Let's go inside out of this hot sun," he said as he put his arm back around Riccan and turned them to enter the house through the back door.

Amanda stayed by Riccan's side as they went into the grand house. Amanda had wondered what type of living accommodations were made for the Elders. She figured she did not have to wonder anymore.

"Do you want to meet in here or somewhere more private?" Daven asked his son as he gestured to the enormous living room overlooking the vast estate at the back of the residence.

"Definitely private," Riccan said emphatically.

Daven looked questioningly at his son's tone but kept his counsel until they could have the privacy his son was requesting. He led the way down several hallways until they came to his private office. He figured his official office would still be a bit too open for Riccan's discussion based on the serious expression he had seen.

"Will this do?" he asked his son with a solemn expression. It was not often his son came home, never with a woman, and never with a serious matter to discuss. He was starting to feel a bit apprehensive.

"This is perfect, Dad. I think we should wait until Mom gets here, so we don't have to repeat the story."

"Are you in trouble, Son?" Daven could not help but prod for some clue as to what was coming.

"No, it's nothing like that, but it's still a pretty serious matter. I think together, you and Mom can piece through the puzzle. We hope you'll have an answer for our particular situation." Riccan did not like to be cryptic with his father, but he really did want to have both his parents present before they got into any of the details.

"Go ahead and sit down and I'll see what's keeping your mother," Daven said, and then he left the room to go search for her himself.

Amanda turned to Riccan and whispered, "Riccan, I'm really scared. Are you sure this is the right thing to be doing?"

"Absolutely, Amanda! You have nothing to worry about with my parents. They are uniquely qualified to hear your story and understand the position you have found yourself in. I promise this will work out as it should." He had planned on saying more, but he caught sight of his parents coming up the hallway, and he hurriedly said, "They're back."

Amanda swiftly turned around so she could meet Riccan's mother. She was shocked at how tiny of a woman she actually was, no more than five feet tall if that. Amanda watched her smile radiantly and rush forward to greet her. Amanda held out her hand for a proper greeting but was stunned when the small woman grabbed her into a hug. Awkwardly she hugged her back.

Riccan smiled at his mother's enthusiasm and introduced the two of them formally, "Amanda Covington this is my mother, Nena Stel."

"It's nice to meet you Mrs. Stel," Amanda said very properly.

Daven and Nena looked at one another with a knowing glance before Nena corrected Amanda by saying, "Please, just call me Nena."

Riccan finally caught on and instructed Amanda with, "In Tuala they don't use the terms 'mister' or 'missus.' I should have thought to warn you about that before we came."

Daven's curiosity was about to consume him that his son would bring someone from Earth to Tuala. This must be a very fascinating situation for this to have happened. He wanted to get their meeting underway immediately, so he said, "Shall we be seated? Riccan has a matter of some grave importance he wishes to discuss with us."

Nena looked at her husband with a look of expectancy. When he just shrugged ignorance of the matter, she glumly sat in the chair next to her husband. She did not like being the last to know something. With a naturally curious nature, she wanted to hear their story in the quickest means possible. "Go ahead; we're ready, honey."

Riccan spoke into the silence and said, "This is really Amanda's story, but, in the end, I believe it will affect all of us in some way. Amanda? Are you ready?"

"I'm not sure where to begin," she looked back at him with fear in her eyes.

"Why don't you get out your journal and tell it to them exactly as you did with me yesterday. I think it's best if they have some history before we get to the part where we'll need their help." He smiled to reassure her.

Amanda nodded stiffly and reached onto the floor to retrieve her journal from her purse. She cleared her throat a couple of times and then opened the small book. With a last glance toward Riccan, she began reading.

Riccan was amazed Amanda was able to get through the entire account without either of his parents interrupting. They must have been more stunned by her tale than he had been. He looked back at his mother and realized her expression leaned more toward fear than surprise, and he asked, "So? What do you guys think?"

Daven was the first to recover his voice and asked, "Can I see the inscription which you found in the text?" He held out his hand for Amanda to give him her journal.

She reluctantly passed the book across the desk. Her fear of the Elders' power was more apparent than she had been willing to admit before. Her fate depended on this Elder and his wife. She looked over at Riccan and saw he was peaceful with his parents and she decided she needed to try to calm her own nerves. For them to figure out their next steps, she would have to be more relaxed.

"Ah, I see," Daven said as his eyes skimmed the page of the journal.

> *"From a far-away land*
> *There will come in time*
> *Intuition is in hand*
> *Strange details known.*
> *With ties to the people*
> *From one of my own*
> *There will be a sign.*
> *Those born to this one*
> *Will transform all.*

Lucinden will pursue
Elders will fall
Then all made new."

"I guess our long wait has finally come to an end," he announced unexpectedly.

Everyone stared at Daven, hoping he would explain his cryptic remark. Nena gasped as she comprehended his words. Daven looked back at his wife and nodded knowingly. "She's the one, Nena."

"The one what?" both Riccan and Amanda spoke in unison.

"The one prophesied in the Unity Song. You remember the words to that song, don't you, Riccan? Please sing it for us," Daven requested.

Riccan had to go back through his memories before he finally recalled the phrasing of the childhood song:

"Crystal around the neck,
Follow the next step,
Changes today,
Changes tomorrow,
We all become one."

Amanda listened to the words, but still did not comprehend the Elder's implications and said, "I don't understand."

Daven weighed his words before answering. After a moment of consideration he finally said, "If you put the words of the Unity Song with the new directive from the ancient text, I believe we have a powerful argument for a change coming to our world on Tuala. I believe, Amanda, that you are the key to those changes. Your experiences are quite unique and show you have great intuition for the people of Tuala. I am going to arrange for you to meet with Jehoban. I believe that is the path in which you are next bound. Will you agree to meet with Jehoban?"

"I would love nothing better," Amanda answered before she fully grasped the idea she was actually going to be in the presence of the Creator of the Universe. Her adrenaline started to pump through her blood, and her hands began to shake. She realized she was actually becoming terrified of her own destiny. This was not what she had had in mind when she set out to return to Tuala. She just wanted to have her children back, if they were even real, and then begin a family with Riccan. She did not know she would become the answer to some ancient prophecy.

Nena could see Amanda's fear beginning to blossom and suddenly interrupted the silence with, "Nothing will be getting done until after we've had a good meal together. We haven't seen Riccan in ages and I, for one, would love to hear what he's been up to since his last visit."

Daven had thought his wife's sudden change of subject was slightly out of character until he, too, looked at the stricken expression on Amanda's face. Once again, he appreciated his wife's ability to know the right thing to do in any situation. He followed her cue and said, "Nothing needs to be decided tonight. Let's go sit down to a family dinner, and we can worry about this other matter at a later time. We've waited thousands of years for a solution to present itself, a few more days or even weeks will hardly make any difference." He hoped what he was saying were actually true. Time might be of the essence, but Amanda needed to be willing to do her part. If he scared her away from her destiny, then he could hardly be qualified to remain an Elder.

Amanda felt a huge weight lift from her shoulders when she realized Riccan's parents were not going to whisk her away to an uncertain future. She would have a little time to get familiar with the idea of meeting Jehoban before it became an actuality. Releasing her breath in a rush, she looked over at Riccan and noticed he also appeared to be more relieved.

Daven rapidly wrote down the new passage and then stood up and said, "Is anyone other than me hungry?" Daven reluctantly handed the journal back to Amanda.

Everyone laughed and stood up as well. With a lightened mood, they walked in pairs to the private family dining hall.

Amanda was relieved to see it only seated six people so it would not be a stuffy and uncomfortable dinner at an immense table. With the smell of food wafting from the open door, Amanda felt herself grow hungrier with every step.

They sat at the table, Riccan was on Amanda's immediate left. His parents sat directly across from them so they would be able to converse with ease. For some unaccountable reason, Amanda no longer felt ill at ease with Riccan's family. They had proved they were willing to accept Amanda for who she claimed to be and did not hold it against her. *Except for being the key to a prophecy*, Amanda reminded herself sarcastically. She pushed that idea aside and determined to have a good time visiting with Riccan's parents.

Nena began the conversation with, "So how did you two meet, officially, that is?"

Amanda tipped her head to indicate this story was for Riccan to tell.

Riccan explained the search and rescue mission and their success. He said they met for dinner later that night. He saw his mother's expression of expectation and knew she was a hopeless romantic. He ended with, "I've only known Amanda for two days now, although, I must admit with everything she's shared with us, I do feel as though we've known one another a lot longer."

Nena clapped her hands together and declared, "I think it's just wonderful. You two are perfect for one another!"

Daven rolled his eyes at his wife's overreaction. "Let's not put the cart before the horse, Nena. Let them get to know one another first!"

Nena did not want to let it go and declared, "Amanda has already decided. Haven't you, Amanda?"

Feeling very much put on the spot, Amanda managed to blush violently but was saved from answering by the delivery of the dinner. She had never been so relieved to see food in her life. If she were forced to answer she would have said yes, but she wanted Riccan to be on the same page first. It was definitely too soon for him to have made a decision.

Amanda was thrilled to be eating the most flavorful food ever in Tuala. She had forgotten how incredible the dishes could be. Eating until she was way too full, she finally pushed her plate away and said quietly to Riccan, "I don't think I can eat another bite."

He smiled at her as he continued to put food on his plate when he went back for a third helping of the foxl stew. There had been times when he was away from Tuala for extended periods of time that he had come back and eaten more than he should have. He understood her desire in wanting to try it all.

Now that their hunger had been assuaged, the conversation began again around the table. Amanda fervently hoped the talk would not return to the budding relationship between herself and Riccan. She wanted to see where they would go naturally and not because the idea was forced on him by his parents, well, his mom really. She looked across the table and smiled at the woman she was just thinking about.

Nena returned her smile with a knowing look in her eye before looking away to her husband as he began to speak.

"Are you planning on going back to Earth tonight?" Daven asked Riccan while he also included Amanda in his gaze. He hoped they would say no and spend some time at the Residence with them.

"Yes, Dad. We still have to figure out a way for Amanda to be able to leave on a more permanent basis. Her mother is very reluctant to see Amanda leave the house for obvious reasons," he said as he squeezed Amanda's knee under the table in sympathy.

Amanda jumped a little at the unexpected touch, but then she tried to relax since she did not want Riccan to remove his hand from its current location. She was thrilled he would even be bold enough to make a move in the first place.

Nena defended Amanda's mother by saying, "You can't blame your mother, Amanda. I'd be a bit overbearing if something were to happen to Riccan. It's what a mom does for her children. They are a constant presence in a mother's mind."

Amanda felt a stab of guilt that she could possibly have children of her own and yet they were only occasionally on her mind. *Does that make me a terrible mother?* Amanda thought to herself. Soon enough she would get the answers she sought from Jehoban Himself, as daunting as the idea was, she was willing if it were to give her some peace of mind for her faulty memories.

Riccan spoke again into the silent room. "We should probably think about heading back soon. We've already spent a few more hours here than I had anticipated."

"Sorry," Amanda apologized. She knew her storytelling took too long.

"It's not your fault, Amanda. We finished what needed to get done," Riccan reassured.

"I guess this means the ball is now in my court," Daven stated.

"Our court, honey. We'll work on this puzzle together," Nena informed her husband.

"Always, my dear, always," Daven agreed as he nodded loving affirmation at his partner in everything.

"So, should we set up a regular meeting every morning this week to go over what our next steps might be?" Riccan inquired of his parents.

"We can plan for that, but hopefully it won't take all that long," Daven replied.

Riccan pushed his chair away from the table and stood up. "Thank you for dinner; it was as wonderful as always."

Amanda hastily put in, "Yes, thank you. It was a pleasure to meet both of you. I guess I'll be seeing you again tomorrow."

Both Daven and Nena stood up and prepared to walk out with the young couple. Nena reached out to hold her husband's hand as they matched paces, Daven shortening his stride to his wife's slower speed.

Amanda could see the couple were madly in love with one another. She hoped one day to find the same sort of relationship with her significant other. She looked over at Riccan and wondered if he were going to be that man. With the example of his parents as he was growing up, at least he would know how to treat his partner.

Daven and Nena gave them both hugs on the edge of the back patio, opting to stay out of the way of the telepod as it took off. They walked down the stairs and across the broad expanse of lawn to get back to the telepod, knowing they were closely watched the entire time. Amanda felt slightly self-conscious, but also cared for at the same time. She understood Riccan had been very lucky in his upbringing to have parents who so obviously adored him. Her own parents had loved her just the same, but their love had been divided among their three girls. She thought there might be some difference because of the division.

They boarded the telepod and took their seats. The windshield was facing the patio, so they both waved farewell to Riccan's parents who promptly waved back. Riccan sped through the start-up procedures and entered an additional step for timing their return so Amanda would not get back to her parents' house too late.

Blackness overtook all of their senses as they teleported back to Earth. Amanda began to understand this was the first of many trips to come in her near future. She took several deep breaths and relaxed into her new world.

They popped back into existence in Riccan's garage. Once they touched down, and the telepod was deactivated, they went back into the house. As they walked through the kitchen, Amanda looked at the time on the microwave. She was certain her wristwatch would be off since they had spent so long in Tuala, but she was more than a little startled to see it was as late as it was. She had hoped to spend some time discussing the events of the evening with Riccan, but now she had to hurry home or face her mother's wrath.

"I have to get going," Amanda said almost apologetically.

"I know," Riccan agreed. "Feel free to come over as soon as you're able tomorrow morning. I'll be ready whenever you get here."

"Okay," Amanda replied lamely. She could not help but feel disappointed by Riccan's quick agreement for her to go home, but she was encouraged by his invitation to return early the next morning. She covered her yawn and turned to go to her car. The drive home would not take too long, but she felt so tired she almost wished she could just curl up in the guest bed upstairs.

"Text me when you get home safely, okay?" Riccan asked with concern for how tired Amanda appeared to be. He should have realized the time transfer would be harder on her since she was still recovering her stamina from the coma.

"Okay," she agreed as she tried to stifle yet another yawn. She decided she would definitely need to drive with the window down to keep awake.

Riccan walked her to the car and offered, "Do you want me to drive you home? You seem too tired to drive."

"No, I'll be fine. I'd rather not have to answer any more questions from my mom. I'll be back tomorrow," she added as she got into her car and rolled down the window. She started the engine and waved out the window as she drove away.

CHAPTER 19

Nena knew her husband almost better than she knew herself. She could tell the appearance of Amanda had made him very concerned. They had discussed the prophecy on many occasions, but they had both agreed it would probably be many generations in the future before it came to pass. Now they were faced with helping Amanda fulfill a prophecy which would probably take Daven's position away if the newest passage were to be taken at face value.

They had returned to Daven's office where he was seated at his desk with the paper in his hands. "I'd like to read that passage for myself, if you don't mind," Nena requested as she held out her hand for the text.

"Sure. I hope you can read something into it that I've missed. It sure makes a dire prediction for my position. You know I love my job serving the people. I'd hate to lose it because the times are changing," he despaired as he handed her the paper.

Nena turned her chair so the light from the window fell onto the page. She rapidly read the entire passage and then went over it again slowly line by line. By the end, she was convinced she had an idea which might put a new perspective on the writing. "I don't think it's saying all Elders will be gone." She put the paper down on the desk between them and pointed to the line above the Elders' section, "You see right here, this is talking about

Lucinden. I think he is going to make a push for power by corrupting some of the Elders. I think those are the ones who will fall. You could never be swayed by Lucinden so your position will be safe."

Daven wanted to believe his wife's interpretation was true. Her idea made a certain type of sense. The more he reviewed it in his mind, the more convinced he became she was right. "I love how you always see the bright side of things, Nena," he praised.

"It's only because I believe people are inherently good. I can't believe our entire social structure will be removed just because changes are on the horizon." Nena looked back at the text to reaffirm her original opinion on the interpretation of the prophecy.

"How long do you think I should wait before requesting an audience with Jehoban for Amanda?" Daven asked into the silence.

"We should spend a little more time getting to know her first, I think."

"Is it because you think she's the one for Riccan or because you want to delay the inevitable because she's the one to bring about change?"

Nena took a few moments to consider the question before she answered, "I think it's a little bit of both. She is the right one for Riccan. She's from Earth but has experienced, in her own unique way, life on Tuala. She's now from both worlds the same as Riccan."

"What if we do discover she had twin girls while she was in Tuala?"

"It would be great! We'd be grandparents that much sooner!"

Daven was not surprised she would eagerly embrace the immediate increase in the family. She loved children. He was only sorry he could not have given her more for herself.

"I guess we'll play it by ear. When they come tomorrow, we can spend some time getting to know Amanda and see if they have any ideas about the meaning of the newest prophecy. I'm sure Riccan is busy thinking about what it all could mean."

"I wouldn't be so sure of that since Amanda seems to be an interesting distraction from his usually sedate life," Daven teased.

Naturally, Nena took him seriously and agreed, "I think you're probably right!"

~

AMANDA HAD NOT APPRECIATED how much of a toll the trip had taken on her until she woke up after ten o'clock. She woke up slowly and stretched on the bed. She rolled over to see how much time she would have to get ready before she would have to leave and then saw what time it actually was. Immediately she shot out of the covers and ran across her room to get into the shower.

Naturally, she would oversleep on what could possibly be the most important day of her life. Raking the shampoo through her hair, she kept castigating herself for not setting the alarm. She skipped the conditioner and did not bother to shave either since she only wanted to get moving out of the house.

She was on the road only ten minutes after waking up. After driving for about ten minutes, Amanda thought she should check to make sure her journal was in her purse. Without taking her eyes off of the road, she reached over to investigate. Immediately she noticed a problem: her purse was not in the car.

"No, no, NO!" she yelled in the car as she frantically looked for a place to turn around. Not wanting to get pulled over without her license she had to manage her speed while she still hurried back to the house. Never before had she forgotten her purse, today was not going very well. She hoped it would begin to improve once she got going again. If the day continued in the same manner, then she was in for a lot of trouble.

Amanda decided there was nothing to be done with the time which had already been wasted. She was going to make the best of the time remaining. She turned up the radio and sang along with one of the new songs which had come out while she was 'away.' In no time, she turned into Riccan's driveway. As she was reaching to press the intercom, she saw the gate was already opening on its own.

Thinking Riccan must be trying to leave, she waited for a few seconds for his car to appear. When no car showed up, she cautiously rolled forward until she could see the whole driveway was clear of traffic. Somehow, Riccan must have programmed the gate to open for her car. She smiled at the implications of the small act of trust on his part.

After parking, she walked in the front door as he had instructed her the day before. She felt a little stealthy since this was not her house, but she boldly walked through the foyer and into the living room. Riccan was seated at a barstool at the kitchen island.

"Sorry, I'm so late," she said as she came up beside him. Riccan jumped with surprise even though Amanda had not consciously tried to be quiet.

"I didn't hear you come in," Riccan said as he looked up from what he was reading.

"Is that the Elder's Instructional Guide?" Amanda asked as she pulled up the bar stool next to him.

"Yeah, I was looking through it to see if anything else had changed since I'd looked at it last," he said with a sigh.

"It looks like you've been at this for quite a while. Have you noticed anything so far?" Amanda thought he looked more tired than she had felt last night. If he were too tired it would not be safe for them to travel in the telepod.

"Thankfully, no," he replied as he shut the book and pushed back from the island. "Do you want some coffee? I haven't had anything to eat or drink this morning, and I'm famished. Did you eat?"

"I would love some coffee, and no, I haven't eaten yet either. I forgot to set my alarm, and I rushed out of the house before it got too late to come see you."

Riccan smiled at his guest and asked in a teasing voice, "Would you like fried foxl and scrambled eggs? I hear they're your favorite."

"I can't imagine where you heard that," she teased back feeling her cheeks grow warmer. "I have it on good authority you were trained by the best in your culinary skills. It would only be fair for me to judge the results for myself."

"Such pressure! Give me a second to concentrate," he said as he visualized the ingredients to be combined for the dishes he had offered. Within just a few seconds, two plates appeared on the counter, the perfectly cooked food steaming and smelling delicious. "Bon apatite!" he declared as he presented Amanda with her breakfast. He sat down next to her after shoving the book across the island so it would not get any food spattered on it.

"Oops, I forgot the coffee!" he declared and then smiled as the cups of steaming black liquid appeared beside each of their plates.

"It never gets old!" Amanda shook her head in wonder.

"Didn't you learn how to do it, too?"

"I'm only good with simple things like a glass of water. In fact, I only discovered I could do that when I needed water to wash down my migraine pills." Amanda picked up her fork and began to eat, blowing across the food to cool it before putting it into her mouth.

"We'll need to work on your skills, it would appear. My parents are both very good teachers. When we go see them today, we can ask them to give you some lessons."

Amanda was embarrassed to ask his parents for such help and tried to argue, "They have better things to do than teach me to use my birth crystal. Besides, where would I use those talents here on Earth? It would most likely end up getting me into trouble."

Riccan looked at her strangely and finally said, "Were you and I both at the same meeting with my parents yesterday? I got the distinct impression from my parents that you are going to be a very important person on Tuala. You are going to need to know how to access the power of your crystal. You're going to need lessons and who better than my parents who already know your destiny."

Amanda choked on the bite she was swallowing and had to cough several times before she managed to say, "My destiny? Don't you think you're being slightly dramatic, Riccan?"

"You were the one to whom the new prophecy was shown. I think that makes this your destiny," Riccan replied matter-of-factly as he shoveled another huge bite into his mouth to chew.

"I'd rather think I have some say over my own destiny. I don't really like the idea that my life is being planned for me without my consent," Amanda replied sullenly as she took another bite of the fried foxl.

"Oh, I'm sure you'll have a say in it. However, I believe your answer will be yes because that's the type of person you are. We still don't have all of the facts, but we'll work on that as well."

"Yeah, like when I meet with Jehoban. Riccan, I can't believe I agreed to meet with Him as easily as though I were going to a doctor's appointment. He's the Creator of the universe for Pete's sake. What was I thinking?" Amanda was rapidly losing her appetite and began pushing the eggs around the plate with her fork. She looked over at Riccan with a stricken expression.

"Like I said, you'll do what you need to do it when the time comes. I have faith in your ability, Amanda. You should have more faith in yourself. Don't play with your food, just eat it. When we're done here, we can head over to my parents' house," Riccan admonished as he finished the last of his food and put down his fork. He wrapped his fingers around the coffee cup and inhaled the rich aroma as he watched Amanda over the rim of the cup.

Amanda almost told him she had lost her appetite, but then she recalled how exhausting the day before had been for her. She decided she would need the nourishment to help her with building her stamina. She forced herself to finish the meal, feeling guilty for not giving it the appreciation it deserved since it was actually quite delicious.

"It may not have looked like it to watch me eat, but your cooking is absolutely fabulous. Thank you for breakfast," she said apologetically.

"I understand your concern for the future, but we can only live in the moment. Try to keep that in mind as we move forward, okay?"

Riccan's statement had a profound impact on Amanda at that moment, and she burst into tears.

"What happened, Amanda? Did I say something wrong?" Riccan touched her shoulder with concern for her abrupt change of mood.

She wiped the tears from her eyes and smiled weakly as she replied, "No, you said exactly the right thing. I need to focus on the moment and not worry about anything else. Don't worry, Riccan, I'll be okay in just a minute." She wiped the tears from her hands onto her jeans and then reached for her own cup of coffee. She was slightly embarrassed for her mood swing, and she wondered if this were a side effect of being in a coma. To hide her momentary confusion, she brought the coffee to her lips and sipped cautiously.

They sat together in silence, both contemplating what events would transpire when they finally got a move on the day. Amanda was concerned about taking people's time away from their important duties. Riccan was concerned about Amanda's journey if she were the key to the prophecy. Both ended up finishing their coffee at the same time and then smiling at one another as though it were a private joke when their empty cups both clanked onto the counter top at the same time.

With a thought, Riccan took care of all of the dishes. He grabbed the ancient text and said, "I need to go put this away, and then we can get going. Are you ready?"

Amanda nodded as Riccan looked at her and then he turned to take care of the old book. Amanda wondered if she were ever going to be ready to take on this new task. When she had been planning it in her head it all seemed so simple: find Riccan, go to Tuala, see if she really did have children of her own, find Neal, and come back home to live out her life on Earth. She laughed at how naïve she had been. She should have known life was never as simple as she imagined it to be.

CHAPTER 20

There was far less fanfare when they arrived on the lawn at the Stel Residence. Nobody came out onto the terrace to greet them so they walked into the back door unannounced. Riccan led the way into his father's private study. He was not surprised to find both of his parents waiting for them as though they had known when they were arriving; they had been doing that very thing for as long as he could remember. One day he would have to find out their secret of always knowing.

"Good afternoon, Riccan, Amanda," Daven said to both of them as they made themselves comfortable in the chairs they had occupied the previous day.

"Have you made any progress interpreting the newest prophecy?" Riccan asked first thing. He never was one for making small talk.

"Your mother has an interesting interpretation on the part about the Elders. She believes Lucinden will make a play for power which involves corrupting some of the Elders. The ones who fall prey to Lucinden's predations are the ones who will fall."

"It seems as though that's been going on for some time. Why would the prophecy appear now?" Riccan asked.

"I think it comes back to Amanda." He gestured toward where Amanda was seated.

Amanda could feel the color rising in her cheeks. She wished she could have more control over her complexion even as she had to agree with Daven's assessment.

"Riccan was saying he thought I was the one responsible for the changes to come to Tuala because I was the one who discovered the newest predictive text," Amanda said as she looked over at Riccan for him to agree with her statement.

Riccan nodded confirmation and then said, "If Amanda is to be the key, then she'll need additional training with her birth crystal."

"Oh! I hadn't thought about that," Nena gasped as she glanced over at Amanda and asked, "Do you really have your own birth crystal?"

"Yes," she affirmed as she pulled up on the chain until the crystal rested on the outside of her shirt.

"A clear diamond! I should have guessed," Daven exclaimed.

"What would make you say that?" Amanda asked with genuine interest.

Daven immediately switched into teaching mode to answer Amanda's question. "The hue of the crystal directly corresponds with the abilities of the wearer as well as the amount of protection needed. Diamond characterizes innocence, love, and healing. They range in color from white, yellow, blue, pink and black. The lighter the crystal, the quicker the wearer is to access the elemy for healing.

"Since you have a clear, or white as it's named, you will be able to heal and comfort people easily. The diamond is also known for being an amplifier stone which simply means you can amplify the abilities of those around you.

"Riccan, have you noticed such an occurrence when you used your powers around Amanda?" Daven asked his son as he finished his explanation.

"I hadn't really considered it before, but, yes, it was easier to make breakfast this morning. Usually, when I'm as tired as I was, it would have taken me twice as long to get it all put together." He grinned at Amanda thinking there was something else which was special when she was with him.

"But wouldn't that mean I'd strengthen the powers of bad people just as easily?" Amanda asked with a sudden intuitive leap.

"Yes, to an extent. Your ability is geared more toward your own intentions. If someone's ideas are going against your own, then you would unconsciously shield your power away from them. It works on people from Earth to a certain extent. You may have noticed you probably got your way more often as you were growing up," Daven assured Amanda.

Amanda chuckled as she could recall her sisters both griping about how their parents always did what she asked. Now she finally had the real reason rather than thinking her parents just loved her more. She had been foolish and self-centered even to think such a thing of her parents. She nodded agreement with Daven, and he continued to expand on his ideas.

"We should set up a schedule to find out where Amanda's abilities lie and then work on strengthening her weaknesses. I have time for an evaluation today if you want to go forward with this idea."

Amanda was shocked to have this come up so soon, but she could not come up with any argument to the contrary so she agreed by nodding her head.

Nena looked over at her son and said, "I think they won't need an audience for this evaluation. Why don't we go to my private office and we can get caught up on all of the things which have kept you too busy to come visit! Shall we?" she asked as she stood and offered her arm to her tall son.

Amanda watched the mother and son leave the room, smiling at their easy relationship. She hoped her own relationship with her parents would become as easy in the near future. She shook her head to clear her thoughts and looked back to see Daven watching her intently. "I'm ready whenever you are."

Daven began the evaluation and soon discovered Amanda was quite adept at the first four levels of training, usually reserved for when children first entered school. These levels included: pulling energy from the crystal, moving it to another location, putting the energy back into the crystal, and creating a breeze. He moved on to the second-grade level and found her to be equally skilled in both boiling and freezing water, both creating and extinguishing a flame, as well as moving an object and her ability to memorize vast amounts of information rapidly. Knowing she had only had training in her dreams he was even more impressed. He was starting to get a better idea of what Amanda's role would be in bringing about changes to their world, but he kept his counsel to himself.

Before he began assessing her skills with the middle school level lessons, he asked her, "I seem to recall when you were reading your journal you had said you and Juila had created meals together. Was it Juila who was doing it or was it yourself?"

"I'm not sure." She considered the question and her memories and replied, "I think it was a joint effort." She sat silently while Daven made some notations on his patil regarding her progress. She suddenly could not contain her next question. "Since everything else from my dreams appear to be real, do you believe that Jena and Juila are also real here in Tuala? Do you think I have children here?"

Daven stopped typing to look at Amanda's troubled expression and said, "With you, I believe anything is possible. I'm sure you can get your answer when you meet with Jehoban." He had meant to be consoling and did not realize he had created another hurdle for Amanda to cross.

She was terrified at the idea of meeting with Jehoban, but she would be willing to do just about anything to find out if her children actually existed. "I'm scared," she finally managed to say.

"I understand your apprehension but consider the one you are planning to meet with. He already loves you and wants the best for you. Think of Him as a parent who only wants the best for His children. If you have any concerns or questions, just ask Him and He will do His best to answer what you need to know."

"What I need to know may not be what I want to know!" Amanda suddenly laughed at the audacity of the whole situation. She tried to see Jehoban as Daven was describing Him. It would take some adjustment, but she felt she could probably come to terms with Daven's assessment.

"I see you are already starting to comprehend," Daven praised. "Now let's work on the next level of your assessment, shall we?"

Amanda readily agreed since she really enjoyed working with her crystal. She felt as though her own body were being energized as she used her crystal. The next level was on healing and Amanda had not ever received any training from Alena or Rasa. She listened intently as Elder Daven explained the process of accessing the elemy and finding the lifeline.

"You have the ability to heal yourself or others with this technique. It is much harder to heal yourself than others, I must caution. Sometimes, when you are in extreme pain, it can alter the way you use the energy and produce an unwanted result. It's always better to seek out a wise-woman for serious matters."

Amanda nodded as she listened.

"So, go ahead and close your eyes and seek out the part of you which is connected with the elemental energy, or elemy, as most call it now."

Amanda remembered the lessons she had overseen of Elder Debbon teaching the wise-woman class. She had witnessed the concentration required for this to be successful. She chided herself for allowing her own distracting thoughts and immediately closed her eyes.

She felt the flow of energy surrounding her crystal and imagined herself following that energy to its source. She could imagine herself sinking far down into the ground until the energy floated freely around her body. For the first time in a long time, she felt completely energized.

Knowing she had achieved her goal she traced her life-line back to herself. She opened her eyes and beamed at her instructor. "I've never felt anything so wonderful in my life!"

Daven had witnessed the truth of her statement so many times in the past that he knew she had accomplished the level he had asked of her. He noted her easy success on his patil.

"Now we'll move on to creation. This is where we'll take a field trip into the kitchen. Normally this would be done in a location where the student is more familiar with their setting, but I doubt you'll have any trouble anyway." He stood up from his desk and felt his knees and back crack as he straightened himself from sitting so long. "Besides, this is a good time to take a break to eat. We can accomplish two tasks in one!"

Amanda chuckled at Daven's last comment and could not help but add, "Unless you find my creation to be inedible. I've never professed to be a good chef."

"You're in luck, I have a strong stomach and an untrained palette," he replied hastily and led the way from the room.

Amanda had never seen this part of the Residence and was impressed with the opulence of it all. She could see why they would be worried about the newest prophecy saying the Elders would fall. If this were her home, she would not want to lose it either.

They arrived in the kitchen which had several women working at different stations. Amanda realized they were preparing the various dishes for the evening meal. It occurred to her that these women could have used their power to create the dishes and she wondered why they did not. Finally, she could not contain her question and asked, "Why don't they just create the dish like you're asking me to do?"

"That's a fair question, Amanda. Some people prefer to have their meals prepared in the 'old fashioned' way while others have simply not learned the skill for which you are being tested today," he answered patiently.

"Some of us just enjoy working with the food and making a masterpiece," one of the cooks spoke up from across the room with a smile as she continued to chop vegetables.

"And then there's that reason," Daven admitted with a smile for Amanda. "Melba, since you have decided to participate in this conversation, can you gather a few supplies for me?"

Melba wiped her hands on her apron and replied, "Sure. What are you looking to make?"

"I'd like Amanda to make a basic vegetable soup."

"Just one moment," Melba said as she started gathering supplies and putting them on the sturdy table in front of where they had stopped.

Amanda felt slightly nervous as she watched the pile of supplies grow in front of her. She had never made soup before, and yet now this was to be her first test. Daven had said this was simple and she wondered what he would consider complicated. She felt lost.

Melba saw Amanda's face and asked, "Honey, have you ever made soup?"

"No."

"Would you like me to tell you the process?" she asked kindly.

"I would be forever grateful!"

Amanda listened as Melba listed the steps needed to make the ingredients ready for the dish. There were several things which could be accomplished at the same time if a person were preparing this the traditional way. Amanda wished she could just let Melba take over so she would not have to embarrass herself with a horrible first creation.

"That's all there is to it, my girl," Melba finished.

"Yes, that's all," Amanda said disconsolately.

"Thank you, Melba, for your very thorough instructions," Daven said and then turned to Amanda. "Go ahead and give it a try."

After reviewing each of the steps listed by Melba, she closed her eyes and concentrated on seeing each of the food items being in their final product. She felt the energy drawing from her birth crystal, and suddenly her confidence level increased. This was not going to be very hard after all. The recipe was complete in her head, and the finished product appeared on the table. Unfortunately, Amanda forgot to visualize the bowl in which it would be placed, and the broth and vegetables poured in every direction across the surface of the table.

"Oh, this is terrible!" Amanda cried as she tried to stop the food from dripping all over the clean floor. "I'm so sorry! Is there a rag I can use to sop this up?" She looked around desperately to locate anything she could use to clean her enormous mess.

When she looked back at the table, she was stunned to see it was spotless again. Immediately she looked up at Daven's pleased expression and said, "Did you do that? I need to learn how to do that!"

"Yes, we'll get to that level in a bit. Now, try to make the soup again. This time, make sure you correct your error." Daven crossed his arms and waited for his student to try again.

Amanda's face turned red, and she promptly closed her eyes so she could pretend she was somewhere else. She repeated each of the steps in her mind and found the process was easier the second time. When the dish was complete, Amanda purposefully envisioned a large serving bowl for her creation to reside. Without incident, the dish was present on the table. Amanda opened her eyes and sighed with relief.

Daven laughed at Amanda's expression and said, "Let's try your soup, shall we?" He picked up two spoons and handed one to Amanda.

They dipped their utensils into the broth, both tasting the soup at the same time. Amanda thought it could use a bit more seasoning.

Daven nodded approval and said, "Nicely done. I think we can cross this lesson off the list." He turned to Melba and said, "Please serve this at dinner this evening."

"No, please don't! It's not very good," Amanda pleaded.

"Melba will take care of it," Daven assured. "Let's take a walk while I explain the next lesson we are going to tackle. Are you feeling well enough to continue?"

"I'd feel better if you told me you'd throw the soup away. Otherwise, I feel perfectly fine to go over the next skill." Amanda looked back over her shoulder to see what was going to happen to her soup. She saw Melba tasting the broth and smiling in satisfaction.

Mortified, Amanda turned her attention to where Daven was walking. She realized he had been talking and she had not heard him. Feeling like a terrible student, Amanda interrupted Daven by saying, "I'm sorry. I was so distracted by Melba tasting the soup that I didn't hear what you just said."

"It's no matter; I was just making small talk until you were ready to continue. A good teacher will always know if their student is paying attention. It appears you are now ready?"

"Yes, you have my undivided attention," Amanda assured him as she watched carefully where they were walking. The last thing she would need now would be to trip and fall to complete her list of mortifying actions in front of Riccan's father.

"We are moving on to the task of distance notation. Are you familiar with the process?"

"I've heard of it, but I've never tried to do it."

"Good. The process is rather simple. First, you imagine where you would like your writing to appear, and then you visualize what you want to write. Then it's as simple as creating a meal; you imagine it completed at the remote location."

Amanda groaned at the reference to cooking, but she understood what he was telling her to do. She nodded her understanding, but was unsure if he wanted her to try it.

"Did you bring your journal today?" Daven asked as though he had read her mind.

"Yes, it's in my purse in your office."

"Perfect. Imagine a short sentence which would be relevant to today's teachings and place it in your journal. Let me know when you've finished." He continued walking silently. They had passed through the double doors of the grand living room and were now outside on the patio.

Amanda stopped walking and rested her hands on the railing which overlooked where they had parked the telepod. She was trying to think of what she would like to write in her journal and finally decided on the right phrase. In a few moments, she felt as though she had completed the task. She turned to Daven and said, "I'm done."

"Wow, that was quick! Are you sure you've never done this before?"

"Very sure, and maybe I didn't even complete what I think I did," Amanda replied with a touch of humility.

"Let's just go back to my office and take a look," Daven said as he turned around and led the way.

CHAPTER 21

When they entered the office, Daven strolled to his side of the desk while Amanda returned to the chair she had used earlier. She reached into her purse and retrieved the journal. Without opening it up, she handed it across the desk to Daven. "It should be on the last page," she instructed.

Daven opened the small book to the last page and burst out laughing as he read the last passage, 'Please don't serve my soup at dinner!' He closed the book and chuckled some more as he returned the journal to Amanda. He made a few more notations on his patil and then considered the next skill they would try to tackle. Normally it would be navigation, but he was more interested in seeing if Amanda were at all sensitive to a person's aura.

Amanda got the distinct impression she was not going to win the battle over the soup so she shrugged with good grace and put her journal back in to her purse. If Elder Daven wanted to poison everyone with her terrible soup, she would just let him. Really the joke would be on him and not her. She had tried to warn him!

"Amanda, are you familiar with what an aura is?" Daven finally decided to ask.

"I've heard of them, but I always thought they were a figment of the imagination. Are you saying they are real?" Amanda realized Daven was serious with his inquiry. Naturally, she would have to adjust her Earth thinking before she would comprehend there was so much more available to the human brain than she was raised to believe. It was the way Tualans thought of their environment and their interactions within it which had first drawn her to want to stay in Tuala.

"Not only are they very real, but they are also quite useful. A person's aura can tell a lot about a person. Like the colors of the birth crystals, the colors of the aura have the same meaning. An aura can change color as the intent of the person changes. Naturally, we can't wander around in 'aura mode' always analyzing the people around us, but if used correctly, it can help in making decisions in life."

"Like if the person you want to marry would be the right fit?" Amanda asked and then blushed again as she realized she had been thinking about Riccan and she was discussing this matter with his father.

"Exactly," Daven continued as if the thought had not occurred to him, "The skill is learned when you become educated in seeing the space around a person rather than the person themselves. Once you learn to access it, you can also expand the aura for easier analysis. Does that make sense?"

As Amanda listened to the explanation, she realized something she had missed earlier. Her daughter had told her that her crystal matched what she saw in her mother. Juila had also mentioned something similar when she was referring to Riccan and her together. Excitedly she explained what she had been thinking to Daven and finally asked, "Do you think Juila was reading our auras?"

"It certainly sounds as if that were the case. I'd certainly like to meet your children someday."

"Me, too," Amanda said sadly. "Do you think Jehoban will know about them if I were to ask?"

"I have no doubt about it, Amanda," he answered assuredly. Seeing his student's attention was once again wandering he decided, "I think we are done with today's lessons. Let's go find Nena and Riccan."

Amanda's attention was once again focused on the idea of being able to be with Riccan again. She had not realized how much she missed him. Eagerly she stood up and asked, "Where do you suppose they've gone?"

"We'll start with Nena's office, she said that's where they would go," Daven replied.

They walked in silence again. Amanda felt comfortable with Daven, and the silence was comforting rather than awkward. She looked around at the paintings on the walls. The look was similar to the wall of family paintings she remembered from Barla's wall. It seemed it was a tradition for people on Tuala to have the portraits done to remember certain times in the family histories.

Daven reached a closed door and opened it after a quick tap. He smiled and opened the door wider as he had discovered both Nena and Riccan were still visiting with one another.

Nena smiled at seeing her husband and asked brightly, "How did the evaluation go, honey?"

Daven continued into the room until he came up behind his wife's chair. He put his hands on her shoulders and leaned down to kiss the top of her head. Once his greeting was completed, he finally answered her. "Amanda is quite skilled with the use of her birth crystal. It's amazing to believe she has never received any training except in her dreams."

An odd expression came over Nena's face as an idea struck her. She turned her face up toward her husband and said, "Do you think Amanda could be an intuitive?"

Daven lightly squeezed her shoulders before moving over to the side of the desk and resting his hip on the top as he considered his wife's inquiry. He had only ever heard of a natural intuitive before so he did not have any comparison for Amanda's obvious skill. He finally shrugged his shoulders and replied, "I don't really know. It might be another question which will have to be asked of Jehoban. He would definitely know."

Amanda groaned as if this conversation actually hurt as she said, "I don't want to be special. I'm just an average person on Earth."

Nena took pity on Amanda and tried to comfort her by saying, "We all have special talents, my dear. Don't try to deny any gift you've been given by Jehoban. It doesn't honor Him or yourself if you won't accept who you were born to be."

Amanda stared across the room at Nena for the wise words she had just imparted to her. She looked over at Riccan and said, "You seem to have gotten your wise sayings from your mother. Now I'll just have to come to terms with it myself."

"That's right, Amanda. The sooner you accept yourself for who you are, the easier and more fulfilling your life will become," Nena agreed.

Amanda wanted to change the subject and asked Riccan, "So what have you been doing while we were away?"

"I was telling Mom some of the adventures I've recently been on which had kept me away from Tuala for longer than when I was in school so long ago," Riccan replied.

Daven wished he could have heard the stories as well and asked, "Were you successful in any of your searches?" He knew Riccan had been following up on leads for locating the other twelve crystal skulls. They had thought they had discovered one a few anons ago, but it had turned out to be a replica and not an original.

"No real progress even though I do have several new leads to check out some time soon. I don't think there are many of the crystal skulls on Earth anymore. It seems as if our best leads have come from our Tualan contacts."

"Did you track down all of our relatives to see if any of them remember more about the family legend? People are usually more than willing to share a tale they think is so far-fetched as to be unbelievable. The crystal skull would definitely fit into the bazaar category of stories," Daven inquired.

"I've only managed to talk to about half of the people on the list we created. Our family seems to move around more than most other families. Also, they don't seem very concerned with leaving forwarding addresses more often than not. It's very frustrating!"

"Maybe you'd have better luck if Amanda were with you. She appears to be a natural amplifier and possibly an intuitive, both qualities which could be of great assistance in your search," Daven reasoned.

Amanda still managed to blush even though Daven's statement were more than likely true about her abilities. The more she considered the possibilities of her talents, the more she believed she could have something special. She also liked the idea of being able to spend more time with Riccan. What better way than to travel the country with him on his unusual quest?

Riccan considered his father's idea and turned to face Amanda as he asked, "I'd love to have the company. Would you want to take a few trips with me?"

"I think it would be a lot of fun. I don't know how much help I'd be on Earth, but I'd be more than willing to offer whatever assistance my skills would lend you." Amanda's heart skipped a beat with the idea, and she had to contain her desire for a little jump for joy.

"We should probably think about heading back," Riccan said as he glanced at his watch.

"Oh, you must stay for dinner. Amanda has created a dish for you to try," Daven teased as he winked across the office at Amanda.

"Ugh, you've got to be kidding. I think Riccan's right, we've got to get going," Amanda protested.

Nena did not understand the byplay which was occurring and innocently asked, "Did Amanda get to the creation lesson today?" She looked back and forth between her husband and Amanda.

"Yes, and further than that too. Riccan, please say you'll stay?" Daven practically begged.

Amanda was shaking her head back and forth.

Riccan smiled at Amanda's discomfort and was curious to see what she had created. In an instant, he changed his plans for the evening as he said, "I guess we'll have enough time to eat, but then we'll have to leave right afterward."

"Traitor," Amanda mumbled to Riccan as everyone got up to go to the dining room.

Riccan just smiled as he gestured for her to leave the room ahead of him.

They sat at the table, and the kitchen staff immediately began serving them their meal. Amanda watched as each item was placed on the table and was relieved to see her soup was not among them. She began to smile at Daven that the joke was on him when Melba appeared in the doorway holding the white soup taurine containing the dreaded vegetable soup.

"Ah," Daven announced as Melba placed the dish directly in front of him. "We'll start with Amanda's creation." He dished up a bowl for everyone and passed them out.

Melba managed to catch Amanda's eye as she was leaving the room. She winked at Amanda and gave her a small smile as she returned to the kitchen.

Amanda started to get the idea that Melba had added a few spices to her horribly bland soup. She started to have some hope that everyone would not laugh at her first creation.

They paused for a short prayer of thanks for the food and then everyone picked up their soup spoon to begin the meal. Amanda was first to dig in and taste the liquid. She was both surprised and pleased to note the pleasant aroma as well as the flavors blossoming on her tongue. It was actually more than merely edible; it was downright tasty. Amanda said a prayer of thanks for Melba's assistance and then she dipped her spoon for another bite.

Daven had tasted the soup and declared, "Well done, Amanda."

Nena and Riccan both agreed as they promptly finished their portion of the soup.

Talk around the table turned to other family matters and Amanda was relieved not to be part of the conversation. She was able to relax and enjoy the rest of the meal. She laughed at some of the family anecdotes, usually to Riccan's despair.

As promised, when the meal was over Riccan announced they had to leave. They all walked together to the back patio where Riccan's parents, once again, remained at the railing to watch them leave. Amanda lengthened her step to keep up with Riccan. He was obviously in a hurry to get going.

Once they had returned to Riccan's garage on Earth, Riccan turned to her and said, "I really would love it if you could accompany me on a few of my trips. I want you to go for yourself, not for any ability for which you might possess. I don't want you to feel in any way obligated because my father put you on the spot."

"I'd love to go with you. I've known you a lot longer than you've known me. Believe me, I'd be going for purely selfish reasons. I enjoy spending time with you," Amanda admitted. She had said more than she intended, but she could tell the words meant a lot to Riccan.

"Well, you get the job of telling your parents. I'd like to take a short trip tomorrow. We'd be gone for two days. Do you think you could swing that?"

"What about going back to Tuala tomorrow? Don't I have more lessons to learn with your father?" Amanda hoped she had not offended Daven to the point where he no longer wanted to instruct her in more lessons.

"As we were walking out my father suggested we come back in a couple of days. He has some matters he needs to take care of," Riccan answered easily.

Amanda felt foolish for only thinking about her own needs. Of course, Daven would have other obligations on his time. Amanda was not his only consideration, and she had been selfishly taking him away from his duties as an Elder. "Okay, I'll figure out something to tell my parents."

"Good, I'm looking forward to taking a trip with you!" he said as he palmed the side door open from the control panel. "It's a little after seven o'clock Earth time. I think we should call it an early evening so you can wake up a little bit earlier tomorrow. Do you think you can get here by nine o'clock in the morning?"

Amanda smiled at his little dig in her oversleeping that morning, and she said, "I'll see what I can manage. Obviously, I can't make any promises. For some reason, when I'm with you, I'm more exhausted than normal."

"Time travel and interplanetary travel has that effect on people with a weak constitution," he teased back.

"Are you saying I have a weak constitution?" Amanda smiled as she tried to come up with a good comeback. She laughed out loud as she had to agree he was probably right so she conceded, "Okay, you got me there. Just give me a few more months to regain my strength. The doctor did tell me I still have the body of an eighteen-year-old so that would make me half your age and very resilient."

"Touché, Amanda!" Riccan laughed.

Amanda turned serious again and asked, "What should I pack for our trip?"

"Nothing formal or anything. What you're wearing right now is perfect for where we're going," he answered as he appraised the way her clothes fit on her slim body. He looked away before his mind could take the next leap.

Amanda appeared not to notice him suddenly shifting his gaze. She was too excited for a new adventure. The idea of telling her parents was slightly daunting, but she was, after all, an adult. She could decide to take a trip if she wanted. She would make this work.

Amanda pulled into her parents' driveway at half past seven. She almost skipped up the walkway and let herself in the front door. She was still smiling when her mother suddenly appeared from the living room.

"Amanda! Where have you been? I tried calling you at least a dozen times and yet you never picked up your phone. Do you know how worried I've been?" Diane rushed forward and hugged her daughter even though she was upset. Her daughter had come home safely, and she had to keep reminding herself it was all going to be okay now.

Amanda had not thought to check her phone. She knew it would not function in Tuala anyway. She pulled it out of her purse and noticed the screen showed thirteen missed calls. "I'm sorry, Mom, the ringer must have been off. I didn't mean to worry you. I've been with Riccan."

"That's what I was worried about. We have no idea who this Riccan man is. He could be dangerous, Amanda. I don't think you should be spending so much time with him. Why don't you stay home for a few days?" Diane reasoned with her daughter.

"I wish I could, but something has come up. I'm going on a business trip with Riccan tomorrow. We'll be gone for two days." She tried to sound confident even as she was quivering inside. She almost felt defiant as she told her mom the plans she had already made.

"No, Amanda! You can't go, it could be dangerous."

Amanda could not help but chuckle at how ludicrous her mother was being as she answered, "Riccan's not dangerous. Please have some faith in my ability to read people."

Chris walked up at that moment and put his hands on Diane's shoulders as he said, "Diane, Amanda is a grown woman. She doesn't need your permission to go."

Amanda was so thankful for her reasonable father, but she decided not to push her luck as she said, "I promise to answer my phone whenever you call, Mom."

Diane was clearly unhappy, but she knew she had lost the battle when her husband sided against her. She simply said, "Make sure the ringer is turned on." She pulled away from her husband's hands and walked stiffly away into the kitchen.

"I didn't mean to upset her," Amanda whispered to her dad.

"I know, honey. She just needs some time to adjust to your independence. She'll come around eventually." He looked into the kitchen to see his wife holding herself up on the edge of the kitchen sink as she stared out the window. *I hope she'll eventually come around,* he thought to himself as he smiled reassuringly at his youngest daughter.

Amanda went into her room to let her parents talk without her. She had to pack a small suitcase, and she still had not decided what she would take with her. Amanda decided to listen to the messages her mother had left on her phone. She sat on the edge of the bed and pushed the key to play all of her messages.

By the end of the thirteenth message, she felt truly awful for how frantic her mother had sounded. She had gone from concerned to angry to downright scared over the course of the day without hearing from Amanda. She would have to ask Riccan if there were any solution to the communication problem so her mother would not have to endure another day like today.

If her intuition were correct, she already knew the answer to be negative. She added the question to the growing list of the things to ask Jehoban. At first, she had thought it might be too trivial for the Creator of the Universe, but then she convinced herself He would not want any of His children to suffer. Her mother was definitely suffering right now, and she would do anything to take that pain away, even if it meant asking Jehoban.

Having another inspirational idea, she pulled out her phone and texted Riccan: 'Can you pick me up tomorrow? My mom would like to meet you before we go on the trip.' She hit the send button and went out to tell her mom the change in plans.

CHAPTER 22

The next morning Amanda was awake and getting ready to go by eight o'clock. After showering she toweled her hair dry as she walked into the kitchen to get her breakfast ready. She was halfway tempted to try to create the dish using her power, but she was too paranoid about her mother catching her at it. In the end, she opted for a bowl of Cheerios.

She draped her towel over the chair back and sat down to eat. When she was almost finished, her mother came into the kitchen to talk.

"Are you sure you have to go on this trip?"

"Yes, Mom. I want to go. I need a change of scenery as well as something constructive to do," Amanda answered patiently and took her last spoonful. She took her bowl to the sink, rinsed it out, and put it in the dishwasher. Her mother was being conspicuously silent, so she turned to find out if she had left the room.

Diane had seated herself at the table and watched her daughter intently. There was something different about Amanda which she could not put her finger on. She tilted her head and considered what it could be before finally realizing she now had an air of confidence she had not displayed since she was a teenager.

"What are you thinking, Mom?" Amanda asked while she returned to the table to sit across from her mother.

"I was just trying to figure out what it is about you which is different. You're more confident than you've been in a long time. I guess you spending time with Riccan is doing that for you. I don't know."

"I'm sure Riccan's company helps because he doesn't treat me any different than anyone else. He doesn't watch me for signs of weakness or think I'm incapable of anything. I'm not saying that to make you feel bad, Mom, I know you love me. He just doesn't try to limit me, and I've found it quite refreshing. I'm learning new things about myself every day when I'm with him, and I'm grateful for it."

Amanda fervently hoped her mother's feelings would not be hurt with her admission, but she had spoken nothing but the truth. The skills she learned under Daven's tutelage were filling her with self-worth as well as confidence. She had not thought about it consciously, but her mom had obviously seen it.

Diane nodded and then finally said, "I've seen it myself. I can't say that it doesn't scare me to see you being so independent, but your father was right when he said I'd have to let you learn to live your life. I'm sorry if I've been too overbearing. I just love you so much."

Amanda reached over and patted her hand resting on the table and said, "I know that, Mom. I love you too. Thank you for trying to understand my situation. I didn't feel the seven years of fright which you did, so it's as though I'm just carrying on from where I left off. Granted, I'm a bit more tired than I was back then." Amanda chuckled to try to lighten the mood and was rewarded when her mother smiled in return.

Diane glanced at the clock on the microwave and asked, "So tell me a bit about Riccan before he shows up on our doorstep."

Amanda spent the next ten minutes telling her what she knew about Riccan, his job, his volunteer service, and his friendship in general. She tried to make their friendship sound casual, but her mother was obviously not fooled.

"I take it you're pretty smitten with him then?" she asked casually. She had followed Amanda into the bathroom so her daughter could continue to get ready while still allowing her to talk to her mom.

"I do care a great deal for him," she started and then raised her hand to stop her mother's protest. "I know I've only known him for a short time, but there's more to it. Someday I may even tell you about it."

Diane raised an eyebrow at her daughter's last statement. *What could she possibly mean by that?* she asked herself. *I guess I'll have to wait until she feels it's the right time to tell me.*

Amanda heard the knock on the front door and raced out of the bathroom to answer the call. She grinned broadly when she saw Riccan standing nervously on the stoop. "Come on in, Riccan." She turned around and saw her mom had followed her across the house. She began the introductions by saying, "Riccan Stel, I'd like you to meet my mother, Diane Covington. Mom, this is Riccan."

Diane extended her hand and Riccan took a hold of it and shook it briefly. He smiled at how much Amanda and her mother looked alike. There was no denying that Diane was Amanda's mother, she was merely an older version of the same person, although with shorter hair.

"It's very nice to meet you, Mrs. Covington. I hope you won't be terribly inconvenienced because I'm whisking Amanda away on such short notice. Her skills are very important to the success of this trip."

"And just where are you taking my daughter, Mr. Stel?" Diane said with very little politeness in her tone.

Amanda looked at her mother to see if she should interject herself into the conversation.

Riccan answered with a grin, "We're going to New Orleans."

It was now Amanda's turn to be surprised. She had no idea they would be going as far as that. She had imagined a short road trip, to do what, she was still unsure.

"What is in New Orleans?" Diane continued to grill Riccan.

"Mom…" Amanda began.

Riccan cut off Amanda and said, "It's okay, Amanda. I should have told you yesterday so you could share with your parents. I'm searching for a lost family member. My family has been trying to track down some family stories, and I believe my great-uncle may have some answers."

"Where will you be staying?" Diane asked.

"Royal Sonesta New Orleans on Bourbon Street," he answered easily. He had expected to be questioned closely. Now he wished he had planned to sit down with her parents before whisking her away. He could understand her parents having qualms about the suddenness of the trip.

"You'll have a separate room, right?" Diane inquired.

"Mom!" Amanda was mortified at her mother's question.

"Of course, Mrs. Covington. I don't have any plans on trying to take advantage of Amanda's friendship. Please believe me when I tell you she will be safe in my care." Riccan managed to keep the smile from his face as he realized just how ridiculous his last statement sounded.

"I've instructed Amanda to keep her cell phone ringer turned on so we can contact her. Be assured we'll be calling her a couple of times per day," Diane warned. She wanted to make sure Riccan knew they would be keeping tabs on their daughter.

"I understand. I'm hoping we can be back tomorrow or the next day at the latest. If our plans change at all, I'll be sure to have Amanda keep you updated."

"That sounds reasonable," Diane answered. She wanted to be able to find a reason to keep Amanda home, but she discovered she was actually beginning to like this man her daughter was leaving with. He had a certain charisma which was infectious. At least now she understood the draw her daughter had toward the man.

Amanda could see her mother and Riccan were getting along, so she raced out of the entry and grabbed her suitcase from her bedroom. She hurriedly returned to where they still stood looking at one another, and announced, "I'm all ready to go whenever you are."

"Let me take that for you," Riccan said as he reached forward and grabbed the suitcase from Amanda's hand. He turned to go back out the door and stopped himself to say, "It was a pleasure meeting you, Mrs. Covington. I'll have Amanda text you my phone number so you can call me if you want."

"Thank you, that'd be appreciated. It was nice meeting you as well."

Amanda held out her arms as she approached her mom to give her a big hug. "I promise to keep a lookout on my phone for your calls. I'm not used to having a cell phone yet, but I'll try really hard. Wish me luck!"

"Good luck. Come back as soon as you can!" Diane said as she felt a horrible sense of déjà vu as her daughter once again left her on the doorstep while she traveled to parts unknown with a man. She hoped this journey would not have such a disastrous end. Diane managed to smile and wave at her daughter as Riccan closed the passenger door and Amanda waved from her seat. She watched them drive away. As soon as she shut the front door, she broke down into tears of despair and heartache for what might happen.

"I'm sorry about that, Riccan," Amanda said as she looked out the side window, too embarrassed to look at Riccan.

"No, I'm the one who's sorry. I should have considered your parents' feelings about this trip. To them, I'm a total stranger, and they would deservedly be scared for your safety. I should have made some time to meet both your mother and father before stealing you away."

Amanda chuckled and asked, "Is that what you're doing? Stealing me away?"

"It kind of feels that way!" Riccan chuckled.

"Are we really going to New Orleans to find your lost family member?"

"Yes, we are. There are a couple of other things I'd like to check out while we're there, but essentially, the trip is to locate my great-uncle, Roderick Rockwood."

Riccan had to pay attention to the road since he was navigating his way to the FL-836 toward the Miami International Airport. The drive should take only about a half hour as long as traffic did not get too stacked up along the way. Their flight was scheduled to leave before noon so they would have to hurry to get checked in on time.

He merged onto the FL-953, leaving only a couple more miles to travel until reaching the busy airport. He followed the signs to parking and managed to find a spot which was not too far out of the way. Riccan wheeled the two bags to the American Airlines ticket counter.

Amanda believed he had picked the wrong line when he entered the First Class line, but she tagged along anyway. The attendant asked them for their identification to which Amanda and Riccan both presented their driver's licenses.

"Do you have any baggage to check today, Mr. Stel?"

"Yes, two bags," Riccan replied.

"Oh, it's okay, Riccan. I can take mine with me, you don't have to pay to check it," Amanda swiftly countered.

"Both of your bags will be checked for free since these are First Class tickets," the attendant corrected Amanda.

She felt her face blush as she realized Riccan had known what he was doing when he chose the check-in line. She appeared to be the only one who was left out of the loop. "Oh, well, then never mind," she mumbled as she looked down at the floor between her feet.

Riccan pocketed the two tickets as the attendant took their bags from the scale and threw them on the conveyer belt behind her ticket counter. "Let's hurry up and get through the TSA checkpoint so we can get to our terminal."

'Hurry' is a relative term, Amanda thought to herself when she saw the number of people standing in line to get through the checkpoint. Once again she was shown how little she knew about air travel when Riccan steered them to an empty line she had assumed was for airport staff.

She was amazed when they practically walked right through the checkpoint when they used the First Class line. Amanda thought this was definitely the way to travel as they swiftly left the crowd behind them on their way to their assigned terminal.

They waited at their gate for almost an hour before they got the call to board. Naturally, they were able to board the plane first, and Amanda sat down at the window seat in row two in her enormous seat. Riccan sat down next to her and smiled at her obvious joy.

The flight attendant asked them if they would like a drink before take-off and they both ordered a tomato juice. When she returned with their drinks, she offered them both a blanket and pillow.

Amanda felt like a queen as she sipped her drink while the rest of the plane's occupants filed by to take their seats at the back of the airplane. It seems as though hundreds of people were getting on this flight as the people continued to move by their seats. Finally, the plane was full, and the passenger loading door was sealed. They pushed back from the gate and taxied to the runway. The takeoff was as smooth as the two-hour and twelve-minute flight.

Amanda tried not to act surprised when the stewardess took their breakfast order and served them their food on real plates, with real silverware, and also their very own salt and pepper shakers. The luxury of First Class was definitely a step up from any Coach flight she had ever taken.

Their flight arrived on time in New Orleans. Riccan had made arrangements for a rental car, and they loaded their bags into the back. Amanda wondered how often Riccan traveled to make everything appear so effortless. She imagined with his history, he would be well-traveled.

Riccan drove them to the Royal Sonesta and pulled up to the valet parking. He popped the trunk and did not even seem to notice when a bellboy opened the trunk and removed their two bags. He handed the keys to a waiting attendant, gave him his name, and then handed him a rather large tip.

They walked into the lobby with the bellboy trailing behind them. Riccan spoke with the front desk clerk.

"Welcome to the Royal Sonesta. Do you have a reservation, sir?" asked the attendant brightly with a smile plastered on her face.

"Yes, the Presidential Suite for Riccan Stel," he answered easily.

Amanda gulped when she heard which room he had reserved. She was slightly concerned when he only mentioned the one room, but she trusted he would take care of their sleeping arrangement. At that moment she realized she would not mind sharing a room with Riccan.

The desk clerk smiled a bit brighter as she handed the two room keys across the desk to Riccan. "Just take the elevator to the fifth floor, Mr. Stel. If you need anything at all, please feel free to contact the concierge. Have a nice stay."

"Thank you," Riccan replied as he took the room keys and turned away from the clerk. He grinned down at Amanda and led the way across the lobby to the elevator.

Amanda had so many questions bubbling in her mind, but she refused to ask them in front of the bellhop who stood doggedly behind them. She entered the elevator and stood beside Riccan as the bellhop made room behind them for their bags. The ride up was short as well as the walk down the hall to their room. Amanda watched Riccan tip the bellhop once they were in their suite and then he shut the door.

"Well, what do you think?" Riccan asked as he looked around the gorgeously appointed rooms. He could appreciate the marble floors, crystal chandeliers, oriental rugs, and silk drapes. He walked through the entrance and into the sitting area where a grand piano stood in the corner.

Amanda gave up trying to seem unimpressed. The place was gorgeous and far more opulent than any place she had ever stayed before. She wandered through the rooms and discovered there were actually two bedrooms, each with its own en-suite bathrooms with giant soaking tubs. After coming out of the second bedroom suite, she noticed they had a dining room as well as a living room. This place had to be at least as big as her parents' house.

"I think it's a bit much for just the two of us!" she exclaimed.

"I could arrange for us to be moved to a one bedroom unit with two queen beds if that would make you more comfortable," he teased.

Amanda shook her head and laughed as she said, "Oh, I'll try my best to make do with these accommodations. And to think, when I asked you what to pack you said 'nothing fancy.' Thanks for the offer though!"

Riccan turned serious and announced, "Why don't you take your bag to whichever room you pick for yourself and get unpacked. We should make the most of the rest of the day to see what we can find out in town."

Amanda grabbed her bag and returned to the last room she had investigated as she preferred the colors of the room. She put her suitcase on the end of the bed and opened it up. She took out the few clothes and hung them in the walk-in closet. She looked at the few clothes in the giant space and had to laugh at how ridiculous it all seemed. She took her bathroom items and placed them around the sink.

She returned to the living room to find Riccan had also finished unpacking. "Okay, where are we off to now?"

"Do you have on comfortable walking shoes?" he asked as he looked down at her feet.

"Sure, are we going to walk instead of drive?"

"I've found it's easier to get people to answer your questions if you're more approachable. What better way than to be among the people?" he asked as he walked to the front door.

CHAPTER 23

Once on the street, Amanda was amazed at the number of people and businesses on Bourbon Street. She had heard of it before, but she had never visited. This was an exciting journey for her.

Riccan spoke with a few of the local people and got negative replies to his inquiries. They kept walking until they got to a street vendor. Riccan's attention was immediately drawn to the items which were displayed for sale on the black velvet-covered table. Riccan was thankful the vendor was busy with another customer and did not see the expression on his face.

Amanda bumped into Riccan as he suddenly stopped. She felt a burst of energy, causing her to look around in confusion. She glanced up at Riccan and asked in a whisper, "What is that? Do you feel it?"

"Good, you feel it, too. I'd like you to pretend to be interested in those necklaces while I check something out, okay?"

Amanda smirked at Riccan's covert instructions and did as he asked. The vendor immediately believed he would soon have another sale and turned his attention to her.

Riccan reached forward and put his fingers against the smooth crystal of the skull resting off to the side of the wares to be sold. Immediately, he felt the hair on the back of his neck stand on end. One part of his quest had been discovered; now he just had to figure out a way to purchase the item.

Amanda finally shook her head and thanked the vendor for his time. She returned to Riccan's side when she had seen he was ready to speak to the vendor.

"I'd like to purchase this skull," Riccan said casually to the vendor.

"Oh, that piece. I'm still not sure if I'm going to sell it. It seems to draw customers to my booth, you see," he replied. He could tell the man was quite interested in the piece and was planning on making the price double if not triple by seeming to be reluctant to sell.

Riccan instantly caught on as well as Amanda. She plucked the sleeve of his shirt and said loudly enough for the vendor to hear, "Let's go, honey. You don't need that thing; it's kind of creepy anyway."

"I guess you're right," he played along.

They started to walk away when the vendor called them back. He did not want to lose the sale so he said, "I guess I could part with it. What kind of a price were you thinking to offer?"

"Since my girlfriend isn't very excited about me getting it, I'd probably only offer about fifty bucks for it," he hoped the price was not too high.

The vendor's eyes widened slightly, and he readily agreed, "Done! I'll just wrap this up for you." He picked up the skull and put a couple of pieces of tissue paper around it. He opened a plastic bag and gently placed it inside before handing it over to Riccan. He accepted the fifty dollar bill and said, "You two have a great day now."

Riccan had not trusted the vendor, so he never took his eyes off of the skull. He was sure if he had not been as diligent in his purchase, the vendor might have tried to switch the skull for an inferior copy. As it was, he put his hand in the bag and felt the same electric energy as he had the first time. He grinned at the vendor and said, "You have a great day, too!"

They walked at a leisurely pace until they reached the end of the block. Riccan suddenly hailed a cab, ducking into the vehicle even before it fully stopped. Amanda could not understand what had gotten into Riccan to end their walk so abruptly. She refrained from asking questions until they were alone.

The cab dropped them off at their hotel where they went up to their room immediately.

"What was that all about?" Amanda could not contain her curiosity anymore.

"We were being followed. I think the vendor planned on getting this skull back," he replied easily.

"How did you know we were being followed? You never looked behind us or even looked around?" Amanda was more than a little curious.

"I created a modified shield around us as soon as the vendor handed me the bag. The shield was created to allow me to know the intent of the people just outside of the shield. There were at least two people who were assigned to get the crystal back. They didn't have any qualms about using lethal force to retrieve it," Riccan stated simply.

Amanda held back a shudder of fear and had to sit down on the couch before her legs gave away to her panic. She decided to change the subject and asked, "Can I take a closer look at your purchase?"

He opened the bag and pulled out the wrapped skull. He peeled back the tissue and set it down on the coffee table in the living room. The sun shone down on it and hundreds of rainbows formed on the ceiling and walls around them.

"This is one of the thirteen, isn't it?" Amanda inquired as she leaned forward to inspect the intricate carving on the solid, flawless piece of clear crystal.

"It is. You felt the energy as well as I did. Heck, maybe your ability to amplify power is the reason we both felt it so strongly," he suggested as he sat down on the couch next to Amanda so he could also admire the piece of art.

"So this makes two skulls of which you know the location. Are you also searching for the other eleven?"

"Yes."

"What will you do when you have them all collected?"

"I don't know. I just have this burning need to gather them together. Can you believe this, Amanda? I've been searching for years to locate even one, but as soon as you are with me, we find this one within a matter of minutes. Either you are my lucky charm, or you are the key to locating these," he pointed to the skull and then looked seriously at Amanda.

"I've never had a desire to look for them, Riccan. Let's just chalk it up to beginner's luck on my part. I don't need another title of 'skull finder' added to the growing list your father is creating," Amanda said.

She started to have a sinking feeling Riccan was probably right about her ability to amplify power. The crystal skull contained massive amounts of power which she had felt calling to her even as she walked by the vendor's booth. She would have discounted the whole feeling had Riccan not stopped right in front of her, forcing her to acknowledge it herself.

"In any event, I think we should avoid walking anywhere near that vendor for the duration of our stay. I'd hate to think what he would do to get this prize back into his possession. I'm going to put it in the room safe, just in case." He rewrapped the crystal and deposited it in the security box. He used his key to lock the door before coming back to where Amanda stared across the room in deep concentration.

"What are you thinking?" he asked as he sat down again.

"I'm not exactly sure. I had a fleeting thought, but it's gone now. If I remember what it is, I'll tell you." She shook her head softly, wishing the thoughts would return. "My mom just called. She wanted to make sure we had arrived safely. She said she'd call back after dinnertime. What are our plans now?"

"Let's order something from room service for lunch. What sounds good?" Riccan asked.

They did not venture out for the remainder of the day. Riccan was too spooked to risk Amanda on the streets. He would return to New Orleans without her if they were unsuccessful in their search the next day. He was in no real hurry now that he had discovered the second crystal.

They spent the evening talking about their families and friends as they were growing up. Riccan retold some of the stories Amanda had heard before. She did not bother to tell him she already knew them as she just enjoyed hearing him talk. There were a couple of times where the stories they told were so funny Amanda had tears streaming down her face as she could not contain her mirth.

Diane called again as planned. Amanda wandered around the room as she talked. She was still uncomfortable with the convenience of the cell phone. Their conversation covered basically the same as it had before, Amanda assured her mom that she was safe and not to worry. She hung up and smirked at Riccan at her mother's obvious tactics.

Finally, it was time to go to bed. Riccan leaned forward and kissed her cheek as he had done from her final dream with him. She felt as though history were repeating itself and she smiled up at him. "Good night, Riccan," she whispered before she turned and walked into her separate room.

The next day Riccan decided on a different plan of action. After Amanda had spoken with her mother, they drove their rental car to the last known location of his great-uncle, Roderick. After driving a few extra blocks to locate a parking spot, they left the vehicle behind and started out on foot.

The houses were all set back from the road and had their yards surrounded by wrought iron gates. The yards were very stately with the magnolia trees in full bloom.

Amanda could see herself living in any one of the houses. She could imagine herself and Riccan sitting on the covered front porch, swinging gently in the afternoon mugginess while sipping on iced tea. She could easily envision the moisture dripping from the sides of the glasses as they were tipped up for a drink.

Her reverie was interrupted when Riccan said, "Let's ask this lady if she knows of Uncle Roderick." They crossed the street and leaned on the fence while Riccan tried to get the woman's attention as she swept her porch steps. "Excuse me, ma'am!"

The woman looked up, slightly startled and then smiled when she saw the handsome couple at her gate. She walked forward while still carrying her broom. "Hallo, how may I help you folks?"

Amanda noticed the woman's odd accent and wondered from where she had originated.

Riccan asked, "I'm searching for my great uncle. His name is Roderick Rockwood. Have you ever heard of him?"

"Oh, sure, Son. He lives up the block two houses on the left. I'm sure he's sitting on the front porch smoking his pipe. It's what he does best," she chuckled.

"That's wonderful! Thank you so much for your help," Riccan spoke kindly.

"It's no bother. Have a nice visit, you hear!" she said as she turned away to continue her sweeping.

"She seemed awfully nice," Amanda whispered as they began walking in the direction the woman had told them.

"That's the way folks are around here. This would be a great place to raise a family," he replied. As soon as the words came out of his mouth, he wondered what had made him say it. Settling down and starting a family had never been a consideration for him before he had met Amanda. She was definitely changing him in a way which would make his mother happy.

Amanda silently agreed with his assessment of the neighborhood as it coincided with her earlier thoughts. They walked in silence until they reached the house for which they had been searching. True to the woman's words, there was a man sitting on the front porch smoking his pipe.

Riccan yelled, "Hello, sir! Would you mind if we chatted for a bit?"

"Come on up, Son. I'd love to have some company," he yelled back from the porch.

Riccan opened the gate, waiting for Amanda to walk through before he closed it behind them. From a distance, the old man had reminded him of his grandfather. As they got closer, he could see an even stronger resemblance.

After they went up the stairs, Riccan said, "I'm looking for my great-uncle, Roderick Rockwood. I'm hoping we've come to the right place."

The old man pulled the pipe from his mouth, blew out a mouthful of smoke, and cocked his head. Before he confirmed or denied his identity, he asked, "And who might you be, Son?"

"My name's Riccan Stel. My parents are Daven and Nena Stel. My father's parents were Edwin and Murisa Stel. Are you familiar with any of these names?" Riccan asked gently.

"Sit down, boy. You should introduce your lady friend as it's impolite to leave her out of the conversation," the old man announced.

"My apologies, this is Amanda Covington. She's a friend of the family," he added as he smiled at Amanda. He promptly sat down in the rocking chair next to the man.

Amanda reached forward and took the old man's leathery, but warm, hand in her own. She felt a spark of kinship as she smiled broadly. "It's a pleasure to meet you, sir." When the man finally let go of her hand, she sat down in the third chair on the porch next to Riccan.

"I've often wondered how long it would take you to find me, Riccan. I'd heard from other family members that you were talking with one person after another. Time is definitely not on your side since we're all so old now. What is it you've traveled so far to ask of me?"

"So you are the Roderick Rockwood I've been searching for?" Riccan wanted to make sure of his identity before he went any further.

"Didn't I just say so? I'm too old for you to beat around the bush, boy, ask your questions," he said with a chuckle before he plugged the pipe back into his mouth.

"I'm writing an accounting of the family legends. I'm told you may have some ideas or facts about a certain crystal skull which had been handed down through the generations. I'm looking to find out where it came from and to whom it was originally given. I don't care how ridiculous the story sounds, it's still a part of our history, and I'd like to get it documented while there are still people alive who remember," Riccan announced.

"Why would you want to waste your time on such a silly legend?"

"Like I said, it's still a part of the family history. Besides, I think it will be a good story to tell my children someday," he answered as he tried to make light of how serious he took the story.

"You have children, do you?" Roderick asked.

"None yet," he said and glanced across at Amanda before continuing, "But I'm hoping to someday."

"Well, since you came all this way, I guess I could tell you what I know. It seems an awful waste of time, but I don't have much else going on these days," he began. He took another drag from the pipe and exhaled the smoke before continuing.

"The story I'd been told, and mind you I think the whole thing is hogwash, is the skull was a gift to my great-grandfather Thomas Rockwood," he spoke slowly and then coughed as the smoke went down wrong. Once he caught his breath again, he said, "This story could take a while. Let me go inside and get us each an iced tea. The day is far too warm for a long story without refreshments." He levered himself up using the arms of his rocking chair and ambled to the front screen door.

Amanda did not want to see the old man try to carry out three glasses and hastily offered, "Let me help." She stood up and held the screen door for Roderick to lead the way to the kitchen.

Riccan could hardly believe they may actually have a decent lead on getting to the bottom of where the skull originally came from. Each family member he had already spoken with said they only remembered their grandfather having it, but nothing more. Riccan was on the verge of entering the house to see what was taking the two so long when he heard Amanda laughing as she backed up to the screen door as she held the tray of iced drinks out in front of her.

Amanda waited for Roderick to be seated before she leaned over and offered him the first glass of tea. She smiled as she turned to offer the second one to Riccan. After both men had taken their glasses, she set the tray down on a small wicker table and took her own glass. She settled herself in her chair again and cradled the cold beverage between her hands.

Roderick took a long gulp of his tea and smacked his lips together. "Nothing better to wet the mouth than a good tea! Now, where were we?"

"You said your great-grandfather Thomas Rockwood was given the crystal skull," Riccan supplied.

"Oh, yes, yes. It seemed Thomas was quite a philanthropist in his time. He was born and raised in France in 1776. He was always willing to help his fellow humans when he came across a family which was quite destitute. He offered them a place to stay in his barn until they could get themselves back on their feet. Naturally, it caused quite a scandal because of who the guests were. The townsfolk did not approve of Thomas' decision, and many stayed away from his house until the guests were gone. The family ended up staying for over a year because their littlest one became very ill during the bad winter.

"Thomas hired a doctor to treat the little girl, and she eventually recovered. Thomas also hired a blacksmith to repair the family's wagon so they would have a place to keep dry as they traveled."

Amanda's curiosity got the best of her. "Why were the townspeople so against the family in need?"

"Oh, didn't I mention that part? They were gypsies, girl. Everyone of that time knew you couldn't trust a gypsy, so it put Thomas in a hard situation socially. Anyway, eventually it came time for the family to move on and the man of the family approached Thomas with a gift of the crystal skull."

"Did you ever hear the name of the gypsy man?" Riccan asked.

"Well, now, I'm not sure. Let me ponder that for a moment," he replied as he took a sip of his drink and shut his eyes to concentrate better. He took a couple of puffs from his pipe.

The smoke drifted toward Amanda making her regret her choice of a seat. She did not dare wave the smoke away from her face for fear she would offend the old man. She had to hold her breath until the worst of the smoke cleared from around her head.

Suddenly his eyes flew open. "His name was Sampson Scamp! Silly name, I know, but that's why I remembered it. Let's see…his wife's name was Celia!" He smiled triumphantly at Amanda and conspiratorially whispered as he tapped his forehead with his weathered finger. "I've still got it going on up here."

Amanda grinned back and said, "I never doubted it for a moment!"

"Do you know if Sampson happened to say from where he'd gotten the skull?" Riccan asked.

Roderick squinted his eyes as he reviewed his memories. "To the best of my recollection, he told Thomas he had received it in trade from another gypsy."

Riccan felt his hope drop with this new piece of the story. He believed it to be difficult enough to locate a gypsy family, but now he had another unknown gypsy to try to locate. Shaking his head at the disappointment, Riccan decided to change tactics. "Did the gypsy Sampson say anything to Thomas about the skull?"

"Oh, yes, he gave him a great story. He told him there were thirteen matching skulls. He said they contained great power and if they were ever brought together in one place, they had unimaginable power. There was some babble about opening the gates to other worlds and such nonsense," he scoffed and took another drink of his tea.

"Can you try to remember the exact wording for the opening of the gates?" Riccan pressed.

"You can't be taking this stuff seriously, can you?" Roderick looked intently at Riccan.

"I just want an accurate account for the historical document on it. Can you recall the exact phrase he was told?" Riccan did not want to seem too desperate for the information because he did believe exactly what the gypsy said to his family about the powers of the crystal.

"Okay, give me a moment to try to remember." He lowered his head and puffed some more on his pipe.

Amanda and Riccan stared at one another for several minutes before Roderick finally raised his head and spoke again. Riccan was beginning to wonder if the old man had fallen asleep and he was thankful he had not reached over to shake his arm.

"This is the best I can do: 'When the descendants of the Watchers bring these all together then the gates between the worlds will be open for all to pass through without a loss.' I told you it was all a bunch of hogwash," he scoffed.

"Okay, that talks about all of the skulls together. Did the gypsy say anything about the skull when it was by itself?" Riccan continued his line of questions.

"Sure, he said it brought luck and prosperity to the owner. He, naturally, did not believe this to be true because of the calamity which had befallen his family after he had taken the skull in trade. His daughter very nearly died, after all." He lifted his glass and drank until the ice clinked against his false teeth.

"Can you think of anything else which might pertain to the crystal? Anything at all?" Riccan asked one final time.

"Only that it's just a legend. The skull was lost many generations ago if it ever existed at all. It's getting rather late, kids. I think I might head in for a nap before supper. Feel free to stop by if you're ever in town again. You can leave your glasses on the tray when you're done." He stood up slowly and carried his glass and pipe into the house. He let the screen slam shut behind him.

They both only had a couple of sips remaining, so they finished quickly and put the glasses where Roderick had instructed. They descended the stairs and left the yard through the garden gate. The house was well behind them before they began to talk. Both were going over the things which had been revealed.

"That was certainly enlightening," Riccan began.

"Had you heard any of that stuff before?"

"No, it was all new to me. All the other relatives just scoffed when I asked about it and told me to find something better to do with my time. Just think, if we hadn't found Roderick today, we might never have heard the story at all. He's so old; I can't imagine he'll be around for very much longer. My guess is he knows even more, but I just didn't know what to ask for with him."

Amanda pondered the conversation and then concluded, "I don't think he knew any more than what he told us. My guess is he liked to listen to his great-grandfather tell stories when he was young. He was probably the only one who believed Thomas because he was so young."

"Maybe you're right," Riccan conceded as they continued the walk back to their rental car. As they were driving back to the hotel, Riccan realized they had completed their task for this journey. If he had been smarter, he would have figured out a way to drag the process out longer so he could stay away with Amanda. "It looks as though we'll be heading home tomorrow morning."

Amanda sighed and stared out the window at the scenery they were passing. The old buildings were so stately, and the people were so friendly. She wished this trip could have lasted at least a bit longer. Her mother would be thrilled for her to return early. She thought of a way to delay the inevitable. "Do you want to find out where the vendor got his crystal skull from? He may have a fresher lead?"

He liked the idea Amanda was proposing, but he was unwilling to risk Amanda's safety just for some additional information. He finally replied, "It's just too risky. Those guys coming after us were not going to take no for an answer. I'd rather just cut our losses and head home with another piece of the puzzle in our hands."

After another sigh, Amanda had to agree. "I guess you're right. I still wish this could have taken a little longer. What do you suppose Roderick meant by the 'descendants of the Watchers?'"

Riccan shook his head and said, "I don't know, but you can be sure I'll try to research it as much as possible."

Amanda stayed quiet for the rest of the journey since it did not seem as though Riccan wanted to talk. She went over the interview several times to see if anything else seemed particularly strange. She smiled inwardly that the gypsy's surname was Scamp. It seemed ironic because of the type of people they were.

CHAPTER 24

Once back at the hotel, they ordered dinner through room service again. Amanda would have preferred to eat in one of the open-air cafés she had seen, but she could tell Riccan wanted to lay low until he had his crystal skull safely tucked into the secret room at his house. She could understand his reticence, but it still did not keep her from wishing it could have turned out differently.

When the meal was finished, Riccan went to the safe and took the crystal skull out. Once again he set it on the coffee table in the living room. Looking anxiously at Amanda, he asked, "Do you feel any power emanating from it now?"

Amanda nodded emphatically. She had felt it the moment they had walked back into the hotel room. With it right before her, she could almost see an aura of power surrounding it. Suddenly an idea hit her. "Riccan, can you see someone's aura?"

"Yes. Can't you?"

"I haven't gotten that far with my training with your father. Is it my imagination or does this crystal have an aura?" Amanda looked excitedly at Riccan.

He drew power from his birth crystal and set up the parameters for aura detection. As soon as it was in place, he gasped as his eyes fell on the skull. "It's as bright as any rainbow I've ever seen. It has every color in it, but it also has a shadow of black. That's odd; I wonder what that means."

"Do you think the skull you already have will match this one's aura?"

"I don't know, but you can bet I'll be checking as soon as we get back home. I'm halfway tempted to try to catch a flight home tonight."

"I wouldn't be opposed as long as you said I could spend the night at your house instead of sending me home," Amanda agreed with her condition set in place.

"It's a deal!" he announced. He jumped up from the couch and pulled out his cell phone from his pants pocket. He dialed up the airline and within a few moments had made arrangements for their tickets to be exchanged for a flight which was leaving in an hour and a half. They did not have much time to pack their belongings, but they did not have much to begin with.

Riccan checked out of the hotel, and the valet brought the car around. With the baggage in the trunk and the crystal skull in Amanda's purse, they drove as fast as they could to get to the airport. They checked their bags, went through the TSA checkpoint, and immediately boarded the plane.

For the first time during this trip, Amanda was truly excited because she was going to be alone with Riccan at his house for the entire night. This was going to be like it was in her dream. They had a new mystery to solve to which she was going to be a part.

While the passengers were still boarding the plane, Amanda's phone rang. Naturally, it was her mother checking in. She paused before answering the call because she did not want to lie to her mother, but she also did not want to tell her the truth about their trip. Her conscience got the best of her, and she hit the call button.

"Hey, Mom."

"Just making sure you're still okay. How's New Orleans?"

"Hot!"

"Have you made any progress finding Riccan's uncle?"

"Yes, we met with him today. He had some great family stories to share with Riccan."

"Do you know when you're coming home?"

"Probably tomorrow. There are a few other leads we want to check out before I come home."

"Okay, as long you're staying safe."

"Never better, Mom. Oh, sorry, Mom. I've got to go. Love you!" She hit the button to end the call since the stewardess was waiting to take their drink order.

"Sorry about that," Amanda said to the stewardess as she gestured to her phone. She promptly requested a tomato juice.

The stewardess smiled at the passenger and said, "No problem. Just make sure you turn off your cell phone before we take off." The stewardess noticed Amanda's bag tucked into the seat beside her and said, "You'll have to stow that either in the overhead compartment or under the seat in front of you before we pull away from the gate. Would you like me to put it in the overhead bin for you?"

Amanda was not particularly fond of either option, but she decided she would feel safer if the bag was in the overhead bin. She zipped the top and handed it to the stewardess and said, "Thanks." She watched carefully to make sure the contents stayed intact and then nodded to the stewardess as she finished.

The flight was uneventful, and Amanda enjoyed the perks of flying First Class. She and Riccan talked in hushed tones about what they were going to do when they got back to Florida. Amanda was happy to hear he had not decided to send her home after all. She had not believed he would, but there was still a small chance he would rethink the matter and change his mind.

They made it back to Riccan's house within an hour of the airplane landing. Riccan carried their suitcases inside and left them at the base of the grand curving staircase. "We can take care of these later. Let's go to the library," he said as he hurried down the hall.

By the time Amanda reached the library door, Riccan had already opened the secret wall and was entering the room behind. She hurried through the opening while she unzipped her purse. When she got to the table in the center of the room, she had not even reached into the bag when she noticed something was wrong.

Riccan had moved to the far wall and was reaching into the niche to pull out the second skull. His hands touched the cold surface causing him to freeze where he stood. There was a power now surging through the stone which had never been there before. Usually, the energy inherent in the crystal would make the hair stand up on the back of his neck and on his arms. This new energy was nothing like how it had always been.

"Riccan? What's wrong?" Amanda noticed how still Riccan was standing. She promptly put her purse down on the table and rapidly walked around the table. She touched his arm to get his attention and immediately understood what had him rooted to the floor. She felt the immense power as it surged through him and into her.

The combined touch lessened the impact of the energy which allowed Riccan to be able to move again. He brought down the carved stone and together they walked it over to the table. Riccan set it down and took his hands away with more than a little effort.

Amanda was more skittish now as she reached in to pull out the tissue wrapped crystal skull and set it on the polished mahogany surface, careful not to touch the stone with her bare hands.

Now that the two stones were together in the room the power had not just doubled, but rather it had quadrupled. She could just imagine the feeling of the power if all thirteen of the stones were put into the same room. It was not hard to believe these stones contained enough power to open a gate between the worlds.

"It's pretty unbelievable, Riccan. What do you see for the aura of your original stone?" Amanda suddenly remembered to ask.

"One second," he said as he prepared himself to see it. "Wow, it's very similar to the other one except instead of a black band on the outside, my original one has a deep red band. I wonder what that could mean. Do you have any ideas about it?"

Amanda considered before answering, "Maybe it's the only way to be able to tell them apart."

"It could be, but it feels as though we're missing something." Without thinking Riccan reached out and touched both stones at the same time. His whole body went rigid as if he were being electrocuted.

Amanda did not hesitate; she tried to move one of his hands and then she was caught in the same vision:

A woman carried a basket containing all thirteen skulls. She walked up to each person in the line in front of her and said, 'You have been chosen to be a caretaker for this samara.' She reached into the basket and pulled out the crystal which fit easily in the palm of her hand.

'As a descendant of the Witness you are to keep this samara in your family line until the appointed time.' The woman touched the outstretched hand of the recipient, and a band of color wrapped itself around the crystal before sinking into the skull. 'Do you promise to retain custody of this samara until it is called into duty?'

One person after another down the line answered with a nod and the woman placed the skull into each hand and then promptly left the room. The entire ceremony lasted for a quarter of an hour. After the last person had departed, the woman sat down in her wicker chair and held the basket in her lap. Picking up the one remaining skull, she said, 'I, Lillia, promise to guard the master samara with my soul.'

As fast as the vision began it disappeared, releasing both Riccan and Amanda from the powerful draw of energy. They stared at one another in stunned silence as they processed the scene which had unfolded in their minds.

"That was amazing!" Amanda was the first to be able to form a coherent sentence.

"You are the master of understatements today." Riccan felt the need to sit down. He did not have a chair nearby, so he simply sank onto the floor.

Amanda lowered herself to the floor as well and felt the need to touch Riccan again. Instinctively, she put her arms around him and hugged him.

Riccan wrapped his arms around Amanda, immediately feeling a comfort he had never known. Overcome with emotions, he was grateful Amanda had shared the experience with him. Without any conscious thought, Riccan pulled away slightly and turned his face toward hers. He brought his lips down to hers, kissing her for several seconds before he managed to break the contact.

"I could swear I felt you trembling as you kissed me, Riccan. Is there something wrong?" Amanda had thoroughly enjoyed the kiss, but she wanted to know what it had meant to him before she made a fool of herself for thinking it might be something more than a casual gesture.

"I was trembling. That kiss meant so much to me; I wanted it to be perfect. I have to admit I tried to keep myself from having feelings for you, but, after that experience, I know for certain you are the person I am supposed to be with. I love you, Amanda," Riccan answered with raw honesty. He watched Amanda's face intently to see if she had felt the same thing he had in that moment of unrestrained emotion.

Amanda's answer was to lean forward and kiss him soundly on the lips. She wrapped her arms tighter around his shoulders and enjoyed the feeling of being so close to the man she had fallen in love with a long time ago. Finally, they were on the same page with their emotions which filled her with joy to have everything work out so well.

"Is that answer enough for you, or do you need more convincing?" Amanda teased as she rested her forehead on his own, their lips barely separated.

Riccan could feel her breath on his face as she spoke to him. He was thrilled.

His brilliant smile told Amanda everything she needed to know. They kissed again, this time with an air of confidence and mutual love.

Amanda was the first to pull away. She had a horrible cramp forming in her twisted leg and had to massage it to get it to stop. "This isn't the most romantic ending to our first kiss," Amanda teased. "What do you want to do now?"

Riccan helped Amanda to her feet and looked down on the two samaras. "I think we should put these away and then we can go to the living room where we can be a lot more comfortable."

"Are you sure you want to touch those things again?" Amanda looked sideways at the two innocuous looking objects.

"I did say we were going to put them away. You take that one," he pointed to his original stone, "and I'll take this one. We can put them in separate niches in the bookcase." He put his words into action and picked up the stone. This time nothing happened except the hair stood up on his arms.

Not to be thought of as a coward, Amanda promptly followed his motion and grabbed the second stone. She put it back into the original niche and then took her hands back. She could not help but rub her palms on her jeans as though that might remove the electric feeling coursing through her.

Amanda felt much more relaxed when they finally got comfortable on the leather couch. Riccan sat down sideways with his feet up before she curled up between his legs to lean back onto his chest. She had wanted to do this even while she had been dreaming. All of her dreams seemed to be coming true.

"We're going to have to come up with something to tell my parents so we can spend more time like this together," Amanda mused out loud.

"Why don't we get engaged," Riccan suddenly said into the silence.

"Was that your idea of a proposal, Riccan? If so, it was terrible!" Amanda slapped his thigh to demonstrate just how bad it had been.

"Oh, I can do it much better if I know that's the direction you want to go with this," he suggested.

"I'll wait to answer that until I think you're actually being serious." Inside, Amanda's heart beat wildly even as her breath became more difficult to keep steady.

Riccan pushed her forward as he scrambled off of the couch. "Wait right there; I'll be right back."

Amanda watched him rush out of the living room and go up the stairs. Staring with open-mouthed dismay, she had no idea what had gotten into him. Only a minute later she watched him practically fly down the stairs and slide back into the living room in his rush.

He dropped down to one knee in front of her and presented a little black box. He opened the box at the same time he said, "Amanda Covington, would you do me the immense honor of becoming my wife?"

Amanda shifted her gaze from his face to the contents of the black box. Nestled among the velvet fabric was a stunning diamond ring. She had no idea where he had gotten a ring on such short notice, but she had to concentrate right now. She had to answer his question with the only thing which came to mind. "Absolutely! I love you, Riccan!" Throwing her arms around him, she kissed him for several seconds.

Riccan pulled away this time. "Let me make this official so we can resume." Plucking the ring out of the box, he slid it onto her left hand. It was a perfect fit.

Amanda admired the sparkling diamond on her hand, unable to contain her curiosity, she asked, "Where did this come from?"

"It was my grandmother's ring."

"What a beautiful family heirloom. Thank you, Riccan."

"May I assume this proposal was more romantic than the first?" Riccan playfully asked as he got up off of the floor and sat down on the couch next to Amanda.

"Absolutely! You're wonderful…unfortunately this isn't going to help my case with my parents. They're going to say we don't know one another well enough to get married. Maybe we should just go to Reno and elope." Only half-joking with her suggestion, Riccan's response surprised her.

"That's a great idea! We know what's going on between us and we have very unique circumstances which nobody would understand or even believe."

"Riccan, I was just kidding. We can't elope!" Amanda shook her head for emphasis.

"Just think about it for a moment, Amanda. The idea has real possibilities which would make us free to come and go without anybody keeping tabs on us. You said yourself you wanted to be able to spend more time in Tuala and, the way I see it, your parents are the only thing stopping you from doing just that."

"I hear what you're saying...and it's all true..." Amanda agreed and could feel herself being persuaded.

"Good, it's all settled then," Riccan announced as he jumped up from the couch and grabbed his cell phone from his pocket. He called the airline and, within several minutes of conversation and pacing, he had First Class reservations to Reno, Nevada. He would have preferred Las Vegas himself, but Amanda had specifically said she wanted Reno. The city did not matter as much as the legality of the whole affair. His smile beamed as he sat back on the couch and grabbed Amanda's hand. "We're going to do this tonight!"

Amanda smiled uncertainly and said, "Are you sure?"

"Absolutely! I've waited a lifetime to be with you. We already agreed we should be man and wife; I don't see why everyone feels the need to wait for months and months before they finalize the relationship. I'm way more decisive than the average person."

"I should say so! Okay then, tonight it is!" Amanda held onto Riccan's hands and squeezed them to emphasize her certainty. After a few moments of grinning foolishly at one another, Amanda realized they had a huge problem. "Riccan! I don't have a thing to wear for the wedding. We don't have rings! We don't have a license! What are we thinking?"

"Give me a minute, and all that will be taken care of." He walked into the office area off to the side of the kitchen and pulled a laptop computer out of the desk drawer. He walked back to the couch while he flipped open the cover. As he sat down, he pressed the power button before settling the computer on his knees to wait for it to boot up.

His processor must have been way better than her father's because his computer was ready within seconds instead of minutes. Amanda watched as he happily clicked some commands on the keyboard. She leaned over to see what he was searching for and discovered there were hundreds of chapels in Reno. One, in particular, caught her eye and she pointed at it on the screen and said, "Let's use this chapel. I like the sound of it."

"Okay, the Chapel of the Bells it is!" Clicking on the site, he booked a timeslot for their ceremony and then clicked on an ad at the side of the page for their rings. Once the page loaded, he asked, "Do you want a simple wedding band or something flashy?"

"Simple," Amanda immediately replied as she looked down at the flashy ring she had already received. "I don't want it to compete with your grandmother's ring."

Riccan smiled lovingly at Amanda. He was thankful she saw the significance of receiving his family's ring. He clicked on several selections on the screen and said, "Do any of these rings look right for you?"

Amanda scrutinized the rings displayed on the screen and pointed as she spoke, "This one is way too wide. I don't like the color of this one; I prefer yellow gold. Here, this is the one."

Riccan agreed wholeheartedly with her selection. It was a narrow band which was quite understated, but would not compete with the engagement ring. "I think I'll get a slightly larger version of your ring so we'll match." He clicked a few more selections and then chose his ring as well.

Once the sizes were selected, he took out his wallet from his back pocket and entered the credit card information to get the payment detail completed. He entered a note to have the rings delivered to the Chapel of the Bells by their appointed time.

He looked at his watch and saw it was too late to go to a department store to find a dress for Amanda. "We can find a dress for you when we get to Reno. I'm sure they'll have a large selection."

"I don't need anything fancy, but I would like something white," she said as she shook her head at how rapidly and easily this was all coming together. She was starting to get the idea that with Riccan a good phrase for his style would be, 'if it's thought, it's bought.' She smiled at her own idea of Riccan's generosity.

By this time on the next day, he would be her husband. Amanda could hardly wrap her mind around the concept, but she certainly liked how it sounded. She was finally going to marry the man of her dreams, literally!

CHAPTER 25

The trip to Reno was a whirlwind. They had taken a flight from Miami to Reno and hired a car to take them to the chapel. The chapel car drove them to the Reno Courthouse to fill out their marriage license paperwork. The driver asked them if they required any other items for the ceremony. Amanda asked to be taken to a dress shop and before long, they had selected a simple white dress.

The ride back to the chapel was one of anticipation. They held hands in the back seat of the car and kept grinning foolishly at one another. Even though they had been awake for more than twenty-four hours, they were too giddy to feel tired. The driver opened the door once they stopped at the chapel and Amanda exited the vehicle first, followed immediately by Riccan.

Riccan carried the bag which contained Amanda's dress as they walked into the chapel. The woman at the front counter welcomed them with a friendly greeting and then whisked Amanda away to get ready. Riccan realized he was still holding the dress and yelled after them, "She might need her dress!"

The woman returned and, without a word, she grabbed the bag from his hand and went back to the area she had taken Amanda.

Riccan had no idea what he was supposed to be doing. He was already wearing the suit in which he would be married. With no other instruction, Riccan sat down in the waiting area until someone told him otherwise. He glanced at his wristwatch and saw it was about a half hour until they were scheduled to say their nuptials.

An older man walked into the chapel. Riccan smiled and nodded at him, but did not pay him much attention. When the old man cleared his throat for the third time, Riccan looked up to see if he needed any help.

"Sir, are you here for the next scheduled ceremony?" the old man asked Riccan.

"Yes, sir, I am."

"And where is the bride-to-be?"

"The receptionist whisked her into the back room to get ready."

"Ah…very good. We're almost ready then," he mumbled and turned to walk into the chapel room. Suddenly, he turned and asked, "Do you have two witnesses for the ceremony?"

"No. I didn't know we needed them. Do I need to go find some people?" Riccan's mind began to race through different scenarios where he would hire two people to sit and watch them get married.

"It's no bother. I'll ask my daughter to come and sit in. My wife is already with your bride so she can be the second person," he said casually. He saw Riccan's expression and said, "It won't be the first time my family has stood in as witnesses. It really is no trouble."

"Okay, as long as you're sure about it. I don't want to put anybody into an unwanted situation," Riccan said with a sigh of relief. Riccan's tired brain finally made the connection and asked, "Are you the person who will be marrying us?"

"It is my honor to do so," he replied with a broad grin.

"Thank you." Feeling at a loss for words, he looked away toward where the woman had taken Amanda. Movement caught his attention as the drapery opened and Amanda stepped from around the corner. He could not believe how beautiful and radiant she appeared as she kept grinning as she walked toward him.

He stood up as she got closer and said, "Amanda, you look stunning!"

"You don't look half bad yourself," she teased back.

Riccan turned to the woman and asked, "Did our rings arrive by courier?"

"Yes, they did. Let me get the package for you." Scurrying around the desk, she began rummaging through the piles of paperwork. "Ah," she said as she flourished the envelope in front of her. "This is for you."

Riccan stepped forward and took the small envelope. "Thank you," he said as he ripped it open and upended it to drop the two rings into his palm. They looked exactly right. He closed his fingers over the rings and shoved them into his pants pocket.

Another woman walked through the front door which the older woman greeted her warmly. "Dad told me I'd be needed to witness a ceremony," she said simply.

"Oh yes, honey, these are the two who are getting married," she indicated their customers.

The young woman turned to face them with a broad smile. "Congratulations are in order for you two."

Riccan thought she looked like a combination of her two parents. She was petite like her mother but had the large, dark eyes like her father. "Thank you for coming on such short notice," he said sincerely.

"It's no bother. We live above the chapel, so it's quite convenient. Besides, I really do enjoy every wedding. It gives me hope that one day it might be my turn."

Riccan did not know what to say to her last statement. As an attractive girl, he wondered why she would even question if she were to have the chance.

"Okay, honey, why don't you take Riccan into the chapel and then go get seated. It's time to begin. I'll go start the music so Amanda can walk down the aisle."

Suddenly, Amanda found herself standing alone in the lobby. Her nerves started to play havoc with her hands. She noticed they were starting to shake pretty badly. In only a moment, Amanda heard the nuptial music begin so she took a deep breath and began walking. She had just reached the doorway when the receptionist thrust a plastic floral bouquet into her hands. Amanda smiled and held onto the ugly flowers like they were a life-line.

Amanda arrived at the end of the short aisle and turned to face Riccan. Smiling at each other, Amanda was so focused on the fact she was actually getting married that she missed almost everything which was said except the part where she heard Riccan say, "I do."

She repeated everything the minister told her to say and then she also said, "I do." She held out her hand and received her ring beside the engagement ring she had forgotten to take off. Amanda took the band out of Riccan's palm and slid it onto Riccan's finger. Suddenly, the minister told Riccan he could kiss his bride. Amanda eagerly leaned forward to have her husband kiss her for the first time. *Husband! I'm married,* she thought to herself as the kiss continued for longer than it probably should have.

In a moment of pure jubilation, Riccan picked Amanda up and twirled her around.

"Put me down, Riccan!" Amanda ordered while she laughed at his foolish expression.

"I will, for now." He leaned close to whisper in her ear, "But I'm never letting you go once we get out of here!"

"You're so silly! Let's go sign the marriage certificate," Amanda admonished.

They finished filling out the rest of the documents which legally bound them in marriage. Amanda handed the bouquet back to the receptionist and thanked her for her thoughtfulness. Riccan carried the certificate in a large manila envelope as they walked out of the chapel.

Riccan hailed a cab so they could return to the airport to fly back home. He had considered the idea of getting a hotel room for them to consummate their marriage, but he had decided against it. They could be much more romantic if they were in the privacy of his home.

This had been a hasty trip, but the end result was what really mattered to the happy couple. As they waited for their plane to arrive, they sat in the terminal. Amanda leaned against her husband in the plastic chairs. Exhaustion finally won the battle and Amanda slipped into a deep sleep.

Riccan draped his arm protectively around his wife. He kissed the top of her head and stroked her hair with his other hand. Never had he imagined he would be married in such a hurry. One thing he was certain of, his mother would be thrilled. She had already commented on how perfect Amanda was for him. Privately he had agreed, and now he had announced to the world that he had found the woman for him.

Another idea struck him: he had only been married on Earth. They would have to perform another ceremony on Tuala for it to be official everywhere. He was certain his dad would want to perform the ceremony. He could hardly wait to get back to Tuala to make his commitment official everywhere.

To keep himself occupied while they waited for their flight to arrive, Riccan watched the people playing the slot machines in the aisle. It seemed there were many people who were winning and he smiled at their happiness. He kept checking the reader board for the status of their flight and was relieved to see it was still scheduled as 'on time.' He looked out the window when something caught his eye, and he saw an airplane pulling into the gate where they would be boarding. Their plane had arrived, now they just had to wait for everyone to deplane and for the plane to be cleaned and restocked.

Riccan sighed. Everything was coming together so nicely. He could not get the sense out of his head that everything was too perfect. There had to be something which would spoil their happiness. He did not naturally have negative thoughts nor did he particularly enjoy them at the moment either. *I must be overly tired,* Riccan said to himself. *There's no reason to think anything will go wrong now that my life is finally getting started with the right person.*

People streamed out of the now-open gate door. Soon they would be back in the air and heading home. Soon he would be carrying his bride across the threshold of their home. Soon he would be putting his wife in their bed. He had to stop his line of thinking, or he would end up embarrassing himself in public.

Finally, they were back in Florida and driving back to Riccan's house. The sunlight was shining right down on them, but Riccan was struggling to keep his eyes open. He could not believe how tired he had become. He had taken a short nap on the flight, but the attendant had kept interrupting his sleep to ask if he needed anything. He had kept his temper and only said to himself that a sleeping person only needed to be left alone.

It was a close call, but Riccan managed to get them safely home where he parked in the garage. Amanda was still passed out in the passenger's seat. He left everything in the car and walked over to Amanda's door and opened it up. He unfastened her seatbelt and easily lifted her.

With only one stumble on the first threshold, Riccan carried Amanda up the stairs. He set her down gently on the king-sized bed. He grabbed a throw blanket and draped it over her. Riccan was so tired he was barely able to make it to the other side of the bed. Removing his shoes was too much to ask, so he left them on. In only a moment he was fast asleep.

~

HOURS LATER AMANDA WOKE UP. Extremely disoriented, she opened her eyes without recognizing the room. She stretched out her legs allowing herself to roll over on the bed. When her eyes saw Riccan asleep on the bed, everything suddenly came rushing back to her. She lifted her hand and verified the two rings which told her they really had gotten married. For a moment she had the scary idea it had all been another dream. This was her new reality.

She reached over and touched Riccan's tousled hair. A smile formed on his lips and he stirred on the bed. In a moment Amanda was looking into his brown eyes and saying, "Hello, sleeping beauty."

"Hello, my wife," he replied. He stretched out on the bed and groaned. Realizing his shoes were still on his feet he hastily used the toe of one foot to dislodge the shoe of the other until they both dropped to the floor in two loud thuds. "This is not how I ever expected to spend my wedding night. How is it at all exciting if we're both fully dressed?"

"I must admit we don't sound very romantic. We'll have to work on that part of our relationship. In the meantime, I need to see if my mother called. I'm sure I've missed several calls by now. She's going to be furious with me!" Amanda looked around and realized she had no idea where any of her stuff ended up. "Where's my purse, Riccan?"

"I left everything in the car. I was too tired to mess with any of it until we both got some rest," he answered as he continued to stretch himself out on the mattress. He watched Amanda rush out of the room to get her phone.

Amanda skipped down the stairs and out to the garage. She opened the truck door and picked up her purse from the floor in front of the seat. As she walked back into the house, Amanda rummaged one-handed in the purse to get her phone. Just as she was flipping it open to hear the messages she was certain her mother had left, it rang in her hand. She immediately hit the call button and brought the phone to her ear.

"Hello," Amanda answered the call.

"Amanda! Where have you been! You promised to answer every call, and I've left five messages. Tell me you're on your way home," her mother almost yelled into the phone.

"Mom, please calm down. We've had an exhausting day. Besides, Riccan and I are going to come over and talk with you and Dad in a little bit. Is Dad going to be coming home at his normal time?"

Diane did not like how this conversation was sounding. Amanda sounded different from her normal self. Her daughter's questions about her father were not doing anything to ease the sense of dread she felt overcoming her. She reluctantly answered, "Yes, he'll be home at his normal time. What's going on, Amanda? Has something bad happened?"

"No, Mom, nothing bad has happened. Riccan and I will be over after five o'clock. I'll talk to you both then. I've got to get going, Mom. I love you."

"I love you, too. I wish you would talk to me about whatever's going on right now," Diane implored.

"You'll just have to wait, Mom," Amanda said patiently. "I've gotta run, Mom. Bye."

"Bye, honey," Diane dejectedly answered.

Amanda flipped the phone closed and decided she did not want to ruin her mood by listening to her mother's messages. Since she had just spoken to her, it was a moot point anyway. She dropped the phone back into her purse and walked back up the stairs to be with her husband.

Thinking they might do something a little more adventurous, Amanda breezed into the bedroom door prepared to flirt with her husband. Unfortunately, Riccan had other plans as he had fallen back asleep. Amanda tried to be disappointed, but she decided to take advantage of his nap to go into the bedroom she remembered from her dream to freshen up in its en-suite bathroom.

She did not want to wake her husband by using his bathroom. She walked across the hall and into the room she recalled from before. As she walked in the door, she was still amazed at how perfectly her dream had imagined this room. Every detail was exactly as she remembered. She went into the bathroom half-way expecting to find her bathing suit drying on the edge of the tub. Naturally, it was not there, and she shook her head for even thinking it might have been.

She turned on the hot water spigot and began to undress. She folded each item as she removed it and set it on the counter. For some reason, she could not bring herself to drop her clothes on the floor like most people would have done. Steam rose from above the shower door, so she hurried to get in.

Just short of getting under the stream of almost boiling water she turned the cold water spigot until her hand was comfortable in the warmth. She stepped under the flow of water and let it rain down onto her body. It felt like it had been forever since she had last showered. The water felt like silk caressing her skin as it slipped down and pooled at her feet.

The shower must have lasted at least thirty minutes. She twirled around and around getting every part of her so warm her skin turned pink. Finally, she decided she should get to the business of actually getting clean. She soaped up her body, shaved, shampooed and conditioned her hair, and finally rinsed everything clean.

She turned off the water with a sigh and reached out of the shower to pull the plush towel from the hook just outside the door. Her hand met empty air. She reached again and then peeked out of the shower to discover it was truly gone.

"Are you looking for this?" Riccan asked with a devilish grin on his face as he held the towel in both hands while he leaned against the counter top several feet away.

"Yes. And if you know what's good for you, you'll hand it over before I get you all wet!" She hid her body behind the shower door.

"Oh, I know what's good for me. Why don't you be a good girl and come and get your towel." Riccan tossed the towel up and caught it.

"Riccan! Give me the towel," Amanda growled playfully. For some reason, she had become unaccountably shy. This was her husband, after all. He had every right to see her naked body. She could not overcome her shyness and remained behind the door.

"I don't think I will. I'll meet you in the other room," Riccan said as he slung the towel over his shoulder and sauntered out of the room.

"Arghhh," Amanda growled. She was going to get even with him. She launched herself out of the shower, ran, and tackled Riccan just as he got near the bed. Riccan managed to twist himself around as he was falling and she landed squarely on his chest. "Give me that towel. Now look, you're getting all wet, too!"

"It was worth it," Riccan replied as he still would not relinquish the towel. "With what I have in mind you won't need to worry about getting dried off," he said as he pulled her head down to kiss her deeply.

Amanda forgot her frustration and kissed him back just as passionately. She no longer worried about the towel as she began unbuttoning Riccan's shirt. She felt Riccan's hands leave her hair and begin to explore her body. *Now, this is more like how a honeymoon should be,* Amanda thought as their mutual pleasure became more intense.

CHAPTER 26

An hour later Amanda was still snuggled next to her husband in the guest bedroom bed. They had not bothered to go back to the master bedroom; it hardly seemed necessary since they had a bed so handy. Amanda giggled at how silly the whole scene had been, but then she was glad it had not ended up being awkward. This was the first time she ever remembered having sex even though she was still convinced she had given birth to twins.

"That was perfect, Riccan," Amanda whispered.

"So are you," Riccan replied. "I love you."

"I love you, too," she said and sighed.

"That was a big sigh and certainly not what I'd expect from someone who was so obviously satisfied." Riccan twisted his head to look down at her face.

"Oh, well, I got a call from my mom when I went down to get my phone," she began and then was silent.

"So…," Riccan prompted.

"I told her that you and I would be coming to their house when Dad got off of work. I didn't tell her why and I can imagine her reaction to this new turn of events."

"Yeah, I know this will be hard for her. I'll just have to convince her that I'll do my very best for you," Riccan comforted. "You're not alone anymore, Amanda. I'll always stay by your side and help you in times of trouble. It's my job now and one I look forward to performing."

"Speaking of jobs, why are you not going to yours in Durseni?" Amanda finally thought to ask.

"I took a leave of absence for eight weeks."

"How much more time do you have before you need to go back?" Amanda hoped it was still a long time. She wanted to spend as much time with her new husband as she possibly could.

"I still have six weeks left," he replied, hugging her tighter to him. "I can think of some great ways to spend each and every moment of those six weeks."

"I think you'd have to eat eventually." Amanda's practical tone instantly reminded her of her mother's.

"I can just nibble a bit on you." He squirmed down until he was biting on her neck.

Amanda squealed and tried to get away from the onslaught. In the end, Riccan convinced her they could wait a while longer before they needed to face reality. Amanda was quite agreeable to his manner of spending time.

A while later, Amanda reached over and twisted Riccan's wrist so she could see the time. She swatted Riccan's arm and exclaimed, "We're going to be late! Get up; we've got to get dressed." She threw back the covers, almost jumping off of the bed as she raced to the bathroom to get dressed.

Riccan watched with an amused expression while his wife streaked through the room. Her long hair trailed out behind her, caressing her perfectly toned body, making him want to skip meeting with her parents. He knew he would have to face them eventually, so he groaned while he got out of bed. He picked up his clothes from the floor and put them on.

Amanda came out of the bathroom raking a brush through her almost dry hair. "Good, you're ready. I can finish getting ready in the car while you drive." She kept walking through the bedroom and out the door to the hallway. She had not heard any noise from Riccan and looked over her shoulder to see what he was doing and said, "Aren't you coming?"

He chuckled as he stood up from putting on his second shoe. "It's going to be that way is it?" He was teasing. He liked seeing Amanda have an air of confidence. He walked over to her and put his arm around her waist and said, "Let's go."

~

THERE WAS an awkward silence as the four of them sat in the living room facing one another. Amanda had her hands folded in her lap and decided to begin the conversation. She thought she should probably get the worst over first and said, "Riccan and I eloped last night in Reno." She picked up her hand to show her parents the two rings.

"What?" both Chris and Diane exclaimed at the same time.

"I know you both think this is too soon…" Amanda began.

"That's an understatement," Diane interrupted. "What were you thinking? You've known each other for four whole days, and you think that's enough time to make a life-long commitment. Chris, go find out how we can get this annulled."

Chris remained seated and quietly asked, "What was the rush?"

Diane looked at him with daggers and said, "You can't possibly think I'm going to allow this to happen?"

"Well, Diane, the truth is, Amanda is an adult and can do whatever she likes. We don't have to agree with her decision, but we will have to live with whatever she decides," Chris reasoned with his wife.

"Well, I'm not going to sit here and listen to this." Standing up in frustration, she planned to storm out of the room.

"Sit down, Diane," Chris demanded. He looked over at his daughter and repeated his question. "What was the rush?"

"It doesn't feel like we're rushing, Dad, honestly. We know we were meant for one another and couldn't see any reason to delay the inevitable."

"Do you hear what she's saying, Chris. She's been brainwashed. I knew we shouldn't have let her go on the trip. Bad things happen when she goes somewhere with a man!"

"Diane, please stop. You aren't making any sense right now. Just listen to what your daughter is telling you from her heart."

"Thank you, Dad. I promise I did this of my own free will. In fact, it was my idea," she ended.

"Why would you do this to us, Amanda? Did we do something wrong to make you want to get away from us?" Diane implored.

"Mom, it's not like that at all. If I hadn't been in the coma for so long, I would most likely be married right now anyway. I've decided it's time for me to start living my life. I can't wait years and years for you to come to terms with the idea that I've grown up. I'm sorry, Mom. I got married because I wanted to, not because of anything you've done, or not done. I love both of you!" Amanda looked from one parent to the other beseeching them to understand. She reached out and held Riccan's hand for support.

Diane did not answer, but the tears started to fall down her cheeks. She felt certain Amanda was acting out because she felt as though she had missed out on so much. She still remembered Amanda's reaction when she was told about her sisters both being married. This had to be because she did not want to be left behind. She just hoped her daughter would discover the error of her decision before they ended up having children together.

Riccan spoke up for the first time. "I love your daughter, and I promise to care for her and love her. I know it seems strange to you how we seemed to rush the process, but we didn't want to delay the inevitable." He squeezed Amanda's hand lightly to show her he was there for her.

"So, Riccan, since we know virtually nothing about you," Chris began, "Why don't you two stay for dinner and you can tell us all about who you are. Since you're now a part of the family, we should at least know the basics."

Amanda smiled at her father. She knew she would be able to count on his support. He was always telling her to go with her heart, and she would never be unhappy. Thankfully he was allowing her to do just that.

Dinner was a small and tense affair. Diane continued to act coldly toward both guests since she was still angry at being kept out of the loop. Chris did his best to keep the conversation as lively as he could. Riccan and Chris exchanged stories about things which had happened at their jobs. Chris was particularly intrigued by Riccan's engineering occupation. Naturally, Riccan had to modify his working credentials since Chris would have no understanding about telepods.

Eventually, the dinner ended much to everyone's relief. Amanda left the three of them to gather some items from her room. She got another suitcase out of her closet and packed the clothing she had received from Barla as well as a wide selection of the clothes from her closet and chest of drawers. Next, she went into the bathroom and took her favorite shampoo and conditioner from the shower. She stuffed everything into the large suitcase and had to sit on it in order to get it zipped shut.

She rolled the suitcase to the front door and left it there for when they were ready to leave. As she walked back into the dining room, she sensed she had interrupted something. The room was silent, and everyone just looked at one another. Right then, she decided it was time to leave and announced, "I'm ready to get going if you are."

Riccan pushed his chair back from the table and stood up. "Thank you for the wonderful dinner. I hope we get to spend more time together soon."

"When do you have to head back to work?" Chris asked.

"Not for another month," Riccan replied and added, "It'll give me enough time for a proper honeymoon with Amanda." He smiled over at his wife.

"Where are you planning to take your honeymoon?" Chris asked politely.

"I thought we'd probably go to Jamaica," he replied and had to resist winking at Amanda. If they ended up going to meet with Jehoban on Acaim, they would technically be on the island of Jamaica.

"We've never been there ourselves," Chris commented as he also rose from his chair to walk the couple out. "I hear it's really nice there."

"I've been many times, and it's been perfect every time," Riccan said making small talk as they walked to the front door together.

Amanda led the way out, ready to escape her mother's dark looks. The evening had essentially gone much as she had imagined, yet she wished her mother could just find a way to be happy for her. She stopped at the door, turning to hug her father.

When she put her arms around her dad's neck, she whispered in his ear, "Thank you, Dad. I promise you I'm happy." She held on to him for a few seconds longer, feeling him kiss the top of her head. This was the type of reception she would have preferred. "I'm not sure when I'll be back to get the rest of my things," she said to her father as they walked together out to Riccan's truck.

"Feel free to leave some things here so your mom can still think you're coming back. It might make the adjustment a little easier for her."

As they drove home, Amanda was the first to speak and said, "I'm sorry about my mother."

"You don't have anything to apologize for." He glanced away from the road to look at his wife. "I don't blame her for being upset at how quickly everything happened. It's totally understandable. You don't regret our decision, do you?"

"No, never, Riccan!" Then she had another thought and asked, "Do you regret it?"

"Nope! I just wanted to give you an out in case you were having second thoughts." He stared straight ahead and grinned a little. He wondered what his mother was going to say. He was certain the announcement would be greeted much more warmly. "Do you want to head over to my parents' house tonight?"

"I kind of had other ideas for our time tonight," Amanda smirked at Riccan.

"Oh, I like the way you think! When do you think we'll be able to find the time to let my parents know the good news?"

Amanda seriously considered the question and finally answered, "We should probably go over there tomorrow. Your dad said he might have some news about meeting with Jehoban in a few days. It's already been that long. We can't delay the inevitable for too long. Besides, if we need to go anywhere or do anything after meeting with Jehoban, you'll still have plenty of time left on your leave from work."

"Good point," Riccan conceded. The meeting with Jehoban had managed to slip his mind given his other recent pursuits. He reasoned with himself that one more day could hardly make much difference. Besides, his father could reach him on his patil if he really needed them to come to Pantano sooner.

Their evening consisted mostly of them getting to know each other more intimately. They christened Riccan's bedroom and explored each other some more in his enormous shower. Amanda had thought she would be more self-conscience with Riccan, but they felt so perfect for one another it was as easy as going home. She had to keep reminding herself that this huge house was now hers as well. She wondered how much longer she would keep referring to everything as his instead of ours.

Morning came all too soon. They managed to find the time to get together intimately one last time before breakfast. Luckily Riccan was pretty handy with using the elemy to produce their breakfast. He had it appear on the nightstand, so they never had to leave the room even to eat. Without any further reason to stall, except very selfish ones, they finally got dressed and packed a few things to stay in Tuala for a few days.

Now that Amanda's parents were not expecting her to check in with them, she felt a sense of freedom overcome her. Not since she had taken the ill-fated trip with Nealand had she felt so independent. She glanced at her phone to see if her mother had called; she had not. Amanda felt slightly guilty for wanting to get away from her mother's watchful eyes.

Amanda had some trepidation about telling Riccan's parents about the marriage after the reception she had received from her own mother. She did not want to ask Riccan what he believed would happen because she did not want to imagine the scene before them.

The telepod ride to Pantano was uneventful, and they touched down on the grand lawn behind the house. They walked hand-in-hand across the grass and up the staircase to the terrace before anyone came out to acknowledge them. Amanda inwardly groaned when she saw Nena rushing across the terrace to greet them. Riccan squeezed her hand and smiled down at her with a reassuring smile.

"Hello, you two! I'm so glad you came back. We have a lot to discuss. Come on inside; we can meet in your father's office." She grabbed Riccan's arm and tucked her hand into the crook of his elbow. "How long are you two planning on staying this time? Please tell me you'll stay longer than just dinner!"

"Actually, we were hoping to stay for a couple of days, at least. We're curious to see if Father has had the opportunity to speak with Jehoban to arrange a meeting with Amanda," Riccan replied.

"All in good time, Son. I'm thrilled you two are planning to stay for a while. I can't wait to get to know Amanda better!" She had thought to get some type of a rise out of her son cautioning her to mind her own business. When nothing was forthcoming, she looked up at her son and narrowed her eyes as she inspected the look on her son's face. He was definitely up to something. Once she got him alone, she'd pry it out of him if she had to go that far.

"Is Dad working right now?" Riccan tried to sound nonchalant.

"He finished up about twenty minutes ago. Why? What's going on, Riccan?" Nena liked to be the first to know any news, and she could tell there was something brewing.

"We'd like to discuss something with the two of you. In private," he added unnecessarily.

"We have time right now. Here we are, you go on into your father's office while I ask someone to send in some drinks for us." She ushered them into the room and practically danced down the hall on her errand.

His father looked up from his patil when he heard the commotion at his door. He was pleasantly surprised to see the two people and said, "I was just thinking about the two of you. Come in and have a seat. Is your mother coming back?"

"Yes, she went to get refreshments for us," Riccan answered. He sat down at the same time Amanda did. He smiled at his father and kept his own counsel until his mother returned. This was definitely a story he only wanted to tell once. He hoped they would be happy for them, but he just did not know for certain.

Nena breezed back into the room and smiled at everyone as she went to sit beside her husband.

"Okay, now that you are both here, Amanda and I have some wonderful news to share," Riccan began.

"You two are engaged!" Nena burst out.

"Nena, let Riccan talk," Daven chided but wondered if his wife were right.

"Not exactly, Mom. Amanda and I got married yesterday in Reno. We eloped!" He held up Amanda's hand as proof of his statement. He smiled broadly at first one parent and then the other.

CHAPTER 27

Nena recovered first from the unexpected news, "Oh, Riccan, that's just wonderful!" She turned to her husband and said smugly, "I told you Amanda was perfect for Riccan. They have the most complimentary auras!" She jumped up from her chair and came to a stop in front of Amanda and said, "Welcome to the family! I always wanted a daughter, and now I have the best one I could ever imagine!"

Amanda felt tears threatening in her eyes. She had been so worried their reaction would be negative and now she was warmly welcomed into the family. She could not have asked for a better scenario. She stood up to hug Nena. Amanda was surprised when Nena kissed her soundly on the cheek and then patted her arm before turning to sit back down.

She had only just begun. "Tell us everything! Don't leave anything out. Oh, this is so exciting, isn't it, Daven?"

"Yes, this is very good news."

"Dad, I have a favor to ask of you?" Riccan said seriously.

"Sure, Son. What can I do for you?"

"I'd like for you to marry us in Tuala. I want our marriage to be official no matter where we are."

Daven was touched by his son's request and did not hesitate to answer, "It would be my honor."

"When would you like the ceremony to happen?" Nena asked. She was already planning an extensive guest list and thinking of all the details which would have to be taken care of. She would need several weeks at the very least.

"We'd like to have it official today, if possible," Amanda interjected.

"Today? That won't give me enough time to put it all together," Nena objected.

"That's actually the point, Mom. We don't want a big affair. We only want the two of you and any house staff who would like to attend. Seriously, Mom, I can see the wheels turning in your head. No plans, no parties, nothing. We want it just as simple as we had it in Reno," Riccan said adamantly. He knew his mother's penchant for putting together lavish affairs, and he knew Amanda would be uncomfortable being put on display in such a manner.

Nena sat back in her chair and crossed her arms. She was not liking how this was turning out. She only had the one son, and she had imagined his wedding ceremony almost from the time he was born. She felt as though she were being left out of an important rite of passage. Moreover, she thought it was unfair to Amanda for her not to have an extravagant wedding.

Amanda could see how upset Nena had become and tried to reassure her. "This is what I want, too. We are so happy to have found one another; we don't want to waste any time with parties or fancy services. We just want it to be official here on Tuala. I hope you can understand."

It seemed as if Nena no longer had a choice in the matter. She gave in with good grace and decided she would have the entire household staff turn out for the event. "Ok, I promise nothing lavish. Can I have at least until tomorrow?"

"No, we'd like to have Dad do the ceremony before lunchtime. Preferably right now if that would work," Riccan pushed.

Daven knew his wife was about to explode next to him, but he wanted to honor his son's wishes. "Let's have a compromise, shall we? Can it wait until after dinner tonight?"

Riccan looked over at Amanda and raised his eyebrows. Amanda nodded. Riccan turned back to his father and said, "Okay. We can wait until after dinner tonight."

"Oh, this is perfect. Thank you for waiting a little bit!" Nena said brightly as she clapped her hands with glee.

Daven desperately wanted to change the subject and asked Riccan, "Were you able to take that trip to find Roderick?"

"Yes, and I took your advice and had Amanda come along with me. You were right, again, because we were very successful on the journey."

"Tell us what happened," Nena said with intense interest. She leaned forward to the edge of her chair in anticipation of a good story.

"On the first day there, we encountered a crystal skull at a vendor's booth. The power of it literally stopped me in my tracks," Riccan chuckled.

"And I ran right into him," Amanda added with a grin.

"The vendor was reluctant to sell it to me, but he did in the end. However, he sent two henchmen to retrieve it once we were a couple of blocks away. I detected the potential problem, and we caught a cab and got out of there in a hurry."

"Were you able to bring it home?" Daven rested his elbows on the desktop as he leaned forward expectantly.

"Yes. We avoided that area from then on, so we were able to get it home safely. I have it stored with the other one at my house."

"Good! Very good! What else did you discover in New Orleans?" Daven prompted.

"We located Uncle Roderick. He was a veritable font of knowledge when it came to the family legend of the skull." Riccan proceeded to tell them everything which they had learned from their ancient relative.

"That's amazing!" Nena commented at the end of the story.

"Oh, just wait until you hear what happened once we got home," Riccan teased.

"Was this before or after you got married?" Nena asked before Riccan could continue.

"Before; it was the day of our wedding, actually. We went to our house to put the crystal skull in a safe place right away because I felt spooked by the two guys who were after us. Anyway, we got it into the secret room. I was ahead of Amanda, and she had the new crystal in her purse. As soon as I touched the original skull, I felt as if I were being electrocuted; although, it wasn't painful. I couldn't move from the spot I was in until Amanda touched me and helped disburse the electrical charge.

"Then when we had both skulls on the table together we could feel an enormous amount of power being created. I don't know why I did, but I put my hand on both of them at the same time. Amanda and I both had a vision of the woman who originally distributed the crystals to their care-takers. She had said they were 'descendants of the Watchers.'

"It was the same phrase Uncle Roderick used. We can only assume then that Uncle Roderick's rendition of the history of the stone is correct. Now we have a new mystery on our hands regarding the descendants of the Watchers. Do you have any knowledge of such a people?" Riccan sat back and watched as his mother and father both wracked their brains for any ideas.

Daven was the first to reply, "I seem to recall something of the sort during my training to become an Elder. It was a long time ago. I think I read about it somewhere when I was taking a stint working in the archives. I'll keep thinking about it and let you know if I can come up with anything. How about you, Nena? Any thoughts?"

"I remember a story my parents used to tell me when I was little about some angels who were called the Watchers. Do you think they could be the same?" Nena shook her head as she could not think of anything more.

"It's something. I'll look into that angle as well," Daven mused. He made a couple of notes for himself on his patil and then turned back to his son and daughter-in-law.

"Riccan, you forgot to tell them what the crystal skulls are actually called," Amanda reminded him in a whisper.

"Oh, yeah, Amanda just reminded me of another important detail: the crystal skulls are called samaras. Maybe you should do some research on that term while you're at it, Dad," Riccan suggested. He knew his father loved to do any type of research and he was more than happy to let him lead the charge.

"That's really good, Riccan. I'll write that down right now," he said as he turned back to his patil and keyed in several thoughts to check up on at a later date. "Can you think of anything else which might make the search easier?"

"Would you be able to find out anything about the Scamp family from around 1800 from France? It would be a long-shot, but if we could find the family who gave the Scamp's the crystal, we may be able to track down the original owner."

Daven looked consideringly at his son and pursed his lips. "You're right, that would be a long shot. I'll see what, if anything, I can find."

"Since you don't seem to have anything else to share about that, why don't you tell me every detail about your wedding?" Nena demanded.

Riccan laughed and knew they were in for a long spell while his mother grilled them to obtain every last detail. There really was not all that much to tell since it had all happened so fast and without much fanfare. He could tell his mother was disappointed in the lack of planning which had happened on Earth as well.

"I can understand why your mother was so upset, Amanda. I'm sure she had the same plans for your wedding as I had for my son. And to say she wasn't even invited! That was really a low blow, Amanda." She held up her hand to forestall her son's objection to her last statement and continued with, "But I understand your dilemma. Your mother has been coddling you since you woke up, but I'm sure it's only because she loves you dearly."

"I know that's true, and I apologized to my mother for going behind her back to get it done. I know she'll eventually get used to the idea, but she's very stubborn." Amanda shrugged to indicate she really had no choice.

"I wish we could invite your folks to the ceremony here," Nena mused as she looked over at her husband with the question in her eyes.

"I really don't think that's a good idea right now," Amanda spoke up hastily to keep the line of thought from going any further. "My mom is having enough difficulty with the fact that I'm married. You'd only be adding another level of worry for her if she knew I was not on Earth anymore!"

"Okay, if you insist. I guess I'll have to let the idea go," she answered sullenly.

Amanda remembered something which was said at the beginning of their conversation and finally thought to ask about it. "What did you mean when you told Daven about my aura complimenting Riccan's? Are you skilled at aura reading?"

"Why yes, I am. It's a favorite hobby of mine. I enjoy seeing the complexities of each person and how they interact with one another. Have you gotten to the lesson on auras yet?" Nena asked.

Daven answered for Amanda and said, "We had just gotten to that point during our last session together. I was going to ask you to take over that skill with her because I happen to know how much better you are at it than myself. Plus I thought it would give you time to grill Amanda about her intentions for our son. I guess that question has been answered," he chuckled. "We still have time before lunch, do you want to learn a couple more skills, Amanda?"

"I would love to, as long as you have time for it. I don't want to put anyone to any trouble."

"I think we can leave you to your lesson then while Dad and I go get our bags out of the telepod. What do you think, Dad?" Riccan stood up and looked down at his father seated at the desk.

"I think it's a perfect idea!" He stood up slowly and kissed his wife as he walked by her. "Be easy on the girl."

"Oh, you go on, get out of here! Let a real teacher get this lesson done!" she said as she slapped playfully at him as he passed.

Amanda sat on the edge of her chair in anticipation of learning the new skill. She did not know what to expect from Nena as she had from Daven. She hoped she would pick it up easily so Nena would not think she was slow at learning.

"Okay, Amanda, I want you to clear your mind of everything except my face in front of you. I want you to pretend to look through me instead of at me. Let your eyes lose their focus slightly. I find that helps some-times. Tell me when you've done all these things."

Amanda did as she was told. She looked through Nena and relaxed her eyes. She started to see some shimmer around Nena. With a smile of delight Amanda finally said, "Okay, I'm there. I can see a shimmer around your head."

"Really? Well, that's really good. Now shift your vision, so it's looking slightly beside the shimmer to allow it to expand."

Amanda once again focused on the instructions and was rewarded with a light band of colors displayed. "I see several colors around you. There's blue, green, yellow, and a little bit of purple."

"Yes, that's correct! You are quite skilled at this, Amanda. Once you learn the trick to it, you'll be able to just glance at a person and see the aura immediately."

"So what do you do with it once you know the colors?" Amanda asked. She could not see where there was much value in seeing color around people.

"That's where this gets really fun. The colors each have a meaning.

They each describe the mood, intent, or intellect of a person. Like when I saw your aura, I could tell you would be a good intellectual match for Riccan. I think we've done enough of this for right now. As the day goes on, try to see the aura around other people. Try not to be terribly obvious since it can make the other person quite uncomfortable to be stared at."

Amanda chuckled and said, "I'll give it a try. Let me know if you see me making a nuisance of myself."

Nena stood up and said, "Let me show you to yours and Riccan's room." She waited for Amanda to come up beside her and she put her arm around her waist and gave her a little squeeze. "I'm so excited you and Riccan found one another. It's such an amazing story, too!"

"Yes, I agree. The sad part is that I've known Riccan through my dreams far longer than he's known me. I'm glad he could see past the weirdness and trust me anyway. I was terribly concerned he would turn me away and not want to talk with me." Amanda sighed and then smiled and said, "But it all worked out in the end. I still have a hard time thinking I have a husband. It thrills me just to say it and to think he's Riccan just makes it that much more special."

"I'm so glad for you both. We're going to have a lot of time to get to know one another," she said as she steered them down the hall and up a flight of stairs.

Amanda had not been paying much attention to where they had been walking. Now she took notice and realized they were in the family's private portion of the Residence. The downstairs was very plush and formal whereas the upstairs was more homey and informal. Amanda decided she preferred the upstairs better.

After passing a few doors, Nena turned them to a door which was slightly ajar. "Here's your room," she said as she pushed the door fully open. "Oh, good. The men have already brought your luggage upstairs. Let's get your things unpacked and hung up so they won't be too wrinkled."

Amanda was not sure how she felt about Nena seeing all of her stuff, but she decided she would have to get used to having another overbearing mother. At least Nena was not concerned about Amanda's every movement. She walked over to her suitcase and unzipped it. She began pulling out the articles of clothing while Nena hung them up in the closet. They made quick work of it as a team. Finally, Amanda pulled out the outfit she had received from Barla. She shook it out and admired it once again in the streaming sunlight.

"What's that you have, Amanda?" Nena asked with a curious expression on her face. She tilted her head and squinted her eyes before she asked, "Where did you get this?"

"My Aunt Barla had it made for me. I remember it from my dream, and I was wearing it when I was found by the paramedics on Earth. They sent it home with me when I finally left the hospital."

"Amanda, are you sure you're not mistaken?"

"Of course I'm sure. This is the outfit I remember."

"There's something strange going on. Can I take a look at that?" Pulling the garment from Amanda's slack fingers, she moved closer to the window and pulled back the cuff of the sleeve to reveal the maker's mark. "Oh, no! It's as bad as I thought!" she whispered to herself.

"What is it?" Amanda went to join her at the window.

"I haven't seen this mark on anything for over fifteen years."

"What does it mean?"

"I'm not sure just now." Nena realized she should not tell Amanda what she knew until she had more facts. "We should go down and find the men." She promptly hung the outfit in the closet next to all of the others as though it were no different.

Amanda was still wondering what Nena had meant when she had seen the outfit from Barla, but she soon forgot to think about it when she saw Riccan walking toward her from the far end of the hall. "Thank you for bringing up my bag. Our room is lovely," she said when they came together to hug and give one another a light kiss on the lips.

Nena pulled Daven to the side and said quietly, "We need to talk alone." She gave him a significant look and watched as Daven nodded confirmation of her request.

Riccan noticed his parents talking softly to one another and suggested to Amanda, "Why don't I show you around the grounds?"

"Sure, I'd like that," Amanda readily agreed.

∿

"HAVE you heard anything back from your request to Jehoban?" Nena asked urgently.

"Not yet. Why?" Daven tilted his head in question at his wife's sudden urgency.

"I just discovered something very odd in Amanda's wardrobe. I think Amanda needs to see Jehoban as soon as possible."

"Okay, let's go to my office and see if there is a reply. Shall we?" Daven offered his arm to his wife. They walked together at a stately pace.

Daven sat down at his desk and turned on his patil. He clicked on the message button and waited a few seconds for it to refresh the messages. "Oh, look! We have a response."

"Well? What are you waiting for? Open it up!"

"No, I think we'll wait to see what it says until Amanda is present."

"Let's go get them and drag them back here then!" Nena was oddly insistent.

"What's gotten into you?"

"Something odd is going on, and I want some answers. It seems as though Jehoban is the only one who will be able to supply the answers I'm looking for when it comes to Amanda's history. There's more to her story than even she knows." Nena jumped up from her chair and marched out of the office.

It had been a good long while since she had last used Riccan's birth crystal to locate him, but she felt it was imperative she find him immediately. After only a couple of seconds, Nena saw the couple down by the pool. She marched to where they were and waved as she got close enough. "We have a message from Jehoban! Come to your father's office."

Riccan nodded confirmation and changed direction to make a beeline for the Residence's side entrance. He was just as anxious as Amanda, but he did not want to show his concern to his wife. She was already nervous enough about the encounter.

After only a few minutes everyone was, once again, reconvened in the office. Riccan began the conversation by asking, "Okay, Dad, what does the message say?"

Amanda sat on the edge of her chair. While she did not know what to expect, she had a feeling, for good or bad, her life would never be the same after she met with Jehoban.

Daven clicked on the message and leaned forward as he read the message out loud. "I'm glad to hear Amanda has returned. I've been waiting a long time for her to come visit."

THE SHADOWS OF DESTINY

BOOK TWO OF THE CHOSEN

CHAPTER 1

Amanda's heart stopped momentarily when she heard Elder Daven say that the Creator of the Universe, Jehoban, had been expecting her to visit with Him. Amanda had always thought of herself as an ordinary woman from Earth. Through the past months, years really if she were being completely honest with herself, she had discovered her life was extraordinary indeed. Now, as she sat next to her husband, Riccan, on another world, called Tuala, she was faced with the biggest challenge of her life.

She had thought she was prepared to ask Jehoban the questions about her past which had been plaguing her, but now she was no longer certain. With panic rising in her, Amanda looked over at Riccan and immediately felt calmer. His beautiful brown eyes were full of love and trust. She reached out and grabbed his hand.

Riccan wished he could take his wife's place. She was so petite and still rather frail from having come out of a seven-year-long coma only eight months before. He wondered if she were strong enough, both physically and emotionally, for the interview.

Riccan took his eyes away from his wife's to look across the desk at his father, Elder Daven. In his capacity as Elder, he always seemed more formidable, but in actuality, he was a tall, older man with white hair and brown eyes like his own. His father was gentle, kind, and compassionate.

Riccan was certain his father would not be sending Amanda to an interview which would cause her harm. He had to hold on to that belief as he asked, "When does Jehoban want to meet with her?"

Daven turned his gaze back to the patil to continue reading the message on the screen. He answered quietly, "He said she should come as soon as possible."

Daven's wife, Nena, who sat beside him during this meeting gasped and raised her tiny hands to cover her mouth. Her blue eyes got wide with concern, and she immediately looked over at Amanda to assess her reaction to the news. Suddenly she brightened and said, "This will at least give me more time to plan your wedding ceremony!"

Amanda did not like Nena's response to the immediate summons. In fact, now her heart began racing thinking this was an imminent interview and not just a far-in-the-future idea. Again, her husband squeezed her hand to offer comfort.

Riccan thought of an idea which would make the interview easier and asked his father, "Does the request say Amanda is to attend the meeting alone? Would I be able to go with her?"

"I'm sorry, Riccan, this is for Amanda, alone, to do."

"I guess this means we'll have to delay our wedding ceremony, Dad," Riccan said.

"Why? Don't you think I could wait until tomorrow morning to go see Jehoban?" Amanda demanded.

"Do you really want to put Jehoban on hold while you do something of your own? When Jehoban requests an interview as soon as possible, you stop whatever you're doing and go. We have to trust that He knows what is best for you, Amanda. Besides, we were already married on Earth, the one here in Tuala is just a formality for Tualan custom."

"I know," Amanda sighed, "I guess I'm just trying to delay the inevitable. When do you want to leave?"

Riccan stood up and pulled Amanda up by the hand he was still holding and replied, "Right now. The telepod awaits us outside."

Nena rushed around the desk and pulled Amanda into an embrace as she said, "I promise you, everything will be okay. I'm sorry if my reaction startled you, I was just surprised at the quick timing. Jehoban is good, and you'll get all of your questions answered." She leaned up on her tiptoes and kissed Amanda on the cheek before turning back to take her own husband's hand.

Daven had stood up by then and said, "We'll walk out with the both of you." They were quiet for a few paces before Daven asked his son, "Do you have the proper coordinates for landing on Acaim?"

"Yes, I've been there many times, remember?" Riccan had visited his grandparents on Jehoban's island frequently until the time of their deaths several anons before. He had a very clear mental image of the landing square even though his telepod was equipped with the newest technology for auto-pilot navigation. It never hurt to use the mental telepathy as backup when operating a telepod.

Riccan's parents remained on the back terrace balcony and said goodbye. Riccan leaned in to kiss his mother's cheek and said, "Don't get any ideas for the wedding, Mom. Just because it's going to be delayed does not mean we want it to be elaborate. We want a simple family affair. Promise me you'll remember that."

"I promise," she said with a slight frown. Her son knew her too well, and now she could not plead ignorance to his wishes. She watched him turn and walk away with his new wife.

Riccan and Amanda descended the flagstone steps down to the grand lawn. Amanda stared ahead at the waiting telepod. It was a marvel of engineering, both designed and built by Riccan. It was a racing red exterior color, which was unusual for the air transportation on Tuala. Amanda liked it because it stood out and practically screamed it was different.

As they got closer, Riccan activated the remote to open the large folding door on the side. They moved up the ramp and through the passenger section of the craft to their seats in the cockpit. Amanda sat in the right seat and fastened her seat belt harness. She looked out the front window to see both of Riccan's parents, her in-laws now, were waving farewell. Amanda forced a smile on her face and waved back.

Riccan sat down in the left-hand seat, fastened his seat belt, and palmed the door closed by using the button on the control panel. Riccan began the telepod's start-up procedures. He touched the plascreen to turn it on, and then he activated the telepod's crystal drive. The vessel rose several inches above the ground soundlessly and hovered in place until Riccan was able to verify each green light on the screen.

He switched screens to be able to enter the course they would be traveling. He typed in the coordinates and pressed enter. Immediately, the course was locked and loaded. With a nod of readiness to Amanda, Riccan pressed the button on the screen to begin the teleportation to Acaim.

Three seconds later they appeared over a flat, grassy field mere inches above the ground. Riccan issued all of the shutdown procedures and unfastened his belt. He turned to Amanda and asked, "Are you ready?"

"No, but it appears I don't have much choice, now does it?" Amanda asked crossly. She did not know why she was taking out her fear on Riccan. He was probably the most supportive person she had ever met. As her husband of one whole day, he definitely did not deserve the sharp side of her tongue. "I'm sorry, Riccan. That wasn't fair of me to take this out on you. I appreciate your offer to stand by my side throughout."

"You'll do fine. I'm sure of it. Besides, Jehoban is an amazing man. Just think, in only a few hours, you'll have the answers to all of your questions. Don't you think that will be worth the fear you're feeling right now?"

"Yes." Amanda smiled at Riccan's attempt to see the bright side of the interview. "Let's get this over with before my heart bursts from the adrenaline of fear."

Riccan palmed open the side door and gestured for her to precede him out of the telepod.

Amanda swiftly unfastened her belt and got out of her seat. She could not get over the feeling that she was going to meet her executioner. In a way, it would be true because the life she had known thus far was not one of reality but just a dream. She hoped she would find out the truth about her history from the best source possible. Jehoban seemed to be the best answer for everything in her life.

Amanda walked down the ramp and stood on the grass. She had only taken two steps before she stopped, turned around, and waited for Riccan to close the side door. She had decided she would keep Riccan as close as possible for as long as possible. Maybe he would even be invited to the interview once Jehoban saw how desperately she needed the support.

Together they walked across the grassy landing field toward a gated area. The closer they got to it, the details became clearer. The gate was unlike anything Amanda had ever seen. It almost looked as though it were made from a single, enormous pearl. She turned and looked questioningly at Riccan.

"There are a lot of marvelous sights to behold here, Amanda. This pearl gate is just the first of many wonders." He put his arm around her waist and continued walking through the gate.

Amanda reached out and touched the pearl surface to satisfy her curiosity. It was definitely real and not just a painted surface. Her curiosity was aroused, and she actually found herself looking forward to seeing the next wonder. She did not have to wait long. The walls of the grand palace were made of a translucent blue stone. Again, Amanda touched the surface to see what it would feel like. The stone was warm from the sunlight and smooth as glass. She wondered how it had been put together so seamlessly until she laughed at her folly.

"What's so funny?" Riccan asked with a smile on his lips. He was glad to see his wife had begun to relax.

"I was just wondering about how perfectly this wall was put together. Of course, it would be perfect if Jehoban made it. I'm assuming He did make everything here," she replied as she gestured with her hand to encompass everything they could see.

"You're right. Nothing here was made by man. All of it is the perfect creation of Jehoban," Riccan agreed with her. "We're going in the door just up there," he said as he pointed to a gold colored door.

When Riccan reached forward to open the door, Amanda realized it was not just gold colored; it was real, solid gold. There were intricate designs carved into the surface of innumerable animals, trees, people, and even telepods. Amanda thought it seemed like a utopian type scene. Her fingers again touched the surface and could find no flaw.

Just inside the door were two teenaged girls. They turned to face the visitors and Amanda could see they were actually identical twins. They were around fifteen or sixteen anons old, with long, blonde hair, blue eyes, and the same height as Amanda. They both smiled, and the one on the left spoke, "Welcome to Acaim. We'll be taking you to see Jehoban. Riccan, will you please wait in the waiting area. We'll bring her back here when she's done with her interview." She pointed to an area with a small fountain and several places to sit for Riccan to make himself feel at home.

It was clearly a dismissal. Riccan smiled at the two girls. He leaned down and kissed Amanda on the cheek before saying, "I'll go count fish until you return."

Amanda smiled at her husband's lame attempt at humor and replied, "I hope I won't be long."

"No bother, take your time. This place is very beautiful." He walked away to go check out the area he had never seen before.

"Right this way, Amanda," the other girl spoke for the first time.

Amanda could not help but think these girls would be what her daughters would look like when they got older. She was fascinated by them and their level of confidence. She took strength from their easy ways. Finally, she asked, "How did you know our names?"

"Jehoban told us you two had arrived. He instructed us to greet you both and bring you alone to see Him," the first girl answered. "We don't have too much farther to go. You need not be worried about the meeting. Jehoban is very excited to finally meet you."

"What did He mean by saying He had been expecting me? We only just decided to try to meet with Him," Amanda asked in confusion as she reviewed the original invitation mentally.

"Our timing is not the same as His. He knows all things which were, are, and will ever be," the second girl seemed to recite the phrases from memory.

"Right," Amanda said with a tinge of awe.

They continued down several grand hallways where the walls were seamless and beautiful in their perfection. Amanda saw several alcoves set with plush furniture for intimate conversations. She began to wonder what type of room she was being led to when they arrived at their destination.

The girls each opened one of the two doors to the grand chamber. Amanda was not sure if she were to enter ahead of them or to wait to be guided. She hesitated and looked from one identical face to the other.

"Go ahead and enter, we will be following you," the first girl replied.

Amanda took a hesitant step forward and then another. She hastily looked around the room to find anybody, but the room was empty of any occupants. She turned back to the girls, who were literally one step behind her, and asked, "Are you sure this is the room?"

The girls both smiled and nodded.

Amanda looked back ahead and almost missed a step as she now saw an older but very handsome gentleman seated at a small table which had not been there mere moments before. She did not want to seem impolite, so she stretched out her hand when she got close and introduced herself. "Hi, I'm Amanda. Thank you for taking the time to meet with me."

The man with the kind eyes smiled and took her hand in His own warm ones. Instead of shaking it He just held it in a comforting way. "The pleasure is mine, Amanda Stel. Please be seated." He turned to the two girls and said, "Thank you for bringing Amanda to me. Please take a seat at the table as well. I'd like you to witness this meeting as a teaching tool."

For once, the girls looked flustered. Amanda hid a small smile to see she was not the only one to be in awe of this man. They sat next to one another across the table from Amanda. For some reason, Amanda felt comfort knowing she would not be left alone with the all-powerful Jehoban.

"Please sit down right here," Jehoban requested as He pulled a plush chair out for Amanda to be seated.

She hurried to comply with His request. He perfectly positioned the chair at the table so Amanda could comfortably lean on the table if she had been relaxed enough to consider it. Instead, Amanda sat rigidly straight in anticipation of the interview.

Jehoban walked a step or two before reaching His own seat and taking a considerable amount of time getting Himself situated. He wanted to give Amanda a few moments to relax before their conversation began. There was much to discuss with her.

"Again," Jehoban began, making Amanda jump, "I want to thank you for coming to see me. I have waited a very long time for this meeting to take place."

Amanda could not contain her curiosity and asked, "Why have you been expecting me? I'm just a normal human from Earth." She really could not understand His insistence on her being special somehow.

"It's true, you are from Earth, but that is not all you are," He said carefully. "You are much more than you appear to be, Amanda, much more. Before I tell you anything further, please ask me the questions you have on your mind?"

The most important question came immediately to mind, "Did I really have twin girls when I was in Tuala?"

"Yes."

Amanda waited for more and realized that was all He was going to say.

She scrambled for another question and asked, "Is Barla really my long-lost aunt?"

"Yes."

"I'd like to go and see her. Do you have any objections to my meeting with her as soon as this meeting is done?"

"Patience, Amanda. Now is not the time for that to be found out by Barla. I will let you know when you may tell her." Jehoban stopped talking and waited for Amanda to ask the next question.

She could not understand why she could not start her relationship with her aunt. It seemed cruel to keep her out of the family. Amanda could see how this interview was going to go. She would have to come up with a question which required something other than an answer of yes or no. Since Jehoban seemed to be done with that subject, she moved on and asked, "Why is my meeting with You so important?"

"Because you are the key to the changes coming to Tuala and Earth. You are the link between the two dimensions."

"I don't understand. There are lots of people who travel between the dimensions. Why am I any different from them?"

"Because of your heritage. You, alone, are uniquely qualified to make the difference."

"The difference to what? Please tell me exactly what about my heritage makes me qualified for your plan?"

"You are the descendant of one of My own."

"What does that mean? Who are your own?" Amanda was starting to feel frustrated with His abbreviated answers which only led to more questions.

"The angels are My own. You are descended from one of them. Have you never wondered why you have received so many gifts?" Jehoban tilted His head and looked at her curiously.

Amanda paused to understand this new revelation. She had two sisters. Were they equally qualified? She asked Him.

"No, your sisters share your same parents, but only you inherited the gifts."

Amanda remembered her genetics lessons in high school and realized she had a twenty-five percent chance of getting something different from her sisters. Both she and her oldest sister had brown eyes, whereas their middle sister had green. It had to work in the same manner with the gifts

Jehoban was talking about. She nodded her head to indicate she understood.

She asked the last questions she had wanted to ask. "What really happened to me when I first came to Tuala? Was all of it a dream?"

Jehoban sat back in His plush chair and considered her questions. "Dreams are an extension of our reality. You have shown a remarkable aptitude for making a reality of your dreams. After all, you are now married to Riccan, right?"

Amanda touched the two rings on her left finger and smiled before saying, "I am."

"Let Me tell you about your time on Tuala. The story is complicated but simple at the same time. You must let go of everything you think you know about your history and open your mind to what I am going to tell you."

Amanda was shocked she was actually going to hear about her past. She hoped she was ready for any revelation which Jehoban might reveal. She mentally prepared herself and then nodded twice.

"Your initial memory of sailing with Nealand was accurate. You were on Earth when the two of you encountered a severe storm at sea. The two of you, as well as the yacht, were transported to Tuala. Petre MacVeen discovered both of you and towed your ship to the nearest Elder who happened to be Elder Vargen."

Amanda was starting to see how her version was very different from reality.

Jehoban stopped to let the truth sink in before He continued. "Elder Vargen confiscated everything from Petre citing his ruling on anything considered *old soul* is the property of the Elders. Petre was unhappy with the treatment he received and submitted an official complaint to the First Elder Debbon."

Amanda was glad to know Elder Debbon was still involved in the story and she had not been completely wrong. "How come I don't remember any of this?"

"Petre had drugged both of you with resh until he could try to sell you. Elder Vargen continued to keep you both drugged while he took you both prisoner. He separated you immediately after he read both of your minds. He took Nealand to the research lab where his skills with engineering could be exploited. Nealand never remembered he had lost you. He is now a slave to the drug, resh."

"Are you saying Nealand is still here?" Amanda's heart rushed with excitement. If she could get him back to Earth, his family would finally have some closure. They would not have to believe their son had died at sea. Amanda would no longer have to carry the guilt of his disappearance.

"Yes, he's still here. Hear the rest of your story before you make any plans to rescue him."

Amanda was properly chastised and tried to set aside her ideas for Neal until she heard Jehoban out.

"Elder Vargen also read your mind, Amanda. He saw the truth of your ancestry, even if you were unaware of it because it leaves a marker in your subconscious. He wanted to keep you and breed you until he could create his own personal version of the one from the prophecy. Elder Vargen believed if he could train the one from the prophecy from birth then he would have control over the outcome of the world."

"Was he right? Would his plan have worked?"

"No. It is not his place. He will never be successful."

"You mean he's still trying?"

"Absolutely. He will always seek to be the best, to be First. He will never achieve his goal."

"Why don't you just stop him?"

"He has his uses. Please listen. Elder Vargen kept you drugged to the point of comatose with the drug resh. Each mesan he tried to impregnate you when you became receptive. Finally, around the seventh mesan, he was successful. He called in a wise-woman to watch over your pregnancy. When she told him you were having twins, he was elated. He believed he would have twice the chance of getting the prophet he desired."

"Was the wise-woman Alena?" Amanda hoped it had been her.

"No, the wise-woman was named Copa."

Amanda scanned her memories of anything related to Copa. Finally, she remembered she was the wise-woman who had helped Ninan when he had been bashed on the head by Petre.

CHAPTER 2

"The mesans went by, and your pregnancy progressed normally. Because you were having twins, your labor came on a mesan earlier than Elder Vargen expected. He did not check up on you anymore because he only wanted your children. He told the wise-woman to tell him when you had delivered the twins.

"The wise-woman had become sympathetic to your plight over the eight mesans she had sat vigil with you. She decided Elder Vargen would never get his hands on your children. When your labor had progressed to the point where she knew it was going to happen, she teleported you to an abandoned house she knew of near where she had grown up. She had intended to move you to the new location to prepare you to be sent back to Earth with your twins, but your labor came on faster than she had anticipated.

"In the end, Copa made the hard decision to keep the children and only send you back to Earth. She could not risk the transfer for the newborns since she wasn't even certain it would work to send you. She did her best to heal your body of the residual effects of the delivery. She dressed you in the clothes Elder Vargen reserved for his *old soul* slaves, and she translated you to Earth.

"As she was afraid of, her skill wasn't very precise. You ended up arriving on Earth in the ocean. As you were still delirious from the resh, you were tossed by the waves until you were almost drowned. By the time you were rescued you had been dead for almost ten minutes. They revived you and kept you alive with machines, but your mind took much longer to heal."

"Yes, seven years actually. I'm surprised I didn't sustain any permanent brain damage." Amanda was even more thankful her mother had not given up hope sooner.

"Yes, seven anons may seem like a long time; however, it also kept you safe from harm from Elder Vargen. Everything happens for a reason."

"Are you saying Elder Vargen would have attempted to abduct me to try again?"

"Yes."

"What happened with my children? Did Elder Vargen find Copa and take them back?"

"No. Copa was very resourceful in keeping the children safe. She met with Captain Issyn to ask for help. He sailed the three of them through the Gulf of Thulen to the Port of Cresdon. During the voyage, Jena became very sick. It wasn't something Copa had ever seen before, and she was unable to access the child's life-line in order to heal her. By the time they docked, Jena had slipped into a coma, and Juila was crying continually.

"Copa took the twins to Barla's home to figure out what type of help could be procured for the sick child. Barla and her assistant, Alena, doted over the infants and Barla told Copa how these twins looked so much like her own daughter, Rasa.

"Alena's boyfriend, Bryon, offered to fly the twins to Elder Debbon's isle to have him heal Jena of her mysterious illness. Bryon, Alena, and Copa stayed with the twins at Elder Debbon's Residence since it took him almost a week to determine the cause of Jena's illness. He discovered that both children were actually sick, but Jena was the only one showing the symptoms. He treated Juila first which made Jena almost immediately better. Next, he treated the residual symptoms of Jena.

"When the healing was complete, he asked Copa why neither of the children had birth crystals. The power of the crystals would have helped to prevent the children from getting sick in the first place.

"Copa finally admitted she did not have access to her ceremonial box since she had to leave so precipitously. Elder Debbon took pity on the older wise-woman and performed the ceremony that very evening. It was a small gathering of Bryon, Alena, and Copa."

When Jehoban paused to take a breath, Amanda commented, "That sounds quite different from what I remember it being."

"Yes, and yet it is the same ceremony you remember. Jena received a black diamond crystal, and Juila received a dark red ruby crystal. It was also during the ceremony that Debbon saw the futures of the two girls and he knew they were special.

"Once the ceremony was complete, the five people returned to Ahn and Barla's house. Copa had realized she would not be able to raise the children on her own since she knew Elder Vargen would be keeping tabs on her. She needed to find a safe house for the girls to keep them away from the Elder's plans.

"Barla began to make arrangements for the children to be entered into her orphan program. She really had intended to adopt out the girls, but they were so charming and reminded her so much of her own daughter, she decided to raise them herself.

"As had happened with Rasa, the girls entered school and were tested for their skills. My representatives were contacted, and arrangements were made for the children's education to be continued on Acaim.

"The girls were teleported to Acaim two weeks later…"

Amanda forgot to whom she was speaking and cut Him off by asking, "My children are here with you? Can I meet them?"

"Patience, Amanda. To answer your question, yes, they are here. Let me finish telling you the history of your children. As I said, your daughters were brought here to be educated by me. I had the perfect person in mind to raise them. I asked Rasa if she would take responsibility for her cousins and she readily agreed.

"They grew to be inquisitive children and learned quickly and easily the ways of the elemy, just as I had known they would. They were placed in the special studies classes with a few other students. I believe you know about those classes."

"Yes, I'm familiar with them," Amanda spoke quietly, and Jehoban continued.

"The girls had only been on the island for a few days before I received a visit from Elder Debbon. As he was walking to my reception chamber, he met Jena in the courtyard. Immediately he had a vision of his family and her being joined together. He stopped and talked with her, and the intuition grew stronger. When he finally met with me, he realized what he needed to do.

"I have always admired Elder Debbon's ability to read people and know when they would be a good match for one another. When he asked me if he could betroth his son to Jena, I knew it was the right thing to do. As you know, betrothals normally are organized before the children are six mesans old. Jena was clearly older than that so special dispensations had to be made.

"A deal was made where Elder Debbon would start a school for Elder children where they would all come together for a semester each year. The descendants of the Elders could range in age from six anons to sixty anons. They would be instructed about becoming an Elder which the Elders themselves didn't have time to teach their kids at home. Mind you, the school was merely supplementary education and not designed as the entire teaching.

"It was arranged for Jena and Juila to go to the school since they were My students. Jena would be able to be introduced to Willian, the son of Elder Debbon. If they had any chemistry, then the betrothal agreement could be finalized.

"Another request of mine was for Rasa to be one of the administrators in the school since she was not yet ready to go into active Elder service, but she could keep brushed up in the techniques. Rasa was given a level of authority similar to that of being an Elder. She would also be able to keep an eye on the twins to make sure all of my mandates were being adhered to.

"In the end, Jena and Willian became good friends, and they were betrothed. She spent several mesans per anon at the Residence of Elder Debbon so she could get to know the family and them to know her. It was the best arrangement to be made.

"We also discovered the extent of the link between Jena and Juila during their separations. Anything learned or experienced by one of the girls was immediately known by the other. Neither child experienced any loss in education since they learned simultaneously."

Amanda thought it odd that she was not disturbed by the idea of her daughter being betrothed. She decided it was because she had already accepted the reality from her dream. She asked the next question which came to mind, "What level have they achieved by now?" Amanda was beyond proud of her children's accomplishments. She had known they were precocious and she was grateful for Copa, Alena, and Barla's assistance in getting them the best education possible. She even forgave Copa for not sending her children with her to Earth. Most likely, they would not have survived the journey.

"They have completed all of the levels. They continually seek new and ingenious ways to use the elemy. I am very proud of them, as you will be, too, when you get to know them."

"When will I get to meet them?" Amanda asked again.

"You already have," Jehoban replied cryptically.

"I don't understand. I've only been to Elder Daven's estate and here. I haven't seen any girls who are seven anons old. How could I have met them?" Amanda continued to wrack her brain for any chance meetings, but came up completely blank.

"You are seeking for the wrong thing, Amanda." He turned to the girls who had sat silently across the table from Amanda during this whole discussion. He gestured toward the girls and said, "I have the honor of presenting your daughters, Jena and Juila."

Amanda smiled and believed Jehoban was playing a joke on her. She looked from Jehoban's serious expression to the two teenage girls. Her initial reaction that they looked like her twins finally hit her: these were her girls. Both girls smiled at her from across the table. Then reality came crashing in and convinced her otherwise, and she argued, "I don't understand. My girls are only seven. These girls are clearly older than that."

She turned to the girls and asked, "How old are you? When is your birthday?"

Juila answered, "We are fifteen. Our birthday is Tebet 28, 3434."

Amanda turned from the girls back to Jehoban and asked, "What date is that in Earth time? How can you explain this?"

"It is October 28, 1982. You entered Tuala through unusual means. The electrical storm triggered an opening, but it did not have any guidance for time. You were teleported back in time nine anons when Elder Vargen took you hostage. When Copa sent you back to Earth, she did not have the proper means to time your return. She sent you forward in time to Earth, one week, in fact, after you had disappeared in the storm."

Amanda tried to do the math in her head, but she finally gave it up for now. She looked at her daughters again without any judgment, and she smiled. The girls continued to grin back at her. "I've missed so much of your lives. I can't wait to make up for lost time."

"Mama," Juila spoke up, "we saw you often."

Amanda looked back to Jehoban with a very confused expression.

Jehoban chuckled and answered the unspoken question. "What Juila is trying to tell you is that I arranged something very special for them while they were dreaming at night. They shared your same memories from when you were in the coma. Everything you remember about them is what they remember about you."

Amanda could feel tears forming in her eyes because Jehoban had thought to give them such a special bond with their absent mother. She was so terribly grateful. "May I give you both a hug?" Amanda asked the girls.

They both nodded and stood up. They came around the table.

Amanda stood up and put her arms out. She openly sobbed when her two daughters each hugged one side of her. She felt complete now. Her family was whole.

After a few minutes, they released each other.

Jehoban cleared His throat and said, "Girls, I'd like a few moments alone with your mother. Please wait outside, and I'll call you in when I'm ready."

"Very good," they replied in unison. They both turned and walked out of the room.

Amanda watched them go and noticed their steps matched with one another. They really were very close. She suddenly had a terrible thought which she kept herself from asking until after the door was shut again.

"You said Elder Vargen impregnated me. Does that mean Elder Vargen is their father?" She was trying to decide whether Elder Vargen or Petre MacVeen was the worse choice of a parent. She decided it was a terrible decision and hoped neither was the biological father.

"I knew this would be your next question. It's why I sent the girls away. I have the answer to your inquiry, but I need to know if it will make any difference to you in the end."

Amanda did not want to answer immediately. She wanted to be sure her answer was as truthful as possible. She had already come to terms with Petre MacVeen as the father and realized she loved her children for themselves regardless of their paternity. Finally, she answered, "No, it makes no difference to me. However, I would like to know for my own personal reasons who their real father is."

Jehoban had watched her inner conflict and knew she was telling Him the truth. He decided her life would be more complete if she had an answer, so He said, "Their real father is Riccan Stel."

Amanda sat in stunned silence. Finally, hoping her assumption was wrong, she asked, "Do you mean he was in on Elder Vargen's plan? Is Riccan not who I really think he is?"

"Your husband is exactly who you think he is. He is destined to be the next Elder of Pantano. I have great expectations for him, and you have nothing to fear for his future. He was just as much of a victim to Elder Vargen as you were yourself."

"Tell me what happened, please," Amanda asked quietly.

"On one of Riccan's journey's to get answers about the samara, he had been drugged. He never knew what happened to him. One moment he was eating dinner in a private dining room in Corpus Christi and the next thing he knew, he woke up in an unknown hotel room. One of the wait staff was actually an employee for Elder Vargen. She was paid to drug Riccan's food and procure his seed."

Amanda knew exactly how Riccan would feel if he knew what had happened to him. He would feel sick to his stomach and violated. He would feel rage and then, finally, it would turn to acceptance. She wished he could remain ignorant of the entire event, but that would mean he would never know the truth about his children. She would never want to do that to him. She would want his parents to know their biological grandchildren.

"I can see you understand the dilemma. Should Riccan remain ignorant or should he know he's a father? I will leave that up to you. Whatever you decide, I offer My assistance to help you through it."

Amanda was touched by Jehoban's offer and said, "Thank you. It means a lot to know I have You on our side."

"You may not thank Me when you hear the rest."

"The rest of what? What more could there be?" Amanda dreaded the tone of Jehoban's voice.

"When you first arrived you had concerns about your role in the prophecy which was revealed to you in your dream. I must tell you that you are instrumental in making that prophecy into a reality."

"What are you saying? What are you expecting from me?" Amanda asked hastily.

"That I cannot tell you. You must do those things which feel right for your life. I will not tell you how to live your life. You do have free will, and I will not take that away from you."

"But what if I don't understand what you need from me?" Amanda instantly became concerned with His cryptic message.

"I will tell you this: re-read the prophecy which was revealed to you in the Elder's ancient text. Keep in mind that you are the key and then follow what your heart tells you. You have all of the people lined up to help you once you begin to take your own personal journey. Call on Me if you have any questions or concerns and I will do My best to guide you."

"If I'm to be the key to the prophecy, how will I know what to do? I've only been active in Tuala in my dreams. None of it was real. How am I supposed to achieve anything?" Amanda was feeling overwhelmed with the responsibility which was being placed on her shoulders.

"Your most developed talent is your intuitive nature. Everything you dreamt of with the people you interacted with on Tuala was accurate except for your personal interaction with them. You were absolutely correct with the emotions and motivations of each person you knew from the Tuala in your dreams."

Amanda tried to wrap her mind around Jehoban's revelation. She had never thought of her intuition as a gift: it was just a part of who she was. She realized she had taken the ability for granted her whole life. Now that she knew its real nature, she would explore the possibilities it could provide for her future. Amanda had quite a few things to consider for her future. The first concern was for her daughters.

"What will happen with my daughters now that I know about them? Will I be able to visit with them?"

Jehoban laughed out loud at Amanda's assumption. "No, you will not be visiting with them. They are your children, Amanda. They will be leaving with you. Their education is complete, and they have been expecting you to come and get them. They are ready."

Amanda could not believe her luck. She burst into tears of happiness. Finally, she would have everything she had always hoped, but never dreamed, she would have. Her family would be complete. She chuckled as she thought about her girls' ages and said, "The only thing which makes this whole story difficult is that I'm technically only ten years older than my girls. That will be hard to explain to people."

"I could make you older, if that is your wish," Jehoban suggested.

"NO! I was just commenting out loud. I'm fine with my age as well as my children's ages. If anything, we could tell people that the girls are Riccan's from a previous relationship. I'd hate to have to deny them as mine, but if the situation came up, we could always temporize."

Jehoban was pleased with Amanda's ability to roll with the punches. He knew she was the right person to lead the charge for change in Tuala and Earth. Her qualifications were very unique and, so far, she had achieved everything she was meant to achieve. "I have nothing further for you unless you have more questions," He said into the silence.

Amanda stirred from her thoughts and blushed as she looked up into Jehoban's face. She replied, "I have nothing more to ask. You have been tremendously generous with Your time, and I thank You wholeheartedly for raising my girls to be so perfect." She stood up to leave, not wanting to overstay her welcome.

Jehoban also stood but did not move to walk her out. "Remember, I'm only a thought away."

The door at the end of the room opened, and the girls smiled as they waited for their mother to join them. Amanda swiftly walked toward her children. They shut the door behind her and then linked an arm through at each of her elbows. Amanda smiled first at one girl and then the other. She had never thought she could be as happy as she was at that moment.

"You two will have to tell me what your real lives have been like. I'd like to know more about your cousin, Rasa, as well. Goodness, there isn't enough time in the world to hear all the things I want to know about you two!" She squeezed her elbows tighter to her waist to feel her daughters' arms closer to her. She hoped they would have enough time to get to know one another before life began to interrupt her utopia.

They walked back to the room where they had left Riccan. He sat at the edge of the pond and tossed small crumbs for the fish to rise up and eat. He seemed content and relaxed as though it had only been a few minutes instead of the half hour she had spent with Jehoban.

"Riccan," she spoke across the room to get his attention.

He looked up, grateful to see his wife again. He stood up and brushed his hands together over the water to rid them of the food crumbs. Walking toward Amanda, he could tell there was something different about her. She had a new confidence, even more than she had shown after their wedding. He hoped she would have good news about her interview with Jehoban.

"I'm glad to see you're looking so happy," he said as he came close enough to kiss Amanda on the cheek. The girls had not let go of Amanda's arms, so Riccan commented, "And you appear to have made two new friends."

"Riccan, the most amazing thing has happened. These two girls are not new friends; they are my daughters!" she announced with a huge grin on her face. She knew precisely what was going on in his head since she had had the exact same ideas only a little while earlier. "I know you're thinking they're a little bit old, but Jehoban explained I was teleported through both time and space. They were born nine anons before I'd believed they were. Oh, I have so much to share with you, but I'd like both Nena and Elder Daven to hear it all at the same time. Can we please go back to the Residence?"

Riccan was speechless. He stared at the girl on the left and then the girl on the right and then compared them both to Amanda herself. The girls were the same height as Amanda. They had the same shaped eyes, even though theirs were blue to Amanda's brown. They had the same smile, even the same shaped teeth. Now that he knew to look for it, he could see the resemblance among the three. Finally, he nodded his head and said with enthusiasm, "Lead the way!"

They began to walk to the golden door when Amanda realized something important. "Girls, don't you need to gather your belongings before you come away with us?"

They smiled the same smile, and Juila answered, "We gathered it already when Jehoban dismissed us from the room. Our bags are already in the telepod."

Amanda laughed at their presumption but was glad they had thought ahead. With a light heart, she said, "Let's get going!"

CHAPTER 3

The trip to the Residence lasted three seconds, just as it should have. Amanda could not believe how she had been so scared to meet with Jehoban and yet she had received more blessings in her life because of it. She did not feel she deserved to be so happy, but she was more than willing to accept it. Life had no guarantees, and she was not going to take this time for granted.

The four people exited the telepod with smiles of delight. The women led as Riccan followed, laden with their baggage. He still had a hard time understanding how the girls could be so much older than Amanda had realized. Eventually, he just shook his head and had to trust Jehoban knew what He was talking about when it came to Amanda's family.

That's when it hit him; he was slightly jealous of Amanda's newfound family. He did not feel as important in Amanda's life because her children now took up her heart. They had only been married for one day, and he was no longer her sole focus. Riccan felt terrible for even stealing any of her joy and tried to lessen his own feelings to be able to focus more on Amanda's happiness. After all, he had promised her parents to do everything in his power to make her happy.

As they ascended the stairs and came closer to the back patio, Riccan looked up and saw his parents had come out to greet them. He grinned in anticipation of their reaction to the addition of the two girls. His mother had pressured him for anons to get married and have children. Nena wanted to be a grandmother, and now she was, times two.

"Who're these two beautiful ladies," Daven asked as he held out a hand for introductions.

Amanda said simply, "These are my daughters." She turned to the girls and said, "This is your grandfather, Elder Daven, and your grandmother, Nena."

The girls smiled, and Juila was the first to hold out her hand to greet her grandfather. She was surprised when Daven used his hand to draw her into a hug instead of the more formal handshake. He looked over to Jena and asked, "What are you waiting for? Come hug your grandfather!"

Jena laughed and joined her sister in the embrace.

Amanda had been watching Nena instead of the trio getting to know one another. Now that she knew what to look for, she recognized the analyzing look Nena had used to scrutinize the auras of the girls. Nena tilted her head, and a look of confusion crossed her eyes before she put a smile on her face and said, "Where are your hugs for your grandma?"

Riccan had finally made it up the stairs, and he pretended to pant under the weight of the bags. Amanda laughed and immediately offered to help him. He declined and said, "I'll take these upstairs and meet you all in Dad's office." He kept walking. He knew the way his parents could carry on unless someone brought them back to reality. His mother could keep them on the patio asking question after question without realizing the day had slipped by.

As if taking the hint, Daven suggested, "Why don't we retire to my office? It seems as though Amanda has more news to share from her visit with Jehoban."

Amanda nodded agreement and said, "You guys have no idea!"

Nena looked over her shoulder as she had taken the lead to go back inside the house and said, "I might have a good idea!"

Amanda wondered if she really did. If so, it would make it easier to explain to Riccan. She was still trying to decide if she were to let Riccan know anything until they were in private. After his mother's cryptic state-ment she decided right then and there to tell the *whole* story after all. If she kept any of it to herself, Riccan could hold it against her for keeping valuable knowledge from him, and she would have to agree with him. She had to be fair and hope he would take the news well.

They had made it to the office and were waiting for Riccan to return from upstairs. Nena kept staring at the twins and smiling broadly. Amanda had saved a seat next to herself so she could be holding Riccan's hand when she told him he was their father. She recalled her own reaction to the news; she could only imagine Riccan's. The more she thought about it, the more nervous she became.

Her daughters would find out at the same time who their father was. She hoped they would be as excited about the news as Amanda had been.

Finally, Riccan rushed into the room and said, "Sorry it took me so long. Did I miss anything?"

"No, Riccan, we waited until you got back. Please sit here next to me." Amanda patted the empty chair, and she took Riccan's hand as he settled into the chair.

Amanda began to talk. She told them about Jehoban's desire for her to study and figure out the latest prophecy and then to follow her heart.

Daven nodded agreement and saw his wife doing the same. They had known Amanda was the key since she was the one who had revealed the prophecy in the first place. They would help Amanda as much as they were able.

"Jehoban told me my greatest gift is my intuition. Maybe you could tell me how to cultivate that talent to make it more immediately accessible. He seemed to be telling me I was going to be using it a lot during this quest." Amanda paused to consider the meaning of Jehoban's words.

Finally, she got to the part about the twins. She had purposely saved it for last since it would have the greatest impact on everyone in the room. "I had been mistaken about the timing of the birth of my children." She stopped and looked significantly at the teenagers and added, "Obviously."

Everyone, including the girls, chuckled at her statement.

Amanda continued, "Jehoban told me about how malleable time can be. When the electrical storm transported me to Tuala, it also sent me back in time nine anons. Almost everything about my recollections of my time in Tuala is untrue; however, Jehoban told me my intuition about the people I met along the way is entirely accurate."

Amanda paused to let her statement sink into their minds. Daven was the first to nod his agreement. Since he was an Elder, he was more conversant with Jehoban's methods. Nena also nodded. Amanda added a little pressure to Riccan's hand before she began the next part of her story.

"Jehoban told me I was held captive by Elder Vargen…"

"That dirty Elder," Daven hissed. He was scowling fiercely and planning on how he would petition for his removal through First Elder Debbon.

"Apparently Elder Vargen took us from Petre MacVeen and incarcerated us for questioning because we were *old souls*. Jehoban told me Nealand is still being held captive and is being given resh to keep him compliant to continue supplying information for Elder Vargen's engineering program."

Another hiss escaped from Daven's lips. He was very unhappy to hear these revelations. There had to be something he could do to shut down Elder Vargen's farce of his questioning tactics.

"I asked Jehoban if He knew the paternity of my children. I was obviously mistaken about my memories. He told me the truth of what had transpired." She turned to her girls and asked, "Do you want to know who your real father is? I won't share what I know if you don't want to know."

Jena and Juila looked at one another. They spoke with silent telepathy between each other. Most people called it a twin link, but it was more like they shared the same thoughts. After only a moment's consideration, they both turned their gazes back to their mother and nodded in the affirmative.

She held her husband's hand slightly tighter and said, "Jehoban told me your father is my husband, Riccan." She took her eyes from her children to look at her husband. His eyes widened in surprise and then she could see he was trying to figure out the logistics.

"How is that possible?" Riccan finally asked.

Nena gasped and held her hand to her mouth with surprise. She had thought the girls' auras were familiar, but now she could definitely see the connection. After all this time, Nena finally had her grandchildren. Real flesh-and-blood grandchildren of her very own. Her heart began to beat faster as the realization hit her hard. The tears began to flow down her cheeks as she realized her dreams had finally come true.

"Do you remember a time in Corpus Christi…?" Amanda began to ask.

Riccan's face turned red as he recalled exactly the time to which Amanda was referring. He had been so confused about his unaccounted time. For a long time, he had played it off as having eaten bad food. Eventually, he managed to not think about what had happened. Now, he had to know the truth. "What happened to me?" he asked in a whisper.

"You were drugged by the waitress at the restaurant. She was employed by Elder Vargen to harvest your seed for impregnating me. Elder Vargen wanted the most powerful opportunity for creating his very own prophet to raise under his tutelage."

Daven was truly outraged now. Amanda was concerned for his health if he did not vent his feelings soon. She understood his reaction since it was his son who had been so tragically taken advantage of.

"Riccan, I'm sorry for having to tell you this news. I know exactly how you must feel, but just know, these beautiful girls are your own flesh and blood. We truly are a real family!"

Riccan listened to his wife's wise words. He felt his heart soften and knew he could love these girls no matter what, but now they were not a reminder of his wife's past, they were also a part of his future. When he thought of all of the time he had missed out on their growing years, he felt his anger rise again. Then he thought it was a waste of time to lament the past; he had his entire future to get to know his children. He felt as though he were on a roller coaster of emotions.

Finally, he decided to make the best of an awkward situation, and he smiled at his children. He did not know what to say to such a revelation, and he could see they were equally affected by the news. The only thing which came to mind was to go over and hug his girls. He stood up, took the two strides to reach them, and dropped to his knees and said, "Welcome to the family." Holding out his arms, the girls lunged forward to hug their father, unable to contain their tears of joy.

Amanda felt tears streaming down her cheeks at the powerful reunion playing out in front of her. She was glad she had decided to tell her husband everything she had discovered. If the girls had said they did not want to know, she was not sure how she would have told her husband the truth. Amanda was certain only good would come of this news.

Nena jumped up from her chair and hurriedly walked around the desk. She, too, kneeled on the floor and wrapped her arms around her son and granddaughters. She had hard feelings for what Elder Vargen had done to her son, but she was even more thankful for the outcome.

Daven was pleased to see his son's acceptance of the girls. He asked the next obvious question, "Where will the four of you live? We have room here."

Nena lifted her head from her son's back and added, "Absolutely. You can all stay here while we sort through the many details."

Riccan shook his head and said, "I believe it's time the girls saw the other part of their lives. We'll take them back to our house on Earth. We need some time to get to know one another. While I have time off of work, I want to spend every waking moment with my new family."

Nena could feel her influence slipping and said, "But you'll wait a few days before you leave, right?" She desperately wanted to spend more time with the girls.

"I don't think so," Riccan began. He realized this decision was not his alone so he looked at Amanda to see what she wanted to do.

"I'll abide by whatever decision you make, Riccan," Amanda said simply.

"We'll leave after dinner then," Riccan announced.

"No, Riccan. Please reconsider!" Nena cried out.

"I'm sorry, Mom, this news changes everything. Please understand my needs in this matter as well. We will come back in a couple of weeks. I promise." He kept his eyes on his mom. He understood her feelings, but he had to think of his own family first.

Nena stood up and looked down at her son and said, "I understand what you're saying, but I don't have to like it." She turned around and walked back to her chair. She sat down and folded her arms across her chest. She shrugged off her husband's consoling hand while her temper simmered.

Daven was embarrassed by his wife's behavior and immediately asked, "Jena, Juila, why don't you tell us about growing up on Acaim? Did you know I grew up there, too?"

The girls' moods brightened, and Juila began to talk. "We were raised by our Aunt Barla. She treated us just like her own children, and we loved growing up at the dock. We would go to the port station and play on the docks. We learned how to fish and even how to sail in a small skiff. Our older foster-brother, Gravin, taught us how to use the elemy. He was a great teacher. We were so excited to begin school, but we knew we were prepared because of Gravin's teachings.

"We didn't know to limit our crystal knowledge during the initial evaluations, and then the school contacted Barla. She cried when they told her that we would be taken to live on Acaim. She had thought she would finally have girls to raise to adulthood, but it had not worked out that way for her. We were given two weeks to say goodbye. Arrangements were made for us to be raised by our cousin, Rasa, even though she was only eleven anons older than us, we were almost six. She was seventeen and very patient with all of our antics." Juila turned and smiled at Jena as though they were having a private conversation remembering the past.

Jena continued the story, "We were like wild banshees when we first got to the island. Without Barla's constant supervision, we invented new ways to get into trouble. Eventually, Rasa figured out all of our tricks, we still don't know how, and then we started to calm down enough to begin our special schooling. During most of the mornings we went to school with all of the other children, but then we had several classes after school which taught us new skills with our birth crystals. These additional classes were the best part of our day. There are endless uses for the elemy, and we wanted to find them all!"

Juila reached up and touched her crystal lovingly.

Amanda remembered Jehoban's comment about her children's education and asked, "Jehoban mentioned you had completed your education, how far did you get?"

"We finished all of the levels of crystal study if that's what you're asking. We opted not to continue with post-study because we knew our future was still in limbo," Juila replied.

Daven wondered at the last statement and asked, "Why would you say that?"

Juila realized they did not know a key piece of information and said, "We knew our mom was going to come and get us eventually. We wanted to be ready to go when she did."

It was now Riccan's turn to ask the next obvious questions, "How did you know about your mom? Did you know about me, too?"

Juila continued to answer, "We were told by Jehoban about our mom. We had dreams about her at night, and we experienced the same memories she had while we were sleeping. Jehoban wanted our mom to be a part of our lives. When we asked about our dad, it was a different story. Jehoban said it was to be revealed at a later time if it ever came to pass at all. We had learned to be content with Jehoban's obscure answers because we knew He always wanted the best for us."

Riccan could not help but feel as though he had been purposely separated from their lives. He did not like it at all. He felt left out and more than a little hurt by the omission. There was plenty of time for him to get to know them, but it would have been better if they could have had the memories.

Juila could see her answer had upset Riccan, and she added, "Jehoban did not know if Amanda would exercise her free will to meet and marry you. It was His plan, but Amanda had to do her part first. Amanda already knew about us, and that's why we shared her memories of us, even though none of them was a reality for any of our lives. Since you were unaware of us, Jehoban did not want you to have strange dreams about twin girls in case you mistook us for the person who you should marry in the future."

Riccan could see where she was going with her logic. It did not lessen the hurt of being excluded. He decided he would have to learn to accept it or get bitter from the disappointment. He plastered a smile on his face and determined to make the best of it as Jena continued their story.

"We finished school as early as we could in anticipation of reuniting with you." She looked over at Amanda. She realized she still had a hard time calling her 'mom' since she had never had anyone to call by that title. In time, she knew it would become more natural.

Nena finally became calm enough to ask, "So now that you have been reunited, has it changed your educational plans? You really should consider continuing to post-study."

Juila answered, "It depends on what Mom and Dad decide to do. We'd like to check out schools on Earth just to see how it differs from what we've already experienced."

It struck Amanda that they now had to consider their children's needs rather than their own. It was a new feeling of responsibility she was unused to having. "We should enroll them in the high school back home. The school year hasn't started yet so they'll have a few more weeks to get oriented before they begin."

"Good point," Riccan agreed. He was still reeling from being called 'Dad' for the first time. Jena had said it so offhandedly it had taken him a moment to realize she had been talking about himself.

Daven cleared his throat and said, "I think everybody is missing something very important."

"What?" Amanda and Riccan spoke at the same time.

"We need to have a crystal ceremony linking the two parents to the two children. We should perform the ceremony immediately."

Nena perked up at the idea of a ceremony. She wanted to be able to put together a lavish affair but knew it would not be accepted, so she did not even offer it. She stood up and said, "I'll go get the staff ready. Maybe we should combine the crystal ceremony with a matrimonial."

Riccan raised his eyes at his mother's suggestion. It was actually a really good idea, and he turned to look at Amanda to see if she also agreed. When Amanda raised her eyebrows and tipped her head to indicate it was his decision, Riccan said, "That's a perfect suggestion, Mom. Our children can be at our wedding and then we can have the crystal ceremony for our children. It's a little on the late side, but I'd feel better knowing it was all taken care of before we went back to Earth."

Daven said, "So, it's all settled." He waved his hands at the office's occupants and said, "Why don't you all run along now. I've got a lot of things to take care of before I can perform the ceremonies before dinner."

Nena was already at the door and smiled at her husband. She turned, opened the door, and walked down the hall to gather the supplies Daven would need for the dual services. She stopped each of the staff she encountered and told them about the afternoon's activities and to tell anyone else they encountered. She expected all of the household staff to be present for the big events.

Riccan resumed holding Amanda's hand and offered his other to Juila. Amanda extended her hand for Jena's and, as a family, they left the office behind and went to explore the grounds outside. Riccan felt a peacefulness descend upon him which he had never felt before. Even though it was accomplished by bizarre means, he had the family he had always wanted.

CHAPTER 4

Nena had all of the details put together in record time. The staff had gone into action, transforming the main reception room into the ceremonial room. Nena approved of all of the decorations as well as the light repast for the guests.

She had changed her outfit to one more appropriate to the occasion. When she was changing, she remembered the clothing Amanda had brought from her time on Tuala. At least now she had the answers for where the outfit had come from. She wondered if they should keep the clothes at the Residence as evidence of Elder Vargen's transgression against both Amanda and Riccan. Nena decided to ask Daven about it before the children and grandchildren left.

Riccan and Amanda had gone to their room. Amanda changed into the same dress she had worn for her wedding in Reno, thankful now that she had thought to bring it along. She watched her husband dress in the same suit he had also worn before. She walked up beside him as he stood in front of the mirror adjusting his tie. They were a handsome couple. Riccan was tall with broad, muscular shoulders. He had short dark hair with the most expressive brown eyes she had ever seen. She was considerably shorter than he since she only came up to the middle of his chest. She felt positively small next to him.

Riccan brushed Amanda's long, brown hair from her shoulder. He adored his wife. She was so fragile looking, but he knew it was a deceptive exterior to her steely resolve. Not only was she beautiful, she was also extremely intelligent, which he found equally exciting. He kissed the top of her head and looked at her face in the mirror as he asked, "Are you ready to marry me all over again?"

"Every day, if I had to!" Amanda replied and squirmed around in his arms to put her arms up around his neck and bring his face down to hers for a long, passionate kiss.

"Hey, now! Keep this up, and we'll miss our own ceremony!" he laughed as he managed to pull himself away from her kiss. "Let's go check on the girls. If they're ready, we can all go down together."

They stayed close to one another as they walked across the hall. Riccan knocked on the door and waited until he heard an invitation to enter. He opened the door, and they peered into the room. The girls were on the far side in front of the long mirror making sure their hair was perfectly positioned. Riccan thought they looked nervous. He realized he was as well.

"Are you two almost ready?" he asked with a grin. They looked perfect, and he could not see any difference in their appearance as they continued to fuss with their hair.

Juila threw her hands down and said, "I give up. Come on, Jena, let's go."

Jena smiled at her sister and turned to leave with her.

Amanda was so proud of her beautiful daughters she had to say, "You two look perfectly beautiful."

They beamed with the praise and then said, "You two look pretty great yourselves."

With the compliments finally taken care of they descended the stairs where Riccan led the way to the ceremonial room. They were the last to arrive. All of the room was filled with the household staff lining the walkway. Riccan and Amanda walked in first followed immediately by the girls. The four halted their forward progress when they stood directly in front of Elder Daven. They kneeled on the floor, and Riccan looked up and smiled at his parents.

Elder Daven waited until his son and daughter-in-law were both seated on the floor in front of him before he began the wedding ceremony. With a return smile for his son, he began the ceremony.

"We have gathered here today to mark the special bond between our son, Riccan, and his newly betrothed, Amanda. As Riccan's parents, we have an obligation to demonstrate the importance of a loving relationship and to teach both our son and his espoused to respect one another unconditionally. Each union blessed in this manner is to be held in the highest regard.

"Nena, as Riccan's mother, do you promise to watch over this union and teach them to the best of your ability the rewards of a loving relationship?"

"I will."

"And I, as Riccan's father, do promise to guide this union into becoming productive partners of our world. I also have the responsibility as an Elder and representative of Jehoban to teach them to use their skills together in a manner which will benefit society and make us proud to call them our son and first-daughter. As the two of them join together in this union, I will make sure they understand the position they hold in society and will prepare Riccan to also become an Elder when he is ready. I am equipped to undertake these tasks with love and devotion."

Daven reached down and mixed several ingredients into a bowl and added a few dollops of liquid to make a paste. He used his finger to stir the contents until it was completely blended. With the green paste on his finger, he drew a line across Riccan's forehead and then Amanda's. He dipped his finger again into the bowl and then drew a circle on the backs of both of their hands.

He set aside the bowl and wiped his finger on a small towel. Next, he opened his ceremonial box, which was a beautifully ornate box with many gemstones set into an elaborate design of leaves and flowers, and pulled out two delicate rings with a clear diamond set flush into each one. He placed first one ring on the middle finger of Riccan's right hand and then placed the other ring on the middle finger of Amanda's left hand. "These rings symbolize the everlasting bond between them. If at this time, a new birth crystal should be required for either Amanda or Riccan I would ask that it be made clear that this is the wish of Jehoban."

After waiting a few seconds to see if Jehoban would make a reply to his request, Daven announced, "With no indication of a change their crystals shall remain unchanged. By the power vested in me by the name of Jehoban, I declare these two citizens to be bonded for life."

Riccan and Amanda kissed one another hastily, stood up, and then moved to the sides so their daughters could come forward and kneel directly in front of Elder Daven.

"Friends, family, and neighbors, we have also gathered together for the important task of linking the protective crystals for these two young ladies to their parents. Riccan and Amanda, as their parents, do you agree to allow me to look into your children's minds to link their individual crystals to your own?" Daven waited for both Amanda and Riccan to reply before continuing.

"Yes, we do," Amanda and Riccan replied in unison.

"We will begin with your firstborn," Daven said as he dipped his finger into the green liquid of the bowl in front of Juila. He marked a line in green across Juila's forehead and chanted, "I mark Juila's forehead to be able to divine the thoughts and intents of this being." He dipped his finger again in the bowl and marked a circle in green on the back of each of her hands chanting, "I mark each of Juila's hands to be able to divine the actions for which she will be responsible in her lifetime."

The room was utterly silent as Daven held each of Juila's hands in his own. With his eyes closed, he began to rock back and forth with a thin smile on his lips, as he spoke, "*Allah dari langit, silakan me panduan dalam penyelidikan. Membuat saya benar bacaan dan kristal tugas tepat.*"

Amanda remembered the meaning from her dream and immediately translated it to, "Creator of heaven, please guide me in this quest. Make my readings true and the crystal assignment precise."

They all sat in silence as Daven continued to rock silently. Amanda again recalled her dream and wondered if Daven saw the same thing Alena had seen. Although now she knew Elder Debbon had performed the ceremony. Perhaps he had seen the same things which Daven saw now.

"This child has had many obstacles in her youth. She will grow to be strong and independent. She will have a strong sense of right from wrong," Daven finished, and he released her hands.

"I see no indication of a change in crystal in this child. Amanda and Riccan, please place your hands on Juila's shoulders and repeat after me, "*Saya memberikan ini untuk Anda dengan cinta.*"

Amanda did as she was told and saw Riccan had also put his hand on Juila's other shoulder. Amanda tried to pace her words with Riccan as she recalled the meaning of the phrase, *I give this to you with love*. The phrase was not entirely accurate since Juila had already been given the crystal by another, but she supposed the intent was the same and that was good enough for her.

Daven used a warm, wet cloth and cleaned the green liquid from Juila's forehead and hands. He rinsed the cloth in another bowl of clean water. Daven removed the cloth, picked up the cup and handed it first to Riccan and then to Amanda. It was minty as Amanda remembered from before.

Daven announced, "I give you this water to drink. By the drinking of the liquid which contains your daughter's essence, you will seal the bond between your lives and Juila's."

Amanda finished the liquid and handed the empty cup back to Daven, and he announced, "With this child, Juila, safe and protected from harm, we will now turn to her sister."

Repeating the same ceremony, Daven dipped his finger into the green liquid in the bowl in front of Jena. As he marked the line across Jena's forehead he chanted, "I mark Jena's forehead to be able to divine the thoughts and intents of this being." Then he continued by marking the circles on the back of each hand chanting, "I mark each of Jena's hands to be able to divine the actions for which she will be responsible in her lifetime."

Again he held each of Jena's hands in his own. With his eyes closed, he began to rock as he petitioned Jehoban to guide him. Suddenly, Daven gasped his eyes popped open; he locked eyes momentarily with Amanda, and then purposefully shut his eyes to continue to see into Jena's future.

"This child's life will be an amazing journey. She will always have those around her who love her unconditionally." Looking down at her birth crystal, he added, "I see no indication of a crystal change for this child."

They repeated the process of putting their hands on Jena's shoulders and saying the phrase, *Saya akan kasih Anda di manapun Anda berada."* Amanda remembered the phrase had changed to *I will love you wherever you are*. She had hoped this part of the ceremony would have changed so her daughter would not be taken away from them. It appeared her destiny was set.

Amanda watched as Daven wiped Jena's forehead and prepared the second cup of liquid for them to drink. She received the cup from Riccan and brought it to her lips to drink. After the first gulp, she tasted a drastic difference; this drink was bitter instead of minty as Juila's had been. She finished it rapidly and returned the cup to Daven.

Daven then spoke to everyone in the room. "With this child, Jena, safe and protected from harm, we can all celebrate."

The four stood up from the floor and hugged one another. They received their first kisses of congratulations from Daven and Nena who were the closest to them. Riccan led Amanda and his girls down the walkway lined with people. They stopped at each person and received kisses and blessings for their future. When they reached the last person, Riccan announced, "Let's eat!"

Everybody laughed, and the formality of the occasion seemed to dissolve immediately. People began to mingle and talk among themselves. Soon, the household staff had disbursed to their assigned stations. Finally, only the six of them remained in the room.

Elder Daven took Riccan and Amanda off to the side of the room and said, "I must give you some instruction regarding the link to your children's birth crystals before you leave. Would you like to do that right now?"

Riccan looked back toward their children and saw they were being entertained by his mother. He decided his mom should have this time alone with them before it was time for them to go. He shrugged and said, "I don't see why not."

The three silently left the room and returned to Daven's personal office. After everyone was seated, Daven started with a grave expression, "What I am about to tell you must never be repeated to anyone, ever. Do you agree?"

Amanda knew what Daven was going to tell them and readily agreed. She could see Riccan was having a harder time and hoped her example of agreeing would convince Riccan likewise. After a moment's consideration, Amanda saw her husband nod his head in the affirmative.

"Good, you are now both parents. It bears a great responsibility. Now that your crystals have been linked to those of your children, I have the pleasure of telling you how you can monitor your children. They will never know about your ability, and you must never reveal it to them."

Riccan leaned forward, curious to hear what his father was about to share.

"As you know, the crystals cannot be removed until the girls reach the age of eighteen. The color of the stone can change with age, friends, or activities. As their parents, you should be watching their colors carefully to monitor their safety. This next part is the most important of all of the functions of the crystal: parents can both see and hear what their children are doing through their crystals."

Riccan suddenly sat back and exclaimed, "So that's how you guys did it! I always thought you were just amazingly intuitive to always show up whenever I got myself into trouble."

Amanda laughed at Riccan's reaction.

He turned to her and said accusingly, "You already knew about this?" Then he remembered she had inadvertently told him about the power when she had recounted her dream about losing Jena. He had not connected the search for Jena with a parent's ability to spy on their children. He had to laugh at himself for missing such an important clue. To be fair, he had been slightly overwhelmed and amazed by Amanda's story to even think about a minor detail such as that.

Amanda still grinned broadly as she nodded.

Daven was intrigued and asked, "Did you learn about it in your dream?"

"Yes. Alena taught me how to access the crystals of each child. I think you'll only need to teach Riccan how it's done," she replied. She kept feeling the mirth bubbling up as she remembered Riccan's reaction to his father's statement. She hoped she had not offended Riccan by her reaction. It did please her to finally know something before Riccan did.

"Tell me how it works," Riccan said. He wanted to have the same knowledge as Amanda.

Daven spent the next half hour going over the basics of accessing the crystals. Riccan concentrated on the color of Juila's crystal and was pleased when he could see she was still talking animatedly with his mother.

"Concentrate on each detail until they become clear. The more you practice this technique, the easier and quicker it will be. I think this will be even more important once you are back on Earth. The elemy seems to be slightly weaker in that realm, so I urge you to become proficient as soon as possible."

Riccan knew what his father was talking about concerning the strength of the elemy. He had grown up on both worlds and knew the difference. He hoped his prior experience would help him to overcome the deficiency.

Following his father's instruction, he sharpened his focus on each detail. He was able to expand the view of the crystal to include both his mother and his other daughter. He could hear their conversation as clearly as though he were next to them. Riccan opened his eyes and smiled his success as he announced, "I think I've got it. Is there anything else I should know about which nobody thought to share with me?"

Daven smiled knowingly and answered, "You'll find out plenty of things as time goes along. It's a part of being a parent. You'll also discover things about your daughters which you will wish you didn't know. However, I think ultimately, it creates a stronger bond between a parent and child. Riccan, you have had many life changes lately. Be careful to ease yourself into it, so you don't become overwhelmed. Don't be too hard on yourself when you make mistakes as a parent. It's a part of the job to make occasional blunders. Learn from your errors and just move on."

Riccan nodded solemnly at his father. He had not expected to get this type of a conversation for many years to come. Now he wondered if they would have other children by conventional means, or if the girls would be enough. He decided time would tell.

Daven slapped his hand down on the desk and announced, "I'm hungry. I think we should adjourn for dinner."

"Amen," Riccan agreed with a grin and stood up to go.

Daven also stood and then said, "Remember, if you have any questions about raising your girls, your mother and I would be more than happy to discuss it with you. We've had a little experience."

Riccan chuckled and said, "I'm sure I kept you both on your toes during my teen anons!"

"Infant, toddler, pre-teen, teen, and adult anons is more like it! As you'll find, it's a never-ending job. It's also one you would never forego, either. It's the hardest job you'll ever love to be a part of." He smiled lovingly at his son. He was so proud of the man he had become.

They rejoined the three women in the ceremonial room. Nena turned and asked, "Did you have a productive meeting?" She winked at Riccan conspiratorially since she knew what the conversation had entailed.

"Yes, Mother," Riccan said to his mom. "It was very informative!" Riccan had another horrifying idea and, pulling her off to the side, he whispered, "Wait, does the parent link through my birth crystal still function?"

She laughed, and her eyes continued to sparkle with mirth as they all headed out to the dining room for dinner.

CHAPTER 5

The girls were excited to finally travel to Earth. Unexpected events had transpired to keep them in Tuala for twelve days from the time they first met their grandparents. They had heard all kinds of stories, but they had never themselves been able to go. When Riccan had told them to gather their belongings to take back to the telepod, they accessed the elemy to telekinetically transport their bags rather than waste time doing it by hand.

When Riccan asked them, "When are you going to get started on your packing?"

Juila replied with a sheepish grin, "Our stuff is already on board the telepod."

Riccan tilted his head in confusion and asked, "Did you use the elemy?"

Both girls nodded affirmation.

Riccan had to hide his pride in their accomplishment as he said, "You know you'll have to curb your abilities when you're on Earth. What the people of Earth consider magic will not be received well and you will be thought of as strange."

"That's what we've been told so we have decided to use our abilities as much as possible until we leave Tuala," Jena responded.

Juila piped in, "I think it'll be fun going back to the old-fashioned way of doing things."

Riccan wondered how long she would think it fun. There were many times he was so tired and had to slog through doing something manually which he knew he could accomplish effortlessly and in a fraction of a second using the elemy.

It could be quite frustrating at times how ignorant the people of Earth could be to the possibilities available to them if they would just open their minds to it. He could not count the number of times he had said the same thing to himself about Earth, but it was not going to change until the people changed. He could not see that happening any time soon.

Finally, they were all settled in the telepod. Riccan was still smiling at how eager the girls were to get to Earth. They had barely taken the time to say goodbye to their grandparents in their desire to get going.

Riccan initiated the start-up procedures and could feel the telepod rise from the ground in readiness for the transfer. He keyed in the coordinates to land inside his garage. He had found it to be easier to find a large garage to land in rather than try to keep the telepod cloaked from the airport radar. The maneuver took more precision, but he had designed the software himself and had confidence in its ability to deliver results.

After asking if everyone were ready and receiving an emphatic 'yes' from behind him, he smiled as he activated the flight plan. The world turned black as they traveled between Tuala and Earth in the length of five seconds. Normally, the transfer between locations on Tuala only took three seconds, but, for some reason, going through the veil between dimensions took an extra amount of time.

He was used to the time delay, but he realized he had forgotten to share the vital piece of information to his newest travelers. When they reappeared in his garage, he could hear gasps of fear behind him. He turned around and asked, "What's wrong?"

"We thought we were lost in between!" Jena exclaimed.

"Why did it take so long?" Juila asked at the same time.

Riccan smiled and explained the logistics of the transfer. They both nodded their understanding, but Riccan could not help but feel he had made his first mistake. Just one moment of explanation could have saved them from being scared. He would have to learn to take more time to be sure they knew what to expect, especially now that they were on Earth.

He could not afford for them to draw attention to his house with their inadvertent mistakes.

"Okay, girls," Amanda announced, "this is the garage of our home on Earth. We park here to avoid causing any type of scene outside. You can have your pick of rooms upstairs. Feel free to explore the house and the grounds. We'll be in the living room when you're done."

Riccan palmed open the door and spoke hastily, "Take your stuff with you!"

The girls immediately turned around and picked up their bags and ran toward the garage door to the house. They were eager to see what type of home awaited them. Would it be like what they were familiar with in Tuala or would it be crazy different? Juila was first to the door, but Jena was the first to enter.

By the time they reached the kitchen, they knew this place was special. It was so opulent and inviting. The kitchen counters were granite, and the island was positively huge. All of the appliances were stainless steel and intimidating looking. They had never had to use an appliance before, so this was definitely going to be an adventure.

They walked past the kitchen into the living room. Their attention was caught by the wall of windows off to the right. The view of the yard was amazing, and the Olympic-sized pool was a sparkling blue wonder to behold. Juila was very fond of swimming, whereas Jena had a slight fear of the water. She did not mind putting her feet in or wading in the shallow end of a pool, but deep water was not her thing.

They finally turned away from the view outside to notice the over-sized furniture of the living room. The couches looked positively luxurious, and they faced a huge, flat-screened television hanging on the wall above a massive fireplace.

They had turned in almost a complete circle when they noticed the front entrance and the grand curving staircase leading to upstairs. With their bags still slung over their shoulders they began to race to see who would find the best bedroom first. Jena was the first to reach the stairs, but Juila was faster and reached the top before she did.

They were giggling like little girls as they opened one door after another down the long hallway. There had to be at least six guest bedrooms. Finally, after looking over their selection for the third time, they settled on two bedrooms which were side-by-side, both overlooking the backyard and pool area.

Juila's room was decorated in pink, which happened to be her favorite color. The decorating was done tastefully in a grown-up fashion, not in a childish manner she would have done for herself. She felt very adult in this room. The en-suite bathroom was also luxurious with a huge soaking Jacuzzi tub as well as a shower with multiple shower heads. She could imagine her showers would be pretty quick with all the water available. After putting her bag down in the middle of the king-sized bed, Juila wandered over to inspect Jena's room.

Jena, of course, had selected a room which was decorated in yellow. It also had a very elegant look to it. The furniture was similar to that of Juila's own room. The view outside was the same. The en-suite bathroom was the mirror image of her own.

Juila came within a foot of her sister and said, "Isn't this amazing? I'd always hoped, but never dreamed, this day would actually come!"

Jena nodded emphatically and then lunged forward and hugged her sister. She was thankful they were embarking on this new journey together. She had always hated when she had to go to Elder Debbon's residence and leave Juila behind. Now they were together, and they could stay that way, at least until she turned eighteen. Then she would be obligated to marry Willian unless she was still in post-study.

Reminded of school, Jena asked her sister, "Do you really want to go to high school? What if we hate it?"

Juila shrugged and said, "Then we quit going. We've already finished the equivalent in Tuala, so this is just going to be for fun. Plus we'll get to meet kids our own age if we attend school. How else do you propose to meet anyone?"

Jena wrinkled her nose and said, "As if that matters to me! My life has already been planned. I already know whom I'm going to marry. It's a good thing I like him!"

Juila smiled at Jena and said, "There's nothing in your contract which states you can't go out with other guys until then. You should at least experience one or two boyfriends while we're here. Willian never needs to know about it."

Jena thought about Juila's suggestion, but she just could not get comfortable with the idea. She would not like it if Willian 'played the field' while she was away. It just did not seem fair. She shrugged her shoulders non-committedly. Jena wanted to change the subject, so she suggested, "Let's go downstairs and finish investigating the house!"

"Okay," Juila readily agreed. She knew how Jena felt about dating, but she could not help herself from pushing Jena toward other options. She did not care for the idea of Jena getting married and leaving her all alone. One day she hoped to find a way to get Jena out of her betrothal. She just needed more time to figure it out.

They went down the stairs together, much more composed than they had been when they went up. Now they paused at the bottom to take in the view of the grand foyer with its huge, sparkling chandelier hanging from the center of the thirty-foot ceiling. The front doors were massive, carved double-doors with windows on either side. The marble floors were polished to a reflective sheen.

They walked back through to the living room and waved at their parents. They turned to the left and went down a hall they had not seen before. They found an office, laundry room, bathroom, and then a huge library. The girls both adored reading and were open-mouthed with awe as they saw the walls covered with books from floor to ceiling.

The girls were fairly certain they had read every book on Acaim. Now they had so much to read it felt as though they had found a massive treasure trove. Jena moved to one side and Juila to the other. They trailed their fingers along the shelves as they read the titles of the books on the spines.

Jena was the first to locate the book with the red spine. When she got to it she had a sudden sensation of power. Without knowing what it could mean she called out, "Juila, get over here and tell me what you feel." She purposely tried to shield her thoughts from Juila, a hard feat in and of itself. They were usually so mentally linked with one another that it had become an unconscious thing.

Juila was intrigued when she felt Jena withdraw mentally. Something amazing must have happened for her sister to do such a thing. She hurried across the library. As she neared her sister, she, too, could feel the pull of energy. It was almost as if it were behind the books, but that did not make sense. This was a solid wall. She shook her head and said, "Let's ask our parents about it. Maybe they know what it is."

Their exploring was essentially over, although the library would warrant further research. They walked back to the living room and sat down on the couch next to their parents. It still felt weird to finally have parents like all of the other children with which they had grown up. Now they did not feel any different. They finally fit in somewhere.

Riccan smiled at the girls and asked, "Which bedrooms did you pick?"

Jena said, "The yellow one," at the same time Juila said, "The pink one."

Amanda laughed and wondered if the girls realized they had picked the same colors they had originally been clothed in from Amanda's dream. She still remembered Justan's cute little voice saying Jena's name had an 'e' and so did 'yellow' while Juila's name had an 'i,' and so did 'pink.' The color of their clothes was how Justan could tell the difference between the identical girls.

"Good! What do you think of the house? Will you be happy here?" Riccan continued to ask.

"Absolutely," the girls said in unison.

"We did have a question about the library, though," Jena began and looked toward Juila to see if they should say anything or just let it go. Juila gave her a small nod and Jena continued, "We felt something along the back wall. Do you know what I'm talking about?"

Riccan and Amanda looked at one another significantly. They had purposely not said anything to the girls about the hidden room. It was apparent they would have to tell them something. Riccan decided to let them in on the secret and said, "Let's go back in there and you can show me what you're talking about, okay?"

The girls eagerly led the way into the library and made a bee-line to the shelf with the red book. "Right here," Jena said emphatically. "I can feel a massive amount of energy when I stand right here."

Riccan smiled and reached under the shelf and pressed the release button. The entire wall moved inward to reveal the large room hidden behind the wall.

Jena and Juila both gasped. They had never heard of a secret room or a false wall. This was terribly exciting.

Riccan was the first to enter followed by Jena, Juila, and finally Amanda. Riccan turned and said, "I think it goes without saying that this room is not to be talked about with anyone except the people in this room right now. I have collected artifacts from Tuala and Earth which are exceptionally rare and must remain hidden. Do you both understand how important this is?"

The girls nodded solemnly, but could not keep their eyes from darting from one amazing artifact to another. Jena began walking toward the pull of energy and stopped when she reached the shelves containing the crystal skulls. She looked up and discovered the carved stones and gasped, "Where did you get these samaras?"

Amanda was the first to ask, "You know about them?"

Riccan was about to ask the same question. Jena even knew the proper term for them which meant she could have even more knowledge about their power, uses, or where the others might be located.

"Yes. I studied about them in the ancient text section of the archives. They are almost ten thousand anons old," she breathed as she stared in awe at the two skulls resting beside one another. She had never even hoped to see one, let alone two. The draw of power was definitely emanating from the samaras. The need to touch one was almost over-powering, so she pulled her hands behind her back to resist the temptation.

Juila came up beside Jena and felt the same pull toward the other samara. She had not read the text, but she knew what it had said since Jena had read it. As she reviewed the knowledge, she was becoming increasingly interested in the whole history.

"For what are the samaras used in the ancient texts?" Riccan asked gently. He hoped they would be able to fill in some blanks from their current knowledge.

"There are thirteen samaras total. It is said they are kept by the descendants of the Watchers until the time comes to bring them back together again," Jena spoke as though she were reading it from her memory.

"Why would they need to come back together? What would they do?" Amanda pressed.

"They will join the worlds together permanently," Jena said matter-of-factly.

Amanda and Riccan looked at each other with frowns of concern. If Amanda were the key, then maybe the knowledge the girls brought with them would take them further toward the fulfillment of the new prophecy.

"Did you girls know there has been a new prophecy given?" Amanda asked.

The two both shook their heads in the negative, but their eyes sparkled with anticipation of learning something few others knew.

Riccan went over and pulled out the Elder's Instructional Guide from the cupboard. He set it on the table and carefully opened the front cover to reveal the page with the recently added words:

"From a far-away land
There will come in time
Intuition is in hand
Strange details known
With ties to the people.
From one of my own
There will be a sign.
Those born to this one
Will transform all.
Lucinden will pursue
Elders will fall
Then all made new."

"Mom, didn't Jehoban say your intuition was the key?" Jena pointed to the section of the prophecy speaking to intuition. She continued to talk to Amanda as she said, "And you are definitely from a far-away land."

"There will come in time..." Amanda murmured as she remembered Jehoban saying she had been transported back in time to deliver her children.

"Amanda, what are you thinking? Have you figured something out?" Riccan touched his wife's arm and leaned toward her anticipating her answer.

"I think so," she mused as she worked it all out in her head before speaking. "If I put myself as the person this is talking about it does make a sort of sense. Like Jena said, I come from a far-away land, and I have a powerful intuition. Jehoban said I'd been transported back in time and I definitely know strange details about people who don't seem to even know me."

Riccan considered Amanda's points and thought she was probably on the right track. He encouraged her to continue by asking, "What else?"

"I don't think I told you, but Jehoban said I was special because I was descended from His angels. I, alone, inherited the special gene from my parents. So I guess that would make me one of His own," Amanda continued. "I'm not sure what the 'sign' is supposed to mean, but I can understand the part where is says my children will transform all."

She looked at her two almost-grown girls and suddenly became scared for their futures. She hoped she had not brought them from the safety of Acaim to put them in harm's way for the sake of this prophecy.

"I don't understand what Lucinden will pursue or why the Elders will fall. The part about all being made new would make sense if what Jena said about bringing the samaras together is correct." Amanda shivered at the implications of the prophecy.

Juila had been strangely silent during the exchange between her parents. She had been intensely studying the prophecy. Finally, she startled everyone by asking, "How long have you known about this prophecy?"

Riccan said, "I've only known about it for a little less than three weeks, but Amanda knew about it long before."

Juila shifted her gaze to her mother to wait for her to answer.

"I first learned about it while I was still in the coma," she answered as she tried to put together the time frame. "I guess I knew about it about eight or nine mesans before Riccan."

Juila nodded as though the time frame meant something to her.

Jena came up beside Juila and casually touched her arm to her sister's. Physical contact always seemed to calm them both. Neither said aloud what was going on in their thoughts. They would have to spend some more time going over everything before they would talk about it with their parents.

The girls suddenly felt the need to get away from the samaras. It was almost as if the energy produced from the crystals were making it harder for them to concentrate. Now that they knew they resided in the house, they were going to have to review their knowledge of the legends surrounding them.

Riccan asked, "Does the time mean something to you, Juila?"

She shook her head and said, "I don't know yet. I'm going to have to think about it. I'll let you know if I remember anything important." She grabbed her sister's arm and said, "Let's get out of here!"

They marched out of the room together and left Amanda and Riccan looking after them with worried expressions. "I wonder what that was all about," Riccan said quietly.

"I don't know, but I'm afraid we'll eventually find out. I'm terrified we might know most of what the prophecy is speaking about. It puts the whole mess directly on Jena and Juila's shoulders. I hope we can keep them safe, Riccan." Amanda stared at her husband willing him to do something.

Riccan drew Amanda into his arms and said, "We'll do everything we can to protect our girls. We will be with them every step of the way. I love you, Amanda."

Amanda hugged her husband tightly around his torso and replied, "I love you, too. I'm so glad we're doing this together. I feel so much better knowing you're with me in this."

"Always, baby, always," he murmured into her hair and then he kissed the top of her head. He pulled away and led her from the room.

CHAPTER 6

"What are we going to do," Juila whispered to Jena as they rushed through the living room and outside to sit beside the pool. They wanted to have some time alone to talk about this new problem.

"I say we do nothing right now. You wanted to experience life on Earth. We should keep our mouths shut until it becomes impossible. Until that time, we will go to school, make new friends, and learn everything we can about Earth. It's simple, really," Jena stated.

Juila nodded, but could not keep from worrying that time was not on their side. Everything seemed to be happening so fast; she was starting to feel like she was losing control of her future much like Jena's had been lost with the betrothal.

It was starting to get dark outside, and some clouds had begun rolling in overhead. It looked like it was going to rain. Just as they had the thought, they started seeing small raindrops fall onto the smooth surface of the pool. As soon as they acknowledged the little drops and began to get up from the lounge chairs, the clouds opened up, and the rain began to pour down from the sky.

The girls squealed as they were caught out unexpectedly. They hunched over and began to run for the side door. In the few seconds it took them to get inside, they were drenched and laughing at how fast their situation had changed.

They spilled into the living room and continued to laugh as they hurriedly shut the door behind them. As they turned from the door, they saw their parents grinning at them as they reclined on the couch in each other's arms. It was a happy scene as Amanda said, "Go upstairs and get some dry clothes on. We can visit here in the living room until it's time for bed."

Walking swiftly, the girls did as their mother had directed. They came back down the stairs together and sat on the couch across from their parents. It was a comfortable feeling to have the whole family together.

Amanda wanted to know everything there was to know about her girls, but she did not want to push them for information. She decided to let the knowledge come to them organically through casual conversation.

Instead of asking what she really wanted to know she asked, "What would you two like to do here?"

The girls looked at one another for a moment before Juila replied, "We'd like to go to high school. It would be really fun to meet kids our own age and see if there are any differences."

"Okay, we can arrange that. Tomorrow is Saturday, but we can go down to the school and get you registered on Monday. Oh," Amanda suddenly realized they would not have any prior educational history or vaccination records. She turned to her husband and asked, "What did you do for proper documentation?"

"Oh, that's easy," Riccan replied easily. "We make it ourselves. We use the elemy to create fake documents."

"That seems like cheating," Amanda scolded.

"What's the alternative, really?" Riccan asked back.

Amanda shrugged and conceded his point. She did not like the idea of making forgeries, but there really was no alternative.

"We will say they've been in boarding school in South Africa. They'll be less likely to look into it if they're from out of the country and they won't know if the documentation is correct or not because of it."

The girls nodded excitedly.

Amanda had to smile at their naivety. She told them, "You'll have to brush up on your geography if you plan on pulling this off. Riccan, why don't you show them how to use the internet to look up the details for their fake history."

Riccan stood up and gestured for the kids to follow him to his study. After a few minutes of instruction, the girls were eagerly looking up different facts and reading the screen intently. He returned to the living room and sat with his wife.

"You don't like this idea, do you?"

"Not particularly. But, like you said, what choice do we have?" Amanda could see so many things going wrong with this plan even as she tried to see the bright side of it. She did want her kids to meet people their own age. It would be good for them to learn about Earth relationships.

Riccan leaned in close to Amanda's ear and said, "This would be a good time to practice looking in on the kids now that they're preoccupied."

Amanda nodded and said, "You go ahead. I'm too worked up to try just now." She sat silently and watched Riccan concentrate on their daughter's crystals. She could tell when he was successful by the bright smile which crossed his face. Curious, she also accessed the children's crystals and could see they were laughing at some fact they had seen on the internet.

At that moment, Amanda realized she had used a talent she had only learned during her dream. Elder Daven had not reviewed it with her even though she had listened in when he was instructing Riccan on its process.

She felt her confidence rising as she realized there was a lot from her dream which was actually real even if her interactions with the people had not been. *Maybe*, she wondered to herself, *I should try to find each of the people from my dream and find out how they fit in with this puzzle. Maybe they are the missing pieces.* Amanda wondered if this were what Jehoban had been instructing her to do when He had said to listen to her heart.

Amanda would think about it some more when she was not so tired. These last few days had been very exhausting with all of the revelations and experiences. She was not likely to forget how her life turned around on the day she met with Jehoban.

As if reading her mind, Riccan asked her, "I meant to ask you something earlier, but I forgot with all of the recent changes in our lives."

Amanda was startled out of her reverie and asked, "What were you going to ask?"

He smiled mischievously and inquired, "What does Jehoban look like?"

Amanda was about to reply confidently until she actually began to think about the answer. Instead, she chuckled and replied, "I think He had kind eyes."

"Ha, it's not just me then. You don't remember either!" He laughed out loud.

Amanda laughed, too, and said, "I see what you mean when you said you didn't really know what He looked like. I spent a half hour with Him, and I still don't know!"

Riccan turned serious and said, "Amanda, you were with Him for half of the day. Did it really only seem like a half hour?"

"Seriously? I was gone that long?" Amanda was amazed all over again. She knew Jehoban had told her time was malleable, but she did not realize He was manipulating it while she met with Him.

"He's rather imposing, don't you think?" Riccan asked.

"Rather!" Amanda agreed emphatically. She wondered if the girls would know what Jehoban looked like since they had been raised on His island. At some point, she would ask them, but for right now, she wanted nothing more than to go to bed with her husband. She took matters into her own hands and stood up from the couch.

Offering her hand to help Riccan up, she said, "Let's tell the girls we're heading to bed now. I'm tired." She kept his hand in hers as they walked down the hall to the study. She leaned in the doorway and announced, "Don't stay up too late. We're heading to bed now. We'll see you in the morning."

The girls turned at the same time and smiled the same smile as first Jena and then Juila said goodnight. They turned back around and typed a new search and hit enter.

Amanda believed the girls would be quite late in getting to bed. She shook her head and sighed at how youthful her children were. She was feeling older and older with each passing day. *How am I going to explain the ages of the children to my parents?* she asked herself with dismay. *Eventually, they'll have to be told the truth. I'll figure something out, but it's not going to be tonight!*

Riccan put his arm around Amanda's waist as they ascended the stairs. He wondered if Amanda were too tired to have a few moments of intimacy. He kissed her neck playfully and was rewarded when Amanda turned to kiss him on the lips. The simple kiss turned passionate, and Riccan realized he had his answer. Without another thought, Riccan scooped Amanda up from the floor and carried her the rest of the way to the bedroom.

Amanda squealed with delight and then covered her mouth as she realized they were no longer alone in the house. They would have to curb their enthusiasm when the girls were around. That did not mean they had to be celibate, but they would have to remain aware of their children's whereabouts. She was thankful for their easy access to their birth crystals. It would surely help their current situation.

THE RAIN CONTINUED through the night, but when the morning came, the sun came out bright, sparkling on the raindrops which covered everything. Juila was the first to wake and had a sudden thrill at remembering they were now on Earth. She jumped out of bed and stared out her bedroom window to see if the morning looked any different than the ones on Tuala. There were slight differences in the intensity of the sun; otherwise, all was the same.

She had been sitting in her window seat for only a few minutes before she could feel her sister's mind waking for the day. Without waiting for an invitation, Juila left her room and silently entered Jena's bedroom. When Jena's eyes opened, she smiled to see her sister looking down at her. Together they moved over to Jena's window seat to watch the sun evaporate the water and create a slight mist until the breezes blew it away.

"We're going to see the high school in a couple of days. If we don't like the looks of it, we can tell Mom we don't want to go," Jena decided for them both.

Juila simply nodded. She had already decided she was going to like it. Of the two of them, Juila seemed to be the more adventurous one. She wondered if it were because she did not have a betrothed to think of and she was free to make decisions for her life on her own.

Once again, Juila had to tamp down her growing anger over Elder

Debbon's claim on her sister's life. It was definitely unfair. It was even harder for her to understand why Jena did not seem to mind the marriage arrangement. She tried to imagine if the roles were reversed, but she shook her head in disgust. It would never have happened to her; she would not have agreed to it.

Jena looked at her sister and wondered why she put so much effort into hating her life's choice. She genuinely liked Willian, so it did not seem too much of a hardship to spend the rest of her life with him. She wished Juila would be more settled with her decision.

The girls seemed to snap out of their reverie at the same time and decided to get dressed and go downstairs for a relaxing weekend. They went downstairs and ended up reclining in the library chairs. There were so many books which they had never even heard of that it was an exciting adventure. When they finally emerged for food, they imagined breakfast would be some exotic Earth food and then had to laugh as their dad served them fried foxl and scrambled eggs. It was nothing different than they would have had on Tuala except it was seasoned better than they were used to.

Both Saturday and Sunday ended up being spent the same way. Research in the library in the mornings and afternoons to be followed by family time in the evenings. They asked many questions about school since they were anticipating seeing it for the first time the next day.

Eventually, Monday morning arrived bright and sunny. After using their own bathroom facilities, they had decided to get dressed. Their thoughts were continually linked. They did not know at what time their mother wanted to get going so they rushed.

Juila looked in her closet and wondered what outfit would be the most appropriate for school. For the first time, she worried about fitting in with the other students. She had always been part of the elite group of students and never had to worry about what the other children thought. This was going to be a new, and possibly awkward, experience. Just the idea of it thrilled her.

Finally, Juila just picked the outfit she liked the best. She would ask her mom if it would be sufficient for school. If not, maybe they could go shopping to buy new clothes, if they did that sort of thing here on Earth. There was so much they still needed to learn about Earth customs. If she thought about it too much, she would be overwhelmed. She decided to take just one situation at a time until it all became more familiar.

Juila left her room at the same time as Jena. Most people would think it odd how the two sisters were so in tune with one another. They did not know any differently, so it seemed as natural as breathing. When Juila saw the outfit her sister had picked out, she began to chuckle. It was the same as her own clothes except in a different color.

Jena smiled back at her sister's thought and walked over to her. They linked arms, like they often did, and went downstairs to find something to eat. Three plates were already set out for them on the kitchen island counter.

"Are you ready to check out high school today?" Riccan asked to make conversation. He was not sure what teenaged girls talked about.

"Sure," Jena replied and then asked, "If we don't like the looks of it, do we still have to go?"

"Nope! This is meant to be educational for you, but you've technically already finished school, so you don't have to attend if you don't want to." Riccan knew the anxiety the girls were feeling; he had felt the same thing on several different occasions as he grew up in different parts of America. He tossed an envelope across the island toward them.

"What's this?" Juila asked curiously.

"Those are the documents you'll need to enter American school. You should look them over and memorize the details so you'll know them should anyone ask about your history," Riccan replied casually. He had been through this same scenario as well when he was young.

Juila opened the envelope and dumped the paperwork out on the counter beside her plate of food. She discovered the two small blue books were passports. After leafing through the pages, she found several stamps indicating they had been to several countries in South Africa. She set those aside and picked up the next item which turned out to be birth certificates. For some reason, this document meant the most to her because it listed both their mother's and father's names. This made her feel official in the family, and her eyes started to blur with tears.

She put down the certificates and picked up two small, tri-folded papers. Unsure of what they were supposed to be she held it up and looked questioningly at Riccan.

"Those are your vaccination records," he answered. He could still see a confused look on her face and remembered they had never needed any shots to prevent illness. Those types of viruses did not happen on Tuala, or else they could be cured instantly by a wise-woman. "Vaccinations are shots which are given to people several times during the course of their life to prevent illnesses which have killed hundreds of thousands of people on Earth over time. The shots are required of all students before they can be admitted to school."

"That makes sense if these illnesses are as deadly as you say. It would be terrible to have your classmates dying," Jena said reasonably.

"It's not quite as bad as that," Riccan said as he tried to control the laughter he felt at his daughter's matter-of-fact reasoning.

"Oh, that's good," Jena said with a relieved sigh.

This time Riccan did chuckle and then said, "The last paper there is documenting the levels of education you have received. Each student must complete a requisite number of classes in each subject in order to be eligible to graduate. You are both considered Junior level students so you will be placed in eleventh grade at the school. That's the typical grade for your age."

"'Junior' seems to be a strange name for a grade." Juila smiled at the different title.

"Okay, I see you need an immediate education in high school terms. Students in ninth grade are called 'Freshmen', tenth graders are called 'Sophomores,' eleventh graders are 'Juniors' as we just discussed, and finally, the twelfth graders are called 'Seniors,'" Riccan explained carefully. He knew he would not have to explain it again since the girls had already mastered the memorization skill during their crystal training. They had that advantage on him since he had finished his crystal training after he had finished high school on Earth. He was certain they would be exemplary students and was eager for them to test their skills against Earth's standards.

"It makes much more sense when you put it that way!" Juila decided.

"Good! Now put the papers back into the envelope and be sure to give them to your mother when she comes down. She should be ready soon," he said. "Eat your food before it gets any colder.

"Where are you going?" Jena asked as she realized their father was not going to go with them.

"I have some research to do, and then I need to write some new software code for my telepod," he answered easily. "I'll be in my study if you need me."

"Oh, okay," Jena said sullenly. She had envisioned them going everywhere together and did not really want to be separated from either parent. Then she chastised herself for being so foolish. They were going to be going to school every day, and their parents definitely would not be there. They had already finished school. Then another idea struck her as she watched Riccan walk away. "How will we get to school if you're going to be tinkering with the telepod?"

Riccan smiled and answered, "You'll take the truck. On Earth, they don't know anything about telepods, and you'll have to remember to never mention any terms from Tuala."

"How will we know what not to say?" Juila asked suddenly.

"You'll learn when the students look at you like they have no idea what you're talking about. It'll only happen a couple of times before you start to catch on," Riccan assured them easily.

"I hope so! I'd hate for the other kids to think we're strange," Juila countered.

"It's one reason I wanted you to be from South Africa. They would have different words and customs from what the kids here would be used to. Most of the time they'll just think it's a cultural difference and they won't be far from the truth, when you think about it," he finished and then continued walking toward his office.

Riccan knew the learning curve would be steep, but he had confidence in the girls' abilities to overcome the obstacles. After all, this was something they wanted to experience. After their initial nervousness wore off, he was certain they would find kids to make friends with rather quickly. They were beautiful girls, so they already had an advantage.

Just before he stepped into his office, he heard Amanda speaking with the girls. He smiled and set his mind on his task of fixing the telepod to have anti-collision capabilities. His mind had been haunted by Amanda's dream of them crashing and dying because of a collision with another flying airplane. On Tuala there had not been a need since the crystals seemed to have spatial awareness and never hit one another. He thought of it like the negative charges of a magnet and how impossible it was to push them together.

If he were to be carrying his family back and forth between Earth and Tuala, he wanted to make sure they would all be as safe as possible. He wondered why he had never thought to implement the improvement before but then shook his head to clear those thoughts and began designing the code for the process.

CHAPTER 7

Amanda smiled when she saw her daughters were already eating their breakfast when she came into the kitchen. "I'm glad to see you're almost ready to go," she said and then saw the extra plate of food and asked, "Is this for me?"

The girls nodded as they both had food in their mouths.

"Riccan is so good to me," she said as she picked up the fork and also ate.

When the meals were finished, Amanda gathered the plates and set them in the sink. She still had not mastered the skill to clean them and put them away. She knew Riccan would not mind taking care of them later.

The girls had been watching their mother's actions and asked, "What happens to the dishes now?"

"Oh," Amanda said, "Riccan will take care of them."

"Why don't you do it?" Jena asked.

"I haven't mastered the cleaning skill yet. I've only discovered I have power in the last few weeks. In time, I'll learn how to do it for myself," Amanda admitted. She felt slightly foolish at having to explain her deficiencies to her overly skilled children.

"If you show me where the dishes end up, I can do it for you," Juila offered kindly.

Again, Amanda was at a loss. She had never actually looked in any of the cupboards since Riccan was always the one to prepare and clean up the meals. She smiled and said, "Let's look together."

The girls hopped off of the bar stools and eagerly investigated the kitchen's cupboards and drawers. In no time at all the girls had memorized the layout. Juila did as she offered and the sink was now empty of dirty dishes.

Amanda beamed at how easily the girls used their skills. She hoped they would not use them at school accidentally. She would remind them of it again before they actually attended school. Today was purely a day to register and look around, so she was not as concerned about any mistakes being made. Looking at her watch, she asked, "Who's ready to check out the school?"

The girls immediately nodded and faced her as they said in unison, "We are!"

"Let's go then," Amanda announced as she turned to go to the opposite garage where the Earth vehicles were parked. Amanda was amused by listening to her children's exclamations of surprise at their newest mode of transportation. They did not know what to make of the strange wheels and the loud engine. Amanda thought the engine was rather quiet herself, but, compared to a crystal drive, which was nearly silent, she could understand their concern.

She drove them slowly out the driveway and through the streets of the town. Everything was new and amazing to the girls, and she wanted them to be able to take the time to appreciate the details. After driving for fifteen minutes, they arrived at Coral Reef Senior High School. The parking lot was nearly empty except for a few different makes and models of cars which created even more exclamations from the girls. Amanda parked in the visitor's parking near the main entrance and turned off the engine.

"This is it," she announced unnecessarily. She opened her door and got out. She waited at the front of the truck for the girls to get out of the passenger side doors and meet up with her. Amanda held the envelope with their documents even as she wondered how Riccan had made them on such short notice.

The trio walked into the reception office after walking through two sets of double doors. The woman at the main desk greeted them warmly.

"Hello. How may I help you?" she asked.

"I'd like to register my girls for school," Amanda replied easily.

The receptionist looked swiftly from Amanda to the twins and then back to Amanda. She could hardly imagine this woman was their mother; she barely looked old enough. *They must be her step-children*, the woman said to herself. "Just one moment and I'll give you the packet of papers to be filled out," she said and bent down to gather the documents.

Amanda was surprised when the woman set down two rather large stacks of paper, one for each child, which would need to be filled out in their entirety. One of her least favorite things to do was to fill out forms, and now she had twice the amount to complete. "Wow," was all Amanda could think to say as she picked up the documents and went to sit in a chair along the back of the room.

After leafing through the separate pages, Amanda decided she would rather take the papers home and fill them out. Or rather, she'd have the girls fill out their own paperwork so they could familiarize themselves with the facts the school found important to know. She stood up, stuffed the papers into her oversized purse, and asked the receptionist, "I think we'll take these home to fill out. Do you think we could get a tour of the school before classes begin?"

"Oh, sure! This next Wednesday is an open house. We will have many volunteer students coming in to take you around," she answered cheerfully.

"That's perfect!" Amanda was pleased to hear they had not missed out on anything important for the girls to be successful in their first Earth school. "What time is the open house?"

"It's from six to eight in the evening. We'll look forward to seeing you then."

"Great! Thanks," she turned away from the counter to go back to the truck, and the twins followed her more slowly.

The school was much larger than they had anticipated. They hoped they would not have too much trouble finding their way around. They were not sure what an 'open house' was, but their mother seemed pleased to hear about it. The three got back into the truck, and Juila asked, "What's an open house?"

"It's an event held at the school for new students. They introduce you to some teachers and students and then take you on a tour of the buildings and classrooms. They will tell about how the daily schedule is handled and answer any questions you may have," Amanda absently answered as she navigated the busy streets back to their house.

Once they got back home, the girls returned to their daily ritual in the library.

Amanda pulled out the bundle of papers and left them on the kitchen counter to deal with later. She looked outside and saw the blue water of the pool and decided a morning swim would be a perfect activity. She went upstairs and changed into her bathing suit.

Tuesday evening Amanda instructed the girls to take a seat and gave them each a pen to fill out their own school admission forms. "If you have any questions, feel free to ask," Amanda instructed as she sat on the stool next to Juila.

Riccan took the last bar stool on the far end next to Jena. Over the next couple of hours and hundreds of questions later, the girls managed to slog through the stacks. They now had an appreciation for the information they needed to know about themselves. Amanda was glad she had thought to have them do the work themselves. It was a good first learning tool.

By the end of the forms session, the girls were itching to do something active. Amanda suggested they all go out to the pool to enjoy the last of the day's sunshine. The girls readily agreed, and everyone rushed to change into their bathing suits.

When they were all walking out to the pool deck, Riccan compared the figures of their children to his wife's. They had almost the same figure which, for some reason, surprised Riccan. He kept trying to see any of his features in the children, but, over and over, he could only see Amanda's traits in the girls.

One thing he thought odd was the fact the girls each had bright blue eyes, whereas both himself and Amanda had brown eyes. He knew how genetics worked, but he would have thought brown eyes would have had a better chance. His mother had blue eyes, and Amanda's father had hazel eyes. They both carried the recessive blue-eyed gene.

Juila jumped right into the pool as well as Amanda. Riccan watched as Jena simply sat on the edge and dangled her feet into the cool water. He jumped in which splashed water all over Jena. He had believed she just wanted to get in slower and yelled, "Get in, Jena. Quicker is easier!"

Jena simply shook her head and said, "I'll be fine right here."

Juila yelled from the middle of the pool, "Jena's afraid of the water." She turned and kept swimming.

Jena felt her cheeks turning pink at her sister's rude comment. She could not refute it, but she did not need it announced either.

Riccan saw her embarrassment and swam closer to her and said, "It's okay, Jena. Swimming's not for everyone. Do you know how to swim?"

"Not really," Jena admitted. It was part of the problem, but certainly not all of it.

"I could teach you if you ever wanted to learn," Riccan offered, but did not want to push.

"Thanks. Maybe some other time. I just want to enjoy the sun right now."

"Okay. Just ask when you're ready, alright?" Riccan reminded her as he pushed himself off of the side of the pool and easily swam the length of the pool and back.

Jena watched at how her father made it look so simple. She thought she might give it a try if her dad were right beside her to keep her safe. She moved her feet back and forth in the coolness and shivered at the thought of drowning. *Maybe not*, she said to herself as she changed her mind on learning to swim.

The family continued to swim while Jena sat on the edge. For the first time, she actually considered facing her fear of the water to join in on the fun. Instead, she thought about the fact they were on Earth, about to begin school, living with their parents, and basically living the life they had always dreamt of having.

She watched as everyone swam over to where she was sitting. They got out and invited her to join them in the hot tub. She eagerly stood up and climbed down into the warm, bubbling water.

Amanda asked, "So what kinds of things did you like to do for fun in Tuala?"

Juila answered, "We did a lot of things. Jena's favorite thing is to read anything she can get her hands on. We rode horses pretty often. When we got a little older, we learned how to fly a telepod, which was really fun." She looked at her sister to continue the list of activities.

"Let's see," Jena mused, "we used to make up games with the elemy. Remember Elemy Tide, Juila?"

Juila laughed and then had to share the story, "We created a great big swath of elemy and let it roll across the ground. The last person standing would be the winner. It was a great idea until some of the house staff got caught up in it and we got in trouble for reckless use of the elemy."

Riccan could well imagine the ideas these two could come up with given their inquisitive natures. He laughed at the misfortune of a game which actually sounded as though it could be quite fun. He suggested, "We might have to revive Elemy Tide here at the house. We just have to make sure all of the staff are off that day!"

Amanda chuckled at Riccan's jest about having staff. She had yet to see a single person working at the house. She asked Jena, "What is your favorite thing to read? I think you've noticed your father has quite the library amassed here at the house. There might be some things you haven't read yet."

Riccan could relate to Jena's need to read. He felt the same way about books which was why he had started collecting them.

"I'll read anything, really. I like anything having to do with crystal skills. It's amazing how much has changed over time about how we use our crystals. The people used to do just about everything with them and then something changed. Either it became out of fashion, or the people just forgot how, I'm still not sure, but more and more things were learned to do by hand and not with the elemy," Jena stated.

"That's an interesting observation," Riccan mused. Between his father and himself, they had probably read every book on Acaim. He had never put together the idea which Jena was proposing. Now that he gave it more consideration, he could tell what she was saying was true. The people used to be more reliant on Jehoban and the skills He gave them. Now the people tended to be more selfish and believed their abilities were better on their own. He wondered what other insights Jena had put together with her unusual heritage.

Jena blushed at her father's praise. It had seemed a rather obvious observation, but nobody seemed to appreciate the scope of it except her dad. She wondered if he liked to read as much as she did, his library seemed to suggest his interest.

"How often did you fly the telepods?" Riccan asked. If they really enjoyed flying, one or both of them might be interested in learning to fly his Cessna. It would be a fun activity for them to bond over. He still did not know how to relate to teenage girls. He was sure there would be many connections he could make if he asked enough questions.

"We just began learning last anon," Juila said.

"We use the term year instead of anon on Earth," Riccan corrected. "Likewise, month is used instead of mesan, and decade instead of declan."

Both girls nodded at the impromptu language lesson. Juila asked, "What other terms should we know about?"

Amanda and Riccan looked at one another and tried to think of things they would need to know. Naturally, they drew a blank and Amanda suggested, "Why don't we correct you as you go along?"

"You were talking about learning to fly the telepods?" Riccan prompted.

"Yes, we were finally certified to fly solo. Of course, the units we trained in were not nearly as nice as the one you own. I'd love to get a tour of your telepod sometime," Juila said to Riccan.

"Oh, no. You don't know what you just asked for, Juila!" Amanda rolled her eyes toward her husband. The telepod was his pride and joy, and he loved nothing more than to show it off to anyone willing to hear about it.

Riccan smiled broadly and countered, "It's more fun to share with someone who appreciates the intricacies of the craftsmanship."

"Oh, I can appreciate the amount of work you put into it, but you lost me when you started talking about the size of the crystal drive and how it's connected to the power controls," Amanda teased back.

"What size crystal do you have in there," Juila asked, genuinely interested.

"Ugh, not you, too!" Amanda turned to her other daughter and asked, "Are you going to abandon me in this as well?"

Jena smiled at her mother's playful banter and reassured her, "Nope, you'll be safe with me. I find the whole thing rather tedious and boring. I'd rather read the manual on how it works rather than poke around the structure looking at it."

"Hmm, that doesn't sound much better, Jena. It looks like I'm the odd man out in this discussion," Amanda said.

The girls looked at their mother strangely at her last statement. Amanda realized they did not understand the colloquialism of 'odd man out' and said, "It just means I'm the only one who's not interested."

The girls nodded, but were still uncertain how the phrase could mean what she suggested if she were a girl.

Riccan laughed at their serious expressions while trying to understand the strange phrase. He remembered having the same thoughts as he learned the oddities of the new culture. He replied to Juila's question about the crystal with, "Since it seems to be such a boring topic, I'll tell you all about it when I give you a tour later."

Juila nodded eagerly. She was glad she had a common interest with her father. She had been scared her parents would not like any of the same things as she and her sister. They had spent many a day discussing what it would be like to finally be reunited and if it would be awkward. So far, it had been as easy as breathing, and they were still waiting to find where the difficulties would lie.

The evening went by swiftly, and soon enough it was time for bed. The family went up the stairs together, distributing hugs and kisses all around, before the two pairs went their separate ways.

Juila followed Jena into her room and sat down on her bed while Jena changed into her nightgown. She had been troubled by the knowledge they shared between them regarding the samaras and wanted to discuss it with her sister.

"When do you think we should tell our parents about the samaras?" Juila asked.

"I'd like to get to know them and Earth first before we go and change everything," Jena replied smartly.

"Do you really think just telling them about it would keep us from staying here?"

Jena stared at her like she had gone crazy and folded her arms as she considered answering her sister. "I don't really know, and I don't want to find out. Please just drop this for now, okay? We have plenty of time before circumstances will force us to talk about it."

"Jena, what are you not telling me? Did you find out something new in the archives?"

"Maybe, but I'm not sure what it means yet. I'll tell you about it when you need to know."

Juila hated it when Jena put her off like that. Her sister did have a powerful, intuitive nature, but sometimes she had to have all the pieces before something made sense. This must be one of those times. She still did not have to like it.

Jena smiled to get her sister to think about something else. "What did you think about those school forms?"

"Could you believe all of the questions they ask just to let you go to school? I thought we were never going to get through those stacks." She was silent for a moment and then changed the subject again as she wondered aloud, "I wonder what gets served for lunch at the school."

Jena had found the forms rather fascinating. It gave her a better idea of what was going to be expected of them when they went there the next day for the open house. She did think the number of hours the students attended school was rather ridiculous. On Tuala, they only had classes in the mornings, except for the special classes they had added on to learn about their crystal skills. Those only lasted for an hour or two in the afternoons, depending on how complex the course of study.

CHAPTER 8

Wednesday evening arrived all too fast. The girls were nervous about what to expect. After driving to the school, Amanda followed the eager girls, while holding the folder containing their admission paperwork. They checked in at the front desk where Amanda handed the forms over to the same receptionist they had met previously.

"Welcome to our open house. Thank you for the forms. I'll get them processed before classes begin. We start school on Friday, August 7th this year." The receptionist smiled at Amanda.

She snapped her fingers at a young girl to get her attention. The girl stepped forward and was told, "Sofia, please take these people on a tour of the school." She turned back to Amanda and said, "Sofia will escort you. Please wear these visitor badges while you are here. When you are ready to leave, return the badges to my desk." She handed them each a rather large plastic tag which had to be pinned to their clothes.

The woman stared as the girls clumsily pinned the badges. It was then she realized their clothing was very odd. She wondered what their story was and could not wait to read their admission papers. This job was perfect for her inquisitive nature. Very soon she would have the answers to her questions. She watched the four ladies leave her office as her phone rang.

Sofia led the way out of the front office before she said, "I'm in the eleventh grade. What grade will you be in?"

Juila answered, "The same as you." She was glad to have already met someone their own age.

"Are you two twins?" Sofia could not help but ask.

The girls looked at one another and then giggled before answering in unison, "Yes!"

Sofia chuckled, too, and said, "I thought it was pretty obvious, but I had to ask. Cool outfits, by the way."

The girls looked down on themselves comically and wondered what 'cool' meant.

Amanda saw the confused look and made a mental note to tell them common lingo for them to learn. She also appraised their clothing and decided a shopping trip would also happen on their way home. The girls would have to fit in better. Amanda was so used to Tualan clothing she had not even thought about how different they must look.

They walked to the end of the hall and Sofia began telling them about the layout of the school. She enjoyed talking to people about the facilities.

"How many students attend here?" Amanda asked.

"Around two thousand," Sofia answered easily.

The girls looked at one another uncertainly and gulped before returning their attention to Sofia's tour. They had never heard of so many students attending school together, making them wonder how they would ever manage to find their way around to their classes with so many people surrounding them. If they were going to pull this off, then they were just going to have to figure it out!

The tour lasted a half hour, and the girls got to experience the crush of students as the other new students were touring the classrooms and filling the open air hallways on their way to their next stop in their own tours. Sofia rushed to get them over to the cafeteria, "This is where my part of the tour ends. Take a seat, and there will be a presentation given by some of the faculty."

Amanda understood what was happening, but the girls were confused. They had thought the tour would last longer and did not know why Sofia could not just stay with them. As they entered the large lunch room, Amanda spoke to Sofia, "Thank you for the tour. It was very well done. Maybe you'll run into Juila and Jena when they start school."

"I'll be on the lookout for them," Sofia replied with a smile as she turned to leave them. She was certain she had another tour group waiting for her in the office.

After another thirty minutes of questions and answers in the cafeteria, they made their way back to the main office. They left the visitor's badges on the top of the desk and went back outside through the double set of doors. When they got back to the truck, Amanda asked, "Do you two want to go shopping for school clothes?"

"Aren't these clothes okay?" Jena asked with confusion and then remembered Sofia's comment about them being 'cool' and asked Amanda about it.

"The word 'cool' refers to something being different, but nice in its own way. She was saying she liked your clothes, but it reminded me you will need to have clothes similar to that of the other students so you won't always stand out," Amanda replied.

Juila started to laugh at something she remembered. "Did you hear the receptionist thinking Mom had to have been our step-mother since she doesn't look old enough to be our biological mom?" she asked her sister as she twisted around in the passenger seat to see her sister's face.

Jena laughed and agreed it was funny.

"What are you talking about? I didn't hear her say anything about that?" Amanda asked with a confused expression on her face.

"She didn't say it out loud. She sure thought it loud enough though," Juila answered easily.

"Are you saying you can hear people's thoughts?" Amanda asked with concern.

"Sure, everybody on Acaim does it," Jena stated.

"Well nobody does it here. You might want to curb that skill before you find yourself getting into trouble," Amanda directed.

The laughter died down as the girls digested this new twist. They had never considered not reading somebody's mind. It could be fun to try and figure out what a person was thinking without seeking it out for themselves.

Amanda stopped at one of the large strip malls and parked the truck. They entered the first clothing store, and Amanda watched with amusement as the girls picked through the various items. They laughed at the different patterns and colors. Jena pulled one particularly ugly shirt off of the rack and asked, "Do people really wear stuff like this?"

Amanda laughed and replied, "Unfortunately, yes. Those people are usually only wanting to draw attention to themselves. I think we'll stick with more conservative colors and styles if you don't mind!"

Jena agreed with her mother's opinion.

Several hours passed as the girls amassed bags of clothes and school supplies. Amanda was never one to like shopping, but the girls seemed to be having lots of fun, so she enjoyed the process for their sakes. It was almost time for bed when they finally arrived back home. They were all exhausted but pleased with their new purchases.

The girls laid out all of their new outfits around the living room floor and matched tops to bottoms. They excitedly examined one another's choices and decided they would probably share the majority of it.

Riccan came out of his office when he heard a commotion from the other room. He walked around the corner and took a step back at the masses of clothes around the whole room. "Wow, somebody's been busy!" he declared as he spotted Amanda and walked over to give her a kiss welcoming her home.

"We'd like to give you a fashion show," Juila declared.

Amanda laughed and said, "Okay. Let's save it for tomorrow, shall we? I'm exhausted!" Amanda dropped onto the couch and sighed with relief as she set her feet up on the coffee table. Now she remembered why she hated shopping, her feet and back ached abominably. She looked out the window and saw the hot tub beckoning her.

THE NEXT AFTERNOON the girls hauled their bags of clothes back down the stairs and dropped them on the living room floor. Jena and Juila were both broadly smiling as Jena announced, "It's time for the fashion show!"

Amanda smiled at their enthusiasm and said, "Take your clothes into the study and change in there. We'll be sitting here on the couch to review."

The girls spent the next hour traipsing through the living room modeling their newest looks. They giggled and pranced along and acted like the young girls they still were. Amanda and Riccan thoroughly enjoyed the afternoon activity. Finally, the girls announced the last change of clothes and Amanda's stomach growled loudly.

"I believe it's time for lunch," Riccan announced. "Do you want me to make something or do you want to go out for pizza?"

Amanda considered and then said, "I think pizza would be a fun experience for the girls. I wish it were faster, though. I'm starving!"

"I can call in our order so it'll at least be started while we drive down there," Riccan suggested.

"That would be perfect!" Amanda smiled up at her husband who had already started to walk across the room to get the phone. "You know what I want. You should order a couple of different selections for the girls to try. They don't even know what they like yet," Amanda suggested.

"Good point," Riccan replied. He decided to order three pizzas with different toppings on each half to give them a good selection from which to choose.

Only a few minutes later they were piling into the 4-Runner and leaving the house. The girls had chosen to wear the last outfits they had tried on to go out in. Amanda approved. Riccan drove, Amanda was in the passenger seat, and the girls both sat in the back seat.

Again, the girls kept their faces plastered to the windows to take in all of the scenery along the way. They commented on the palm trees and other greenery which was different from what they knew in Tuala. The traffic signal lights were another thing they commented on, which prompted another lesson so the girls would understand how to avoid getting run over by a car should they be using the sidewalks.

Amanda was beginning to appreciate the number of things she took for granted from being raised on Earth. There was so much for her children to learn. She did not envy their position. When she had thought she was in Tuala, she had felt at a loss for the differences, but she had just been in a dream. Her girls were in reality where their mistakes could have serious consequences. If she thought about it too much, she might not let them leave the house!

At the restaurant, the girls' reaction to the new food was as fun as Amanda had expected. As it turned out, Juila preferred the beef and pineapple, which was Amanda's favorite. Jena preferred the taco pizza, which was Riccan's favorite. The other versions were also tried and eaten. They ended up with several to-go boxes and had a lively ride home.

The girls kept a constant chatter from the back seat. Riccan had taken a circuitous route home so they could see more of the town in which they resided. Several jumbo jets took off from the nearby Miami International Airport which caused the girls to stare in awe at the enormous, winged crafts with the loud engines.

Riccan smiled at their concerned comments and said, "Just wait until I take you flying in my Cessna!"

"What's a Cessna?" Jena asked.

"It's a type of airplane used here on Earth. It's their equivalent of a telepod," he explained.

Amanda snorted at his simplistic explanation. She knew there was no comparison between the two aircraft. Soon enough the girls would be able to come to the same conclusion.

Riccan grinned at his wife's reaction and shrugged his shoulders, "It's the best explanation I can think of until they can see it for themselves."

"I guess," Amanda laughed.

CHAPTER 9

The morning of their first day of school finally arrived, and the nervous girls attempted to eat their breakfast. Neither really had much appetite, but their mom had insisted they give it a try. Their school bags were packed and waiting by the garage door.

Finally, Amanda gave up on watching them push their food around and announced, "Let's get going. I want to make sure we have all of the admission stuff taken care of before the first class starts."

Immediately, the dishes in front of the girls disappeared. They both had taken care of their own dirty bowls with an instinctive thought. They hopped off their chairs in unison and walked with matching strides toward the garage.

Again they parked in front of the main office, and the girls piled out of the vehicle with their bags in tow. As soon as they walked up to the reception desk, Amanda noticed the girl who had given them the tour sitting in a chair off to the side.

Sofia had been waiting to meet with the new girls. She had felt an odd connection with them and had decided she was going to try to be their friend. Meeting them in the office had seemed like the best way to get their friendship started. She knew what it was like to be new to a school. Her own parents had moved to the United States only five years before.

When she started going to the grade school, she had not even known English.

Jena and Juila had been looking at the receptionist and had not noticed the young girl waiting for them. Amanda rested her forearms on the credenza and waited for the receptionist to get off the phone. She leaned toward her girls and said, "Why don't you go and say hi to Sofia? This could take a while."

The girls suddenly looked around and finally spotted the only person they knew at the school. They both smiled the same smile and walked over to the girl. "Hi, Sofia," Juila said when they got close enough.

"Hi. I hope you don't mind me waiting for you two," she said, suddenly feeling shy.

"No way! It's good to see someone we know," Jena spoke hurriedly so the girl could stop feeling guilty. *Oops,* Jena thought to herself, *Mom told us not to read people's minds.* She smiled and sat down next to Sofia.

Juila sat down on the other side of Sofia and said, "I don't think we told you our names before. I'm Juila Stel, and this is Jena."

"Your mother had mentioned your names, but I'm pleased to meet you, Juila and Jena," she responded and looked at each girl as she said their names. "My name is Sofia Castillo."

"I noticed your words sound different from other people we've met. Are you from a different place?" Jena asked kindly.

Sofia tried to figure out what Jena was talking about when she realized she meant her accent. She laughed and said, "Yes, my accent is from Argentina where my family is from originally. We immigrated to Florida five years ago when there got to be too much fighting in our home country. My parents thought it would be safer for me to grow up in America and get a better education."

The girls both nodded but did not understand all of the things they had been told. They had decided, before arriving at the school, that they would not ask too many unusual questions. Instead, they would make a mental list of things to either look up on the internet themselves or ask their parents when they got home. Sofia just supplied the first two things on their list.

They spent the next ten minutes visiting with Sofia while their mom finally got to start talking to the receptionist. Eventually, their mom turned and gestured for them to come up to the desk. They rushed across the room, wondering what was going to happen next.

The receptionist stood up and held out a piece of paper and asked, "Which one of you is Juila?"

Juila raised her hand slightly and said, "Me."

The receptionist set the paper down in front of her and said, "This is your class schedule. And this," she handed her a separate slip of paper, "is your locker combination. You and your sister will be able to share a locker, so the combination is the same for both of you."

Juila hastily looked down at the schedule of classes and saw there were seven. 1. College Writing, 2. Biology, 3. American Government, 4. AP US History, lunch period, 5. College Algebra, 6. English III, and 7. Health.

Jena received her list of classes and immediately noticed they were slightly different than her sister's: 1. College Writing, 2. Biology, 3. Spanish I, 4. American Government, lunch period, 5. College Algebra, 6. English III, and 7. Health.

The receptionist said, "The room locations are listed next to each class. If you have any trouble with any of them, come back to me, and we'll see if we can move you to something else. Have a nice day!" The phone rang, effectively dismissing them, as she sat down to take the call.

Sofia came up behind them and asked, "Can I see your schedules? We might have some classes together. I can also show you where your locker is located."

The girls turned their schedule papers around, and Sofia looked at them carefully. Her expression changed when she saw she had at least three classes with each girl. She told them and then asked what locker number they had been assigned. "Cool, that's really close to mine. We don't have much time before first period, so we should get going."

Juila and Jena both turned and hugged their mother goodbye. They were eager to get started with school, but also sad to be separated from the mother they had just found. Sofia urged them to hurry, so they rushed their farewell and followed their new friend.

They turned down several hallways and arrived at their locker. Sofia showed them how the combination lock worked and they got to look inside a school locker for the first time. It seemed awfully small for two people to share.

Almost as if the students materialized from nowhere, the trio was surrounded by masses of kids walking in every direction. Jena wished they could have gotten to their first class before the crush of people kept them from being able to see how to get to the room. Thankfully, Sofia shared the same class, so she walked with them.

They milled through the room and found open seats before the final bell rang. Juila noticed that Sofia was sitting two seats ahead of her in the next row over. It seemed silly, but Juila was grateful to have at least one familiar face other than her own sister.

The teacher began lecturing on writing techniques, and Juila soon discovered the lesson was nearly identical to the class she had already completed on Tuala. She was glad at least this one class would not be too taxing on her time. Jena might have other ideas since she never did care for free-writing. Her twin much preferred to read other people's writing to making stuff up on her own.

When class let out, Sofia practically ran them to their class since she did not share it with them. They waited at the front of the room to be assigned their seats at the tall, black lab tables. Both of the girls were eager to find out what this class covered as they were fairly certain they did not have the equivalent on Tuala. The teacher walked backward and pulled a rolling a cart into the classroom containing jars with floating dead animals in them. Jena had to jump out of the way before the teacher bumped into her.

Just as the teacher moved past the twins, he stopped and said, "Oh, hello there, girls." He looked at both of them carefully and asked, "Are you twins?"

The girls nodded and said, "I'm Juila," and "I'm Jena," at the same time.

"I see," he stated and then said, "just pick any empty table. After I pass out the specimens for today, I'll be passing out the textbooks."

The girls thanked the teacher and wove their way around the desks and standing students until they got to their table. They pulled out the lab stools and sat down. Soon, the teacher deposited one of the jars onto their table as well as a tray of various metal implements. Jena leaned forward to peer into the yellowish liquid. She turned up her nose and whispered to Juila, "I think it's a frog."

"Yuck," Juila replied. "I wonder what we're going to do with it."

They had not been as quiet as they imagined since a young boy at the table in front of them turned around and announced, "You're going to cut it up and identify its parts." He grinned when he saw the looks of disgust on their faces. He noticed how pretty they both were and asked, "Hey, you're new here. Where did you transfer from?"

Juila was the first to regain her composure and replied politely, "South Africa."

The kid laughed and said, "Good one! Really, where did you come from?"

Jena answered with more authority, "We really did just come from South Africa where we've had all of our schooling, up until today."

The boy looked at her more seriously and said, "Wow, that's cool. I've never met anyone from Africa. I thought they were all supposed to be black there. You guys don't look black at all."

Now it was Juila's turn to laugh. The studying she had done on the internet paid off as she declared, "South Africa is mostly populated by white people who descended from Europe and England hundreds of years ago. You should look it up on the internet."

The class bell rang, and the teacher started to lecture about the different parts of the frog they were to identify before the end of the day's class. He passed out a worksheet with numbered arrows so they could write in their answers. As he went by the girl's table, he dropped off two rather large, hardbound books. He said, "We're working on chapter three right now. You'll find it will help you figure out the answers to the worksheet."

"Thank you," they replied in unison.

The teacher gave them another stare before he moved on to the next table to hand them the worksheet.

"You get to fish it out," Jena declared.

"Fine. You get to be the one to cut into it," Juila rebutted.

Jena wished she had offered to remove it from the container.

Juila unscrewed the lid to the jar and almost gagged when the smell of formaldehyde rose from the container. She looked around to see what the other kids were doing and then used the tongs to pull the stiff frog from the disgusting liquid. She immediately dropped it onto the desktop before replacing the lid on the jar. It lessened the smell, but with everyone in the room doing the same thing, it lingered like a disgusting funk around them all.

"You cut, and I'll mark the worksheet," Juila offered sweetly.

Jena replied, "Thanks." She picked up the scalpel she had seen the other kids use, and cut into the frog. Soon enough, her fascination with the different organs captured her attention and she no longer cared about the smell or the fact she was dissecting something which used to be alive.

The rest of the day went by along the same vein. At lunch, they sat with Sofia and a friend of hers, named Valentina, and then had one more class with Sofia before the day ended. As the last bell rang for the day, Jena and Juila wondered what they were supposed to do. They had never discussed how they were getting home. At their locker, they debated the problem between themselves, "Do you think we should call Mom and find out if she's coming to get us?"

"I don't know. I would have thought she'd have mentioned if she were coming to get us," Juila stated.

Sofia walked up to them and said, "Are you going to ride the bus home?"

"There's a bus that goes to our house?" Jena asked with a surprised expression.

Sofia could not help but giggle and said, "Almost all of the kids take a bus to get home. Where do you live? Maybe I can help you figure out which one gets you closest to your house and then you can walk the rest of the way from the stop."

Jena felt rather stupid with her first question about the bus. She nodded for Sofia to help them while Juila told her their address.

Sofia brightened and declared, "You only live a couple of blocks from me! Come on; we can all take the same bus." She began weaving her way expertly through the throngs of kids milling around. She walked through a gate in a chain-link fence and down the row of bright yellow busses. When she got to the one with the number fifty-seven she turned and said, "This is our bus. We take the same one home every day. Bus forty-eight comes around and picks us up in the morning at the same place fifty-seven drops us off." She mounted the three large steps and started walking down the aisle.

The girls looked at one another and then shrugged their shoulders as they decided. Jena declared under her breath, "We wanted the Earth experience." She followed Sofia's example and entered the bus.

Not to be left behind, Juila speedily followed. They found an empty seat near the back of the bus and sat together across from Sofia. The only other vehicle the girls had ridden in was the 4-Runner, so this was definitely something new. They had no idea vehicles could get so large. Still, more and more students filed into the bus until all of the seats were taken.

The driver shut the door and pulled forward along with the line of other busses. Jena stared out the window at the passing scenery while Juila struck up a lively conversation with Sofia.

Sofia asked, "I heard someone say you were from South Africa. Is it true?"

Juila nodded and said, "I guess you could call us immigrants then, too!"

"When did your family move here?" Sofia continued to question.

"Oh, they've lived here all along. It's just the two of us who were in boarding school in South Africa," Juila said. She really did not like lying to Sofia since she seemed like such a nice girl. "We just came home on July 17th," she said. She was proud she had remembered the name of the month correctly.

"Why didn't your parents go with you?"

"It's a long story, but the short version is that my dad is an engineer and has to travel a lot. My mom was in a really bad accident a long time ago, and she was in a coma for seven years."

"Oh, wow! She sure seemed fine when I met her at the open house," Sofia could hardly believe that such a nice woman could have been hurt badly enough to be in a coma for so long. It probably explained why she still looked so young, though.

"Yeah, we missed out on a lot, but we're finally a family again."

"What are your parents' names?"

"Amanda and Riccan Stel."

"Are you kidding? The Riccan Stel as in the NHRA drag racing Riccan Stel? The same man who volunteers his airplane and time for search and rescue missions?" Sofia's voice rose louder and louder with each question.

Several students were now turning around to see what the commotion was all about.

Juila blushed and replied, "I guess. He's just our dad." She did not know what NHRA drag racing was, but she knew he had participated in the telepod races in Tuala so she could well imagine he would also partake of a similar sport on Earth.

"That's so cool, Juila. My dad just loves to watch your dad on TV," Sofia kept talking excitedly.

The students who had turned around to listen were now whispering to their seatmates and then to the kids in front of them. Pretty soon the entire bus knew who Juila's dad was. She was not sure if she should be proud or embarrassed because everybody seemed to know of her father.

The bus made at least a dozen stops before Sofia announced the next stop was the one for them to exit. It seemed such a strange concept to drop kids off at the corner of the road. For some reason, it did not seem entirely safe. Yet, Sofia did not seem to think anything of it at all.

The girls let Sofia lead them down the aisle and off the bus. Once the bus had driven away, Sofia announced, "I'll walk you to your house since you're probably not very familiar with the neighborhoods yet." She took off down the sidewalk clearly expecting the girls to follow.

Jena and Juila were glad to have the escort since they had no idea where they were dropped off. Some landmarks seemed vaguely familiar, but they were eager to have the company along the way to keep them on the right track.

Sofia kept thinking to herself how exciting it must be to have a famous dad, but she decided to keep it to herself since it seemed to make her new friends slightly embarrassed. Instead, she changed the subject back to school and asked, "So how do you think your first day in an American school went? Was it easier or harder than what you're used to?"

"Some of the stuff we'd already taken, like the writing class. The biology class is totally new and pretty fascinating," Jena spoke up finally. She was furthest away from Sofia and had to look around her sister to talk as they walked.

"Oh, yuck. You guys are dissecting frogs, aren't you? I could smell it from two halls away. It's so disgusting. I still think it's weird that the teacher has you do it on your first day even though you haven't covered any of the subject yet," Sofia commented.

"I liked it," Jena muttered to herself and kept walking.

Juila had heard her sister and asked her own question of Sofia, "What have been your favorite subjects?"

"I really enjoy English, Health, and Math," she answered and then amended part of her answer, "although I really struggle trying to learn all of the parts of the body in Health."

"Oh that's really easy," Juila stated. "We already memorized every body part from our previous schooling. If you need any help with it, let us know, and we'll try to give you some tricks to make them easier to remember."

"That'd be awesome. Thanks. You know I'm going to take you up on the offer, right?"

"Yes, that's why I offered," Juila said seriously, not realizing Sofia was trying to be funny.

Sofia laughed anyway at just how strange the girls reacted to normal sayings. She could really get to like these girls. There was something new and refreshing about them. Even though they were stunningly gorgeous, it was almost as if they were completely unaware of it. They were very approachable, and that was what Sofia found so pleasant about them.

Juila had been reading Sofia's thoughts and became embarrassed by the praise. Naturally, she could not refute Sofia's ideas since she never actually said any of them out loud. This was another case where she should probably stop invading people's privacy and leave their minds alone. It was just so hard to not take a look when she was curious about the people of Earth.

They had been walking up one very long street for quite a while when Jena began to notice certain houses and landmarks which looked extremely familiar. Before she knew it, they were standing outside their gated driveway.

Sofia had driven by these houses many times, but she had never been able to see this particular house since it was not visible from the road. Wishing she could invite herself over, she refrained and instead said, "Well, now you know your way home. I guess I'll head over to mine."

Juila had not given up on the mind-reading yet and heard Sofia's yearning to come inside so, she asked, "Do you have time to visit for a bit? We can call your parents and let them know where you are."

Not wanting to seem too eager, Sofia smiled and said, "That would be great. Thanks."

CHAPTER 10

Amanda had dropped the kids off at school for their first day and immediately drove back home. She wanted to discuss some matters with Riccan while the girls were away. Most importantly, she wanted to know what Riccan's plans were for when he had to head back to work after this next week was over. Were they going to live apart for the week and then come back together for the weekends? She sincerely hoped that would not be the case, but she did not know how the girls were going to have the Earth experience if they all went back to Tuala.

She parked the truck back in the garage and walked to Riccan's office. She walked through the doorway knowing he would be in there only to discover the room was empty. Amanda shook her head and whispered, "Where are you?"

After walking through the living room and kitchen, she thought he might be out in the other garage with the telepod. He had been working on some new technology for the telepod, after all. She opened the garage door and was not surprised to see the room was completely empty. Without thinking twice, she walked confidently across the floor and put her hand up to where the entry pad would be located on the side of the cloaked telepod.

With her hand held out in front of her, she took step after hesitant step until she was past the spot where the telepod would normally be resting. It was at that moment she had to admit the telepod was not just cloaked for security, it really was gone from the garage. She laughed at how she must have looked, walking through the empty garage with her outstretched arm. Now she really did not know where Riccan had gone.

Maybe he's somehow testing the new software, she thought to herself. She went back into the house and fixed herself some breakfast, the old-fashioned way since she had not yet mastered the skill of creating it from the elemy. The power seemed to work easier on Tuala, so Amanda had decided to only practice the skills when she was in Tuala. Until she had a better handle on accessing the power, she would not frustrate herself by trying and failing, on Earth.

After the simple meal consisting of a bowl of cereal and some toast was ready, Amanda sat on a stool at the island and ate in silence. Her mind kept coming back to allowing the girls to stay on Earth while she was able to divide her time between the two worlds. If the girls were in school all day, there was nothing to keep her from working in Tuala during the day as well. Maybe she could work with Riccan again. She had adored her job during her dream. It might just work out.

She took another bite of food and chewed absently while her thoughts kept returning to her girls. It was still unbelievable that they were as old as they were. There was still so much she wanted to know about their lives which she would probably never know. Then there was the betrothal agreement with Elder Debbon's son. Now that she was back among the living, she should probably make an effort to meet the future family of her daughter's.

Speaking of family, she still needed to find a way to tell her own parents about the girls. Somehow it seemed to be the biggest hurdle she had yet to face. Even telling them she had gotten married, seemed simpler than explaining why her children were only nine years younger than she was. It actually scared her to even contemplate how that conversation would go. Her father would accept and believe whatever she told them, but her mother was always one to ask the hard questions.

Maybe her parents would actually end up being the key for her to continue her life in both worlds. When Riccan was growing up, he had lived with various relatives while attending school. Her daughters would love to get to know their Earth grandparents. Amanda was not even considering leaving her children for weeks or even days at a time, but she did want them to have a safe place to stay until they got home from work in Tuala.

She dipped her spoon back into the bowl and discovered she had finished eating. It seemed almost a waste of food to not even recall having eaten it. She smiled at herself and stood up from the stool. With the bowl in her hand, she turned to take it to the sink to clean it when she came face-to-face with a woman she had never before seen. The bowl immediately dropped from her hands, crashing into a million little pieces on the floor.

Amanda screeched a small startled scream as her hands flew to her mouth in surprise. "Who are you? And what are you doing in my house?"

The woman looked equally surprised and answered swiftly, "I'm Riccan's housekeeper. I come to clean every other Friday. Who, may I ask, are you?"

Amanda could not help but chuckle at how ridiculous the whole scene looked now and replied, "I'm Riccan's wife. I guess we still have a few things left to talk about." She held out her hand to the maid and introduced herself. "My name's Amanda. I'm sorry I screamed when I saw you."

"It's understandable, given the circumstances. I wasn't aware Riccan was even dating anybody, not to mention contemplating marriage. My name's Mary." She shook Amanda's hand as she spoke. She had hoped one day to introduce her daughter to the most eligible and handsome bachelor, and now it appeared she had waited too long. "Let me get this mess cleaned up," she said and turned to get the dustpan and broom from the cleaning closet.

Amanda felt terrible that her first meeting with a staff member also caused her more work. She realized Riccan had not been kidding about having staff and she was going to have to find out the schedules of all of the help so she would not be startled again by a stranger in or around the house. It would not help to hover while Mary cleaned up the mess, so she picked up the big pieces and her spoon and walked over to the sink. She threw the broken pieces in the garbage under the sink and then washed the spoon by hand, dried it, and put it away.

She was glad she had not tried to practice her crystal skills now since she could easily have been seen. Going into the secret room was definitely out of the question. There had to be something she could do until Riccan finally came home. She felt uncomfortable sitting around the house while Mary worked around her. Making up her mind, she grabbed her purse and went back to tell Mary she was leaving.

The drive to her parents' house was uneventful. She hoped her mother would still be on talking terms with her. They had not had any conversations since she had left their house after telling them she had gotten married. It felt like her whole life had changed all over again since that night. There had to be a way to convince her mother the truth about her girls. The trouble she kept running into was the age of the girls; it seemed to be an insurmountable obstacle.

She pulled into the semi-circular driveway and stopped outside the front door. Her parents had changed the front yard recently to make it easier to get in and out of the garage. She liked the change since it meant her parents were up for something new. Her news was definitely in the category of new.

The walk to the front door seemed to take forever. Amanda knew she was dragging her feet since she was not exactly sure what she would tell her mother about the girls. Then an idea struck her, and she realized the answer was simple. She took the last few steps eagerly and knocked on the front door.

Her mother answered right away, and a smile crossed her lips when she saw it was her youngest daughter. Everyone had always said Amanda looked the most like her and she tended to agree. Amanda, however, did not share her temperament; hers was totally that of her father.

"Come in, honey. What are you doing knocking? This is your house, too," she stood aside and gestured for Amanda to enter the house.

"I just didn't know how I'd be received since I dumped my big news on you the last time I was here," Amanda stated simply.

"Oh, honey, I was just surprised. You'll always be welcome in our home. We love you!" Diane hugged her daughter to emphasize her words. "Right now, I'm wondering why you're here alone. Where's your husband? Oh, that still seems weird to say!"

Amanda chuckled and said, "He had a few things to take care of with his vehicle. I thought I'd come over and talk to you about Riccan's family."

"Oh, has something gone wrong with them? Are they giving you a hard time, too?" Diane would be relieved if she weren't the only one to get mad at the sudden news of them getting married.

"No, no, it's nothing like that. They were thrilled to hear the news," Amanda replied easily. She missed her mother's hurt expression as she had looked down to try to decide how to go about the next part of her conversation with her mother.

"So, what's the problem with his family?" Diane prompted.

"Nothing's wrong, really. I just found out Riccan has two teenage girls and I thought you and Dad might want to get to know them, too. I know you already have grandchildren, but they are a part of my family, and I just wondered…" Amanda trailed off and looked across at her mother.

"We'd be thrilled to meet your step-daughters. When do you think you can bring them over? Or would you rather we come to Riccan's house? We've never even seen your new place. Maybe we can have a family gathering at your house. What do you think?" Diane was already planning what she would wear. She had an idea that Riccan had money, but she was not entirely sure.

Amanda smiled at her mother's enthusiasm and had to decide what scenario would work best. Maybe having the meeting at her new home would make it easier. At least her mother would be so impressed with the scale of the house that she might not notice the resemblance the twins had to herself. After all, the twins had blonde hair and blue eyes while she, herself, had brown for both.

"I'd like for us to do it as soon as possible. I'm not sure if tonight will work since I haven't even run the idea by Riccan, but for sure we'll get together this week. I'll call and let you know, okay?" Amanda wished she had thought of this before she took the girls to school. If they could get the introductions done tonight, then she would not have to worry about it any longer.

"We can be ready whenever you get it figured out. You know we don't plan much in the evenings anymore." Diane had started walking toward the living room so they could sit down and be more comfortable while they visited. She hoped Amanda would stay for a few hours so she could be certain her youngest child was truly happy.

Amanda sat down on the couch where she had spent so many afternoons during her recovery. She could still imagine her thick journal sitting open in her lap as the sun from the windows lit the pages containing all of her memories from while she was in the coma. One day, she had promised to share her journal entries with her mother. That day might soon be approaching if they could see the twins were actually her own children. It might be the only way to actually convince them of a version of the truth, as strange as it may seem.

CHAPTER 11

Riccan hardly had to spend any time at all writing the code for the computer program in his telepod. Once he had gotten started it almost seemed as though he had written it before. He considered if that were an actual possibility, but shook his head in dismissal and finished up.

Once the thumb drive contained the program, he swiftly took it out to the telepod. It was a simple matter to upload the file to the main system on the telepod. It helped that he had designed and built the telepod in the first place, so he knew every word of the existing program. Of course, he would not know if his newest program worked correctly unless he took it out and tested it.

He would have to figure out a way to test it without actually putting himself or anyone else in danger. He buckled himself into the pilot's seat and contemplated his options. The initial start-up procedures went smoothly, and all of the indicator lights on the dash remained green. He set a destination in the navigator and used the manual start switch to make the transfer. Riccan wanted to make sure he had the manual control in his hand in case something went wrong.

The location he had selected was known to be a place where birds liked to congregate. He figured if the program would avoid a collision with the avian species then it would definitely work with a larger obstacle. He did not like the idea of anything dying for the sake of testing the equipment, but he hoped the software would avoid any loss.

The telepod floated several inches off of the garage floor since the system had been activated. Now he pressed the button to telekinetically transfer his craft to the location he had selected. Everything went black, and his senses could no longer register anything during the three seconds it took to move through space to his target destination.

Normally, he would simply reappear, seemingly out of thin air. This time was different. He could begin to have the use of his senses when everything blacked out again, and again, and again. Riccan began to worry he had created a stutter in the program which would eventually be fatal. Just when he thought all was lost, he reappeared at his destination. He looked out the window and saw a flock of birds had just passed by where he had intended to emerge.

Riccan whooped a cheer out loud and pumped his fist in congratulations that his system had done exactly as he had designed it. He had not anticipated the need for multiple avoidances, but the system had performed perfectly. When he looked down on the console he saw the transfer had taken a full nine seconds: six seconds longer than a Tualan transfer, and three seconds longer than a transfer between Earth and Tuala.

He had spent enough time hovering in his present location, so he entered the coordinates to go to his parents' Residence in Tuala. He initiated the transfer and waited the six seconds to travel the vast distance. The telepod entered his destination and hovered above the immense lawn in the backyard of the Residence. Riccan speedily initiated the shutdown procedures and opened the main door.

While his parents were not expecting him, they always welcomed him. He walked briskly across the lawn and up the stairs to the back verandah. Nobody had come out to see him, so he entered the Residence through the glass double doors into the grand living room. Again, there was nobody around, and he continued to walk down the hall until he reached his father's private office. The door was open, and the room was empty.

Riccan had never been to their home without encountering at least a few house servants. He was starting to get worried something bad had happened. He began to run down the hall until he reached his mother's private office. It, too, was empty. This was not good. Something had gone wrong. Riccan full out ran to the kitchen. There was always somebody in the kitchen.

He burst through the swinging door and literally came face-to-face with Melba, the head maid of the household. He grabbed her shoulders to keep from running physically into her whole body with his own.

"Riccan! What's wrong?" Melba managed to gasp as she caught her breath from the surprise.

"I was going to ask you the same thing. How come the house is empty? Where are my parents?" Riccan asked in a rush.

Melba looked relieved to find no emergency really existed and answered calmly, "Your parents were invited to speak with Jehoban, so I gave the staff a much-needed day off."

Riccan could hardly believe what Melba told him. Jehoban did not simply request an audience of anybody. Something urgent must be happening. He had to find out what was going on and, right now, his best source of information stood right in front of him. He gestured for them to sit down so he could ask her some questions.

Melba accepted his invitation by moving over and easing herself down on one of the barstools. She had never seen Riccan so rattled, and she wondered what had happened to get him so worked up.

"Do you know what Jehoban wanted to talk to them about?" Riccan began after he took a deep breath.

"No, they didn't happen to share that particular detail with me. Would you care for some steena tea? You seem a little shaken," Melba offered. She always thought steena tea cured anything.

Riccan imagined Melba would make the tea by hand, so he gladly accepted. If she were distracted by cooking, then he might get more answers out of the usually close-mouthed servant.

To his great surprise, Melba actually created the two cups of tea using her crystal power. In all the anons he had known her, he had never seen her use her powers. He had begun to believe she did not actually possess the skill, as she had always said it was better to do it by hand.

Melba noticed his reaction and could almost read the thoughts as they passed through him. She smiled because she had managed to startle Riccan. He had always been one step ahead of her as he grew up. He must really be worried about something to put him off his normal game.

"Thanks," Riccan managed as he tried to cover his reaction. He picked up the cup and blew across the surface to avoid scalding his lips, or tongue, on the hot liquid. He cautiously sipped and closed his eyes at how perfectly Melba had brewed the herbs.

"What's going on, Riccan? Is there trouble coming?"

Riccan looked up into Melba's eyes and replied, "Not that I know of. I just came to speak with my parents about my telepod, but when I couldn't find a single person here, I thought something terrible must have happened."

Melba smiled as she realized everything was just a misunderstanding and began to relax. She picked up her hot tea and took a healthy sip. It could never be too hot for her. It was nice to have an excuse to be off of her feet. It had been a long time since she had visited with Riccan and right now seemed the perfect opportunity to find out more about his mysterious new wife. Rumors had been spreading among the staff, and she did not like not knowing the truth of things.

"How did you and Amanda meet?" Melba asked directly.

Melba was aware of his connection with Earth, so he did not have to worry about upsetting her with the knowledge of Amanda being from Earth. He answered, "I met her during a search and rescue mission back on Earth. She volunteered to go up with me in my airplane to be the spotter to find a missing boy."

"It sounds as though she shares your passion for helping people then," Melba said as she fished for more details.

"You might say so. Amanda has actually known me much longer than I've known her. She is a very special person. Jehoban said as much when He met with her last mesan," Riccan replied with more than a touch of pride in his wife's abilities.

"So I've gathered," Melba muttered as she took another sip of her tea.

"How long ago did my parents leave?"

"They received a special message first thing this morning before they even had breakfast. They left immediately. One mustn't make Jehoban wait, you know."

"Yes, I do know." He took another sip of the now pleasantly warm tea. He took another, larger sip and set his cup down. "I should get home then. It sounds as though we have no idea how long my parents will be gone. Amanda should be arriving home soon after dropping the kids off at school. Thank you for the tea, Melba." Riccan stood up and walked out of the kitchen without looking back.

Riccan rushed back through the hallway and then outside to his waiting telepod. There really was no reason to rush, but he could well imagine Melba keeping him trapped in the kitchen all day with the number of questions she was bound to have about Amanda and the girls. Besides, if he really needed to, he could time his trip back to Earth, so he would not have missed any time at all. Naturally, this would not be needed for the small amount of time he had been away.

The telepod functioned perfectly, and he returned to the garage on Earth. As was his habit, the telepod was in cloaked mode as it transferred into the tight space. He did not want to run the risk of the craft being seen by any of the people who worked in or around the house. This time, it was lucky he had used the cloaking feature since Mary was actually in the garage when he popped back into existence.

Mary could swear she could hear something as soon as she opened the garage door. She did not normally enter this garage because it gave her a bad feeling. That feeling was reinforced when she could feel the energy from the telepod being disbursed through the concrete space. There was nothing to be seen, but she could still feel something was not right. She hastily dumped the shards of the bowl into the trash bin and raced back into the house.

Riccan watched Mary as she looked around the garage with a scared expression. He was sorry to have made her afraid, but he was glad the cloaking device worked exactly as he had designed it. He waited a few seconds before he completed the shut-down procedure and opened the side door. Riccan exited the vehicle and palmed the door to close.

Instead of going back into the house via the garage door, Riccan went out the man door at the back of the garage. He decided he would stroll through the yard and enter the house through the living room doors. Mary would be less suspicious of him if he were only taking a walk rather than coming in from the garage she had just seen was empty.

Riccan began to whistle as he walked down the cobbled pathway. The day was beautiful, and he could imagine spending some time alone with his wife. He believed she had already returned home from taking the kids to school.

He chuckled at how mundane and ordinary his life had become in such a short time. In fact, he did not even think he had told Amanda about the household schedule. He made a mental note to tell her about the people who were expected and on what days so she would not be startled by any strangers.

Riccan walked into the living room from the glass doors in the back, still whistling. He saw Mary scrubbing the kitchen counters, and he called out, "Hello, Mary."

She whipped around, caught her breath, and said, "Hello, Mr. Stel. So you up and got married, did you?"

"So you met Amanda? Where is she?" Riccan was not surprised by Mary's direct speech. He was thankful she did not like to beat around the bush. She always spoke exactly what she was thinking.

"Yes, I met her. She left a bit ago saying she had an errand to run." Mary scrubbed the island in front of her now that she was turned around. She always wondered why the kitchen was so clean, especially with a bachelor in the house. She had imagined he must eat out a lot, but she often found homemade leftovers in the refrigerator.

"Okay, thanks. I'll be in my office if you need anything." Riccan retreated to his private space. He did not like the staff to think he was watching them work. Once he was seated at his desk, he decided he'd call Amanda on her cell phone. There were some things he wanted to talk to her about without the children home.

The phone rang twice in his ear before it went to voicemail. He left a message and then speculated what Amanda could be doing which would prevent her from answering the phone. He wished he could check her birth crystal like he could the children's. It would certainly simplify things if it were possible.

Riccan decided to do some more research on the gypsy families in France until he heard back from Amanda. He had no idea that almost an hour had passed, he was so engrossed in reading random articles on the internet. When his phone rang, it startled him.

"Hello," he answered.

"Hi, Riccan. It's me, Amanda," his wife said over the line.

Riccan laughed that Amanda really thought she would have to tell him who she was. He would know her voice anywhere. "I know who you are! Where are you?"

"I'm over at my mom's house. Hey, I wondered if we could invite my parents over to meet *your* daughters. I hoped we could do it tonight if you don't already have plans."

"Sure, tonight works great. The girls will certainly be excited," he answered easily. He pondered how Amanda had managed to tell her mom about the girls until he realized she had stressed the word 'your' when referring to the girls. Riccan smiled at Amanda's craftiness in getting her parents involved in the girls' lives without really telling them who they were. After all, they were his girls too.

"Great! I'll tell my mom right now. I think sometime around six o'clock would be good. I'm almost ready to head home, so I'll see you in about a half hour. I love you!"

"Sounds good. I love you, too. Drive carefully." He wished he could install anti-collision software on his wife's car so he would not have to worry about her getting into an automobile accident. She had already had enough bad things happen in her life. The line went dead, and he hung up the receiver.

Amanda was amazing at problem-solving. This matter with the children just proved it to him all over again. Only Amanda would think up such a good excuse for two teenage girls to suddenly be a part of their life. Now he was certain Amanda's parents would inquire about the twins' mother. He did not want to lie about it, but he was not sure how to answer it honestly. He would have to ask Amanda about it when she got home.

Just then Mary popped her head into the office doorway and said, "I'm finished for the day. I saw you had two guest rooms in use upstairs. Are they going to be used for a while?"

"Yes, my two daughters are going to be living here now," Riccan replied, feeling a sense of pride in claiming them as his own.

Mary's eyes grew wide, and she exclaimed, "I was not aware you had any children."

"Yes. Their names are Juila and Jena. They're fifteen years old and twins, obviously."

"Will wonders never cease?" Mary said as she shook her head. "First you suddenly get married, and now you have two girls. Your life has drastically changed since I was here last. I hope I can keep up with all of your changes."

Taking pity on her, he said, "There shouldn't be anything additional happening in the near future. We might have to talk about changing your schedule to once per week now that there are three women also living here. Thank you for your hard work, Mary. Have a great week."

"Thank you, Mr. Stel. Just let me know if you want me to change my schedule. I can begin when you give the word. I wish you the best of luck with your teenagers. They can be a handful on their best days!" She smiled to take the sting out of her words and backed away from the door. She began to wonder if she should ask for a raise if the girls turned out to be as messy as normal teenagers tended to be; her job might be getting considerably harder.

Riccan considered Mary's reaction to his sudden marriage and addition of his children. There might be several more people in his life who would have similar reactions. He should probably think about trying to let them know in a less startling way. He added it to the list of things to talk to Amanda about when she got home.

Now that they had the house to themselves, maybe they should spend some private time upstairs. They seemed to have many great conversations as they lay naked in each other's arms. The idea had great potential and managed to keep his mind quite occupied until he heard the garage door opening.

He smiled and stood up from his desk. The object of his desire was about to enter the house. He left his office and walked toward the far door. When the door opened just before he reached it, all thoughts or concerns left his head as the woman of his heart smiled at him and walked into his outstretched arms.

He would do anything for this beautiful woman. Right now, he was going to show her how much he loved her. He leaned down and passionately kissed her. Her response left him wanting more. He lifted her into his arms and carried her up the stairs to their bedroom. This was still their honeymoon, after all!

CHAPTER 12

Just as Riccan had imagined, they enjoyed one another's company greatly, and now they were relaxing in bed with one another. He stroked her arm and tried to imagine himself with anyone else and failed utterly. There were so many reasons for him to be thankful; Amanda had dreamt about him and sought him out. He had no idea how he had gotten so lucky, but he was not going to take any of it for granted.

"So," Riccan spoke softly, "what's this about the girls being mine now?" He smiled as he looked down on Amanda.

"It's the truth. They are yours," she smiled up at him and added, "I just didn't happen to mention that they are mine as well."

Riccan knew what Amanda had been doing. "I know you want your parents to meet them. Don't you think they'll see a resemblance to you though?"

"I'm actually hoping they do," Amanda admitted. "It would sure make life easier to handle if they actually knew the truth about everything. I think my dad would be okay with it all; it's just my mother who has a hard time adjusting to bizarre situations."

"This definitely fits that bill," Riccan agreed.

"I just feel so bad for all of the hardship I've put them through for so long. It's made even worse because I didn't even know they were hurting. I lived a whole other life while they were sitting at my bedside, praying for me to wake up. I stole seven years of their lives, Riccan. Can you understand how guilty that makes me feel?" Amanda closed her eyes when she felt the tears threaten.

"I do understand, Amanda. You'd do the same for your children, I'm sure. Your parents love you, and they'll love the twins as well. Right now they'll believe them to be my children alone, but eventually, we'll tell them the whole truth. One day, they'll be ready for it."

"I sincerely hope so," Amanda sighed. She had to sit up since the impending tears were making her nose stuff up. She breathed deeply and looked down at her husband. "I wouldn't change a thing, though. It's all worked out fine so far. We have our children, and we have each other. We can get through this together."

Riccan smiled at her optimism. He fervently hoped everything would turn out as she imagined. He decided to change the subject and asked, "How did the girls seem when you dropped them off at school?"

"They were clearly excited. Oh, and the girl who gave us the tour at the open house was waiting in the receptionist's lobby to help them navigate the school. Wasn't that nice of her?"

"Very," Riccan agreed. "Maybe she'll turn out to be a good friend for them."

"I hope so, she seems very nice," Amanda mused. Her mind returned to the dinner planned with her parents for that evening.

"I guess you met the housekeeper this morning," Riccan stated breaking into Amanda's thoughts.

"Oh, Riccan, that was just terrible. I discovered Mary standing right in the hallway when I finished my breakfast. She scared me half to death, causing me to drop my bowl, which shattered all over the floor. She had no idea who I was and, likewise, I didn't know who she was. It was so embarrassing."

"I'm sorry; it slipped my mind to tell you. She's the only staff member who comes into the house, and she only comes on every other Friday morning. I also have three groundskeepers who come once a week on Wednesday mornings. They take care of all of the grounds as well as the pool. When they come again, I'll be sure to introduce you to them so you won't have another scare like this morning."

"Speaking of this morning, where were you when I came home?" Amanda suddenly asked.

"Oh, I finished writing the anti-collision software for the telepod, and I wanted to try it out," he said offhandedly.

"Really? How do you go about testing something like that?" Amanda suddenly had dire visions of his telepod popping into existence in front of an airliner, and she shuddered.

"I went to a location which is known to have a large bird population. I figured it would be relatively safe if I accidentally impacted a few birds if the software didn't work."

"Safe for you, but what about the birds? Poor little guys," Amanda teased.

"Well luckily enough for them, the software performed perfectly. No animals were harmed in the testing of the equipment, and I successfully avoided all collisions," Riccan announced with pride in his accomplishment.

"Well good. We wouldn't want any lives to suffer for progress. I'm glad you developed the software so fast. It will be one less thing for me to worry about when we travel. Speaking of which," she paused to gather her thoughts. "What are we going to do when you have to go back to work?"

"I was thinking about that same thing today. I only have one more week off, and I still don't know. I want the girls to be able to live here and learn what they want to about Earth. But I have commitments to my job as well. It's a hard call to make. Do you have any suggestions?"

"I do have one suggestion, actually." Amanda leaned forward and ran her fingertips down his naked chest.

Riccan grabbed her hand and shivered at the way the light touch had made him feel. "I like the way you're thinking..."

"I was actually hoping you'd hire me to work for you again," Amanda smiled teasingly. She saw he was considering the idea and went on to say, "With the children in school all day, I can't see why we shouldn't work together in Tuala. We can come home in the evenings just like any other working parents."

"I actually like your idea a lot," Riccan said as he tried to imagine how he could turn it into a reality. "I can make a few inquiries on my patil later. Hopefully, we can get something worked out before I have to go back."

"Thank you, Riccan. I loved working for you before. I'm sure I won't have any trouble with it again."

He smiled at her belief in her dream reality. He mentally shrugged when he realized she had been so accurate in her dream about the new prophecy and also about her relationship with himself. Maybe she was right to believe it could work out so nicely.

"What would you like to serve for dinner tonight?" Riccan changed the subject to a more urgent matter.

"I have no idea. I was hoping you'd have a suggestion and possibly you'd fix it as well. I'm actually pretty miserable in the kitchen," Amanda confessed.

"I see. You waited until after we were married to tell me I was going to starve to death unless I continued to make the meals?" Riccan teased.

"You've done pretty well for yourself. I can see the evidence right here," she playfully pinched the taut skin on his tummy.

"Oh, really? For that, you're going to pay." Riccan rose up and loomed over the top of her. He swooped down and kissed her neck playfully until she began to squirm and giggle underneath his body. Conversation officially ended as they began kissing with renewed passion.

❧

ELDER DAVEN HAD NEVER RECEIVED a direct summons from Jehoban before, and he wondered why, at this point, he was being asked. Not to mention, his wife was also requested to attend the meeting. Something was definitely afoot, and he was wary of what it might mean for his family. As soon as he had opened and read the message, he called for Nena to get ready to travel.

Luckily for him, Nena seldom asked questions until after they were on their way to whatever emergency happened. She had known Daven long enough to trust him when he said they needed to leave immediately. Once they were in the telepod and she saw the location he had entered, she raised her eyebrows and continued to keep her own counsel until they were safely transported to their desired location.

They touched down on the landing grounds before Nena finally asked, "What's going on, Daven? Has something bad happened?"

Since he did not know himself, he honestly replied, "I don't have the first clue. We received a summons this morning to meet with Jehoban. I believe we'll find out shortly, however." He could see one of Jehoban's assistants walking toward their telepod. Daven tipped his head toward the window and said, "It looks as though our escort has arrived. Let's go find out what's going on, shall we?"

Nena smiled at Daven's attempt to remain calm and collected. She could tell he was just as curious as she was herself. She unfastened her seatbelt and stood up to leave the telepod first. She could feel her husband right on her heels.

Daven palmed the side door to close and turned around to meet the guide. As she approached closer, he discovered it was none other than Rasa, the cousin to his new grandchildren. For the first time, he could see the marked resemblance between the twins and Rasa. She had darker blonde hair, and she was older, but the resemblance was clear. He smiled and asked, "To what do we owe this great honor, Rasa?"

"Elder Daven, Nena," Rasa addressed the two of them formally as she stopped in front of them. "I haven't been told the reason for your requested visit, only that I'm to bring you to the meeting once you have arrived. Shall we?" She gestured for them to walk with her as she turned to go back the way she had come.

"Are there others in attendance?" Daven asked as he walked beside the petite woman.

"Yes," Rasa answered simply. She did not volunteer anything further.

Daven did not press her for any further information. He would simply have to remain patient, and soon all would be revealed. He squeezed his wife's hand as she remained strangely silent walking beside him along the garden pathways.

As many times as he had walked along these grounds, he never lost his wonder in their beauty. Jehoban had created a perfect paradise, and he had been honored to grow up among it all. He still remembered how disillusioned he had been when he first traveled away from Acaim. He had been surrounded by such beauty for his whole life; he had naturally assumed the whole world was equally as radiant.

They entered the palace through one of the many intricately carved, golden doors. Daven could feel an inner peace settle through himself. There was nothing to fear when Jehoban was near. He could feel His presence even without knowing exactly where He was in the palace.

The courtyard they passed through was new since he had last visited. He looked around with wonder at how perfectly serene the setting felt.

There were both potted and planted shrubs lining the spotless, polished pathway. Everywhere he looked he could see flowering plants in every shade making a kaleidoscope of color all around him. He took a deep breath and enjoyed the floral scents throughout the enormous courtyard.

They left the enclosure and entered an inner hallway. Rasa had set a pretty brisk pace, and Daven lengthened his stride to keep up. The assault on his senses continued as he found the windows had been replaced with fantastic stained glass scenes. Again, the light from outside shone through the colored glass to make a rainbow of colors dance through the hallway. He divided his attention between where they were going and above his head to try to figure out the theme of the windows.

Nena stopped Daven from running into Rasa who had stopped at an inner doorway. Daven felt himself almost blush when he realized he had almost run over the girl while he was gawking at Jehoban's latest creation. "Sorry," he mumbled as they stood at the closed doorway.

"It's understandable," Rasa smiled. She opened the door and instructed, "Go ahead and pick a seat. The rest of the guests will be here shortly."

Daven was surprised to find Elder Debbon was already seated at the grand table. His wife, Chelesa, was also present, which made Daven wonder what this meeting could really be all about. This was obviously not a meeting of the Elders since the wives were present. He could not imagine what could possibly be happening.

He pulled out a chair for his wife next to Chelesa's seat. He acknowledged Elder Debbon with a nod before he sat down in the chair beside his wife. Somehow it did not seem proper to converse until Jehoban began the meeting. It seemed Elder Debbon had felt the same way since he merely nodded in return.

A few minutes later the door opened to admit Bryon and Alena Kesh. They both walked silently and reverently through the room and selected seats next to Elder Debbon. Alena had been taught the skills to be a wise-woman by First Elder Debbon, so she felt most comfortable being near him.

They remained silent in the room. Jehoban did not appear to commence the meeting. There must be someone who was still expected. The people at the table seemed to be preoccupied with their own thoughts on the imminent meeting.

Again the door opened. This time Rasa entered the room ahead of her parents, Captain Ahn and Barla. The newest members seemed startled to see the people assembled in the room. Rasa motioned for her parents to take two of the remaining four seats for themselves.

Rasa broke the silence and stated, "Everyone is now present. I will request Jehoban to come to start the meeting." She closed her eyes and stood still as she used the power in her crystal to speak directly with Jehoban. She smiled slightly and then opened her eyes before she took one of the remaining chairs next to her mother. "Jehoban will be here momentarily," she announced unnecessarily.

As if her statement had created the truth, Jehoban appeared at the head of the table, directly in front of everybody. Chairs immediately scraped across the floor as everyone rushed to stand in the presence of the Creator. Jehoban smiled at His children and said, "Please be at ease. I have a very important matter to discuss with you all."

A rustle of activity followed Jehoban's greeting as the people resumed their seats and Jehoban also sat down. He turned to Elder Daven and asked, "Elder Daven, did you bring the prophecy as I requested of you?"

"Yes, my Lord," he replied as he fumbled to retrieve it from his tunic pocket.

"Please be so kind to read it aloud for everyone present to hear."

Daven placed the piece of paper on the table in front of him and cleared his throat before he began to read:

"From a far-away land
There will come in time
Intuition is in hand
Strange details known
With ties to the people.
From one of my own
There will be a sign.
Those born to this one
Will transform all.
Lucinden will pursue
Elders will fall
Then all made new."

He finished speaking, and the room remained silent as the people processed what they had just heard.

Jehoban spoke one ominous sentence. "The time has come."

Alena was the first to respond to Jehoban's simple statement. "How can we help? I'm assuming you have brought us all together because we will each have a part in fulfilling this prophecy."

Jehoban smiled and nodded as He said, "Alena, you are as quick and as wise as ever. Yes, you are correct. However, I'm not going to reveal to you what each of your roles will be in this. Your actions must be of your own free will."

Elder Debbon had closed his eyes to recite the words to himself. He was troubled by the fall of the Elders and asked, "May I ask if all the Elders will fall, or only ones who have been swayed by Lucinden?"

"I will let you decide how to answer your own question," Jehoban replied. "Look around this room and know the people who are present. Follow your hearts and this will turn out for the good and Lucinden will not have the final victory. Trust in yourselves and in the people here today. When you are approached to do your part, you will remember this day, and you will be ready."

"It sounds so simple," Barla said as she frowned with concern. She could not imagine how she had been included in this elite group of powerful people. This was turning out to be quite the mystery to solve. She only hoped she would be able to do her part in making the prophecy come to fruition.

For the first time since reading the new prophecy, Elder Daven spoke, "I believe the person who will come in time is my new daughter-in-law, Amanda. She married my son last mesan. She is from Earth and has intimate knowledge of every person in this room."

A chorus of disbelief rose around the table. Daven raised his hand and said, "Amanda has a unique ability. She was transported back in time and delivered a set of twins who also happen to be the biological children of my son. I will let her tell her own story, if and when you ever get the chance to meet her. I believe the twins will also play a role in these changes. Their names are Juila and Jena."

Barla gasped as she realized Elder Daven was speaking of the two girls she had raised until they were nearly six anons old. She began to see why she had been included in this extraordinary meeting. If those talented girls were the offspring of a woman from Earth, then she knew they were in for quite an adventure. She looked forward to meeting their mother and hopefully, the girls as well. Barla turned her gaze back to Jehoban and realized He was no longer in the room with them.

"Jehoban has left us," Barla announced. The room went silent as each person confirmed what Barla had stated.

Elder Debbon, as First of the Elders, took over the meeting. He stood up and said, "I think it's safe to assume we should keep the matters of this meeting private. If Jehoban had wanted more people to know about this prophecy, then He would have invited them to the meeting. Now that we know something is coming, and Jehoban has confirmed the time has come, then we must be willing and able to assist Amanda, Juila, or Jena whenever they come to us for help."

Debbon felt a sense of pride that his son was betrothed to one of the people who would bring this prophecy to pass. He had watched Jena grow up from a little girl, and he respected the power she possessed. Now it made sense why Jehoban had granted his request for the betrothal. It had not made sense at the time, but now he believed he understood. He was more likely to help someone he already knew than a perfect stranger.

Debbon had an idea and asked, "Can each person tell how you are acquainted with either of the children? I can start. My son is betrothed to Jena, and she has been coming to my Residence since she was six anons old."

Chelesa spoke for the first time and said, "Jena is a delightful girl. Her sister has also been to our home on several occasions. They both are extremely talented with their gifts. This has been adequately demonstrated by the fact Jehoban selected them to be taught by Him personally."

After Chelesa finished speaking, Barla immediately said, "I raised the girls from babyhood until they were taken to be taught by Jehoban. Ahn and I think of them as our own children."

Ahn nodded his head and added, "I arranged transportation of the babies for wise-woman Copa before they came to live with us."

"I was assisting Barla with her orphanage when Copa brought the babies to her," Alena added, "after they had developed a severe illness. I also had the honor of being present at their birth crystal ceremonies."

"I also was present at their crystal ceremonies, and I transported the infants to Elder Debbon for their healing and then back to Captain Ahn and Barla's house so they could be adopted into a loving home," Bryon added.

Rasa spoke for the first time saying, "I had the honor of watching over the girls for the past declan when Jehoban asked me to care for them when they came to Acaim for their teaching."

Debbon added, "I have seen into the girls' futures, and I believe Elder Daven is correct in that they will play a key role in the fulfillment of this prophecy. At the time, the revelations had not made sense, but now it is very clear. Elder Daven, we know your connection with the girls. Do you have anything you'd like to add?"

"Nothing at this time," Daven said as he looked over at his wife to see if she wanted to say anything. When she shook her head, he continued, "I will make copies of the prophecy and distribute them to each person present so you will have your own copy to keep safe. Jehoban has instructed us to follow our hearts in this matter. We must be vigilant in following His instructions."

Elder Debbon nodded his head and added, "We must keep in contact with one another to make sure we all know what is going on in order to make sure this matter proceeds as Jehoban has planned."

The people around the table fervently agreed. They were about to be involved in changing the future of their world.

CHAPTER 13

Sofia kept her mouth from dropping as she walked up the driveway
with the twins. The house was even grander than she had imagined it would be. The front had two-story columns, and the house
was symmetrical, even down to the two three-car garages on either side
of the house. She could only imagine how the inside would look
compared to the perfect landscaping on the outside.

The girls chatted away as they approached the front entrance. They
did not seem to notice Sofia's reaction to the property. Her own house
would almost fit in the circular driveway. She could not imagine living in
a house as large as this one. The girls had seemed so down-to-earth she
would never believe they were so rich.

Jena opened the front door and led the way up the stairs to their
rooms. Sofia walked behind Jena, and Juila brought up the rear. She
almost missed a step since she was looking out over the foyer with its
polished marble floors and grand chandelier. Finally, she could not
contain her amazement and stated, "This place is absolutely beautiful!"

Juila merely smiled. She had, once again, gone against her own edict to
keep her mind to herself. She had been reading Sofia's mind since they
had first entered the gated driveway. It had been fascinating to see the
house through someone else's eyes. Now she had a new appreciation for

the luxury she had simply taken for granted. Living on Acaim had accustomed her to being surrounded by beauty.

They walked into Jena's room since she was in the lead. Sofia looked around the spacious room and said, "This bedroom is fabulous. You are so lucky. You don't even have to share. And, oh, you have your own bathroom. Sweet!" She walked into the bathroom and strolled around the entire area. She ran her fingers along the cool, smooth granite sink top and turned to stare into the shower. It had more body spray nozzles on one wall than she had showerheads in her entire house.

She returned to the bedroom and shook her head; if only she could live the life of these girls for just one day.

"What do you think," Jena asked even though she had already read all of Sofia's thoughts for herself.

"I just love everything. The colors and designs are perfect. Is your room just the same, Juila?"

"It's similar, but mine is pink. The bathroom is identical," Juila answered. "Do you want to see it?"

"Sure!"

They trooped to the next room over, and Sofia was not sure which one she preferred. They both had their own touches which made them equally nice. "I love them both!" she declared finally.

The three girls laughed, and Jena said, "We should go downstairs and eat leftover pizza. Our parents should be home, too, if you want to meet them. Well, I guess you've technically already met our mom, but you can meet our dad if he's done with his project in the study."

Sofia could hardly believe she was actually going to meet Riccan. Her father was going to be so jealous. He would probably make her recount every detail of her meeting until she was thoroughly sick of his questions. She answered simply, "That would be great!"

They thudded down the stairs and raced toward the kitchen. The twins were absolutely starving. They were not used to the commotion they had been subjected to at the school, so their minds had been on high alert all day.

They pulled the pizza box from the refrigerator and then realized they would not be able to use their powers to heat it up. They had not yet learned how to use the microwave. They looked at one another, at a loss over what they were supposed to do. It would seem very strange, indeed, to tell their new friend they did not know how to use a microwave.

Unbeknownst to them, their mother had been monitoring their birth crystals. She could tell they were suddenly distressed and she came out of the study with Riccan right behind her. "Hello, girls. Hello, Sofia. It's nice to see you here. Do you all want some pizza? Here." She held out her hand and took the box from Juila. "Why don't you sit down at the island and I'll get this ready for you."

Juila and Jena were not sure how their mother had known they needed assistance right when they did, but they were vastly relieved to be rescued from a potentially embarrassing situation. Seeing her father standing nearby she took it upon herself to introduce their friend. "Dad, this is our new friend, Sofia. Sofia, this is our father, Riccan Stel."

Riccan held out his hand and took Sofia's small hand and shook it as he said, "I'm pleased to meet you. I also want to thank you for taking such good care of my girls both before and during their first day."

"It's no problem. That is part of my volunteer service. I enjoy getting to meet with new students," she demurred. She kept watching Amanda. Now that she knew of her seven-year ordeal in the coma, she was interested to see if she displayed any differences. She certainly looked only a few years older than her daughters. It was definitely strange.

Amanda listened to the conversation behind her as she got out several plates and placed two large pieces of pizza on each one. She put the first plate in the microwave and hit the pizza button. When the microwave beeped, she put the plate in front of Sofia first and then repeated the process for her girls' plates. She hoped the girls were paying attention so they would know how to use the microwave on their own.

"I have good news," Amanda announced as she set the last plate down in front of Juila. "My parents are going to come over for dinner tonight. Sofia, you're invited, too, if you want to stay for dinner." Amanda thought it would be rude not to invite her, but she secretly hoped she would decide to go home.

"Thank you for the offer, Mrs. Stel, but I have to get going home soon. I was just going to walk the girls to their gate, but then they invited me in. I was terribly curious to see the house, so I decided to come over." Sofia finally stopped herself from rambling. She had not meant to say so much, and now she was slightly embarrassed. To hide her confusion, she picked up the pizza and took her first bite.

"Well, we'll have to plan for another time then." Amanda smiled at their guest. She was thrilled it had worked out as she had planned. It would be hard to explain that the girls had never met their grandparents who only lived one town over from their house. She turned to Riccan and said, "Do you want to finish our research in the office?"

"What research?" Riccan asked.

Amanda walked around the island and winked at her husband.

"Oh," he amended lamely, "That research! Sure. Let's go."

Amanda stifled a chuckle as she reached her husband and grabbed hold of his arm and almost towed him back to the study. Once they were in the room, she said, "Really, Riccan! Sometimes you can be pretty dense."

"What did I do? I just wanted to visit with the girls. What's wrong with that?" he asked sincerely.

"When the girls have a friend over, the last thing they would want to do is hang out with their father. You've got a lot to learn about teenage girls," she teased.

"I guess so," he agreed. He sat down in his desk chair and asked, "So what would you like to research since we're now stuck in here until Sofia leaves apparently."

"Have you done any searches on the word 'samara'?" Amanda asked.

"No," he admitted. He opened his laptop computer and typed in the term. They did not have any luck except one obscure entry which said the old term for samara was key. Riccan thought that was an odd coincidence. Could the samaras be a key of some sort?

"That was a bust," Amanda said as she stretched her back out from leaning over the desk while she scanned the screen. "What have you found out about the gypsy families? Anything?"

"Not much. The Scamp family line seemed to die out around 1920. I haven't been able to trace anything beyond that time period."

"Huh," Amanda said as she tried to think of some other angle in which to look. "Has your dad found anything out on his end?"

"I haven't asked him lately. I went over there today," he began.

"You did? When? I thought you said you were testing your newest software," Amanda accused.

"I was, and then I went over to see them," he replied defensively.

"What were they up to?"

"I don't know. I went inside, and there wasn't a person there. I began to get very worried something bad had happened until I ran into Melba in the kitchen. Apparently," Riccan began and decided to sit back in his chair and cross his arms to continue the story and continued, "my parents got a request to meet with Jehoban before breakfast. They left right away and had not been back. Melba took the liberty of letting the entire staff have the day off since my parents were going to be gone."

"Did Melba know why Jehoban wanted to talk to them?" Amanda asked, full of curiosity.

"She didn't, but she was sure interested in sitting me down in the kitchen to ask all kinds of questions about you!" Riccan smiled at Amanda's grimace.

She was remembering the batch of soup she had forgotten to put into a bowl while Melba was watching. The whole experience with creating had been humiliating. She did not like it when she was not good at something, and then to have an audience witness your failure was even worse.

"I hope you kept your answers short," Amanda commented.

"I did. Hey, maybe we should have Melba make dinner for your folks tonight?" He suddenly brightened at the idea.

"Would she want to come here to prepare it, do you think?" Amanda was not so sure it was a very good idea if that were the case. She really did not want an audience for her parents to meet the children.

"It could be. She's always been asking to come see my house on Earth," he mused.

Amanda watched her husband's expression as he considered the possibilities for dinner.

"I could always call a restaurant to cater for us," he proposed.

"I think that's the best idea I've heard yet," Amanda smiled at Riccan's final suggestion.

Riccan leaned forward and tapped a few keystrokes on the computer and got a list of places which could cater at the last minute. Together, they picked an Italian themed dinner menu, and Riccan placed the order.

Amanda could hardly believe the cost of the food; however, Riccan did not even seem phased by the price. She was certainly going to have to get used to having a lot of money. Riccan never even seemed to consider money to be an issue, and his house and lifestyle showed it was not a problem.

A few minutes later, Juila popped her head around the doorframe and announced, "We're going to walk Sofia down to the end of the driveway. We'll be back in a minute." She smiled and immediately disappeared.

Amanda grinned at Riccan to see if he thought the new friendship of the girls' was cute. She saw his return grin and knew he was thinking the same thing. She stood up and asked, "Do you want to go sit in the living room. My guess is the girls are going to want to share their ideas about school when they return. It'll be much more comfortable out there than in here."

"You're so brilliant!" he stated as he shut his computer and stood up. He grabbed her hand, and they walked out of the office together. Riccan could almost feel the energy pulsing from Amanda's hand. Either she was excited to hear about her children's day, or she was nervous for the dinner party with her parents tonight. He hoped everything would go as she planned, but he secretly wished her parents could know the whole truth and ease his wife's mind.

They settled in their favorite spot on the living room couch. Amanda rested her back against her husband's side, and they waited for the girls to return. The front door opened and the twins laughed their way through the foyer and into the living room.

"How was your first day?" Amanda asked.

"It was great!" Juila replied. "Some of my classes are going to be interesting. We don't have anything like Biology class in Tuala. The American Government will also give me a good idea of how the political system is structured, at least here in America."

"How about your classes, Jena?" Amanda shifted her gaze to ask her other daughter.

"I have most of the same classes as Juila, and a couple with Sofia, which is really nice. I think I'm going to enjoy the English class the most," she answered and then considered the other classes before adding, "I think the Spanish class will be the most challenging. You know we only have English in Tuala, so I've never even considered learning another language."

"Of course," Juila added, "Whatever Jena learns I will also learn through her and vice versa. I wish we could have had all separate classes so we could have twice the amount of classes from which to gain knowledge." The sisters looked at one another, and both nodded in agreement.

Riccan smiled at their overachieving attitude. He appreciated their desire to learn everything, but they were going to have to pace themselves or find out people here on Earth did not appreciate being shown up in school.

Juila remembered what her mother had announced earlier and asked, "So what's this about your parents coming over for dinner tonight?" She had been under the impression that they would probably never get to meet their maternal grandparents because of the discrepancy of their own ages to their mother's. How do you explain such a thing to people from Earth who know nothing about an alternate universe right under their noses?

Amanda smiled and said, "I told my mom that you both were Riccan's children. I hated not being able to tell her that you're mine as well, but this is going to have to be the start. I want you to know them. If they happen to see you two resemble me, then we can go from there. I hope you two aren't upset with my small deception."

Together they shook their heads, and Jena said, "I hope we can eventually tell them the truth. It would be so much more fun to have family who lives nearby to go and visit regularly."

"I'd like that, too," Amanda agreed. "Your father has ordered Italian food for dinner. It should be here around 5:45 pm and your grandparents are supposed to be here around six. They've never been here before."

"Oh, this is so exciting. What should I wear?" Juila suddenly became nervous. She hoped her grandmother was the same as she remembered from her own mother's dreams when she was growing up. They had often talked about the dream where they had lived with their grandparents when they were two. Since they had only ever lived in Tuala, it seemed such a grand fantasy. Now it could possibly become a reality, and it was nerve-wracking.

"They're not that big on formalities. What you have on right now will be fine," Amanda tried to assure them.

"No, I want to wear something special. Maybe that pretty dress we picked out." Juila turned to Jena to see if she agreed. "Why don't we go upstairs and get it figured out together?"

Jena smiled at her sister's sudden desire to be fashionable. Naturally, she agreed, and the two of them practically skipped across the living room, foyer, and up the stairs.

Amanda got tired just watching all of their energy. She still had not recovered her full endurance since waking up from the coma, and she was glad to be resting on the couch with her husband. She wished her entire life could look like this exact moment. Relaxing together in perfect harmony seemed a pleasant fantasy. She sighed deeply and asked, "What do we need to do to get ready for the dinner tonight?"

"Nothing, really. Once the food arrives, then we can get out the serving trays. Until then, all we need to do is set the table for six," Riccan declared.

CHAPTER 14

Riccan reprogrammed the front gate to automatically open when a car pulled in front of it. He did not want to have to stand around waiting for the caterer to call in on the intercom nor did he want to make Amanda's parents feel even more uncomfortable by making them wait out front. He had asked Amanda if she had given specific instructions on where his driveway was located. Some people had a hard time finding the place for the first few times they came over.

Amanda smiled at Riccan's growing nervousness. She had always seen him so calm and collected. Somehow watching Riccan pace through the living room caused her to be able to relax as they waited for the time to pass by slowly.

They both jumped when the front doorbell rang. Riccan reached the door in record time and escorted the caterers into the kitchen. They took over from there and created plates of food which would be presentable for the table. Riccan left them to it, grateful they wanted to get it taken care of. He returned to his pacing in the living room.

The caterers left after only about ten minutes of preparation time. They had moved the meal into the dining room. All was in readiness except for the guests of honor.

Riccan looked at the clock on the microwave again and groaned because only two minutes had passed. He wished they had made the dinner plans for earlier now. Another thought struck him, and he suddenly asked, "Who will we say is the mother of the girls? I don't want to lie to your parents, and I'm sure you don't want to, either."

Amanda opened her mouth to reply when she was interrupted by the doorbell.

Riccan turned and looked at her with alarm.

"I guess we'll have to play it by ear," Amanda suggested as she got up from the couch and rushed to the front door. Riccan had not made a move to do so, and she did not want to leave them standing outside for too long.

She opened the tall front door and smiled broadly at her parents. They looked slightly in awe of the house, and she tried to make them feel more comfortable by asking, "Did you find the place okay?"

"Yes," Chris answered as he leaned forward to kiss his daughter on the cheek, "Your directions were perfect. We were expecting something a little smaller, though."

"Sorry to burst your expectations." Amanda giggled. "Please, come in!"

Amanda grabbed her mother's hand and led her inside. She hurriedly hugged her and asked, "Can I take your coat and purse?"

Her mother handed her the purse and then removed her jacket, all the while she was looking at how luxurious the house appeared on the inside. It relieved her to know her daughter had a nice place to live; they had gotten married so fast she did not know what to expect of Riccan's success. Not that it mattered a great deal to her, it was just comforting to know her youngest daughter would be well taken care of.

"Didn't you say Riccan was an engineer?" Diane leaned in and asked Amanda in a whisper. "I didn't think engineers made so much money."

Amanda restrained her laugh as she replied, "He has family money, too. This isn't all from his job."

Diane nodded seriously. "That makes more sense then. Oh, hello, Riccan. Thank you for having us over for dinner." She leaned around Amanda and stretched out her hand to shake Riccan's.

He laughed and moved closer to hug Diane. He said, "I think we're beyond handshakes now, don't you?"

Diane laughed and said, "You're probably right." She hugged him for a few seconds and then they parted. "You have a beautiful home, Riccan."

"Thank you. Just wait until you meet the girls. They should be coming downstairs soon," Riccan replied. He was also anxious for this meeting to go well.

As though his words foretold their actions, the girls appeared on the top landing of the stairs. They looked down on the guests and squealed with delight. Together, they raced down the steps and came to a halt right in front of Chris.

Chris had initially been startled by how swiftly the girls had appeared, but then he was even more startled when he looked down at their faces. They were blonde-haired, blue-eyed versions of his own daughter. He became very confused and asked, "Amanda, what's going on here?"

Amanda refrained from answering. She wanted her mother to come to the same conclusion.

Diane had seen the children come down the stairs, but she had not gotten a very good look at them yet. She took a couple of steps to be by her husband's side and had the same impression as Chris. Trying to be a bit more polite about it, Diane stretched out her hand toward Jena and said, "It's nice to meet you. My name's Diane. This is my husband, Chris."

Jena took her grandmother's hand and smiled broadly at her.

Diane felt an immediate connection with the girl as soon as their palms touched. It almost felt as if she had been shocked but in a more pleasant way. The girl introduced herself but made no indication of having felt the tingling in her palm. Something very strange was going on in this house, and she was going to get to the bottom of it soon. When Jena released her hand, she extended it toward Juila and felt the same sensation. Juila also introduced herself.

Chris turned to his wife and asked, "Do you see what I see?"

"Of course, Chris. We'd have to be blind not to. Now, let's not be rude," she said hastily. She turned to her daughter and said, "I hope we aren't too late for dinner."

"Nope, you're right on time. In fact, the meal is on the table already. Shall we go sit down?" Amanda answered as calmly as she was able.

Riccan said, "If you'll follow me, we can get started right away."

The group filed into the dining room, each selecting their own seat. Chris and Diane sat across the table from the twins. Amanda and Riccan sat across from one another at the heads of the table.

Chris could not seem to stop staring and noticing how much the girls looked like his own Amanda. It had to be a coincidence. The girls were clearly too old to be Amanda's children. Besides, he would have known if his daughter had had any kids. The resemblance was remarkable, though.

Diane had been thinking along the same lines. She had begun to believe Riccan had been attracted to their daughter because she probably looked quite similar to the children's mother. It made perfect sense when she thought of it that way. She would ask Riccan about the girls' mother and get to the bottom of the mystery.

Small talk was maintained throughout the meal. Chris and Diane asked Riccan more about his work. They talked about the classes the girls were taking in school. By the time the food was consumed, the talking had also drawn to a close.

Riccan suggested during the lull, "Shall we move our conversation to the living room where we can be more comfortable?"

Chairs scraped back against the floor as everyone got up from the table. Riccan led the way with Amanda entering the room last. This was the other part of the evening which Amanda had worried about. With no other distractions, she wondered if her parents would start to notice the similarities of the girls to herself.

Diane inspected the interior design as they walked from the dining room to the living room. Everything was finished superbly. There was not a single thing she would have done differently. When they entered the living room, Diane noticed the view looking out over the backyard. She immediately walked to the windows and stopped to admire the landscaping. "This place is absolutely stunning, Riccan. Do you maintain it all yourself?"

Riccan laughed and replied, "I'm afraid I'm not that talented nor do I possess enough patience. I have three landscapers who take care of it all for me."

"Can you send them over to my house?" Diane teased. She wished she had enough time to tame all of the plants which grew profusely in the perfect Floridian climate. She enjoyed working in her yard; she found it therapeutic in fact, but there was never enough time to make it perfect. This garden setting was inspiring.

"Let me know when and I'll send them over," Riccan replied since he had taken her statement literally.

Diane realized his mistake and attempted to backtrack by saying, "Oh,

I was just teasing. I enjoy working in my yard. I might even steal a few ideas from your patio if you don't mind."

"Not at all. We can take a walk outside if you would like," Riccan offered. It was seldom he was able to show the gardens to someone who truly appreciated the work which had gone into it.

"I would love that. Plus it would give the meal a chance to settle before we sit down," Diane replied.

Jena and Juila had been watching the exchange. They still did not know quite what to make of their grandmother, but they were certain their grandfather was a kindred spirit. His questions at dinner had made them more curious about what Earth could offer. He seemed inquisitive about almost everything. They wondered what he would say about where they were truly from. It would be fun to watch his expressions as he processed the ideas.

Chris decided to walk with the twins once they got outside. The more he heard them talk, the more convinced he became that they were somehow his daughter's children. Their mannerisms were identical to Amanda's at their age. He decided to ask them, "Where does your mother live?"

The girls clearly had not been expecting the question, and neither seemed inclined to answer. Something had to be said, so Jena finally spoke up, "She has been absent for most of our lives." She hoped that would be sufficient to discourage more questions. They underestimated Chris' curious nature.

"So is she much like Amanda?"

Again the girls looked at one another before Juila simply nodded her head. They did not want to have to lie to their grandfather, but they also did not want to be the ones to tell him the truth. One rule which was not broken was do not tell people from Earth who you really are. At least they believed this to be a hard and fast rule.

Chris continued by saying, "I think it's really strange how you two look just like Amanda did at your age. How old are you two?"

Juila could feel her heart start to beat faster as she answered, "Fifteen."

Chris shook his head and said, "You see, it just doesn't make sense. Amanda is clearly not old enough to be your mother, but then we have physical evidence to the contrary. How would you two explain something such as this?"

Jena smiled and answered honestly, "Timewarp. Definitely!"

Chris laughed along with her and said, "I'm starting to believe something like that must have happened. Is Amanda your birth mother?"

Another significant look passed between the girls. Jena said, "You should talk to your daughter about this." At the same time, Juila nodded her head in confirmation.

Chris took pity on the situation in which he had put the children and finally let up. He said, "Don't worry, I'll definitely be talking to Amanda about this. It feels like something pretty significant happened quite a while ago and I'm desperate to know just exactly what it was. Diane always told me curiosity killed the cat, but I think in this case, my curiosity will bring me two new grandchildren."

Juila desperately wanted to get out of this conversation and announced, "I'll go get Amanda for you!" She ran ahead and grabbed her mother's arm. She leaned close and whispered, "Grandpa has figured it out. Not all of the details, of course, but he's certain we are your children. Can we sit them down and tell him the truth?"

"I think we're going to have to do that. Do you want to go on ahead or do you want to join me?" Amanda asked as she turned around and walked back toward her father.

"I'll come with you." Juila was fairly buzzing with excitement.

When Amanda was facing her father, she said, "Let's go sit by the pool." She led the way while she considered how she was going to tell him the truth. Without having it all figured out, she sat on one of the pool chairs and looked at her father.

Chris sat sideways in the adjacent chair so he could face his daughter.

The girls pulled a third chair over, and both sat in it together facing their mother and grandfather. This was going to be an interesting conversation which they did not want to miss.

Without waiting for Amanda to start the conversation, Chris asked, "How is it these girls are yours, Amanda?"

"If I simply said they are, but that I can't share the details, would that be enough for you?" Amanda asked hopefully.

"No. I would like the whole truth. Unlike your mother, I'm willing to accept facts for what they are. Start talking," he stated matter-of-factly.

Amanda closed her eyes wishing he could accept a simple answer and yet knowing he would not be her father unless he were asking questions.

She decided to share a simplified version of the truth and said, "It all started when I went sailing with Neal. We got caught in an electrical storm, and it transported us to another world called Tuala." She stopped to see if her father believed her so far.

Since he did not react in any way other than staring at her, she continued, "I just recently discovered that not only was I transferred to the other world, but I was also pulled back in time by nine years. I was held captive and impregnated by a crazy leader of their community.

"Eventually, a woman took pity on me and tried to rescue me before the girls were born. I had already gone into labor, and the girls were swiftly delivered. The wise-woman, what we'd call a healer or maybe even a doctor, sent me back to Earth without the children. They were raised by my Aunt Barla as well as by Jehoban."

"Okay," Chris said and then looked away to try to absorb it all. "Now I understand why you wanted to keep your answer simple. Okay," he said again. "How long were you and Neal sailing before the storm?"

"Just over a week."

"How long were you being held captive in Tuala?"

"I'm not exactly sure, but Jehoban told me it was several mesans, that's what they call months there, before Elder Vargen had me impregnated. Then it was another eight mesans until the girls were born."

"And then the healer sent you back to Earth?"

"Yes."

"So that's why you were missing for a week? Was the healer not very good at transporting you back to Earth?"

"It's not something a wise-woman would normally do. She tried her best. She actually sent me forward in time. Imagine if she would have gotten it right and I would have been returned while I was ten on Earth. There would have been two of me then."

"That would get confusing, now, wouldn't it?" Chris chuckled. He thought about what else to ask and came up with, "Who is this Aunt Barla?"

"She is Mom's sister, Aunt Barbara. She was transferred to Tuala when everyone thought she had drowned. She's married and has two children of her own. She raised Jena and Juila until they were almost six. At that age, they were evaluated for their skills, and that's when they went to live with Jehoban." Even as Amanda was telling her father about the crystal skills, she regretted her choice of words. She knew her father would only have more questions.

"Who is Jehoban?"

"He's the Creator of the Universe. We call Him God," Amanda answered simply.

Chris raised his eyebrows at this latest revelation. Finally, he asked, "Amanda, do you believe this is true?"

"Yes. I've even met Him."

"Well, then, that's good enough for me," he replied and patted Amanda's knee. "You know I'm going to have a lot more questions, right?"

"I wouldn't expect anything less from you!" Amanda laughed.

Chris turned to the twins and said, "I guess that makes you two my biological grandchildren and I couldn't be happier!" He held out his arms for the girls to come and hug him. They leaned forward, and he wrapped his arms around them, and said, "Welcome to the family." He kissed each one on the top of the head, and he felt tears form in the corners of his eyes.

"How long have you known about the girls?" Chris asked as he kept his arms around the twins.

"I knew about them even while I was in the coma. It was only last month Jehoban told me they were older than I imagined. He told me about being abducted and held captive. He also let me know my children were with Him. I didn't know it at the time, but they were in the room listening to the whole story as He told it to me. Okay, I knew they were in the room, but I didn't know they were my children. I was expecting seven to nine-year-olds so I never even considered the possibility." Amanda was having a hard time explaining her thoughts coherently. Luckily, she knew her father would either understand or request clarification.

"Did you have a lot of memories from when you were in your coma?" Chris asked.

"Yes. I wrote it all down in my journal."

"I'd like to read your journal," her father said simply.

"I wouldn't mind it, but I have to tell you that the memories I had are not what really happened. It's hard to explain, but Jehoban has told me I'm to be involved in some sort of prophecy. I wrote it down at the end of my journal," she ended, not knowing what more to say. She was thankful she had spent time since her meeting with Jehoban to write down the history as Jehoban had told her it had happened.

"That's okay; I'd still like to read what you remember. Did you meet Riccan in your dream?" he asked as he suddenly realized it was what Amanda had meant about knowing him better than they thought when she had told them they had gotten married.

"Yes, I've known Riccan for a long time. It's just he doesn't remember what I do. All of the memories I had of him and his family are all true. He could not deny the things I knew about them all," she admitted.

"That's fascinating. Have you met his parents? Where do they live?"

"Well, that's where this gets complicated..." Amanda did not know if she should continue.

"I'm pretty good with complicated," Chris prompted.

Amanda had to laugh at that comment since it was so true. She decided to tell him the truth, "Riccan's parents are both from Tuala. We went to Pantano, where they live, and told them about our getting married and the new prophecy."

CHAPTER 15

"Okay, so you said the first time you went to Tuala was by accident in an electrical storm. Then the healer used her power to send you back to us. How did you and Riccan travel to Tuala to see his parents?"

"Oh, my," Amanda said and looked over at Jena and Juila. They were both smiling, on the verge of laughing actually, at the predicament into which she was getting herself.

"Come on, Amanda. You've told me this much. I can't imagine it would be so hard to explain," Chris complained.

"Okay, fine. We flew in Riccan's telepod," she said in a rush.

"Seriously? Is it here? Can I see it?" Chris looked around like it was parked in the yard somewhere.

Now Amanda could not help but laugh at her father's reaction. Naturally, he would want to see a bona fide spaceship. She sighed and said, "We keep it in the garage."

Chris stood up and said, "Let's go check it out!"

Amanda reached up and took hold of his hand, pulling him back down to his seat. "Dad, can't we take this one step at a time? Think about it. Mom doesn't know anything about this, and I doubt she'll take it all as well as you have. Read my journal. After you're done, we can talk about all of this some more."

"But I want to see the telepod," Chris practically begged. "What if Riccan leaves with it and then I'll never get the chance to see it?"

"We're not going anywhere, Dad." Amanda laughed at his sullen expression. Seeing he needed a little more convincing she said, "We just enrolled the girls in school. They want to have the Earth experience. We're going to be here at least until the end of the school year. You'll have plenty of time to see the telepod."

Chris had to be content with her answer. He had to admit if they just up and left the yard then Diane would start to ask questions which Amanda would feel compelled to answer. He was not sure how much of the truth Diane could handle. He would try to ease her into the idea about Amanda's past. It was going to take some time.

He turned his head to look at the girls and asked, "So what do you think of the Earth experience so far?"

"We think it's amazing. We have so much to learn!" Juila answered happily for both of the girls.

Chris laughed at her enthusiasm and said, "Yes, I bet you do!"

He was silent for a few minutes while he processed all of the details his daughter had shared and then asked, "You said the children were evaluated for their skills. What does that mean?"

"Shortly after a child of Tuala is born, they have what's called a birth crystal ceremony. They receive a necklace with colored crystals which they will wear for the rest of their lives. The crystal allows the people of Tuala to access the elemental energy of the earth to do things which would seem magical to us here on Earth."

"Can that magic also be performed on Earth?"

"Yes."

"Can I see the necklaces?"

Amanda was not sure if her children wanted to share theirs, so she hastily said, "I received one, too." She reached into the collar of her shirt and pulled the chain up until the pendant was resting in her hand.

Chris leaned forward and inspected the intricately woven chain which held an equally elaborate pendant from which a quarter-sized tree-shaped design and leaves of clear crystal was suspended. "How did you end up with one, Amanda?"

"I'm not exactly sure. I know how it happened from my dream, but I forgot to ask Jehoban how it happened in reality." Amanda realized she had yet another question for the Creator of the Universe. She could hardly believe she could contemplate taking His time to answer her silly questions. It should be enough simply having the necklace, but she had inherited her father's curiosity in knowing all the facts.

"Are you able to use your crystal to access this elemental energy?"

"Yes. The people of Tuala call it elemy for short," Amanda answered. She looked around swiftly and could see her mother was occupied with Riccan and then concentrated on pulling a sphere of energy out of her crystal. She let it hover for a few seconds before allowing it to melt back into the crystal.

Chris' eyes got big as he watched the ball come out of the crystal. He was not sure for what use the ball could be used, but it was impressive nonetheless. The fact his daughter had done it with her mind alone was equally remarkable. "What else can be done with the crystal and elemy?"

Juila piped in excitedly, "Anything! Jena and I have been studying for years to find out if there are any limits to what can be accomplished. So far we haven't found any."

Chris turned his attention to the girls and asked, "So you two are comfortable using your crystals? Are yours the same as your mother's?"

The girls shook their heads, and each pulled their chain to show their grandfather their individual crystals.

Chris leaned forward and could see the chains were all the same, but the colors of the crystals were vastly different. Jena's was so dark as to be almost black, whereas Juila's was a deep red color. Each stone had a brightness which almost made them appear as though they had been lit from within. He had not noticed it so much with Amanda's stone since it was perfectly clear and he had believed it was because the sun was shining outside.

Amanda had been watching her father intently and offered, "The stones are actually real gemstones. They are considered commonplace on Tuala so nobody would consider stealing them. Here on Earth, however, they would be very valuable. Jena's stones are real black diamonds. Juila's are rubies. Mine," she looked down on the beautiful crystals and continued, "are flawless diamonds."

"So what's to keep them from being stolen?" Chris was suddenly alarmed for the children possessing such wealth.

"The crystals have a power of their own in protecting the wearer from harm. The necklaces cannot be taken off of the children, even the children cannot remove them until they're eighteen," Amanda explained.

"That's a relief," Chris sighed. "You three are going to have to show me more of what the crystals can do when we have more time." He looked over at his wife, and added, "And more privacy."

Jena leaned forward and said, "I think that would be really fun. You'll be amazed at what we can do. Maybe we can teach Mom a few things, too?" She looked over at Amanda and received a smile and a nod.

"I'd like that, too," Amanda agreed.

Chris was growing more and more excited. These children had a wealth of information available, and he wanted to know everything they had experienced in Tuala. More than ever, he wanted to see the telepod and anything else related to this other world they had known all of their lives. He had always believed there was more than could be seen and now he had proof.

Amanda imagined she could see the wheels turning in her father's head. He had always been such a curious person, and this topic presented a whole new area for him to explore. "We're going to have to take this kind of slow, Dad. I'm still not sure how to let Mom know any of it. She's always been so skeptical of everything."

Looking over at his wife, Chris could not help but agree with Amanda's opinion of her mother. They were polar opposites in their interest in new technology. Diane only cared about it if it had a positive impact on her own life; otherwise, she could care less. Chris did not mind if an idea were simple or complex, he was intrigued by any invention. He wanted to take everything apart to see how it functioned and he would talk to anyone about a new idea.

They had to suspend their conversation as Riccan and Diane started to make their way toward them at the pool. The silence became awkward since they could not come up with an alternate conversation before the pair joined their group.

"This must have been an interesting conversation for it to cease when we came near," Diane commented as they stopped behind Amanda's chair.

Chris spoke up and said, "The girls were telling me stories of their childhood. They had just finished with one when you arrived."

Diane could tell there was more to the story than her husband was sharing, but she decided to let it go. She had not been able to get any information about the girls' mother from Riccan, and she was feeling rather frustrated. She said, "I think we should be heading home, Chris, I feel a headache coming on."

"Oh, Mom! Can I get something for you?" Amanda stood up with concern.

"No, I probably just need to get home and go to bed. I'll be fine shortly."

"I really loved having the two of you come over. We'll have to get together again soon," Riccan spoke to both of Amanda's parents.

"It was a fascinating evening," Chris said as he looked down at his grandchildren. He had stood up to stand by his wife's side. The only reason he looked forward to going home was because Amanda had said he could read her journal. He was certain there were many fascinating details to be discovered, even if not all of them would necessarily be true.

"I'm glad to hear that," Riccan replied with a meaningful look toward Amanda. He wondered what had transpired while he had been entertaining Diane. Once they left the house, he was certain to talk with his wife and children about what they had discussed in his absence.

Amanda looked away from Riccan and a small grin formed on her lips. She remembered her promise to her father and said, "If you'll excuse me, I have something to get upstairs for Dad."

She turned and rushed back into the house. She practically ran up the stairs and into her bedroom. Amanda walked around to the far side of the bed and kneeled to open the nightstand drawer where she kept her journal. It would raise too many questions for her to simply hand it to her father right in front of her mother, so she had to figure out a way to disguise it.

Suddenly an idea dawned on her. She took the back stairs down to the first floor and rushed into the library. There was a book on twentieth-century inventions she had seen earlier. After rapidly scanning the shelves, she located the book and pulled it off the ledge.

It was not a perfect fit, but the dust jacket from the book fit well enough on her journal as to pass an initial inspection. Besides, her mother would never look twice at a book of inventions. It was the perfect detail to keep her secret until her father could help her devise a way to tell her mom the truth.

Amanda hurried to go back outside but came to an abrupt halt as she found the group had moved into the living room on their way to the front door. She thrust the book forward and said, "Dad, here's the book on inventions I was telling you I had for you to read. I'm sure you'll enjoy it immensely."

Chris automatically took the book from Amanda's outstretched hand. He looked at her quizzically and then down on the cover of the book. He started to open it to see what she was talking about when she stopped him.

"Dad, you can't start reading it here! Mom wants to get going home. When you get to your office at home, you can read it in peace and quiet. I know how much you like learning about new things."

Finally, Chris realized Amanda had disguised the journal so her mother would not get suspicious; he mentally kicked himself for being so dense. He smiled and said, "I'll look forward to it. When I'm done with it, I'll bring it back to you. I'm sure such an interesting book would need to be put back into the collection."

"Dad, you're so silly! I love you. Enjoy the book." She leaned forward and kissed him on the cheek.

He put his arms around her and hugged her tightly. She was a fascinating child who had always entertained him. Now she was proposing a new adventure in which he would be included. He could not wait to get home.

Amanda stepped away from her father and put out her arms to hug her mother goodbye. She kissed her cheek and said, "I hope your head feels better soon. Thank you for coming to dinner."

"Thank you for inviting us. We had a lovely time," she said. She turned away from her daughter and addressed her newest grandchildren, "I'm happy to have met the two of you. I'm sure we'll have plenty of opportunities to get to know one another." Diane still did not know how to tell the two girls apart.

Part of her headache was trying to figure out the mystery of why the girls looked so similar to her daughter; eventually, she would figure it out. She would see what Chris had managed to ascertain while he had been talking with the girls and Amanda.

They returned to their car with a few more farewell waves, and finally, they were on their way home. The ride was silent. Each person was consumed with their own ideas of how the evening had gone.

After they pulled into their driveway, Chris asked, "Do you need me to get you any medicine for your headache?"

"No, honey. I think I'll just take a hot shower and then go to bed. Enjoy reading the book Amanda loaned to you," she said as she looked down at the boring-looking book. She would never understand how such things could continue to be of interest to him. She kissed him on the cheek and turned to head into their bedroom.

Chris walked into his office and shut the door. He normally left it open, but for this reading, he thought a little forewarning of any company would be wise. Once he sat down at the desk, he laid the book down in front of him. After only a moment's pause, he lifted the cover and held the book flat as he looked down at his daughter's distinctive print, the all-capital letters she had adopted since studying architecture in high school. This was her story.

After only a few minutes of reading, Chris no longer saw the printing. He was fully engrossed in the story she told. When she had given him the short version at her house he had never imagined so much could have happened to her while she was asleep in her coma. Now he realized she had lived a whole other life during their time of mourning.

He was so thankful Diane had insisted they keep her on life-support. What if he had gotten his way and Amanda had been allowed to slip away into death. At the time, he had believed it would be more merciful than letting her waste away for years; now he knew he had been so wrong. Guilt built up inside him, realizing he could have lost his daughter because of his impatience.

Circumstances could not have worked out any better; Amanda had everything restored to her life. She had the husband, literally of her dreams, and now she had her children back. Granted, her life was considerably more complicated than he had ever dreamt it could be for a child of his, but he was certain she would not change it for anything.

Page after page revealed more details about this new world. The complexity of the society fascinated Chris, making him wish he could meet these people who had influenced and helped his daughter along her journey. He felt a deep hatred for Petre and was thankful that man was beyond his reach.

Chris' curiosity was being satisfied on so many levels and yet there were still so many questions. *Why were Amanda's memories so different from what Jehoban had told her had happened? What was the purpose of this other world? Were there more worlds yet to be discovered and explored? How did his daughter fit into the whole scheme? Why did the Elder want to impregnate her? Who was the father of the twins? How did Riccan feel about this whole thing? Would I ever be able to visit Tuala?*

He turned the page and found the prophecy his daughter had told him about. He was curious to see how Amanda's theory about herself being involved actually played out as he read each of the lines. By the time he finished, he agreed with his daughter's assessment. Either she or her daughters were going to be involved further in the changes to come to both Earth and Tuala. He hoped they would all stay safe during the process.

There was not much he could do to try to stop them from their destiny, but he did have the ability to help them wherever he could. The first step would be to convince Diane of Amanda's past. He knew it was an uphill battle. He was willing to risk everything to help keep his daughter safe. If she weren't torn between secrecy and honesty, it would free her mind to worry about the bigger problems on her horizon.

As he read the last few entries, Chris had at least one answer to his numerous questions. Riccan was the biological father of the two girls. He was glad to know they were a family in every way. At least one thing had worked out right.

Chris closed the book and took a deep breath. His hand rested on the cover as he sat back in his chair and tried to imagine all of the trials his daughter had gone through. She must have been so scared and feeling so alone. He wished he would have insisted she talk to them sooner. He should have been there for her more. He would be there now.

RICCAN CLOSED the front door and turned around to confront his guilty-looking family. "What happened while I was distracting your mother? Don't try to deny anything either. I saw all of your heads together as you were having a deep discussion."

Amanda smiled and said, "I'd never try to deny it, honey. Let's sit down." Amanda told Riccan all about what she had discussed with her father. She continued to smile at how well her dad had taken the news.

Riccan patted her knee and said, "One down and one to go. Do you think your dad will work on your mom or is it still up to you?"

"I gave Dad my journal to read so he'd have an idea of what he's dealing with. He said he'd work on Mom. I know he's more optimistic about the outcome than I am."

Amanda grew silent as she recalled her conversation with her dad. Another thought came to mind, and she asked Riccan, "What were you and Mom talking about?"

It was his turn to wickedly smile as he said, "She was trying to get me to tell her about the mother of the children. She's convinced the woman must look very similar to you, Amanda. She thinks I married you so fast because you look like someone I lost."

"Did you correct her?" Amanda demanded.

"I tried, but I couldn't get a word in edgewise." Riccan raised his hands in defeat. "Your mom is very stubborn and determined. I'm starting to worry you inherited those traits from her." He tried to look terrified of the possibility but ended in laughing at Amanda's expression.

"I showed Dad a sphere of elemy from my necklace," Amanda suddenly announced.

"Really? What did he think?" Riccan was suddenly interested in Chris' reaction.

"Of course, he was fascinated. He's determined to see your telepod, and I'm sure he won't rest until he gets a ride in it," Amanda admitted.

"I don't have any problem showing him my pride and joy. We can make it a family affair if you want?" he teased and received exactly the reaction for which he had hoped.

"Oh, please, no!" Amanda sat back and shook her head. "You and Juila can have the honors of that conversation, but leave me out of it!"

"Okay, I promise to spirit your father away and leave you to entertaining your mom," Riccan relented.

"Hmm, how come I feel like you've let me out of the frying pan, but left me in the fire?" Amanda accused.

"Hey, you said you wanted to be left out of it. I'm just being the dutiful husband and doing as you asked," he raised his hands to show his innocence.

The evening seemed to be winding down, and the girls had homework to get done. They stood up and said, "We're going to head upstairs to work on homework and then go to bed. We love you." They took turns kissing each parent and then left the room.

Amanda and Riccan stayed silent as they watched their daughters leave the room. Not for a second did they believe the two of them were simply going to do homework. Without discussing it with one another, they both concentrated on their daughter's crystals. It seemed natural for Amanda to look in on Juila while Riccan gravitated more toward Jena.

The girls marched up the stairs and did not say a word to one another until they sat down on Jena's bed. Juila asked, "What do you think of Grandpa Chris?"

"I thought he was awesome. I'm so glad he believed our story. I think Mom is going to be so much happier with him helping, too." Jena leaned forward as she spoke quickly with her sister. They really did not even need to speak out loud, but they had realized as they were growing up that it made other people uncomfortable for them to just stare at one another silently as they conversed in their minds alone.

"Agreed! Did you hear what he was thinking?"

The girls giggled at the memory, and Jena added, "He had so many questions which he didn't ask. I'm not sure Mom knows what she got herself in for when she said they'd talk again after he read her journal!"

The laughter died down, and they were silent for a moment with their own thoughts. "Do you think we should ask him for help with our problem?" Juila suddenly asked.

"I don't know yet. I don't want to worry about that right now," she said as she stood up from the bed and picked up her backpack. She pulled out her Spanish textbook and said, "I need to study this Spanish if I plan on passing the class. I suggest you work on the Biology. We could both use some help on that subject!"

Juila wrinkled her nose at the thought of the disgusting class. She would be glad when the term was over, and she could take something more tasteful. Juila got up off of the bed and went to her own room. She got the Biology book out of her bag and threw it on her bed.

Amanda released her hold on Juila's crystal and reached out to touch Riccan on the arm. She waited for him to refocus his eyes on her own before she asked, "What problem do you think they have?"

"I don't know. One thing is for sure; I'm going to have to talk to them about reading people's thoughts. It's considered very rude, you know. I wouldn't have expected it from either of them. From the sounds of it, they make a regular practice of fishing into people's minds. It's just not done!" Riccan's voice was getting louder the longer he talked about it.

Amanda squeezed his arm and said, "Hush, Riccan. Do you want to let the girls know we were looking in on them? We need to figure out the right time to bring this up. We need to have a plan of our own. Besides, I already told them not to do it at school." While she did not like the idea of the girls' rude behavior, she was more concerned that they had a problem they did not feel comfortable sharing with either of them. She would have to work on building trust with them, apparently.

CHAPTER 16

Alena had a hard time concentrating on her patient load now that she had met with Jehoban personally. She could hardly believe she was going to be involved in something so important. When she had helped care for those twins so long ago, she never imagined it would change her own life, let alone the lives of everyone in Tuala.

She pushed away from the patil where she had been reviewing patient records. It was no use trying to work when her mind was clearly elsewhere. She got up from the desk and went into the kitchen.

She had not been paying attention to the time and walked into the hallway just as her children came bombarding through the front door. "Oh," she exclaimed rocking back on her heels to avoid a collision with Justan, her oldest son.

"Sorry, Mom," he said as he stopped in front of her. He leaned forward and gave her a quick hug and kiss.

"It's okay. You just startled me." She smiled across at him. He had grown so big this year, and she could now look him in the eyes. She could hardly believe he was in his fifth year of school. He had yet to decide what crystal electives he wanted to take in school. She fervently hoped he would look into healing.

Just behind Justan was his betrothed, Andera. She was such a lovely girl with her long, wavy, blonde hair and blue eyes. She looked so dainty next to Justan. They were the same age and also about to be choosing her new electives in school. She had already affirmed her intention to go into healing. Maybe her decision would prompt Justan to follow her.

Alena looked beyond the two youngsters and asked, "Where's Kyelon?" Her youngest son was usually pretty close to his older brother. He had a more sensitive nature and was easily teased by other kids. He had learned early on that being close to Justan kept the other kids away from him.

Justan answered, "He stopped off at Tana's house to see if she needed any help." The couple linked arms and continued on into the living room to begin their afternoon studies.

Alena usually liked to watch their progress in the crystal skills, some-times offering helpful hints for improvement. Today they seemed to want to be alone, so she walked to the kitchen instead. She had to look in the refrigerator to see what they would be having for dinner anyway. She had wanted to make foxl stew, but she could not remember if they had used the last of the vegetables. She might be making a last-minute trip to the market.

Alena could not believe Bryon had chosen to go into the office after their meeting ended. She would have liked to talk this matter over with him. Of course, she understood his responsibilities at Kirma Shipping and Receiving, but this matter seemed slightly more important.

Bryon had mentioned the idea of them getting together with Captain Ahn and Barla soon. Maybe he was onto a good idea with his suggestion. If the four of them worked together, then they might be able to figure out a way to be of more assistance to either the twins or their mother.

Captain Ahn and Barla had gone straight to their home after the meeting on Acaim. Even though it was a weekday and Ahn should have gone down to the dock, they needed to digest all of the things which had been revealed to them that day. They had asked Rasa to accompany them home, but she had declined as usual.

This was one time in particular where he would have wished she had come home. There were so many questions he had about Juila and Jena. His most vivid memories of the girls were when they were so young. He wanted to know what had happened with them in the past nine anons and what they thought about this new prophecy. Rasa had seemed reticent to even talk about the girls she had practically raised.

"Were you able to get any information about the twins from Rasa?" Ahn could not help but ask.

"Only that they've been reunited with their mom and they're now living on Earth," Barla replied.

"I wonder if Elder Debbon knows about that particular turn of events. If Jena left without his knowledge then there will certainly be a problem," Ahn declared.

"You know how I've felt about that betrothal since the moment I found out about it. I hope Jena gets to experience whatever she wants while she's on Earth. Elder Debbon has presumed too much on that girl already. She is way too good for his lousy son," Barla continued with her diatribe. Another thought struck her, and she asked, "Have you ever seen how Willian looks at Jena? He is obviously jealous of her talent. I think Jena would make a better Elder than Willian, regardless of the fact that Elder Debbon is First."

"You shouldn't talk that way, Barla," Ahn cautioned. "I know how you feel, but you never know who might be listening in to our conversations." He had noticed over the anons, on the few occasions when they had the opportunity to see Jena when she was visiting with Elder Debbon's family, the discord between the two betrothed children.

"I know, Ahn. I'm sorry. I just am so sick of the Elders thinking they deserve so much more just because of their position in society," she apologized. "Just think, Ahn, we were included in the same meeting as two of the Elders. We are going to help change the world."

"I hope it will be for the better," Ahn said quietly as he turned away.

CHELESA WAS NOT EXCITED about the prospect of her first-daughter being involved in this mess. She could not see any way to make this situation better. Her husband had kept his cool during the meeting, but he had seriously lost his cool on their trip home. She had taken over control of their telepod just to make sure they actually made it home.

It had been hard enough to keep Willian from being jealous of his betrothed; now she feared it would be impossible. She wished Willian put as much effort into his crystal studies as he did in being resentful of Jena's skills and the fact that she was selected to live on Acaim whereas he was not. Chelesa had never thought the day would come when she would rather have had her son taken away to live with Jehoban than keep him home for herself.

If the two kids had grown up together on Acaim then maybe Willian could have grown to love Jena. What she found so sad about the whole situation was that Jena truly was in love with Willian even with all of his harsh words and actions toward her. She was such a sweet girl. If there were a way to break the betrothal, she would have done it long ago.

She could hear her husband stomping down the hall toward her private study. Normally she was able to calm him with words of reason, however, this time she was in need of calming herself. This was bound to be a loud meeting. It was a good thing Willian had not yet returned from school to be present for the upcoming tirade.

The door to her office flung open, and Debbon stormed through the opening just in time to miss being hit by the door swinging shut after it bounced off the wall behind it. "Can you believe this?"

"No," Chelesa agreed with him. She was about to tell him to sit down before she realized he would be better off pacing, it would help him burn off some energy.

"I asked to see Jena before we left. Do you know what I was told?" Debbon planted his fists on her desk and leaned toward his wife. "She's no longer on Acaim."

"What? Where is she?" Chelesa was horrified by this news. How could she be kept safe if she were no longer on Acaim? There had to be some mistake.

"She's with her mother on Earth! On Earth, Chelesa! And her sister went with her, too!" He resumed his angry pacing as he tried to figure out what to do next.

"Her mother? Are you saying she went with Elder Daven's daughter-in-law?" she asked in confusion.

"Yes. What are we going to do about it? We have to maintain control over Jena if we are going to keep her interested in our son," Debbon stated. He had such hopes for Jena being the one with power when his son finally became eligible to be an Elder. He loved his son, but he had to admit Jena would make the better Elder out of the two of them.

For once, Chelesa felt a ray of hope shining on their family. If Jena were out of reach then maybe Willian would discover his own power instead of feeling the need to compete with Jena. If he had more confidence in his own ability, he would excel in his studies. Chelesa could not think of anything constructive to say so she kept her mouth shut. She felt certain Debbon would come up with his own plan.

NENA PONDERED her knowledge of the whole situation regarding her new daughter-in-law. She was glad they had been able to perform both the marriage service as well as the adoption ceremony. She felt better knowing both Riccan and Amanda were able to access their children's crystals to help keep them safe.

She was sitting in her office with her elbows resting on the desktop. Her head was being supported by her hands as she went over every detail she knew about the prophecy. Now that Jehoban had told them they were to be involved in the fulfillment of it, she felt an added responsibility in doing her part. Her mind was plagued by an elusive thought. There was something important she was missing. The more she tried to push the thought to the forefront of her mind the more her head began to ache.

"This is ridiculous," she said out loud, even though she was the only one in the room. She pushed herself up from the desk and decided to go take a walk. Maybe the refreshing air outside would help her to recall the missing piece to the puzzle.

As she left her office, Nena did not encounter any house staff while walking through the empty halls and grand living room where she opened the glass door to go out to the terrace. The sun shone brightly, which made her squint as she left the dim interior of the house. She continued across the stone terrace and down the stairs to the great lawn. The tops of the trees were blowing wildly in a breeze which could only be felt up high since the air was calm and still where Nena was walking.

The prophecy had stated the Elders would fall. She had to make sure this part of the future would not affect her husband's position. He was so good at his job, and the people adored him. It would be nice to discuss this matter with Daven, but he was resolving an issue with some of his constituents.

If she had to predict which Elder would fall, she would guess Elder Vargen and his supporters. His assault against the people of Earth would surely anger Jehoban. She hated even thinking that way against an Elder, but he had brought it on himself by holding people prisoner. She was certain they did not even know the extent to which he went to extract knowledge from people. Now they had proof the Elder had drugged their own son to take his sperm. How much lower could an Elder get than to do something so dastardly?

She had to leave that line of thinking, or she would never get anywhere. Nena could feel her blood pressure rising just thinking about how her son had been taken advantage of in the name of progress for Elder Vargen. She closed her eyes and took a deep breath. She counted slowly to ten as she released the breath out of her nose. Her anger had somewhat simmered, and she opened her eyes and once again appreciated the beauty around her.

Maybe she should contact the wise-woman, Copa, to see if she knew more about the things Elder Vargen was involved with. If she had helped Amanda escape all of those anons ago, then she might be willing to work against Elder Vargen's continued research in Earth technology. It was not much, but it was something into which to check.

She wished she could have spent more time with both Jena and Juila. The extra twelve days they had spent with them had been a blessing; however, the time had slipped by so fast. Because the girls had been students of Jehoban, she knew they had displayed remarkable talent with their crystal skills. She would like to talk to them and find out where their particular strengths lay. If she knew that information, then she might be able to figure out what their possible role in the fulfillment of the prophecy would be.

Maybe she and Daven should plan a trip to Earth. It had been over a declan since their last visit. If they stayed at Riccan's house, then they would have ample opportunity to get to know the children and Amanda better. Even as the thought was forming, Nena knew it was a terrible idea. Her son was still on his honeymoon, and he would certainly not appreciate having his parents underfoot while he was amorous with his wife.

The walk had done the trick of clearing her head of her negative thoughts. She turned around and retraced her steps through the gardens. She would go back to her patil and continue researching any angle for the prophecy. Maybe Riccan was on the right track in trying to locate all of the samaras.

If she could locate some on her own, then Riccan would have fewer to search out. She smiled as she imagined herself finding the remaining eleven and offering them up to Riccan. Nena had never understood his deep-seated desire to locate them all, but now she wondered if it were his part in the fulfillment of the prophecy. Jehoban had told them to follow their hearts. Riccan's heart was set on locating all thirteen crystal skulls. The idea definitely had possibilities. Maybe.

CHAPTER 17

Sofia saw the girls walking down the hallway heading toward their fifth-period class. She rushed over to talk to them with a huge smile on her face and said, "Guess what I got?"

The two stared back at her and wondered what could be happening to get Sofia so excited. Since they had no idea, Jena was the first to ask, "What?"

Sofia held up a small plastic card with her picture on it and smiled even brighter. "Can you believe it?" she said.

The girls had no idea what the card signified and merely smiled politely because of their friend's obvious happiness. "What is it?" Juila asked.

Sofia's smiled dimmed slightly at Juila's question before she declared, "It's my driver's license! Isn't it awesome?"

Still, the girls were at a loss and shook their heads with confusion.

Now Sofia's smile disappeared completely as she demanded, "Don't they drive in South Africa? It's not like it's a different planet! Geez. Here I thought you two would be more excited."

Jena and Juila both burst out laughing at Sofia's statement about it being a different planet, and Juila stated, "You have no idea how different it is!" Juila spent a moment searching Sofia's mind for the significance of the driver's license and realized it was a very important thing for a sixteen-year-old to obtain one, so they could drive a vehicle without a parent in the car. She had noticed Sofia's absence from their Algebra class; she had been down at the DMV getting her license. She then said, "That's really cool, Sofia. Do you have a car to drive?"

Relief showed on Sofia's face as the girls finally seemed to understand what she was showing them. She answered, "Yes. My parents bought me a used Chevy Sprint. It's kind of ugly, but I love it!"

Jena smiled and said, "You'll have to show it to us sometime."

"How about after school? I can give you a ride home so we won't have to take the bus."

"Okay," the two girls replied in unison. The warning bell rang for them to get to their classes and they parted ways.

Without speaking out loud, Jena asked her sister, *Did you know about this before?*

If I did, do you think that would have been so awkward? Juila scowled at her sister.

I wonder if we can get a driver's license, too.

It seems the only criteria is that you be sixteen. Since our birthday is in a couple of mesans, we should ask our parents about it when we get home.

Agreed! Jena was overjoyed at the prospect of exploring Earth without any adult supervision. It seemed an extremely daring and fun thing to do.

Juila tilted her head and wondered why her sister would suddenly want to feel daring and fun. It was normally Juila's role to be both.

I can be, too, Jena defended herself.

Ha, Juila replied. They wound through the rows of chairs until they reached the back of the room and sat down in their English class.

Jena's feelings were hurt, and she turned her body away from her sister as if it would do any good. Their shared minds kept them closer than any sisters ever could be. Jena continued to stew over her sister's opinion of her stuffy behavior. Before the class was half over, she had to admit there was some merit to Juila's opinion. She imagined the fact she was betrothed had changed her outlook on life.

That's for sure, Juila suddenly piped in.

Shut up. This is my revelation, Jena defended. After a few more minutes of futile thoughts, Jena relented and asked, *What would you suggest I do?*

Act more like a teenager and less like an old married woman! Juila did not hesitate to reply.

I don't have much choice in the matter, now, do I? I'm going to marry Willian as soon as my schooling is done, Jena declared.

So decide to go to post-study. You can delay the marriage until Willian grows up more and becomes less jealous of you, or maybe he'll find someone else he'd rather marry!

Juila! How can you even suggest such a thing? I'd never break the betrothal; it was sanctioned by Jehoban Himself. I'd bring disgrace to both of our families if I acted as you are suggesting. Jena turned her head to stare at her sister to see if she were serious or just trying to get a reaction out of her. Jena's eyes got wider as she realized her sister was deadly serious. *No, Juila, I won't do it*, she said again, this time with less conviction.

The class bell rang and startled Jena out of her thoughts. She was thankful Juila had been paying attention in class so she would not have missed the lecture. Never before had she even considered being with anyone other than Willian. From the moment she had met him, she had been smitten by the brooding dark look of the serious youngster.

When she had smiled at him when they first met, he seemed to light up inside. He had eagerly partnered with her at school. Normally she would have simply picked Juila as her partner, but the teacher had said they needed to partner with someone they were not related to in the class. Willian had a brilliant mind, and he had shown off quite a bit during their crystal skills lessons. Well, Jena had to admit to herself, he had at first. Over time he had more and more often deferred to her own knowledge rather than his own. Now Jena wondered if Juila could be right about his jealousy. It seemed silly for him to be envious of her skills when he possessed nearly as much talent on his own. Maybe she would never truly understand boys. This was more complicated than she had originally believed.

After their last class let out, they walked with Sofia out to the parking lot. Jena looked behind them at the rows of busses and hoped they were doing the right thing. After all, Sofia had only received her driver's license that day. What if she did not really know how to get them home safely?

Juila turned and frowned at Jena and said, *Point proven! You are a fuddy-duddy.*

Shut up, she replied and started walking faster so she would not have to see Juila's smug reaction even if she could clearly hear it in her head.

Sofia was oblivious to the mental conversation passing between the two girls. Her sole focus was on getting to drive. She was eager to show her car off to Jena and Juila. "Ta-da," she said as she reached the side of an ugly green car and held out her hands to show off the vehicle.

"This is so cool, Sofia," Juila enthused even though she agreed with Sofia's original statement that the car was not great to look at.

Sofia unlocked her door with the key and opened it up. She reached in and hit the power lock button even as she said, "Get in on the other side. We should hurry if we're going to beat the busses out of here. I'd hate to have to stop at every other block all the way home."

The girls skipped around to the other door, and Jena automatically took the back seat. Juila sat up front and fastened the seat belt. *At least the car smells fine inside*, she thought to herself. Jena chuckled softly in the back seat. Juila looked around the interior and noticed it was different than the truck her mother usually drove them around in.

Sofia turned on the ignition and pushed her foot down on the clutch as she shifted the manual gear to put it into reverse. She slowly added gas as she released the clutch and promptly killed the engine. "Oops," she said nervously as she returned her feet to the brake and clutch before restarting the ignition.

Juila started to think Jena may have been right about Sofia's ability being slightly lower than what would be considered safe. She did not even have to turn around to see Jena's smug expression.

The car moved out of the parking space, and Sofia shifted the car into first gear. They lurched forward a couple of times before she added enough gas and then they were moving into the line of traffic trying to leave the school. After several minutes of not-so-great driving, they turned onto the main road where Sofia was able to shift into both second and then third gears which handled much more smoothly than first.

At the first traffic light, Sofia flipped on the radio and began singing to one of her favorite songs. Juila wondered if Sofia should have any type of distractions since she did not seem to know how to handle the car very well yet. The light turned green, and they lurched and stumbled forward until they shifted into second gear and the traveling smoothed out again.

Eventually, they reached the gate outside of the Stel residence. Juila got out of the car and entered the manual code to open the security gate and returned to the passenger seat. There had been several moments where she had wished they had taken the bus, but one look at how happy

Sofia appeared behind the wheel, she decided they would have to trust Sofia would better with more practice. Besides, if the twins were in the car with her, their crystals would help to keep them all safe from harm.

Sofia pulled to a stop in the circular driveway at the front door. She left the engine running and asked, "Do you want me to pick you up for school tomorrow?"

"Sure," Juila answered brightly.

Jena remained silent until after she got out of the back seat. "Drive careful," she said as she leaned down to speak to their friend across the car. She closed the door and sighed in relief now that the terrible ride was over. There had been at least two occasions she was sure their crystals had intervened in an impending accident. She hoped Sofia would be so lucky when she was by herself.

They watched Sofia lurch her way around the circular driveway before she found another gear and sped around the corner and out of sight. "That was terrifying," the girls said in unison and then burst out laughing. They turned and walked to go inside the house.

They found their parents sitting in the living room.

"How was your day?" Riccan asked with an eager expression.

"Fine, until the ride home," Jena said solemnly.

"Did you have trouble on the bus?" Amanda asked.

"We didn't take the bus. Sofia got her driver's license today, so she drove us home," Jena continued.

Juila nodded agreement and added, "She's the worst driver ever! I swear the only thing which kept us from getting into at least two accidents were our crystals."

Amanda frowned at this news. She did not like thinking her daughters were in any danger.

"And the worst thing is, Sofia is picking us up tomorrow to take us to school," Jena finished with a sigh as she dropped herself down onto the couch.

"Oh, my," Amanda said as she looked at Riccan to see if he had any suggestions.

Riccan shrugged his shoulders indicating he could not help.

"Should we call Sofia and tell her we'd like her to practice more on her own before she drives our girls anywhere?" Amanda asked.

"Mom, it would hurt her feelings. We can't do that. Besides, I think we are the only people who can keep her safe," Jena declared.

Riccan finally spoke, "Jena's right. The girls won't be in any danger. Sofia will be better off with them in her car. What made her driving so bad?"

"I think it might be her car. It kept lurching forward and dying," Juila declared.

Riccan started to laugh at his daughter's description and then asked, "Did she have a lever between the seats she kept moving around?"

"Yes! What was it?" Juila asked.

"It's called a stick-shift which manually changes the gears in the transmission so the car can travel at different speeds. It sounds as though Sofia needs to get a better feel between the clutch, which is the far left pedal on the floor, and the gas, which is the pedal furthest to the right. You have to have a perfect balance between the two or else the car won't run smoothly."

"That's an understatement," Jena murmured.

Everyone burst into laughter at Jena's comment.

Riccan continued, "I promise she'll get better. A manual transmission takes a bit of time to get used to, but she'll learn."

Juila brightened and asked, "Can we get our own driver's licenses?"

Amanda groaned. She should have seen this coming. The girls were the right age to be thinking about such a thing. Somehow, she had imagined them staying dependent on their parents for their mobility. Amanda liked her time alone with the girls in the car.

"Sure," Riccan answered for both of them. He could understand Amanda's hesitance, but the girls were here to experience everything Earth had to offer. Driving was definitely a skill to know. "I can start giving you lessons in the driveway after dinner. All of our vehicles are automatic transmissions which means you only have to learn two pedals on the floor; one pedal to go faster and the other to stop or slow down."

"That sounds safer. Why wouldn't Sofia's parents get her that other kind of a car?" Jena asked.

"A lot of people think young people should learn in Sofia's kind of car so they're able to drive anything in any situation. It's a good practice, but we don't need you girls learning that just now. I hope you don't mind,"

Riccan said as he looked closely at his daughters to judge their opinion on the matter.

"I think we have plenty of other things to learn that we don't need to be burdened with a manual transmission," Juila declared.

"Great, then we agree." Riccan slapped his hand on his knee. Riccan changed the subject and asked, "Would either of you like to test out a theory of mine with the samaras?"

All three girls looked at Riccan with a questioning expression.

"What theory?" Amanda asked cautiously.

"Remember the aura's I saw on them?"

"Yes," Amanda answered slowly.

"I think they might mean something. I want the girls to have a look and tell me what they think about it," he answered simply. He did not want to say too much because he wanted their own opinions.

Juila was the first to stand up. She had been thinking about the crystals as well, but she had not wanted to go into the room alone. She led the way into the library and stood to the side as her father unlatched the secret door.

Riccan walked into the room behind the bookcase and stopped only two steps into the room. He held out his arm to keep the others from entering any further. "Stay right here and let me know what you feel?"

The girls did as asked and concentrated on the energy they could easily sense emanating from the two samaras. Jena took an involuntary step further into the room. She gasped and said, "It seems like one of them is calling to me. Do any of you notice anything?"

Amanda could feel her heart start to race. She could sense the energy of the two skulls, but it did not appear any different to her. She shook her head and found herself saying, "Follow your heart." Even as it came out of her mouth, she wished she could take it back. What if the samaras were evil and only wanted to harm her girls. She stayed silent and watched as her two girls slowly advanced on the bookcase containing the two niches where the stones resided.

Riccan reached over and took Amanda's damp hand in his own. He felt the same nervous energy as his wife. There had been a nagging feeling Riccan had been ignoring. He was about to find out if his theory were true.

CHAPTER 18

Jena slowly reached up and pulled the newest samara from its resting place. She looked as though she were radiating with the pulsing energy of the stone. She turned and said, "It's beautiful."

Juila had seen her sister draw out the stone and saw the same visions which the skull had shown to Jena. Finally, unable to stop herself, she reached up and touched Riccan's original samara. Just as Jena had felt a completion of her soul, Juila felt the same thing. It was almost as if the stone were an extension of her own thoughts and abilities. Except the stone seemed to draw more out of her, making her want to expand her knowledge even faster.

Riccan watched with avid excitement as the girls had each picked up the samara which had the aura matching perfectly with the birth crystal of each daughter. He wondered if the stones were actually keyed to an individual person based on the aura's color and the birth crystal of the owner.

"What's going on, Riccan? What was your theory? Is this what you had in mind?" Amanda had so many questions; she could hardly pause long enough for Riccan to answer.

"Did you notice who picked which samara?" Riccan asked cryptically.

"What are you talking about?" Amanda demanded.

"I'm talking about auras. Remember how I saw the black aura on the stone we found in New Orleans?"

"Yes."

"Jena felt drawn to that stone. Her birth crystal is black," Riccan answered rapidly.

Amanda finally started to understand what he was saying and continued with, "And Juila picked up the samara with the ruby red aura… just like her own birth crystal. Do you think it's significant?"

"I don't know yet, but it could be." He continued to watch as his children seemed to be in communion with the individual samaras. Neither girl appeared to be in any distress, quite the opposite really. Both girls looked positively blissful as they stared into their own samara.

"Should we try to put a stop to this?" Amanda asked as the girls continued to silently hold the crystals for another ten minutes.

"Let's give it a few more minutes," Riccan suggested. Another thought came to him, and he asked, "How did your studies come with my mother in the aura skill?"

Amanda was surprised at the turn of conversation and answered, "I was able to see it if that's what you mean."

"Good, look at your daughters' auras and tell me what you see."

Amanda frowned at Riccan and then turned her attention to the children. After a few moments of concentration she gasped and said, "Riccan! Do you see what I see?"

"Yep!" Riccan was transfixed by the bright auras surrounding their children. "Okay," he said, "I think we should try to get the girls to put down the crystals now. I don't want them to tire themselves out the first time they experience the raw power of the crystals."

Amanda frowned as she asked, "And how do you propose to do that, Riccan?"

"I'm not exactly sure, but I wouldn't recommend touching either the girls or the crystals." He smiled at the memory of the last time they had come into physical contact with the crystals.

"How about a distraction? A bright light or a loud noise, maybe?" Amanda suggested.

Riccan leaned closer to Amanda and whispered in her ear, "How about we look in on their birth crystals to see what's actually going on with them?"

Amanda was not so sure it was a good idea, but she was curious to know what they were learning from the samaras. "I'll take Juila," Amanda whispered back to Riccan. He did not reply, he simply nodded. Amanda concentrated on Juila's red birth crystal. She visualized the unique band of colors which surrounded it and soon became lost in the additional bands of color encompassing it. She became mesmerized by the swirling colors and almost forgot to concentrate on individual details to make the images become clearer.

Images raced across her awareness too fast for her to recognize any details. She was starting to get dizzy with the confusion of it all until she decided to step her focus back slightly so she could see the bigger picture. It was as if Juila were receiving instructions from the crystal. Instinct took over, and she focused her power to cloak her daughter's birth crystal from the power of the samara.

As if on cue, Juila took a deep breath and removed her hand from the stone on the shelf. She took a step back and gazed in wonder at the leering skull looking back at her. There was so much she still needed to learn, but she had seen enough in the few minutes that she was willing to wait quite a while before trying to touch it again.

Juila looked over at her sister and saw she was still enthralled by the magic of her own samara. That was how Juila now viewed the stones. They each owned the stone they had touched. The idea felt so right. Without even thinking, Juila's thoughts entered Jena's mind and asked, *Can you put the samara down? I think we've learned enough for now.*

Jena seemed to shudder, but her arms moved jerkily upward until the stone was, once again, resting back in the niche in which it had been found. Her hand immediately rose and grasped the birth crystal around her neck. She knew her heart was racing with the exciting images she had seen. She needed to feel the calming power of her own crystal for a few moments. Jena took a deep breath and took her hand away from her necklace.

Juila smiled at Jena's reaction. She had felt the same way. Suddenly her happy smile turned to a look of astonishment. She pointed and said, "Jena! Look at your crystal!"

Jena immediately pulled her crystal forward on its chain until she could easily see it in front of her. Her gasp alarmed both of her parents and they came rushing forward. She held it out for them to see how it had changed. All of her life she had been plagued with a black stone denoting a hard life full of danger. Now her fingers were cradling a deep amethyst stone instead.

"What does that mean?" Amanda asked with alarm. From one of her deepest memories, she recalled a conversation she had had with Barla. The stones could change color with the circumstances of a person's life. It was more typical for a stone to get darker with a person's life choices. Jena's stone had already been as dark as it could possibly get and the fact that it was now lighter could only mean her daughter had taken the first step in making her life better, safer even.

"It means Jena has made the correct choice in claiming that particular samara," Riccan declared.

Juila rushed forward to hug her sister. She was so happy to see her sister one step away from the dangerous life promised to her. This had to be the start of a great adventure. Juila tightened her grip as she felt her sister start to slump toward the floor. "Help me, Dad! I think Jena is fainting!"

Riccan rushed forward just in time to catch his daughter. He easily picked her up and carried her from the secret room. It was probably better to get her away from the overwhelming power of the samaras, even if it could make her safer. Jena had clearly reached her breaking point. Riccan only hoped he had not mistakenly pushed the girls too far. The last thing he wanted was to hurt their minds with the power of the samaras.

When he had linked with Jena's birth crystal, he had been amazed at the power coursing through his daughter. She had seemed to be reveling in the energy as it moved all around and through her. Jena was far stronger than he had ever suspected. He looked down at her serene face and realized she was still so young. He should never have asked them to test out his theory. As his father had warned, he had made mistake number two.

He placed her on the couch in the living room. He wanted to make sure they had good lighting to see if she were going to need additional medical attention. Healing had never been his strong point, but he could easily get his father to their house if need be. Elders were taught healing skills before being elevated to the Elder status.

Riccan wished he had actually attended any of the supplementary meetings which had been offered for the children of the Elders. He had always had something else going on in his life at the time, so he had missed them each anon. The only healing practice he had received was the training he had gleaned in high school to achieve his crystal proficiency in the subject. If he were ever to be elevated to the status of Elder after his father either stepped down from office or passed away, then he would have to get more serious about that particular training.

He watched his daughter's pale face to see if she were in any distress. He focused his thoughts to find Jena's life-line to assure himself of her health. Everything appeared to be in order. Riccan believed she had just been overwhelmed by all of the sensory input from the stone and then the added shock of her birth crystal changing color. It had all been too much, and she had passed out.

A few minutes had passed, and Riccan was starting to get worried. Just as he was about to go contact his father, Jena's eyelids began to flicker. He leaned over her just in time to see her eyes open all of the way. She turned her head to find her sister and then started to sit up.

"Stay down, Jena," Riccan advised cautiously. "Let your body adjust while you are lying down. We'll give you a couple more minutes and then you can sit up. Are you feeling strange anywhere? Dizzy? Disoriented?"

Jena considered all of his questions and determined she felt fine. She shook her head and said, "I think I was just overwhelmed. I feel great, actually!" To appease her father, she remained on the couch in the supine position. She looked again at her sister and asked through their mental link, *Did you see everything I saw?*

I think so, it was amazing, wasn't it? Juila smiled down at her sister. She moved between her parents and sat down on the couch next to Jena's head. She stroked Jena's hair and enjoyed the soft feel beneath her fingers.

Jena closed her eyes as she relaxed, *I'm glad we learned all that we did. At least we know we have two more anons to go before we need to worry about what's to come.*

True, but we have a lot to learn in that time, Juila admonished.

I think we'll enjoy the process, Jena smiled even with her eyes closed.

Juila looked up from her sister's serene expression and said to their parents, "I think she's okay now." At her father's nod of approval, Juila helped her sister to sit up.

"Can you tell us what happened when you held the crystal?" Riccan asked as he sat down on Jena's other side.

Amanda settled onto the arm of the couch to hear what her daughters would say about their experience.

"It was really strange," Jena began as she tried to put into words the ideas and pictures she had seen so swiftly. "It was almost as if I were watching a movie, except faster than anyone could keep up with it. As soon as I picked up the samara, I knew it was made for me to have."

Riccan nodded his head in agreement. He had wondered if the stones were actually keyed to an individual and his daughter's statement seemed to confirm his initial belief. Now he just had to figure out who the owners would be of the other samaras. More to the point, he had to locate the other stones before the owners could be identified. There were eleven more of them out there. Eleven more people who would be instrumental in changing history.

Juila spoke up to give her sister a chance to form her thoughts. "I felt the same draw to the samara I held. Was that the theory you had in mind, Dad?"

"Sort of," Riccan answered. "I had seen the colors of the auras of the two skulls. I don't know why it took me so long to put it together, but their auras matched your own two birth crystals." Riccan pointed to his children's necklaces and then reconsidered as he saw Jena's was now amethyst instead of black. "At least they used to," he said gently.

They had been so concerned with Jena they had not thought to check the samara to see if it had changed. Amanda stood up from the couch arm and said, "I'll go check it out and see if the samara changed also." She was thankful for something constructive to do. She had felt so helpless seeing her daughter so pale and still. Amanda had never even learned the rudimentary skills in healing.

Amanda rushed down the hall and into the library. The door had been left open in their rush to help Jena, so she simply walked into the hidden chamber. She did not make the mistake of getting too close to the powerful stones. She stood at the entrance and focused the energy from her own birth crystal toward the samara in question. Instantly, she felt a pull toward the skulls, but she resisted the temptation to step forward.

She held out her hand to keep herself next to the bookshelf door. As she continued to focus, the aura began to form around the skull. The rainbow of colors shifted and shimmered until they settled into the traditional rainbow. Where the black had been obvious before, it had now turned into the purple amethyst matching her daughter's new stone color. Relief coursed through her to know they matched. For some reason, the idea of them being different from one another seemed to upset her sensibilities.

To satisfy her curiosity, Amanda moved her focus to the samara Juila had chosen. The aura came into focus easier than Jena's had. It had remained unchanged despite the encounter. She sighed in relief and pulled the elemy back into her birth crystal. She turned and left the secret chamber. This time Amanda was careful to pull the wall closed behind her to disguise the room from any unknowledgeable person. Secrecy was the key to their continued peaceful existence on Earth.

She returned to the living room and shared her observations with her family. Riccan simply nodded as though he had expected as much. The girls looked at one another but said nothing. Amanda kept feeling as though her daughters were speaking with one another with their thoughts, but it was only an intuition rather than a known fact. She smiled inwardly at her choice of words. Jehoban had told her to trust her intuition so then she must be right about the twins.

"So what was it like? You said it was like a movie. Did you see specific images?" Riccan pressed to get answers.

Jena shook her head and said, "I don't think it's something that can be explained. It has to be experienced in order to understand. I did feel as though my powers were being augmented. That's something you could understand. It felt as though I were standing in the center of all the lei lines which ever existed. The power shifted and refocused when Juila touched her own stone. It was better when Juila was involved. Alone, it was quite overpowering."

Riccan continued to nod approvingly as Jena kept speaking. He wished he could have felt the same sensations. His observations of Jena through her birth crystal must have paled in comparison to what she had personally felt. *Maybe*, he thought, *I'll find a stone of my own. Then I'll know the personal connections Jena and Juila had felt.*

Riccan also felt a small sense of betrayal. The samara had been in his family line so long; he had begun to believe it had been meant for himself. Now that his daughter had laid claim to it, he wanted to find another one. *Could there be more than one samara for a family? Of course, there could,* he admonished himself, *both of your daughters have one! Now I just have to find one keyed to myself!*

Driving lessons were canceled for that evening. After dinner was over, the girls were positively drooping over their plates. Amanda suggested they go up to their rooms and go straight to bed. They had school early the next morning, and it would not do for them to fall asleep on their desks.

The girls were unresisting of the suggestion and trudged up the stairs as though their legs were weighted down with concrete. They had never known the exhaustion they were currently experiencing. Juila was thankful her bedroom was closest to the stairs. Her mind stayed linked with her sister's to make sure Jena reached her bed safely.

Juila was unsure if her tiredness were because of her experience with the samara or if she were feeling Jena's exhaustion through their twin link. In either event, sleep would be the best cure. As she stretched out on her bed, she rested her head on the pillow and immediately began to dream. The dreams were a slower replay of the scenes she had seen before.

This time she recognized some of the people. She felt relief when Captain Ahn and Barla appeared in front of her and hugged her. She had not known she had missed the couple so much until that very moment. Captain Ahn moved behind Barla and placed his hands on her shoulders. Her foster parents disappeared and were replaced with Elder Debbon and his wife, Chelesa. She did not feel as comfortable with Jena's future family.

Juila rolled over onto her other side, and the dream shifted yet again. This time Rasa appeared for an instant before she turned and blew away like dust. Out of the dust appeared two strangers, a man, and a woman. They were nice-looking people who smiled in Juila's direction but did not say anything. They turned and walked away. From behind Juila, she could feel movement. She whipped around and discovered Elder Daven and Nena approaching her with their arms outstretched to support her.

She found herself falling; she could not control the movement. In another moment, Juila bounced on the mattress, and her eyes popped open. Juila looked around her room to make sure she was truly alone. The dream had seemed as though it was trying to tell her something, but she was too tired to try to figure it out. She closed her eyes again and tried to fall back to sleep. Unfortunately, sleep alluded her, so she fell back onto a childhood habit; Juila linked her mind to her sister's, took a deep breath, and relaxed back into a peaceful sleep.

CHAPTER 19

Riccan returned to work a week after the girls started school. Amanda had pressed for him to try to get her a job in Durseni with him. He originally had thought it was a good idea until the incident with the samaras had let him know they had more important things to do than work. He had his obligation to his job, but Amanda was free to continue to research the locations of the remaining samaras without the encumbrance of a job.

When he returned home after his first day of work, Riccan pulled Amanda aside and finally confided his thoughts. "I thought it would be better for everyone if you didn't get a job."

"What? I loved working with you, Riccan." Amanda looked up at her husband with a hurt expression. She saw the look on his face and inquired, "What's really going on?"

"I argued with my boss, Ela Nena, today. I told her I had gotten married," he said and then stopped talking to look away in embarrassment.

"Why would she be mad at you for that?" Amanda could not fathom what could possibly be wrong with getting married.

"I think she's jealous of my being happy. I don't know. She's a hard one to read. Sometimes I don't really like her very well." Riccan sat down on their bed as though he were too exhausted to remain standing.

Amanda sat down next to him and put her hand on his knee to comfort him. "What else happened today?"

"I suggested to Ela Nena that you could come and work for me and she about took my head off. She became so unreasonable and irrational, almost as though she were another person entirely. Needless to say, I think it wouldn't be a very good idea to bring you into the mess at my work."

"I see," Amanda said quietly as she continued to go over what she remembered from her dream about the office politics. She had to believe everything happened for a reason. She was going to focus on what this turn of events could mean for their future.

"I hope you're not too upset," Riccan said as he took his wife's hand from his knee and held it in his own large hand. He would like nothing better than to spend every waking moment with this woman, but she had better things to do than placate a jealous boss in Durseni. "I was thinking maybe you could use your free time in researching the missing samaras."

"That's a good idea. I just have no idea where to start looking." She squeezed his hand and glanced up at his eyes.

"Jehoban had said you should use your intuition for the fulfillment of this prophecy. Why don't you let the idea simmer in your brain for a while? I'm sure something will come to you."

"Okay, I'll give it a try," Amanda said. It was then that she realized she would be spending quite a bit of time alone while the girls were in school and Riccan was at work. She would have nothing but time on her hands. She had really set her heart on working with Riccan, but she had to admit he had a point about keeping her time free to focus on the prophecy. Jehoban had said she was the key to the whole thing; it was time to put some effort into finding answers.

SCHOOL CONTINUED to be a marvel of new ideas for the girls. They excelled in their classes, and they grew in popularity. They had a new group of friends which they hung around with every day. Behn Wilson was the first new friend they had made. He was the oldest one of a set of triplets, which immediately created a bond with the girls. He had been in their Biology class and had sat at the next desk over.

Juila had been confused by an assignment and Behn had offered to help them with the steps needed to complete the work. Since that day, Juila had searched for excuses to speak with the tall, handsome boy. She liked his dark, soulful eyes and his expressive eyebrows. Jena often poked her in the ribs to get her attention back on their school work rather than on Behn's appearance.

Behn had begun to walk the two girls to their classes. Eventually, they were having lunch together, and that was when the girls were introduced to the other two in the set of triplets, Valentina and Jon. Valentina was almost as tall as her brother, Behn, but she had blonde hair with brown eyes. She often teased Behn for his nerdish ways even though she was just as smart as he. Jon was leaner than Behn, slightly shorter, and considerably quieter than his siblings. Jena wondered if it were because he was not as smart or if he were just more reserved in his conversational skills. She tended to believe it was the latter.

There seemed to be some sort of relationship budding between Jon and Sofia. Neither of them talked about it at all, but the chemistry between the two was very entertaining. Sofia was outgoing and outspoken, and she tended to tease Jon into talking or joking around. Eventually, Sofia admitted she had a crush on Jon and asked Juila's advice on whether she should ask him, or wait to see if he would ask her, to the homecoming dance which was being held in a few weeks.

Juila had not been much help on the subject since they did not have dances on Tuala. She had been unaware of the upcoming event and did not have any advice to offer. Sofia's question had started her thinking about Behn asking her to the dance.

Juila felt so comfortable around Behn that she often forgot about their fundamental differences and even convinced herself it did not matter that she was from Tuala. She imagined herself in a relationship with Behn, kissing his full lips, looking closely into his beautiful eyes until she got poked in the ribs and scowled at by her sister.

It also helped that the triplets were new to the school as well. They had moved from the town of Pinecrest several months before the twins had arrived. Juila was interested in their experience in coming to the new town and school. She often compared their experiences to her own.

Behn and Jon introduced Jena and Juila to their two good friends, Ryan Perino and Luke Thompson. They were both very athletic and spent a lot of time in the gym perfecting their perfect physiques. They were obviously not as smart, book-wise at least, as the triplets, but they were fun to hang around.

The group often spent time outside of class joking around and laughing with one another. Now that their group had grown so large, they were always with a friend and never alone. This was exactly what both Juila and Jena had been hoping for when they had asked for the Earth experience.

Finally, it came down to the deadline for the school dance. If the couples were going to be attending, then they would have to get over their nervous fears and just start asking. Juila was the first one to be asked. She had casually mentioned her desire to go when she and Behn were standing in the line to get their food at lunchtime. She wanted to see if he were at all interested before she put the question out there.

He smiled at her attempt at being subtle and let her off the hook. "I love dancing. Would you like to go with me?"

Juila looked up at him and immediately looked away before answering. She could feel her cheeks burning, and she hoped he would not notice.

Behn noticed and thought it was adorable. He nodded and then prompted for an answer, "Well?"

Juila looked up and smiled broadly and said, "I'd love to."

"Really? I mean, that's great. We're going to have so much fun." He shut his mouth before anything else really stupid could come out. He looked back at the choices of food before selecting his burger.

Juila let herself smile at Behn's comments. She had wondered if he were going to ask her and she had hoped he would. She did not know he had already turned down several invitations in hopes of this outcome. She picked up her last dish and together they turned to sit down with the rest of their group already seated at the big round table.

As they got close, Juila announced to her sister and Sofia, "Behn asked me to the dance!"

The girls smiled and congratulated the two. Sofia tried to ignore the pointed stares from Juila letting her know it would be a good time to ask Jon who sat right next to her. Sofia did not want the invitation to seem as though it were an afterthought. She would wait for a better time or not go at all.

Valentina perked up and announced, "Ryan asked me to go with him, and I accepted."

Ryan seemed suddenly engrossed in the plate of food in front of him. He smiled as he received pokes in the ribs on both sides as both Luke and Jon teased him about not telling them.

Jena had been considering whether Luke would ask her to go with him, but she could not get over the idea that she would be cheating on Willian. She thought it would be a fun experience, but not enough so if it made her betrothed angry. She was well aware of Juila's opinion on the matter since she had almost set up a mantra in her own head about experiencing everything Earth had to offer.

Jena had been very concerned about Willian as of late. She had expected to have heard something from him in the time they had been away, but still, there was nothing. She hoped nothing had gone wrong or that he was not upset with her leaving without discussing it with him. There was nothing in their betrothal agreement which said he was entitled to that type of consideration, but Jena would have liked to at least discuss it with him before they left.

Juila, once again, interrupted her thoughts with a pleasant, *shut up.* Jena smiled at her sister and then purposefully shut her out of her mind. It was something she had learned to do which bothered Juila to no end. Juila scowled back at Jena and then turned her attention to Sofia who was telling a rather rowdy story.

At the end of Sofia's story, she announced, "It has come to my attention that there is a birthday coming up."

Heads turned around to look at each person, and finally, Jon asked, "Whose birthday is it?"

"Juila and Jena's!" she announced proudly.

The twins did not know what to expect. They did not have any expectations since they had not been raised on Earth.

"You guys are going to have a party, aren't you?" Sofia continued.

"I don't know," Juila stammered. "We'll have to ask our parents about it."

"Let me know what they decide. I'd love to plan the event for you," Sofia offered kindly.

CHAPTER 20

True to her word, Sofia helped Amanda put together a grand party for the girls. Only their core group of friends were invited as well as Chris and Diane. Jena had fretted over the entire event and wondered if it were a good idea at all. She did not like to be the focus of attention, and this party was centered solely on her and her sister.

The party was scheduled for their actual birthday which happened to fall on a Wednesday. The guests began arriving right at six o'clock. The first to come over were Chris and Diane. After kissing the two girls, the adults went to talk with Amanda and Riccan.

Chris pulled Amanda aside and furtively returned her journal. He whispered, "I understand what you meant about 'complicated' now. Please let me know if there is anything I can do to help you in your quest. I think you're right in thinking the prophecy centers around you and your girls."

Amanda received the journal and tucked it under her arm until she could put it away upstairs. She hugged her father and said, "Thank you for your support. You can't know what it means to Riccan and me."

"I'll work on your mother," Chris promised.

Amanda smiled unconvincingly at her father. She did not hold out much hope for that conversation going very well. She looked over his shoulder and smiled at her mother talking with Riccan across the living room. Her father was much more optimistic than she would ever be with her mother.

The doorbell rang again, and Amanda excused herself to answer it. When she opened the door, she came face-to-face with three teenagers who all had a similar family look while each had different coloring. Something about the boys caught her attention; they reminded her of someone, but she just could not place where. "Come in! You must be Behn, Jon, and Valentina." Amanda welcomed them into the house.

The trio stood on the porch and stared at Amanda for longer than was comfortable. Behn was the first to recover by smiling and said, "Hi! I'm guessing you're Amanda's mother."

"Yes, I am. I'm glad you guys could come. This is the first birthday the girls have had in the United States," Amanda replied as she stepped aside to allow the group to enter. She had almost felt like the kids had shown a flicker of recognition toward Amanda and yet she was certain she had never met any of them on Earth or on Tuala. She shut the door and turned around to see the newest group of kids tilt their heads toward one another as though they were having a private conversation.

"Did you see her? She could be our mother's sister! They look just alike!" Valentina whispered as they walked into the foyer.

"That's what I was thinking, too!" Jon agreed with his sister. His memories of their time with their mother was not nearly as sharp as his siblings, possibly because he had spent so much time being sick.

"It has to be a coincidence," Behn reasoned. "It's not as if she's a long-lost relative or anything." He turned away and saw Juila heading toward them. He waved and moved away from his siblings to greet her. As she came close enough, he leaned in and gave her a quick hug and said, "Happy birthday, Juila!"

"Thanks, Behn. I'm glad you guys could come." She looked past him to wave at his brother and sister as they were still lingering in the foyer.

Valentina and Jon suddenly ended their discussion and came over to wish Juila a happy birthday as well.

"Go on inside and get a snack. We are still waiting for a few more guests before we begin," Juila said. She wanted to stay with Behn, but she thought her mother might need something. There was something about her mother's expression which puzzled her. She moved away from the triplets and touched her mom's arm. "Are you okay?" she asked.

"I could swear I've seen those kids before, but I can't place where. And you know what else is strange? It seemed as though they knew me when I answered the door. Weird, huh?" Amanda tried to shrug off the strange feeling.

The doorbell rang again, and Juila moved past her mom to greet the new arrivals. A squeal of delight erupted from Sofia as she stood outside. Beside her were Luke and Ryan. Sofia rushed forward to hug Juila, and practically cheered, "Happy birthday, Juila!"

The boys smiled at Sofia's exuberance, and each said a much quieter, but heartfelt, wish for a happy birthday as they entered the house. Luke asked, "Where's Jena?"

"She's just over there in the living room. Head straight and turn to your left. You won't be able to miss her," Juila grinned. She had read Luke's mind, and she liked the thoughts he was having toward her sister. There might be hope yet in getting Jena away from the dreadful Willian.

Sofia grabbed her arm and Ryan's and started to tow them into the living room. She declared, "Let's get this party started!"

Juila could not help but laugh at Sofia's attitude. Their friend had put a lot of time and energy into decorating the living room, kitchen, and back patio for this event. There were streamers, balloons, and banners every-where which made the normally opulent space very festive. She had really outdone herself, and both Jena and Juila were glad their friend had offered to help their mom in getting it all ready.

Sofia got the music started in the living room. She had a mixed music cd and was pleased to hear how good it sounded on the surround sound speakers both in the room and out on the patio.

During the natural progression of the evening, the kids gravitated toward one another, and the adults did likewise. Since it was such a nice evening, the adults convened on the patio and let the kids dance, talk, and mingle without their interference.

Amanda noticed her mother paying particular attention to the birthday girls. She seemed to be appraising them in some way. Eventually, Amanda's curiosity got the best of her, and she asked, "Mom, why are you looking at the girls so strangely?"

Since it was just the four of them outside Diane did not even attempt to be subtle as she replied, "I read your journal which you conveniently disguised as the innovation book. I figured since Chris was allowed to read it, then I would be able to as well."

Amanda felt bad about attempting to deceive her mom, and she replied, "I'm sorry, Mom. I just did not know how to tell you the truth. Now that you know everything, I'm sure you can understand my predicament." Amanda looked pleadingly at her mother and hoped she would not stay angry for long.

Much to everyone's surprise, Diane declared, "I'm thrilled to finally have everything answered! I know I can be hard to convince about certain things, but it's fairly obvious those girls are yours, Amanda. Anyone with eyes could see that much!"

Amanda could not believe her mother had come to be on her side so easily. She jumped up from her chair and hugged her mother as she said, "Thank you, Mom! I love you so much!"

"I love you, too, honey." She patted Amanda on the back until Amanda pulled away and returned to her seat.

Amanda wiped the tears of joy from her eyes. "Everything is perfect now!" She looked over at Riccan and could see he was very pleased with the night's revelation. "No more secrets, Mom, I promise!"

"Does this mean I get to see the telepod soon?" Chris asked eagerly.

"Telepod?" Diane questioned and looked over at Riccan as she asked, "Do you have one here?"

"Yes. When the party is over, and the kids all leave, we can go take a tour if you would like," Riccan suggested.

Chris smiled as though he had just opened his very own birthday gift. He had no idea Diane had read the journal. He felt guilty that he had left it out where Diane would have had access to it. He should have been more careful with Amanda's secret. In the future, he would be more vigilant.

Sofia popped her head out the patio door and said, "I think we're ready for the cake now."

The adults looked guiltily at one another and immediately stood up to come inside. Riccan led the way, and Amanda followed on his heels. They went to the kitchen refrigerator, and Riccan pulled out the half sheet cake and opened the box on the counter.

Amanda got out the candles and started to arrange them on the top of the cake. She put sixteen of them on each side so each daughter would have her own set of candles to blow out. Since this was their first birthday, she wanted to make sure they had the proper experience.

Riccan began to light the candles, and the guests started to move toward the kitchen. Jena and Juila were pushed toward the island first so they would be able to reach the candles. They stood there admiring the beautiful cake and wondered what they were supposed to do next.

Suddenly, everyone burst into song, startling the birthday girls. They looked around with bewildered expressions that everyone seemed to know the same song. Amanda smiled at her children even as she continued to sing the song. When the song was over, Amanda announced, "You each blow out the candles on your own side of the cake. If you do it in one blow, then your wish will come true."

"What wish?" Jena asked seriously.

The guests laughed.

Amanda leaned forward and replied, "Whatever wish you ask for in your mind. Now hurry up and blow these out before they melt the cake!"

Alarmed at the idea of everything melting, Juila closed her eyes, made a quick wish, and then drew in a deep breath. She wanted to be successful so her wish would come true.

Jena scowled at her sister before she also took a deep breath. Together they both blew out the candles on their own sides of the cake. No flames survived, and a plume of smoke rose up causing the girls to back up and fan the smoke away from their faces.

Riccan pulled the cake back toward him and started pulling the candles out so he could cut it to serve. "Amanda, can you please get out the ice cream?"

After everyone ate their fill of the dessert, the evening wound down rapidly. There were no gifts to open since the girls had requested that none be brought. The two groups of three left at nearly the same time. Within a few minutes, the house was strangely quiet.

Chris turned to Riccan and said, "Can we see the telepod now?"

Riccan rolled his eyes toward Amanda and said, "You were right!"

Everyone laughed as Riccan led the way to the telepod garage. He opened the garage door and reached into his pants pocket to get the remote for the telepod. As he stepped down into the garage, he hit the button on the remote to deactivate the cloaking shield. As if from thin air, Riccan's red telepod appeared in the garage. It had every appearance of being a spacecraft as it was rounded, without wings, and no wheels on which to rest.

Chris paused at the garage doorway and admired the functional piece of art. He had never seen anything like it, and he was beyond amazed at how excited he was to be one of the few people from Earth to see it. He stepped down into the garage and looked back to see how Diane was reacting to this new revelation. Chris was not disappointed to finally see Diane react to an innovation.

Diane could hardly believe what she was seeing. While she had read the journal and she wanted to believe the children were Amanda's, somehow none of it seemed real until she personally saw the telepod appear in front of her. She had no way to refute what she had seen, and now she was going to have to be more open-minded with everything her daughter and new family shared with her. This was going to be quite the mental adjustment for her. She reached forward and took hold of Chris' hand for support.

They took a few steps into the garage to allow room for Amanda, Juila, and then Jena to step down out of the doorway. Suddenly there was a commotion behind Jena.

"Hey, you guys! Sorry to barge in, I forgot my purse…" Sofia said from the garage doorway. She had gotten her first glimpse of the telepod, and she became speechless. Her eyes got huge, and she finally managed to ask, "What is that thing?"

Riccan whirled around and saw the problem immediately. Now he had to decide how he was going to handle the situation. He had a couple of options: he could mind wipe Sofia, so she did not remember seeing the telepod, or he could lie and say it was a top-secret engineering project for work. After seeing the scared expressions on both of his daughters' faces, he opted for the latter.

Riccan took a step back toward the garage door and said, "It's a project from work. You can come and take a look at it, but you must promise not to tell anyone you saw it. I could get into a lot of trouble at work if they knew I was showing this to anyone." He knew how stupid he sounded as he was obviously showing the vehicle off to Amanda's parents.

"I'd love to look at it, but I've got to get home," Sofia replied. "I won't tell anyone about it. I promise. Again, I'm sorry for letting myself in. I knocked on the door, but nobody answered."

Jena turned around and walked back toward Sofia. "That's okay," she said as she came back up next to her. "I'll help you find your purse." She steered her away from the garage and back into the kitchen.

"Where did you leave it?"

Sofia seemed to be having a hard time concentrating. She took a few seconds to answer, "I thought I left it in the dining room."

Jena spent a few moments reading Sofia's thoughts. She wanted to make sure their friend would actually keep her word and not share their secret with anyone. Everything they had wanted to achieve on Earth could be ruined if Sofia could not restrain herself with this knowledge. Luckily, Sofia's thoughts coincided with Jena's wishes. She had no desire to ruin her relationship with the girls by getting their dad in trouble. Sofia was going to remain silent.

"Let's go look in there again, shall we?" Jena asked as she kept walking through the kitchen. She could have used some of her own powers to take the memory from Sofia's mind. She was glad she would not have to resort to such measures.

They walked into the dining room and looked around. Beside, and slightly under, one of the chairs they located the missing purse. Jena picked it up and said, "I found it!"

"Oh! Thank you!" Sofia gushed as she came forward and hugged Jena for helping her. "My mom would have been so upset if I had actually lost my driver's license." As if the scene in the garage had not happened, Sofia asked, "When are you and Juila going to get yours?"

"We hadn't really thought about it much lately," she answered with a shrug of her shoulders.

"It was all I could think about from the time I turned fifteen and got my permit. Anyway, I've really got to get going. Happy birthday, Jena! I had a great time. I hope you did, too."

"It was really great, thanks to all of your help!" Jena replied and gave Sofia another quick hug. "I'll walk you out."

Together they left the dining room and moved across the foyer to the main entry. Jena opened the door for Sofia and waved at her as she got into her car and drove away. Jena leaned against the doorframe and closed her eyes with relief. Their secret was still safe, and they could remain on Earth for a while longer. She closed the front door and retraced her steps back to the garage in time to see Chris and Diane entering the telepod.

Chris saw there were several rows of seats covered in a soft, smooth leather. All of the interior was covered in either fabric or some foreign substance, so none of the metal framework showed, even on the floor. "What type of material is this?" Chris asked with his hand still touching the wall.

"We call that plasfilm. It's a durable and flexible type of plastic film," Riccan replied.

Without waiting for permission, Chris continued into the craft until he could see the control panel. It came as no surprise, none of the panel looked even remotely familiar. He sat down in one of the front seats and stared at the construction and design of the cockpit. "Is this what you do at your company?"

"Yep, she's my pride and joy. She has all of the latest technology, most of which has yet to be seen by anyone outside of our company."

"This is amazing, Riccan." He ran his fingers along the sleek dashboard and wondered what it would look like during flight. "How fast does she fly?"

Riccan smiled and answered, "Faster than anything else on Earth or Tuala. I haven't had the opportunity to really test her paces, but I imagine she'd surprise everyone. I discovered a new way to align the crystals, so they're even more responsive even when a lesser crystal is used. The control panel is mostly handled the same way as the conventional tele-pods, but the displays are all located within the plascreen. On other tele-pods, each function has its own light on the board; this one integrates them all to one screen, so there's less chance of missing something vital. There's even a built-in safeguard against pilot error which is almost equivalent to an auto-pilot."

"Amazing! Can I see the power system?"

"Certainly, it's at the back of the main cabin." He backed away from the cockpit and walked the few paces, past Diane, Amanda, and the girls, to the rear of the craft. He turned a few knobs and pushed aside a panel to reveal the intricate design of the main crystal and the brackets suspending it. The brackets had wires attached to them to power the various compo-nents throughout the vessel.

"It's such a simple and clean design." Chris kneeled on the floor and wished he could see a schematic of the ship to see how it really worked. The whole idea of powering a vehicle with a crystal was such a novel concept, and he wanted to know more. The biggest problem he was running into now was he just did not know what questions to ask since he knew nothing about this technology.

"I wish I knew more about this technology so I'd be able to ask intelligent questions. Unfortunately, I'm at a complete loss except to say it's beautiful in its simplicity," Chris said as he looked up at Riccan from his kneeling position at the panel.

"Would you like to go for a ride?"

"Do you really have to ask? I'd never turn the opportunity down!"

"Let's get buckled in and we'll go." He turned around and saw Diane's expression. "Do you want to take it for a spin, too?"

She was torn between curiosity and fear. All her life she had let fear win every battle, this time she determined to face down her fear. She looked over at Amanda and said, "I think I'd like to go for a ride, as well!"

Amanda could not contain her surprise and blurted, "Really?"

Diane chuckled and said, "I've decided to support you in everything. Remember?"

"Well then, okay!" Amanda backed up and pointed to one of the passenger seats. "You can sit here, and I'll sit next to you."

Diane hastily sat down and buckled the conventional seatbelt. It brought her comfort that at least some things were the same. Even though her heart was racing with fear, she was going to take this ride if it were the last thing she did.

Amanda sat down and buckled up while the twins selected the seats immediately behind them. There were three seats per row and two rows of seats. The telepod could transport eight people in its current configuration, but it could be reconfigured to haul fourteen should the need arise.

Riccan kneeled and replaced the panel over the power system. He then returned to the cockpit and sat down in the left-hand seat. At that moment Riccan recalled Amanda's story about him taking Chris for his first ride. He decided to use the same route from Amanda's dream for this maiden voyage.

Chris managed to figure out the fastening system of the right-hand seatbelt and smiled at Riccan to indicate his readiness. He watched intently as Riccan began the start-up procedures.

Riccan touched the plascreen to turn it on, and then he activated the telepod's crystal drive. The vessel rose several inches above the ground soundlessly and hovered in place until Riccan was able to verify each green light on the screen.

"We're going to teleport to a location away from any people. It would be hard for me to explain my presence on Earth if the press made a big deal of a UFO sighting. The Elders frown on any publicity, and I tend to agree with them. I'm pretty sure you'd like a demonstration of how we normally travel. Are you ready?"

"Absolutely."

"Okay, I'll warn you that during the transfer you won't have any sensory input. Some people have a hard time with that even when they know what to expect. My best advice is to keep track of your breathing and remain calm."

"Deep breathing and remain calm…I got it. Let's go!"

Riccan turned in his seat to make sure Diane had heard his warning about the sensory deprivation. The last thing he wanted was to make it so Diane never wanted to travel in a telepod; he needed her support for Amanda's sake.

Diane had been listening intently to her son-in-law and husband talking up front. She only had one question, "How long should we expect to not feel or see anything?"

"It should only last three seconds, but it will feel longer the first couple of times," he warned.

Diane nodded and took a calming breath. She had already committed to doing this crazy stunt. Now she just had to see it through to the end.

Riccan faced the front of the craft again and glanced one last time at Chris before he touched the activation switch to start their journey. As promised, everything went dark and silent. Riccan mentally counted to three, and they emerged into the bright daylight right on time.

"The ride is so smooth it doesn't even feel as though we're moving." Chris stared out the windows with a boyish grin pasted on his face. All he could see out the window was water far below them.

Riccan was thrilled to have an avid flyer in the seat next to him and asked, "What do you think, should we see how fast she can travel in manual mode?"

"Absolutely! Let's go. Whoa!" Chris' breath was taken away as the scenery below became a blur and nothing could be identified as they flew east. At this rate, he was certain they were traveling as fast as a space shuttle. Never in his life did he imagine he would travel at such a rate of speed. He also wondered why he was not feeling any G-forces. "I can see we're moving really fast, how come we don't feel it as well?"

"I activated the anti-gravity force before we began. If I hadn't done that, we would have passed out well before now. I think we might have found her top speed."

"What is it?"

"Just under 20,000 miles per hour. At this rate, we'll circle the Earth in just over a minute. Did you ever imagine you would travel the world tonight?"

"Not in my wildest dreams!" He leaned forward to see if anything could be seen below, but everything remained a blur until Riccan suddenly stopped the telepod. Chris looked over at Riccan and asked, "Where are we?"

"We are a couple of miles off of the Pacific coast."

Amanda glanced over at her mother to see how she was reacting to this new experience. Amanda reached out and patted her mother's hand as it rested on the arm of the seat. Her mother's knuckles were white as she held on tightly.

Diane turned to look at her daughter with wide eyes as she heard Riccan tell Chris just how fast they were traveling. She was thankful she was unable to see out the windows. It was bad enough with the knowledge alone; she did not need the evidence of actually seeing the blur of land below them.

"It's time to transfer to the house. Everyone get ready," Riccan advised as he programmed the plascreen to take them back to the garage in Florida. He pressed the button to switch from manual to mental control and took his hand from the controller. With one more movement, he clicked on the final destination, and everything turned black, and all feeling ceased.

Three seconds later they appeared back in the garage mere inches above the cement floor. Riccan performed all of the shutdown procedures and reaffirmed the cloaking shield's activation had held during the transfer. Since they were landed, Riccan was able to finally check on his passengers. "Are you okay, Chris?"

"I'm sure I'll never be the same, Riccan. That was the most amazing adventure I've ever been on. Amanda tried to explain this type of travel, but words do nothing to describe the reality."

Riccan smiled at Chris' answer and then turned to get Diane's take on the trip. "What did you think, Diane?"

"It was definitely a unique experience. I'm not sure I'd like to do it regularly, but I understand how convenient it could be to travel so fast," she replied honestly.

"I thought it was amazing, Dad," Juila announced from the back of the craft. She jumped up from her seat and took the few steps to the front console. "You're going to have to show me how all the controls work! This 'pod is so much better than anything we flew in back home!"

"A girl after my own heart." Chris beamed up at Juila.

"Mine, too," Riccan said. He smiled up at his daughter and told her, "We'll definitely go out soon, but I think your grandma would like to get her feet back on solid ground."

"You got that right," Diane laughed as she unfastened her seatbelt and stood up. Her legs were slightly shaky, and her palms were sweaty. She was glad she had gone on the flight just so she would know what Chris was sure to talk about later. She could already hear the conversations which Chris would initiate based on this one experience. For once, she would have to agree the trip had been fantastic and amazing.

Riccan palmed open the side door from the main console and waited for his daughters, wife, and mother-in-law to exit the vehicle before he stood up himself. He had enjoyed taking them up for a ride and showing off his favorite engineering project. Chris shared his appreciation for the craft which made it more fulfilling.

CHAPTER 21

The homecoming dance was held the weekend after the twins' birthday party. The girls were glad to have something else on which to concentrate. The party had been really fun and a great success with their friends, but they had been uncomfortable being the center of attention for the whole evening.

All the dresses, suits, and transportation were eventually purchased or planned for the dance. Since there were so many of them, Sofia had suggested they rent a limousine to take them first to dinner and then later to the dance.

Riccan had arranged the limousine. He had instructed the driver to pick up each of the boys and then bring them all to the house. It may only be a school dance, but he was still a father of teenaged girls and wanted to make sure some ground rules were laid down before they left for the evening.

The couples were official: Behn and Juila, Luke and Jena, Jon and Sofia, and Ryan and Valentina. The pairings had worked out rather nicely, nobody was left out, and everybody seemed content with the person with which they were going to the dance.

The night of the dance finally arrived, and all of the girls had come over to the Stel house to get ready. They had the most bathroom space of all the families, so it seemed the natural choice. The noise emanating from the two upstairs rooms was quite apparent downstairs.

Amanda and Riccan had laughed and smiled at the level of excitement being demonstrated by the girls. Each of them remembered their own experiences with the school dances and were glad both of the girls had decided to attend. They had wondered if Jena would take a date or if she would rather go stag.

Amanda had the camera ready. She was going to make sure this occasion was properly documented. She had taken all four of the girls dress shopping, which had been quite the experience of its own. Luckily, each of them had selected modest dresses which she had readily approved.

Riccan had purchased the boutonnieres for the boys as well as the corsages for the girls. He had explained to Amanda that he wanted to make sure the flowers were perfect and did not want to leave it to chance. These days, the boys might not think about it, and he wanted to make sure each of the girls felt perfect and special, and not excluded because the boy had lamed out.

There was a knock on the front door. The limo had arrived, and the boys were waiting outside. Riccan went and opened the door. He invited the nicely dressed young men into the foyer. For once, he was glad to have an imposing and grand house. The boys were properly formal when they introduced themselves to Riccan.

Behn had been perfectly polite as he put out his hand and shook Riccan's hand. He had been told that Riccan was wealthy, but he had not appreciated the truth of the matter. Even though they had all been to the house for the birthday party, they had been focused on the birthday girls. They had not taken any time to appreciate the surroundings. He tried to keep himself from looking around. Behn stood to the side as the other three guys with him each took their turns greeting Riccan.

Jon was an NHRA enthusiast, so he was particularly enamored with the popular racer. He immediately began asking Riccan about racing and the tension in the room dissipated.

They walked as a group into the living room where they received their second surprise. They met Amanda armed with her camera. The boys took the time to notice that not only was she terribly young-looking to be the mother of Jena and Juila, she was also very beautiful in the same manner as her daughters. That she was their mother was not even a question, the girls would eventually look exactly like their mother when they got older.

Amanda stood up and shook each boy's hand as the formal occasion warranted. Amanda was pleased to see the outfits the boys had selected. They were each dressed in a suit jacket, button-up shirt, and a colored cummerbund. The girls must have given the boys a clue as to the color of their dresses since each boy had a fair match to their date's outfit. Amanda picked up the boutonnieres from the console table and carefully pinned the single flower on the lapel of each boy.

She picked up the camera she'd had to set down because of the boutonnieres and began ordering the boys to pose for pictures. There were several poses at which Amanda laughed as she snapped the pictures because the boys were beginning to hear the girls giggling upstairs and their expressions were priceless.

When Amanda finished with the picture taking, she put the camera down and said, "I'll go see if the girls are about ready." She walked out of the room as all of the boys watched her go. It felt nice to be appreciated by so many handsome men. She ascended the stairs and followed the noise.

She walked into Jena's bathroom and saw all of the girls sitting on the bathroom countertop putting on their mascara and fixing their hair. She had forgotten how much work went into getting all gussied up for a formal event. "The boys are here. Are you girls almost ready?"

The girls giggled some more and Jena said, "Yes. We could spend all night in here!" Even though she had agreed to this, and excited about it, she also wanted to get it over with. She felt guilty despite Juila's persistent reminders that she was not married yet.

A mere ten minutes later, Amanda led the beautified girls down the stairs. She had expected the boys to be waiting at the bottom of the stairs like you would see in a movie. Unfortunately, this was not the actuality. With a puzzled expression, she continued to lead the girls through the foyer and into the living room.

Now she could clearly see what had distracted the men. Riccan had turned on the TV, and all of the boys were avidly watching one of Riccan's recorded races. The surround sound in the room was perfect for the deep growl of the high-performance engine as the truck did a burnout before the racing began. The boys all cheered and talked at once about how cool it sounded and how fun it would be to drive the truck.

The girls watched with growing scowls as they stood unnoticed at the edge of the living room. They were less impressed with the races and were beginning to wonder why they had spent so much time getting ready only to be ignored.

For the first time, Amanda used her power from the crystal to turn off the TV. Riccan looked down at the remote in his hand comically before he turned and saw the lineup of perfectly dressed girls all scowling at them. He had the grace to look embarrassed, and he cleared his throat and said, "I think you boys are needed right now. We can watch the races another time."

Instantly, the boys leaped up from the couch, and each hurried over to his date. Their compliments were sincere, but it was a little too late to make a good first impression.

Riccan came forward with the corsages and handed one to each boy. He watched as they opened the plastic container and then awkwardly put them on the girls' wrists. He was glad he had thought to purchase the flowers since it seemed none of the boys had even considered it.

Amanda decided to interrupt the commotion by picking up her camera and having the pairs pose for individual pictures. Once those were done, she had them all line up in front of the grand fireplace, and she took a group shot. The girls looked elegant in their solid-colored satin dresses as they stood next to their dates in their formal-looking suits.

"The limo is waiting outside to take you all to dinner," Riccan reminded them. While he had enjoyed getting to visit with the boys, he was anxious to have the house back to just the two of them.

Juila and Behn led the group away followed closely by Jena and Luke. Valentina and Ryan followed Sofia and Jon out the front door. Riccan and Amanda stood at the entrance and waved as the group filed into the limo and eventually drove away.

When they had turned the corner of the driveway and were no longer visible, Amanda elbowed Riccan in the ribs, turned around, and went back into the living room. She was upset with Riccan's stunt with the racing.

"Hey," Riccan called out to her. "What's wrong with you?"

"Really? You have to ask," Amanda spun around and accused.

"What did I do?" Riccan asked innocently.

"You had to show the boys your races? Really?"

"What was wrong with doing that?" he asked. Jon had inquired about the racing, and the girls had taken so long to come downstairs he thought it was a brilliant idea to keep them entertained until their dates were ready.

"Do you imagine having the boys so engrossed with watching you race that they didn't even notice the girls entering the room would make them feel special and appreciated?" Amanda crossed her arms as she pointed out the obvious.

"I hadn't thought about it that way." Riccan paused and considered the situation from the girls' point of view. It had been rather insensitive of him to distract the boys' attention away from the event for which they had come over. Suddenly he realized one other thing, and he accused, "You turned off the TV using your power, didn't you?"

"Yes! And I'd do it again in a heartbeat!" Amanda replied heatedly.

Riccan walked carefully toward Amanda and held out his hands in a placating manner until they were resting on Amanda's shoulders. "I'm really sorry, honey. I wasn't thinking. I'm just another dumb boy who doesn't know the right thing to do all of the time. Can you forgive me?"

Amanda had a hard time keeping the smile from curving her lips at her husband's ridiculous speech. Finally, she relented and said, "No more showing races until after the special events are over. Deal?"

"Deal!" Riccan replied and leaned down to kiss Amanda in apology. The kiss turned passionate just as Riccan had hoped. He leaned forward and scooped Amanda up into his arms and turned. He carried her as she giggled all the way up to their room. He kicked the door shut behind them and set her gently down on the bed. Their evening consisted of Riccan making amends for his gross error in judgment.

Amanda was thoroughly convinced of his sincerity.

CHAPTER 22

The group had a great time at dinner. They ordered their dishes and talked animatedly until the server brought their meals. An awkward silence fell on them all as they concentrated on eating their food elegantly. Even though they ate lunch together every day, there was something different about being all dressed up and trying to maintain the formality of the occasion.

Juila decided she preferred casual to formal. They would have had more fun if they had simply opted to go to dinner and then the movies. She mentally sighed and thought, *I asked for the Earth experience. I guess this is one of them.*

Jena smiled and added, *I'm glad you're finally seeing this my way.*

Not even. I just wish we could be more relaxed, she replied heatedly.

I just hope this whole evening doesn't backfire on both of us, Jena said with a scowl.

We're supposed to be having fun tonight. Try to do your part, Juila admonished.

Jena grinned unnaturally at her sister and Juila could not help but laugh at her sister's comical expression.

As if the laugh had allowed the tension to dissipate, the kids began to relax and become more casual. They told stories to one another about their previous school experiences and enjoyed each other's company. The dinner took almost two hours with all of the laughter and discussion and yet nobody seemed to notice the passing of the time. It was fun to be in a large group outside the constraints of the school structure. They would have to do this more often.

Eventually, they requested the bill and then spent the next five minutes figuring out how much each boy would pay for themselves and their dates. Juila had to keep her mouth shut on the whole matter. She had only needed one glance at the receipt before she had tallied everybody's totals including their fifteen percent tip.

The group trouped back out to the waiting limo. The girls giggled as they stumbled over their dresses while they found their seats in the car. It was unanimously decided that the idea of a limo was much more elegant than the actuality of one. The hump in the middle of the floor caused the long-legged boys to have to sit in an awkward position. There really was no elegant way to get to the seats furthest from the door. In spite of it all, the kids still managed to have fun.

The drive to the dance hall was only about seven minutes. The driver pulled up in front of the venue and came around to hold their door open. The kids exited the vehicle with as much grace as they had entered it.

As they walked up the path to the entrance, the girls straightened their skirts and checked their hair both with their own hands as well as the opinion of another girl in the group. The boys tugged on their jackets to get them to fall just right and then stuck their fingers in their collars to try to ease the strangulation they were experiencing with their ties. It would have been obvious to any casual observer that these kids were not used to the types of clothing they were sporting on this occasion.

They checked in at the front desk and then entered a second door inside. The room had been decorated in the theme of a nineteen-seventy disco hall. There were several mirrored balls hanging from the ceiling sparkling light in every direction. The refreshment tables were covered in tie-dyed cloth, and the plates and napkins carried the same theme.

The dance was well on its way. There were over five hundred kids their own age already on the dance floor. It was a different experience to see all of the same people as they normally would in class except now they were all dressed so elegantly. They were like different people.

Juila could well understand as she felt special herself just because of the clothing. Only Jena would know how altered they would feel since they had been wearing dress-up clothes since the first day of school. None of the clothes they had originally brought from Tuala had been worn since they had toured the school and Sofia had commented on them. It made them both slightly home-sick to not have any reminders of their heritage.

Juila chided herself for such thinking. Earth was as much their heritage as was Tuala. They just had not experienced the ways of Earth until now. Their father had spent much more of his childhood in both places, so he had not had to feel as out of place as they did.

Again, Juila had to shake her head to stop thinking about their home in Tuala. This evening was supposed to be all about the here and now. She smiled up at Behn and asked, "Do you want to dance?" She had seen enough of the dancing to realize the kids were just moving around to the beat of the song. There did not seem to be any formal types of movements, so it seemed safe enough just to wing it.

"I'd love to," Behn answered with a smile. He took her hand and led her out to the dance floor.

Just as they were beginning to dance, the music shifted to a slow song. Behn moved forward and put his hands around her waist, drawing her close to his body. She had not been expecting this and swiftly looked around her to see what the other girls were doing. Only a second late, Juila put her arms around Behn's neck and leaned in to rest her head on his shoulder. This was much nicer than the fast dance. She liked how Behn felt and smelled.

As they turned slowly in a circle, Juila saw that each of the other couples from their group had joined them out on the dance floor. Jena seemed particularly stiff in Luke's arms. Juila hoped Jena would relax or else Luke would think there was something wrong with himself. Of course, Jena would not be able to tell him she was already betrothed. It was just not something done here on Earth anymore.

Behn interrupted her thoughts as he whispered, "You look very beautiful tonight, Juila."

"Thank you," Juila managed to reply while she blushed. "You don't look so bad yourself."

"Thanks," Behn said as he chuckled. "Is it just my imagination, or does Jena seem uncomfortable?"

Juila winced. She had hoped she had been the only one to notice since she and her sister were so close. "Jena's never been on a date before. She's just nervous."

"What about you? You don't seem nervous. Does that mean you've been on dates before?" Behn teased.

Juila was grateful for the low lighting since she knew her cheeks had begun to blush violently. She shook her head slightly and replied, "No, you're my first date ever."

Behn smiled and thought Juila was teasing him. Surely this beautiful girl had been dating for quite some time. "I find that very hard to believe."

Juila looked up at him earnestly and said, "You really are my first. Jena and I have always been in a private school, and dating was not allowed."

"Well you don't seem nervous, or maybe you just hide it better than your sister," Behn suggested.

"That must be it because I feel terribly out of sorts when I'm around you," she admitted shyly.

"You don't have to be nervous. It's just me under all these fancy duds," he teased again.

Juila continued to blush. She could just imagine what was under his fancy duds and the idea made her miss a step in the dance. She accidentally stepped on his toe, and she instantly apologized, "Sorry!"

"I guess I should have opted for the steel-toed version of these dress shoes," Behn joked.

"Do they really make those?" Juila thought it sounded like a great invention.

"No, I was just kidding. These shoes are so stiff I doubt I'd feel you even should you stand on top of them."

They were quiet for the rest of the song. They swayed in time to the slow music and held one another close. Every full turn showed them all of their friends. Jena did not ever seem to loosen up. When the music stopped, Juila unwrapped her arms from around Behn's neck, took his hand, and said, "Let's go rescue Luke from Jena. I'm going to have a talk with her and see if she can start to have a good time."

Behn thought that seemed like a good idea. They rushed to where they had last seen the couple. The area had rapidly become crowded as all of the dancers were taking this break to get refreshments from the table behind where Luke and Jena had just been dancing.

Juila used her twin link to easily guide Behn through the crowd. Only a few seconds after the music had ended, Juila let go of Behn's hand and grabbed Jena's arm and started to haul her away toward the bathrooms. Juila could hear Behn talking with Luke to excuse their abrupt departure.

"What is wrong with you?" Juila whispered loudly as she kept them moving in the direction of the women's restroom, which now had a line forming out of the door. "Could you be any more aloof with Luke? He's going to think he did something wrong unless you start acting like you're having fun."

"I'm sorry, Juila. I'm trying, honest. I just feel like such a traitor to Willian. He never asked for any of this, and I don't want to hurt his feelings." Jena looked down to avoid looking into Juila's eyes. She hoped her sister would stay out of her mind or she would see what she was really thinking.

Juila could tell her sister was being evasive, so she linked her thoughts and discovered the truth of the matter. Her eyes got big and round, and she gasped, "Jena! You like Luke!"

"Shh," Jena looked around furtively to see who had heard her sister's outburst. "I can't like Luke, Juila, and you know it."

"Whether you want to admit it or not, you have feelings for Luke. And these feelings are quite different than what you feel for Willian. Maybe Willian does have something to worry about," Juila teased.

Jena blushed even more as she glared at her sister. "Stop talking, Juila! You have no idea what you're saying."

Juila nodded with a knowing expression. She and her sister shared their minds as if they were each their own. Juila knew exactly what she was talking about. Now she just had to figure out a way to exploit this relationship so Jena would break her betrothal with Willian. The hold Willian had on Jena was abominable.

In this strained silence, Sofia and Valentina joined them in the line. They were both happy and smiling.

"This evening is going to be amazing," Sofia gushed. "Jon is such a wonderful dancer. Never once did he step on my feet."

"Ugh," Valentina said to Sofia. "I don't know what you see in my brother. He's always been so annoying as we've grown up."

Sofia smiled at Valentina and said, "That's his job as your brother. He's been very romantic with me."

Juila asked Valentina, "How's your date with Ryan going?"

Valentina looked away and smiled before she answered, "Better than I had hoped. I think he actually does like me. When he asked me to go, I thought he just did it because he wanted to hang out with the group."

"What?" Juila and Jena both exclaimed at the same time.

Jena piped in, "Ryan is definitely into you, Valentina."

"Do you really think so? He's been so perfectly polite. I thought maybe I was just reading too much into it," Valentina replied.

Sofia nodded solemnly and turned the question back onto Jena and Juila, "And how are your dates going?"

"Wonderful," Juila answered right away.

"Fine," Jena replied at the same time as Juila's answer.

Sofia tilted her head and considered Jena's answer. "I thought you liked Luke."

"I do. Maybe a bit too much," Jena admitted.

"The evening has just begun. Just relax and let yourself enjoy the music. If you and Luke are meant to be, then it'll happen. Just have fun," Sofia offered.

"I'll do what I can," Jena murmured as she stepped into the now-open stall in the bathroom. "I just hope this evening won't make me regret my choices," she said quietly to herself.

After the bathroom break, Jena did try to have more fun. She talked animatedly with Luke, and he seemed to notice the difference in his date as well. He had fun, and they danced with every song for the rest of the evening.

Before they knew it, midnight had arrived, and the music finished for the night. They did not want to end the evening, so they asked the limo driver to take them to an all-night diner. They pushed two tables together, and all sat around it talking about the other kids they had seen at the dance.

There had been some excitement in the middle of the evening when two boys got into a fist-fight over the same girl. The boys had both been banned from the hall for the rest of the evening. The two girls, who were best friends, did not seem to care much and they ended up spending the rest of the night together on the dance floor, laughing and having a good time even without the boys.

Each couple had ordered milkshakes and French fries. They dipped the fries in the shake and laughed at each story being shared. Jena accidentally dropped her napkin and leaned over to pick it up. Her necklace came free from under the bodice of her dress and came to rest outside the concealing cloth.

Sofia leaned forward to look at the gemstones. She suddenly said, "Jena, I could have sworn your necklace was black. In this light, it looks almost purple."

Jena placed her hand over the birth crystal and tucked it back into her dress. "It changes color with the lighting," she said nervously.

With almost everyone looking at Jena, nobody saw the look of confusion which passed between Behn and Valentina. They would be discussing this later.

Almost casually, Behn turned to Juila and asked, "I noticed you also wear a necklace. Is it the same as your sisters?"

"Not exactly. The chains are the same, but my crystal is red," Juila said. This line of questioning was making her nervous. Nobody had ever mentioned their necklaces before, and now they were both under scrutiny, it seemed.

Behn pressed on, "Can I see yours?"

With no other choice, unless she wanted to appear rude, Juila pulled the pendant up from under her dress and held it out for Behn to look at it.

He leaned close and inspected it from a couple of angles. Finally, he sat back in his chair and smiled as he said, "It's a beautiful pendant. Did you get it as a gift?"

"Yes, both of our necklaces were gifts," Juila answered honestly. She was not about to admit she could never remember a time without it. She wished someone else would come up with something else to talk about.

As if on cue, Valentina said, "It's getting late, and my feet are killing me. I think we should probably call it a night and head home."

Juila agreed wholeheartedly. She had not wished the evening would end on such a note, but she was also tired. She flagged the waitress down and asked for the bill. This time, when the bill was presented, Juila told each boy the amount he would have to pay so they could get going as soon as possible.

The limo dropped off Behn, Valentina, and Jon first as their house was the closest to the diner. Behn had leaned in and kissed Juila swiftly before he got out. Juila had not been expecting it, but she could still feel the tingle on her lips from where his had touched hers. Her fingers rose to her lips as she sat in wonder at her first kiss.

A few minutes later, the limo stopped again, this time in front of Luke's house. Luke kissed Jena on the cheek and told her he would see her at school on Monday. Ryan got out as well since he had driven over to Luke's house and his car was still there. Ryan said goodbye to everyone left since his date had already been dropped off.

The next stop was at Sofia's house. The girls had never been to her house and were excited to see where she lived. From what they could see in the dark, the house was quite small, and the neighborhood was not all that decent.

"We'll see you Monday," Jena and Juila yelled out at the same time as Sofia walked up her walkway just before the driver shut the door. The girls refrained from speaking until the driver opened the door for them at their own house.

"Thank you," Juila told the driver as she exited the vehicle. "I'm sorry we kept you so long."

"No problem. Your father expected as much." He smiled and tipped his hat at the girls. He walked around the front of the limo and drove away.

The girls watched him go and then turned to go into the house. Their parents had left the porch light on and the door unlocked. They expected to walk into a quiet house, but their parents had waited up and were sitting in the living room.

"How did it go?" Riccan yelled across the distance.

Juila jumped since she had not anticipated the question and then turned away from the staircase to go into the living room instead. She pulled off her high heels as she walked through the foyer and sighed with relief at finally being free of the terrible contraptions. It was beyond her comprehension why women would choose to wear the torture devices for more than special occasions.

"We had so much fun," she said as she dropped wearily onto the couch. She watched her sister's slower progress into the living room.

"How about you, Jena? Did you have fun?" Amanda asked her other daughter. She could tell the two girls had had different experiences at the same event.

"It was fine. Remind me never to wear new shoes to a dance. I think I have at least three blisters on each foot," Jena said as she took small, careful steps over to sit on the couch between her sister and her father.

"Here, let me take a look," Riccan said as he held his hand out for Jena's foot. He leaned forward and inspected the red blisters and tender skin around them. In an instant, he used the elemy to sooth the irritations until they were again smooth, perfect skin.

"Oh, that's wonderful," Jena sighed with relief as she exchanged her other injured foot for the freshly healed one. Mere moments later she was able to relax in comfort on the couch. It was strange that she had not even considered healing herself. Since they had been on Earth, their usage of their crystal powers had curtailed to almost nil.

Juila had watched the scene unfold next to her. When her sister was sitting comfortably again, she stretched her leg across her sister's lap toward her father and asked, "Can you do mine, too?"

Riccan laughed and performed the same service for both of Juila's feet. Hers were not nearly as badly wounded as Jena's had been. He asked, "Did you not dance as much as Jena?"

Juila laughed as she brought her legs back under herself on the couch, "I'm sure I danced more. My shoes just fit better, I guess."

The girls spent the next few minutes sharing their stories of the evening with their parents. Jena seemed more reserved about the event, and Amanda wanted to know what was going on.

"You seem sad, Jena. What's wrong?"

Jena looked away as though she were embarrassed.

Juila answered for her. "She's decided she likes Luke. Since she's betrothed to Willian, she feels guilty for having had a good time."

"It's just not fair of me to do this to Willian," Jena defended herself snippily.

Riccan could understand the feelings of both of his girls. He spoke quietly, "Jena, a betrothal is a contract for a future relationship. It doesn't mean you're not allowed to experience other relationships until the time comes for you to honor the contract."

"See! That's what I said," Juila stared accusingly at her sister.

"That's not exactly what you said. You're hoping I'll break the betrothal and not marry Willian at all," Jena accused.

Riccan was startled by this allegation. He asked, "Is that true, Juila?"

Juila had the grace to look embarrassed and looked away as she answered quietly, "Yes."

"Why wouldn't you want your sister to marry Willian? The betrothal was sanctified by Jehoban. It's quite an honor."

"It may be an honor, but Willian's not the right person for Jena. He's jealous of her abilities, and she caters to all of his insecurities. It's disgusting to watch them together. Jena dotes on him, and he takes advantage of her skills. I hate Willian!" Juila finished loudly.

"Is Juila right, Jena? Do you think Willian is jealous of you?" Riccan asked softly. This could be a serious matter into which he would need to look. If the two people involved in the betrothal did not like one another, then it was not a blessing to keep them bound to the contract.

"I *like* Willian," Jena said quietly. Before she would have said she loved him, but after her evening with Luke, she was not so sure she knew what it was to be loved by someone. Luke had treated her gently and with respect, more so than Willian ever had. Willian had never even tried to be romantic with her. He was always so consumed with his role in society and making sure he did everything so properly. Jena did not feel treasured and protected like she had with Luke.

"Liking someone is a far cry from loving him. At your age, I'd think you'd know if you wanted to marry Willian. Has he ever talked about the two of you getting married?" Amanda asked. She was not sure how this whole betrothal thing usually unfolded, but she had seen Alena's children, and they had admired one another from the time they were little. If Jena were not feeling that same connection, then she would have to look into getting the contract vacated, if that were even a possibility.

"Sure, he's talked about me being his wife." Jena started out certain with what she was saying until she really thought about the talks she and Willian had actually had. His exact wording had been when Jena was his wife; then she would have to be sure to curtail her inner dialogue with her sister. He would not have Juila interfering with their relationship.

"Hah!" Juila cried out as she read her sister's mind. She had not known about that particular conversation until just this moment. "Tell them the truth, Jena, or I will!"

Reluctantly Jena talked. She looked down at her folded hands as she realized her whole life had been devoted to someone who did not appreciate who she was as a person. Willian was only interested in her power and how it would elevate his status. She felt tears slipping down her cheeks and dripping onto the satin fabric of her dress.

Riccan pulled her into his lap as though she were a small child. He wrapped his arms around her and whispered into her hair, "Don't worry, honey. We'll get this mess fixed. I'm sorry I wasn't around to take care of you when you were little. If we'd known about you, then we might have kept you from all of this trouble." He was not certain this would have been true. He could not imagine too many people who would turn down the offer of a betrothal with the child of an Elder.

Amanda felt terrible for the pain her daughter had endured. She was glad she had her sister to lean on in times of trouble. She looked over and saw Juila was crying the same as her sister. They were very close, and what one felt, the other did also. Both of her children had been hurt by this unfortunate union. Hopefully, they could resolve the issue without creating an enemy from either the Elder or his son.

Amanda patted Jena's arm, and she said, "I don't want you to feel bad for having feelings for Luke. If the two of you are meant to be, then we'll take it from there. I don't ever want you to deny your feelings just because you feel an obligation toward someone else. Love is a powerful emotion which has been gifted to us by Jehoban. Never deny yourself love out of obligation. It's not fair to you or your partner."

Jena sniffed the snot back up into her nose and swallowed. She pushed the wet streams of tears off of her cheeks, and she moved off of her father's lap. The crying had released a lot of pent-up tension she had not realized she had been harboring. She felt better already.

Her parents were wise, and they would know what to do. Jena no longer felt alone in the betrothal. Juila had always done her part to help her, but Jena always knew Juila was powerless to really do anything about it. Juila would always be viewed as the jealous sister. Her parents could make a difference.

"It's late, girls," Amanda said. She stood up and walked over to stand in front of her children. She held out a hand to each of them and helped them up from the couch. Amanda hugged the two of them at the same time and said, "I love you both. You can always talk to us about anything. We want both of you to be happy, no matter what!" She gave them a last squeeze and then released them. She took a step back and smiled at them.

In unison, the girls said, "We love you, Mom."

"Hey, don't leave me out of this!" Riccan hastily stood up to include himself in the family hugs. He stretched out his arms and hugged the girls tightly as they rushed to him and hugged him around the middle. They were the same height as their mother, but they seemed so much smaller because of their vulnerability. He could not imagine his life getting any better than right at that moment.

Jena reached up and pulled his head down. Jena kissed one of his cheeks while Juila kissed the other. "We love you, too, Dad!" they spoke together and laughed.

The girls pulled away and started to leave the living room before Juila turned back around and announced, "We'll see you in the morning."

"Not too early," Amanda moaned as she realized it was almost two o'clock in the morning. "Sleep in!" she yelled at their hastily retreating backs. They raced up the stairs and into their rooms. Their loud footsteps on the floor let both of their parents know where they were in the process of getting to bed.

Amanda turned to Riccan and asked, "Is there anything we can do about this betrothal?"

"I don't know right now, but you can bet I'll be talking to my dad about it. If Juila is right and Willian is just using Jena, then obviously we're going to have to put a stop to it before it goes any further."

"What a mess," Amanda sighed as she leaned into her husband's side. She loved it when his arms wrapped around her and made her feel safe and secure. She wanted this same feeling for both of their children.

"We'll work this out together," Riccan promised. He took his wife's hand and led her up to bed. Even though they had spent the evening home alone, they had worried for their girls. It had been a long day, and they were both ready to get some sleep.

CHAPTER 23

Over the next two days, Behn and Valentina kept their heads together trying to figure out how Juila and Jena had the same type of necklaces which they had. They knew the two of them and Jon had been adopted when they were eight years old. Other than that, they had no idea where their birth family had been from or where to look to find them.

The last memory they had was their mother crying and walking them through the woods in the dark. Jon had been very sick and yet there had been no help for him. Their mother had pleaded for the people in their town to help them, but they had been turned away.

They had fleeting memories of an older man who seemed to be the leader of their community. He was a mean man who took pleasure in scaring the children whenever they came near him. He had told them if they were bad then they would be left out in the woods to be eaten by the animals. To this day they did not like being out in the dark alone.

They argued over whether or not to talk to Jena and Juila about their past. Behn was all for telling them about it, whereas Valentina was ashamed of being adopted and did not want to have anyone look at them with pity as they had in their last school. She was glad they had moved and were able to get a fresh start where nobody knew their history.

They did not even bother to ask Jon about his opinion on the matter.

He had absolutely no memories of their life before their adoptive family. He had been so delirious with fever for so long it had burned the recollections from his mind. In a way, Jon had an easier time adjusting because of it, but he also felt left out when his siblings talked about the 'time before.'

"Come on, Val, I swear it'll be different this time," Behn pled.

"Why, because Juila is cute and you have a crush on her? What happens if you two decide to break up and she tells everyone how pathetic we are?" Valentina asked snidely.

"First of all, Juila and I aren't even going out. It'd be kind of hard to break up, don't you think?" he smiled winningly.

"You know what I mean, Behn! I want to stay free of the stigma which has followed us our whole lives!"

"We're older now. What if Juila or Jena can tell us about the necklaces? They are the only things we have left from our mother. What if we could find our mother? Isn't that something you've said you've wanted to do?" Behn tried to reason with his sister.

Valentina lifted the leather strap out of her t-shirt and held the fiery orange crystal in her palm. She looked down at it and felt a sort of peace come over her. It might have been a memory or a dream, but Valentina could remember the crystal glowing with power. She imagined that power helping her through troubling times.

With a frustrated sigh, she dropped the crystal so that it swung just above her cleavage and she said, "Fine! We can talk to them, but only if Jon is not around."

Behn smiled. He knew he had won when Valentina had held her crystal. For some reason, whenever she had a difficult decision to make she held her crystal. Behn seldom even thought about the leather thong suspending his smoky gray crystal.

"And don't even give me that crap about you and Juila not going out. After the dance, I saw you kissed her on the lips. I also saw her expression after you got out of the limo," Valentina accused.

"You did?" Behn asked with sudden interest. "What do you think she was thinking?"

"Duh! She's fallen for you," Valentina smirked and stood up to leave the room. She liked it when she knew something, and he did not. She would draw this out as long as she could. She walked to Behn's bedroom door and opened it.

"Val, you can't just leave now. You have to tell me everything. What did you girls talk about when you were getting ready?" Behn asked.

"Girls' code, Behn. I can't share that with you," she said over her shoulder as she left the room and closed the door behind her. She could hear a shoe hitting the other side as Behn had become frustrated and thrown the closest object he could reach. She smiled as she walked back to her own room.

Maybe she should think about going out with Ryan again. He had certainly been more attentive than she had expected during the dance. She actually had fun, even though she had only agreed to go to keep her brothers out of trouble.

~

MONDAY MORNING PROVED to be awkward at school. Juila could not forget about Behn's kiss and wondered if it had meant he wanted to go out with her, or if he only wanted to kiss her goodnight. She did not know how to act around him and ended up making a fool of herself.

Behn only smiled at Juila's silliness. He really did like Juila, and he was going to ask her to be his girlfriend. With the way she was acting, he was not sure she wanted the same thing from him even though his sister had insisted it was true. Behn had thought to ask her at lunch, but she sat between two girls and kept averting her eyes from him. There never seemed to be a time where he could get her alone, and he found it very frustrating.

When the first bell rang letting them know they had ten minutes until their next class, Behn cornered Juila alone at her locker. Suddenly, he was at a loss for what he wanted to say.

"I had fun at the dance with you," he said lamely. He was so mortified he wished he had just kept walking and not opened his big mouth.

Juila looked up through her eyelashes as she admitted quietly, "I did, too."

With renewed hope that his statement had not sounded too ridiculous, Behn continued with, "I was wondering if you'd want to go out with me again sometime?"

Juila tilted her head up and looked at him straight in the eyes as she replied, "I'd love to."

"Really?" he exclaimed before he cleared his throat and continued more calmly, "How about a movie tomorrow night?"

"Sure. Do you want to make it a double date? Maybe you could have Luke ask Jena. I'd hate to leave her home alone. You know what I mean, right?" Juila asked. She really did not care about leaving Jena alone since her mental link would keep her in touch. She just wanted Luke to see Jena again so she would quit obsessing over her non-existent relationship with Willian. A date would be a perfect distraction.

"Yeah, I can probably arrange that. I'll let you know after the next class," he said as they started walking toward their classrooms.

When they got to the hallway where they would have to part ways, Behn took the liberty of kissing Juila on the cheek before he turned and hurried away. Juila stared after him until she realized several students were watching her and smiling. She blushed furiously and ducked into her Algebra class where she immediately sat down in her seat.

Jena was already at her desk. She could see Juila's blush and did not even pause before entering her mind to find out what was going on. A second later, Jena accused, *You did not ask Behn to set me up!*

What if I did? Don't you think Mom and Dad would have an easier time permitting me out on a date if you and I are together? You know how much I wanted to see Behn again. Don't you dare ruin this for me! She sat facing forward and tried valiantly to shut Jena out of her mind. Hopefully, she had not seen the part where she wanted her to forget about her betrothed.

You'll pay for this, Juila! Jena spat out mentally and then withdrew her power from her sister's head. She fumed over Juila's presumption on her time while at the same time she wondered if she would have as good a time with Luke during a less formal occasion.

The final bell rang, and the teacher began the day's math lesson. Jena was grateful for the distraction. She loved math, and her thoughts were swiftly absorbed in the new equations and formulas.

Their next class, English, flew by and still the sisters did not talk with one another. They walked into their final class of the day, Health. A new, male anatomical structure was standing next to the teacher's desk. The two girls looked at one another as they could see it was a very correct structure which made them blush and giggle as they walked by it to their seats.

To their great mortification, the lesson for the day was on sexual reproduction. While all of their classmates had been learning about it since the third grade, this was a new experience for the twins. They did have an idea about the differences between male and female bodies which they confirmed when they had entered the room and seen it for themselves. However, the only experience they had in their past was during their healing sessions they had learned about the different body parts, but not how they interacted with the opposite sex for reproduction purposes. They could heal a body, but they were ignorant of anything more than that.

As the class went on, they found themselves alternately fascinated and embarrassed. It turned more humiliating when it became apparent to their classmates that this was their first experience with the topic. The teacher had called on Jena for her view and Jena had to admit she had no opinion. Their teacher had also seemed flustered and then hastily called on another student to give the correct answer.

Finally, the bell sounded, and the abominable class was over. With flaming red cheeks, the two girls fled the room and sought refuge at their locker. When both Behn and Luke approached them, they had no idea what they were walking into.

"Hey, Juila," Behn called when he got close enough. He saw Juila's strange expression as she turned and saw him walking closer. "What's going on?" By then he had reached the two girls and stopped beside their open locker door.

Juila's eyes darted down to his crotch and then hastily away.

"We just had a particularly informative lesson in Health class," Jena admitted.

Behn smiled as he realized what this week's lesson entailed and asked, "Sex Ed?"

"Yep!" Jena replied hurriedly, ducking down to get her book bag from the bottom of the locker.

"It's not anything we haven't already heard before," Behn stated matter-of-factly.

"Maybe for you," Juila finally managed to speak.

"Really? You two have never had that discussed in school before?" Behn could hardly imagine where they had grown up to miss out on such a big subject. It was hard to believe South Africa could be so far behind on the subject as to neglect it from the curriculum. "If you have any questions, I'd be happy to answer them," he offered cheerfully.

Juila's cheeks flushed even more, and she managed to say, "I think we got the idea." She, also, grabbed her book bag and slung it over her shoulder. She slammed the locker door shut and turned the combination lock so it would not be on the last number entered. She looked around for Sofia so they could get going home.

"Are you looking for Sofia?" Behn asked.

"Yes," Juila said simply.

"I saw her down by the doors to the buses. She asked me if I could give you a ride home today since she and Jon were going to go out."

"They are? When did that happen?" Juila was shocked that Sofia had not told her herself. This was news which girls usually shared with one another. She decided to find out what had happened before the evening was over. Meanwhile, she felt a thrill of excitement with the idea of riding in Behn's car. She looked over at her sister and asked, "Are you okay with the idea of Behn taking us home?"

"Sure. Why not? It beats riding the bus," Jena admitted. She looked over at Luke who had been silent this whole time and wondered if he were going to be riding with them.

As if he had heard her question Luke said, "I can ride in the back seat with you, Jena."

"Okay," she replied lamely.

They walked out to the parking lot and got into Behn's silver Nissan Altima. It was a much nicer car than Sofia's, and his was an automatic.

Juila sat in the front seat, and Jena took the place behind her. Luke got into the car behind Behn, and they drove in silence until they left the school grounds and started going faster on the main road.

"So," Luke said quietly to Jena as he leaned over closer to her, "I was wondering if you'd want to go to the movies with me tomorrow night. Behn and Juila are going, and I thought…"

Jena rolled her eyes before she turned her head to answer Luke, "I know Behn put you up to this."

Luke looked down and smiled a little before he looked back up into her eyes and said, "Behn suggested it, but I really wanted to do it myself. I'm glad for the opportunity, that is, if you want to go with me."

Jena felt bad she had been so rude to him. He really did look as though he wanted her to go with him. She relented and said, "I think it'll be fun. We can make sure those two," she thumbed toward the two up front, "don't get out of line."

"Sounds like a plan," Luke sat back in his seat with a pleased expression on his face.

They dropped Luke off at his house first and then continued on to their house. Juila was torn between the excitement of being alone, sort of, with Behn and the embarrassment of not knowing what to talk about. She decided the group dating idea had been easier since there was always someone willing to chat.

They got to the gated driveway and had to stop as the gate was not programmed to open for Behn's car. Jena got out of the backseat and entered the code before getting back in on the other side for the ride up the driveway.

The ride took an unexpected turn when Behn pulled up to the front of the house and turned off his engine. He turned to the girls and asked, "Do you mind if I come inside? There's something I wanted to talk to both of you about...privately."

The girls looked curiously at one another, and both shrugged before Juila said, "Sure, I don't see why not."

"Are your parents home?" Behn asked.

"Probably. Do you want to talk with them as well?" Jena asked from the back seat as none of them had made any move to get out of the car.

"I'd rather not, at least not right now. It's a pretty private family matter," Behn replied cryptically.

"We can talk in my room," Jena offered. Hers was the furthest away from their parents' room and from the stairs. They would have the most warning if their parents decided to come in to talk with them.

Behn nodded and grabbed the door handle. He hoped this was the right thing to do. He had a good feeling about it, and his intuition was usually pretty accurate. He stepped out of the car and smiled at Juila over the top of the car. She smiled in return, and he knew this was going to work out just fine.

They trooped upstairs without having seen either parent. Not that Behn wanted to be secretive, but he wanted confidentiality. He was surprised to find Jena's room so spacious. He was glad it was large enough to have its own seating area so they would not have to sit on the bed together. He chose the window bench and sat down with his back resting on the side wall and his leg crooked up on the bench seat.

Juila sat across from him on the window seat while Jena pulled a chair closer from the formal seating area. They did not know what to expect, so they remained silent until Behn felt comfortable enough to talk.

He cleared his throat uncomfortably and then began, "I wanted to ask you about your necklaces."

The girls looked at one another with alarm. This had not been what they had expected. They could not share their story without getting them all in trouble.

Behn saw the look they shared and then decided to try to ease their minds. He pulled up the leather thong from below his shirt and exposed the smoky gray crystal suspended from the same intricate filigreed silver-work as the girls' own stones. "I was hoping you could help me learn about my own necklace, you see."

The girls did see. They were both alarmed and curious. Surely it could not be a real birth crystal. The crystal was suspended not by an ornate chain, but, instead, a leather thong. They had only ever heard of them on an ornate chain designed to match the crystal's mount.

CHAPTER 24

Juila was the first to recover from the shock of seeing the pendant. She leaned forward and saw it did look authentic except for the lack of chain. She asked, "Where did you get this?"

"I got it from my mother when I was very little," he replied. "Both of my siblings have them as well, but theirs are different colors than mine. When I saw you both had the same style of crystal, I thought you might be able to help us."

"What kind of help are you seeking?" Jena asked suspiciously.

"We want to find our mother," Behn said and looked down at the crystal still held in his left hand.

"I thought you lived with both of your parents," Juila said. She had not met their parents, but she had heard them talk about them often enough.

"We weren't born with the last name of Wilson. You see, Valentina doesn't like people to know that the three of us were adopted when we were eight," he answered.

"Oh," Juila said lamely.

"What makes you think we can help you find your birth mother?" Jena leaned forward and asked.

Behn shrugged and replied, "All of our lives, we have searched for signs. Up until we saw your necklaces after the dance, we had never seen anyone with anything similar. It's the only thing we have left of our mother. Maybe, if you can tell us where you got yours, then we can go and ask the seller if they remember our mother or us."

Again, the twins exchanged looks, knowing there was no seller of these necklaces; they were gifts from Jehoban. They needed to find out how Behn and his siblings had gotten theirs.

A simple test needed to be performed. Jena asked, "Can you take it off so I can look at it more closely?"

Behn looked away as though he were embarrassed and he shook his head slightly as he answered, "It won't come off. All three of us have tried over the years without success. I know it sounds crazy…"

Jena shook her head and asked, "Do you mind if I try?"

"Go ahead," Behn leaned forward so she could have better access to the leather strap.

She reached up and touched the leather. It felt normal beneath her fingers as she slipped them under the strap. She tried to lift it off his neck, but it held fast. She tried a second time with no better success. Jena took her hands away from the leather and raised her eyebrows in question as she went to touch the crystal itself.

Behn nodded approval.

Jena touched the stone and received a literal shock of recognition. The crystal knew who she was and responded to her touch. It was definitely a real birth crystal from Tuala. Jena did not doubt it anymore. She smiled and let go of the crystal. It swung back down onto Behn's chest.

Behn looked at Jena in amazement. Nobody had ever been able to touch the stone before. He had been sure Jena would have been frustrated until he saw her fingers lift up the stone. She had looked as though she were concentrating on the stone, communicating with it almost. It had been very strange.

She looked up at Behn and smiled. She stated simply, "It is the same as ours."

"Are you unable to remove yours as well?" Behn asked hopefully.

Both girls shook their heads.

Behn released a sigh and said, "Finally! Now we don't have to feel so embarrassed about these things." He tapped the crystal in accusation. "What is it? What do you know about them?"

Juila spoke first, "It's called a birth crystal. You were most likely given it when you were only a day or two old. Your mother would have presented you at the crystal ceremony."

Behn looked at her in confusion and said, "It sounds like something from a cult."

"On the contrary, it's more like a culture," she answered easily. This was not a conversation she should be having with Behn. They were going to have to get her parents involved if they were going to discuss this further. Juila was not comfortable discussing Tualan culture with Behn unless he really was from Tuala himself. If he did not remember it, then she was not sure she would be able to help him in his quest to find his mother. "I think we should include my parents in this discussion. I can't share anything more with you about the necklace unless they want me to."

Behn frowned in confusion, and he said, "Okay if you think so."

Juila stood up and said, "Let's go find them downstairs."

"You mean right now?" Behn was not so sure about this anymore.

"There's no time like the present," Jena stated as she also stood.

Behn had no choice but to follow as the two girls left the room to find their parents. At the bottom of the stairs, the two girls split up to search for them.

Amanda was found in the living room. Riccan was located in his office. Juila led Riccan into the living room where they had all sat down to wait. Jena spent the next few moments letting them know what she had discovered and then fell silent to see what Behn wanted to add to the conversation.

Riccan looked at Behn with new appreciation. If Behn were from Tuala, then he would be a good match for Juila. The problem then came about where Behn's parents were and why the children were separated from them. This was a new mystery which he thought would be rather fascinating to puzzle through.

"Tell me what you remember from the time before you were adopted and you all were still with your birth mother," Riccan prompted as the room remained silent.

"I think we had a pretty typical childhood. We played a lot with one another since we were all the same age. I don't remember too many other kids our own age. I do remember an older man who I think was the leader of the community. I think his name was Grobin or something like that. We were pretty poor, and our house was made from logs. During the winter it was pretty cold and drafty.

"One particularly bad winter, Jon got really sick with a cold. His lungs were bad, and he had a hard time breathing. He coughed all of the time. Our mom was sick with worry, and she asked Grobin for help many times. He came over to our house and stood over Jon with his arms crossed.

"After a few minutes, he turned to my mom and said, 'You have too many kids anyhow. It won't hurt if you lost this one. I'm not going to risk any of our men to go get you a wise-woman.'" Behn scrunched his face as he remembered the right term from his memory.

He looked up and said, "I know this sounds crazy. Sometimes I think I must have dreamt it all up until I talk to Valentina and she remembers the same thing."

Riccan had been surprised to hear the term for the healer from Behn. He had been uncertain before, but, with that one phrase, he had no doubt about Behn's story. They were from Tuala. "I've heard stranger things. Please continue," Riccan urged.

"My mom clutched her stomach when Grobin left our house. She was crying loudly, and she kept looking around the house as though she were trying to figure out what she would do next. Suddenly she stood up and rummaged inside a high cupboard. She took out something we'd never seen before and turned back to us kids. 'Get your things together. We're going to get you kids to safety,' she'd said as she held the wrapped bundle from the cupboard to her chest.

"We didn't know what she meant for us to do. We didn't really have much of anything, so we just stood there and looked at her dumbly. She moved around the house and picked up a jacket for each of us and told us to put them on. She didn't yell or scream or anything other than sob quietly.

"She helped Jon to sit up and put his coat on carefully. Then she urged him to his feet and told us we were going for a walk. We didn't know what she was talking about since it was cold and dark outside. She opened the door and herded us ahead of her. As we walked and stumbled through the woods, Mom kept giving us directions to turn or to keep heading straight. We held on to one another and kept Jon between us to keep him upright.

"Finally we came to a creek and followed it for some time. Mom had us spetch the creek until we were standing on a small island in the middle. She didn't follow us across. I heard her mumble as we walked, 'Corva said it would come to this. I hope she knows what she's talking about.'" Behn looked up and asked, "Does any of this mean anything to you?"

It had been forever since Riccan had heard the Tualan term 'spetch.' He instantly translated it to 'jumping over the narrow area of the creek.' Riccan nodded slightly and asked, "Can you please tell us the rest?"

"Okay, we stood on the island, and our mom unwrapped the bundle she had been holding. It was dark outside, but I could have sworn it was a small skull she held. The picture of it in her hands still haunts me when I'm sleeping. She held it out in front of her, and she yelled, 'Outside Ascension,' and then everything turned black. I couldn't feel anything or anybody around me for several seconds.

"We must have fallen asleep because the next thing I remember we were sitting just outside of a cave and it was daylight. We had no idea where we were, but we knew we had to get help for Jon. He was delirious by now, and he was so hot that his eyes kept rolling back in his head. Val and I each took one of Jon's arms and slung it over our shoulders. We walked and stumbled until we found a house. When we knocked on the door, an old lady saw us and immediately brought us inside. She called an ambulance, and they took Jon away.

"We went into the foster system since we didn't know where our mother was and, eventually, Jon was reunited with us. We were moved through at least seven houses before we were all adopted by the Wilson family." Behn sat back on the couch and waited to see what Riccan and Amanda would say.

The room remained quiet while everyone absorbed the details of Behn's story.

Amanda was the first to have a question when she asked, "You were so young when all of that happened. How is it you remember it so well?"

Behn easily answered, "I've dreamt about it often. I used to think it was a reoccurring nightmare until I started talking to Val about it. She remembered it almost the same as I did. When we talked to Jon about it, he gave us a blank stare. He says he doesn't recall anything until the time we were adopted."

"Traumatic events can do that to a person," Amanda reassured Behn. She had certainly had her own share of traumatic events to draw knowledge from in her past. She still could not recall the details of Jehoban's version of her time in Tuala. "It doesn't mean the events didn't happen the way you remember," she continued.

Riccan suddenly jumped up from the couch and left the room. Nobody seemed to know what to make of his actions, so they sat quietly in their seats until he returned several minutes later. He had his hands behind his back as he entered the room.

"I'm going to show you something, and I want you to tell me your first thought when you see it. Okay?" Riccan said as he stopped directly in front of Behn.

Juila stiffened immediately because she could feel the power of the samara as her father entered the room.

Riccan brought the samara around to the front of him and waited for Behn's reaction.

"That's what my mother was holding! How did you get it?" Behn looked up excitedly from the stone to Riccan's face and then to Juila's.

"This is a different skull than the one your mother had. We have been told there are thirteen of these in existence. We are searching for them all. Maybe we can work together to find your mother and to locate the missing samara," Riccan proposed.

"That's what the skull is called? A samara?" Behn asked. For the first time, he had hope for finding their missing mother. She had seemed so distraught the last time they had seen her. They hoped she had not been punished for sending her children away. Grobin had never been enthusiastic about himself or his brother, but they had often seen the leader of the community watching their sister intently.

"Yes. We are attempting to locate all of them," Riccan said as he put the crystal skull down on the coffee table in between them all.

Juila looked down and saw the hair all along her arm was standing on end. She used her other hand to try to brush it down. The attempt was futile. As long as the stone was close, she would feel the power affecting her own birth crystal.

"Do you feel anything with that skull near?" Juila suddenly asked Behn.

"No. Why? Do you?"

"Yes." She turned to Riccan and asked, "Is that the one I was holding earlier?"

"Yes. I wondered if you'd know the difference," Riccan smiled as Juila had confirmed a suspicion of his. Jena did not appear affected by the proximity, but Juila seemed anxious and on edge. "I'll go put it back," he offered. He scooped the skull back up and left the room again.

Juila shivered slightly as the energy pulsed one last time around her and then released its hold. She felt it dissipate back into the earth and she was able to concentrate once again on Behn's amazing story. She no longer believed in coincidence. Everything happened for a reason, and it was up to her and her family to discover why Behn's family had come to Pinecrest when they had. "I'd like to talk to Valentina to see if she remembers any details you haven't shared," Juila said to Behn.

"She may or may not want to talk about it. She just wants to be normal like everyone else," Behn shrugged.

"I think you'll find that to be impossible. Have you ever thought weird things happened which you could not explain?" Juila asked suddenly.

"Like what?"

"I don't know. Anything strange really."

"I can't think of anything in particular. I'll have to get back to you on that one," Behn said with a smile. He had no idea what Juila could be getting at, but he sure did want to spend more time with her now that she and her family knew their secret.

Riccan returned to the room and sat down on the couch next to Amanda again. He had been gone longer than was necessary to return the crystal to the secret room. He spoke up and said, "I sent a message to my father asking him to come to see you, Behn."

Behn gave him a bewildered look.

"My dad is what you'd consider a counselor or a mediator. He specializes in helping people solve problems."

"Is he a shrink?" Behn was suddenly suspicious.

"Definitely not! But I do believe he is our best hope for getting to the bottom of your mystery, Behn."

"Did he say how long it would take him to get here?" Amanda asked quietly.

"He said he had to finish up something and then he'd be right over. I think he'll probably time it anyway," Riccan whispered.

As if their conversation had produced the man, they heard the door to the garage open and then close. They heard footsteps. As they turned around, they could see a tall, older man wearing Tualan clothes walk through the kitchen and approach the living room. He smiled as he saw his son and took the few remaining steps to greet him warmly with a hug.

Riccan had stood up from the couch and turned to receive his father's affectionate welcome. He kept his hand on his father's arm as he turned and made introductions. "Dad, I'd like you to meet Behn Wilson. Behn, this is my father, Daven Stel."

Daven stepped forward and offered his hand out. "It's a pleasure to meet you."

They shook hands and Behn was overwhelmed with how fast Riccan's father had made it to their house. It had only been a matter of minutes. Did Daven live on the property then?

"Thank you for coming out so quickly to hear my story," Behn said as he took Daven's hand in his own. From the moment their palms touched, Behn felt an overwhelming sense of calm and easiness come over him. This man would be able to help him, of that he was certain.

Daven used his mental skills to read Behn's thoughts. They needed to be sure Behn was someone to be trusted and not someone sent from Lucinden to cause them harm. Ever since the new prophecy had been revealed, Daven had the idea that Lucinden would start making moves to block their progress. It seemed rather coincidental that Behn would appear when he had. They had to be careful of everybody they let into their circle of trust from now on.

His quick, but thorough analysis revealed Behn's story to be true and accurate. He had seen the samara his mother had held. He knew the three kids had originally been from Tuala. He could not know why they had been sent to Earth or why Corva would have warned their mother to such drastic measures. There was more to this story, but Behn did not know the answers.

Daven nodded his head toward his son before he sat down on the couch between Amanda and Jena.

Riccan spoke to Behn. "If you won't mind, please share your story with my father." He knew it was unnecessary since his father had already gotten what he needed. He wanted Behn to relax and feel as though he could trust Daven. The only way they would accomplish that was with time.

CHAPTER 25

Behn retold his story and watched Daven intently. He could not tell what the older man was thinking, but he was encouraged to keep talking by the slight nods of his head. He finished recounting all of the details and then waited to see what would be done.

Daven cleared his throat and said, "I think we should tell him the truth."

"You are the Elder. I had to leave this decision up to you," Riccan affirmed.

Daven nodded toward his son and turned to Behn, "You and your siblings have had quite the adventure. I'm afraid it has only been the beginning for each of you, however." Daven turned back to Riccan and said, "I think you were right to bring me into this. I believe Behn's memories are significant to what we're trying to accomplish."

"What are you saying? It sounds as though you're saying we're in some sort of danger." Behn looked hurriedly from Daven to Riccan and finally to Juila.

Daven accessed the elemy and released a sense of calming in Behn's direction. They did not need Behn to be scared; he had experienced enough fear in his lifetime already. Behn was going to help them bring another samara into play. They had to determine where his mother had been living before they could ask for her help.

"It could be. I need to get more information before I can be sure," Daven replied softly. "What is your birth mother's name?"

"Vinia," Behn replied. It had been forever since he had last spoken her name. It felt good to claim her once again.

"What about your father's name?" he persisted.

"We never knew. Our mother never spoke his name," he said, slightly embarrassed at not knowing his own father's name.

"That's okay. Do you remember the name of the town you lived in? Or any towns nearby?"

"No. We lived in the woods along with all of our other neighbors. Nobody ever left the area; we were pretty self-sufficient."

"You said the community leader's name was Grobin. Was he married? Do you know the names of any other neighbors?"

Behn was going to reply rapidly, but then realized he did know another name. "I don't think Grobin was married, although he seemed to pay a lot of attention to all of the women of the community. He usually walked around with another man whose name was Mosan. I guess you'd call him his right-hand man."

"That's good. Can you think of anyone else?"

Behn shook his head slowly as he reviewed all of this earliest memories. He realized then that all of the names he did remember were strange and he asked, "Why are all of the names I remember so odd?"

Davin considered his question, and instead of answering him directly, he asked a question of his own, "Have you ever heard the name Tuala?"

Behn started to shake his head until he realized he had heard it before. His birth mother had used to say the phrase 'what on Tuala' when she was confused. Behn smiled at the new memory and looked up at Davin and said, "Yes! My mother used to say it."

"Good," Davin declared. "I believe you come from a place called Tuala. It's pretty far from here, but we can take you there if you want to go. I'm afraid we'd have to blindfold you, however, until you are ready for more of the details."

Behn was willing to try to find his mother, but he thought the blindfolding part was just a bit strange. He did not know who this man was and Juila seemed eager for him to trust him. He did not think she would try to mislead him in any way. Reluctantly he nodded his agreement.

"Great! Let's go!" Juila exclaimed as she immediately stood up from the couch. She was eager to see how this would play out.

"What? You mean right now?" Behn looked concernedly from Juila to Daven.

"There's no time like the present. Isn't that what they usually say?" Daven joked as he, too, stood up more slowly. "We could wait for a different time, if you'd rather," Daven suggested when he could see Behn was getting scared.

He really did want to have answers. These people seemed to know something. "I just don't understand the necessity of the blindfold," he hurriedly spoke.

"It's just a precaution for your safety if we find out you aren't really from where we believe you're from," Daven spoke reasonably. Daven used the elemy to push Behn to come to the same understanding.

Without knowing why Behn found himself nodding in agreement. He slowly stood up and watched as all of the other people in the room also stood and began walking out to the garage through the kitchen. They stopped just before the door and turned. Riccan produced a handkerchief from his pocket and motioned for him to come up next to him.

Behn stood still as Riccan fitted the fabric over his eyes and tied it around the back of his head. He did not know why exactly he had agreed to this whole bizarre scheme. It almost felt as though he were moving slowly through a dream and he kept waiting for himself to wake up. The only problem was he knew this was real. He had set this in motion when he had asked the twins about their necklaces.

Juila came up beside Behn and held onto his arm. She pulled him forward and said, "We're going to take one step down into the garage." He stepped forward until he felt the threshold of the door and then he stepped down. It was a different sensation to be blindfolded. He could hear the people moving ahead of them as they talked and stepped through the garage.

"Here's a slight incline as we get in the vehicle," Juila said.

Behn wondered what type of vehicle had a ramp. He was sure he was going to have to duck, but nobody said anything about it, so he continued up the slope and felt the floor flatten out. He felt Juila stand in front of him and turn him with her hands on both of his arms.

"Sit straight down," Juila instructed. She could not help but smile at this strange adventure.

"When can I take off the blindfold?" Behn asked after he sat in the plush leather seat.

"I don't think it'll be too long," Juila assured him. "From what I could tell, it's not that far to where you're from if Grandpa is correct."

"We'll know shortly," Amanda said from directly behind him.

Behn was startled by Amanda. He had not known she had been near him. It was quite disorienting with the blindfold. He could hear Riccan and Daven whispering ahead of him, but he could not make out what they were saying.

Riccan had taken the left pilot seat and motioned for his father to take the right co-pilot seat up front. After they had fastened their seatbelts, he began initiating the start-up procedures. He looked behind him to make sure everybody was safely on board and then palmed the side door to shut soundlessly. The control panel came to life, and all of the indicator lights were green.

With the telepod powered up, they were hovering several inches off of the ground. The crystal drive was silent. The next step would be to enter the coordinates for their destination. He leaned closer to his father and asked, "What should I enter for the destination?"

"Do you recall a place called Roanoke? It's a small island community several hundred gania north of Pantano on the coast. I think, based on Behn's description of the people, we should begin our search there," Daven replied softly.

Riccan was surprised to hear where they were going. The people rumored to live in that area were not very friendly to strangers. They had odd beliefs about magic and witchcraft. He was not feeling very positive about this adventure now. He trusted his father to know what he was doing, so he entered the location into the telepod system.

He moved his hand to the manual control and looked one last time at his father before he hit the activation button. Daven nodded, and Riccan hit the button. Everything went black, and all sensation was lost.

Behn felt disoriented as though he were experiencing the nightmare from his childhood. He could not explain why he suddenly felt anxious even though he was still sitting in the plush chair. That was when he realized he could no longer feel the chair beneath him. Just as he was getting ready to rip off the blindfold to see what was really going on, sensation returned, and he breathed a sigh of relief. "What just happened?" Behn asked.

"Nothing," Juila reassured. "It won't be too much longer, and we'll be there."

That did not make sense. In the amount of time he had been sitting in the chair, they would only have been able to get to the end of their driveway. This was certainly getting strange. Besides, he did not even think they had moved yet considering he had not heard the car start up, let alone move.

Riccan set the telepod down in a clearing on the beach near the ocean. He scanned the view from the window to see if there were any people around. After issuing all of the commands to power down the craft, he pressed the button to open the side door for them to exit. He was absolutely going to cloak his vehicle once they had all exited. He did not like the feeling he got from this place.

Riccan removed his seatbelt, stood up, and led the way to the side door. Daven followed swiftly on his heels. As he came up beside Behn, he said, "We're there. Unfasten your seatbelt." He turned to Juila and said, "Be sure to lead him out carefully."

Juila looked strangely up at her father. For some reason, he seemed nervous, and that did not inspire great feelings in herself. She complied with her father's request and hurried Behn from the craft and down the ramp.

Once everyone was out of the telepod, Riccan palmed the control to shut the door, and then he pressed a button on his remote to cloak the telepod from view. Even though it was not the first time Juila had watched the procedure, it was always fascinating to suddenly be able to see through what she knew to be a solid aircraft. The technology was truly amazing.

"Go ahead and remove the cloth, Behn," Daven ordered from nearby.

Behn was more than happy to comply. This whole journey had been very confusing. Surely they were still in the garage. It had only been a few minutes at most, and they had never even moved. He looked around himself in utter amazement as he took in the waves from the ocean crashing onto the beach not more than twenty feet away. He spun around and saw the tree line along the edge of the beach. He continued to turn around and finally asked, "What happened to the car?"

"Don't worry about that just now. Does any of this look familiar to you?" Daven asked.

"No," Behn answered. He balled up the cloth and shoved it into his front pants pocket.

"Let's walk up into the trees. Maybe something there will trigger a memory," Daven suggested as he took the lead.

They walked in silence for ten minutes. The ocean was no longer heard behind them, and the forest had grown quite dense. Behn was starting to feel the anxiety creeping up inside him of his childhood fear of the woods. He scolded himself for being so stupid since it was broad daylight and he was with a group of people. *What could possibly go wrong?* He almost laughed out loud at his question. In every scary movie, the main character would always say something so stupid just before all hell broke loose.

Another few minutes passed, and then they were following a stream. Behn realized suddenly that it did look familiar to him. He wanted to cross over to the other side but did not know why. He called out to Daven, "Can we cross somewhere? I think this looks familiar."

Daven nodded and kept walking a bit longer. They came to a narrow section of the creek, and they were able to jump from one bank to the other with little trouble. Daven turned and asked, "What direction feels right now that we're on this side of the water?"

Behn paused to consider. He turned his head to the left and then the right before he answered definitively, "To the right." They set off in the direction he had specified. With each step, he felt closer to his childhood memories. They came to a small trail, and Behn said, "Turn left onto this path."

Daven led the way through the narrow passage in the underbrush. He used his elemy to feel for any people around them who were not a part of their group. Unless the people here could shield themselves, they were utterly alone for quite some distance.

Behn found himself walking faster as they moved through the woods. Soon he found he was striding next to Daven himself. He recognized more and more around him. This was feeling so right. Somehow, Daven had managed to bring him home. His mother was probably sitting in their cabin waiting anxiously for his return. He took the lead and almost started running as yet another twisted tree triggered a memory.

Several turns later, Behn stopped dead in his tracks. Directly ahead of him was the home he remembered. It was exactly the same as it was in his dreams. He turned to make sure the others had caught up to him before he walked slowly forward. His mother would be so excited to see him again.

Daven walked beside Behn. He already knew the cabin was empty. The people who used to live in this area had moved on. They were going to have to do some more research to find where the people of this community had gone.

Behn reached the cabin door and somehow could not bring himself to just open the door and walk in. Instead, he lifted his fist to the door and knocked loudly. He waited and waited. He knocked again, but still there remained silence from inside the cabin. Finally, Behn lifted the latch and let the door swing in with its own weight.

He saw dust swirl as the wind from outside lifted it from the table and other furniture in the room. He could tell it had been vacant for quite some time. A terrible sense of loss overwhelmed Behn's heart. He had believed he would see his mother and now it was just a dead end.

"This is the home from my childhood," Behn said as he turned and looked at Daven. "What happened to my mom?"

"I don't know, Behn. I'll do some research to see if I can find out. At least now we know where to start," Daven said as he patted the distraught Behn on the shoulder.

"Where are we? What's this place called?" Behn demanded.

"Roanoke," Daven said as he tried to turn Behn around to go back to the telepod. He did not want to stay around here too long. He had a strange feeling they were being watched even though he could not sense any people nearby.

"Wait, I want to look in the cabin really fast," Behn said as he shrugged away from Daven's hand.

He entered the cabin and ran his hand along the dusty table. He saw dishes lined up on the shelf above the counter by the front door. As he moved further into the cabin, he opened the cupboard where he remembered his mother retrieving the glass skull. The shelf was empty. He turned and saw several cots along the far wall, including the one where

Jon had been so sick with fever on that last fateful day. There was nothing for him here anymore. He wanted to leave.

Behn turned around and rushed past the surprised Daven and Riccan. He kept walking until he was beyond everyone who had come on this adventure with him. The woods surrounded him again, and he could feel tears of frustration falling from his eyes and down his cheeks. He brushed them away angrily with the backs of his hands and kept on walking until he reached the creek.

Instead of turning to the right, he turned left. He was going to find the last place he remembered being with his mother. It could not be too much further up the stream. It had seemed a long way in the dark, supporting his sick brother, but now he was nearly an adult. His strides were sure, and soon enough he came upon the fork in the stream. He stopped and stared at the small island where his whole life had changed.

He flinched when he felt a hand touch his arm gently. He looked down to his right and saw Juila looking up at him with concern in her eyes. "This is the last place I remember my family being together," he said as he pointed to the island.

"We'll find your mother, Behn," Juila said quietly. She knew what it was like to not be with her parents. Her whole life had been adrift up until recently. She could relate, but she could not share her own journey with Behn. Not yet. She waited a few more minutes in silence and then said, "Let's go back home. We can work on a plan to find your mother."

Behn nodded and took Juila's hand. It felt good to have someone who cared and wanted to help him through this situation. They walked slowly back to where the others had waited for them on the original trail. Together they led the group back to the beach.

Juila kept walking along the shore. She knew where they had left the telepod even though she could not see it. Finally, she stopped and pulled Behn around to face her. "I think you should put the blindfold back on now."

Behn looked at her with a confused expression, "Right here? In the middle of nowhere?"

Juila smiled and nodded as she said, "Yes. We will explain it later, but today you're going to have to trust me."

He shook his head slowly and pulled the handkerchief from his front pocket. He offered it to Juila so she could put it on him.

The other people of their group had caught up to them, talking all around him. Riccan called out from a short distance and said, "Let's get home, kids."

Juila once again held his arm and led him to the waiting vehicle. They walked up the ramp and sat in the same plush seat. Juila fastened his seat belt, and he waited.

He listened intently for the sounds of an engine or any movement at all. This time, he felt when the door closed since the breeze from the ocean no longer entered the vehicle. With intense concentration he thought he could feel a slight movement, but nothing close to what it would take to get them off of the beach.

When all of his senses disappeared, he no longer wanted to be a compliant passenger. He reached up and ripped off the blindfold. Everything was still gone, and he turned his head from side to side desperate to see, hear, or feel anything. Another few seconds passed before they were suddenly back in the garage.

Behn looked around the inside of the telepod with huge eyes. This was unlike any vehicle he had ever seen. He turned and saw Juila looking over at him; her eyes were as big as his.

"Dad, I think we have a problem," she called up to the front of the craft.

Behn shifted his attention to Riccan getting up out of his seat and walking back toward him. He wished he had left on his blindfold.

Riccan stopped in front of him and said, "I think we can probably tell him everything. We've established his origin, after all. Come inside; we have a lot to discuss." Riccan turned and walked down the ramp. He did not turn to look back to see if Behn were complying.

Behn undid his own seatbelt and scrambled out of his seat. He took the few steps to get down the ramp and then turned to see what kind of vehicle in which they had traveled. His jaw dropped as he looked back on the big, red, spacecraft.

Juila grabbed his arm and began pulling him away from the vehicle and toward the garage door. "Come inside, Behn. We have a lot to talk about and not a lot of time."

He looked down at Juila with wide eyes. She did not seem disturbed by the mode of transportation. He had trusted her before, and he would continue to do so. He smiled down at her with renewed appreciation.

Behn felt himself stepping away from the vehicle and toward the door. Even as he turned to take one last look behind him, the strange craft disappeared from view. He gasped and tripped slightly. "Did you see that?" he asked Juila incredulously. "It just disappeared!"

Juila laughed at Behn's statement and replied reasonably, "We can't very well leave the telepod in full view for anyone to see! Of course, it disappeared. Come on, let's get inside."

"No, of course not," Behn repeated sarcastically. "That thing is called a telepod? Where did it come from? What's going on, Juila?"

"Quit asking questions. You're about to find out. Now move your body inside the house!" Juila tugged on his shirt sleeve to emphasize her statement.

Behn looked over his shoulder one last time to verify the garage was indeed empty before he took the last few steps to leave the garage. He stepped through the doorway into the house, uncertain of what was about to happen, but certain he was motivated to find out.

CHAPTER 26

Behn sat down in the chair opposite the couch where Daven, Riccan, Amanda, and Jena had taken seats. He looked up at Juila as she came over and sat on the arm of his chair. It was comforting to have her so close for this conversation. He had so many questions going through his mind and yet he could think of nothing to say.

Daven had been watching the teenage boy carefully. This would be a hard discussion for him since he had no idea he was actually from Tuala. Everything he knew had been from his time on Earth. He decided to begin with Behn's connection to Tuala: his necklace.

"You came to Juila and Jena seeking answers regarding the link between your necklace and theirs. I believe we have proven to you that we are able to help you in your search for your mother. This situation has been complicated by the fact you and your siblings have been displaced, not only from your family but from your world." Daven paused to let his statement sink in.

Behn's eyes darted from his lap to Daven's face. He had known something remarkable had transpired, but he had never imagined he had just been in a different world. "What did you just say?"

"You are from a place called Tuala. It is an alternate reality on Earth which coexists with Earth. It is a rather complex idea to comprehend, but both realities exist at the same time, but are very different one from the other."

"Tell me about this Tuala, then," Behn demanded.

"Tuala is the original creation of Earth. Jehoban lives in Tuala with His people."

"Who is Jehoban?" Behn interrupted.

"He is the one you call God."

Behn sat back in shock. This had to be a fantastic story and not his reality.

"With the exception of Amanda, all of us are from Tuala. We are here on Earth searching for either experience or for the fulfillment of a prophecy. With what you have shared about your mother, I believe you are destined to help us with the prophecy which has only recently been revealed."

"What are you saying?" Behn asked in confusion.

"Your mother has a samara. We believe the samaras are instrumental in bringing the changes needed to Tuala."

"Wait! What are you talking about? What is this prophecy? What does my mother have to do with any of this?" Behn could feel his anger rising. He did not like the idea of these people only helping him to find his mother because they wanted something from her.

Juila touched his shoulder and spoke softly, "My mother discovered a new prophecy in an ancient text. My parents took that new scripture to my grandfather to ask his advice on the matter."

Daven nodded and picked up the story by saying, "Jehoban called a group of us together and told us the prophecy was valid and each of us had a part in making sure it came to fruition. We have been charged with a great mission, and I hope you will help us. Don't answer right now; I want you to think about what this could mean for you and your siblings. You each have a necklace which connects you to Tuala. You have the power available to you through your connection."

Daven pulled his own birth crystal from his tunic pocket and dangled it in front of him.

Behn could hardly believe this old man also had a necklace much like his own. He could not help but ask, "What is this power you are talking about? What does the necklace have to do with it?"

"The crystal is a gift from Jehoban to His people. It is a bond between the land and the children which allows the people to use the earth's elemental energy to do fantastic things." To demonstrate, Daven pulled a sphere of energy from his own dangling crystal. He allowed it to travel in a circle around his crystal before it sank back into the stone.

Behn's eyes grew big as he saw the amazing sight before him. There could have been no way for Daven to trick him. Both of his hands were clearly present, and nobody else in the room had moved. "What does that prove?" he finally asked.

"It proves there is magic in your crystal. You can access that magic to change your life. You are not like the other people here on Earth. You are a child of Tuala. You have untapped potential and talent. We would like to help you explore your talents and achieve the goals Jehoban has set out for your life."

"Why would you want to do that for us?" Behn was stalling for time. His mind was reeling with these new ideas.

"Because I'm a representative of Jehoban. The people of Tuala call me an Elder. I have studied alongside Jehoban, and I understand His will for the people," Daven replied simply.

"An Elder," Behn whispered. He could vaguely remember hearing that title as a child. His mother had wanted to seek out an Elder to help heal Jon from his ailments. Grobin had denied his mother's request. "How come I don't recall anybody using the magic from these stones before my mother made us leave?"

Daven nodded and considered Behn's question. He eventually answered, "From what I know of the people with whom you were raised, they are a different community. They are very superstitious and did not allow people to use their talents."

"If they were so superstitious, then how did we come to have the crystals in the first place?" Behn asked reasonably.

Daven liked how Behn's mind worked. He was able to assimilate information rapidly and ask intelligent questions. He answered, "I'm not sure. It's something which I will be looking into when I get back home."

"In Tuala?" Behn asked.

"Yes. I live in Tuala."

"And you're saying we traveled in the...I think you called it a tele-pod...in the garage to Tuala?" Behn was trying to make sense of the pieces of information he had ascertained. He looked at Juila as he finished the question. He still had a hard time believing he had traveled in a spaceship.

"Yes. Your mother lived in a community called the Roanoke Colony."

An idea popped into Behn's head. He could not remember where, but he had heard of that colony before. When he left this meeting, he was going to do some research of his own.

Daven watched Behn closely. Finally, he offered, "If you'll allow me, I could show you how to access your own crystal."

"I think I'd like that," Behn replied. The easiest way to convince his sister of this day's crazy events would be to show her evidence of its truth.

Elder Daven rose from the couch and took the few steps around the coffee table to stand in front of Behn. He kneeled and put his hands on Behn's head. He spoke softly, "Open your mind. I believe you have already learned what I have shown you, but you have let the knowledge slip to your subconscious." Even as he spoke, he sent tendrils of inquiry into Behn's mind. Almost immediately he found the memory he was after and pulled it forward so Behn could access it. He removed his hands and stepped away to return to the couch. The rest of the work was up to Behn.

Behn had thought it was strange for the old man to put his hands on his head, but then a forgotten memory stepped forward in his mind and shocked him into gasping out loud. "How did you do that?" he asked.

In his mind, he could see his mother sitting across the small wooden table from him and his two siblings. She was laughing at one of their attempts to do something with their crystal. Jon had decided to take the lead and performed perfectly the sphere of energy Daven had just shown him.

'You did it,' his mother had exclaimed as she clapped her hands in approval. She had turned to Behn and Valentina and said, 'Okay, now it's your turn.'

Valentina was the next to produce the expected result, and then finally, Behn achieved the same level of success. Behn had looked up at his mother and smiled at his own success. He remembered exactly the feeling he had when his mother nodded in approval.

He looked up at the people sitting across from him and announced, "I remember doing it! My mom taught us how to access the energy in the crystal when we were little!"

Riccan and Daven both nodded with understanding. Each of them had been taught by their own mothers when they were little, before entering school. It was expected for the children to have a rudimentary knowledge of their crystal's power by the time they entered school. At eight, Behn and his siblings would have learned several levels of skill.

"You have the memories; you just have to recall them," Daven instructed. "Don't try to force your memory, let it come on its own."

Behn nodded seriously. He had a lot to consider from today's revelations and wondered how much of what he had learned today he would share with his sister. Maybe once he could use the energy in his crystal he would talk about it with her, until then, he would wait. Too much was at stake for him to mess this up by revealing too much, too soon.

This whole afternoon had the qualities of a very elaborate dream. He looked up at Juila and realized she was implying she, too, was from Tuala and not Earth at all. Was the story about South Africa just that: a story? Everything was so confusing. Behn leaned forward until his elbows rested on his knees and his hands hung down in front of him.

"Okay, let me get this straight. All of you, except for Mrs. Stel, are from Tuala. You are living here because you want the girls to experience Earth. You are telling me that I and my brother and sister are all from Tuala as well and the place you took me was not here on Earth, but in Tuala?"

"Yes. You've summed it up pretty accurately," Amanda spoke for the first time.

"Where do you fit into all of this?" Behn asked her.

"It's quite complicated. Eventually, I will be moving to Tuala permanently. For right now, we will stay here for the girls to finish school," she answered.

"Tell me more about this prophecy and how you think I fit into it," he asked.

Amanda retold the story of discovering the new scripture and quoted it perfectly so he would understand their mystery. "We think the crystal skulls are a part of what will make the changes take place. It's still unclear how, but the more samaras we discover, we hope we'll uncover more clues. If your mother possesses one of the samaras then she may be a part of this as well.

"We would help you find your mother regardless of her custody of the crystal skull. I had enough help finding my girls, and I want to do the same for you as well." She smiled and stopped talking.

"I'm confused. When did you lose Juila and Jena?"

"It's another long story. Let's just say for simplicity's sake, we have been reunited after sixteen years apart." She patted Jena's hand and smiled lovingly over at Juila.

"Sixteen years? That's as long as they've been alive! Hopefully, I'll get to hear the story sometime." He shook his head at the idea of being apart for as long as that. He was even more grateful for the memories he had of his mother; it was more than Juila or Jena had of their own mom. He had only been separated from his mother for half of his life.

"It is going to take some time to take in all of these details," Amanda cautioned.

"You're telling me!" Behn said. He needed some time alone to think. He stood up and said, "I'm going to go home now. You can be sure I'll be back with a ton more questions, but you've given me plenty to consider."

"I'll walk you out," Juila offered as she stood up from the arm of the chair. She had been worried when Behn had removed his blindfold. She had dire predictions of her grandpa Daven swiping Behn's mind. She was glad it had all turned out so well. Now she would not have to keep this huge secret from the one person she had begun to care about on Earth. In fact, it was ironic that the person to whom she had been attracted had also originated from Tuala.

She walked by his side, and neither said anything until after Juila had closed the front door behind them. "Are you going to be okay?" she inquired.

"Yeah, I asked for it, didn't I?" he chuckled. "I just had no idea what I was getting myself into when I wanted answers about your necklace."

"If you want help learning to use yours, Jena and I are very good at it," she offered shyly.

"Really? You'd help me?" He had stopped walking and turned to face her.

"Of course. Your journey has been more perilous than my own. I had plenty of help along the way, and I'd do the same for you. I can teach

Valentina and Jon, too, if you wanted." She plunged her hands into her pants pockets to hide how nervous she suddenly felt.

"I'd rather keep this to myself until I can really prove it to Val. She is really set on keeping things status quo with our adoptive family. I understand her need, but we have a mother out there who is probably wondering about our well-being."

Juila nodded understandingly. It was Behn's call as to what to share with his siblings. She would help wherever he needed. She offered, "Why don't you come over after school every day and we can give you private crystal lessons in the library?"

"I'd like that," he replied. "Hey, are we still on for the movies tomorrow?"

"As long as you're not too freaked out after all you've discovered about me today." She looked up at him with hope in her eyes.

"As it turns out, you and I have more in common than I ever would have guessed. Hopefully, you're not too freaked out about me coming from some strange colony," he joked.

Juila laughed. She was glad he could make a jest about it. She had fresh hope for them actually having a future together. "I'm good with weird!"

"Me, too," he laughed along with her. He really needed to get home even though he wished he could stay and talk more with Juila. Not knowing what else to do, he leaned forward and kissed her on the cheek. He pulled away and smiled as he turned to get into his car. "I'll see you at school tomorrow!"

"Yep, I'll see you, too," she called after him as she lifted her hand to wave. As he drove away, she frowned at how lame her reply had sounded. There were so many other things she could have said, but, no, she had to say something dumb. She walked back into the house to see what her family had discussed during her absence.

She came into the living room and looked around in confusion. "Where's Grandpa?"

"He went home," Riccan replied. "How did Behn seem when you walked him out?"

"Pretty normal, actually. He's going to come over after school every day so we can teach him how to use his birth crystal." She looked over at Jena and said, "He doesn't want to tell either of his siblings about any of this until he has learned to use his crystal."

Jena nodded with understanding. She had been reading Behn's thoughts and knew he was going to be okay with this new information.

Juila turned back to their parents and said, "Behn and Luke are also going to be taking us out to the movies tomorrow night. I hope that's okay."

Amanda smiled at her beautiful young daughter and said, "I think it's a great idea. Behn will need something normal to do after spending an afternoon learning to use his crystal. I may have learned while I was dreaming, but the lessons were tiring nonetheless."

CHAPTER 27

"Hey, Behn. Where have you been?" Jon asked when he came into Behn's room and found him resting in bed on his back.

"I gave Luke, Jena, and Juila a ride home," he answered.

"You sure were gone a long time. What took you so long?" Jon persisted. He could tell Behn was keeping something from him. Eventually, he would work it out of him.

"I stayed at the girls' house and visited with their family. I didn't realize it had gotten so late," he replied lamely.

"What did you talk about?"

Behn realized there was not much he could share with Jon unless he wanted to tell him the truth. Even then he did not think Jon would believe him. Not yet anyway. He had to answer, so he said, "Riccan's dad came over, and he talked about his family."

"It sounds kind of boring," Jon said as he plunked himself down on the bed next to Behn. "Did you ask Juila out already?"

"Yes. We're going to the movies tomorrow night with Luke and Jena. Why?" He looked over at his brother. It was not like him to be so curious about Behn's personal life.

"Val and I had a bet going."

Behn rolled over and propped his head on his hand and asked, "What was the bet, and who won?"

"I won, naturally. We bet on how long it would take you to ask her out again. Val thought you'd wait until the end of the week," he replied with a grin.

"I'm glad to hear I'm so interesting to the two of you. You both need to get a life!" He rolled onto his back again and then decided to turn the tables on his brother when he asked, "So when are you going to go out with Sofia?"

Jon actually blushed as he turned his head away toward the door. He wished he had kept his mouth shut.

Behn poked him in the ribs to try to get him to answer.

"I don't know. I don't think she's really that into me."

"Why would you say that? I thought the two of you did something after school today."

"We did. We went to the frozen yogurt shop. Sofia hardly said anything the whole time we ate. As soon as we finished, she couldn't get me home fast enough." Jon shrugged his shoulders. "I don't understand what happened."

"It might not have had anything to do with you. You should call her and find out."

"No thanks," he said and shuddered at the thought of getting the cold shoulder over the phone as well. It would only make the whole situation worse. It was better to just let it go.

"I'll ask Juila about it tomorrow," he suggested. "I'm going to be spending the afternoons at their house for a while. Juila asked for my help with some studies."

"Sure! Studying! Ha!" Jon poked Behn in the ribs and then jumped off of the bed before his brother could retaliate. He beat a hasty retreat out of the bedroom just as something hit the back side of the door. He laughed loudly for Behn to hear and then returned to the living room to watch his favorite TV show before dinner.

Behn turned his head back up toward the ceiling. He really wished he could talk to someone about all of the things he had learned that day. The longer he thought about it all, the more fantastical it all seemed. Things like this did not happen to adopted kids, not unless it was part of a fantasy fiction movie.

He really did remember his mother teaching him to use his birth crystal.

That was a memory he had forgotten. Could he do it on his own? He suddenly needed to try. Behn sat up on the bed and crossed his legs in front of him. He pulled the crystal out from under his collar and nestled it in his palm.

His thoughts began to focus on the childhood memory and how it felt to succeed in making the energy come out of the stone. He continued to stare at the crystal and willed it to do something. Just as he was about to give up, he felt a pull of energy. A small light appeared outside of his crystal.

"What are you doing?" Val asked from the doorway.

Behn dropped the crystal and looked up guiltily. He had no idea what she had seen, so he tried to sound casual as he said, "Nothing. I was just looking at the mounting of the crystal."

"Bull, I saw you doing something. Spill it!" Valentina walked into his room like she owned the place.

"You're reaching, Val. Besides, Jon told me about the bet you had going. Don't you have anything better to do than keep tabs on me?" He decided to use a diversionary tactic since she seemed determined to stay in his room and make trouble.

"I was just messing with Jon to cheer him up since his disastrous outing with Sofia. I don't get that girl. Jon is a perfect gentleman. Any girl would be lucky to go out with him." She sat down on the bed where Jon had vacated.

"Yeah, Jon's a good guy. I told him I'd ask Juila about it tomorrow. There had to have been something else going on," Behn agreed.

Val turned and looked at him and asked seriously, "What were you doing with your necklace, Behn. Don't tell me it was nothing, either."

"I was just looking at it, Val. Our mom gave this to us when we were little. Don't you think it's a little strange that we can't take them off?" He sidestepped her question with one of his own.

"It is weird." She pulled her own pendant out from under her collar. Today it was a bright green as the sunlight touched it. She was always surprised to see how different it could be colored depending on the ambient light. Its color ranged from purple to red to brown to bright, almost lime green. "How come mine changes color and yours and Jon's stay the same?"

"I don't know. It's another mystery." He looked down at his gray stone.

It always looked the same, and he was glad. "Hey, have you ever heard of the Roanoke Colony?"

"What are you talking about?" she asked, surprised at his sudden change in subject.

"I heard someone talking about a Roanoke Colony today, and I couldn't place where I'd heard it before. Do you have any ideas?"

"Have you looked it up on the internet?" She stood up and walked over to his desk where his computer was already turned on.

"No, I hadn't gotten that far," he admitted. He was just as happy to let Valentina do the research. His mind was too preoccupied at the moment.

Valentina sat down in the chair and typed out a few words in the search engine. She hit the enter button and waited a few seconds for the results to appear. She scanned the results and summarized her findings, "It looks like it was an English settlement founded by Sir Walter Raleigh in August of 1585 on the coast of North Carolina. The original one hundred or so colonists suffered from a lack of food supplies and attacking Indians and returned to England a year later. Another hundred people decided to try to settle the same place again in 1587 with John White. White returned to England to get more supplies when the war with Spain delayed his return to Roanoke. By the time he finally returned in August 1590, everyone had vanished."

She finished talking and asked, "What's this about, Behn?"

He had been wondering the same thing. He shrugged his shoulders and said, "It must be a different group."

"Who?" Valentina demanded.

"I heard some kids talking about finding the lost Roanoke Colony over spring break," Behn lied.

"That sounds stupid," Valentina replied. She got up from the computer and turned to leave the room. She called over her shoulder, "Dinner should be ready in about ten minutes."

"Okay, thanks," he called out to her as she left the room. He fell back onto his pillow and contemplated this new information. What if the colonists from 1587 had accidentally stumbled on a way into Tuala? Could there be gateways between the worlds? Is that the reason the people on Tuala were so scared to use the powers of the birth crystals? It would make sense if they had kept to themselves and still believed as the people from the 1500's believed. The people of that time had been a superstitious lot. It could go a long way in explaining their fear of outsiders.

He would have to ask Juila what she thought about his new theory. It did not sound any more outlandish than the one about him coming from a different world. It seemed everything was plausible these days.

ELDER DEBBON HAD EXPERIENCED one frustrating event after another this day. He was glad to finally go to his house and get away from all of the petitioning constituents. If he had been forced to see one more sniveling petitioner, he could not account for how he would have reacted. Petre MacVeen had been the last person he had seen during the day, and he was always trying, even on a good day.

Petre had actually accused him of delaying his decision on a matter he had disputed over a declan before. Petre wanted compensation from Elder Vargen for a stolen artifact. Elder Vargen had denied having ever received anything. Without proof, Petre could not present a case worthy of judgment. It was a simple matter where no evidence of wrongdoing appeared to exist.

He teleported himself directly into his office at his home several gania away from his work Residence. Many Elders chose to live in the Residence where they worked. Debbon had found it better to separate the two houses for his own peace of mind.

Debbon sat down wearily at his desk and rested his head in his hands. He used the elemy to relieve his head of the pulsing ache behind his eyes. It had been a long time since he had been so upset.

There was a brief knock on his office door before it was flung open. His son, Willian, stood framed by the doorway. He stalked into the office and put his fists on the other side of Debbon's desk. "How long has Jena been gone?"

Debbon looked up at his son uncomprehendingly for a moment. How had Willian found out? "What are you talking about?"

"I just came from one of the special sessions. Rasa told me both Jena and Juila are on an extended vacation. Where did they go? When are they coming back? How come I wasn't asked before Jena left?"

Debbon did not like the way his son talked about Jena like she was personal property. He scowled back at his son and ordered, "Sit down!" He pointed to the chair behind Willian and refused to say another word until his errant boy complied.

He used the few moments of rebellion to compose his thoughts before he answered his son. "I met with Jehoban a couple of mesans ago. He reunited the girls with their mother. They are spending time with her for a while. You were not consulted because Jehoban had made the decision."

Willian still looked rebellious despite the fact Jehoban had been the one to choose. "You've known about this for mesans, and yet you didn't think to tell me? I want to know where Jena is so I can go visit her. Don't you think I should meet her mother as well?"

"No, Willian. I think you should let Jena have this time to herself. There will be enough time with her once you are married," Debbon reasoned.

His son scowled at being denied. Jena was his betrothed. She belonged to him, and he should be her first priority in everything. It did not matter that Jena had never known her mother. She should depend solely on him and nobody else. "I want to hear it directly from Jena. Send her a message that I want to talk to her."

Debbon stood up and walked around his desk. "I'll not be ordered around by you, Willian. If you want to send Jena a message, then I suggest you get on your patil and make it happen. *If* she replies to you, then you'll have your answer." Debbon was angry enough to strike his own son. He balled his fists to contain himself and walked stiffly out the door of his office. He had sought sanctuary in his own home and yet he had managed to find discord there as well.

BEHN AND LUKE picked up the girls from their house right at seven-thirty in the evening. The movie was scheduled to begin at eight, so they had a few minutes to kill before they had to get going.

Riccan pulled Behn aside and asked him, "How are you feeling today?"

Behn smiled at Riccan's question and replied, "I'm fine. I just wish I could have come over today after school to have the girls give me my first lesson. I never knew keeping a secret from my brother and sister could be so complicated!"

Riccan chuckled. He was an only child, so he had no experience with which to compare. "Hopefully, you won't have to keep it from them for too long. They may actually have memories which you don't have which may help us in the search for your mother."

Behn shook his head and replied, "I don't think so. Val and I have talked about our dreams and memories at length."

"Just consider it, Behn." Riccan patted his arm and then turned to kiss his girls goodbye. He wished he could have spent more time with them, but he had ended up working late and was too tired to time it home. "What movie are you going to see?" he asked Juila.

Juila turned to Behn and raised her eyebrows in question.

Behn chuckled and answered Riccan's question, "It's an Adam Sandler comedy called The Waterboy. I hear it's pretty good."

Riccan chuckled again since he had seen the movie trailers and knew it was about a young man who wanted to play football. He was not sure what the girls would think of the subject matter, but it really did not matter so much as the company. "Have fun, you guys. I expect you both to be home before midnight."

As much as he tried to play the stern father, he knew he could always check in on the girls through their necklaces. He had the sudden idea that Behn's mother could still be monitoring her children on Earth through their crystals. He would have to ask his father if it were a possibility.

Amanda came away from her daughters to stand by Riccan's side as the two couples left the house. She tweaked him in the side and said, "You sound like a very concerned father."

"Hey, I do what I can!" he replied as he smiled down at his beautiful wife. "Have you talked to your parents lately?"

"Sure. Was there something in particular in which you wanted me to talk to them about?" Amanda wondered what Riccan was thinking.

"Your father had said he would be mulling over the new prophecy. I just wondered if he had come up with anything different than what we've been working on."

"Hmm, nothing new on that front. Riccan, it's made me so happy to have my parents in-the-know about our lives." She hugged him closer in her happiness.

"I know. I'm glad for it, too. Now we don't have to watch everything we say or do around them. Have the girls planned any trips to your parents' house?"

"Not yet, but they keep asking about getting their driver's licenses. How did our girls grow up so fast?" Amanda started to laugh. Normally parents would say that of their children as they slowly watched them age, their children had been given to them already almost grown.

Riccan laughed along with her. "I know exactly what you mean!"

"I hope the girls enjoy their first movie theater experience," Amanda said as they moved from the foyer to the living room. They had planned their own movie night in the privacy of their house.

"I'm sure they'll love it."

"I know Juila will. I'm more worried about Jena. She seems more sullen lately. Do you think it has anything to do with Willian? I'm surprised we haven't heard anything from him."

Riccan looked at Amanda as though she had just said something remarkable. He shook his head at how stupid he had been the whole time the girls had been with them.

"What is it, Riccan? What did I say?"

"Willian may have tried to reach Jena, but I've never shown her my patil here at the house. She has no idea she can access her personal account and still converse with Willian. If he's left her any messages, she would not have known about them."

"Why hasn't Jena asked about how to get in touch with him then? Don't you think it odd?" Amanda did not have a good feeling about her daughter's betrothed. The more she heard about the relationship, the less she liked it.

"I wonder if Rasa has access to the girls' personal accounts," Riccan mused softly to himself as he changed the direction of his steps from going to the living room to heading down the hall to his office. Riccan left Amanda behind in the living room and said, "I'll be back in a couple of minutes. I want to check something out."

From another secret compartment in the wall, he opened the access to his own patil. He touched a couple of buttons on the touchscreen and dialed up Rasa's code.

In a few moments, Rasa's face showed life-sized on the screen. "Hi, Riccan. How's everything going? No trouble, I hope."

"I hope not, either," Riccan replied. He went on to share his concerns about Willian and waited to see what Rasa had to say.

She frowned before she said, "We just held another Elders' children summit. Willian was asking after Jena, and I told him that she and her sister were visiting with their mom. He tried not to show it, but I could see he was furious. Apparently, Elder Debbon had not seen fit to tell his son that Jena has been living on Earth. I didn't tell him that part, either. What would you like me to do?"

"Do you have access to Jena's personal patil account? If Willian has tried to contact her, then I'm afraid he could get quite upset at thinking he was being ignored all this time."

"I see," Rasa said. All too clearly she saw how much trouble this could bring Jena. Willian was a hot-headed child who had no qualms about taking out his frustrations on the quiet and gentle Jena. "I'll send you both of the girls' account information. I'll leave it up to your discretion to handle whatever information you find in their accounts. Good luck!"

Rasa did not envy Riccan's and Amanda's positions in this whole matter. They appeared to have drawn the short stick as far as she was concerned. Everyone else had been given more time with the girls rather than their own parents. It was unfortunate. She would do whatever she could to make things easier for everyone involved.

Rasa tapped out a few commands and accessed the information she was seeking. She copied the data and pasted it into another link on her patil. "Okay, I just messaged the links to you. Let me know if you need anything else."

"Thanks, Rasa. We really appreciate it," Riccan replied and disconnected the call. He opened his messenger box and retrieved the links. He touched Jena's link first. For the next few minutes he waited for all of the messages to load to her inbox.

As each new message popped in it showed the sender's name. One after another, after another, and another showed Willian as the sender. There were more than one hundred messages from Willian alone. Riccan scrolled down to the earliest message and opened it. The message seemed innocent enough. Willian was asking after Jena's wellbeing since he had not seen her in a few days. The date confirmed it was right after the girls had gone with them to his parents' house in Pantano.

He clicked on the next message and could tell Willian was peeved at not being answered in the previous missive. Each subsequent message became more rude and blunt. This was not how a man talked with his betrothed, or anyone, for that matter. This was very unacceptable. By the time he opened the last message, he was fuming with anger.

Someone was going to have to teach this kid some manners. Riccan no longer cared that Willian was the son of an Elder. As far as Riccan was concerned, Willian was a spoiled, incompetent brat who did not deserve his daughter. This was going to come to an end.

He jumped in his seat as he felt a hand touch his shoulder. He looked up and behind him and saw his wife looking down on him with concern.

"What have you found out, Riccan?"

"Just that Willian is not going to be betrothed to our daughter much longer!" He stood up and shut the cupboard to hide his patil. He had to take a walk to control his raging thoughts. Riccan took Amanda's hand in his and led her from the office.

They walked outside on the garden paths, and Riccan told his wife about the messages. Riccan recounted the gist of the messages he had read to Amanda. By the time he told her about the final message, he was fuming all over again.

"He had the audacity to tell Jena that if she did not answer him within the next twenty-four hours that he would request her to be sanctioned for abusing their relationship! Can you believe his audacity? If anyone should be sanctioned, it should be Willian. The amount of verbal abuse in those messages was inexcusable."

Amanda was not sure what the sanctioning would entail, but she could easily share in Riccan's anger. She asked, "When was his last message sent?"

"Only a couple of hours ago," Riccan replied as he kicked a fallen palm frond from the path angrily.

"What can we do about this, Riccan? We can't let it continue, and I don't want Jena to read any of those messages."

"I already took the first step by forwarding each of the messages to Elder Debbon, my father, and Rasa. I have aired my concerns and have asked for their advice on the matter." Riccan felt as though he had not done nearly enough to defend his daughter's honor from that bastard.

"So I guess we just wait and see what comes of it then." Amanda put her arm around Riccan's waist to show her support of the steps he had taken thus far.

CHAPTER 28

The next morning, Amanda found herself alone in the house. The girls were at school, and Riccan had left for work. Taking Riccan's advice about using her intuition in trying to locate the missing samaras, she decided to go into the office and do some research of her own.

After much thought, she decided to look into a part of her dream which did not seem to fit with the rest of the story. Why had she dreamed about Cannon Memorial Asylum? She typed the name of the asylum into the search engine and waited to see what the results would tell her about the facility.

As she scanned the articles, she learned it was located in North Carolina, built in 1962. Then she came across an article which showed the medical group which ran the asylum had been bought out by another company. With the merger of the two sections, Cannon Memorial was slated to be shut down in the beginning of 1999.

She clicked on the article and read the details of the merger. More importantly, she wanted to know where Dr. Gascon was going after the facility was shut down. She wanted to make sure she stayed clear of any place where he was actively doing business. Further review of the article showed Dr. Gascon had retired from institutional practice to go into private practice and consultation for coma patients. Apparently, he had not let go of his fascination with his multi-dimensional theory.

Now that Dr. Gascon was no longer an issue, Amanda felt the overwhelming urge to visit the place of her dream. She could not say what had led her to the idea, but she was willing to take the leap of faith that she should follow her intuition. She scrolled through the several articles until she located the phone number for Cannon Memorial. She wrote down the number and turned off the computer.

She had left her cell phone in the living room, so she left the office to make the call. Amanda dialed the number and expected to get an answering machine. To her surprise, someone picked up the call.

"Cannon Memorial, may I help you?" a woman's bored voice asked.

"I was wondering if the facility were open for a walk-through," Amanda asked.

"There isn't much here anymore, lady. The facility's going to be closed in several weeks. The patients and their records have already been moved to their new facility."

"That's fine. Perfect, actually," Amanda spoke. She rapidly wracked her brain for what to say to the person for why she wanted to tour the empty facility. "I'm working on a documentary, and I need to see how a mental facility is set up."

"Whatever makes you happy, lady. Our building is open from eight to five during the week. We close for lunch from noon to one for the few staff who are still closing things up. Feel free to come over and walk the empty halls."

"Great! I'll plan on coming up tomorrow then. Thank you!" Amanda hung up the phone and could not control the thrill of excitement she felt coursing through her body. She knew she was onto something important. Maybe she would even find the next clue to lead them to a samara. She chuckled at her last idea, but remained hopeful, nonetheless.

After a moment's thought, Amanda had another idea. She opened her phone and dialed her mother's number. After two rings the call connected.

"Hello?" Diane answered the phone.

"Mom, it's me, Amanda. Hey, are you busy today?"

"Not really. What's going on?" Diane could tell her daughter was excited by the tone of her voice.

Amanda had begun to walk back into the office to look up flight information even as she was formulating her plan. "Do you want to go on a trip with me?"

"A trip? Where are you thinking of going and when?"

"I'd like to check out Cannon Memorial Asylum today. The only way we could do it would be to catch a flight to Charlotte. We can rent a car and be there before they close. What do you think? Are you in or should I go alone?" Amanda had pulled up flight records and saw the next scheduled flight left Miami at 9:55. If they hurried, they'd be just in time.

"You can't go alone! I'm going with you. How much time do I have to get ready?" Diane could not imagine letting her daughter step foot in that nuthouse after what she had read in Amanda's journal. For that matter, she could not imagine Amanda even wanting to go there herself.

"I'll pick you up in twenty minutes. We're going to have to hurry to make the 9:55 flight. We'll come back tonight, so we won't need to pack anything. See you in a couple of minutes." Amanda hung up on her mom and then dialed the number for American Airlines. Even as she raced through the house, grabbed her purse, and ran to the garage, she talked with the ticket agent and arranged the flights.

By the time she had reached the highway, everything had been arranged. She reached her mother's house in record time and was thankful her mom was waiting on the sidewalk. They were on their way again within a matter of seconds.

Diane could not help but smile at Amanda's infectious mood.

They were just in time for the flight and boarded the plane only twenty minutes after arriving and checking into the flight. Diane was surprised to find they had been booked in First Class. She had only flown a few times in her life, and it had always been in Coach.

The flight was just over two hours long and had been very pleasant. Amanda rushed them off of the plane and through the airport to the car rental area. It was only twelve-thirty, but they were going to have to drive an additional two hours to get to the asylum.

She was glad they had been fed on the airplane so they would not have to stop for food until dinner. She had booked their return flight for eight-fifteen that evening. They were going to be crunched for time, but she believed they could accomplish all they needed to get done.

They made good time on the interstate in their economy rental car.

Amanda imagined Riccan would have picked a luxury car for the trip, but she thought this car would be just fine, plus her mom would probably have been uncomfortable in anything nicer.

"What do you hope to find at the asylum," Diane asked Amanda now that they were alone. She had been dying to ask questions while they were flying, but it just had not seemed private enough on the airplane. It seemed as though the flight attendants were always lurking nearby to cater to their every whim. It had been quite annoying, really.

"I'm not sure. Jehoban had told me to go with my intuition. My gut is telling me that Cannon Memorial holds more to this story than just making it so I would wake up from the coma."

"What about Dr. Gascon? Doesn't he work there?" Diane recalled her reaction to Dr. Gascon once she had read what the man had done to Amanda from the writings in her journal. When she had met the man at Amanda's last appointment with Dr. Medin, she had wondered at Amanda's response to the doctor. Now she knew how truly evil the doctor was and she did not want her daughter anywhere near the crazy man.

"Oh, didn't I tell you? The asylum is closing down. Dr. Gascon has retired to private practice. There won't be any doctors or patients at the hospital. It's one of the reasons I wanted to get in there before they won't allow visitors into the facility." Amanda kept her eyes focused on the road as she spoke. She did not want to miss any signs indicating turns for their route.

"Well, that's a relief!" Diane said as she looked out the side window and enjoyed the passing scenery for a while. The silence continued until Diane repeated her initial question. "What do you hope to find there?"

"I hope there's a clue to finding another samara," she answered simply.

"How will you know?"

"I'm hoping I'll feel it like I did with the one we bought in New Orleans."

"Oh." Diane could not understand what her daughter meant by feeling it. The whole thing about the necklaces and the elemy was a mystery to her.

Once Amanda turned off of highway NC-181N she pulled a piece of paper out of her purse and handed it to her mother.

"What's this?" Diane asked as she unfolded the paper.

"Directions to the asylum. I don't want to get lost now that we're this close. Tell me what my next turn will be, please." Amanda kept watching for signs.

For another hour, her mother made sure they were driving on the correct roads. Finally, they pulled into the parking lot of the asylum. The imposing red brick building was straight ahead of them, and Amanda suppressed a shiver of fear. She was more thankful than ever to know there were no doctors or patients remaining in the building.

They got out of the car and went to the entrance. Amanda could not help but feel the door would be locked and this trip would have been a waste of time. She put her hand on the handle and pulled the door open. She waited for her mother to enter first while she held the door open.

A reception desk was the first thing they encountered. A woman, probably the same one Amanda had spoken to earlier, sat at the desk. They walked up to her and Amanda leaned on the credenza type desk to say, "I called earlier about taking a tour of the facility."

"Yes, I remember. I thought you said you were coming tomorrow?" she asked with a slightly annoyed tone.

"Change of plans," Amanda said brightly.

"Suit yourself. Put on these badges. Be sure to return them to my desk before five o'clock, or you will be locked in the building all night," she answered sharply.

"Okay," Amanda said as she picked up the two badges and handed one to her mother. She turned and addressed her mother, "Are you ready for this?"

"As ready as you are!" Diane answered. She could tell her daughter was nervous and possibly afraid. She clipped the badge on her shirt and followed her daughter down the long corridor.

They stopped at an elevator and waited for it to open. Amanda was trying to decide if she wanted to investigate the basement or the fourth floor first. She was more afraid of the basement so she thought she would rather get that out of the way first. Besides, she only had one room in which to look in the basement. There were several places on the fourth floor which held her interest.

The doors opened, and they stepped into the large enclosure. The doors closed and Amanda picked the button marked with a B. They waited for several seconds as they felt the elevator drop down the shaft and come to an abrupt stop at the bottom. The doors opened to the dark hallway, exactly as Amanda remembered it being.

Amanda took a deep breath and stepped out of the elevator. The sooner she got this done, the sooner she could go back up to the daylight. She marched down the hall until she reached the last room she remembered from this dreadful facility. When she reached the room in question, she pushed the door open and peered inside before committing herself to entering the space.

Once she was satisfied the room was empty, she tentatively stepped inside. Most of the equipment had been removed; however, the chair to which she had been strapped was a prominent feature in the corner. She shivered with the recollection of being involuntarily strapped to the chair before having electroshock therapy administered.

She pulled her stare away from the chair and began to methodically search the room for any clues. She opened the empty cupboards and drawers without any success. It was a relief, really, since it meant they could get out of the creepy room. She could not get over the sense of being watched the whole time they were in there.

Diane had stood in the doorway, making sure nobody shut them in the room. She watched as Amanda searched everywhere and was glad when she was done.

"Let's get out of here," Amanda said as she marched past her mother to head back to the elevator. She punched the elevator call button and was even further relieved when the doors immediately opened. Amanda stepped in first and waited for her mother to join her. She pressed the button for the fourth floor and did not breathe until the doors clunked solidly shut on the view of the basement corridor.

She let out her breath loudly and said, "I had to get that over with first. I'm glad it's over now."

"Was that room like you remembered?" Diane asked.

"Exactly like my memory. Of course, there was more equipment, but the chair was the same," Amanda replied and shivered again.

"I'm sorry, Amanda. I don't know what this is all about but seems like you had some pretty scary dreams while I was sitting with you at the hospital. If I had known, I would have tried to comfort you more." Diane felt helpless to help her daughter through this venture.

"It's enough that you're here with me now, Mom. I'm really thankful not to be doing this alone," she said as she reached over and hugged her mom with one arm over her mother's shoulders.

"Me, too," Diane agreed.

The elevator door opened to a well-lit corridor. The two of them stepped out and looked first one direction and then the other. Amanda could see the nurse's station and thought it was as good of a place to begin as any. She walked confidently toward the desk until a powerful force hit her and stopped her dead in her tracks.

Diane bumped into Amanda since she had stopped so suddenly. "What is it, Amanda? What's wrong?" She looked around them with wide eyes, anticipating danger from any direction.

"Don't you feel that, Mom?" Amanda whispered.

"Feel what?" Diane demanded.

"That power! It's so strong! How can you not feel that, Mom?" Amanda turned her body until she was facing the direction where the pull felt the strongest. She began walking slowly to keep her senses trained on the source of the energy reaching out to her.

Diane trailed after her daughter. She could see Amanda was concentrating intently and did not want to disturb her concentration with unnecessary questions. She smiled at herself because she knew if Chris had been there, he would have been seeking answers to a million questions and talking non-stop.

Amanda stopped walking when she came to a patient room. She looked up and almost laughed when she saw it was room 426. The very room from her dreams. With a small push, the door slowly swung open to show the small cot still in place on the far wall and the small table next to it. She had spent so many hours sitting on that very bed. She had also relearned how to use her crystal on that last fateful day.

Amanda took a couple of steps into the room. She turned around to say something to her mother when her attention was caught by the comic strips taped to the wall. It had been a small detail she had written about in her journal, but now it seemed important. The facility did not have any decoration whatsoever. These comics had no place on the wall. She reached up and pulled them from off of the wall.

"What do you have there, Amanda? Is it a clue?" Diane asked as she came up beside her daughter to see what she had found. "Comics?" she asked with a puzzled expression. She looked back at where they had been taped to the wall and gasped out loud. She pointed to the hole in the wall, but could not manage to say a single word.

Amanda looked over to where her mother was pointing and could not believe what she was seeing. Inside the wall was one of the missing samaras. She stepped forward and reached in and took hold of the samara.

As soon as her skin came in contact with the ancient crystal, Amanda began to see visions. There were too many of them going by too fast to be able to really understand what she was seeing. By instinct, she concentrated her own crystal's power to try to direct the flow of information. Several minutes passed as Amanda stood transfixed by the samara. Finally, the trance dissipated.

Amanda turned and looked at her mother with wide eyes, "I know now what I have to do next!"

THE DESTINY OF HUNTERS

BOOK THREE OF THE CHOSEN

CHAPTER 1

Amanda held the samara in her hands as she turned and looked at her mother. She had seen so many visions of what was to come and now she knew what her next step should be in her journey.

"What is that thing, Amanda?" Diane asked. She had been worried when her daughter had remained immobile for so long while holding the strange clear, crystal skull.

"This is a samara, Mom," Amanda said as she continued to hold it in both of her hands, completely amazed because she had found it in the first place. Coming to the Cannon Memorial Asylum had merely been based on a hunch from her memories on which she had followed up. She had hoped to find a clue to lead her to a samara, instead she had found the object itself.

"What is a samara?" her mother asked with a skeptical expression on her face. She looked up from the strange object to her daughter's face. Amanda looked positively radiant, healthier than she had looked since before her seven-year coma, in fact.

"There is a legend in Tuala about there being thirteen of these skulls. Each samara was given to a different individual to hold through time to keep it safe until they would be needed again. We believe with the revelation of the new prophecy that these samaras are the keys to the success of accomplishing the prophecy."

Amanda had tried to simplify the complicated task for her mother, but she was sure it would only lead to more questions. At the moment, she knew the stone in her hands was the reason for her coming to this facility. Since she had custody of the object, they should probably leave before someone questioned them. "I think we should get out of here, Mom," Amanda said as she reached for her voluminous purse which was hanging from her shoulder. She carefully placed the samara in her bag and took a step toward the door to the hallway.

Diane seemed to think Amanda's suggestion about leaving seemed a rather perfect idea. She had not liked the feel of the building since the moment they had parked in the parking lot and looked up at the imposing brick structure. It was hard to imagine people had actually been kept here, both voluntarily and involuntarily, while they were being psychologically evaluated or studied. She followed Amanda into the hall and matched her pace as they walked back to the elevator.

They left their visitor badges with the unfriendly receptionist and walked out the front door. They both took a deep breath in relief as they exited the building and crossed the parking lot to their rental car. There was an uneasy sense which both of them could feel even as they were getting farther from the building.

Amanda dug the key out of her purse and brushed her finger against the samara as she did so. She received another burst of energy, more intense than a static shock, but not painful. It was more surprising than anything and she swiftly grabbed the key and withdrew her hand. She clicked on the remote to unlock the doors even as they were still approaching the economy class car.

As Amanda dropped down into the driver's seat, she tossed her purse onto the back seat. She put the key in the ignition and started the engine before she even had the front door closed. As soon as she saw her mother's door shut, Amanda shifted the car into reverse and backed out of their parking space. The sooner she left the premises, the better she would feel.

She pulled onto the main road leading away from the asylum and drove without any regard for direction for a good five minutes. Suddenly she pulled on the blinker and turned off of the road.

Diane was shocked at the sudden change and gasped, "What are you doing, Amanda?"

"I needed someplace private, away from the asylum, to check out the samara a little closer," she replied even as she pulled into a parking space and turned off the ignition. Amanda had chosen a small playground in which to stop the car. She reached back and pulled her purse into her lap.

She did not want to risk any further revelations from contacting the crystal with her skin so she folded the bag down until the sun sparkled on the smooth surface of the top of the skull. Something had been nagging at her mind since she had first touched the stone. If her husband were correct, then she could find out who should be the correct owner of the samara by checking the color of the aura surrounding it.

She looked down on it in concentration. As her mother-in-law, Nena, had instructed, she focused her thoughts around the object instead of staring directly at it. Within a few moments, a rainbow of color shimmered from the surface and then one color dominated all the rest: vibrant green.

Amanda nodded confirmation of her original idea, and closed her bag back up over the crystal. She returned the purse to the back seat and started to reach for the key still dangling from the ignition.

"Wait a minute, Amanda. Before we go anywhere, I want you to answer some questions," Diane spoke suddenly.

Amanda was surprised by her mother's outburst. In actuality, she had been so focused on the samara she had forgotten how much of this story her mother still either did not know or did not comprehend. She had to spare some time right now to help her mother understand so she would remain an ally. "Sure, Mom. What do you want to know?"

"What did you do just now?" She had not planned on asking that question first, yet it was the first thing which came out of her mouth so she had to go with it.

"I was checking to see what color of aura this stone has."

"You can see auras now? Since when?" Diane began and then interrupted her own question to ask, "Wait! Do you have another stone?"

"Yes. Riccan had one handed down through his family line from the seventeen hundreds. Then, together, we found another one on our trip to New Orleans. With the addition of this one from the asylum, we have found three of the thirteen."

Diane simply nodded as she added this new information to all she had recently assimilated from reading Amanda's diary. She was still trying to wrap her mind around the idea of there being an alternate plane of reality on Earth which was called Tuala. Amanda insisted she had met people there while she had been in a coma for seven years.

Then when she had finally awoken, she had found Riccan who was someone whom she said she had met in her dream. The facts about Riccan had been too accurate to refute. Riccan admitted he was from Tuala which verified all of Amanda's ideas about her supposed dream. This was becoming quite complicated.

"What will happen when you find all thirteen?" Diane finally asked.

"You read the prophecy, Mom. We are going to follow what it says," she said slightly annoyed because her mom could have such a hard time understanding all of this.

"Please tell me the prophecy again."

Amanda sighed and then closed her eyes to remember it exactly before she spoke,

> *"From a far-away land,*
> *There will come in time,*
> *Intuition is in hand,*
> *Strange details known,*
> *With ties to the people.*
> *From one of my own,*
> *There will be a sign.*
> *Those born to this one,*
> *Will transform all.*
> *Lucinden will pursue,*
> *Elders will fall,*
> *Then all made new."*

Diane stared at her for a moment before she said, "I don't see how the skull thing fits into the poem." She looked into the back seat uneasily as she spoke about the samara.

"To be honest, Mom, neither do I. When I met with Jehoban, He told me to use my intuition to solve the riddle. I had a hunch about room 426 at Cannon Memorial Asylum being so specific in my dream memory. The idea led me to find this samara. I think if Riccan and I can find all of the stones, then we will be one step closer to solving the mystery."

Amanda waited several minutes to see if her mother had any more urgent questions before she said, "I think we should start driving back to Charlotte. We have to catch the 8:15 flight this evening to get back to Miami. We still have just over two hours of driving before we get to the airport. Can you ask me questions while I drive?"

Diane had too many ideas rushing through her brain to ask any coherent questions so she merely nodded consent.

Amanda started the car and navigated her way back to the main highway. She followed the signs directing her to Charlotte. Because they were on a long stretch of road, Amanda knew her mother would start in with the questions again. Normally she would expect such a grilling from her father because of his inquisitive nature, but her mother needed reassurance that Amanda was going to be okay in this strange, new journey.

"So who exactly is Jehoban?" Diane asked in the silence.

"He is the one we call God. He lives on an island He calls Acaim. We call the same island Jamaica."

"And you believe this to be true?" Diane could not help but feel it was sacrilegious to speak of God so flippantly.

"I do, Mom. I've met with Him personally," Amanda said as she glanced away from the road to assure her mom of the truth of her statement.

"So what does He look like?"

Amanda chuckled as she recalled having this same conversation with Riccan a few weeks before. "He is indescribable. When you are with Him, you know it is He. As soon as you are away from Him, you forget every detail you promised yourself you'd remember."

"Okay, that's odd," Diane had to admit. "So who is Lucinden then? I read where you mentioned him a couple of times in your journal, but I was never clear who he really was."

"He is the devil. He used to be one of Jehoban's angels, but he decided he could do things better with the people if he told them what they should do for him. Needless to say, Jehoban wanted His people to retain their free will, so He banished Lucinden and all of the other angels who believed as Lucinden did from Acaim. They usually stay to themselves and only come out every once in a while to stir up trouble and strife."

"From the sound of the new prophecy, Lucinden will make a play for power. Are you sure you want to get yourself involved in something which takes the devil head on? I don't think this is such a good idea, Amanda. Why don't you leave this up to the people of Tuala?" Diane shivered to think of her daughter pitting herself directly against the devil. She could not see any outcome where her daughter would win against such a powerful source of evil.

"In case you hadn't noticed, Mom, my daughters and my husband are the people of Tuala. This directly affects their futures, and by extension, my own as well. I can't leave this to chance, not when Jehoban told me I was the key. I have to try, Mom. Surely you can understand." Amanda gripped the steering wheel harder to try to contain her rising anger at her mother's reluctance to see she had no choice in this matter.

"Tell me more about Barla, then. You wrote about her being my long-lost sister. Do you think it's true as well, or just a fabrication of your dream?" Diane wished with all her might for her sister, Barbara, to still be living even though she had been presumed drowned back when she was a teenager.

"I asked Jehoban about my relationship to Barla. He confirmed she is actually my Aunt Barbara. Can you think of why she would have changed her name?" Amanda had always wondered.

Diane smiled at a childhood memory and nodded as she replied, "When I was really little, I used to call her Barla because it was easier to say than Barbara. The nickname stuck, but only within our house. At school and everywhere else she went by Barbara. I can only imagine she was homesick when she said her name was Barla."

"She misses her family on Earth. If it weren't for the problem with the gates between the worlds erasing the memory of any person from Earth when they travel in either direction, Barla would have made the attempt to come and visit. She could not risk forgetting her family and happiness she has found on Tuala by attempting to navigate through the Ascension Gate."

"Why don't you lose your memory when you and Riccan teleport in and out of Tuala, then?"

Amanda reached up and pulled the diamond pendant out from under the collar of her shirt. As she held it in her hand, she said, "This is why.

The people of Tuala each receive a birth crystal which allows them to retain their memory during travel."

"Why doesn't Barla get one then?" Diane was struggling to understand the complexities of Tualan life.

"I think she's scared of being found out for being an *old soul*. The people of Tuala have been trained to be scared of Earth's people. They are scared enough to turn them in to the Elders. Many of those people are never heard from again. Barla could not risk her family for the sake of the chance of getting a crystal." Amanda felt another stab of guilt for having received her own crystal when Barla deserved one as well. She still had to find out from Jehoban how she had happened to get her own birth crystal.

"Do you think you can intervene on her behalf? I mean, if you are on speaking terms with Jehoban, can't you just ask Him to send her a crystal of her own?" Diane asked. She realized she was still struggling with the idea of her sister being alive. For so long, she had been thought of as dead, it would be wonderful for her to be able to come home and visit with their mother and brother.

"It couldn't hurt to ask," Amanda said as she considered her mother's request. It seemed such a simple idea. She wondered why it had not occurred to her before.

"What happened...," Diane began to ask when Amanda's phone began to ring in her purse in the back seat.

"Can you get my phone, Mom?" Amanda asked.

Diane reached into the back of the car and pulled Amanda's purse into her lap. She opened the purse and saw Amanda's phone just under the crystal skull. Without thinking, she went to move the skull out of the way. As soon as her fingers came in contact with the stone, she felt an odd tingling sensation. She jerked her hand away and cried out in fear.

"What happened, Mom?"

"That thing did something to me!" Diane could feel the adrenaline coursing through her body. Her hands began to shake even as the phone continued to ring.

"Here. Let me get the phone then," Amanda said as she reached toward her bag even as she tried to keep watch on the road ahead. The car swerved slightly.

Diane cried out, "Watch out for the truck, Amanda!"

Amanda diverted her sole attention back to the road and brought the car into the center of the lane again. She took the purse from her mom's lap and said, "You steer."

Diane gladly took over steering the wheel as Amanda rummaged in her bag. She did not want anything further to do with such a weird artifact.

Amanda pulled the phone out of the bag. The phone stopped ringing even as she flipped it open to answer it. She saw from the caller id that she had missed a call from Riccan. Immediately she realized she had left the house in such a hurry she had forgotten to leave a note explaining where she had gone. She was certain Riccan would be upset with her lapse in judgement.

She had not even considered the fact the children would be left home alone. Well, not exactly alone, they would have had Behn over for his daily crystal lesson. What if something had gone wrong during their lesson and one of the kids got hurt? She should have been home or made arrangements for someone to be there. This thought was irrational since there was nobody who would understand what her children could do with the elemental energy through their birth crystals. They would be called out for the aliens who they were.

Amanda needed to call Riccan back. She did not want to be driving while talking on the phone. She searched for a place to pull over so she could make the call. She saw a sign for a rest area in two miles. It would have to do. She set the phone in her lap, dropped her purse on the floor by her feet, and resumed driving the car.

"Who was it?" Diane asked.

"Riccan," Amanda answered with a sigh.

"Is something wrong with you two?"

"There will be when I call him back. I forgot to leave a note and I never even considered the kids being home alone."

Diane started to laugh.

"What?" Amanda asked harshly.

"You! Your children are sixteen, Amanda. I hardly think they'd burn the house down or do anything else foolish. They are the most responsible teenagers I've ever met," Diane commented. Then she considered the rest of what Amanda said and agreed, "You should have left a note for your husband, though."

"I'm going to call him back as soon as we get to the rest area in the next couple of minutes," Amanda said. She realized her mother was right about her girls. They were almost adults and they were very responsible. Their necklaces also kept them from true harm and she could always use those necklaces to look in on them if she were truly curious as to what they were doing.

The next minute was driven in silence. Amanda considered what she would tell Riccan and tried to judge how upset he would be about her disappearance. She saw the exit up ahead and signaled to get into the far right lane. She slowed down and pulled to a stop in one of the parking spots furthest from the bathrooms. She put the car in park and turned off the engine.

With a sigh of resignation, she flipped open her phone and pressed the speed dial number one and put the phone to her ear. She listened to it ring twice before her husband answered.

"Amanda! Where are you?" Riccan asked without saying hello.

"Mom and I are in North Carolina. We should be home around ten o'clock. I'm sorry I didn't leave you a note. I got so excited to check out a lead that I called Mom and then we left immediately this morning."

"North Carolina? A lead on what?" Riccan was trying to figure out what Amanda had been up to. None of this was making much sense.

"I found another samara, Riccan. I'll explain it all when we get home. We're flying American Airlines on the 8:15 flight out of Charleston. Can we talk more about this when I get home?" Amanda knew she was rambling, but she wanted Riccan to know she was safe.

"Sure, honey. I'm just glad to hear everything is okay. I was worried when I asked the girls where you were and they told me you were gone when they got home. It just wasn't like you so I got to worrying. I love you, Amanda. I can't wait to hear what happened to you today. It sounds as though it was very eventful."

Amanda was both surprised and confused by Riccan's easy approval of her disappearance. Maybe she had overestimated his concern. "Okay. We're about an hour away from the Charleston Airport yet. We'll probably eat dinner at the airport so we won't have to worry about missing the flight. I'll have to drop Mom off at her house before I can come home. I'll see you in a few hours."

"Okay. Safe travels. I love you."

"I love you, too. Bye."

Seeing Amanda hang up the phone, Diane asked, "Was Riccan mad?"

"Not really," Amanda replied as she flipped the phone shut and returned it to her purse. She did not want to have her bag on the floor at her feet so she moved it into the back seat again. She started the car and navigated her way back onto the highway.

Her mind was reviewing the conversation she had just had with Riccan. *Was he angry and just hiding it well? Did he not really care where she had been, yet wanted to know when she was coming home? Now I'm just be ridiculous.* She shook her head at all of her nonsensical thoughts and decided it would all be okay once she got home with the samara.

They returned the car to the rental place at the airport and checked in for their flight. Just as Amanda had told Riccan, they ate dinner at the airport. They found a small deli-style shop and bought sandwiches and bottled waters.

"What are you going to do now?" Diane asked Amanda before she took another bite of her chicken sandwich.

"I'm going to give the samara to Riccan and see what he thinks about it. Afterward, we'll have to play it by ear," Amanda answered. She had an idea what would be coming next, but she did not think her mom would want to know about it. Her mom already tended to worry too much, and this next plan could potentially be dangerous. Amanda did not need to hear another lecture on keeping safe. She had no intention of getting hurt, she had far too much to live for because she had her daughters and her husband to care for.

CHAPTER 2

The flight to Miami was uneventful as well as the drive to Diane's house. Amanda thanked her mom for going on the trip with her and promised to call her the next day. Amanda drove the twenty minutes to her house while she composed how she would tell her husband about her adventure. She hoped Riccan would understand.

She drove into her garage and turned off the engine. With her purse in hand, she walked into the house and down the hallway toward the living room. She imagined Riccan would most likely be waiting for her on the comfortable leather couch. Her suspicion was correct.

Riccan spotted his wife, stood up, and took the last couple of steps which separated them. He wrapped his arms around her and kissed the top of her head. He spoke softly, "I missed you."

"I missed you, too. I'm sorry about not leaving a note," she began.

"Enough, Amanda. I trust you to take care of yourself. I can hardly wait to hear about your adventure. Let's sit down." He took her hand and led her to the couch.

Amanda looked around and asked, "Where are the girls?"

"They are upstairs studying. I told them you'd be home late. I didn't mention anything about the samara," Riccan said as he winked at her. "To whom do you suppose this one will belong?"

Amanda smiled at Riccan's excitement. She opened her purse and held it out for him to take out the samara as she said, "Why don't you tell me?"

Riccan looked from the bag to Amanda's face with a puzzled expression. "Do you already know?"

"I have a suspicion. I don't want to say anything until you confirm my idea. Go ahead and pick it up," Amanda encouraged as she shook the bag slightly to get his attention back on the samara.

Riccan could feel the energy pulsing from the stone even before Amanda had opened the bag. The sensation was unlike what he had experienced with the two other skulls kept in their secret room off of the library. With a slight amount of hesitation, Riccan reached into the bag with both hands and cradled the crystal.

Amanda watched as her husband's expression turned to one of wonder. She knew now she had been correct: this was Riccan's samara. Several minutes went by as Riccan seemed to commune with his stone. His face underwent several changes as he watched the scenes unfold in his mind alone. Amanda had some idea of what he was seeing, but she knew it would be more clear and easier to understand for Riccan since this samara was keyed to him specifically.

Finally, Riccan took a deep breath and slowly released the air through his mouth. His eyes looked up into Amanda's and he said, "This one's mine."

"I knew it!" Amanda clapped her hands together like a little child with her glee.

"Where did you find it?" Riccan had to put the crystal down on the table to be able to concentrate on Amanda's tale.

"At Cannon Memorial Asylum in North Carolina. It was in room 426. It was the room from my dream, Riccan, behind the comic strips which were taped to the wall. I always thought the comics were an odd addition to the room. As it turns out, it was my clue for finding it." Amanda smiled triumphantly at her husband.

"What made you even think to look at the asylum?" Riccan was always surprised at how her mind worked, this was no different.

"I used my intuition. Why would it have been part of my dream? It didn't fit in anywhere so I thought I'd check into it. As it turns out, the asylum is being closed down. The only people remaining there now are a few support staff and some movers."

"It worked out well, didn't it?" Riccan asked.

"I'd say! You can't know how nerve-wracking it was going back through all of the rooms I remembered from before. The basement was the worst! We went there first and got out of there as fast as we could. Luckily, I could feel the pull of the crystal as soon as I walked by the room. When I touched it, I saw a lot of visions of future events. What did you see?"

"Probably the same as you. There was a lot of it which didn't make sense. I'm sure it'll become clear as we go along." Riccan looked over at his own samara and suddenly realized he knew exactly how his daughter's had felt when they had held the crystal which was meant for them personally. It was a feeling like no other, one of wholeness. He had not even realized he had been missing anything until the samara completed him.

"I saw something else when I held your samara, Riccan," Amanda spoke into the silence.

"What was it?"

"I saw myself going back to Tuala to rescue Nealand from Elder Vargen."

Riccan was not sure how he felt about this turn of events. He felt secure in his relationship with Amanda, but Nealand had been her fiancé. Would this undertaking bring the two of them back together again? "When do we go?"

"We don't go, Riccan. I only saw myself there. You stayed here with the girls," Amanda answered softly. She hoped Riccan would understand and not try to make this harder than it was going to be already.

"I see," Riccan replied simply as he digested Amanda's statement. He did not like the idea at all, but he could also not see any other way around it. He had his work to do, and the girls had settled in nicely at their school. "What did your mom say about this?"

"I didn't tell her. I knew she would only worry and think up reasons for me to stay home. As soon as I saw the vision, I knew it was the right thing to do. My parents suffered for seven years while I was in the coma. Imagine how much harder this has been for Nealand's family. They don't even have a body to mourn. He's alive, Riccan, and I can bring him home and reunite him with his family." Amanda searched Riccan's face for understanding.

"I understand what you're telling me and I admire your willingness to risk everything to help him. Other than Nealand's family having closure, what will this do for the completion of the prophecy?" Riccan hoped this question would keep Amanda from pursuing the dangerous expedition.

"I'm not sure. Just like when I went to the asylum, I went based on my intuition. When I saw myself taking this journey, it felt like the right thing to do. You'll just have to trust my instincts on this matter."

"I do trust you, Amanda. It's Elder Vargen whom I don't trust. He already imprisoned you once. What's to keep him from doing it again?" The more Riccan thought about it, the less comfortable he became.

"We'll have to pray for my safety. I'm going to go, Riccan." Amanda squeezed her hand on his knee to impress upon him how important this was to her.

"When do you go?"

"Tomorrow."

"What? No, Amanda. We need to make plans to ensure your safety. I'll message my dad and see what we can do to keep you safe. How would you get there? How will you get him home?" Riccan would say just about anything to keep Amanda from leaving the next day.

"You're right, Riccan. I am getting ahead of myself. I'd like you to teach me to fly your old telepod. It still has the portable gate in it, right?"

Riccan breathed a sigh of relief since he had managed to stall his wife's journey. Training her to fly the telepod would take several weeks so he readily agreed by saying, "Yes, it does. When do you want to start your lessons?"

"I'd say right now, but I'm too tired after all of today's traveling. Maybe tomorrow after work. What do you think?" Amanda stifled a yawn.

"I love you! Tomorrow it is," Riccan said as he hugged his wife fiercely. "Let's go to bed. You seem exhausted."

"Don't you think you should put that away first?" Amanda asked as she pointed to the samara on the coffee table.

Riccan chuckled and said, "You're always so practical. Yes, I'll go put it away right now." He picked up the skull shaped stone and marveled again at how right it felt in his possession. He stood up and walked with Amanda into the library. They went to the far wall and pressed the release mechanism under the shelf to open the secret passage into the room behind the bookcase.

He walked into the far side of the room and set his personal samara in the next niche over from the other two already in their possession. *Three down, ten to go*, he thought as he turned around to take his wife upstairs to go to bed.

~

DAVEN WAS SURPRISED to see he had a message from his son. Normally, Riccan would just show up at their house rather than use the patil to contact him. This must be something extraordinary for him to deviate from his normal routine.

After he read the message, he understood Riccan's need for his assistance. Amanda's newest idea would be very dangerous and Daven would need all the time he could get to try to make it as safe as possible. He would have to try to distract Elder Vargen away from his pet project at the Old Soul Engineering Facility so Amanda could extract Nealand from his clutches. Even then, it was going to be an uphill battle to extricate his prisoner.

He sat back in his chair and folded his hands together across his stomach as he considered all of his options. Maybe he should get Elder Debbon involved in this as well. As the First of the Elders, Debbon would have the most sway over Elder Vargen's time. There had to be a valid reason to call a meeting of the Elders.

It would appear he would have at least two weeks to put something together. If Riccan could make the telepod training take longer, then it would be easier. He would have to come up with a couple of different options depending on the time constraints.

Daven sat forward and changed the patil screen to compose a message to Elder Debbon. He considered what he would say and then opted for the simplest message possible: Amanda needs our help. Please contact me at your earliest convenience.

After the private meeting both he and Elder Debbon had been summoned to with Jehoban they had all agreed they would assist Amanda and her daughters in any way to help fulfill the prophecy. This request was bound to be the first of many.

~

JUILA WAS IMPRESSED with her boyfriend's progress in learning the different levels of crystal skills. She could tell he had been accessing more of his memories as he rapidly attained mastery of yet another level. When they had first started two days ago, Behn had been reluctant to open his mind enough to allow the energy to easily course through him. His lack of belief in himself had been his own worst enemy.

Their first session had been an impromptu one after they had gone on a double-date to the movies. They had dropped Luke off at his house so it was just Jena, Juila, and Behn left in the car. Behn had not been able to come over after school like he had originally planned. Since they were alone together, Behn asked, "Is there something simple you could teach me tonight so I can start working on it on my own?"

Juila and Jena looked at one another and spoke silently though their twin link. Jena nodded as Juila replied, "We need to start at the beginning. Do you remember what Daven showed you?"

"You mean how the ball of light came out of his crystal?" Behn still found the sight to be truly amazing. The fact he actually remembered doing it himself for his own mother, meant even more to him. If he could relearn such skills, then he felt he could accomplish anything.

Juila nodded confirmation and went on to say, "It's the first lesson taught to little children before they go to school. It demonstrates the wearer of the necklace understands the power contained in the earth. By creating the ball of light, you demonstrate the ability to harness the power to your will." Juila looked up into Behn's dark eyes and saw he knew what she was saying. She believed he had probably heard similar words from his own mother as she taught him when he was little.

Behn did remember. He just did not know how to accomplish the task. "How do I make it happen?"

"Hold your crystal in your hand," Jena told him.

Behn reached into the collar of his shirt to fish out the circular pendant. He looked down at the smoky grey crystals suspended on a shaped tree. The symbol always made him think of the tree of life and now he understood it was to represent exactly as he believed. This necklace was a symbol given to the children of Tuala from Jehoban. The

Creator of the Universe wanted His children to have a link to the power of the earth.

"Okay, now what?" Behn asked impatiently.

"Concentrate on the individual crystals. Imagine where they came from. Imagine the power of the earth which created their beauty. Feel yourself link to the power within," Juila said as she leaned forward to see if Behn were following her instructions.

Behn honestly tried to do as Juila had asked. He looked at the crystals and knew they had been created by a massive force in the earth. However, it was as far as he could get. He did not know how to link with the power. He could not remember what the particular aspect of it had felt like. Finally he shook his head in frustration and said, "This is impossible. I don't feel anything!"

"It takes practice and patience. I think you are trying too hard," Jena offered.

"Think of it like a meditation," Juila suggested. "Keep working on it tonight. If you are still unable to do it on your own by the time we meet after school tomorrow, then I can try to link with your mind to show you."

Behn's eyes abruptly left his crystal to look up at Juila. She had already proved she could be trusted with his biggest secret, but she was offering to get inside his head. He was not sure he was comfortable with the idea. He saw her blue eyes widen as she registered his reticence. Hurriedly he said, "I'll work on it tonight. Hopefully, it won't be necessary."

CHAPTER 3

The next day, Behn came to their house after school. They went to the library and sat down in the oversized chairs. Juila closed the door to the library to keep their lesson private should any of their father's help happen to come into the house. It would not do to be found out until they were ready to return to Tuala. They still had many things to learn about Earth culture before they would be ready to go home.

"Okay, Behn. Show us what you have learned so far," Jena spoke into the silence.

Once again, Behn pulled up his necklace from under his shirt. None of them kept their birth crystals out where the people might see them and ask questions. Behn's pendant was on a leather strap instead of the ornate chain which each of the girls owned. He took a deep breath and focused deeply on his crystal. After several minutes had passed and bead of sweat had popped out on Behn's brow, he sighed and had to admit defeat. He had been just as unsuccessful the entire evening before.

"Do you want help?" Juila offered. It physically hurt her to see him trying so hard and still not understanding the process. If he just let her show him, then he could speed up his progress.

"No!" Behn cried out. "Just give me a few more minutes. Tell me what it feels like so maybe I can be more successful."

Stop it, Juila. Can't you see he's scared? Jena thought to her sister. To Behn, Jena spoke aloud, "The elemy has a tingly feeling. Once you start to draw it from the earth, you imagine it flowing through your crystal. Then you think about turning the energy into a sphere and pulling it outside of your birth crystal to float a few inches from it. Give it a try."

Behn nodded and appreciated Jena's patience with his lack of progress. He was about to take Juila up on her offer of assistance when he started to feel a tingling sensation. With the notion in his head that this must have been what Jena was referring to, he managed to focus his attention to draw the energy into his crystal.

It was rather pathetic, but he succeeded in creating the smallest sphere of energy imaginable. He looked up with a foolish grin and immediately lost control of the sphere. It began to career around the room until Juila built another sphere around it and kept it from moving.

"Okay, so we've established you are able to create the energy. Now we need to work on keeping you focused on maintaining control once you've unleashed the power." Juila smiled to take the sting out of her words. She was actually pleased because Behn had done this on his own. Hopefully, because he had accessed the elemy, he would not have trouble repeating it for further levels of achievement.

Next they taught him how to move the sphere to a second location at will. This took a little trial and error. Both of the girls had been on high alert to keep any further mishaps from occurring. The last thing they wanted to do was explain to their parents why the house had burned down from their lack of attention to detail when teaching Behn how to use his birth crystal.

Finally they taught him how to return the sphere to his own birth crystal. This step was important for practicing on his own. They had him repeat the process several times before they felt confident letting him go home with his new knowledge.

The next day they moved on to the fourth level of achievement which was learning how to create a breeze. Behn had been pleased with his prior success since he had been able to repeat the steps in the privacy of his bedroom at home without anything going wrong. Now he was not so sure of himself. The breeze seemed to be a different aspect of the energy unlike what he had been doing with the sphere. It seemed more elusive.

Once again, Juila offered to assist him inside his mind. This made him want to achieve it on his own even more. While he really liked Juila and wanted her to be his girlfriend, he was not sure he wanted her in his mind. It just did not seem like the right thing to do. "Can you explain it to me in another way?" he asked Jena. She seemed to be the better teacher of the two of them.

"Hmm," she said as she tried to think of an easier way to say what needed to be done. "Okay, imagine your mind is like a hand passing through the air very fast. What is left behind is the breeze from the disturbed air. Does that make sense?"

"Yeah. Let me try it," he said as he sat still in the library chair. His eyes focused solely on his birth crystal held in his hand. The smoky grey crystals reminded him of storm clouds so creating a breeze should not be a real problem. He could feel the elemy rise up to his pendant and then it seemed to be asking him what he wanted to do with it. He used Jena's description to try to direct the flow of energy to create a soft breeze in front of him.

Jena had a feather held up in front of her to be able to tell if he were successful. The tip of the feather began to sway to the side and then the lower part of the feather also moved as the breeze continued to gain strength. "Easy, now, Behn. You don't want your soft breeze to get out of control. Imagine it remaining a gentle breeze and not a storm."

Behn nodded understanding even though he never took his eyes from his crystal. The breeze gentled and then stopped altogether. He looked up with a satisfied grin on his face and asked, "How was that?"

Juila smiled back at him and replied, "It was perfect. You're learning control which will be a very good thing with the lessons to come. Especially when we get to the fire lesson."

Behn gulped with nerves and then asked, "How many levels are there?"

"Oh, there're only twenty-seven levels taught to ordinary people who want to learn it all. The first ten levels are usually taught to each student by the time they get to the second grade. In middle school you take elective classes, not necessarily in any order. The rest are usually reserved for specific occupations instead of for the general public," Jena rattled off easily.

She loved learning everything she could about the elemental energy. As far as she had been able to determine, there was no limit to its uses except for the imagination. If you could think it, you could conceive it.

Jehoban had always praised them for their intuitive nature when it came to working with the elemy. They enjoyed the approval immensely and sought to keep His attention with their new ideas.

"That's just great. So if I'm to understand you correctly, I've been struggling to do what a first grader could easily do. Right? Boy do I feel stupid." Behn let go of his necklace and let it fall back to his chest as he realized just how dumb the girls must think he was for how slowly he had learned the first three skills.

"Not at all, Behn. You've been doing a great job. It's so much easier to teach children because they don't have any beliefs to keep them from attempting anything we ask. The older we get, the more set in our ways we become," Juila piped in swiftly. She hated to see Behn be so hard on himself. He had been a fabulous student for one so old. The only other person she knew of who had learned to use the crystal as an adult had been her own mother.

"Yeah, Behn. Just wait until you see your brother and sister try to learn this stuff. Then you'll know just how difficult a task we are actually asking you to achieve. Have patience with yourself. I promise you, you are doing a wonderful job," Jena added once Juila stopped talking.

"How many levels have you two learned?" Behn asked sullenly.

The two girls looked at one another guiltily before Jena answered, "We've finished them all and then some. It's kind of our thing, Behn. We've always been intrigued by the whole process and we've made a game out of it our whole lives."

"I guess I've got the best teachers then, huh?" Behn chuckled. If he did not make a joke of it then he would truly be discouraged by the level of achievement they had acquired even though they were the same age as he was.

Juila thought she would propose her suggestion one more time. "Behn, if you'd let me link with your brain, then I could show you how to do everything we know and you wouldn't have to struggle to figure it out on your own. It would save you a lot of frustration." She stopped talking and waited for him to decide what he wanted to do.

Behn had to admit he was tempted to know everything they knew with one fell swoop. Unfortunately, the honorable side of him thought of it as cheating. They had been able to learn it on their own and it had probably made them better for it. He could expect no less of himself. He shook his head slowly and answered, "I appreciate the offer, but I think I'll have to do this the old-fashioned way. It may take longer, but it will mean more to me to do it on my own. Can you understand?"

"Sure," Juila said even as she tried to keep from feeling rejected by him. His reasoning sounded sincere and she supposed she could understand why he would want to take the hard route.

"So…what comes after learning to create a breeze?" Behn asked as he tried to distract the girls from thinking badly of him.

Jena answered immediately, "Boiling water."

"Really? That's kind of cool," Behn said with excitement.

"Yes, but it's actually very hot," Juila joked.

The three teens laughed together and the tension in the room dissipated.

"Do you want me to go get some water from the kitchen?" Behn asked as their chuckles died down.

"No need," Jena said and held out her hand. In an instant, a glass of water was grasped in her fingers. "Use this," she said as she set the cup down on the table between them.

"How did you do that? Is it something I'll learn, too?" Behn was very impressed with the display of seeming magic. He was starting to appreciate why the girls said they had been excited about the training they had received in Tuala. For once, he wished he had remained on Tuala so he would have been able to learn these things as a child with his mother and siblings. His adoptive family had been wonderful, but it never took away their dream of finding their mother someday.

"Same process, different skill. It's number twelve on the list. Something we call 'creating' where something is created from elements already around. We use it for putting together meals, mostly. It takes us seconds to put together a gourmet meal where it would take someone from Earth thirty minutes or more. We reverse the process to clean up the mess afterward. But, we're getting ahead of ourselves. We need to teach you how to boil the water," Juila said and then turned to Jena to give Behn the directions.

"Okay, Behn, focus on the water. Imagine its molecular structure and each molecule moving faster and faster around each other. Now, just like the breeze you created, imagine stirring the water until the water begins to form bubbles as the vaporized gas is released."

Behn listened to Jena's instructions. The way she described it sounded so simple. He probably could have figured it out himself as he loved chemistry and understood how the boiling process worked. He directed his focus to the glass of water and did as Jena had explained. Within a few seconds he could see the water was starting to form bubbles. The process seemed to stall as he lost his focus with his excitement so he renewed his focus on the contents of the glass until it was boiling continually.

He smiled like a little boy and announced, "I did it!" He looked up at Juila first and then over to Jena. They both smiled proudly in return. "What's next? I can really do this!"

"Of course you can do this, Behn. It's your birthright. Freezing water is next," Juila spoke in a matter-of- fact tone.

Jena continued her instructions by saying, "Okay, Behn, focus on the hot water. Again, imagine its molecular structure and each molecule moving slower and slower around each other. Now, just like the breeze you created, imagine your finger stirring the water until the ice crystals begin to form and cling to one another until it is a solid mass."

Behn was seeing a pattern of instruction and then had a question of his own before he attempted the next task. "How do you explain molecular structures to children in the second grade? You did say this was a task a second grader would learn, right?"

"The children of Tuala are more in tune with the energy in the earth. They don't need to learn about molecules to understand the process. It's hard to explain, it's almost as if they use their intuition without hesitating. People from Earth need to know how something works before they can accomplish it, whereas the people from Tuala just expect something to work because they think it. It's a terrible explanation, but it's the best way I can think to say it," Juila spoke kindly. She hoped Behn would understand the difference.

He was starting to understand the vast difference between the two worlds. He hoped when he finally got to go back there, he would not feel too out of place. These lessons were bound to help him make the adjustment easier.

Behn nodded and shifted his gaze from Juila to the still steaming glass of water. He tried to use his intuition and expectation instead of the process which Jena explained. With absolute belief in what he was attempting, he managed to freeze the water so fast, the glass surrounding the liquid broke into pieces with the sudden change in temperature. He looked up guiltily. "I'm sorry for breaking the glass. I didn't mean for it to happen!"

Both of the girls were starting to chuckle. Behn looked at them as though they had lost their minds. What about this situation could possibly be funny?

"Don't worry about it, Behn. I can fix the glass. Tell me what you did different?" Jena asked.

Behn shrugged his shoulders and then answered slowly, "I guess I used my expectations instead of my reasoning. It appears to work much faster."

"Exactly. I'm glad you understood what I was trying to tell you. You'll find each lesson will be easier since you've discovered the mental shift needed to complete a task," Juila spoke with pride to Behn. He had been an eager student. She imagined his desire to learn had something to do with it, but she also knew he was starting to access the parts of his brain which had developed on Tuala until he was eight and was sent to Earth by his mother.

CHAPTER 4

Nealan hated mornings. They always started with an intense headache and his eyes felt as though they had been scratched with sand paper. It seemed as though each day took longer for him to feel better than the one before. He pushed the covers off of himself and looked over at the woman who had started sharing his bed over a mesan ago.

He pulled his legs to the side of the bed and groaned as his feet hit the floor. The joints in his knees were aching as well as every other joint in his body. He wished he could explain the pain away by the weather turning, but where he lived was a temperate climate year around. The only thing which would make him feel better was the cup of steena tea he would have at work.

After looking at his timepiece, he realized he was going to have to rush if he were going to be at his job on time. Even though he found his work to be fulfilling, it always seemed as though there were something else he should be doing with his life. Try as he might, he never could figure out what was missing. Until he had his morning tea, it was pointless to even consider using his aching brain.

There were five minutes until Nealan had to report to his shift so he stopped off at the commissary to get his usual blend of steena tea. He had tried getting tea to have at his house, but the blend never seemed to relieve his aching body like the ones here at work did.

The old woman had a sad smile on her face as she handed him the cup of hot liquid. "Have a good morning, Nealan," she said.

"Thanks," he mumbled as he turned away from her and took a sip of the hot tea. With experience, he knew he would not feel any relief until at least a quarter of the liquid had been consumed. He wished the woman making the tea would make it cooler so he could imbibe it quicker. With slow steps and small sips, he moved in the direction of his cubicle in the office building.

Several people acknowledged Nealan as he passed and he merely grunted in reply. None of them seemed to take offense at his lack of enthusiasm. In fact, the other people seemed to be feeling the same way he did this early in the morning.

He reached his desk and sat down gingerly in the high-backed chair. With a sigh of relief to be off of his aching legs, he cradled the tea between his hands and enjoyed the warmth of the cup on his fingers. After a few more sips, he would have to log into his patil and begin his day.

VINIA FELT Nealan get out of the bed. She pretended to remain asleep since she hated his morning attitude. The first time she had attempted to talk to him in the morning, she thought she had made a grave mistake in moving in with him. After all, she had her daughter to think about. If Nealan were a mean man, she would not be able to stay with him.

By the time Nealan came home from work, he had been like a different person. He was the man she had fallen in love with and wanted to spend her time around. Over the past mesan she had seen the same problem emerge every day and then be gone by the second hour after rising. It was the most peculiar change in personality.

She had once asked him if he had seen a wise-woman to see if there were anything which could be done about it. Nealan had not been very happy with her suggestion so she stopped asking. Instead, Vinia had inquired of a wise-woman on her own. What she had learned did not make her very happy.

Her suspicions were confirmed when they had received a special delivery from Nealan's work on the first weekend after she had moved in. They had sent him a cup of the blend of tea he preferred. After Nealan had consumed most of it, his mood had improved immensely. Vinia had asked if she could try his drink. Being in a much better mood than when he had started the beverage, he gladly offered her his cup.

She sniffed the minty smelling liquid before she took a small sip of her own. At first, she believed it to be a strong blend of steena tea until an aftertaste lingered on her tongue. Within a few minutes she could feel herself becoming very sleepy and her fingers began to tingle. She hastily drank several glasses of water to dilute the drug which had been placed in his tea.

The wise-woman had told her the symptoms of resh addiction. She said it was very uncommon in people of Tuala, but not impossible. She had also told Vinia about the taste and effects of the drug on someone who was not used to its potency.

She would have left that very day if it had not been for her daughter. They needed a place to live since they were no longer near the people from their village. Nealan was a very amicable person and she was happy with him most of the time. She wished he had more interest in her daughter. He mostly just ignored her, which Vinia preferred over him expressing an unnatural desire to be around her alone which was why she had left her village.

As if the thought of her daughter had awoken her, she started to babble from her crib in the second bedroom. Vinia pushed back the warm covers and slid her feet into her slippers before leaving her bedroom to go across the hall to retrieve her little girl.

The moment Vinia opened the bedroom door the little girl held out her arms and said, "Mama!"

"How's my little Danika this morning?" she asked as she crossed the room and picked up the standing girl in her arms. "Are you hungry?" Danika nodded solemnly and Vinia had to laugh at her reaction to the question. She must have been quite hungry since she was over an hour later waking up than usual. She must be growing again, Vinia thought to herself as she walked into the kitchen with Danika in her arms.

Even as she entered the kitchen she had created the warm cereal to feed Danika. She sat her down in the high-chair and put the tray in place. Vinia grabbed the bowl from the counter behind her as she pulled up a chair and began feeding Danika. She would normally have let her eat on her own, but she did not feel like cleaning up the large mess she was most likely to make.

Danika had other plans for her breakfast. She kept shutting her mouth just as Vinia brought the spoon to her lips. Her other new tactic was to turn her head at the last second and then giggle as her mother would put the spoon of cereal on her cheek.

Finally, Vinia gave up and set the bowl and spoon down onto the tray and said, "Okay, I get it. You want to do it yourself. Right?"

Danika picked up the spoon easily in her fisted hand and plunged it down into the bottom of the cereal bowl. She brought it up heaping with dripping food. She shoved it toward her mouth just as nearly all of the food dripped off of the not-so-level spoon.

Danika's expression when she put the empty spoon in her mouth was comical. Vinia laughed at her daughter's mishap and then decided she was hungry as well. She encouraged, "Try it again, dear. Watch the spoon as you pick it up. You might find more food on it that way."

The little girl seemed to understand what her mother was saying since she was much more successful on her second attempt. As she happily munched on the soft mush, she made happy noises and her other hand slapped the tray in front of her. Her little feet began to flop up and down as she continued to fidget around while she ate.

Vinia created a plate of scrambled eggs and fried foxl and inhaled the wonderful aroma before she picked up her fork to eat. Just as she was about to take her first bite, she was interrupted by a knock on the front door. She set down her fork and said to Danika, "Mommy will be right back."

She had no idea who would be calling at this hour of the morning so she opened the door cautiously. To her surprise, she found the wise-woman, Copa, outside. She stood for a moment with her mouth hanging open in shock before she remembered her manners and said, "Copa, I never expected to see you here. Come inside, please!" She stood to the side and gestured for the elderly woman to come into her house.

Copa swiftly entered the house and looked around to see who else was about. "Are we alone?"

"My daughter's in the kitchen eating. I should check on her," she said as she started walking back to the kitchen. "What brings you here?"

"I heard you were here from the local wise-woman. I wanted to find out how you and your children were doing," she said as she followed the younger woman into the kitchen.

"My children," Vinia said quietly. She sat down wearily in the chair and said, "Please take a seat, Copa. I was just going to eat breakfast. Would you like me to make you something as well?"

"No, my dear, I'm fine. But, please eat your breakfast while it's still hot. I can't stay long," Copa said cryptically.

Vinia ate her food hurriedly. She felt as if she were being rude eating in front of her guest. She saw Danika had managed to spread her food far and wide, but she also appeared to be satisfied enough to be finished. With a few thoughts, she had all of the dishes cleaned and put away as well as Danika made presentable again.

She picked Danika up out of the chair and said to Copa, "Let me get Danika set up with some toys in the living room and we can have a few minutes of privacy to talk about whatever has brought you here."

A few minutes later Vinia sat down on the couch next to the tiny, old woman. "Tell me what has brought you here, Copa."

"I did not tell you before because it did not matter," she said cryptically.

"What did you not tell me, Copa?" Vinia was confused as to what the wise-woman was trying to tell her.

Instead of answering her questions, she asked her own, "Where are your other three children, Vinia?"

Vinia looked down at her folded hands and spoke quietly, "I had to do as you suggested."

Copa looked up at her in alarm and asked, "What brought it about?" Her visions were only possibilities of the future, by no means a certain outcome. She had hoped this vision would not come to pass.

"I overheard Grobin talking about taking Valentina as his wife. His *wife*, Copa, not his betrothed. Valentina wasn't even eight anons old yet. Mosan scoffed at him and said he was crazy. Grobin insisted she was plenty old enough for what he had in mind. Mosan continued to laugh at Grobin which upset Grobin to the point where he said he would do it the next day." Vinia stopped and took a deep breath to calm her racing heart.

"Also, Jon was very sick. When I asked Grobin to bring in an Elder or a wise-woman to help him, he scoffed and said there were too many men in the colony as it was. He had the audacity to say it would not matter if Jon died and then he left. It was the last straw.

"I grabbed the samara you gave me and took the children out into the woods where you had shown me was the strongest place. I said the words you told me to say, and then the children were gone. They had disappeared as though they had never existed.

"Copa, please tell me they are still alive! I have tried and tried to reach them through their birth crystals, but I have never even felt a spark of life from any of them. I have worried continually about whether I did the right thing."

"It will all be fine, Vinia," Copa said and patted Vinia's hand comfortingly.

"It hasn't seemed like it. I had Danika early because of all of the stress I had been under. Grobin was furious with me when he came calling the next morning. He told me his intentions with Valentina and I told him he would never touch my daughter. He actually struck me across the face with his fist before he tore apart my house looking for the children. Grobin insisted I tell him where he could find Valentina, but I told him she was forever out of his reach. Finally, he left and I sat down on Jon's cot and cried until bedtime. I was so alone."

"He didn't find the samara when he searched your house, did he?" Copa asked hastily.

"No, I hid it in the woods before I returned home from sending the children away," she replied and held back a shiver as she remembered the feel of the power as it surged through the crystal skull when her children disappeared. She had wanted nothing more to do with it and hid it in a small hollow near the stream and covered it with rocks, branches, and dried leaves.

Copa seemed to brighten considerably with Vinia's confession of hiding the stone. She knew Vinia had no idea of the significance of the stone and she was not about to reveal it to her for fear of Vinia's mind being read by Elder Vargen. When she had heard Vinia had been living within Elder Vargen's jurisdiction she had been afraid he would feel the power of the samara and investigate. She could not let the powerful artifact fall into the corrupt Elder's hands. All would be lost if it were ever to happen.

"How is your little one?" Copa asked.

"She is fine now. Like I said, she came early, almost a mesan early. Grobin seemed inordinately pleased to see I'd had another daughter. When she started walking at about seven mesans he kept showing up wherever she was playing. While I watched him I could see he was planning something for Danika and I was not about to stick around to see what vile plot he could concoct for her. In the evening, I packed up all the belongings I could carry and I walked away from the colony for the last time."

"You did the right thing, my dear," Copa said as she again patted Vinia's hand. Even as she touched the woman, she was reading her mind. She could see the truth to her words and knew if she had stayed, Danika would have been taken by Grobin as his betrothed. Her mind saw the scene as clearly as if it had happened in reality.

It was a gift and a curse to see the possibilities of people's futures. She was glad Vinia had acted as fast as she had. Unfortunately, Vinia had put herself in a position of another hard decision. She only had a short time yet until the decision would have to be made. It would turn out to be a curse and a blessing, but it had to be of her own accord. Time would tell.

"I'm glad to see all has turned out well, Vinia," Copa said as she stood slowly from the low couch. "I must be on my way. Should you have need to speak with me in the future, please contact your local wise-woman and let her know your need to reach me. She will be able to get a hold of me and I will come to you." She had walked to the front door by this time and she put her hand on the knob before she said her last words, "I'll see you again soon."

"Okay," Vinia said even though she was very confused with how their conversation had gone. She had no idea why she had told Copa all of the sordid details of the colony she had left. She had never planned on telling anyone how bad it had become in the backwoods community. There was something about the particular wise-woman which encouraged a person to share even the most intimate details about a person's life. She slowly shut the front door she had been holding like a life-line as the woman disappeared around the corner of the block.

"That was really weird," she mumbled to herself as she leaned her back against the closed front door. She felt a sense of relief at telling someone where her children had gone. If anything happened to her, then there was at least one person on Tuala who would care about the location of her children.

It was then she realized Copa had not answered her question about not being able to sense the children's birth crystals. No distance had ever kept her from seeing her children. She guessed the distance across the realm into Earth was too far for the power of their crystals. It made her sad to think they would not know what had really happened. They had not even known they had a sister on the way.

Danika had been the only thing keeping her going after the children had been sent to Earth. At first, it was just keeping herself healthy to keep the baby thriving. Then after she had been born, she had to maintain a good diet to nurse the baby. Afterward, it had been about keeping her baby safe from the lusty intentions of their colony leader.

She sat down on the couch and turned sideways to watch her daughter play on the floor contentedly. She was glad to finally have a house and some security. Even Nealan's mood swings were better than any alternative she could have had if she had remained living with the colony.

Her use of her birth crystal had been frowned upon in the colony. They believed it to be witchcraft to use the power which was their birthright. She had never agreed with their belief even as her own mother had not. She had learned everything she knew from her mother.

She had begun to teach her own children in the privacy of their house. Vinia had been very diligent in letting her children know the skills they were learning with their necklaces was not to be shared with anybody in the village. She had been so proud of their ability to learn so rapidly.

Since they were on Earth, she supposed they had forgotten all about what she had taught them, even though they had only been gone for just over an anon. Her biggest hope was them finding a good family to take them all in as a group. The idea of them being separated from one another was another personal nightmare of hers.

At almost eleven mesans old, Danika was a very bright and inquisitive child. She had more opportunity to interact with children her own age which helped her develop social skills. Back in the colony, her other children kept mostly to themselves because they were considered an oddity. Triplets were not common. Danika was not going to live that kind of life, Vinia would make sure of it.

CHAPTER 5

Elder Debbon read Elder Daven's message regarding Amanda's need for help. He wondered what assistance he could render for a woman he had never met. With his curiosity piqued, he typed up Daven's patil code and waited. A few seconds later, Daven's face appeared on his screen.

"Elder Daven! I'm glad you picked up. I just read your message. How may I be of assistance?" Debbon asked with a smile on his face.

"Elder Debbon, I'm afraid this has become quite complicated. Amanda is going to attempt to take back a person from Earth who is being held by Elder Vargen in his Old Soul Engineering Facility. Do you have any ideas on how we may assist her in this quest?"

This was clearly not what he had been expecting to hear. He could not see any benefit to this particular mission and he asked, "What is the purpose of this journey? How will this help fulfill the prophecy?"

"I'm unclear, Elder, but Jehoban said we would need to render our assistance when requested. There has to be a reason, or she would not be asking for help," Daven replied uneasily. He did not like how Debbon was scowling through the patil.

"I'm aware of Jehoban's request, Daven. There's no need to remind me. I just want to make sure we are not being taken advantage of for personal gain. As First, I must put my position above all perceived wrongdoing, you understand," Debbon replied tartly.

"If this were any other person, I would handle it myself. Elder Vargen has done some disgraceful things to my family and I'm not in the position to impede him in any way. Please just consider how we may assist Amanda when she is ready to make her move."

"What is our timeline?"

"I imagine we will have at least two weeks. Riccan is going to have to teach Amanda how to fly a telepod first," Daven said with a grin.

"Really? That's interesting. I've never heard of someone from Earth learning the skill. What do you think the chances are of her succeeding?" Debbon asked with a chuckle.

"Knowing Amanda's talent in picking up new skills, her chances are pretty good. I doubt it will even take the two weeks Riccan has planned. I'll keep you posted."

"Sounds good. Until then, I'll see what I can come up with. Good day, Daven."

"Good day, Debbon," Daven said as he clicked off the connection on the patil.

After the screen went blank, Debbon switched the patil back to the messages program. He had taken a few days off to spend time with his wife, Chelesa, and he had a backlog of messages. There were several petitions from constituents which would take quite some time to go through so he printed them off and put them in a stack for later review.

For the next half hour he continued to read through his messages until he got to one which surprised him. He clicked on the communication and read the brief, but terse, note. At first he believed Riccan Stel had exaggerated his displeasure of the letters his daughter had received. However, upon reviewing the notes written by his own son, Debbon was no longer feeling upset with Riccan.

On the contrary, he was furious with his own son for the manner in which he had been addressing his betrothed. Clearly, he had not shown his son the proper way in which to address a woman, let alone the one who was going to become his wife. Willian had spoken to Jena with disrespect bordering on ownership rather than with affection. This was not at all acceptable.

When he had told his son to write to Jena, he had never expected his son to become so aggressive in his attempts to contact her. Clearly she had other things to do rather than sit around and wait for Willian's next missive. But for his son to threaten sanctioning had gone too far. He was going to have a stern conversation with his son.

He pushed away from his desk and stalked out of his office. He could not remember a time when he had been as upset as he currently felt. Instead of translating himself to his estate several gania away, Elder Debbon decided he could use the walk to clear his mind of the uncharitable thoughts. His mind was so troubled, he failed to see several patrons waving and trying to get his attention.

When he finally reached his estate, he was sure of what he would say to his son. Unsure of where Willian would be at this hour, Debbon went to his wife's office down the hall from the front door. He knew he should talk over his plan with Chelesa before they discussed the outcome with their son.

Debbon knocked on the office door and waited for Chelesa to ask him in. Only a moment later, Chelesa opened the door herself and a smile lit up her face as she saw her husband had come home from the Residence. It was so infrequent for him to do such a thing and she warmly welcomed him into her office.

Debbon wished he had some good news to discuss with her since she was clearly in a good mood. Unfortunately, this discussion could not be put off. They should have been monitoring their son's correspondence. Because of their inattentiveness, they were being taken to task for their son's inappropriate behavior.

"What's going on, Debbon?" Chelesa asked as she walked around her desk and sat down to face her husband.

"Nothing good, Chelesa," he replied as he wearily sat down. The walk had been very long and he was exhausted.

"Oh no! What happened?"

"It's about Willian. He has gone too far this time."

"What are you talking about? What has Willian done? Is he hurt?" She was starting to get worried until she realized her husband seemed downtrodden and discouraged. She would have to wait for Debbon to tell her in his own way whatever had transpired.

"I was going through my messages on the patil at the Residence when I came across a message sent several days ago from Riccan Stel."

Chelesa cocked her head sideways as she tried to recall who he was. Suddenly she remembered and asked, "Isn't that Jena's father?" It was still hard to believe Jena had parents to take into account now. There had been so many anons where she and her sister were considered orphans.

"Yes and he's very concerned about Willian's letters to Jena. He forwarded to me the correspondences which Jena's account had been receiving. Apparently, the girls have been so busy with learning the ways of Earth and attending school that they have yet to ask about having access to a patil."

"Okay, so what seems to be the problem?"

"At first Willian's letters were considerate and inquiring about Jena's time away. However, as each letter went unanswered, Willian became increasingly angrier. By the final letter, Willian was threatening to have Jena sanctioned because of her inattentiveness."

Chelesa gasped with shock and her hands flew up to cover her mouth. Her eyes had grown wide with disbelief and she said, "No! Debbon, what are we going to do?"

"That's what I wanted to talk to you about. How would you feel if we withdrew the betrothal agreement until Willian can correct his behavior?" Debbon knew this was a drastic proposal, but their son needed to have wake-up call on how inappropriate he had acted.

Chelesa controlled her expression since she could hardly hope this could be happening. As far as she was concerned, the betrothal had been a mistake from the beginning. Their son had been too intimidated with Jena's abilities and training and he had become bitter and mean. She did not like saying such mean things about their son, but she had to be honest with the reality of what had transpired over the anons. "I'll support you in whatever decision you make in this matter."

"Okay, then that's what we'll do. Where is Willian?"

Looking down on her timepiece, Chelesa replied, "He should be coming home from school in about a half hour. We have time to get something to eat if you're up to it."

"I could think of no better way to spend the time than with my wife," Debbon said and smiled across the desk at Chelesa.

She stood up and walked around the desk. As she got close to him, she held out her hand. She always felt so close when they walked hand-in-hand. As far as she was concerned, nothing could be more right than when they were connected in such a way. Right now, they needed to feel the connection between them since they were going to have a hard discussion very soon.

Debbon took her hand and felt the same feelings as she did. He knew they were the same because he often looked into her mind. The practice was normally frowned upon, but he and Chelesa had decided long ago he would be able to do it whenever he needed reassurance. At this moment, he was satisfied with his wife's thoughts since they mirrored his own.

Eating a late lunch did help them to calm their anger. When they heard the front door open, they knew it was time to clear up this unpleasant matter. As one, they rose from the kitchen chairs and walked toward the living room where Willian was sure to dump off his school gear and sit down to practice his crystal skills until dinner.

Willian expected to see his mother appear in the doorway, but his eyes widened when he also saw his father. His pleased expression abruptly changed to one of concern when he noticed neither of his parents seemed happy. "What's going on? Why are you home so early, Dad?"

"We need to have a family discussion. Do you want to follow us into my office?" Debbon said. Without waiting for a reply, he turned around and expected everybody else to follow him.

His mother remained standing in the doorway for a moment longer and then she turned away. Willian could not imagine what had happened which would create this type of scenario. Never in all of his life could he recall his father coming home from work early, let alone calling a family meeting. Something must have happened at his work. He hoped his status as First Elder had not been challenged. He walked down the hall and thought all manner of things which could have occurred, none of which had to do with him in particular.

"Sit down," Debbon commanded as Willian entered the office.

His brow furrowed at his father's tone, but he sat down immediately. He looked over at his mom and noticed she was no longer making eye contact with him. Instead she sat in her chair with her hands folded in her lap with her head down and her eyes looking at her hands. This must be a truly serious matter since his mother now seemed uncomfortable. "What is it, Dad?"

"A matter has come to my attention which is of great concern to myself and your mother regarding your correspondence with Jena. Do you have anything to say about this before I continue?" Debbon wished his son would have a valid reason for his terrible notes.

"My letters to Jena? What are you talking about?" Willian asked with genuine confusion.

"Can you tell us about the letters which you have sent to Jena since she's been gone?" Chelesa asked quietly.

"Dad told me to send her messages. I've sent her quite a few and she has never responded to a single one. I'm pretty sure something bad has happened to her. Can you look into it, Father?"

"I think your sudden concern for her wellbeing is a tad overstated. Don't you think you'd rather have her sanctioned for her inattention to you?" Debbon interrogated.

Willian's complexion turned white as he realized his father had actually seen the last message he had sent just three days before. He knew even as he wrote it that it was a bit drastic to say, but he had been so angry he hit send before he could reconsider his choice of words. "I didn't mean what I said, Dad, honest. I was angry because Jena hasn't replied to me or even tried to contact me ever since she went to live with her mother."

"Well, Jena's father didn't see any humor in it either. He has asked for something be done with you, Willian. We have come to a decision in this matter." He paused to let the last statement sink into his son's mind before he continued. "We are going to withdraw the betrothal agreement. It has become clear this relationship is not working out."

Willian stood up so fast his chair fell over behind him. His face turned red as his anger replaced his embarrassment and he yelled, "You can't do that to me, Dad. Jena is mine! I've put far too much into this relationship for you to just throw it all away."

"Have you considered Jena's feelings in this matter?" Chelesa asked.

"Jena's feelings? What does that have to do with this? She's my betrothed. I'm all that should matter to her. I'm not going to let you do this, Father!" Willian did not wait for any further discussion. He turned on his heel and stomped out of the office.

A few moments later, they heard the front door slam. Chelesa looked up at her husband and said, "I guess our discussion went as well as we could have expected."

"Yes, I quite agree. We'll have to see what Willian does next. Hopefully once he calms down he'll apologize for his appalling behavior."

CHAPTER 6

Amanda sat outside in the sunshine next to the Olympic sized pool. She had spent the morning stewing over what her next steps should be in rescuing Nealand from Elder Vargen's clutches. She was going to need a lot of assistance. She closed her eyes and said aloud, "Jehoban, I'm going to need Your help in this more than I've ever imagined."

When she opened her eyes she was shocked to see she was no longer poolside on Earth. Instead she had been translated to Acaim where Rasa stood a few feet away from her with a smile on her face. Amanda was sure her expression was pretty comical. She was hardly dressed appropriately to meet with Jehoban.

"Rasa! This can't be happening! Look at what I'm wearing!" Amanda said as she looked down and saw she was wearing a loose-fitting white robe with gold tassels hanging from the sleeves. "What in the world?" Amanda asked with eyes wide as she looked up to see Rasa chuckling softly.

"It seems as though you are out of excuses, Amanda. Come, Jehoban is waiting. You asked for an audience and He has made Himself available for you," she said softly as she pulled on Amanda's arm to get her moving.

They walked through several courtyards which were all different than the one she had seen the last time she had been to the palace. Amanda wondered how often the scenery changed and how the people could manage to know where they were if everything changed so often. She had to think rapidly about all of the things she needed to talk to Jehoban about this time. She had been in so much awe the last time she had forgotten as much as she remembered.

Rasa came to a stop at another solid gold door which was intricately carved with birds and flowers. She opened the door and gestured for Amanda to enter the room. Rasa followed Amanda inside and the door shut quietly behind them.

Amanda was self-conscious about taking the lead, but Rasa had seemed to want her to go first. She could see there were three chairs sitting around a small, round table. This appeared to be a much more intimate meeting than her previous one, for which she was grateful. Just as she reached the chairs, Jehoban appeared in front of her. She bowed her head and said, "Thank you for the quick answer, Jehoban. It is much appreciated."

"You're quite welcome, Amanda. Please find comfort in one of the chairs and ask Me what you will," He said kindly and He picked the furthest chair to the left.

Amanda felt uncomfortable choosing the chair right next to Him, yet it would seem rude to change her mind since she knew where He would be sitting. She sat down and saw Rasa had joined them in the third chair. She had thought this would be a private meeting, but she found she did not mind having the moral support of her cousin.

"First, I would like to request a birth crystal to be given to my Aunt Barla," she began.

Rasa made a small sound as she heard the request and her hand went to her mouth as she tried to contain any further noise.

Amanda looked over at Rasa and continued, "I don't know why, but I believe it will be imperative for Barla to learn the skills which can only be taught to one who has a birth crystal."

"I have waited for Barla to ask for one, however her fear has kept her from even hoping to ever get one. I will grant your request."

Rasa could hardly believe this was actually happening. She had always hoped this moment would happen, but never in her wildest dreams had she thought it would come about in this way. She could feel tears of happiness falling from her eyes and dripping down her cheeks. She smiled gratefully at Amanda for this wonderful gift.

"What else may I do for you, Amanda?" Jehoban asked.

"Can you tell me how I came to have my own birth crystal? I know what I dreamt, but I know it could not have been true," she said and then shut her mouth before she could ramble on any longer.

Jehoban paused for a moment as he considered Amanda's request. There could be no benefit to her knowing, but because she had thought to help another before helping herself, He decided to answer. "It is really very simple," He began and then paused for a moment as He thought over what she really needed to know.

"When the wise-woman Copa decided to send you back to Earth while you were pregnant, she petitioned Me for a crystal of your own to give you safe passage. Obviously, I granted her request and she took with her the single necklace. She had no idea you would deliver your twins before she could complete your transfer to Earth. While you were still delirious with the drug *epeny*, she performed your birth crystal ceremony. It was unconventional since you were an adult as well as basically unconscious, but I had already sanctioned it.

"She wanted you to have the crystal for safe passage to Earth, but also for a safe delivery of your children. She knew they were special and they would need you to be protected during delivery. Copa had no way of knowing your children were already on the way even as she was performing the ceremony since you were still a month from your due date." Jehoban stopped talking.

Amanda took a moment before she realized she had heard all she was going to hear about her own birth crystal. The story really had been simpler than she had guessed, but it made sense since Jehoban had told her. There had been no other opportunity for her to have anyone give her a birth crystal. Elder Vargen certainly would not have wanted her to have one of her own. The fact he had kept her practically unconscious spoke volumes for how nervous she must have made him.

"I only have one more question," Amanda said quietly and then cleared her throat before continuing, "Can you help me get Nealand home? I can't get out of my head the need to go and rescue him from Elder Vargen's

Old Soul Engineering Facility. Obviously, I don't want to meet up with Elder Vargen again after my last encounter with him. Is there anything you can do to help me in this matter?"

Jehoban nodded with a pleased expression on His face, "Because you seek to help another I will do as you have requested. I will not tell you the means in which I will assist you, but you must have faith I will do as I have promised. You are a fine woman, Amanda. I am pleased with the progress you have shown. Thank you."

Amanda looked down in embarrassment and felt herself blushing furiously. She felt Rasa touch her hand and she looked up at her shyly.

"Jehoban has left us, Amanda. I assume you were finished," she said with a slightly questioning tone.

Amanda simply nodded. She could not imagine being in Jehoban's presence every day since He was such an imposing figure. She looked at Rasa with renewed admiration. Amanda wondered if Rasa knew how lucky she had been to grow up in such a great atmosphere. Looking at Rasa's quiet confidence, she believed Rasa did know how fortunate she had been.

"Let us get you back home before you are missed," Rasa said as she stood up from the chair. Her heart was still beating rapidly with the knowledge of her mother finally receiving her own crystal. She wondered what color she would get. She looked forward to the surprise as she walked back to the door they had entered.

Amanda followed Rasa quietly with her head down and her fingers playing with the fringe on her sleeves. She felt worn out as though she had just run a marathon. She was so happy she had said her prayer and even happier to know it was all going to be granted. With no explanation for why she had been chosen for this great task other than her heritage was perfect she felt quite overwhelmed with the enormity of the task.

They stopped in one of the courtyards and Rasa turned to face her. She held each of Amanda's arms in her hands and said, "Please close your eyes, Amanda. I'm going to send you home now."

"Thank you, Rasa. I'm glad you could be with me today. It meant a lot to be with family," she said in a rush and hugged her cousin swiftly before she moved away from her again.

Rasa smiled in return and said, "Thank you for thinking of my mom.

I'm not sure if she'll be more happy or scared, but I'll be relieved either way! Now, close your eyes."

Amanda closed her eyes even as she continued to grin foolishly. She could not feel any difference in herself, but she felt a breeze on her skin where the robes had covered her before. She opened her eyes and stared in wonder at how swiftly and easily she had slipped across space to be back in her yard in Florida. "Wow," Amanda said out loud as she stared out at the pool and landscaped yard while standing in her bikini.

~

RASA WAS THRILLED when Jehoban called her into another meeting immediately after sending Amanda home. She could feel there was something stirring in the air. Naturally, she believed it would be about her mother receiving her own birth crystal. Walking with an air of humility, she entered Jehoban's personal chambers quietly.

A few feet from Him, she stopped and kept her eyes focused on the floor a few inches in front of her toes. She spoke softly, "I have come at your request, My Lord. How may I be of assistance?"

"I would like to discuss a matter of some delicacy, Rasa. Please sit down and be in comfort," He said kindly.

Rasa hastily glanced up at Jehoban since she was surprised to hear the topic of discussion. She sat down with alacrity and composed herself to be ready for any situation in which her Lord might require her. Without saying anything, she waited for Jehoban to continue in His own time.

Jehoban watched His student with the pride of a parent. She had so much potential and promise. All of her schooling had led her to this moment and yet He worried for her. "I have decided the time has come for you to pursue your next step."

Again, Rasa kept her head down and this time she nodded very slightly. She knew this day would eventually come, and yet she still wished to have more time in the presence of the Creator. She did not like the idea of moving away from Acaim and no longer feeling the power of the earth beneath her feet. No other place in all of the lands had as many lay lines flowing underneath it than did the land where Jehoban lived.

"Elder Wilken has come to me with a particular problem and I wish to ask your assistance in the matter," He said and then remained silent.

Rasa knew Elder Wilken to be a very wise, old man. He was well-respected by his peers as well as by the people of his jurisdiction. His only child, a daughter, had married, but had remained childless. Suddenly, Rasa understood where Jehoban was taking this conversation and she was pleased, scared, and troubled at the same time.

"I see you have come to the same conclusion as I have," Jehoban said simply. "Do you have questions?"

"Only one. Why me? There are any number of students here who would make an excellent match..." she stopped speaking when she looked up and saw Jehoban shaking His head slowly. "I'm sorry for questioning. It is just an unexpected turn of events."

"I want you to meet with Elder Wilken in the next day or two. From there I want you to go home to the Port of Cresdon. Your mother has no idea what is in store for her, but you are the perfect person to deliver the gift." Jehoban reached into His tunic pocket and withdrew a birth crystal. The golden circle contained a gold filigreed tree with brilliant light blue crystals set as the leaves. He held it out for Rasa to reach up and take from Him.

She smiled as she stared at the blue stones shimmering in the sunlight. Today she held her mother's future in her hand as she put her fingers around the stone and felt the weight of it as Jehoban released His hold. "Do you want me to perform the crystal ceremony for my own mother?" She could hardly believe she would be the one to do the honor.

"I can think of none other Barla would trust more. Her fear has kept her from this for far too long. I'm glad Amanda has interceded on her behalf. Now we will right a wrong."

"When would You have me leave?" Rasa asked as she tucked the necklace gently into her own tunic pocket.

"Today would be best. Spend today and tomorrow in Manzanit with Elder Wilken. Let him know you are My choice for his successor. He will understand the next steps to be taken. Go and pack your things. Your journey has just begun." Jehoban turned and walked a few steps to lean against the window sill. He looked out on His island and was pleased with all He saw.

Rasa rose from her chair and began to leave the chamber. When she reached the door, she turned her head and said, "You have been so good to me, my Lord. Thank you for all of the opportunities which you have given me. I will do my best to make you proud of me." She saw Jehoban nod and she left the room.

Jehoban waited until the door closed behind Rasa before He spoke quietly, "You've been a blessing, Rasa."

CHAPTER 7

Rasa did not know how long she would be away from Acaim, so she worried over what to pack for her journey. Finally she decided to take her ceremonial robes as well as her ornate box. She selected several changes of clothes and carefully folded them and put them in her duffel bag. There were only a couple of personal items which she would take with her.

With no further decision to be made, Rasa picked up her full bag and walked out of her room. She looked back and wondered if she had spent her last night in the room or if she would be returning for a while yet. For so long, she had been certain about her life. She had been a student of Jehoban since she was six anons old. Now she was twenty-seven and her life was about to be turned upside down.

Since she was going to the Residence of an Elder, Rasa opted to have a telepod take her to Manzanit rather than translate herself. She wanted to make a good impression, and translating was perceived as being too showy for the older generation.

She walked across the perfectly manicured grounds until she reached the telepod landing site. There were usually several telepods waiting to take passengers anywhere in the world. Today there was only one.

When she came close enough, she saw the driver was a younger

543

gentlemen with whom she was unfamiliar. "Are you taking passengers, or are you waiting for someone to return?" she asked.

The man straightened up and spoke politely, "I'm at your service, my lady. Where would you like to go?"

"Manzanit, please," Rasa spoke as she was helped up the ramp and to her seat. She had held her bag in front of her and shook her head when the man gestured to take it from her. When she sat down, she gently placed her bag on the floor by her feet. She looked around and noticed the telepod was an older version, she only hoped the crystal drive was still sound and the driver was competent.

The man passed her as he moved to the front of the telepod and palmed the side door closed from the main console. He fiddled with several of the controls as he began the startup procedure. The telepod rose a few inches from the ground in preparation for transport. The man leafed through a book of coordinates and mumbled a few things to himself before he moved his hand over to the manual control.

The world turned black as the telepod disappeared from the grounds on Acaim to travel through the space between to bring them to their destination. Rasa counted to three and was relieved when the telepod once again appeared around her. For a moment she had the overwhelming feeling something had gone terribly wrong.

The operator palmed open the side door and announced, "We are at our destination. Please disembark."

Rasa thought his phrasing seemed slightly off even as she unbuckled her seatbelt. She picked up her bag and stood up to leave. When she turned and saw outside of the 'pod she realized they were not at the destination she had requested. Suddenly, the alarm bells in her head began to chime in earnest. Instead of saying anything to the contrary, Rasa pretended everything was normal and she stepped off of the telepod in front of the operator.

What he did not expect was her ability to translate herself at will. Even as he reached forward to grab her arm, she seemed to disintegrate in front of him. His fingers closed on empty air and he cursed violently at how easily the woman had escaped from him.

He did not look forward to telling his Master of his failure in his simple mission. He slapped the outside control to close the door to the telepod and he stalked away from the vessel before he did something he would later regret.

❦

RASA HAD LEARNED from experience to heed her intuition immediately. She sensed the danger she was in and instantly took action. Even though she had left the situation behind her, she still monitored the man's thoughts. A shiver passed through her as she discovered the man had worked for Lucinden. Never before had Lucinden attempted to send one of his minions onto Acaim. Apparently the real games were about to begin.

Even as she walked the short distance to the Residence in Manzanit, she was working on what she was going to tell Elder Debbon about what had just occurred. Everyone who had been at the meeting with Jehoban would have to be warned about Lucinden's new involvement. She had composed the message she planned to send when a patil became available and filed it away in her memory for later.

At this moment, she needed to concentrate on presenting her best self to Elder Wilken. There had been several occasions where the good Elder had been present on Acaim and Rasa had found him to be a pleasant man to be around. She hoped she would prove to be as capable an Elder as he had been for his people.

When she reached the front door of the Residence, she struck her knuckles three times on the door and then waited for someone to answer her call. A few moments later, the door was opened by a middle-aged woman.

"May I help you?" she asked.

Rasa smiled politely and said, "My name is Rasa and I am to meet with Elder Wilken at Jehoban's request. Is the Elder available?"

The woman's expression turned to one of confusion. She had never heard a response such as this woman had given and the Elder was not at the Residence. She immediately stood aside and said, "Please do come in. I'm sorry to say Elder Wilken is not in Residence presently, but I can try to get a message to him. If we had known you were coming..."

Rasa put her hand on the woman's arm and said, "It's of no concern, I only found out from Jehoban a little bit ago. I can wait for Elder Wilken's return. Do you know how long he will be out?"

"He went out into the district to adjudicate. There's no telling when he'll be back," she said as she began to wring her hands with worry. She had a healthy fear of Jehoban and did not want herself or her master to fall on bad terms with the Creator. She had to do something to make this situation better. "Please come in and make yourself at home. Is there anything I can get for you?"

"There is one thing…do you have a patil I could use? A situation came up on my way here which I need to report," Rasa inquired.

"Absolutely. Please follow me." She was relieved to hear she only needed to use a patil. If the woman were planning to tell Jehoban about being kept from meeting with Elder Wilken she would not have needed a patil to do it. She led the woman to a private office kept in reserve for dignitaries and closed the door behind Rasa as she entered.

Rasa was relieved to be able to take care of the matter regarding Lucinden immediately. She knew she could have waited, but she preferred to have everyone on alert as soon as possible. As she sat down to type out her message, she had no idea the amount of turmoil she had set into motion in the Residence around her.

The maids were aflutter with gossip about what this meeting could be about. Had Elder Wilken finally decided on a successor? Was there about to be a change in the Residence? Were any of the staff to be let go?

The head maid immediately dispatched an urgent message to Elder Wilken's head assistant who always traveled with the frail Elder. She hoped to have a response before Rasa had finished with her messages. Until then, she had the kitchen staff prepare a light repast and hot steena tea to offer her when she emerged from the office. She went to stand at the ready outside of the office door.

Rasa decided to notify Elder Debbon first. She turned on the patil and touched the screen to compose a new message. She typed up the message she had memorized on the walk and hit send. Next, she decided she should probably give her mother warning of her visit. She would hate to arrive at their house to find out they, too, were gone for an undisclosed period of time.

She did not want to tell her mother the actual nature of her visit. She wanted to see her mother's reaction when she showed her the birth crystal Jehoban had picked for her. Rasa supposed her mother would not suspect an ulterior motive for Rasa to visit the home of her childhood. Barla would be excited enough just by the fact Rasa was coming home at all.

"Mom, I think we should plan a small family reunion. I'll be at your house in three days. Please ask Gravin to come home as well. There are many new things on the horizon and I think we should attempt to get together one last time before we are all too busy to meet. I love you. Rasa." Rasa read over her missive and thought it sounded upbeat enough. She hit the send button and then turned off the patil.

Now she officially had nothing to do until Elder Wilken returned. She contemplated the idea of staying alone in the office, but thought it would probably be considered rude. With a sigh, she stood up, walked across the room, opened the door, and began to leave the room when she was startled by the maid.

"Let me show you to the living room," she said as she appeared at Rasa's side.

"Thank you," Rasa managed to say as she tried to hide her jumpiness.

The older maid led the way into a large and airy room with plush furniture and a gorgeous view overlooking the district. "Please make yourself at home. I have ordered some snacks and tea for you. Ah, here it is now," she said as she moved aside for two other women to bring in the hot teapot and the plates of snacks. She gestured for them to set them down on a side table near one of the more comfortable-looking chairs.

Rasa sat down next to the table and realized she was quite ravenously hungry. "Thank you. It all looks so lovely. I'm sure I'll be very content to await Elder Wilken with this food and the gorgeous view."

"I'll let you know as soon as I've heard anything from him," the maid said as she left the room.

Rasa selected an item from the tray of edibles and popped it into her mouth as she poured herself a cup of the hot tea. She stood up and walked to the wall of windows and looked out over the countryside. It was hard to imagine when Elder Wilken stepped down from his office, this would be her new home and the people of this land would be her responsibility.

She had spent the past twenty-one years training for this moment and, yet, the idea scared her half to death. There were bound to be mistakes made, but she hoped her intuition would help guide her to the right decisions.

Furthermore, she knew this post was highly coveted because of the potency of the ley lines beneath this part of the country. Even at this moment, she could feel the surge of energy ready for her beck and call. It was almost as good as the power available on Acaim. She hoped her promotion to this post would not cause contention among the Elders.

It was then she realized there would have to be an assembly of the Elders to promote her as the successor to this post. She was certain there would be a lot of anger and tension at the meeting. Not only would she be the first female Elder, she was also going to be receiving the best location, second only to Acaim.

Rasa felt a moment of clarity when she realized Jehoban's plan for her new post was designed to distract the Elders long enough for Amanda to extract Nealand from Tuala. She chuckled out loud at the devious manner in which Jehoban planned to help Amanda without seeming to interfere with the order of things on Tuala. She was still smiling when she heard someone clear her throat behind her. She turned swiftly to see who had wanted to get her attention.

The head maid said, "I'm sorry to interrupt, but I've received word from Elder Wilken. He will be back at the Residence within the hour. Is there anything I can get for you while you wait?"

"No, I'm fine. I've been enjoying the view as well as the wonderful repast you have prepared for me. Thank you." Rasa meant every word she said and hoped her sincerity came through.

The maid smiled in appreciation of the compliment and curtsied before she turned and left.

Rasa wandered over to the pastry tray and picked another appetizing bite and popped it into her mouth. She had picked a strawberry tart and it practically melted in her mouth. If this were the type of food they served to guests, she could only imagine the fare for the Elder.

She toured the rest of the living room to see what other grand sights there were to be found. She discovered a large globe of Tuala which had inlaid precious stones for each jurisdiction. The beauty and precision of it was nothing short of a masterpiece. It appeared Elder Wilken had an eye for art as well developed as his skill in working for the people. She had no idea how much time had passed while she had been sipping on her tea and admiring the craftsmanship of the Residence.

She heard a commotion in the hallway and walked toward the doorway to see what was occurring. Just as she entered the opening, she came face-to-face with Elder Wilken himself. She smiled brightly and said, "I hope I haven't come at a bad time and caused you any major inconvenience."

"Nonsense, my dear girl! Jehoban sent you at the perfect time. I hope you have been comfortable while you waited for my return." He leaned forward and kissed Rasa on the cheek before he walked past her and over to the coffee table. He picked up another of the strawberry tarts and ate it with great enjoyment. "My chefs do make the best pastries! Come, come. Let us sit and talk for a while!" He lowered himself into the chair Rasa had originally used.

Rasa pulled another chair closer to the other side of the table so she could continue to sample the pastries as they discussed Elder Wilken's plans for Rasa's future. She sat down and happily ate a chocolate truffle. She smiled at the old gentleman across from her and waited for him to start. This had been initiated by him, after all.

"Let me begin by thanking you for agreeing to take on this job. I have several more anons before I am wanting to step down, but I felt it was important to make my decision for you public. As the first woman Elder, I want people to adjust to the idea slowly. When it finally comes time for you to step into this role, the community will already know you to be fair and equitable."

Rasa sighed with relief and said, "I'm glad to hear you say you want to stay on for a while yet. There is much I need to learn from you before I will be ready to lead the district."

Wilken chuckled at Rasa's deprecation of her skills and said, "I doubt you will have any trouble in the matter. Jehoban has spoken highly of you and your skills for two declans now and I have watched you personally as you have handled the school for the Elders' children. Even so, I still feel young at heart, but my body has other ideas. A person never knows when his time will come to an end and I want my district to be at peace because they will continue to be guided with a wise hand."

"Thank you for your trust, Elder Wilken. What did you have in mind for me while you continue to serve in your post?" Rasa was intrigued with this new challenge. This was turning out better than she could have ever hoped.

"I would like for you to move into the Residence so you can be a part of the everyday proceedings. Before I hand down my decisions, I want you to share your opinions on the matters. In this way, I can help to guide you toward the way things are done in this district. Also, the people will see you sitting with me and they will learn to trust you as they have trusted me for the past eleven declans."

Rasa nodded even though she was surprised to hear Elder Wilken had been in this post for as long as he had. She knew the Elders lived longer lives, yet she had not appreciated the scope of it until it was shoved right in her face. "That makes sense. I only have one problem with your plan."

"And what would that be, my dear?" Elder Wilken smiled and picked up another pastry.

"Jehoban has asked me to go to my mother's house in three days' time to take care of a very important matter. I'm not sure how long I will be gone, but I'll do my best to return quickly." Rasa blushed slightly as she thought about the task she would be performing for her mother. She could never tell anyone about it since her mother was from Earth.

"I'd never presume to think my tasks are more important than those set by Jehoban. By all means, do as He requests and return to me when you are able. In the meantime, I will begin the formal written process for making you my successor. You do accept the post, right?" Elder Wilken stopped himself to verify Rasa's willingness to proceed.

"Absolutely, Elder Wilken. It would be my greatest honor to learn from you. Could I ask you a question, though?" Rasa was reticent to even ask, yet she wanted to be certain of something before her acceptance was firm.

"Ask what you will. I never want you to hold back any question from me."

"Why is your daughter not your first choice as the successor?" Rasa looked down into her teacup.

"From the time she was very little, Pluska declared she only wanted to marry and lead a simple life. This was further confirmed by her utter lack of desire to learn how to use her birth crystal. It appears she has very little aptitude for accessing the elemy which, in itself, would render her incapable of holding this position.

"She has led her life just as she planned with one exception: she never was able to conceive. Her grand design was to have many children. She hoped one of them would be a suitable candidate for succession, but this was not to be.

"Pluska has been a sweet child and I could never be disappointed in her decision to do something else with her life. She has been happy, and it's all I could ever ask for my only child. I suppose I'm as much at fault for not remarrying and having more children. When my wife died delivering Pluska, I just could not ever come to terms with the feelings of betrayal should I marry again." Elder Wilken fell silent as he considered the choices he had made for himself. He could not fault himself because his heart had always led his decisions.

Rasa nodded and said, "Thank you for sharing. I'm sure some of it was difficult to bring out into the open. I understand better where you are coming from and I can honestly say I have no other reservations about accepting this honorable post."

"I appreciate your concern. Since we are embarking on uncharted territory with you, I would not want anyone to argue there was a more suitable candidate other than yourself. I assure you, there is no other person who has even the smallest claim to the Manzanit post. You will be undisputed. Besides, who are we to argue against what Jehoban has put into motion?"

Rasa smiled and nodded confirmation. She had spent enough time around Jehoban to know just how true his statement had been. Jehoban always had the best plan and the people were wise when they complied to His plans immediately.

With a whirlwind of activity, Rasa found herself being settled into a massive bedroom upstairs. When Elder Wilken had spoken to the staff, the head maid had retrieved Rasa's bag from the study and shown her to the room she would be using until she became an Elder herself. She was embarrassed to have forgotten about her bag in the first place, and had been deep in thought as the maid led her to her room.

She unpacked the few things she had brought. She hung up her clothes in the wardrobe and set her ceremonial box on top of the chifforobe. With her hands still resting on her jeweled box, she looked up at herself in the mirror and could not believe her life had just changed. With her upbringing, she trusted Jehoban to know this was her path, now she just had to believe in herself the same way He did.

The next two days were a blur of activity. Elder Wilken and she probably spent seventeen of the twenty-four hours of each day working together. They had eaten every meal together, sat through several disputes of the local dignitaries, and spoke at length about how the district operated on a normal basis.

Rasa was glad to know she would have a break from the amount of information she had been amassing. When the third day arrived, Rasa went down for breakfast as usual. She sat at her normal seat and enjoyed Elder Wilken's company.

When the last morsel was consumed, Elder Wilken said, "Please tell your parents I'm very pleased with your progress. They have to be very proud of you. I'll miss you until your return. Please don't stay away for too long." He smiled at the girl he had begun to feel was more like a daughter to him than his own Pluska. They shared so many of the same ideas and he was doubly pleased with Jehoban's decision to send her to him.

Rasa held her head down at the Elder's praise and said, "I'll be sure to pass along your greetings. As to the post, they have yet to learn about it. I was reticent to say anything to them until I was certain you would want me to stay."

"Ha! I knew from the moment Jehoban suggested you that you would be perfect. These last couple of days have proven His wisdom. Go home with a clear conscience because I find you more than acceptable. You are the perfect choice and I dare anyone to argue against it!"

"I'm sure there will be plenty of arguing at the assembly, but it does please me to hear you say you approve of me. I will do everything in my power to keep your esteem. I think I'll head out in the next few minutes."

"Good. It means you will return that much sooner!" Elder Wilken winked at her.

Rasa laughed and stood up from her chair. "I'll go pack now. If I don't see you before I go, then I'll say I can't wait until I can return and continue learning under your tutelage."

She left the room, went upstairs to her room, and gathered her meager belongings as well as her ceremonial box. She checked her tunic pocket to confirm the birth crystal was still where she had left it. Her heart skipped a beat as she realized she was about to change her mother's life.

With a happy heart, and a clear conscience, Rasa teleported herself directly from her bedroom. She had considered taking a telepod, but after her last experience, she was unwilling to risk it. This ceremony had to happen and she was not about to put anything to chance.

CHAPTER 8

Barla had been over the moon when she had read the message from Rasa about coming home. She had immediately contacted her son, Gravin, and implored him to come home. It had been since Rasa was six that they had all been in the home together. Barla was sad to think it had actually been as long as that, but now they would have their family reunion.

Gravin had arrived the day before. He had stayed in the bedroom he had used as a child. Nothing had been changed in it since the day he had left home. He was enjoying the last few anons of his retirement to the fullest and seldom made time for his parents.

Other than the few letters and calls through the patil, Gravin had not had any contact with his sister since the day she had been chosen to be taught by Jehoban. He still felt the jealousy rise up in him at his lost opportunity. It should have been he being sent away and learning all of the secrets from Jehoban.

Then he considered the fact he would not have been able to spend the amount of time fooling around if he had been chosen. Rasa was twenty-seven and still learning and living on Acaim. Maybe it was not as grand as he had always believed it to be. Rasa had more responsibility on her shoulders than he ever thought would be comfortable. Maybe it had worked out for the best.

Gravin had never seen his mother this nervous for a guest. He did not realize Rasa had only been home once since she had originally left. Now he was wondering what had brought her to come home at all, let alone requesting a family gathering.

The next morning, Gravin was relaxing alone in the front sitting room when Rasa translated herself directly into the room. He had known the mode of transportation was possible, but he had never seen it done, let alone seen his sister display any of the various and amazing talents she had surely acquired in her anons of study.

He stood up with alacrity and came forward to greet her. "Rasa! What an unexpected entrance! Impressive, though!"

"I'm sorry, it was terribly rude of me to come home this way. I assumed this room would be empty during this time of day. Nobody ever used it before," she said hastily as her nerves started to get the best of her. "Where's Mom?"

"She's making breakfast in the kitchen," he answered and then offered, "Would you like me to take any of your things upstairs to your old room?"

She hated to tell her brother no, but she could not let another person carry her ceremonial box. "Is it where I'll be staying?" she asked.

"Yes and I noticed your room has not changed since the day you left, just as mine hasn't!" he grinned at her.

Again, Rasa was relieved to receive this information so she would not have to offend her brother. With a thought, she transported her belongings into her room. "No need to bother with my things."

"Wow! Rasa, you are going to have to teach me some of these tricks. My life could become so much simpler with them." Gravin spoke with utter awe now.

"Let's go see Mom, shall we?" Rasa said as she led the way out of the room. She was thankful they still lived in the same house and she was able to navigate the corridors and find her way to the kitchen without assistance. She only paused briefly in the front hallway to look up at the family portrait and see the little girl she had been looking back at her.

Gravin nudged her to continue walking and said, "Do you miss the old days?"

"Sometimes. Our futures are bright, though, and we can be glad for it," she said as she resumed walking to the kitchen.

As expected, Barla screamed with delight when she saw Rasa enter the kitchen. She wiped her hands on her apron and rushed forward to hug her daughter. She pulled away and then brought Gravin forward to hug them both together. Her children were home and her heart was thankful. Now they just had to wait for Ahn to come downstairs for breakfast for the family unit to be complete.

Even as she thought it, she heard Ahn's footsteps as he came down the stairs. More greetings were issued as Ahn grabbed Rasa up off her feet in a bear hug. Barla could not stop smiling with joy to see her husband interacting with their two children. Nothing could get better than this moment.

"Breakfast is almost ready," Barla announced cheerfully. She turned back to her task and finished beating the eggs to scramble them in the frying pan.

"I've already eaten, Mom," Rasa announced so her mom would not prepare a fourth plate.

The three of them sat at the table and exchanged pleasantries until Barla could join them.

A few minutes later, Barla brought the three plates to the table and set them down. She looked over at Rasa and asked, "Are you sure I can't get you something?"

"I'm sure, Mom. Sit down and eat while it's still warm." She patted the chair next to her and smiled up at her mother. Rasa could feel the weight of the birth crystal in her pocket as it rested on top of her thigh. She would make the announcement as soon as they were done eating and the dishes cleaned.

The meal was eaten swiftly as it seemed nobody was as interested in eating as much as they wanted to hear stories about both Rasa and Gravin. The last morsel was scraped from a plate and Rasa could contain her excitement no longer. She was not about to wait for her mother to wash the dishes by hand. With a thought, she had the dishes cleared from the table, washed, and put back in the cupboard.

Everybody at the table looked at one another with comical expressions until Rasa said, "Come on! We have more important things to discuss than waste time on watching Mom do dishes. Let's go to the living room." She scraped her chair back and stood up.

Her eagerness was infectious and the family followed her orders. Barla removed her apron and left it on the island as they passed by it. She was the last to leave the kitchen and looked ahead of her to see her entire family walking together. She almost had to pinch herself to find out if she were dreaming.

The family began seating themselves in their favorite spots, but Rasa remained standing. She could not sit down until she had said what she had come home to do.

"Aren't you going to sit down, darling?" Barla asked. She wondered what had Rasa so worked up. She hoped nothing bad had happened, but as she looked closer, she could only see excitement in her daughter's movements and expression. "What's going on, Rasa?"

"There are a few things, but only one which I think is the most important." She did not know any other way to broach the subject so she reached into her pocket and pulled out the birth crystal with the bright blue stones. She came close to her mother and said, "Jehoban has requested I perform the ceremony for you to have this birth crystal. Will you let me do the honors?"

Barla's eyes widened with a mixture of surprise and fear. This was a dream she had known would never come true. She did not deserve the honor and yet her daughter was telling her it was hers for the taking. There was no way to say no so she simply nodded as tears formed in her eyes and fell down her cheeks.

"Mother, this is amazing!" Gravin jumped up from his chair and fell to his knees in front of his mom's chair and hugged her tightly. He looked up at his sister and asked, "When can we do the ceremony?"

"As soon as everyone is properly dressed. I brought everything I would need to perform the ceremony." She could feel tears of her own as she witnessed her mother's raw emotions of gratitude.

Only twenty minutes had passed since Rasa had requested the ceremony. Each person had gone to their own rooms and changed into their most formal attire for this most auspicious occasion. Nobody seemed to care this event was several declans late, it was happening now and it was all that mattered.

Rasa opened her ceremonial box and gently placed her mother's necklace inside. She would honor all of the normal traditions in requesting and presenting the crystal even though everyone had already seen it. She closed the box and ran her hand along the top lovingly. The sparkling jewels covering the outside were only a sampling of the beauty which Jehoban created for His people.

She picked up the box and carried it down to the living room where they would meet again to perform the service. She picked the far end to set up the two cups of liquid and the small squares of cloth. She kneeled on the floor and made sure all was ready before they began.

Almost as if on cue, Ahn entered the room dressed in his best suit. His manner was somber, but his expression was one of delight. He sat down in the first seat on the right. Next to enter the room was her brother. Gravin was also attired in a nice outfit. He had not known to bring anything formal, so he wore the best he had. He sat down across from his father and turned to watch his mother enter the room.

Barla wore her finest white dress. She had never worn it before and often wondered why she had kept it at all since it was too fancy to wear to any occasion. Now she knew she had been hoping for this very moment even if she had never admitted it to herself before. She walked across the room and kneeled on the floor in front of her daughter.

"Family we have gathered together for the important task of giving the protective crystal to Barla. Barla, do you agree to allow me to look into your mind in order for me to assign a unique crystal?" Rasa waited for her mother to reply before continuing.

"Yes, I do." Barla wondered what Rasa would see of her future.

Rasa dipped her finger into the green liquid in the bowl beside Barla's knee. She marked a line in green across her mother's forehead and chanted, "I mark your forehead to be able to divine the thoughts and intents of your being." She dipped her finger again in the bowl and marked a circle in green on the back of each of her mother's outstretched hands chanting, "I mark each of your hands to be able to divine the actions for which you will be responsible in your lifetime."

The room was utterly silent as Rasa held each of Barla's hands in her own. With her eyes closed, she began to rock back and forth as she spoke, *"Allah dari langit, silakan me panduan dalam penyelidikan. Membuat saya benar bacaan dan kristal tugas tepat."*

Barla recognized the same words from her own children's ceremonies so long ago and easily translated Rasa's phrase with, "Jehoban of creation, please guide me in the quest. Make my readings true and the crystal assignment precise."

They all sat in silence as Rasa continued to rock silently. Rasa had never probed an adult mind in this manner. She was finding it both difficult and fascinating as she had to shuffle through her mother's consciousness while trying to see into her future.

Rasa finally spoke again. "Your life has many challenges to come in the future. Gentleness is apparent in your very nature as well as a strong sense of right from wrong." Rasa finished and released Barla's hands. She had seen some wondrous things in her mother's past and future and she was more than a little alarmed at the visions. To hide her sudden apprehension Rasa opened the hinged lid of the ornate box on the floor.

The lid obscured her view of the contents, yet Barla knew the box contained the protective crystals. Barla had already seen her crystal and wondered if Rasa had taken it from her pocket and put it into the box.

Rasa did not hesitate as she reached into the open box. She brought forth the same pendant she had already shown the family. She purposefully closed the box as she deftly threaded the crystal onto a delicate, but ornate, chain which was procured from an almost hidden pocket in her tunic.

She then handed the necklace to Barla and continued the slightly-altered formal procedure, by saying, "As you place this crystal of protection on yourself, say, *Saya memakai ini dengan restu dari Tuhan.*"

Barla repeated the phrase as she placed the necklace around her own neck. She silently translated the phrase as 'I wear this with the blessing of Jehoban.' Knowing with certainty this was true, she felt a sudden warmth inside her heart and the prickle of tears come to her eyes as she realized she had been accepted by Jehoban.

Rasa took a new warm, wet cloth and wiped the green liquid from Barla's forehead and hands. She rinsed the cloth in another bowl of clean water. Rasa removed the cloth, picked up the cup and handed it to Barla and announced, "I give you this water to drink. By the drinking of the liquid which contains your essence, you will seal the bond with your new birth crystal."

Barla brought the cup to her lips and drank down the mint flavored water and then returned the cup to Rasa. To conclude the service, Rasa then spoke to everyone in the room, "With Barla safe and protected from harm because she is united with her birth crystal we can all celebrate."

Barla stood and turned to face her family. The three most important people in her life came and hugged her from all sides. Never before had she felt so loved. This moment was possibly the best one of her life. Her blessings kept multiplying and she offered a silent prayer of thanks to Jehoban for His mercy.

There was not a single dry eye in the room and they could not have been any happier about it. Finally, they sat down and used tissue to clean themselves up a bit. Barla could not contain the question which had been plaguing her so she asked, "What made Jehoban want to give me a birth crystal at my age?"

Rasa answered, "Amanda met with Jehoban and asked for it be given to you."

"Amanda? Why would she do it? She doesn't even know me." She continued to ponder the many questions in her mind.

Rasa considered her mother's questions. She knew the truth about Amanda being related to them, but her mother had no idea. This was not her place to say anything, of that she felt certain. She finally answered what she could by saying, "When you meet her, you can ask her yourself. There are many surprises in all of our futures."

Barla raised her eyebrow at her daughter's cryptic remark. Once again, she wondered what Rasa had seen of her past and future. She knew better than to ask, but her imagination could still think about it.

Ahn piped in with his comment, "I'll be sure to give her a big kiss for asking Jehoban on our behalf."

Rasa turned to her brother and asked, "How long are you able to stay home?"

"A few weeks. Why?"

"We need to train Mom on how to use her crystal. I'm sure she remembers the lessons from when we were little, but it's quite a different story when you are the user and not merely the observer!"

"That's right. Mom, now you won't have to do everything by hand. Imagine how much more time you'll have when you're able to just think everything done." Gravin was eager to begin the lessons, but he believed Rasa would be the better teacher and he said as much to his sister.

"Oh, Gravin, I have it on good authority that you are an excellent teacher. I wouldn't be where I am today had it not been for your training. I have a few days off so we can do it together, okay?" Rasa held her brother's arm in her hand and squeezed it lovingly.

CHAPTER 9

Riccan decided he would make a family affair of teaching Amanda how to fly the telepod. He planned to instruct her first in his newest telepod and then give her his older one to use for her missions in Tuala. When he got home from work, he was going to tell them all about it.

With Behn having just left the house from his afternoon crystal lesson, the girls seemed to be in good moods. Amanda had spent the day researching different ideas about leads on the ten remaining samaras.

Riccan was glad to be away from the office where he had experienced a particularly bad day with his boss, Ela Nena. She had decided to give Riccan a few extra duties as well as a tighter deadline for several of his projects. He was starting to believe Ela Nena was purposely being harder on him because he had gotten married. There was no other explanation for her sudden change in attitude toward him.

He walked into the kitchen from the garage at his home in Florida. The first people he saw were his two girls getting themselves a snack while they sat at the kitchen island. "Hey, you two. What's to eat?"

"We were just trying to decide that ourselves. Maybe since it's getting so late, we should just plan to make dinner," Jena suggested.

"How about foxl stew? I haven't had it for ages and it sounds delicious," Juila exclaimed.

Riccan asked, "Do you want to make it yourselves or would you rather I just put it together?"

The girls both looked at him and batted their eyelashes innocently.

Riccan laughed and said, "Alright, alright, enough of the puppy dog eyes. I'll make dinner. You're going to love my grandma's recipe for it, too."

The three of them began to laugh just as Amanda appeared in the hallway from the study. She walked forward and smiled at the happy picture her family made as they enjoyed one another's company in the kitchen. "What's so funny?" she asked as she reached the island.

"Hi, honey," Riccan said as he leaned forward and kissed her on the forehead. "The girls were just convincing me to cook dinner for the family. They were practicing their best powers of persuasion by batting their eyelashes at me."

"It appears to have worked," Amanda declared. She took a seat at the island and prepared to await what was sure to be a fabulous meal.

"When are you going to learn to create, Mom?" Juila asked in the sudden silence.

"She already has," Riccan commented even as he began to compile in his head the list of food items he would need to make dinner.

Juila turned her gaze from her father to her mother with eyes wide with amazement. "You have? When? I've never seen you do it."

Amanda rolled her eyes at her husband's gross overstatement of her abilities. "I've created one dish in my lifetime and it was barely edible. Your father is a much better chef than I'm afraid I'll ever be."

"And she's content with letting me do all of the hard work," Riccan added with a wide grin on his face.

"Hard work! Ha!" Amanda scoffed.

The entire family laughed.

Within a few minutes Riccan had a large pot of stew prepared and placed in a large kettle in the middle of the island. The girls prepared the table by getting out dishes, silverware, and napkins. Naturally they used their talents to do the work.

Amanda sat in awe of her family's easy use of the elemy when she could barely manage to do anything without great effort. Even then, the results were far from predictable. It was obvious she should spend at least part of each day working on getting better with her crystal skills.

She had been so consumed with finding the samaras that she had neglected to train. Obviously, Jehoban had entrusted her with her own birth crystal for more than just allowing her to fit into the Tualan society. He must have wanted her to use all of her abilities to their fullest. She owed it to Him to be her best.

The family ate dinner without much conversation. As always the food was excellent and everyone praised Riccan for another successful meal. When the pot of stew was empty, the girls took it upon themselves to use their powers to clear the dishes and put everything away.

Riccan sat back on his stool and sighed with contentment. "I was thinking we should all go out in the telepod so Amanda can start to learn how to use it. What do you think?"

Amanda was pleased to hear the suggestion about her learning to fly. However, she was not so certain their daughters should be going with them in case her navigational skills got them lost in between spaces. It would be bad enough knowing she had caused her husband's demise, but she could not reconcile the idea of taking out her entire family in one flight.

"I don't know, Riccan. I wouldn't think it would be such a good idea. What if something went wrong? Maybe the girls should stay home for the first few flights."

Riccan began to laugh at Amanda's concern for killing her family. He knew his telepod was built with safeguards against her fear and told her as much.

Amanda was relieved to hear about it, but she still could not fully release her fear for them all being together.

Jena could see her mother's internal struggle as she watched her expression change. "Juila and I have homework to get done tonight. Maybe we can go another time." *Mom is scared to have us go. She doesn't need the distraction while she's trying to learn something so important. Back me up on this, Juila,* Jena hurriedly spoke in her mind to Juila.

"Jena's right, Mom. We can't go tonight. Sorry, Dad. It's going to have to be the two of you tonight. I'll look forward to a future flight, though."

"Okay. I guess it's settled," Amanda said brightly. She pushed herself off of the stool and looked over at her husband. "I'm ready to go whenever you are."

"I'm ready. Let's go," Riccan said even as he leaned over to kiss each of his daughters on her forehead as he moved past them to go out to the garage. "Be good. I'm not sure how late we'll be."

"We'll be fine, Dad," Jena smiled as she reassured him.

"I know," Riccan smiled and put his arm around Amanda and turned them both to leave.

"I love you both," Amanda called over her shoulder as she let herself be led out of the house.

"Love you, too," the girls replied in unison.

Riccan opened the garage door and they stepped down onto the concrete pad. The telepod was in cloaked mode, as it always was whenever it was on Earth. "I think I'll guide the 'pod to Tuala and we can start your lessons where we won't have to worry about being seen."

"I love the way you think," Amanda said. Secretly she was glad to be able to carefully watch the steps he took to get the craft ready for flight before she would be called upon to do the same.

Riccan palmed open the side door and stood to the side while the ramp unfolded for them to enter the craft. He let Amanda enter first and get herself settled in the right-hand seat reserved for the co-pilot. He followed her and took the left seat. At the same time they put their seat-belts on.

Riccan used the remote to shut the side door and waited a second for the door to completely shut, creating an airtight seal. He looked over at Amanda and began teaching her the basics by saying, "The control panel is mostly handled the same way as the conventional telepods, but the displays are all located within the plascreen. On other telepods, each function has its own light on the board. This one integrates them all to one screen so there's less chance of missing something vital. There's even a built-in safeguard against pilot error which is almost equivalent to an auto-pilot, to which I was referring in the kitchen."

"I'm glad to hear you thought about putting it into your telepod," she said as she nodded understanding of Riccan's explanation so far.

Riccan touched the plascreen to turn it on and then he activated the telepod's crystal drive. The vessel rose several inches above the ground soundlessly and hovered in place until Riccan was able to verify each green light on the screen.

He switched screens to be able to enter the course they would be traveling. He typed in the coordinates and pressed enter. Immediately, the course was locked and loaded. With a nod of readiness to Amanda, Riccan pressed the button on the screen to begin the teleportation to Tuala.

Three seconds later they appeared over a flat, grassy field mere inches above the ground. Riccan issued all of the shutdown procedures, turned to Amanda and said, "Are you ready? Press this button right here." He pointed to a plastic circle on the dash.

Amanda pressed it and saw the panels light up in front of both her and Riccan. "Okay, now what?"

"When the display screens clear of all of their test messages, then you'll press the activate button on the touchscreen in front of you." He waited a few seconds and then pointed at the screen, "Right there."

"Can I do it from either screen?" she asked as she reached toward the screen in front of her and hesitated.

"Yes, they are both identically connected to the main system. Good! Do you feel us levitating?"

"Yes. Do I have to worry about us continuing to rise?" She anxiously looked down out of the windshield in front of her.

Riccan chuckled at her reaction and then answered seriously, "No, it's programmed to stay a few inches from the ground. However, if you are operating an older telepod then you would have to pay attention to the altitude from the moment you activated the flight switch. Good question. Now, using the touchscreen, tap on the navigate button and enter Kirma. From the initial location we will then enter a secondary location to go to Pantano so we can stop for a moment and say hello to my parents."

"Why Kirma?" she asked even as she was typing it in.

"It's an area with relatively little air traffic. The actual coordinates are stored in the memory of the telepod. Here, let me show you really quick so you'll have a visual in mind while we travel." He pulled up an aerial map and pointed to the spot. He wanted Amanda to become more familiar with Tualan landmarks.

Amanda leaned closer and could see the topography of the land was slightly different, otherwise, it just looked like land. She nodded her head and asked, "Now what?"

"Look over the entire dash and make sure you don't see anything lit up in red. Red is bad. If you did happen to see anything red, then you would immediately shut down the telepod and begin again. Never take off if there is any sign of trouble."

His advice seemed perfectly reasonable. Amanda once again nodded, looked over the dash, and replied, "It all looks good."

"I agree. Now concentrate on the location where we are heading and, at the same time, press the activate travel button." Riccan did the same thing from his seat just to make sure they actually ended up where they intended.

Everything went black as they teleported between locations. With equal suddenness they emerged over the outskirts of the city of Kirma in the brightness of the evening sun.

"That was perfect. Now I want you to land the 'pod over there in the open field using the manual controls," he said confidently.

"What? I don't have any idea how it works. You've got to be kidding!" Amanda looked over at Riccan with an alarmed expression.

"How do you expect to learn if you only ever watch me? You need to get the feel of the craft as she's flying. Just so you know, I have the same controls on my side so I can make any corrections should I see anything going awry." He put his hand on the manual control and raised his eyebrows to confirm she was going to comply with his instructions.

"Fine, but don't blame me if something happens to your telepod. I warned you!" Amanda spoke more sharply than she intended since she could feel fear spreading through her entire body. Her hand shook as she lifted it to hold the manual control stick. She tried to delay the inevitable by asking, "Don't you think I should try to maneuver the telepod first before I get too close to the ground?"

"Sure, if it'll make you feel more comfortable. Try moving in a lazy eight pattern," he said with a smile on his face. He looked out the windows to make sure the surrounding airspace was clear. The telepods were designed to repel each other when they came into close proximity due to the crystal drives. Still, it was good practice to make sure all was open around them.

Amanda nervously shifted the control slightly to the right and immediately felt the craft roll in the desired direction. She held it in the roll for a moment longer and then moved the control into the opposite direction until they had turned and were facing the direction in which they started. She was starting to understand why Riccan had faith in her ability. His telepod was designed to perform exactly as it was operated. Amanda started to relax. She asked, "What do I need to do to land?"

"Slowly move the control forward. You will see the ground will come closer, but you will also be traveling forward. To keep yourself from going too far forward, simply press the button on the side of the shifter and you will only descend and not advance. When you get within a couple of feet of the ground, begin to release your forward pressure until you are about a foot from the surface."

"I don't know where the bottom of the telepod is, Riccan. I think you should take over." She looked over at him with fresh fear showing on her face.

"Amanda, you need to do this. You won't be able to help Nealand if you are unable to use the telepod to go get him and bring him home. Remember your goal and land this telepod."

Amanda needed the reminder and decided she was going to overcome her fear and set the telepod down as best as she could. She moved the control forward and saw the front of the telepod dip lower. They were about fifty feet above the ground and she did not like how fast the earth appeared to be rising to meet her. She relieved some of the pressure and saw the front of the craft begin to level off.

CHAPTER 10

With one success under her belt, she decided to try descending without the forward momentum. She pressed the button on the side of her control and again pushed it forward. This time she could feel the difference and could see the evidence out the window since they were getting lower at a slower pace. She liked this feeling much better.

"Okay, we're about five feet from landing. Ease up slightly. Good. Okay, let go of the manual control," Riccan directed.

Amanda was concerned about letting go altogether until she realized it was programmed to stay level without user input. She smiled brightly over at her husband and said, "Now what?"

"Now you begin the shutdown procedures. Touch the bottom of the plascreen and select touchdown. Once you feel the brush of the ground, then you hit the main power button right here." He pointed to a push button located in between the two plascreens which was labeled as the master power switch.

Amanda followed Riccan's directions as he gave them. The telepod touched down onto the ground gently. Amanda touched the master switch with a feeling of satisfaction. She had successfully flown and landed and nothing had gone wrong. Surely the operation of a telepod could not be as simple as it seemed. There was hardly anything the operator needed to do except enter the commands. She asked Riccan about it.

"The older telepods are quite manual. There is no automation of any feature so you have to be very diligent in watching all of the controls to make sure you are staying on course. The biggest difference is the older models rely solely on the directions given by the operator's brain. Those pilots need to be very focused on keeping a clear image in their heads so they will actually end up in a secondary location."

"Why do they even allow the older models? They sound dangerous." Amanda could not fathom putting so much faith in her ability to concentrate on the coordinates of a location through the blackness of the transfer. She felt certain she would get distracted by some other thought and then she would be utterly lost.

"They are slowly being phased out. The problem is cost. Most people cannot afford the latest technology. I'm fortunate since I work for the leading designer and I'm able to build them myself. I was able to integrate all of the technology into my own craft to make it safer than anything currently flying."

"Riccan, I have a question."

"What is it?"

"If I'm going to be using your telepod to rescue Nealand, then how are you going to be getting to work every day?"

He tried to hide a smile at her concern and said, "I have a surprise for you, actually. I was planning on telling you after you were done learning to fly, but you have preempted me once again. I have another telepod which I'm going to give to you." He stopped and let his statement sink in.

"Wait. What? Give to me?" Amanda clearly had not been expecting such a gift.

"Now don't get too excited. The one you will be flying is the telepod I designed and built before this current one. It's not nearly as large or as nicely painted. I still have to make a few minor adjustments in the software to make sure you have the best navigation and safety equipment, but otherwise I think you'll find it perfect for your needs."

"So it's not red?" Amanda asked hopefully. She had sort of dreaded flying this telepod because it was so recognizable with its unusually bright color scheme.

"Nope, it's a boring grey," he said sullenly.

"It's perfect, Riccan. I want to go unnoticed and it will do the trick nicely. When can I see it?" Amanda asked eagerly.

"I have it parked in the garage at home already," he admitted shyly.

"Seriously? You are so devious. How did you manage to do it? I don't think even you are capable of operating two telepods at the same time, even with all of your fancy equipment."

"It's not a bad idea, Amanda. I'm going to have to put some thought into it." Riccan considered Amanda's comment seriously. He could already imagine several uses for such technology.

"Riccan! I wasn't being serious, I was just kidding. Are you going to answer me?"

"Oh, yes. Sorry. Lana and I dropped it off today during lunch."

"Lana? Isn't she the receptionist at your work?" Amanda pulled the memory from the deep recesses of her brain.

"Yes…how did you know? You've never met her." Riccan was genuinely intrigued by Amanda's random knowledge of his life.

"She was a part of my dream, too," she answered simply. Amanda was still trying to wrap her brain around the idea of having her own telepod to fly. It was truly amazing. She wished she were able to take her dad flying, but she would have a hard time doing it on Earth. There were too many areas with radar to make it safe, even during cloaking mode.

"Wow. It's so amazing how much you learned while you were sleeping. I know you told me the whole story, but I'm sure it'll be quite a while before I discover all of the nuances you forgot to share," Riccan said as he shook his head in disbelief. A moment later he realized Amanda had been stalling and announced, "Okay, it's time to go visit my parents. Show me what you remember about getting the telepod ready to fly. Be sure to say each step out loud so I will know what you are planning."

Amanda did as asked and was able to perform each step as it should have been. Again, she was amazed at the simplicity of Riccan's design. She had entered Pantano as their destination and told Riccan her plan to hit the activation switch. She saw him nod approval and she pressed the button.

Darkness surrounded them for the three second duration of the flight between locations. Amanda was startled when she realized the coordinates programmed for his parent's house had them materialize mere inches from the ground. She looked over at Riccan and asked, "Do I just press the side switch and tap the forward control slightly? We're already mighty close to the ground."

"Your instincts are perfect. It's exactly what I'd do in this instance." He nodded approval and watched as Amanda did as she had said.

Amanda landed the craft and performed all of the shutdown procedures. She was very pleased with herself and almost jumped up and down in her seat with her glee. Luckily, her seatbelt was still fastened so she had to contain her enthusiasm. She was certain Riccan would have laughed at her if she had done a happy dance.

"Let's go see what my parents are up to, shall we?" Riccan unfastened his seatbelt and watched as Amanda did the same.

They left the telepod and walked across the vast lawn until they got to the stone staircase leading up to the back terrace of the Residence. Amanda suddenly asked, "Why do some of the Elders live in the Residence, while others maintain a separate house for their family?"

"I guess it depends on the district where the Elder serves, or possibly the preference of the Elder himself. Take Elder Debbon, for instance..."

"I was actually thinking about him," Amanda interrupted.

"His district is quite peaceful now, but it was not always so. He decided to have a separate estate where he could get away from the constant demands of the people. When he is ready to go to work, then he translates himself to the Residence. When he is there, the people know they are able to come to him."

"Do you think he keeps a separate place because he's First of the Elders?"

"I'm sure it's part of it. Although he's only been First for about a declan, he's been an Elder for a lot longer."

They continued to climb the steps as Amanda asked, "How long do Elders serve in their position?"

"For as long as they desire. In the past, some have been in office for twenty declans. These days, they seem to only serve for about seven declans, though."

Amanda had stopped climbing when Riccan had said the Elders had served for two hundred years. Surely she had heard him incorrectly. "Riccan, you're teasing me. People don't live for two hundred years," she laughed at how silly it sounded even as she said it out loud.

Riccan had taken two more steps before he realized she had stopped.

He turned and looked down on her with a serious expression, "I'm not joking, Amanda. Elders are known to live for a very long time. Some think it's because they are in contact with the elemy so often, but I'm not sure of the real reason."

"It seems sort of tragic, really. If the Elder lives so long, his wife would grow old and die long before he would," Amanda said as she climbed the remaining two steps to once again be beside her husband.

Riccan smiled at Amanda's assumption and gently corrected her by saying, "On the contrary, Amanda. The wives seem to age at the same rate as their husbands. Maybe it's a gift from Jehoban for the service which the Elders provide. Nobody ever questions it, so I can't say for sure. You sure do come up with interesting ideas. Let's see if my dad has any answers." He put his arm around her shoulders and they walked the last few feet to the back door.

Riccan did not knock, he simply opened the door and gently pushed Amanda into the room ahead of himself. The grand living room was empty so they continued to walk through the room and down the hallway to the private offices.

They ran into Melba as she came around the corner. The head maid smiled at them as they approached.

"What brings you two here today?" she asked with a twinkle in her eyes.

"We were just in the area and thought we'd stop by. Are my parents available? Do you know where they are?" Riccan asked. He had always appreciated Melba's ability to know where everyone was in the Residence at any given time.

"Sure, they are both in your father's office. Do you want me to bring you anything?"

"No, thank you. We won't be staying long," he replied and then started to walk again in the direction of Daven's office. Riccan stopped outside the door and knocked lightly. He waited until he heard his father's voice telling them to come in before he opened the door.

Both Daven and Nena immediately stood up from their chairs as they saw who their visitors were.

"Oh! Riccan! Amanda! What a pleasant surprise. What brings you here?" Nena rushed forward and hugged first her son and then Amanda enthusiastically.

Amanda was always surprised with how small her mother-in-law was and how big her personality made her seem. When she hugged her, she had to lean down. It almost felt as though she were hugging a child, she was so small.

"I was just giving Amanda her first telepod flying lesson. We were in the area and I thought she should know the coordinates to get to your house, no matter what. So we thought we'd come in and say hello before we headed home."

"How did the lesson go?" Daven asked as he looked over at Amanda to answer.

Amanda shrugged noncommittally, and replied, "We're still alive."

Daven and Riccan chuckled while Nena said seriously, "I should hope so. I'm sure you did wonderfully. Riccan, tell us the truth."

Riccan looked lovingly over at his wife and said, "She did great. She's a natural at it. I wouldn't expect any less of her since she's shown such great aptitudes for everything we've shown her thus far."

"I knew it!" Nena exclaimed as she clapped her hands together with glee. "She was so quick to learn how to read a person's aura. She was bound to be good at this as well."

"I thought so, too," Daven said and looked purposefully at his son. He knew Amanda was not going to wait two weeks before she wanted to start her mission to rescue Nealand.

Riccan understood his father's look and nodded his head slightly in agreement. He cleared his throat and asked, "I take it you got my message the other morning?"

"I did. We should all sit down and I'll tell you what's happened since then." He gestured to the guest chairs across from his own and waited until the women had taken their seats before he sat down himself.

"What have you heard?" Riccan asked.

"What are you talking about?" Amanda asked at the same time.

Riccan turned to Amanda and said, "I asked Dad to help me figure out a way to distract Elder Vargen until you can extract Nealand from his district." He repeated his question to his father, "Have you heard something which will help?"

"As a matter-of-fact, I heard something just a few minutes before you two showed up. You seem to have rather convenient timing these days," he said with a smile to the newcomers. "Elder Debbon has scheduled a convocation of the Elders to be held on Selasa, Adar 1st."

Amanda shifted her confused gaze to her husband.

He translated his father's statement by saying, "The Elders are going to be meeting on Tuesday, December 1st. He's saying we'll have fifteen days to figure out a plan before you can have a safe opportunity to find Nealand."

"I see. It's a little longer than I wanted to wait, but I understand." She sat back in her chair and started to plan all of the details she could research before she had to leave. First and foremost, she needed to see if anyone could locate where Neal was living specifically. She sat forward and asked, "Do you have any record of where Neal is living? Surely, he'd have a house or something. I can't imagine Elder Vargen would keep him locked up. Jehoban told me he's with the Elder, but no other details."

Daven turned to face his patil and started to type, "Give me a second and I'll see what I can find." He scrolled down the screen and touched a couple of passages before he smiled and said, "I think I may have found him. There's a man by the name of Nealan who is registered to the work housing for the Old Soul Engineering Facility. The slight change in the spelling of the name would make sense because Tualan men's names all end with an 'n' unless they've lost the honor to keep it. What do you think? Is it him?"

As soon as Daven had started talking about it, Amanda instinctively knew this information was what she needed. She nodded and said, "I'm sure of it. Can you print out everything you've discovered so I can use it to help put together my plan?"

"Absolutely. I've already begun," he said. The papers began to appear below the patil screen. When the last one had finished printing, he tapped the stack together on the top of his desk before he handed the bundle over to Amanda. "Let me know if you think of anything else."

"You know I'm going to take you up on the offer!" Amanda said with a foolish grin on her face.

"I'm hoping it means you'll come visit more often," Daven said in a more serious tone. He knew they had their own lives to live in Florida, but he and Nena wanted to get to know their new daughter and granddaughters.

"The girls will be on winter break in a few more weeks. Maybe they'll want to come and spend some time here at the Residence. Do you think it might be possible? I don't want to mention it to the girls if it won't work out." Amanda had realized the girls would be mostly unattended during the break if she were going to be spending her time helping Neal and Riccan was at work.

"It's a wonderful idea, Amanda." Nena clasped her hands tightly in her lap as she tried to contain her excitement. She had considered going to Earth for a visit, but Amanda's plan was even better. She began to put together a list of things she would like to do with the twins.

Riccan looked over at Amanda and said, "We should probably head home now. I'm going to have to fly the transfer back to Earth so you will know how to do it."

"I can't wait!" Amanda exclaimed.

CHAPTER 11

Jena watched her parents leave and waited a few more minutes before she talked to her sister about what was really going on in her mind. "Do you want to go to the secret room and hold our samaras?" The last time they had held them, they had received massive amounts of information which was too much, too soon. She hoped repetition would make the messages more clear than they had been before.

"I don't know if it's such a good idea for us to do alone. What if something happens to you again, Jena? I'd never forgive myself for agreeing to do this."

"You're one of the best healers I know. I'm not at all worried."

"I wasn't much help last time, now was I?" Juila still felt bad because she had just sat there and did nothing when her sister had fainted and remained unconscious for several minutes.

"You were just in shock. Now we know what to look for and we can be on guard against information overload. Come on!"

Juila could not believe her sister was even asking to do this. Ordinarily Jena was the sister who refused to take any risks and now it seemed as though she had thrown caution out the window. If it meant so much to her sister, then she supposed there could not be much harm in it. She rarely asked for much.

"Fine. Let's go," Juila said with a sigh of resignation.

"Okay!" She jumped down from the stool at the island and began heading toward the library, where the secret room was located.

Even as she neared the room, she could feel the pull of the samaras. It was one of the reasons they had selected the library in which to train Behn. The additional power created by the samaras made it easier for Behn to access the elemy to learn to use his birth crystal.

Jena hurried across the room to the far wall where she pressed the release mechanism under the shelf. The entire wall moved in on one end to allow the two girls to access the Tualan artifacts and samaras located in the room. They made a beeline for the shelf.

Before either one of them had a chance to touch their crystal skulls, they stood open-mouthed at the sight of the third samara. They had not heard about another one being found and they were intensely curious to know to whom it would eventually belong.

"Where did it come from?" Jena asked as she pointed and turned her head to see her sister's expression matching her own.

"I don't know. Maybe it had something to do with the day Mom stayed out so late and Dad had been so worried about her."

"Why didn't they tell us about it? Don't you think it's a bit strange?" Jena was actually more surprised since she had not noticed the extra power which had been emanating from the additional crystal.

"We have been rather busy lately with school, homework, and Behn's lessons. Maybe they were waiting for something special before they planned to tell us."

"I think we should take these into the library so we can sit down while we're using them. This way we won't have to worry about fainting or falling down," Jena suggested.

"We shouldn't touch them with our bare hands, then." Juila paused for a moment as she accessed the elemy to retrieve two bath towels from her bathroom upstairs. She handed one of them to her sister with a grin.

"Good idea." She unfolded the towel once so it would be less bulky when she reached into the niche to pull down the stone. When she had originally seen the first two samaras she had believed they were identical. Since the crystal had 'claimed' her, she could see it looked nothing like either of the other two. She had no trouble identifying her own stone and she could see Juila was equally as decisive.

They took their bundles into the library and each sat in her regular seat. As if they had rehearsed this, they each set the bundle down on her lap and unfolded the cloth from around it. They were so in tune with one another that they each touched the samara at the same time.

Jena's vision of the library disappeared as she began to see scenes unfold inside her head. Since she knew what to expect this time, she purposely slowed the scenes down so she could understand what they were showing.

She sucked in a breath when she saw a woman who looked eerily like her own mother who was also holding a samara. This woman looked distinctly uncomfortable with the object in her hands so it was obviously not meant for her. Jena wondered whose crystal it would become.

The scene changed again so she saw her foster-mother, Barla. Jena clearly saw a bright blue birth crystal hanging from her neck. It was only then Jena realized she had never seen Barla wearing it before and she thought it was an odd sight to see now. There had to be some meaning behind it, she just had to wait until she had more information before she could fit all the pieces together.

Then she saw her cousins, Gravin and Rasa, instructing Barla on using her birth crystal. Jena frowned when she saw this scene. Why would Barla need lessons now? She paid closer attention to Rasa and realized she seemed happier than she had ever seen her before. There was something definitely going on with Rasa's life. Hopefully, she would find out what had transpired. Rasa almost felt like a second, or maybe a third, mother to her. She wanted good things to happen for her.

Like before, there were many scenes which contained people she did not recognize. This time, however, she used her memorization skills to note each detail for future scrutiny. She saw a large group of people come together. It was hard to understand what they were all doing together, but Jena, Juila, and both of their parents were included in the group.

Juila had been having the identical visions of her sister. She was not sure if their minds were linked, their samaras, or both. In any event, they were going to have a lot to discuss when they were finished.

Neither sister had any concept of time as they communed with their crystals. Nor did they hear when their parents were calling their names. They only became aware of anything when the samaras suddenly stopped transmitting to their minds.

The girls looked up, stared in wonder at one another, and then noticed their parents frowning at them from the doorway. For some reason, they felt as though they had been caught doing something very bad and they hung their heads in shame. After a short moment, Jena remembered the other crystal and raised her head.

"Where did the other samara come from? Whose is it? Why weren't we told about it?" Jena had done the asking, but Juila nodded her head at the same time.

Amanda could not be mad at her girls for wanting to explore what the samaras had to offer. She walked forward and sat down in a vacant chair. She motioned for Riccan to join them in the room and sit down across from her.

"We've been meaning to tell you about it, but the time never seemed right. I found the samara in the Cannon Memorial Asylum in North Carolina. You remember the time when I got home really late last week, right?"

The girls nodded.

"I brought it home and we discovered it belongs to your father," Amanda announced happily.

Now the girls' eyes grew wide and they exclaimed happily to their dad, "You got your own!"

"Yeah, it's pretty cool. I know how you two felt since I have been claimed by my own," Riccan said as he recalled the feeling of being completed when he held it in his hands. Recalling what they had walked into, he asked, "What happened with both of you just now?"

Jena spoke up and said, "I wanted us to try out the samaras again. We knew what to expect since the last time and I wanted to know if we could control the flow of information."

"Were you right?" Amanda asked. She was so proud of her daughters and their willingness to try new things. Even though she had missed out on all of their childhood, she hoped she would continue to be a part of their futures.

"Yes, to an extent. It wasn't nearly as confusing as it was the first time. While I wasn't able to exactly direct the flow of information, I was, at least, able to make it slow down so I could take more of it in. There's still a lot of it which doesn't make sense, but at least now I'll be able to put it all together when the pieces fall into place," Jena replied with a confident smile.

"Is there anything you want to share about what you saw?" Riccan asked.

"Not just now, if you don't mind. I'd like to think about it for a while before I say anything. Juila may have seen something she'd like to share."

Everyone looked over at Juila with expectant stares.

Juila shrugged and said, "I think we saw the same things. I don't really know how to explain any of it. I'm sorry."

"That's okay, honey. We can talk about it whenever you are ready. Besides, I think we have some time yet before we'll be called into action," Amanda said cryptically.

"What makes you think so, Amanda?" Riccan asked.

Amanda lifted her eyebrow and said, "Call it intuition."

"Hmph," Riccan replied with a small grin. "Well there's something else I wanted to talk to Jena about."

"What is it, Dad?"

"First, I think you should both put your samaras away. This discussion might take a while."

The girls looked at one another with puzzled expressions, but gathered their towels back around the crystals and walked them into the hidden room.

While they were gone, Amanda asked, "What did you want to talk about with Jena?"

"I think we should tell her about Willian's letters and the steps we have taken with his father. If anything comes of it, I think it would be better for Jena to be prepared."

"Of course. I hope she doesn't get too upset."

"I agree. It's one of the reasons I asked them to put away their samaras. With the power those crystals contain, I would hate to see what she could unleash if she were angry while holding it."

"Good call!"

The girls returned to the room and resumed their chairs. Jena asked, "Okay, what did you want to talk to me about?"

"I did something which I'm not sure you'll approve, but as your father, I'm glad I did."

"What did you do?"

"A few days ago, you and Juila were talking about your relationship with Willian and it got me thinking about how you would normally keep in touch with him. I contacted Rasa and got your access information for your personal account. I wanted to see if Willian had been trying to get in touch with you since you've been gone. I read through his correspondence to you and I must say I'm very concerned about the tone in which he addresses you."

"What did he say? Did you read them while you were at work?"

"No, Jena. I have a patil here at the house. I have to be able to keep in touch with my father, after all."

"You have a patil here? I would have asked to use it had I known. What did Willian say?"

"I figured as much. You'd been here long enough without asking about it that I thought maybe you wanted a break from Willian. When I read through his messages to you, I'd totally understand why. Anyway, he threatened to have you sanctioned because he feels as though you have abandoned their relationship by not responding to him."

"What? Sanctioned! How dare him!" Jena's mind was whirling with confusing thoughts. She could understand his position, but she also had no idea how he could go so far.

"What can we do about it, Dad?" Juila asked with concern for her sister. She hoped Willian had finally gone too far and finally Jena would see him for the controlling creep he actually was.

"I forwarded all of Willian's messages to his father and told him that I'm concerned about Willian's behavior. I asked him to look into the matter and get back to me. As of today, I haven't heard anything, but I'm hoping we can have this resolved amicably."

"Amicably? As in you think Jena should stay with him?" Juila was about to burst with anger.

"Not necessarily," Riccan replied hastily. "We'll see what Elder Debbon has to say about the matter and then we'll take it from there."

Jena felt sick to her stomach. She had never imagined Willian could be so cruel as to threaten her with such dire measures. She knew he could be mean, but not cruel, especially not to her.

"May I be excused? I'm not feeling too well," Jena asked as she crossed her arms over her stomach.

"Sure, honey. Remember we're here to help and protect you. Please don't feel as though you're alone in this matter," Amanda said kindly to her daughter. She hated seeing how hurt she was in this and was at a loss for what to do for her. She stood up and walked over to Jena. Kneeling down, she reached out and held Jena in her arms.

The embrace was too much for Jena and she burst out in sobs. No longer did she feel as though the betrothal were her own burden to bear. She had parents who wanted her to be happy and wanted to protect her. This was what she had always dreamed for her life. After a few minutes, she kissed her mom's cheek and said, "I'd like to be alone for a bit, if you don't mind."

"Absolutely. We love you," Amanda said as she pulled her arms away from her daughter. She stood up and looked down at Jena with a concerned expression. "We'll have to trust in Jehoban to make this all come right. Can you do that?"

"Yes," she said as she stood up and hurried out of the room.

Juila stared after her sister. She tried to link with Jena's mind, but found herself shut out completely. This was very bad. Her sister seldom shut her out unless she were thinking meaningful things about Willian. She hoped Jena would let her back in to help comfort her. She turned to her dad and asked, "What else did Willian say?"

"At first he was inquiring about Jena's time away and when she would be back. Each letter was a bit more abrupt when the previous message went unanswered. By the end, you know what happened. What do you think about the relationship between the two of them? Do you think there's any hope for making the betrothal work?"

"Willian has always thought I was the jealous sister, but I have to be honest and say I have always thought this was a bad idea. At first, Willian was really friendly with Jena. The more time we spent with him, the more I realized he was jealous of Jena's powers.

"At some point I think he decided since he would never be as good as she with the elemy, then he would use her skills for his own advantage. After that point he began to treat her like property rather than as a potential partner. I really despise Willian, and Jena knows how I feel. She also knows it's not because of jealousy on my part, but genuine concern for her happiness.

"Why do you think I've pushed her to date other guys here on Earth? I wanted her to see how real relationships should be. What Willian's shown her is not love, it's twisted." Juila had vented all of her frustrations and she leaned back in her chair and waited to see how her parents would respond to her tirade.

"I see," Riccan said simply. This situation went deeper than he had originally thought. To have Juila vehemently hate her sister's betrothed was not a good sign. Hopefully he would hear something from Elder Debbon soon. He did not want this conversation to end on such a negative note so he said, "I brought home another telepod for your mother to learn to fly. It's in the garage. Do you want to go see it? Your mother hasn't even seen it yet."

Juila knew what her father was trying to do by distracting her with something she enjoyed. She smiled at her father's tactic and found she was interested in seeing the telepod. "Sure, I'd love to see it."

The three of them trooped out of the library, down the hall, through the kitchen, and out into the far garage. They walked past Riccan's usual telepod and stopped a few feet beyond it. Riccan reached into his pants pocket and pulled out a remote none of the girls had seen before. He clicked the single button on it and the cloaking mode turned off.

The girls both exclaimed about the size of the telepod. It was a small four-seater unit which would be perfect for Amanda's mission. They all moved forward and walked around the unit inspecting the differences from the one they normally rode in.

"Can we go inside it?" Juila asked.

"Of course. Go ahead and hit the button on the side," Riccan replied with a smile. He was glad to see Juila's expression change from being so worried about her sister. Until they heard from Elder Debbon, there was little they could accomplish by worrying.

Juila went up to the side of the telepod and pressed the button to open the door. It descended silently and revealed the simple interior. This unit was not luxurious by any means nor was it a stripped down basic model either. Without asking for permission, she stepped up onto the ramp and went inside.

There were two things which interested Juila the most, the power unit, and the control panel. She turned to the back of the unit and uncovered the power unit first. Like the other telepod, this unit had a single crystal drive. The crystal for this one was considerably smaller, but still flawless.

She saw there were some different connections and wondered what components were missing from this telepod.

She replaced the cover and moved to the front of the telepod. After seating herself at the pilot's seat, she looked over the controls. This one had a single glass panel rather than the double of the other one. It was positioned more centrally so each person in the front could easily access it. She was so engrossed in her inspection she failed to notice her father walking up behind her.

"Does it meet with your approval?" he asked as he sat down in the co-pilot's seat.

She chuckled before answering, "Of course."

"This unit isn't as grand as my regular flyer. This was a prototype to the other one."

"Prototype or not, this 'pod is still nicer by far than the one Jena and I learned to fly. I'd love for you to teach me to fly this one someday."

"Maybe because your mother's had her first lesson she won't be so scared to have you fly with us. You can hear me teach her so when it's your turn, you'll already know what do to. What do you think?"

"I think it sounds great. Hey, Mom?" she called out the side door where her mother was still standing.

Amanda came up the ramp and sat down in one of the two passenger seats and asked, "What do you think?"

"Dad said you might let me come fly with you while you're training. What do you think?"

"If your dad thinks it's safe, then I'll defer to his opinion."

"I'm positive it's safe. I have the same software installed in this unit as in the other one. This version is slightly older, but the ideas are the same. The only thing I need to install is the anti-collision software. I'll get that done tonight and take it for a test spin. We can go flying tomorrow after I get home from work."

Juila smiled at her father's enthusiasm. She was looking forward to getting up into the air and traveling again. Even though it had only been a couple of mesans, *months*, she reminded herself since she was on Earth after all, she really missed the feeling of independence which flying gave her. "I think you should take me up in your airplane, too, Dad."

"I like the way you think, Juila! How about this? Once we get your mother ready to fly on her own, we can start teaching you how to fly the

Cessna." Riccan was beyond pleased to have his daughter express an interest in his hobby on Earth.

"It sounds perfect!" Juila agreed with a smile. "Here, Mom. Why don't you sit up front and Dad can go over the panel with you." She stood up and walked to the back seats. She sat in the one beside where her mom was sitting and watched as her mother went up front.

Riccan talked about the controls and both Amanda and Juila listened intently. Juila's mind was recording what her father was saying so she could review it later, but she was also attempting to relink with her sister, to no avail. After a few minutes, Juila gave up trying and turned her sole attention back to her parents' discussion.

CHAPTER 12

Nealan's day had been quite satisfying since he had come up with a new way of cooling an office building. There were so many times he had been consulted for redesigning various components of objects where he had been successful. Today was one of those days.

He absolutely wanted to celebrate when he got home. Again, he was glad he had invited Vinia to come and live with him. The only unfortunate thing about the whole thing had been the fact she had a child. He did not know why, but he really did not like children and babies were the worst. Not only was she messy and loud, she was utterly useless around the house. As far as he was concerned, she was just another mouth to feed; a necessary evil if he were to have Vinia in his bed.

He had to grin and bear it for the sake of Vinia's company. She was the best thing to have happened to him in a long time. He did not realize how lonely he had been until she had quite literally walked into his life.

Remembering how they met, he smiled. He had gone down to the marketplace to stock up on some food when they had run into each other. Normally, he would not have given her a second glance since she had been holding a baby, but there was something about her which caught his attention. He recalled staring at her until she had become uncomfortable with his attention.

To this day, he was still unsure of the connection, however she had reminded him of someone. There was a lot about his past which he could not remember, but he seemed to recall knowing someone who had looked similar to Vinia. He had told her she looked familiar and had asked out to dinner the same night. Luckily for him, she had accepted.

His house was right around the corner. Hopefully the neighbor would be willing to watch Vinia's little girl while they went out to dinner. As he came closer, he knocked on the neighbor's door and waited for her to answer. Within a few moments, a portly old lady opened the door and stared up at him when she said, "What do you want?"

Knowing this was how she talked to everybody, he was not offended. He asked, "Would you be available to watch Vinia's daughter tonight? I'd like to take Vinia out to dinner."

"You would, would you? Hmm," she said as she folded her arms and tapped her foot while she decided on her answer. "I suppose I could manage it. Bring Danika over in twenty minutes."

"Who?" Nealan asked with genuine confusion.

"Danika. You know, Vinia's daughter! Good grief, what is wrong with you?" asked the woman as she turned, walked back into her house, glared at him, and slammed the door in his face.

"Her name is Danika? I thought it was Dana," he mumbled to himself as he shook his head. He took the last few steps to his own home and walked inside with a smile on his face. Vinia had her back to him while she was doing something on the living room floor.

Vinia turned around when she thought she heard a noise behind her. She smiled when she saw Nealan had finally gotten home. She could see he was in a good mood and she was thankful. "Hello, Nealan. How was your day?"

"Wonderful! I think the two of us should go out to dinner to celebrate," he announced happily.

A small frown crossed Vinia's face. She had to consider Danika and it did not sound as though Nealan wanted her to be included. Vinia stood up and faced Nealan as she said, "Danika will have to come with us, Nealan. I can't leave her home alone."

"I already talked to the neighbor and she's agreed to watch her. Come on. Let's get ready to go out." Nealan rushed through the living room and went into their bathroom to take a quick shower.

Vinia stood still as she watched him go past her. She was surprised since Nealan had even taken Danika into consideration without her having to point it out to him. Maybe he was more aware of her daughter than she had initially realized. She was going to have to reflect on this turn of events.

She left Danika playing contentedly on the floor and went into their shared bedroom. She could hear Nealan humming in the shower and she turned to the closet to pick out what she would wear to go out to dinner. She selected a dress she seldom wore and pulled it out of the closet. She laid it out on the bed and went into the bathroom to check her hair.

Vinia had just finished brushing out her long, dark hair when Nealan stepped out of the shower. She looked appreciatively at his perfectly toned body. She liked his chest full of hair and imagined her fingers playing with it. Vinia could tell Nealan was very confident in his looks and had no problem prancing around naked.

One thing she did notice was the fact he had lost weight in the few weeks she had known him. She wondered if it had anything to do with the resh. The next time she saw the local wise-woman she would ask if it were a side-effect of addiction to the nasty drug.

Nealan smiled at Vinia's approving stares. He loved being appreciated. Vinia was always one to boost his self-esteem because she continually told him how handsome he looked. He hastily toweled off and threw the wet cloth over the edge of the tub before walking forward and pressing his naked body up against the back of Vinia.

She squealed with delight at his sensual embrace. Vinia squirmed in his arms until she had herself turned around. She rubbed herself suggestively against him and felt his body respond as she liked.

"Maybe we should skip dinner and stay in," Nealan growled in her ear.

"Not a chance. I'd like to wear my special dress and spend some time with you."

"Fine. Let's get ready then," he said sullenly as he pulled away and left the bathroom. He hated being rejected when he obviously wanted to have sex. As he entered the bedroom he saw the dress Vinia had picked out to wear and his mood improved. Maybe they could leave the girl over at the neighbor's house for a while after they were done with dinner so they could come back home where he could take the dress off of her.

Vinia entered the bedroom and noticed Nealan staring at her dress and asked, "Will this outfit do for this evening?"

"Absolutely," he agreed as he turned to get out his own nice clothes from the wardrobe.

She smiled as she swiftly took off her clothes and slipped the dress over her head while his back was turned. She knew from experience he could easily be distracted by her nakedness and she was hungry. Using the elemy, she zipped up the dress rather than ask for Nealan's help for the same reason.

Finally they were both ready to go. They entered the living room and Vinia dipped down to pick up Danika and rest the little girl on her hip. Nealan automatically picked the other side of Vinia than where she held the child. The last thing he wanted was for her to reach over and touch his nice clothes with her grubby hands or, worse, to spit up on him. He kept a safe distance from her.

Vinia gathered items to take over to the neighbors. She was not sure how late they would be so she included her favorite blanket for sleeping and a few toys along with the usual nappies and snack food items.

Together they walked over to the neighbors and Nealan knocked on the door again. The old woman answered the door with a sour expression on her face which only lit up when she looked at Danika. The woman held out her arms to take the child and Danika lunged into her grasp with a giggle. Vinia set the bag of Danika's things inside the door and smiled at the neighbor.

"Thank you for doing this for us," Vinia said politely.

"You have a precious little girl. I don't mind," she said as she tickled Danika's round belly. She turned around and kicked the door shut behind her.

Vinia and Nealan smiled at their apparent dismissal. They knew their neighbor was not very social and so they had to laugh at her unusual ways. "I guess we should be on our way then," Vinia said with a grin.

Nealan draped his arm across Vinia's shoulders and turned her away from the house. They walked in the direction of the marketplace. He had heard of a place which served cuisine in the style of the east coast. He had never eaten it so he thought it would be something good to try.

When they sat down to eat, the waiter told them the items which were being offered. Vinia sat with a stunned expression on her face. They were going to be eating food which she had been raised with. She looked over at Nealan to see if this had been his plan all along, but he obviously had no idea. She had never told him where she had come from and she still did not plan on it.

She ordered a dish which had been her favorite growing up and waited for Nealan to decide what he would have. They talked for a bit while the waiter placed their orders. She asked him what had happened during the day to make him want to go out for dinner.

"I invented a new way to keep the office building cool during the hot summer season. I don't know why nobody ever thought of it before, but it's going to be a lot nicer going in to work with my improvement," Nealan bragged.

Vinia smiled at his boasting ways. She played to his ego and said, "It's because you're brilliant. They would not be able to do their jobs without your input."

"That's what I was just thinking!"

Their order arrived and they fell into silence as they ate their individual meals. Vinia's dish was just as it should have been. The seasoning tasted as though the cook had been from her very own colony. For a moment she panicked at the thought it could be possible until she realized Grobin never let anyone of any importance leave. The chef obviously knew what he was doing when he put together the special ingredients.

After the meal was over, Nealan made many not-so-subtle hints about his intentions for the rest of their evening. Since his stomach was no longer protesting, he was quite willing to address his physical needs as well. The sooner he got Vinia home and out of her dress, the happier he would be.

Vinia mentally rolled her eyes. She had no idea when she had moved in with Nealan that his sexual appetite could be so uncontrolled. Thankfully, she had gotten a contraceptive from the wise-woman so she would not have to worry about getting pregnant again. She went along with his planned course of events because she was grateful for being allowed to live in a safe home. It helped that he was nice most of the time, too.

CHAPTER 13

Jena could not get the discussion with her parents out of her head. She had always thought Willian could not do anything which would make her actively dislike him. He had his flaws for sure, but the idea of him threatening to sanction her went entirely too far.

She walked with Juila to the classes they shared with one another and never spoke a word. There had to be something she could do to straighten out the whole situation, but for the life of her, she could come up with nothing.

Finally, lunch came around and their usual group of friends sat around the table. Juila sat next to her and Behn was beside her. For the moment, Jena's left-side seat had remained empty until Luke suddenly sat down. Across from them sat Sofia with her boyfriend, Jon, and also Valentina and her boyfriend, Ryan.

"You're awfully quiet today. Is something wrong?" Luke spoke softly so Jena alone could hear.

Just the idea of Luke asking about her mood made her burst into tears.

Luke looked up in alarm at Juila and asked, "Did I say something wrong?"

"No, Luke. It has nothing to do with you. We've had a disagreement in the family and Jena's taking it kind of hard. She's fine, aren't you, Jena?" Juila nudged her sister in the ribs with her elbow.

Jena wiped the tears from her cheeks and sniffled loudly while she nodded her head. She kept looking down into her lap as she replied, "I'm sorry, Luke. It has nothing to do with you. I'll be fine. Just give me a moment to get myself back together."

Luke decided to take an interest in his lunch and picked up his hamburger and took a big bite. When Jena wanted to talk to him, he would be ready. He hated to see her feeling so down. Maybe he should ask her out to distract her from whatever was happening at home. They had had a good time at the movies the week before.

Luke looked around the table and saw everyone else was involved in conversations of their own. Jena seemed composed again. He leaned over and quietly asked, "Do you want to go out to the movies again with me? It could be just the two of us, if you want."

At that moment, the feeling in Jena's head shifted. She no longer felt guilty for wanting to have someone who cared for her. She no longer cared what Willian thought about her actions. He had made the decision himself when he had threatened her. Jena looked up into Luke's eyes and smiled as she replied, "I'd like that a lot. Are you free tonight?"

Luke had not expected her to respond quite that swiftly and was taken aback. After a second's pause, he replied, "Absolutely! I'll check the movie times and call to let you know what's available tonight."

Jena smiled for the second time that day and noticed her appetite had returned. She was looking forward to spending time with Luke. He was always so considerate of her feelings and he always complemented her intelligence. In other words, he was the polar opposite of Willian and she was ready for a change.

Juila looked over at Jena and unconsciously relinked their minds. The thoughts she saw rolling through Jena's mind made her smile. She was so glad Luke had asked her out. She would do everything in her power to make sure their evening happened without any incident or unpleasantness.

By the end of the day, Behn had heard about Luke asking Jena out to the movies. He came up beside Juila and asked, "Do you want to go on a double-date with Luke and Jena?"

"No. I think they should have this time alone. It'll be good for Jena. We can do something on our own, though, if you want."

Behn's expression changed to one of happiness since he thought Juila was turning him down outright. He now understood that she wanted her sister to be on her own and not that she did not want to spend time with him. Suddenly he asked, "Do you want to go bowling?"

"What's that?"

"Something you should definitely try before you go home! I promise you'll have fun. What do you say?"

"Sure. If you think I'll like it, then I'm willing to give it a try. What time do you want to go?"

"I'll pick you up at seven. Okay?"

"Sure, it's a date!"

Behn held out his hand and took hold of Juila's. They walked out to the parking lot since their last class was over. Ahead of them they could see Jena walking with both Luke and Sofia.

Juila used her twin-link with Jena to ask, *What's going on? Is Luke riding with you and Sofia?*

Jena looked behind her and smiled as she answered, *Yes. We're going to drop him off at home before Sofia takes us home. Are you going to ride with Behn?*

I don't know. Let me ask him. She turned to Behn and asked, "Should I ride with Sofia?"

"I don't mind taking you home. Besides, it's a good excuse for staying over for my crystal lesson." He was rather pleased with his simple solution to staying over at their house. So far his sister and brother had not called him out for going home with them every day after school.

Behn's got me, go on ahead, Juila answered. She heard Jena's mental chuckle.

Jena replied, *He certainly does have you.*

Stop it! We'll see you at home! she said sternly in her mind. She smiled outwardly as she walked and was very glad to hear her sister joking around with her again. Jena seemed to be over the worst of her anger over Willian. Maybe now she would move on with her life and dump the loser.

I heard that! Jena broke into her thoughts.

I don't care if you did. I was only thinking the truth.

I know. I love you for it.

Behn drove straight to Juila's house so they were already inside the library before Jena came home. He had seen there was something going on with Jena and he wanted to talk to both of the sisters about it. Instinctively he knew it had something to do with their life back in Tuala. He hoped they trusted him enough to share.

Juila tapped his knee to get his attention. "Are you ready to try the next level?"

"Sure," Behn eagerly replied. "How many more levels do I have to learn before my education is equivalent to a second grader?"

"I wish you'd quit thinking about it that way. Your progress is going great and it's what really matters."

"You keep saying that, yet I can't help but feel I should already know what a second grader knows. The three of us were almost eight years old when we came to Earth. Don't you think we would have already learned all of this before then?"

"It depends. From what Grandpa Daven said about the colony where you grew up, they did not mix with outsiders and they disapproved of using the elemy entirely. I think it's fortunate you learned anything at all given those circumstances, if you asked me."

Behn tilted his head as he considered the validity of her points. Maybe he was being too hard on himself. Still, he wanted to learn as much as he could, in as short a time as possible, before he took the information about their heritage to his sister and brother.

The fact of them being from Tuala and not Earth at all was fantastic enough to believe. He felt certain they would not be able to refute his claims once he showed them his skills with his birth crystal. He lifted the small silver pendant with the tree on it. He had never considered the leaves of the tree which were made of smoky grey crystals to be his link with the land and with Jehoban. The more he learned about using the elemental energy, the more he felt the connection between himself, his necklace, and the elemy in the land.

"Fine. I'll agree to stop saying it out loud. I'm still going to push myself to achieve more than a second grader anyway."

"Well you should. You are very talented with the elemy and I have a feeling you'll go quite far. You just have to focus more on your training and less on getting me to tell you stories. Now, let's get back to work. The next level for you to achieve is putting out fire." She got up from her chair and walked over to one of the shelves in the library. She picked up the large candle and brought it back to her seat. Once she set it down on the coffee table between them, she used her own crystal skill to light the candle. "Now, Behn, put out the flame."

Behn recalled all of the previous lessons and wondered how Jena would have explained the process. Would she say to eliminate the oxygen or create a breeze to blow it out? He decided on the latter and created a quick breeze which snuffed out the flame. Immediately, he looked over to Juila to see her reaction.

"Very good, Behn. You used a breeze, right?"

"Yes."

"Can you put it out in any other way?" She lit the candle again using her mind.

Behn nodded and concentrated on moving the oxygen away from the flame. It took slightly longer, but he could see the benefit in knowing either method. If he needed a flame to go out without the possibility of spreading, then the second option was by far the best one. The flame got smaller until it went out, only to be replaced by a small puff of smoke which rose straight up from the wick.

Juila could tell what he had done the second time. The smoke rising without moving around also told her that the oxygen had been eliminated. The second technique was by far harder to accomplish than the first one he had chosen. She was glad he had used both methods without first asking how it was to be done because it showed he was applying previous techniques.

"That was perfect. I'm going to have you do both methods several more times before we move on." She lit the candle. "Go ahead."

The candle winked out.

Juila lit it.

Out again, much quicker this time.

Faster, Juila produced another flame.

Instantly, it went out.

Several more times they went through it as if it were a game. Finally, Juila laughed and said, "I surrender. You obviously are a quick study on this skill. Do you want a break, or do you want to go on to the next one."

"What's the next one?"

"You get to light the candle!" She smiled as she saw Behn's horrified expression.

"I think we should wait for Jena to get here. If I can't manage to control the flame, then it would be better to have two of you to put it out!"

Juila tilted her head and then had to agree to his wisdom. Then another idea struck her; they should take the next lesson out to the garage where it would be difficult to set the concrete on fire. It was a perfect location, actually, since her father's regular telepod would be in Tuala. They would have plenty of space to work without fear of burning down the house. Even if the power of the samaras would not help augment Behn's powers, he did not need to be particularly strong when learning to create a flame.

She stood up from her plush chair and said, "Let's get a snack." She looked down on her timepiece and wondered why Jena had not gotten home yet. Even as she was having the worried thought, she could sense Jena as Sofia's car turned onto their driveway. She sighed in relief and kept walking until she reached the kitchen.

Behn sat down at the island and wondered what Juila was going to get for a snack.

Juila opened the refrigerator and looked over the meager items. Suddenly she decided she wanted something from home rather than from Earth. With a surreptitious glance in either direction to make sure she would not be seen she created a large plate with scrambled eggs and fried foxl.

Behn's eyes grew wide as he was now looking on a plate of hot food which had not been on the island the second before. This must be what the girls had talked about when they said he would learn to create something using the elemy. This was the first time he could appreciate the utility of it. Normally, he had to wait for food to be prepared. Once he learned how to create for himself, he would never have to go hungry while he made a meal by hand.

The front door opened and Jena walked through the foyer and into the kitchen. She spied the plate on the island and then looked suspiciously at her sister. "Is that what I think it is?"

Juila looked sheepish as she replied, "Yes."

"Juila, you know what dad said about using your powers out in the open."

"I don't see how it's any different than when Dad does it to make dinner," Juila responded.

"It's not any different, but we're here to learn Earth's ways so we're supposed to make the ordinary effort."

"That's all well and good except when I'm craving fried foxl. Besides, don't you think Behn should try some native cuisine?"

"You're reaching, Juila." Jena could not fault her logic. The food did smell delicious. She relented and said, "Where are the forks? It looks like there's plenty for three people." She sat down at the island stool next to Behn and looked up at her sister expectantly.

Juila squealed with delight and immediately three forks appeared on the countertop.

The three dug into the meal.

Behn was first worried he would not like the foxl, but then found he did remember eating it as a kid. There were so many things he had yet to remember. One by one the memories were returning. He only hoped he would have total recall before taking this story to his doubting sister, Valentina.

When the plate no longer had a morsel of food left on it, Juila again used her powers to take care of the mess. She looked smugly at her sister and said, "Now we can resume Behn's lessons. We were far too hungry to carry on before."

"Before? You guys started without me?"

"You took forever, Jena. Behn has proven he can put out a flame. As fast as I created it, he put it out. He used both techniques with equal skill."

"That's great, Behn." Jena looked over at him with a huge grin on her face. She was just as proud of his progress as Juila.

"I thought we might take the next lesson out to the garage. Behn will have a harder time burning down the house if we're out in the concrete. Don't you think?"

"Sounds like you've thought of everything. Let's go."

The three walked out to the telepod garage. The sat down on the floor. Jena asked, "Where's the candle?"

"Sorry! I forgot it in the library." A moment later the candle appeared on the concrete floor in the middle of where they sat.

Behn could only hope to have the ease of skill and accuracy of the girls someday. They used their power effortlessly and he was quite impressed. He no longer commented on it since he could tell it made them uncomfortable, but he still thought it nonetheless.

Jena explained the process for creating the flame and Behn achieved success several times before they decided to call an end to the daily lessons. Jena really wanted some time alone with Juila so she did not want to move on to the next skill.

Behn could tell the girls were done teaching for the day. Before they stood up he turned to Jena and asked, "Has something happened from Tuala to make you sad?"

Jena's eyes shot over to Juila with accusation clear in her mind. Juila shook her head slightly and then Jena looked back to Behn as she asked, "What would make you come to that conclusion?"

"I don't know. Just a feeling I had. I couldn't imagine anything bad happening with either of your parents and you seemed fine with Juila. The only other thing it could have been would be something from home. Tuala, I mean."

"I know what you mean and you're right. Something very bad has happened in our old lives. We should probably explain a custom to you so you might understand the situation better. Are you sure you want to hear this story? It could take a while."

"I want to hear whatever you feel free to share. There's so much I don't remember about Tuala that it makes me sad." Behn looked down at the floor.

"There is a custom which is often followed among upper-class families…"

"And any other class when two families are particularly close," Juila interrupted.

Jena glared at her sister's interruption and said, "Yes, that, too. Anyway, it's call a betrothal. Have you ever heard of the term?"

Behn did recall it, but only from history classes. He was certain it would have a different meaning on Tuala and said as much.

Jena grinned and then said, "It means the same thing in Tuala. Anyway, when I was six years old, it was arranged for me to be betrothed to the son of one of the most respected Elders. In fact he's the First of the Elders so it was a great honor considering we were considered orphans up until this year."

"So you're saying you have a fiancé, Jena?" Behn could hardly believe what he was hearing. This whole thing seemed so archaic and unbeliev-able. He had to be misunderstanding her somehow.

"Willian is my *betrothed*. We have a contract for marriage when we turn eighteen or when we finish school," Jena corrected Behn's choice of word for the relationship.

"I don't see a difference."

"We haven't dated, Behn. We are contracted to marry one another when we're adults. I've been to his parent's house and they have treated me as their first-daughter—that's what the Tualans call the girl in the relationship when it comes to the other family.

"Traditionally, the girl would become betrothed before she's six months old and then go and live with the boy's family to be raised alongside the boy. The reasoning is that both of the children would be raised with the same set of values and they would admire one another and be the best of friends.

"In my case, I've only spent a few months at a time at Elder Debbon's house. Because of my training with Jehoban, I was not able to have the traditional relationship with my betrothed."

"Not that it would've mattered," Juila muttered.

Again, Jena glared at her sister for the rude comment. Then she had to reevaluate her harsh criticism of her sister since she had been right all along with Willian.

Behn interrupted Jena's thought when he asked, "So has something happened with Willian?"

"In a manner of speaking, yes. He has written to me several times since I've been here and I did not know I could access my mail from here. Needless to say, his letters to me were getting more and more demanding. My father intercepted my mail and he was not happy with what he saw. We are waiting to see what will be done, but I think it's safe to say, my betrothal is going to be called off."

"Is that bad? He sounds like a jerk!"

"It is bad. It brings dishonor to both houses when a betrothal is broken. The union is sanctioned by Jehoban and is considered a blessing on both houses."

Behn looked over at Juila and said, "I take it you don't think much of Willian."

"I've never liked him. I think this could be the best thing which ever happened to Jena. Now she'll be free of his unreasonable demands and she can choose someone to love on her own terms as it should have been from the start."

"Wow! I see," Behn replied as he let out a long breath. Juila's anger toward Willian was quite concerning. The guy must be bad news to have gotten on Juila's bad side. She was the most easy-going person he had ever met. "Thank you for sharing your situation with me. If you ever want to talk about it, you know you can trust me." He stood up from the cold concrete and offered both of his hands to the girls to help them up.

"That's something which would never occur to Willian," Juila remarked snidely.

"What?" Behn asked.

"Being chivalrous in helping Jena up from the ground. He would have left the garage and then yelled for Jena to hurry up and quit lollygagging around."

Jena could not argue with the truth so she opted to remain silent.

"You're still going to the movies with Luke tonight, right?" Behn asked suddenly as they were walking back into the house. "I think you have the right idea to go out with a friend while this is getting resolved."

"See, Jena! That's exactly what I've been telling her all along," Juila said to Behn after rubbing it in to Jena.

"Not exactly, Juila. You wanted me to date even before we knew there was a problem."

"I've known there was a problem since we were seven years old. It's just taken this long for you to admit the guy's a controlling jerk," Juila replied heatedly.

Behn knew when it was time for him to make his escape. He leaned forward and kissed Juila on the cheek and said, "I'll pick you up at seven. See you later, Jena." He waved at both girls and hurried through the foyer and out the front door.

"I'm surprised you told Behn about your situation with Willian," Juila said softly to her sister.

"Me, too. I guess I just wanted a fresh perspective on the whole thing." She shook her head and started to walk through the foyer.

"Where are you going?" Juila asked. For once she did not have the link with her sister open.

"I think I'm going to soak in a nice hot bubble bath for a bit before Luke calls to let me know what time he'll be coming over. You should probably link with me to make sure I don't drown since I slept so poorly last night." Jena pulled herself up the stairs with the railing. She was mentally, emotionally, and physically exhausted.

Juila took her sister's advice and linked minds with her. She was sad to see all of the troubled thoughts coursing through Jena's mind. She had no idea how heavily this whole mess had weighed upon her. Carefully, Juila tucked another idea into her mind about how she was going to mess up Willian for hurting her sister yet again.

CHAPTER 14

Willian still had not been home since his father had given him the ultimatum. He was not some child to be taken to task for a stupid misunderstanding. He had every right to call Jena out for her refusal to talk to him for so many mesans. There was no other man who would put up with such behavior and he was not going to either.

As he stalked through the grounds on the estate, he thought of different ways to get even with Jena. If the betrothal were called off, then she would have caused him to lose honor and then his plans to become First Elder after his father would be impossible to achieve. Jena would not be the cause of his downfall.

Short of going to Earth and forcing her to return to Tuala, he could not see a way out of this mess. If they thought he would apologize to Jena, then they had another thing coming. He had done nothing wrong in this whole mess. How come nobody was siding with him? Wasn't he the one who had been abandoned and ignored?

Jena should have come to him about wanting to go to Earth with her mother. Instead, she up and left without as much as a goodbye. To make matters worse, she had been gone for several mesans before he even knew about it.

That was not a very good point to make. As an attentive man, he should have noticed her absence much sooner. Forget the last argument. She should have come to him and asked his opinion about getting to know her mother. Why she needed one at her age was beyond him anyway.

He was not about to go back into his parent's house. It was better for them to worry about where he was so he decided to spend the night at a friend's house. He gathered several items from his room using the elemy and marched off of the house grounds and down the street. His parents could spend some time thinking about him and what he meant to them rather than how wonderful Jena was and how he had supposedly done her wrong.

~

CHELESA HAD BEEN MONITORING her son through his birth crystal. More than once she was grateful for the parental link to their children's necklaces. She was able to clearly see and hear everything going on around Willian. If she really wanted to, she could also use the birth crystal to read his very thoughts.

She knew Willian's thoughts were quite dark at the moment and she did not want to subject herself to such negativity. She left his mind alone and just monitored his whereabouts. When she saw him go into his friend's house, she disconnected the link and looked over at her husband.

"He's going to spend the night at one of his friend's house. Do you think we pushed him too far?" Chelesa was concerned for her son even though she thought the betrothal should have been called off anons before.

"I doubt we even pushed him at all, except to anger. I'm sure he thinks of himself as the victim here and he blames us for not seeing the big picture."

"I think you may be right," Chelesa said as she sank down on the edge of their bed. The day had been long and exhausting and yet she doubted sleep would come easily.

"We need to trust Jehoban can work this out for the good, Chelesa." Debbon sat beside his wife and put his hand gently on her leg to offer comfort.

Chelesa placed her own hand over his and looked up into his eyes as she said, "I'm trying. Sometimes I wonder what path will have to be taken before it comes out alright."

Debbon chuckled because his wife always had interesting insights to Jehoban's methods. Usually she was right. Now he was probably going to have trouble falling asleep while he pondered all the different ways this situation could go and all of the possible outcomes.

~

AMANDA AND RICCAN were off for another flying lesson when Behn and Luke both drove in to pick up the girls. The girls parted ways as they each got into different cars. Juila had purposely chosen not to connect their mental link so Jena would be able to relax and have a good time without worrying what her sister would say.

Luke and Jena went to a comedic movie. He was a perfect gentleman and bought them both popcorn, soda, and several candies. They whispered to one another during the previews and then fell silent as they became engrossed in eating and laughing at the movie.

Behn and Juila went to the bowling alley. They walked into the loud lobby and Juila looked around with wide eyes. She saw all of the wooden lanes and people throwing large balls down their own lanes. She jumped when the ball crashed into the waiting pins.

Behn led them to a counter where a man leaned heavily on his elbows and asked in a bored tone, "What size?"

Behn looked over at Juila to answer.

Juila looked back at Behn and asked, "What size for what?"

Behn laughed and said, "Shoes. What size shoes do you wear?"

"I don't know. My shoes are fine, though. I don't need another pair."

Again, Behn laughed at Juila's naivety. "We have to wear special shoes for bowling. Hand me one of your shoes and I'll look and see what size you wear."

She removed her shoe and gave it to Behn with a puzzled expression. She had no idea the shoe size was printed inside her shoe. Juila leaned forward and tried to see what Behn was looking at in her shoe when they bumped heads. "Ow. I'm sorry, Behn."

Behn was rubbing his head, but still smiling. He turned to the clerk and said, "She'll need a size five. I'll take a ten." He handed Juila back her shoe and then paid the clerk several dollars for the two new pairs. He took them off the counter and led the way to a bench for them to change into the shoes.

The clerk yelled out to them, "Take lane six."

Behn nodded and asked Juila if she were ready to go pick out a ball.

Juila nodded without understanding. She had no idea what to look for in a ball.

Finally, after Behn had his own ball picked out and sitting on the return rack, he came over and helped Juila. He explained, "We are going to be throwing the balls down the lane to try to knock over all ten pins. We get two tries, but you're trying to get it done with one ball. We need to find you a ball which is not too heavy with finger holes which fit your hand well. Here try this one out."

After at least twenty attempts, Juila found a ball which fit relatively well. She put her fingers in and swung the ball like she had seen other people do in the other lanes. This seemed like a very strange activity, but she was up for the challenge.

Behn went first. His ball hit six pins on the first try and another three on the second. He came back to the seat and marked the scorecard. "It's your turn, Juila."

Juila picked up her ball and inserted her fingers. She stepped up onto the wooden platform and tried to replicate what she had seen Behn do. She took three steps and swung the ball. Suddenly, she felt her feet flying ahead of her. She hit the ground hard and the ball went rolling off of her hand.

Behn let the ball roll wherever it wanted to go, his main concern was if Juila were injured. He rushed over to her side, kneeled, and asked, "Are you okay?"

Juila recovered her breath and smiled weakly as she said, "You made this look a lot easier! Why are the shoes so slippery?"

Behn laughed because he knew she could not be seriously hurt if she were complaining about the shoes. "Do you need help getting up?"

"I don't think so. Hey, have you seen my ball?" Juila had gotten to her hands and knees before she realized her hands were empty and the ball was nowhere to be seen.

"I'll find it. Be careful getting up!" Behn called back to her as he stepped down from the platform to locate her missing ball.

Juila was not normally embarrassed in any situation, but for some reason, this had been exceptionally humiliating. She wanted to be good at this because Behn obviously had some skills with it. Immediately, she realized this was how Behn must feel during their crystal lessons. From now on she was going to be more patient and understanding. She never wanted Behn to feel the same as she did when she was lying on the ground.

She got to her feet and scuffed the shoes on the floor to get the feeling of the slippery feeling soles. Because she knew what to expect, she felt confident she would not repeat her previous performance. Behn had found her missing ball and handed it to her. "Thank you." She started to turn around when she called over her shoulder saying, "You might want to stand off to the side, just in case!"

She could hear Behn laughing behind her as she eyed the pins while she stepped forward and released the ball. It was all she could do to keep from using her powers when she realized the ball was not going to hit the pins very well. She held her breath as she watched one pin fall before the ball fell into the gutter. Juila promised herself the next turn would be better.

Since she had seen how it worked, she realized it was just a math equation which needed to be solved. She needed the right angle and velocity in order to get all the pins to fall. As she waited for the return, she stared at the placement of the remaining nine pins. Immediately she saw what needed to be done to make them fall into each other. She took her final turn and jumped up and cheered as all of the pins fell just as she had imagined.

She turned with a huge smile on her face and asked, "Did you see that? They all fell down!" She walked back to the bench and sat down. Behn gave her a high five as she passed him.

The game was close. Both of them were very good at getting the right angle to knock the pins over. The end score was 237 to 243 with Juila in the lead.

"Are you sure you haven't played before?" Behn asked.

"Positive. It's pretty simple when you understand the math." Juila had thoroughly enjoyed the game even though her initial impression had not been so favorable.

Since she had turned in her shoes and put on her original ones, she realized her hip and back were starting to hurt from her fall. As Behn was leading them to the exit, she excused herself and said, "I've got to use the bathroom. I'll be right back."

As soon as she locked the stall door behind her she accessed her own life-line and pulled up several strands of elemy to soothe the parts of her which were beginning to cramp up and bruise. She sighed with relief as the soreness evaporated. She released the elemy back into the earth when she no longer felt any twinges of pain.

She did not heal herself very often since Jena was usually around, but she was thankful she knew how to do it on herself. Her evening could have been so much more painful without the skill they had learned two years before. She opened the stall door and walked out to the sink.

Juila washed her hands with soap since she realized the bowling ball had left an oily sheen on her hands from handling it. She looked up into the mirror and saw a girl who was having a good time with a person whom she could see herself spending quite a bit more time with. She pulled several paper towels from the dispenser and left the bathroom even as she was drying off her hands.

"Ready?" Behn asked as she came close.

"Sure. What are we going to do now?" She looked around and found a trash can and threw her wet paper towels away.

"I thought we'd go to the pool tables to see if you can apply the same skills to make me look bad at that, too!" Behn chuckled at his own joke.

Juila wondered if Behn's feelings were hurt. She could see he was smiling, but was he just using that to hide his true emotions. She went against her own rules and took a quick peek into his mind. With a sigh of relief, she saw he really did not mind if she beat him. He really just wanted to spend more time with her. "I'll try it. Where are they?"

"Just down here at the other end of the lobby. There's a game room for people who don't like to bowl," he said as he led the way.

Once again, Behn explained the rules of the game and the end objective. He racked up the balls and asked, "Do you want me to break or do you want to try it?"

"You better go first. It'll give me a chance to see how it works."

Behn brought up the pool stick and balanced it across the bridge of his hand. With a quick jerk, he pulled the stick back and then forward until it hit the cue ball with a satisfying thud. The cue flew across the table and struck the cluster, causing it to break apart in every direction. The yellow striped ball flew into a side pocket and Behn got to go again.

Juila watched avidly as Behn set up several more shots. She could see this game was not so different than bowling. She could apply the same math to get the appropriate angles to make the balls go wherever she wanted. As soon as she got a turn, she would test out her theory. As Behn took yet another shot, she started to wonder if she were even going to get a turn. She watched as the white ball followed the green striped ball into the corner pocket.

Behn reached in and pulled the cue ball back out and set it on the table. He said, "I scratched, so now it's your turn. Put the ball anywhere you want as long as it stays behind these two white diamonds here on either side." He pointed to the design on the side of the pool table and Juila leaned forward to see what he was showing her.

Just as she had imagined, the game was simple. She finished sinking all of the solid colored balls and then looked up at Behn expectantly. "Do I do the striped ones now?"

Behn laughed again and said, "No. Those were my responsibility. You won. Let's rack it up again and we'll let you go first."

CHAPTER 15

They ended up playing several more games before they called it a night. Behn was satisfied with his one win. He knew it was a fluke, but he would take it anyway. His principal joy was spending time with Juila and hearing her laugh as they executed their plays.

He drove slowly since he did not want the evening to end. They had school the next day so he knew they had to get back to their own homes soon. He did not want to make Juila sad, but he wanted to know the answer he asked, "Is Jena going to be okay?"

Juila looked over at him and nodded. "I'm hoping they'll agree to nullify the agreement and allow Jena to be free to live her own life."

"What went wrong with the two of them?"

"Willian became jealous because Jena's powers were further along than his own. He resented the idea of Jena being taught by Jehoban whereas Willian was being taught by his father."

"I see. Is Willian a really bad person then?"

"I don't think so. I just think he's really bad for Jena. If Willian were to find someone whose skills were not equal to his own, then he wouldn't feel the need to compete or compare. Does that make sense?"

Behn mulled over Juila's ideas and thought he understood what she was trying to say. He said, "I think I get it. How long do you think it'll take for a decision to be made?"

"I have no idea. I've never heard of a betrothal being broken."

"Hmm. Well can you keep me informed of whatever you hear? I don't want to seem nosy, but I do find the whole thing rather interesting."

"Sure." They were silent for a few moments before Juila put the conversation back on Behn when she asked, "So when are you going to talk to Valentina about Tuala?"

Behn smirked and let out a breath before he said, "I'd like to complete the second grade skills first. Then I'll consider telling her."

"I don't think you should wait much longer than that, Behn. It's great you want to show her what you can do, but if you get too far ahead, then it might put her off on wanting to learn the skills for herself."

Behn considered Juila's statement and realized she might have a valid point. Valentina could be touchy about many things and she was terribly competitive with her siblings. "Okay, I promise to talk to her after I've completed level ten, then. I see what you mean about getting too far ahead. I want her to learn everything as I have. We'll have to learn it if we ever want to return to Tuala, right?"

Juila laughed as she replied, "No, Behn. It's not like an entrance exam. Some people never even achieve all of the first ten levels. It's not a requirement, it's just strongly suggested to make life easier for the people."

Behn was relieved to hear this news. He had the idea of everybody doing everything using the elemy and never lifting a finger except to eat. He had to laugh at his naivety. There was still a lot for him to learn about Tuala. Hopefully, Valentina and Jon would be by his side as they learned about all of its secrets.

They turned into the Stel driveway. Behn pulled into the circular drive and stopped near the front door. He shut off the engine and turned off the headlights. They had a few more minutes before he would have to get going.

"I had a good time tonight," they both said in unison and then they both burst into laughter.

"Do you think Jena's home yet?" Behn asked.

Juila shook her head and said, "They're driving home right now."

"How do you know?"

Juila wondered if she should keep the secret or tell Behn. Honesty won out and she said, "Jena and I can link our minds. We hear what one another thinks and we can have conversations over vast distances. It's kind of nice because we can never be lost or alone since we always have one another."

"It sounds kind of annoying to have a sibling in your head all of the time."

"It definitely can be, especially when we're angry with one another. Most of the time, however, it's comforting. We always have someone to talk to."

"If you say so. Would it be the same if you were to link with my brain?"

"No. They called ours a twin link and it's stronger than anyone has ever seen before. What Jena learns, I learn also, and vice versa."

"But you two are in so many of the same classes. Aren't you bored out of your mind then?"

"It can get pretty tedious in school. Next term we're going to ask for completely separate schedules so we can learn twice as much in the same amount of time. We don't have too much longer before we're going to have to return to Tuala."

"Wait! What? Why do you have to return? Why can't you stay here like your father does?"

Juila realized she had said too much. She could not leave Behn wondering what was going on so she gave him a simple answer. "We have a task set out for us to do in Tuala. Once we've finished it, then we'll be free to live our own lives. Until it's accomplished, we're going to have to return to Tuala."

"You make it sound as if you know when you're leaving. Do you?" Behn realized he was going to have to speed up his plan for learning if the girls were going to be leaving.

"We have just over a year left before we leave."

"So you'll be able to finish high school, right?" Behn did not know why it was so important to him for them to finish. Maybe he was just being selfish and wanted to spend the rest of his schooling with them.

"Yes, we will, just barely. Hopefully." Juila hoped she was telling the truth.

Headlights lit up the side of Behn's car as Luke drove up the driveway and came to a stop beside them. Behn leaned over and kissed Juila on the lips and said, "I want to talk about this again when we have more time. Okay?"

"Sure. Thanks for a great evening, Behn. I'll see you at school tomorrow." She got out of the car and shut the door. She looked across the top of the car and watched her sister say goodnight to Luke and exit the vehicle.

Jena joined her sister and together they went into their house.

"Did you have fun?" Juila asked in a whisper as they climbed the stairs.

"I did! How about you? What was bowling like?"

"Oh, my, it was embarrassing! The first time I went up to throw the ball I fell flat on my rear and the ball went flying behind me."

"Are you serious? It sounds dreadful!"

"It was, at first. After I picked myself up off of the ground, I figured out what went wrong. Then it was really fun. I even beat Behn's score and he's been bowling lots of times. Then we played a game called pool. He won once, but I beat him all of the other games. We'll have to go out on a double-date to do both again."

"Sure. It sounds like fun. Besides, I'd like to go out with Luke again."

"Did he kiss you at the movies?"

Jena blushed a little and looked down to the ground even as she said, "Yes."

"Oh! Do tell!" Juila said as she grabbed Jena's arm. Juila had kept her mind to herself all evening long. She wanted her sister to be able to enjoy her evening without having company in her head. The only time she had looked in on her the whole evening had been to find out when she was coming home.

"It was nothing really. Luke kissed me once in the theater just as the movie was ending."

"Was it on the lips?"

"Yes."

"With tongue?"

"Juila, does it matter?"

"Yes, was it?"

"Yes. There! Are you happy?"

Juila smirked and nodded her head. "Did you like it?"

"Yes."

They had reached Juila's room. She stayed in the doorway until she saw Jena go into her own room. With a smile still on her face she turned and walked into her room. There was hope for her sister yet. Willian had some competition and she was sure he would come up short whenever Jena compared the two against one another.

~

BARLA'S TRAINING with both of her children went better than anyone had guessed it would. The only explanation Rasa could give to herself was that her mother had wanted this for so long. Because of the opportunity she had been given, Barla poured her whole being into making her dream the best reality possible. It also helped that she and Gravin were the ones teaching her. Not only did she trust them implicitly, she was so proud of their abilities to be so patient with her fumbled attempts to get each skill done right. Rasa had seen this in Barla's mind when Gravin had been explaining one of the processes. Her mother had achieved the first ten skill levels before Rasa had to leave.

On Rasa's final day, she came down the stairs and asked everyone if they could meet in the living room. She had yet to tell them of her new position with Elder Wilken. She had purposely not talked about it for fear of making her visit home awkward with her brother. All of her life she had known Gravin had been envious of her schooling, but this might be too much for him to bear.

When everyone was gathered again in the living room, Rasa paced nervously in front of the fireplace. She stopped pacing and said, "I told you all that I had two items of news to share with the family. The first thing was Mom's birth crystal. Well, the second thing is that I've been transferred away from Acaim."

"What? Why?" Barla asked with genuine concern. She hoped nothing had gone wrong for such a thing to happen.

"It's good news actually. Jehoban asked me to meet with Elder Wilken and to study with him. I told the Elder I would only be away for a few days and then I would return to Manzanit to resume my studies."

"I don't understand what Elder Wilken could teach you which Jehoban would not be able. What's going on, Rasa?" Ahn asked.

Rasa glanced nervously at her brother and watched his expression intently as she answered, "I'm to be Elder Wilken's successor when he steps down."

Gravin's eyes grew wide as he understood what Rasa had told them all. He asked, "How is that possible? There's never been a female Elder."

"Jehoban said I was to be the first. It was His wish. I could hardly refuse the honor." Rasa clasped her hands in front of her and willed her brother to not be angry or jealous. She wanted the easygoing and carefree relationship they had shared when they were little. These past couple days had made her think it could be a possibility, but only if Gravin would accept her new post.

"This is wonderful and amazing news, Rasa," Barla exclaimed as she jumped up from her chair to come and embrace her daughter. She had always known Rasa would do special things with her life. This had never even been a consideration in her mind, but she could easily accept it since it was Jehoban's wish.

"Gravin, are you okay with this? If you aren't then I'll ask Jehoban to reconsider," Rasa spoke softly to her brother.

"Are you kidding? You can't turn down this opportunity. Besides, it's better you than me in this situation. I'm having entirely too much fun being retired to even consider what you're going to have to go through for the next several anons. Then when Elder Wilken decides to retire, all of the problems of the district will be squarely on you." He came over and hugged his sister and whispered in her ear. "I'm really proud of you. Don't ever give up a dream because of someone else, not even me."

Rasa could feel tears forming in her eyes as she pulled back slightly and said quietly, "Thank you, Gravin. Your support means the world to me."

"I have been jealous of you from time to time..." he began.

Rasa cocked her head sideways, crossed her arms, and raised one eyebrow at her brother.

"Okay, okay! I was jealous for a long time, but I've gotten over it. You have the better temperament for being an Elder than I would ever have. You bring honor to our family just by being asked by Jehoban to take on this task."

"I know and I must admit the whole idea scares me. Elder Wilken said he believes I'll be good at the job so I'll have to trust everyone knows best for my future. I'm going to do everything possible to prove everybody correct."

"When will it be made formal?" Ahn asked.

"Elder Debbon has scheduled a convocation of the Elders to be held on Selasa, Adar 1st so I imagine it will be sometime after that. It's anybody's guess how long it will take for all of the Elders to agree to allow me to be a successor. If I were a boy then it wouldn't even be a discussion."

"Are they allowed to decline the promotion?" Barla asked.

"I don't really know. I would imagine they could, but then Jehoban might step in and override them. After all, this was His decision in the first place. Who are the Elders to say no to something Jehoban has said will be done."

"There are some really stupid people in this world," Gravin muttered.

"Will you be present at the convocation? Is family allowed to attend?" Ahn asked.

"I don't know the answer to either of your questions, Dad. I'll find out and let you know. Meanwhile, I really need to get back to Manzanit. There's so much I need to learn and if I can prove my worth before the convocation, then it will be ever so much harder for the other Elders to disagree with Elder Wilken's choice."

"When do you have to go?" Barla hated the thought of any of her children leaving her again.

"Right now, Mom."

"No, Rasa. Can't you wait until tomorrow? What about my crystal lessons? Surely there's something more you need to teach me."

"I'm sorry, Mom. This can't be helped. Besides, Gravin has agreed to continue to teach you until he leaves. He's very skilled and patient." She looked over at her brother and smiled. "If you get stuck on anything, send me a message on the patil. I'll be checking it several times a day and I'll help whenever I can."

"You don't need to worry about your mother, Rasa. I have a few skills of my own. Gravin and I will continue your mother's training. We love you and want you to do your best with this new task," Ahn said, also standing up so he could hug his daughter.

Rasa found herself surrounded by her family's arms. She had forgotten how good it felt to have family to support her and want her to be happy. Living on Acaim had been wonderful, but nothing could compare to this moment of bliss. "I have the best family!"

CHAPTER 16

Just as Daven had predicted, Amanda only needed ten days before she was proficient in piloting her own telepod. They had begun training in the smaller craft on their second day so she would be comfortable with the systems. There was a sense of urgency for her to get started on her journey to rescue Neal before the first of December.

It was already November twenty-fifth and Amanda was itching to get herself to Tuala. She had it in her mind that she would go and meet Bryon and Alena for the first time. The meeting had the potential to be very awkward, but she could not shake the feeling it was the right thing to do.

Right after Riccan left for work and the girls had been picked up for school, Amanda packed a bag with some snacks and she was ready to go. If only her nerves would calm down, then she could start to enjoy this new adventure. She had already discussed her plans for the day with Riccan so he would know where to look for her should anything go wrong.

Just as she thought she was ready to go, she felt a desperate need to go to the bathroom. Her bowels were quite upset with how nervous she had made herself. She remained in the living room for a few more minutes and convinced herself how ridiculous this whole thing was. She had things which needed to get arranged and she was the only one who had the time to get it done.

She went out to the garage and palmed open the door with the remote even as she was walked toward the telepod. Never before had she attempted this alone. Her heart was racing as she buckled herself into the pilot's seat. She flipped the master power switch and began the startup procedures.

Looking down on the glass panel she saw there was a red button lit up. Immediately alarmed since Riccan had told her anything red was bad, she started to review the potential problems. When she discovered the cause, she could have kicked herself. She had left the side door open. Of course she could not very well take off with the door hanging open. It was at that point where she wondered what other things Riccan had done out of habit which she might forget to do for herself.

She hit the door switch and watched the panel to verify the red light had gone out. Everything was now displayed in green and she took a deep breath to try to calm herself before going any further. Deciding to take one step at a time and not worry about future events, she entered the location of Kirma into the system and pressed enter.

As Riccan had taught her, she looked at the visual coordinates to keep them in mind as she traveled. While technology was a good thing, it was important to remember it had flaws. Even though the system was automated, she always wanted to be linked with the crystal drive to verify she would end up at her desired location.

She touched the screen to begin the transfer and then counted her heartbeats until she entered the outskirts of Kirma. Because she had been so nervous, Amanda had counted many more heartbeats than normal and she had to chuckle at her own self-doubt. Getting back into the piloting mode, Amanda concentrated on landing the telepod on a level patch of grass. She issued all of the shutdown procedures and unbuckled her seat harness.

Amanda picked up her small bag and left the telepod. She palmed the door shut with a satisfying slap on the outside switch and then turned on the cloaking mode with the remote. After she securely put the remote into her pants pocket, she began walking toward Kirma.

She checked her watch and saw it was almost nine o'clock. Bryon would be in his office at Kirma Shipping and Receiving at this time of day. She had decided to go to his work to speak with him in private.

Hoping her memory was correct she began walking toward the end of town where she believed the business was located. It only took about fifteen minutes for Amanda to reach the edge of town. She smiled when she saw the road which looked eerily familiar even though this was the first time she had seen it in reality.

Another ten minutes passed and Amanda was facing the entrance of Kirma Shipping and Receiving. She had only been here a couple of times during her dream. It looked larger than her memories and she started to doubt whether or not this were a good idea. *Don't be silly*, she said to herself. *You came here to accomplish something, now do it!* With new resolve, she stepped onto the business property and walked toward the building where she knew Bryon kept his office.

She went up the couple of steps and opened the door. In front of her was a woman who was in her mid-thirties with dark red hair and bright, green eyes. Amanda looked down and saw the sign in front of her said her name was Frasnia. "So far, so good," Amanda whispered. She stepped into the office and let the door shut behind her.

"May I help you?" Frasnia asked.

"Yes. I'd like to meet with Bryon Kesh, please."

"May I tell him your name?"

"Oh, sorry. My name's Amanda Stel." Amanda fidgeted with the bag she was holding and then forced her hands to her sides so she could relax. Frasnia was exactly as she remembered and Bryon obviously worked here since Frasnia had not seemed confused with her request. All was going according to plan.

"Bryon will be available in a few minutes. Please feel free to take a seat." Frasnia smiled and then turned away as a call came through her patil for her to answer.

Amanda shifted her gaze to give Frasnia some privacy and she wandered over to the waiting chairs. Even though she really did not want to sit down because of her nerves, she thought it would be more polite to appear relaxed. She looked at her watch for something to do and then fidgeted with the bag she had brought.

Since she was sitting here, she was not so sure this was the right way to go about this part of her plan. Bryon was a very busy man and he might not want to be interrupted with some stranger's crazy tale. Amanda was about ready to get up and leave when Bryon's office door opened and he walked out to the lobby to greet her. Amanda stood up. He looked the same. He was extremely tall, very muscular, with dark expressive eyes, and dark hair which he liked to spike up.

"Hello, Amanda. I'm pleased to meet you," he said as he held out his hand in greeting.

"Me, too." She took his hand and hastily shook it.

"Please, come into my office. I'm curious to hear what you have to tell me." He led the way back to his own room and shut the door behind her. "Have a seat. Can I get you anything? Water? Java? Steena tea?"

"Water, please," Amanda replied as she took the offered seat.

Bryon created a glass of water and handed it to her and then he went around the desk to sit in his big, black chair. "I was told to expect a visit from you. What can I do to help you?"

Amanda took a quick sip of the water as she tried to hide her amazement in how easy this seemed to be going. She asked, "Do you know who I am?"

"Sure. You're Elder Daven's First-daughter. I was told to expect a visit from you sometime in the future and to render any assistance which you might request. I'm at your service!" He smiled and leaned forward as he wiggled his eyebrows amusingly.

Amanda laughed at his foolishness and felt herself calming down because she was back in the presence of a friend. She knew the friendship was very different than what she had experienced, but at least this was not going to be as awkward as she had imagined. She cleared her throat and said, "This may seem like a strange question…"

"It's okay. Ask whatever you want."

"Alright. When you were a teenager did you go to Earth?"

Bryon's eyes opened wide. He had expected any number of bazaar questions, but not this one. "Actually, yes. I did. Why is it important?"

"I can explain, but first I have another question. Did you or Linden bring anything back from Earth?"

Again, Bryon was surprised to hear Amanda speak the name of his childhood friend. He had been told Amanda knew strange details about their lives and now he believed it. "Yes. We brought back a crystal skull." He shivered even as he remembered that time in his life. They had been so terrified when they had seen it glow they had fallen all over themselves to get out of the cave and away from it.

Amanda nodded with a small smile on her lips. "Would you have some time to take me to the cave where you two left it?"

He stared at her for a few seconds before speaking. Once again, she had known a detail he had only shared with two other people on Tuala. He knew both of them would never talk to anybody else about it. Amanda had once again proven her ability to know unusual details of his life. He could hardly wait to get home and tell Alena about Amanda.

"Sure. Let me check my schedule really quick." He turned and touched the screen on his patil a few times and then he stood up. He walked around the desk and opened the door to speak with Frasnia.

"Can you clear my schedule for the rest of the day? Something important has come up and I'm going to have to leave. Hopefully, I'll be back tomorrow morning. If not, I'll call you before the end of today and let you know."

Frasnia's brow furrowed in confusion, yet she nodded and said, "Of course. I'll take care of it."

Bryon remained standing where he was, turned back to Amanda, and said, "I'm ready whenever you are!"

Amanda put the glass of water down on his desk and stood up swiftly. "Great! Lead on!"

Wishing he had not chosen to walk to work, Bryon walked over to a small key box mounted to the wall, opened it, and took out one of the sets of keys. "I'll be taking telepod number twenty, Frasnia."

Frasnia nodded calmly even as she grew more curious. She already planned on tracking the telepod beacon to see what her boss was up to. It was not like him to make sudden plans and she was intrigued.

Amanda and Bryon left the office together. They walked across the shipping yard to where the telepods were stored and entered number twenty. Bryon obviously sat in the pilot's seat and Amanda sat beside him. They buckled up and Bryon performed all of the procedures to get them to their location.

Amanda was staring at all of the controls on the panel. This looked just like she remembered from her dream, which meant it was nothing like what she had trained on to get her here. She was glad Bryon had taken the lead since she was sure she would not have gotten them to the cave.

Bryon asked, "Are you ready?"

"Yes. Let's go."

Everything went black and Amanda counted three seconds before they arrived back into the bright sunshine at a different location. Amanda looked out the window and saw the cave she remembered exiting when she had returned to Tuala in her dream. This next part was what had her most anxious because in her dream, the crystal no longer sat in the niche near the gate.

They exited the telepod and walked to the cave entrance. Amanda's nerves were calmed as she could feel the energy of the samara projecting from darkness within. She smiled over at Bryon and said, "Do you want to take the lead, or shall I?"

Bryon desperately wanted to tell her to go first, but the man in him said, "I can go first." He stepped forward while at the same time he created a sphere of elemy to light their way. Immediately, he felt the same sense of strange energy which he assumed was the gate. Just like when he was a teenager, he felt so nervous he could feel sweat starting to form in his armpits and his mouth was getting dry.

Amanda nudged him to continue walking. When they neared the gate, Amanda could clearly see the samara nestled in a niche of the wall. She stared at the skull to check the color of its aura. Swiftly, she determined it to be a dark shade of orange. She turned to Bryon and asked, "What color is your birth crystal?"

Again, Bryon was surprised at Amanda's question, but answered, "It is dark orange. Why does it matter?"

Instead of answering, Amanda created her own sphere of light and said, "Let go of your elemy and go get your samara from the niche."

"My what?"

"That's what the crystal skull is called. It's a samara and this one is yours, Bryon. Go and claim it. I'll wait right here." She could fully understand his confusion and his reluctance to get near the object which projected so much power. She also knew he had been scared of it for a couple of declans which would make this even harder. "Don't be afraid of it, Bryon. I promise you everything will turn out just as it should."

Bryon had said he would do whatever was asked of him, but he had never expected this to be his task. He was scared out of his mind. His feet felt rooted to the floor of the cave and his mind could not convince them to move toward the object of many terrifying dreams since he was a teenager.

Amanda could see this was going to be more difficult than she had anticipated. She said, "Use your birth crystal, Bryon, and feel the energy from the samara and how it interacts with your own crystals."

Even as she was telling him to move forward, Amanda recalled several things at once. First, when her two girls had initially held their samaras they had been held in thrall for quite some time. Second, when she found the skull at the asylum, she had been pulled into several visions of her own. Third, the unsanctioned gate next to where the samara was tucked away may have an unpredictable energy of its own. And fourth, the second time the girls had used their crystals, they had carried them in towels until they were ready to touch them.

"Wait!" Amanda cried out as Bryon took his first step toward the niche.

Bryon whirled around with wide eyes and asked, "What? Has something happened?"

"I'm sorry to scare you, Bryon. I just had an idea. Do you have a large towel at home which you can get right now?"

"You want me to create it right now?"

"If you could, it'd be very helpful."

CHAPTER 17

Glad for any excuse to delay the inevitable, Bryon concentrated for a second before he was holding his bath towel from home. "Will this work?"

"Perfectly," Amanda answered as she appraised its thickness. She nodded even as she walked forward. "Can you create a sphere of light for us?"

Bryon did as she asked and followed her closely.

Together, they walked forward. She directed him to use the towel to pick up the samara from where it had sat for more than twenty anons. She smiled as he turned back to her, allowing him to walk past her to leave the cave. She stayed close to Bryon since he controlled the light around her as they left the cave. The towel completely covered the small skull and Bryon had it tucked under his arm to prevent anything from happening to it.

They got back into the telepod and sat down again.

Bryon asked, "What do we do with it now?"

"Can you take me to your house? I think we should be somewhere safe and private for what comes next."

Bryon did not like the sound of this. He had a bit of a harder time concentrating on the coordinates to his home. Passing the bundle to her, he finally inhaled deeply to calm himself before issuing the command to send them between locations. Bryon kept his mind focused until they arrived at his driveway. He parked the telepod and performed all of the shutdown procedures.

Amanda noticed the house was exactly as she remembered. She still held the samara under her arm as she exited the vehicle. Bryon led the way as they went into the house.

"Alena! Are you home?" Bryon called out as they walked through the living room. There was no reply.

Since they were going to need uninterrupted privacy, Amanda said, "We should go into your office, Bryon. We need to make sure we aren't disturbed for a while."

By now, Bryon's shirt had become soaked with nervous sweat. He could not believe he could be so afraid of something. If anyone would have asked him before today, he could have honestly said he was scared of nothing. Now he knew this to be patently untrue. Without any excuse to refuse, he led Amanda into his office.

"Sit down, Bryon. Get comfortable." Amanda watched him go to his desk chair and sit with his hands clutching the armrests. She set down the towel containing the samara onto the desk. She left it covered and picked a chair for herself. "Let me tell you what I know so far. I don't want you to be so afraid."

"I'm listening," Bryon said. He hoped she could keep talking long enough for her to change her mind about him having anything to do with the thing perched so closely to him on the desk.

"There are thirteen of these samaras in existence. Riccan and I have found and possess three of them. This is the fourth one which has now been located. Thousands of anons ago twelve of the samaras, as they are called, were originally given out to the descendants of the Watchers. They were commissioned to keep them in their family line until the time came for them to once again be reunited for their intended purpose. Over time, families have died out and some of the samaras have been misplaced.

"However, each one has a unique aura and so far, each aura has matched the color of the birth stone of the proper owner. I checked the aura of this samara and it happens to match your own birth crystal. I am further convinced that this samara belongs to you, Bryon. If you would trust my intuition in this matter, I'd like to ask you to put your hands on the samara. You will know immediately if I'm right."

"What happens if you're wrong?" Bryon asked nervously. He had been fascinated by her story, but it was not enough proof to convince him he should take such a risk. He had a wife and three kids to consider.

Amanda could see Bryon's hesitation and answered, "I've handled two of the samaras with my bare hands. While I can't say nothing happened, I can say nothing bad happened. I'm living proof that it won't kill."

Bryon swallowed and nodded agreement. The sooner he got this over with, the sooner he could get away from the thing.

Amanda pulled the cloth off of each side and left the crystal exposed in the center. She sat back and waited for Bryon to make the next move.

Bryon leaned forward and stared at the design for several seconds. From his dreams, he recalled it being much fiercer. Clearly he had let his imagination get the better of him. He rested his elbows on the tabletop and let his hands drop down onto the top of the skull.

Immediately, he felt massive amounts of energy course through his hands, up his arms, and through his birth crystal. Visions of people he knew and strangers passed through his mind faster than he could comprehend. A sense of calm and completeness came over him. He sighed with relief and took his hands away from his samara.

He looked up at Amanda with bright eyes and said, "It really is mine, isn't it?"

Amanda grinned as she said, "It would appear so!" She began to laugh.

"What's so funny?"

"You have no idea how long you were communing with your samara, do you?"

"What are you talking about? I only touched it for a couple of seconds." He looked down at his timepiece and gasped. It was almost noon. "Are you saying I was touching my samara for nearly three hours?"

Amanda nodded. She was glad they had been left alone so he could have a good first experience with the power of the stone. She was also thankful he had been sitting down. If he had first held it in the cave, he could have fallen down into the ascension gate and ended up who knows where. This was the best possible outcome.

They heard a commotion out in the living room and Bryon looked at her with a panicked expression. "What are we going to do with my samara?"

"I suggest you find a safe place to hide it for now," Amanda said calmly.

She wondered who had come home and hoped it was Alena. She had no idea what she'd say to her if it were her, but she hoped it nonetheless.

Bryon carefully pulled the towel up around the crystal and picked it up from the desktop. He opened a drawer and placed it inside and moved several items over the top of it to keep it from being terribly obvious. "Let's go find out who is home." He walked out of the office, down the hall, and into the living room.

Alena and their next-door-neighbor, Tana, were walking toward them. They saw Bryon and smiled and then they spotted Amanda and raised their eyebrows in question. Alena said, "I saw your work telepod outside and wondered what could possibly have happened for you to come home with it. What's going on? Who is your friend?"

"Alena, I'd like for you to meet Amanda Stel," he said with a mischievous grin. He watched his wife's face carefully until he could see recognition of the name sink into her mind.

She smiled brightly and moved forward to greet her. "Amanda, I'm so pleased to meet you. Has Bryon been helping you? Oh, sorry! How rude of me, let me introduce our neighbor…"

"Tana," Amanda said quietly. She held out her hand and smiled at the neighbor.

"How did you know my name?" she asked with a confused expression. She looked from Alena to Bryon and wondered what was going on. Suddenly she felt as though she were intruding on something important. "I should probably get going home. I'll talk to you later, Alena. It was nice to meet you, Amanda."

They remained silent until the front door closed. Alena spoke first by saying, "I guess it's true about you knowing details about our lives. I'd hate to think what you know about me!" She chuckled nervously.

"Everything I know about you is good. Don't worry, Alena."

Alena smiled and turned to her husband as she asked, "Have you offered Amanda any refreshments?" Without waiting for a reply she turned to Amanda and asked, "May I get you something to eat or drink?"

"You wouldn't happen to have any fruit salad, would you? I have it on good authority that yours is the best!"

Alena grinned and said, "You do know the good things, don't you! Come into the kitchen and you can tell us what help you need."

Bryon was bursting to tell his good news, but he knew from experience that he had to let Alena play hostess before he would be heard. He followed them into the kitchen and looked forward to eating some of the fruit salad as well.

They sat at the kitchen table and the salad appeared on the table between them. Next to appear were the plates, forks, napkins, and glasses of chilled steena tea. Alena filled each plate by hand and sat back down in her chair to eat.

The food was as amazing as Amanda remembered. "That was marvelous, Alena. Thank you so much."

Bryon knew he would be able to finally share his news. He leaned forward as he set his fork down on the empty plate. "Amanda came to my work first thing this morning."

"Really?" She looked from her husband over to Amanda. Bryon looked like a child with a secret and she wondered what could have happened.

"We went on a little trip down memory lane. Do you remember me telling you about my adventure with Linden when I was a teenager?"

Alena remembered the story well. She could not imagine why this would be important right now and raised her eyebrows in question even as she nodded affirmation.

"Amanda and I went to the cave and retrieved the skull!"

"What? Why?" Alena raised her voice in alarm. This was definitely not making sense.

Amanda answered, "They are important for the fulfillment of a new prophecy which has come to light."

Alena remained silent as she reviewed the words of the prophecy as it had been written down for her to keep. "I don't understand what it has to do with it."

"So you know about the prophecy?" Amanda could not help but be surprised about them knowing it. She wondered who else knew it and asked, "How did you find out about it?"

"Jehoban called a meeting and everyone present was told the prophecy and that we were to help you when you asked for anything."

"Who was at the meeting?"

"Let's see: Bryon and myself, Ahn, Barla, and Rasa, Elder Daven and Nena, and Elder Debbon and Chelesa."

Amanda listened intently to the names and then she realized an important detail. Each of the people present at the meeting were going to have their own samaras. It was so obvious she had to laugh about it. Bryon had received his today. She wondered who would be next.

"What's so funny, Amanda?" Bryon asked.

"I think I just figured out Jehoban's plan. I don't want to say anything about my suspicion just in case I'm wrong. I do need something from you if possible?"

"Whatever you ask, we will do our best to do."

"Can you find out the birth crystal colors of each of the people at the meeting?"

Alena looked at her husband with a puzzled expression. This was the last thing she had expected Amanda to ask for.

Bryon began to laugh as he put the pieces together just as Amanda had. "We'll get it done, Amanda. Is there some way we can get the information to you?"

"You can send any messages to me through my husband, Riccan, or Elder Daven. Do you have their account names?"

"We can get them, don't worry," Bryon answered even as he continued to chuckle.

"I'd like to stay longer, but I really should get going," Amanda said.

"Really? I wish I could have spent more time getting to know you," Alena said sadly.

"Don't worry. I'm sure there will be plenty of time for it. Maybe even tomorrow. I'm working on something right now which may require some advice."

"Please tell me about it. If I have more time to think on it, I may be able to help you better," Alena insisted.

Amanda realized Alena was right. She could not possibly get Neal out without many people helping her put together a plan. "You're so right, Alena. I need to find out if a friend of mine is being held captive by Elder Vargen at his Old Soul Engineering Facility. If he is there, then I'm going to rescue him and take him back home to his family on Earth."

"Wow! That's a huge task, Amanda. What's his name?"

"Nealand. I always called him Neal, but I think he's going by Nealan here."

"That would make sense," Bryon said.

"When do you propose to get him and how are you going to find him?" Alena asked.

Amanda had to concentrate to remember the date as it was called in Tuala and answered, "On Selasa, Adar 1st. The Elders are all being called to a meeting on that day so it'll at least get him out of the way. I also already know the address of someone named Nealan. If it's my friend, then I'll teleport him back home with me."

"What makes you think he'd want to go home?" Alena asked.

"I hope he'll want to. Jehoban told me he's being drugged with resh and his parents have been mourning his loss for the last seven anons."

Alena hissed at the statement about the resh. She knew how addictive the drug could be to some people. If it were taken long enough, any person addicted to resh would eventually die a slow wasting death. This was more serious than she had first believed. If it were just a mission to bring someone back to Earth then she would have a harder time getting involved. The resh made this a rescue mission indeed.

She nodded her understanding of Amanda's plight. "I'll put some serious thought into this problem and let you know if I come up with anything which might help."

Another thought came to Amanda and she asked, "Do either of you know a wise-woman named Copa?"

Bryon and Alena looked at one another in amazement and turned back to Amanda and nodded. Bryon said, "She helped one of my employees after he was attacked and hurt badly."

Now it was Amanda's turn to be surprised when she asked, "Was he named Ninan?"

"Yes. Do you know him?" Alena asked as she leaned forward.

"No. I had a dream about him," Amanda replied quietly.

Another significant look passed between husband and wife. They recalled from their meeting with Jehoban that Amanda would know things about them which they would find amazing. This was yet another example of her unique talents.

"I do know Copa. She and I have spent a considerable amount of time together since Ninan had been hurt. Are you trying to find her?"

"Yes, I have some things I'd like to talk to her about. I'd like to arrange a meeting with her. Can you tell me how to get in touch with her?"

"Sure," Alena said as she got up from the table and walked over to the kitchen counter. She grabbed a piece of paper and wrote down Copa's call sign for contacting her on the patil. She walked back to the table and handed it to Amanda.

"Thank you so much! I hate to eat and run, but I really need to get going." She folded the paper and put it into the pocket of her pants. Amanda would wait to see Copa until she had spoken to Riccan about it. She had realized how important it was to make sure her family knew where she was since she had stolen away to the asylum.

Bryon asked, "How did you get here?"

"I flew my telepod."

Alena and Bryon had the same amazed expressions on their faces.

Bryon said, "I didn't know people from Earth could learn to fly a telepod."

Amanda chuckled, pulled her pendant up from her shirt, and said, "And I bet you didn't know we could also get our own birth crystals, either. Jehoban is full of surprises these days. I think we should start to expect the unexpected anymore!"

Alena laughed at Amanda's statement and said, "Duly noted! I think our lives will never be the same since you've come around, Amanda."

"I hope it's only for the good," Amanda replied fervently.

"Let me see the paper with Copa's address. Since you have a telepod, I can give you the coordinates to her house." She wrote down the additional directions and handed the paper back with a grin. "I can't believe you can fly a telepod! Do you realize how many Tualans can't even do that?"

Amanda tipped her head at Alena's comment. She could not understand why it would be so hard. Then she remembered her husband had designed her telepod to be very easy and safe for a person to fly. Not everyone had the advantage of such advanced technology. She returned the directions to her pocket.

Bryon asked, "Where did you park your telepod?"

"In the landing field outside of town."

"Come on, I'll give you a ride out there so you won't have to walk."

Amanda rose from the table and said, "Thank you, Alena. I look forward to sitting down with you really soon."

"Me, too!" Alena could not resist reaching forward to hug Amanda.

Amanda returned the hug gladly. She missed her friendship with this woman and hoped it could be rekindled just as she remembered it from her dream.

Bryon could hardly wait for them to be alone so he could ask the question which was burning a hole in his brain. As soon as the side door shut on the telepod, he asked, "All of the people at the meeting with Jehoban are going to get their own samara, aren't they?"

"It seems like it. Please don't say anything about it yet. Okay? I could be wrong."

"I won't speak of it. Do you think it would be okay for me to tell Alena about my samara?"

"Absolutely! I think it'll make it easier for her to know you have one so when she gets her own, then she can be easier about it."

"I was a mess, wasn't I?"

"I won't hold it against you," Amanda teased.

Bryon had the telepod ready for the transfer so Amanda remained silent until they reached the landing field. He opened the side door and said, "I'm glad you came to see me today, Amanda."

"I'm glad, too, Bryon. I have a feeling I'll be seeing a lot of you and your wife in the next few days!" She walked out of the telepod and over to her own. She turned off the cloaking and palmed open the door. She waved farewell to Bryon as she entered her own telepod to go home.

CHAPTER 18

Behn repeatedly practiced the crystal skills while sitting on his bed. He had been careful to shut the door for privacy. He promptly became engrossed in both lighting and extinguishing a candle he had taken from his mom's collection. There was something very satisfying to see a flame appear where there had only been a smoking black wick moments before. He extinguished it again and relit it almost immediately.

He only had two more things to learn before he was going to talk to his sister about what he had discovered about their heritage. Juila had promised to teach him how to move an object the next day. For an instant, he wondered if he could try to do it on his own. Almost in the same thought he decided it would be better to be around someone trained before he attempted it. He was too ignorant in the matter to know what could possibly go wrong so he opted to continue lighting and extinguishing the candle.

He had been so engrossed in his task that he failed to hear his door open. Valentina watched for several seconds before she spoke. "What are you doing, Behn?"

Almost jumping out of his bed with fear, Behn sat up and looked at his sister with wide eyes. "I…I didn't hear you come in," he said lamely.

"I got that. What were you doing with the candle?"

Behn looked at the candle as though it would come up with an excuse for him and then he glanced back at Valentina. Here was his opportunity to tell Valentina everything. If he chose to lie now, it would jeopardize his credibility when he got around to telling her the truth later. He took a deep breath and said, "I think you should shut the door and sit down with me. I've found some things out about our mom and where we came from."

Valentina's eyebrows came down over her eyes as she scowled at him. She followed his instructions and shut the door, but she was slower to go over to sit down. Her mind was thinking furiously about how Behn could have found anything out. All he ever did was go to school and then spend the afternoons tutoring Juila.

What she had witnessed as she stood at his door had nothing to do with family discoveries. Valentina wondered if Behn were using a deflection technique so he would not have to answer what he had been doing with the candle.

She sat down on the bed facing Behn and crossed her arms. "This explanation had better be good, Behn."

Behn faced his sister, but kept his gaze down on the comforter while he tried to figure out where to start. He really needed Val to believe him. It felt like he would only have one opportunity to convince her or else she would shut him out and never hear the truth. The fact that she really did not want to know about their mom since they had such a loving home with their adoptive family complicated it even further.

Finally nodding as he decided what to say Behn looked up at his sister. "Have you ever wondered why we can't take off our necklaces?"

Clearly Valentina had not expected Behn to change the subject. She shook her head in confusion and asked, "What are you talking about, Behn? I want to know what you were doing with the candle!"

"I'm getting to that! Just answer my question about the necklaces."

Valentina blew out a breath with frustration and replied, "You know that's something which has always bothered me, and also the fact that nobody ever really seems to notice we're wearing them in the first place."

"Exactly! We always thought of our necklaces as a gift to us from our mom, but that's only part of the truth. They were actually given to us by a wise-woman at our mother's request. The necklaces give us access to the elemental energy of the land."

"Wait! What are you talking about? What is a wise-woman?" Even as Valentina asked her questions she was starting to have a memory emerge regarding the strange title.

"Let me show you something I've learned to do with the help of my necklace," Behn said. He concentrated on the first skill he had learned and produced a palm-sized sphere of energy above his outstretched hand.

Valentina hastily moved backward on the bed as she stared in amazement at the sphere which had not been there just the moment before. She looked up at Behn's face, but could not make herself say anything.

Behn took this as a good sign and moved the ball of light around the room beside the bed. He was careful to maintain impeccable control of the energy. When he believed Valentina had seen enough he carefully drew the energy back into his birth crystal where it disappeared. He felt a tingle go through him as the elemy returned to the earth.

"What. Was. That?"

"That was a demonstration of some of the things we learned from our mother before she sent us away. Try to think past your fear and astonishment and remember us sitting around a small wooden table with Jon and our mom. We each did what I showed you and when we were done, our mom clapped her hands, smiled, and told us she knew we could do it. Try to remember, Val! This is really important." He stopped talking and leaned forward to show his sister how much this meant to him for her to recall the memory.

It was hard for Valentina to dispute the evidence he had shown her, but for him to say she had done something similar when she was a little kid? No way! She would never forget something so amazing. She was ready to tell him he was mistaken when she suddenly did remember. The scene appeared in her head and she gasped in astonishment.

Behn had been watching his sister's expression. He could tell the exact moment when she believed him. This was going to be easier because she had the memory of their mom back.

"Behn, how did you find out about this? What else do you remember?"

"I remember everything, Val. Juila has been helping me to recall it all."

"Juila? Did you tell her about us? How could she help you?"

"I told you I was going to talk to her about us. She's been training me to use my birth crystal." He picked up the pendant and admired the silver tree with its smoky grey crystals for leaves.

"Okay, now I'm officially confused. How could Juila teach you the things we learned from our mom when we were little? You're not making any sense, Behn."

"She can teach me because she's from the same place we are. She and her family are going to help us find our mom, Val. Isn't that great?"

"What do you mean she's from the same place we came from? I thought she has been living in South Africa. Somehow I doubt that's where we're from, Behn."

Behn could not help but laugh at his sister's line of thinking. He answered, "No, we're not from South Africa and neither is she. We're all from a place called Tuala. Does that ring any bells? Can you hear our mom saying the phrase 'what on Tuala'?"

Valentina rested her chin on her hand as she leaned forward. There were so many thoughts swirling through her brain she was having a hard time concentrating on any one detail. Finally, she did recognize the phrase and she nodded her head in agreement. "Where is Tuala? Is it very far from here?"

Behn chuckled at the understatement. This part was going to be tricky since Val was always so practical. "Yes, you could say it's a world away. Literally."

"Behn, please stop being so cryptic. Where is it?"

"I just told you. Tuala is another world. The way I understand it, Tuala and Earth coexist on different planes of reality."

Valentina laughed out loud and said, "Oh, Behn, you got me. I thought you were being serious!"

Behn looked at her with a serious expression and said, "It is true, Val. Tuala is where we're from. We are not from Earth. Our mother sent us to Earth to protect us. I'm not sure what she was protecting us from, but I mean to find out when we locate her."

Valentina stopped laughing as Behn kept talking. She realized he actually believed what he was saying. "What has Juila been telling you? Maybe I should have a little chat with Juila for filling your head with such lies. And here I thought she was such a nice girl!" She started to get up from the bed when Behn caught her hand and pulled her back down. She looked at his hand and then back up to his face.

"She didn't lie, Val. Let me show you what else we can do with our necklaces. Maybe after you see more, you'll start to believe me."

He jumped up from the bed and ran from the room. He was going to have to hurry if he were going to keep Val from leaving his room. A half minute later he returned with a glass of water. In his rush, he had sloshed water everywhere, but he could not worry about that right now. He set the glass down next to the candle on his nightstand.

Before he showed her what he could do with the water he created a breeze which blew her hair away from her face. Her hands flew up and caught her hair up to keep it from tangling. "That was me creating a breeze. You felt it, right?"

"Duh! What's the water for?" Val asked. Her interest was piqued. She had never seen her brother act like this before.

"That's next. Okay, watch the water in the glass and tell me what you see in a second."

"I don't see anything but water, Behn. This is ridiculous!" Even as the words were coming out of her mouth she thought she could see bubbles forming on the sides of the clear glass. She leaned forward and stared in disbelief as the bubbles became larger until all of it was moving as though it were boiling. She asked, "Is that water boiling?"

"Yes. Now watch this!"

Valentina did watch. Slowly the water stopped boiling and the outside of the glass started to turn white as if it were getting colder. Within another minute the water was a solid block of ice. She stood up from the bed and went over to the nightstand. She picked up the glass and confirmed it was freezing cold. "Behn, what have you done? How are you able to do this?"

"It's not anything special in Tuala. In fact all kids learn how to do this by the time they're in the second grade. If you want, you can come over to Juila's house with me and they can teach you how to do it, too." Behn was excited to see his sister had expressed an interest in what he had learned. Unfortunately, he had read her wrong. She was not eager to learn, she was scared of what Behn had learned to do.

"Behn, you can't be doing this! What if our parents find out? What if the kids at school find out? They'll call us freaks and then we'll never have a moment of peace at our new school. Don't you remember how bad it was at our last school? All of the kids made fun of us for being adopted. I can't go through that again, Behn. I won't!" Valentina set the glass down on the table with a loud thud. She crossed her arms and scowled down at her brother.

"Jeez, Val! What is wrong with you? I tell you we are special and that we can do amazing things because we're from Tuala, and all you can talk about is fitting in at school? Who cares what those kids think! We're almost adults and then we won't ever see them again. I'm trying to tell you that we have unlimited power with our necklaces and you don't even care!"

"Behn, you are going to stop seeing Juila. If you don't then I'll tell our parents you're having sex with her!"

"What? We've never had sex. Good grief, I've only ever kissed her." Behn had no idea what Val was talking about. It never even occurred to him she would lie about his relationship to their parents.

"Do you think our parents will believe you if I tell them otherwise? I'd tell them anything to keep you from going over there for her to feed you full of her own lies."

"They're not lies, Val. They took me to Tuala and I visited the house where we lived with Mom."

Now Behn had her attention. She had seen their old house in her dreams many times, but she could only vaguely remember any details. "What are you saying?"

"I'm telling you the truth. They took me to Tuala and I found our old home. They told me it's called the Roanoke Colony. All of the people were gone so I couldn't ask anyone where our mom had gone. Riccan's dad is going to keep searching for our mom." Behn stopped talking since he could not think of anything else which might convince his sister he was telling the truth.

"Roanoke Colony?" she whispered. "You had me look up that term a couple weeks ago. Is that when you supposedly went there?"

"Yes."

"Are you saying you think those people who disappeared in the 1500's are our family?"

"No, I think we are the descendants of those people. I think they accidentally found a way to go between the worlds and ended up in Tuala without knowing how to get back to Earth."

"Wow, Behn. I really think you've lost your marbles. I can't take any more of this nonsense right now." She stomped out of the room and slammed the door behind her.

Behn knew when to shut up. He had planted all of the seeds and now he just had to wait for some of them to germinate. Even though his sister was mad, she would keep going over everything he had said and done. Eventually, she would come to the same conclusion he had: they were not from this world.

VALENTINA WENT DIRECTLY to her room after leaving her brother. She desperately wanted to believe he was delusional except she could tell there were kernels of truth. Even as she fought to keep the memories from coming she was recalling the lessons with their mother at the kitchen table.

She slammed her fist down onto the mattress of her bed. She did not want to be different! She was so tired of being teased by everyone! Worst of all, she hated that she cared so much what other people thought of her and her brothers.

She hated herself for yelling at her brother and threatening him. He had done nothing wrong and she had treated him as if he had. She had even told him he was crazy. How could she be such a terrible sister?

Finally, she realized she was jealous. She did not like the idea that Juila had been so instrumental in helping him to remember their past. There had been so many times where Behn and she had talked about all of their dreams and what they thought they recalled from 'before.' They always referred to the time prior to their adoption as being 'before.'

What if she were to go and see Juila on her own? Maybe she could get to the bottom of this after all. There had to be some other explanation about where they were from other than that they were from a different world; the whole idea was just preposterous.

With her decision made, she got up from her bed and calmly walked back to Behn's room. She did not even bother to knock. She opened the door and leaned into the room. "I want to go with you to Juila's house tomorrow. I'm going to get to the bottom of this!" She did not wait to hear his reply, she simply shut the door and walked back to her room.

What did she think she was going to accomplish over at Juila's house?

Was she just feeding into Behn's delusion, or should she say Juila's delusion? In any event, she was going to sort it all out until she was satisfied with the outcome.

If they really were from a different world, then it would not matter what anyone from here said about them. They could return to Tuala and start their lives over. She really liked the sound of that until she realized she would have to leave her adoptive parents. She loved them as though they were her birth-parents. They had kept them all together when the orphanage had wanted to separate them. Their generosity was a debt which could never be repaid.

She felt like a traitor for even considering the idea of leaving. While she knew she would not spend the rest of her life living with them, she always thought she would at least live near them.

She wished she had shut Behn's door and never confronted him about what he had been doing. If she had minded her own business, she could keep living her idyllic life without any inner conflict.

Unbidden, she could feel tears threatening because now she was faced with the idea of losing yet another family. First she had lost her mother and now, when her life was back on a good track, she was probably going to lose this family when they found out who she really was. This was the worst day of her life!

CHAPTER 19

Alena wondered if Bryon were going to go back to work or come home after dropping Amanda off at the landing site. She knew something had happened with her husband and she was dying to know what it was. Just as she was about to give up hope, Alena heard the front door open and close. She hurried from the kitchen to confront Bryon only to be disappointed to see it was not him at all.

Justan, Andera, and Kyelon trooped through the foyer with their school bags in hand. They waved welcome to their mother and continued on into the living room. They did not notice their mother's frustrated expression since she immediately hid it from them with a smile of greeting. Of course she loved her children and was always glad to see them, but right now something big was going on and she was not in the know.

Instead of joining them in the living room, Alena continued on to the front door and went outside. Since Bryon had walked to work today, he would either return in the company telepod or he would walk home after returning the transport. Either way, he would end up outside their house and not in the garage. She decided she was too anxious to remain cooped up in the house and she began pulling weeds from the front yard to keep busy.

As she had suspected, Bryon had taken the vehicle back to work and now he was walking swiftly up the sidewalk to their house. Alena brushed off her palms onto her pants as she stood up to go greet him.

He smiled as he saw her outside. Bryon knew exactly what she was doing and knew her mind was definitely not on beautifying the front yard. His pace quickened until Alena came up beside him as she turned and walked with him.

"What happened? Don't keep me in suspense!" Alena grabbed her husband's arm in her excitement.

"It's not something which I can just talk about. Let's go into my office and I'll show you what happened with Amanda today." Bryon smirked at Alena's puzzled expression. Very seldom could he surprise her and he was certain this was not something which she would ever guess.

Alena cocked her head as she tried to figure out what could possibly be in his office which she did not already know about. She tugged his arm to speed him along.

Bryon gladly went along with his wife. He could not remember a time when he had felt this happy. There was something about his samara which had changed him. He could not put his finger on it exactly, maybe Alena could help him to understand what he was feeling. "Have the kids gotten home yet?"

"Yes, they just arrived about five minutes ago."

Bryon frowned slightly. He was not so sure the children should be in the house when he showed the crystal to his wife. It may just be he was being paranoid, but he could not be sure how the power of the samara could affect his family. "Maybe we could have them go to the marketplace or over to Tana's house."

Alena cocked her head sideways and asked, "Is whatever you have in your office dangerous?"

"I'm not sure. I just want us to keep it between us for now. If the kids are at home, one of them might come bursting into the office and see something which maybe they shouldn't know about."

"Okay. There are a few things I need from the market. I'll send them on their way," she replied as they reached the front door and walked inside. The kids were still in the living room when Alena came around the corner. "I'd like for the three of you to go and get me some items for dinner."

Justan looked up in surprise and teased, "It sounds like you're trying to get rid of us. What's going on?"

Alena laughed nervously and replied, "Wouldn't that be just the thing! Your father just got home and he's hungry. Now, you kids need to get yourselves to the marketplace and buy me the ingredients for glawlets. Andera, you remember what goes in them, right?"

Andera nodded even as Kyelon jumped up from the floor eagerly. His favorite meal was glawlets with krumplis and sweetened foxl gravy.

Alena went to the kitchen to get a few taj to give to the kids so they could buy the items. She came back immediately and handed the money to Andera. "Go ahead and get yourselves some treats while you're there."

The three kids smiled as Andera put the money carefully in her tunic pocket. They were already planning which sweets they were going to get. After a flurry of noise and activity, the children trooped out the front door.

Alena wasted no time in turning to Bryon and saying, "Let's go to your office. Who knows how long the kids will be gone."

Bryon chuckled at Alena's eagerness even as he turned to go to his office. He did not even have to turn to see if Alena were following him. He could practically feel her breathing down his neck in her excitement. Bryon walked around his desk and said to Alena, "Go ahead and sit down. I have a feeling you're going to want to be seated when you see what I have in my desk."

Alena complied immediately and wondered what could possibly be so important.

Without hesitating, Bryon opened the drawer and shoved the items off of the top of the towel wrapped bundle. He picked it up and set it on his desk with a flourish and a sense of mystery. Before he exposed the contents he looked up at Alena and remained watching her expression as he pulled the towel away to reveal the skull shaped crystal.

Alena jerked back in her chair and looked up to Bryon with wide, scared eyes. "Bryon! Where did you get that? Why do you have it?"

He was thankful to see he was not the only one to have a natural fear of the object. Now he had to convince his wife that it was actually okay to possess. Without touching the stone, Bryon sat down in his own chair and rested his chin on the steeple of his fingers. "It's my samara, Alena. Amanda had me go back to the cave where I traveled to Earth when I was a teenager. We brought the skull out of the cave and she asked me to bring her here to our house. She convinced me to touch it, and I can assure you this samara was meant for me to own."

"Is that what it's called: a samara?" Alena was rapidly processing what her husband was telling her. She still had no idea what significance this terrifying object would play in their lives and she was not sure she wanted to know.

"Yes. Do you remember the legends we talked about years ago when I first told you about my journey to Earth?"

"Yes. Are you saying those legends are true?"

"Completely true. There are thirteen of these out there somewhere. Amanda said she and Riccan have three of them at their home on Earth. I think we might want to help Amanda locate the other nine of them if we can."

"Right," Alena said with a great amount of uncertainty. She was not sure she was pleased to have one of them in her house, let alone go about the countryside looking for more of them.

"Alena, I know you are scared right now. I was utterly terrified when Amanda first said we were going to go get it out of the cave. As you can see, I'm fine with it now."

"What made you change your mind?"

"Amanda told me that each of the samaras is keyed to belong to one person. She has convinced me that this one is keyed to me. When I touched it, I somehow felt different."

"What do you mean my different?"

"I can't really explain it. Maybe you should connect with my life-line and tell me if you can see if anything has changed."

Perhaps for the first time in her life, since becoming a wise-woman, she was nervous about touching another person's life-line. If Bryon's were connected with the samara now, then she had no idea what kind of power to expect when she touched upon it. She had to do as he asked and she nodded assent. Very slowly and purposefully, Alena crafted a protective weaving around her own self before she allowed her energy to move across to the spark of life she associated with Bryon.

As soon as she realized there was no danger to herself, she followed her senses to explore. Bryon's life-line was definitely larger in diameter before, as if he were now more grounded than he ever had been. The colors were slightly more vibrant, but other than that, it was still her very own Bryon at the core. She withdrew her own energy, unraveled the protection from herself, and returned all of it to the earth before opening her eyes.

"I see what you mean," she answered finally. "Essentially you are the same, just more intense. I guess you'd say you were more deeply connected to the elemy than you were before. Does that make sense?"

"Exactly. I knew you'd be able to explain it better than I!" Bryon grinned at his wife.

"What happened? Did you touch the samara?"

"Amanda insisted. It took everything I had to force myself to put my fingers on it, but then I did and I saw all sorts of visions. There were so many people and places which flashed through my mind I couldn't even begin to explain what I saw. It was amazing, Alena. I can't wait for you to get your own samara so you'll know what I experienced."

Alena shuddered at the very idea. She tried to remain clinical in her approach to this new turn of events. "How long did the visions last?"

Bryon chuckled as he said, "It felt like only a few seconds, but Amanda had me look at my timepiece. Almost three hours had passed. Can you believe it?"

"What did Amanda do all the while you were enthralled with your samara?"

For the first time Bryon looked confused. He had not considered how the time would have dragged by for Amanda. Surely it had been quite boring for her to watch him while he did nothing but stare into his samara. "I think she just sat there and watched me. When I came back to myself, she was sitting in the same chair you are. It didn't appear she had moved."

Alena thought about Bryon's statement and wondered to herself if Amanda had been able to see what Bryon had been seeing. When she met with Amanda again, she would ask her about it. Until that time, there was nothing more for her to think about. Her thoughts were interrupted by Bryon clearing his throat to capture her attention.

"I think we should do as we promised Amanda and make a list pertaining to the birth crystal colors of each person who attended the meeting with Jehoban," Bryon said as he pulled out a piece of paper and a pen. He wrote down Elder Debbon's name and then looked up at Alena with a questioning expression.

"Let's see, when I was in my wise-woman training with Elder Debbon as my instructor, I seem to recall his birth crystal was apricot with an iridescent moon. When his wife, Chelesa, joined the class I think I remember hers being an aqua green."

Bryon jotted down the colors Alena remembered and then wrote down Captain Ahn, Barla, and Rasa's names. "Have you ever seen any of their crystals?"

Alena cocked her head to the side as she considered his question. In all of the time she had spent with Barla while working on the orphan project, not only had she never seen her display a birth crystal, she had also never seen her use any skills associated with one. "I guess I don't know what color Barla's is, but Captain Ahn's is dark grey, like storm clouds, and Rasa's is clear except for two small stones which are a light blue. I remember the sun shining on it during our meeting and I thought it was strange that two of the stones would be a different color."

Bryon left a blank space next to Barla's name and duly noted her husband and daughter's colors. He grinned across the table at his wife and said, "I guess we don't need to write down my own color since I have my samara." He carefully wrote down his wife's name and lavender for the color of her birth crystal. "Do you think we need to find out about Elder Daven and Nena? It would seem to be easier for Amanda to follow up on those two since they are her husband's parents," Bryon asked as he wrote down each of their names and left blank spaces next to them.

"We can see if there's a way for us to find out. If it doesn't work out for us, then Amanda can ask her husband. I'm sure he would know his own parents' colors," Alena replied.

"I guess that's all we can do on this for right now," Bryon said as he set the pen and shoved the paper away from him on the desktop. He looked over at his samara and grinned like a foolish schoolboy.

"Do you think we should tell the people from the meeting about your samara? It seems like a pretty significant discovery."

Bryon shook his head and answered, "Amanda asked me to keep this to myself for the time being. She wants to check out a few things before letting anyone know about it."

Alena nodded even though she was not sure it was the best advice.

However, Jehoban had told them to trust Amanda's instincts. She nodded again as she reaffirmed the decision. "We should probably put that away since the kids could come back at any moment from the marketplace." Alena believed her husband's admission of the crystal belonging to him, but it did not mean she wanted to be staring at the grinning skull.

Bryon chuckled even as he pulled the towel up over the clear crystal. He returned it to its new home in his desk drawer and he moved several paper items back over the top of it. Even as he was closing the drawer, they could hear the sound of the front door slamming.

They stood up at the same time and smiled at one another with conspiratorial grins as they left the office with Alena in the lead. Each of the children carried a bag as they marched into the kitchen. With their backs to their parents, they never even noticed them coming out of the office and Alena was thankful for it.

AMANDA FLEW straight home from the meeting with Bryon. She landed the telepod in the garage and went into the house. Even though she had not been the one to commune with the samara, she felt exhausted nonetheless. She headed upstairs to take a long, hot bath.

As she was soaking in the luxuriant bubbles, she smiled at her achievement of the day. She had joined yet another person with his own samara. There were only nine left to be discovered. They already had a lead on one more with news of Behn's mother.

Now they just had to find out where she had disappeared. When they had gone to the Roanoke Colony with Behn, they had discovered the settlement to have been abandoned. She had no idea why they would have left, but she knew with everyone doing research on it, they were certain to figure it out in short order.

She put Behn's mother out of her mind and focused again on how she was going to get Neal home. When Alena had asked her about whether or not Neal wanted to come home, it had taken her aback. She had never even considered him wanting to stay. What if he had made a life or a family while he had been there? He might be happy in Tuala like her Aunt Barla. Who was she to say he had to come back?

She had almost convinced herself to leave him alone when she remembered one important detail: Neal's addiction to resh. No matter what his circumstances were in Tuala, he was being held captive by the drug. She had learned enough about its addictive nature to shudder at the idea of leaving him to suffer through a life of addiction. No, she was going to bring Neal home. If he wanted to go back to Tuala after seeing his parents, Amanda would gladly take him back.

Her bath had gone cold. She got dressed and went down the back stairs to go into Riccan's study. She wanted to send a message to wise-woman Copa to try to arrange a time to go and see her.

CHAPTER 20

Valentina did not waste any time going over to Juila's house the next day after school. She did have to wait at the gate to be let in since it was not coded to open for her car. She seldom drove anyway since both of her brothers also drove. Eventually the gate swung open and she sped up the curving road and parked by the front door.

She did not have to knock on the door since Juila was already standing in the opening. "What brings you here, Val?"

"I need to talk to you about my brother." She did not see the need to say anything further as she walked over to entrance.

"Come in," Juila said as she stood to the side to let Valentina enter the house. "Do you want to talk downstairs or up in my room?"

"Your room would be better," she replied.

Juila took the lead and walked up the stairs and into her room. She offered for Valentina to take a seat in the sitting area of her room.

Valentina picked a spot and waited for Juila to also sit before she began. "Why are you filling my brother's head full of lies? We've already had a hard enough time in life with our mother abandoning us. Behn has placed his trust and our future in your hands."

It was the last thing Juila expected to hear and was at a loss for words. Finally she answered, "I've never lied to Behn. What are you talking about?"

"Tuala."

"Tuala is real and it also happens to be where you all come from as well as my own family. My parents are trying to locate your mom and when they do, she'll tell you the same thing."

Juila had been so convincing in her speech, Valentina could easily see how Behn had been taken in by her story. She simply stared at Juila and could think of nothing to say to refute her.

"What's in this for you, Juila?"

"Nothing! That's why it wouldn't make sense for me to lie about it. Think about it, Val, why would I risk exposing my whole family's existence here on Earth just to impress my boyfriend?"

Val paused to consider Juila's argument and then reached into her shirt collar to pull her pendant out for Juila to see. "What did you tell Behn this was called?"

"A birth crystal."

"Why would they call it that when it obviously has many crystals?" She looked down on the pendant to see the twisted metal making up the tree trunk and branches. The branches contained many crystals. Hers were mostly clear with some gold and black flecks in them. Sometimes she thought they changed color depending on the light.

Juila lifted her shoulders as she also stared at Valentina's necklace and said, "I don't know, it's just what they're called. The crystals are your birthright and your connection with the energy in the earth. If you want, I can give you a demonstration."

Valentina immediately shook her head and replied, "Behn already showed me the tricks you taught him. I can't see how they can be of any benefit, but I can see how they could get us into a lot of trouble."

"I'd have to agree with you on your last point. Behn has only learned the very basics. Jena and I can do just about anything we set our minds to using the power from our crystals. I really wish you'd let me show you."

Against Val's better judgement, she found herself curious. "Fine! Show me something which will amaze me!"

Juila took only one moment to consider when she grabbed Valentina's arm in her hand and translated them both down to the library. She had used a considerable amount of power to make the transfer as fast as possible.

No sooner had they appeared out of nowhere in the library, Jena came rushing in and asked, "What just happened, Juila? I felt you use a lot of power!"

Juila waited to answer her sister since she was staring pointedly at Valentina.

"Where are we?" Valentina asked with a quiver of fear evident in her voice.

"We are in my father's library downstairs from my room."

Val nodded silently. She had to admit to herself she had asked for a dramatic demonstration and Juila did not disappoint. Still, she could not see how this power would have any use to them on Earth other than to get them in trouble.

"Do you believe me now?" Juila asked into the silence.

"I believe you know something about power. I still don't know what to make of your tale about Tuala. I guess we'll have to find our mom just to get this whole thing straightened out." Valentina saw there was a chair behind her and she sank down into it. Her legs felt rubbery and she was quite shaken by what had just transpired.

Jena looked from Valentina to Juila and asked again, "What's going on, Juila? What have you done?"

Juila turned to her sister and silently spoke into her mind. *Val asked for a demonstration of what we can do with our birth crystals. She wanted something dramatic to make her believe it was more than a parlor trick. I translated us both down here from my room.*

Jena sat down next to Valentina as she heard her sister's explanation. She simply nodded to let her sister know she had heard her. Against their parents' wishes, Jena rapidly scanned Valentina's mind to see where she was at in her understanding of what had just happened. Much to her amazement, Val was already trying to figure out a way for it to be yet another trick. Jena spoke gently, "We haven't shown you any tricks, Val. We are showing you your heritage."

"How did you know what I was thinking? Can you read my mind, too?" Val's eyes got big as she glanced swiftly from Jena up to Juila who was still standing where they had first translated into the room.

"Yes," both girls replied at the same time.

"Seriously? You can read minds?" She grabbed the arms of the chair in panic.

"We don't do it very often here on Earth. Our parents asked us not to.

I just peeked into your mind to see if you were going to be okay with everything Juila has told you. I'm sorry for invading your privacy." Jena realized now what her parents had been trying to shield her from.

Val was trying to decide if she should leave or stay and hear more of what they knew.

Jena spoke softly, "I wish you'd stay so we could answer any questions you might have."

"Are you still in my head? Get out!" Valentina was starting to get angry even through her fear.

"No, Val. I was watching your face. It was easy to tell you were trying to decide what you should do. I promise I won't read your mind again unless you ask." Jena felt terrible for having invaded her privacy in the first place. Val was one of their best friends and she did not want to jeopardize their relationship.

Val searched Jena's face to try to tell if she were telling the truth. Finally she realized she was being a bit dramatic with this whole situation. She had come over to their house for answers and now she was thinking of bolting because it was not going as she had planned. With a deep breath to relax herself, she finally said, "Okay, I believe you, Jena."

Juila hurriedly sat down in the chair next to Valentina and asked, "What questions do you have for us? We want you to know everything, but we also recognize it has to be at your own pace."

Val considered both of the girls' statements. She did have a lot of questions, but she was not sure if she were ready for the answers. One idea did come to mind readily and she asked, "How come your mother looks so much like our own?"

"She does?" Juila asked with surprise. She looked over at her sister and raised an eyebrow in question.

"That's interesting," Jena spoke quietly, mostly to herself. She filed the information away for analyzing later. There had to be some significance to it since not much seemed to be coincidental anymore.

"If your family is from Tuala, why are you here in Florida?" Valentina asked Juila.

"Well, our mom is from Florida. She's what you would call an adopted Tualan. She has been accepted by Jehoban as one of His own since He gave her a birth crystal. I, Jena, and our dad were actually born in Tuala."

Now it was Valentina's turn to be surprised. She had thought their whole family had been from Tuala, now she had learned their mom was not. "Who is Jehoban?"

"He is God. He lives in Tuala."

Val chuckled at their matter-of-fact statement about where God lived. "Really?"

"Yes. We lived with Him on Acaim. He asked for us to study with Him."

"So, you're saying you both lived with God and He taught you how to use your birth crystals?" Val thought this story was getting a bit far-fetched.

"Yes. I know it sounds incredible, but I promise it's all true."

"So the things you learned are the same things you're teaching Behn? What good is it all? I mean, what can you do with it?"

"The only limit we've found is our imagination. If we can think it, we can do it."

"That sounds dangerous if it were to get into the wrong hands. What good will it do you?"

"Here on Earth, we've been able to keep Sofia from being in several accidents," Jena put in hastily.

Val laughed. "I've been in the car with Sofia, and I bet you were very busy keeping her safe."

"We thought it was our duty until she learned how to drive better," Juila agreed.

"How else can it help you?"

"We learned memorization techniques which are very useful with school." Jena looked over at Juila and they both nodded in agreement.

"When we're at home, we can use our skills to make daily life much easier. We can create an entire meal just by thought. We are able to clean up the whole mess with just a thought as well." Juila picked up the explanation.

"Wow that could be useful. But really what is the point of it?" Valentina really could not understand why they would want to be so different.

"It is a gift from Jehoban. We use it in our everyday lives in Tuala. It can be used to heal people almost instantaneously. We are also able to communicate across vast distances with just a thought. Mostly it makes our lives more convenient and safer. The crystals help to keep us from harm."

"Okay, I can see where the healing would be helpful and also the ability to keep you from harm, but the rest just seems superfluous." Valentina did not know why she was still humoring these girls with this subject.

"I guess we're not explaining it correctly if you can't see the value in it. Behn remembered your mother teaching all of you to learn how to use your birth crystals. Do you have any memory of that?" Jena asked.

Valentina wanted to be able to deny it, but she did recall something about it with her mother. Slowly she nodded, but she still could not see why she would want to learn the things her brother had shown her. She did just fine without any parlor tricks. "So if everyone can do anything they put their mind to, why do you need each other?"

"While that may be true, not everyone is as skilled with their crystal use. Just as with any other talent, people have different levels of ability and desire to learn. Some only learn the first ten basic lessons, which we were teaching to Behn. Some people never even achieve those levels because they just don't have the aptitude for it. Other individuals have certain areas of interest, such as healing, where they learn everything associated with that art. Then there are Jehoban's students, such as we two, where we are encouraged to learn as far as our imaginations will take us."

"What will you do with all of your abilities?" Valentina was beginning to see what the girls were referring to with the birth crystals. Just as fingerprints, people were unique in their talents.

"We still haven't decided, but I think I'd like to become an Elder," Jena declared.

Juila could not help but smile at her sister's ambition. She knew only men became Elders, but who was she to say Jena could not be the first woman Elder.

Valentina turned to Juila and asked, "What about you? What will you do when you go back home?"

"I really don't know. I'm sure we'll have many anons, years as you call them, to pick an occupation."

"Only if we continue with post-study," Jena reminded her.

"What's post-study?" Val looked from one girl to the other with a confused expression.

"The equivalent of your idea of college," Jena declared.

"Does that mean you'll be going back to Tuala once you've graduated from high school?"

"Possibly. We've technically already completed high school in Tuala. We just wanted to meet kids our own age so school seemed like the best avenue."

"That's terrible!" Val could not imagine going back to high school once she had completed it. These girls must really want to make friends, she thought to herself. "So you're saying you've already done all the classes you're taking right now?"

"No, that's what's been so wonderful. We don't have anything like your science classes or any other languages. Those classes have been very enlightening," Jena enthused.

Juila also added, "We've enjoyed the history, health, and American government classes. They've given us great insight to what the people here consider important to know."

"So you're saying everyone speaks the same language? That would be convenient." Valentina was really starting to become interested in the Tuala the girls were describing to her. Maybe someday she would go there with them. Suddenly she asked, "How do you travel between here and Tuala? I can't imagine there's public transportation between the two places."

Juila chuckled as she replied, "No, definitely not. However, there are places called Ascension Gates which allow travel between the two places. Those gates are monitored and guarded by the Elders. We use a telepod to travel between, however."

"What's a telepod?"

"You'd probably call it a spaceship. For us, it's just a normal mode of transportation similar to your airplanes. The telepod is much more efficient and quieter..." Jena explained.

"Not to mention a telepod is much faster," Juila interrupted. "If either of our parents were home, we'd show you their telepods."

"Wait! Are you're saying you guys keep spaceships here at the house? Where? In the garage?" She laughed as though she were making a joke.

"Where else would you keep your vehicle?" Jena asked seriously.

Valentina stopped laughing as she realized the telepods *were* kept in the garage. "Seriously? You two are pulling my leg!"

"If, by pulling your leg, you mean we are joking, then we are not. Stick around for about another hour and you can see for yourself," Jena replied.

"What do they do in Tuala?"

"Our dad works there at the Telepod Engineering Company. Our mom is doing some research over there and meeting with various people," Jena replied. She did not want to go into too much detail about their mom's journeys into Tuala since she was working on fulfilling the prophecy.

Valentina remained silent while she took in everything that had been told to her since arriving at the Stel house. She had come over to tell them to quit telling her brother lies and here she was asking them questions about the very place which seemed make-believe. She realized in that moment she actually did believe the girls were telling the truth.

Because she had made her decision to believe them she wanted to know everything. The first step would be to wait for either of their parents to come home so she could see their telepod. "I would like to stay until your mom gets home. I'd like to see her telepod."

Juila nodded approval, stood up from her chair, and said, "Let's get something to eat in the kitchen while we wait."

Both girls nodded agreement and Valentina smiled at the twins as they left the library. They walked through the living room and sat down in the high chairs at the island.

"Would you like to try some food from Tuala?" Juila asked.

Valentina nodded. She wondered if it would be something she would remember from her childhood. If it were, then she would have another proof of the girls' story.

Juila did not even have to think about what she would prepare. Instantly, three plates of scrambled eggs and fried foxl appeared in front of them, complete with silverware and glasses of pika juice.

Valentina sat back in surprise at the suddenness of the arrival of the food. While the girls had told her it was possible, the actuality of the food appearing before her was another matter. She leaned forward to smell the food as well as to look at it better. "What is it?"

Juila told her even as she pulled her own plate forward.

Valentina watched in amazement as the two girls bowed their heads and closed their eyes. She could only imagine they were praying. For some reason, she had not thought them to be very religious since they had come from Tuala.

Juila opened her eyes, picked up her fork, and plunged it into the scrambled eggs.

Valentina took a more cautious approach. She picked up the glass of juice and looked down into it. She smelled it and thought it was almost like orange juice. As soon as she took a sip, she realized it was nothing like orange juice. It was both sweeter and tangier than she expected.

She pulled the plate closer and picked up the fork. Using the utensil to point at the meat, she asked, "What is this?"

"Fried foxl," Jena replied as she speared a bite of the meat and shoved it into her mouth.

"What exactly is it?"

"It looks like a combination of a cow and a sheep with long hair. We use foxl in just about everything we eat. Try it, you'll like it," said Jena with an encouraging look.

Valentina picked up some and brought it close to her nose to smell it. Something about the scent seemed to remind her of something. Maybe it was a childhood memory. She put it into her mouth and suddenly the memory came back, full force.

She and her brothers were sitting at a wooden table with their mother. They were laughing at some joke one of the boys had made. Their mother put breakfast on the table and she served them each their meager portion of food. They were having scrambled eggs and fried foxl just the same as she was eating right now.

Valentina closed her eyes and savored both the flavor of the food as well as the memories which had returned. More and more scenes from her past began to flood her mind. She could feel tears of joy and sadness forming in her eyes. Now was not the time to cry. She picked up the glass of juice and took a large swallow to help clear her pallet and control her thoughts.

A noise came from behind them and they all turned to see what it was. Amanda walked across the living room with a smile on her face. "Did you guys make food and not invite me?"

Juila laughed and replied, "We didn't even know you were home. Where have you been?"

"I was upstairs taking a bath and then I was in your father's study. What are you guys up to?"

"Valentina has asked to see your telepod. We were waiting for you to get home. I thought you'd be another hour or so." Juila was glad her mother had decided to come home early on this day in particular. She wanted to make sure Valentina was thoroughly convinced of her heritage before she went home.

"I take it Behn finally talked to you?" Amanda raised her eyebrows as she asked Valentina.

"Yes, but it's taken me a lot longer to accept it. Would you mind letting me see your telepod?"

"Seeing is believing," Amanda said jauntily. "Once you're finished eating, we can go out together." Amanda reached over and picked up a hunk of foxl from Juila's plate and winked at her as she put it into her mouth.

CHAPTER 21

Rasa was anxious to get back into the swing of things with Elder Wilken. There was less than a week before the convocation for her to learn everything she could. She wanted to demonstrate her ability to handle the position if any of the Elders were to question her before they made their decision.

Elder Wilken often scoffed at her for wanting to learn it all so fast. He had no reservations about his choice of a successor. He had been in his job long enough to know a quality person. If any of the Elders even tried to dissuade him from pursuing this course, then they were going to have a fight on their hands. Not only had Jehoban recommended Rasa for the position, but he also knew she was the best candidate for his post.

Rasa was surprised with Elder Wilken called an end to the day. It was only lunchtime and she was certain there had been several people waiting to discuss a matter with the Elder. She followed him into his grand living room and sat down in her favorite chair.

"I wanted to take some time to talk with you, Rasa," he said as he sat in his own preferred chair overlooking the view outside.

There was a moment of activity as several maids came in and deposited a tea tray as well as a sweets tray. One maid poured them each a cup of hot steena tea while the other one set out small plates for them on which to put their selection of treats.

After they had helped themselves to the desserts, Rasa sat quietly while she waited for Elder Wilken to talk to her about whatever was on his mind. She wondered briefly if he had changed his mind and wanted to break it to her gently. Somehow, she could not convince herself that this would be the case. She had more confidence in her ability than to continue with that line of thinking.

Elder Wilken finally broke the silence. "Are you afraid the convocation won't accept my petition?"

"Yes."

"Why?"

"Because I'm a woman."

"Ah! So you think you need to prove yourself more because of it?"

"Don't you? If I make any mistakes, they'll call me out on it for sure. They'll say it's because I'm a woman and that I don't deserve to be in this post."

"Do you think Jehoban was wrong to send you here?"

Rasa's eyes widened in surprise. She had never doubted any decisions made by Jehoban before, yet she realized it was exactly what she had been doing for weeks now. She looked up at Elder Wilken and replied, "That's what I've been doing. I don't know what's gotten into me. He's always done His best for me. I've always known it to be true. Thank you, Elder Wilken, for making me see what you've known all along."

He smiled kindly at her. He knew it would not take much to get her back on the right track. She had spent so long on Acaim, she had started to take it for granted. Everything had come easily while she had remained there. Now she was starting to face adversity and it was a growing experience for her.

Rasa finally relaxed for the first time since she had returned to Manzanit. She picked up one of her favorite sweet treats and popped it into her mouth. She looked up into Elder Wilken's face and smiled in gratitude for the gift he had just given her.

Elder Wilken smiled back and raised his tea cup in a congratulatory toast before he took a sip of the hot liquid. His late anons were going to be pleasant because he had good company to share. Once again, he wondered why he had not sought out another wife before it was too late. He could have had this type of comradery all this time instead of remaining alone. He silently thanked Jehoban for sending Rasa to him. She was a perfect successor and companion.

⁓

SOFIA HAD OFTEN THOUGHT about the strange vehicle she had seen in the Stel's garage on the night of Jena and Juila's birthday. She had been told it was an engineering experiment for Riccan's work, but somehow she could not get the idea out of her head that it was something more. If it were to be such a secret then why had the whole family been going out to see it?

She looked over at Juila sitting in the passenger seat of her car and decided to ask her about it. Juila was her best friend, after all. Surely they would not have any secrets from one another. "How is your dad's experiment going?"

Juila looked at Sofia with a blank expression.

Sofia clarified by saying, "You know, that thing out in the garage."

Juila's eyebrows rose and she nodded her head, "Oh, it's going fine."

"What's it for and what is he going to do with it?"

"It's a new kind of aircraft. His work asked him to design it. I don't know what they're going to do with it." Juila sincerely hoped Sofia would let it go, she really did not want to have to erase the memory from her head.

"That's really cool. Does it fly? Have you flown in it?"

Juila rolled her eyes. She should have known Sofia would not give up. "Yes it flies, and yes I've flown in it."

"Can I go for a ride? What is he calling it?"

"I don't know if Dad would take a non-family member for a ride in it. He's calling it a telepod. Sofia, you know this is supposed to be a secret. We shouldn't even be talking about it right now."

"Why? Do you think my car is bugged?" Sofia rolled her eyes and laughed at Juila's paranoia.

Juila had to laugh as well and replied, "No, I don't think your car is bugged. However, I do know my father could get in big trouble if anybody found out that you knew about the telepod. Can we please not talk about this anymore?"

Sofia sighed. She supposed this was all she was going to find out about what she had seen. "Fine, I'll leave it alone for now. I might have more questions later, though!"

"You always do!" Juila teased her friend.

Sofia looked over at her friend and realized she had not told her everything. She did not know what it was right now, but eventually she would figure it out. Something big was going on and she wanted to be in on it, too.

Sofia decided to change the subject and asked, "Does Behn come over to your house after school every day?"

"Yes. Why?" Juila did not like how this conversation was going. If Sofia figured out there were a connection between Behn and the telepod, then they were all going to be in trouble.

"No reason, I just wondered. Does this mean that you two are getting pretty close?" Sofia kept her eyes on the road, hoping Juila would divulge more about her relationship with her boyfriend.

"I guess. You know we went bowling the other night, right?"

"Wow, bowling! You two must be serious then!" Sofia teased.

"Really? I didn't know it would mean that! I hope I didn't give Behn the wrong impression!" Juila answered seriously.

Sofia looked over at Juila and saw she was serious which made her start laughing even harder. Sometimes it was easy to forget she was from South Africa because she seemed so normal. Right now, Juila reminded her of just how different her upbringing had been. "I was just kidding, Juila. Bowling is a perfectly appropriate activity for a first or second date. There's no chance of physical activity when you're in a room full of old people throwing balls at pins!"

Juila was relieved to hear she had not made a mistake with Behn and she smiled weakly at Sofia's teasing. She could see where it would be funny from Sofia's side, but right now she felt slightly stupid for being the brunt of the joke. "I have to admit, you really had me going there. Although I couldn't see why bowling would be considered such a serious thing. You guys do have some pretty strange customs here though."

Sofia continued to laugh. She was thankful the light had changed, forcing her to stop driving. She was having a hard time seeing the road through the tears from her laughter. Sometimes Juila acted as though she came from farther away than merely another continent.

~

DR. GASCON SAT at his mahogany desk and peered closely at the pictures he had commissioned. There were so many people who seemed to have become friends with Amanda since she married that Riccan Stel. He wondered why they had felt the need to get married so swiftly, and secretly at that. The whole affair seemed very strange to his line of thinking.

There was definitely something going on with Amanda Covington...*Stel*...he corrected himself with a sneer. He should have insisted on being allowed to interview Amanda before she was released from the hospital. He had too many unanswered questions for his comfort. Surely, Amanda could have spared him five minutes—ten tops—to answer some basic questions.

The private investigator cleared his throat as he waited for Dr. Gascon to finish going through the packet of documents he had gathered. "Is there anything more you require, Dr. Gascon?"

"Yes. I'd like you to continue your surveillance of the Stel residence, the girls' school, and anywhere Amanda goes. I'd like weekly updates." Dr. Gascon did not even raise his eyes from the pictures held in his hands. He did not care what the investigator thought of him. He paid the man to document the movements of a family, not to have an opinion of the assignment.

"I think you'll find the paperwork to be sufficient. I'll just keep following the family's movements as you have asked. If that's everything then I'll just be on my way," he stated as he scraped his chair back away from the desk so he could stand. As he did not get any indication from his client to do otherwise, he turned on his heel, left the room, and closed the door softly behind him.

Dr. Gascon lined up each picture on his desktop and then pulled out the documenting paperwork. He smiled as he read each account of the actions of the Stel household. He noted the schedule of the maid as well as the grounds crew. They might be good people to bring in for questioning. With their low pay and obvious heritage differences, they could probably be easily convinced to cooperate.

Grinning at how his plan was coming together so easily, Dr. Gascon leaned back in his chair and laughed out loud. One way or another, he would know Amanda's story. Each new person who entered their lives would become another source of information available for his plan. His study of the multi-dimensional disorder would launch him back into the spotlight where he deserved. He would once again be vaunted for his expertise and be sought out for his advice.

He picked up the stack of paperwork and began memorizing the names of each person who came into contact with the Stel family. Not only would he know all of the players in this puzzle, he would piece them together as he saw fit. Surely he could find a way to insert himself into some of their lives. He would unravel this mystery if it were the last thing he did!

CHAPTER 22

Willian spent as little time at home as possible. He had checked for messages on the patil and then left as soon as possible. He thought for sure he would have heard something from Jena since he had talked about the sanctioning. Still, there was no news from her.

He was tired of being last on everybody's list of priorities. He had done what his father had said and written to Jena. She had never replied. If she were going to continue on as his betrothed, then she was going to have to start acting like it. If she did not want to be in Tuala, then he was going to have to go to Earth.

There had been many details to work out in order to be able to leave, but he felt certain he had thought of everything. As soon as he was done with his classes today, he was going to pack enough clothes to last him for several mesans. He did not think it would take that long to convince Jena to come home with him, but he wanted to be ready just in case.

Instead of working on the class assignments, he worked on writing a letter for his mother. He was sorry for how she would feel when he left and he did not want her to worry about him. She had always supported him even when his father was hard on him.

When the last class finally finished, he rushed out of the classroom. He ignored several of his friends who were trying to get his attention. He no longer had time for their foolish antics. He had more important things to do than go fishing with them or hang out at their houses. Normally it took fifteen minutes to walk to his house, but he set a brisk pace and got home in less than ten.

He went straight to his room. He was no longer angry since he had decided on a plan of action. Either he would work it out with Jena or he would break off their betrothal. In any event, he would resolve this issue. If Jena knew what were good for her, she would decide to come home with him.

With his bag packed and slung over his shoulder he stood at his bedroom door and looked out into the hallway to see if any staff were around. The last thing he needed was for one of the workers to tell his parents about his plan before he even made it out of his room. All was quiet, he slipped down the hall and out a side door.

Now all he had to do was wait for his father to leave the Residence so he could use the Ascension Gate. He had never actually used it himself before, but he had been present when other people had. It did not seem too complicated and he had learned the basics of it in the special sessions set up for the Elder's successors.

Time seemed to creep by as Willian waited on the docks. There were so many people walking about that he did not stand out in the crowd. His timing was going to have to be exact for this plan to work. He needed to wait for his father to leave the Residence, but make his move before they sat down for dinner and discovered he was missing. One other major consideration was to make sure none of the Residence staff saw him either. The last thing he needed was for his father to return to the Residence and thwart his plan to get Jena back.

Glancing at his timepiece one more time, Willian stood up from where he had been sitting at the edge of the dock. He had spent the whole afternoon watching watercrafts come and go from the harbor. Now was the time for him to complete the first task.

He walked down the side walkway of the Residence. Willian did not want to register his visit with the guards at the entrances so he was going to have to be more creative about getting into the place. He decided the safest route would be through the storage room off of the kitchen.

There were always people in the kitchen, but he felt certain he could sneak around them since they were usually pretty busy getting ready to go home for the night. There were only two staff members who lived at the Residence, so it was pretty easy to believe he could avoid two people.

Gaining access to the storage room proved to be no problem, but it seemed as though the staff were having some sort of meeting before going home. With his ear to the door, he waited for what seemed an eternity for them to finish and finally be on their way. He had a close call when one of the maids came into the storage room to get one more thing ready for the next day. Luckily, he was able to hide behind the door and she left without noticing him crouched in the shadows.

He listened closely to the noises from the other room until he had not heard anything for quite some time. Peeking around the corner of the door, he could see the room was empty. Picking up his bag, he stealthily stepped into the kitchen. There was a moment when his heart skipped a beat when he heard the two maids talking in a hallway nearby. Holding his breath, he rushed across the kitchen and went out the far door into the main section of the Residence.

Once he gained access to the hall, he was able to navigate through the rooms. The Ascension Gate was located in the basement which could be accessed secretly through his father's private office. Willian had only seen it once when he was several anons younger. He hoped nothing had changed since then or his plan would not work. There was another entrance to the gate, but it was heavily guarded and unavailable to Willian without letting his father know his intentions.

Willian stood outside of his father's office door and reached for the knob. As he looked down, he noticed his hand was shaking. When he took this next step, he was either going to get into a lot of trouble, or he was going to win Jena back. He could not see any other option. He opened the door and hoped the room was empty.

Luck remained on his side and he closed the door quietly behind him. He walked over to the bookcase on the far wall, and tipped the special book which allowed the hidden door to open inward. Looking down the steep stairway, he started to feel apprehensive. This had seemed like a good idea until he actually got right down to it.

He almost turned around to go back home until he remembered his father's ultimatum about rescinding the betrothal agreement. If he did not go now, he would lose status with all of his friends. Jena was just going to have to change her mind and come home with him. He created a sphere of elemy to light his way, Willian took several steps down before closing the hidden door behind him. The sound of the door latching seemed so final. There was no turning back now.

Willian approached the entrance of the Ascension Gate. The unfurnished room looked unremarkable, but he could feel the power emanating from the circular doorway across from him. Even though he was trembling inside, he knew this was his chance for making his life right again. If he waited for his father's approval, it might be too late with Jena.

He knew if he took any more time to think over his decision, he would most likely turn around and go home. His anger kept him moving forward until both of his feet stood in the center of the Gate. He spoke the two words which would take him where he had never before gone.

"Outside Ascension," he whispered as he kept a picture of Jena firmly in his mind.

The world seemed to disappear around him. The sensation was similar to taking a ride in a telepod except without the benefit of feeling safe inside a vehicle. Fear started to kick in when the sensation of nothingness continued on for far longer than he had ever known in a telepod. He could feel a scream of anguish forming inside him when he suddenly appeared inside a dark cave.

He clutched the dirt floor with relief at still being alive. Then he realized it *was* dirt and not the polished floor like at his father's Residence. This could not possibly be the right location. He had to have made a mistake during the transfer. Fresh fear overcame him as he realized he could be lost either in time or on another world other than Earth. He had really messed up this time.

WHEN THE AFTERNOON meal was finished, all of the girls trooped out of the house and into the garage. When Valentina came through the door and saw the completely empty space across the concrete she frowned. She looked around in confusion and then she started to get angry. She believed the whole family had been lying to her and she did not appreciate the joke perpetrated on her.

Jena had been watching her friend's expression and touched her arm. "Look across the garage, Val."

Valentina angrily shifted her gaze back across the empty expanse. "I don't see any…"

Amanda tapped the remote and allowed the cloaking shield to dissolve. Where nothing had been before, now saw a very large, greyish-silver craft.

Amanda and her daughters all smiled with contained mirth at Valentina's expression of wonder. Not too long before, Amanda had felt the same way when her dream had become a reality and she had actually flown in Riccan's telepod. She could easily relate to Valentina's stunned look.

"That is amazing," Valentina whispered as she continued to walk forward so she could get a closer look at it. "I mean, one second the garage was clearly empty and then, poof, here is this magnificent flying saucer!"

"Not exactly a flying saucer, but I understand the sentiment," Amanda chuckled. "Let's go inside it." She walked up to the side of the pod and touched the panel to open the door.

Valentina hastily moved to the side to allow the outer section to drop down to the ground silently. She had no idea she was looking at a small model or that it was more modern than most Tualan citizens had witnessed. To her, it was just amazing and wonderful. Without noticing, she found herself standing inside the telepod.

She touched the leather seats in the back and moved forward until she was viewing the cockpit. She was surprised to see it was similar to a modern airplane. Somehow she imagined it would contain controls which only an alien could understand like she had seen in movies.

Valentina turned around and saw the three women staring at her. "This is fantastic. Can you really fly this, Mrs. Stel?"

Amanda chuckled and answered, "Yes, with appropriate training. Of course."

"We learned how to operate a telepod before we left Tuala," Juila piped in.

"Really? How cool. Are all of the telepods like this one?" Valentina stepped back into the main cabin and back down the ramp. She walked slowly around the entire telepod. She could see it was resting on the concrete without any support, nor were there any wheels or wings. It was hard to imagine how it could fly, let alone how it would get into the garage since it was clearly larger than the roll-up door. "How does it get into here?" Valentina asked.

Juila had followed her around the craft and answered, "This is a small version, typical to what a family would use. It teleports similar to what I did with you from my room into the library."

"Wow! If you hadn't shown that to me, I might not believe you right now. You really are from Tuala, aren't you?" Valentina was completely convinced of the truth of their story. Now she just had to come to terms with the idea of herself also being from there.

"Yes, we are, Val, including you and your brothers. Someday soon, we'll take you back there."

"I think I'd like to finish high school first," Valentina said with a nervous chuckle.

"I'm not saying we'd abduct you and leave you stranded there. I just thought you'd like to take a quick look around like Behn did. We won't have to stay long."

"In that case, I think I'd like to go," she said as she nodded slowly as the idea mulled around in her head.

Amanda had come around to the other side of the telepod where the girls were talking. She had heard their last statements and offered, "I could probably take you there on one of my field trips. I usually only stay for a couple of hours at a time. Would you be interested in something like that?"

"Count me in," Valentina declared. She had made up her mind to embrace her history. *In for a penny, in for a pound,* she said to herself. *Maybe I'll even ask the girls to teach me how to use my birth crystal. Maybe.*

CHAPTER 23

Amanda still had not heard anything from Copa by the time Riccan came home from work. It was just as well since she wanted to discuss it with him before she made any arrangements. Again, she was using her intuition in this matter. She was not sure what she needed to discuss with Copa, only that she felt a burning desire to do so.

After their dinner was over, they sat down in the living room. Amanda asked Riccan, "How was your day?"

Riccan ran his hands through his hair and he leaned forward as he took a deep breath and let it out slowly from his mouth. "I don't know what's going on with Ela Nena. We used to get along so well and she let me do my job. Now, I don't know. It's like she's not even the same person anymore."

"Oh, Riccan! What happened?"

"She's just micromanaging me and my team. Every time I turn around, she's either in my department keeping my people from doing their jobs, or she's pulling my team away to do other assignments."

"Why don't you tell her to let you do your job?" Amanda was relieved since she had not gone to work with Riccan. She certainly did not need any further complications in her life. She felt so bad for Riccan for having to put up with such pettiness.

"I can't very well do that, Amanda. They may be my team, but she's my boss. Technically, she has access to every person in the company at her disposal. I'm just going to have to bide my time until Ela Nena gets through whatever is causing her this extra stress."

"Well, I hope she comes to her senses before she drives her star player away from the company," Amanda said as she patted Riccan on the knee.

"Enough about my work. What did you do today?" Riccan looked up at his beautiful wife with an expectant expression.

"I met Bryon and Alena today."

"Really? How did that go?"

"Better than I could have hoped, really. I helped Bryon find his own samara," she said with a grin.

"Seriously? The samara was still in the cave, then?" Riccan was overjoyed to hear of yet another samara being found and put into the hands of its rightful owner. He was still amazed at his wife's ability to locate the artifacts based solely on her dreams and intuition.

"Yes, and it was definitely meant for Bryon. I checked the samara's aura before I had Bryon touch it. Just as we thought, it matched the color of his birth crystal. And speaking of that, I asked both Bryon and Alena to put together a list of the crystal colors for each of the people who were summoned to meet with Jehoban regarding the prophecy. They said they'd put it together and send it to your father. Can you let me know when he receives it?"

"Wait a minute. I think you figured something out on your own, and I'm not sure I follow your line of thinking. What is the connection between the people at the meeting with Jehoban and the samaras?"

Amanda chuckled and replied, "It makes perfect sense. When you add up the number of people at the meeting along with the four of us here, there are thirteen people. There are thirteen samaras. Ergo, each person at that meeting will eventually get their own samara. Why else would Jehoban bring them all together unless He meant for them to work together to fulfill the prophecy?"

When Amanda put it that way, it seemed an obvious answer. Riccan shook his head in amazement at his wife's line of thinking. The more he pondered it, the more he became convinced of the validity of his wife's claim. Also, the fact that Bryon now had his own samara seemed to cement the idea. Whether she were right or wrong, time would tell. When they found the rest of the samaras, they would know for sure.

"So what are you planning on doing now?" Riccan asked.

"I can't seem to shake the feeling that I need to meet with wise-woman Copa. I got coordinates from Alena today. I've also sent her a message on the patil asking for a meeting. She hasn't gotten back to me yet. I wanted to talk to you about it before I went anyway."

"What do you want to talk to her about?"

"Well, I really want to thank her for saving my life and for taking good care of our children. She could have just walked away and left us all to Elder Vargen's devices."

"That's true. Maybe I should come with you to thank her as well."

"I don't think that's necessary, but I will pass along your thanks as well, if you want. I also want to talk to her about my birth crystal. Jehoban told me she had requested it for me to have a safe journey. I want to know why she would even consider it for a person from Earth. I've heard often enough that *old souls* don't get birth crystals. Hopefully, she can shed some light on my questions."

"I can't wait to hear what she has to say. You do bring up a good point about *old souls*. You are the first person from Earth whom I've ever heard of getting your own birth crystal. If you hear from Copa while I'm at work, send me a message on the patil before you go."

"Okay. Although I'm hoping she'll get back to me yet this evening. I'd really love to go see her tomorrow."

"You should talk to her about Neal," Riccan said suddenly.

"Neal? Why would you say that?"

"She obviously spent time in Elder Vargen's facility when you were there. Maybe she knows more about Neal and his situation. She may be able to give you vital information for getting him out of there."

Amanda hugged her husband and kissed him firmly on the lips. She pulled back and held his face in both of her hands as she said, "You're brilliant! Do you know that? I love you so much!"

"Thanks! I love you, too!" He smiled at her enthusiasm even though he was not sure what he had said which would cause her to react so impulsively.

"I've been so worried about the timing of rescuing Neal. The days keep ticking by and yet I've not gotten any closer to figuring out how to get him home. I'm sure Copa will be very helpful in that regard. After all, she got me out, didn't she?" Amanda sat back on the couch and started going over every idea and imagining how her conversation would go with Copa. This had to be the answer. Her hope was renewed. She was certain she would be able to succeed with Neal now.

❧

As LUCK WOULD HAVE IT, Amanda did get a reply from Copa before she went to bed that night. Riccan was with her when she went to check the patil for any unread messages. She clicked on it and read: "I'd love to meet with the one who got away. I'll be at home all day tomorrow should you have the opportunity to come then. Otherwise, let me know when you're available and we'll figure something out. Yours, Copa."

Amanda turned to Riccan and said, "I'm going tomorrow!"

"I never doubted it," he replied with a grin. He kissed her on the top of her head and said, "Let's go to bed now, shall we?"

After shutting down and storing the patil once again in its secret spot, Amanda followed her husband to bed. Amanda was certain she would be too excited to fall asleep, but she wanted to at least make an attempt to sleep for her husband's sake. As soon as her head hit the pillow, Amanda was out like a light.

Morning came swiftly. Amanda was so grateful to have slept soundly so she would have a clear mind for her meeting with Copa. She dressed carefully and made sure her birth crystal was displayed prominently against her black shirt. She really wanted to show Copa how much the gift had meant for her.

Riccan kissed her goodbye and wished her luck with her meeting. He walked out the door and went off to work.

The kids were sleeping in since it was Thanksgiving Day and school was closed until the following Monday.

Amanda rushed downstairs and out to her telepod. She set the coordinates, as they were written by Alena, into the control panel. With her seatbelt fastened and all of the green lights lit, Amanda hit the activation button and began her journey to see Copa.

She reappeared several seconds later in an unfamiliar area. This was nowhere near any of the places she and Riccan had practiced flying. She scanned the ground for a good landing area and saw one not too far ahead of her. She manually steered the telepod over and set it down gently onto the ground. She issued all of the shutdown procedures and unfastened her seatbelt.

Standing in the doorway of the telepod, Amanda surveyed the land and tried to decide which direction she should go first to find Copa's house. It was pretty easy to imagine anyone in the area would know where the wise-woman lived. All she had to do was stop someone and ask for directions.

With her mind made up, she stepped away from the telepod and shut the door as she walked toward the small town. She did not bother to cloak the vehicle since she was in an unfamiliar area and she wanted to make sure she could get back to it. Ahead, there were several rows of houses. Beyond those dwellings was a small group of people talking. Amanda decided to ask one of them where Copa's house was located.

Amanda came closer to the cluster of people and, much to her dismay, they disbursed and went into their homes. She looked around in confusion at how unfriendly the people seemed. Not to be deterred, she knocked on the door closest to her. After a moment, the occupant opened the door the merest crack.

"What do you want?" said a gruff voice.

Amanda could not tell if it were a man or a woman. She asked, "I'm supposed to meet with wise-woman Copa. Can you please direct me to her dwelling?"

A wizened old finger pointed outside the door as the person said, "Up the avenue, turn left at the crossing. Third home on the right." Without waiting for anything further, the door shut soundly.

Amanda could hear a deadbolt being drawn closed on the other side. She could not imagine what had happened to make these people so leery of strangers. She shook her head sadly and turned from the doorway. Following the directions given, she soon found herself standing outside what she hoped to be Copa's house.

With a bit of trepidation, Amanda knocked on the door.

The door opened. The reception was vastly different than she had received before. A woman whom she had no knowledge of ever seeing before smiled at her broadly.

"Amanda, dear. Please come in. You can't imagine how pleased I was to hear from you yesterday. Come in!" Copa stood to the side and gestured for Amanda to enter the house.

Amanda smiled nervously and stepped into the well-kept home. She was instantly reminded of Alena's house. They appeared to be similar in size and Amanda imagined had a separate room dedicated to treating patients.

"You haven't aged a day, Amanda. Please sit down. You must have so many questions."

Amanda thought Copa seemed rather nervous as she prattled on. She took a seat on the worn couch and waited for Copa to join her. "What has happened in town to make the people act so strangely to outsiders?"

Copa finally sat down in a chair across from Amanda. "Oh, that. We've had some trouble with a group of people who have settled in the woods outside of town. They call themselves the Roanoke Colony."

With eyebrows raised at the mention of the people Behn had grown up with, Amanda asked, "What have they done?"

"They keep coming into the village trying to convince the young girls to come back with them. They are getting more aggressive each day and some fear there will be violence soon."

"Have you talked with an Elder about it?" Amanda did not like the sound of how this was going.

"No. I'm sure we'll have to shortly. Enough of that. What brings you to see me?"

"First, my husband and I wanted to thank you for your help in rescuing me and my children from Elder Vargen. I don't know how we'll ever repay you for the danger you put yourself in for me and mine."

Copa continued to stare at Amanda. She had thought Vinia had been the one who would be the keeper of the samara. Vinia and Amanda looked so similar to one another, it was easy to see how she had made such a mistake. Looking at Amanda, she looked exactly as her vision had shown her. "It was my duty, Amanda."

Amanda scowled at Copa's choice of words and asked, "What do you mean by duty?"

"I'm a wise-woman. You were someone in great need. I did what needed to be done. It's that simple," she answered with a self-deprecating shrug.

Amanda did not know what to say. She touched her birth-crystal and said, "Jehoban told me you requested this for my safe travels. Thank you, but why did you think an *old soul* would be given one?"

Copa was surprised to hear about Amanda having spoken to Jehoban over the matter. This situation must have progressed further than she had originally imagined. "What else did Jehoban tell you?"

"He said I'm the key. Does that mean anything to you?" Amanda was reticent to share too much of her mission to this stranger.

Copa nodded softly. The time had come. "I have foreseen many things. I have developed a talent for seeing visions of the future. Long ago, I had one of you."

"Please continue," Amanda urged when Copa stopped talking.

"I will share what I know. Hopefully, you will understand." She paused to wait for Amanda to nod in approval. "I saw you with a group of people. Each one of you held a samara in your hand as you drew together. The power of the samaras was incredible and a light shown up into the heavens. As one, the people turned and walked in every direction to fulfill their task. You were one of the people in the group. Does this mean anything to you?"

Amanda could only nod mutely. She had seen the vision when she had held the samara in the hidden room at her home so many months ago. To hear the same story from this old woman merely strengthened her resolve to complete the task. "I have been searching for all of the samaras. We have found four so far. Do you have knowledge of any others?"

It was now Copa's turn to be surprised. Not only did Amanda believe what Copa had said, she had already begun the quest to fulfill the vision. "Yes, I know the whereabouts of one other. I gave it to a woman named Vinia. When I met her, I believed she was the one to whom it should belong. I see now I was wrong."

"Why would you believe Vinia should have been the owner?"

"It is irrelevant now." Copa fluttered her hand in front of her dismissing the question. "Let me tell you where she has left it."

"Left it? Are you saying it has no guardian?" Amanda's heart began to race as she thought of all of the evil things which could happen should the samara be found by the wrong person.

"Be at peace, Amanda. It is well hidden. There are no people in the area anymore as they are now residing in the woods here. If you allow it, I will share the location with your mind so you will know exactly where it is located." Copa leaned forward and held out her hands toward Amanda's head, waiting for approval.

Amanda had no choice other than to say, "Yes. Please show me quickly."

Copa touched her hands to Amanda's skull and shared her knowledge with Amanda. It was a simple and quick method to deliver vital information without a chance of anyone overhearing. She removed her hands and sat back down across from the young woman.

"Thank you. I will retrieve the samara today."

"Do you have any other questions for me?" Copa could feel Amanda's desire for assistance in another matter entirely. Her skill at reading people was quite acute which made her very good at her occupation.

"What can you tell me about the man who was taken captive with me? His name is Nealand. Jehoban has told me he is still being held captive by Elder Vargen. He also told me he has been addicted to resh," Amanda said hastily.

Even though she should have expected no less from this remarkable woman, Copa was surprised at Amanda's question. Not only did she have knowledge of Nealan, she had been to his house only two weeks before. "Oh, dear! If your friend has been taking resh all of this time, then he is definitely in danger."

"What makes you say that?" Amanda leaned forward anxiously.

"Resh is a painkiller and a sedative for the people of Tuala and is considered relatively harmless. To people from Earth, it is a very different matter. For some reason, your kind are very susceptible to becoming addicted to resh and are not able to keep it from becoming toxic. Over time it poisons the body, eventually killing the addict. If your friend has been taking it as long as you say, I'm surprised he's lasted this long."

"This is worse than I imagined," Amanda mused as she sat back on the couch and considered what she should do. At first, she had thought to give him the option of going home, but this information changed everything. Neal would die if she left him in Tuala. "What can I do to save him?"

Copa thought over the situation and realized there was only one option. "You must drug him senseless with resh and take him home to Earth. Crossing the veil will eradicate the drug from his body entirely. This is his only hope of surviving."

"I see. Where can I get the resh? For that matter, how will I give it to him?" Amanda was beginning to appreciate the complexity of this rescue.

"I can help you with the first part. As a wise-woman, I have a supply of resh. I will give you what you require. As for the second part, Nealan is living with Vinia. Before you ask, yes, she is the same woman who had the samara. Tell her what I have told you and she will give Nealan the drug. She loves him and would not want to see him die."

Amanda thought it all sounded too simple and rather convenient. She should have known her intuition would lead her to the right people to complete her tasks. It still seemed rather remarkable and coincidental to have everything work out so perfectly.

"Let me gather your provisions so you may be on your way," Copa said as she rose from the chair and left the room.

Amanda sat staring after her. For some reason, the thought of Neal living with and loving another person hurt her. She had moved on and married, so she was surprised to find she still cared so much for Neal. She was also thankful for him moving on with his life as well, even though she was about to ruin anything he had created for himself here on Tuala. Although she felt bad about it, she knew the alternative was for him to die a slow, wasting death.

Soon, Copa returned with a small leather bag in her hand. She held it out for Amanda to take. "Tell Vinia to put all of this in a cup of strong steena tea. Make sure Nealan drinks all of it. He should be incoherent after half of the cup and completely knocked out after all of it. Transport him speedily after he's taken it. This dosage could kill him if you don't get him back to Earth swiftly."

Amanda looked down at the leather bag and wondered if she were going to be responsible for Neal's death after all. This plan had to work.

Copa held out two pieces of paper and said, "One of these is the directions to where Nealan and Vinia live. The second one is a note for Vinia. She has to know how serious this situation is and that I believe your help is necessary for him to live. I have also given her the instructions for the making of the special tea so she won't mess it up."

Amanda took the two papers and folded them carefully in half. She could not think of anything else she needed to ask Copa and she was grateful for her assistance. She did not want to take up any more of her time, or bring suspicion to her house for an extended visit. Amanda stood up and said, "Thank you so much for everything. If you ever need anything, please don't hesitate to ask."

"Good luck, Amanda. I wish you the best in your tasks. I'm sure I'll be seeing you again in the future."

"Did you have a vision about it?" Amanda asked with a smile. She enjoyed Copa's company.

"Not exactly. Call it intuition," she said with a wink.

Amanda laughed even as she moved across the room toward the front door. She tucked the bag and the two notes into her pants pocket. The last thing she needed was for Copa's neighbors to talk about her taking strange things away from the wise-woman's house.

Copa followed her to the entrance and gave her a quick hug before she opened the door.

Amanda hugged her back and whispered into her ear, "Thank you."

"You're quite welcome. Safe journeys." She stood in the entrance and watched Amanda retreat down the empty avenue until she turned the corner. "You're going to need every bit of luck," she said to herself as she closed the wooden door with a soft thud.

CHAPTER 24

As Amanda traveled back to her house in Florida, she made up her mind about what she would do next. Amanda had the coordinates for the samara in her head. Since she could tell it was located in a very remote area she decided it would be a good opportunity to take Valentina for a ride in the telepod. For some reason she had it in her mind it was important to have Valentina on board and comfortable with the idea of Tuala.

After parking the telepod in the garage, Amanda entered her house. She went into the office and uncovered the patil from its secret hiding place. Wanting to know if there had been any news from either Daven or Bryon she touched the screen to display new messages. Unfortunately, there was nothing new to read.

Disappointed, she turned off the device and stored it back away. She left the office and walked down the hall to the library. She opened the secret wall to where the samaras were located. Spending time alone with the three they had in the room seemed like something important to do. Just being near them was enough to satisfy Amanda's curiosity. She did not have any desire to touch one and risk being held enthralled for hours on end.

"What are you doing, Mom?" Juila asked from the doorway to the room.

Amanda jumped and turned with a quick intake of breath. "You scared me!"

"I'm sorry, Mom. Did you find anything out today? Is that why you're in here?"

"I did find something out. Do you think Valentina would be available to come over in a little bit? I'm thinking of making a short trip into Tuala and I thought she might want to come along."

"I'll go call her right now. I'd like to come, too. Do you think that would be okay?"

"I don't see why not. I'd love to have the company and you could be my co-pilot since you've already been certified in a pod similar in size to mine."

Juila laughed and said, "It may have been similar in size, but I can assure you the ones we trained in were positively archaic compared to yours!" She turned and hurried from the room to go call Valentina.

Amanda followed more slowly and carefully closed the door to the hidden room. She had been careless when she had come in. Juila should not have discovered her in there since she should have closed it behind her. What if someone else had walked in and seen it open? She did not want to be the one to make the room unusable because other people had found out about its existence.

When Amanda entered the living room, Juila was already talking on the phone and sitting next to Jena on the leather couch. It was clear from Juila's expression that they would be having company for the trip.

Juila held her hand over the mouthpiece and said, "Mom, Behn wants to know if he can come, too?"

"I don't know, Juila. My pod only has four seats. Where would he sit?" Amanda answered reasonably.

"I'll stay home, Mom," Jena offered.

"Are you sure?" Amanda was slightly saddened to hear her other daughter would not be coming along.

Jena nodded with an understanding grin. She knew her sister wanted Behn to come along so she was willing to forego the opportunity to make her happy.

"Tell Behn it's okay then," Amanda said as she sat down next to Jena. "Are you really sure you don't want to come?"

"I'll have an opportunity to work on my homework. Plus I want to find out if the link between Juila and me works across the veil."

Again, Juila held her hand over the mouthpiece of the phone and asked quietly, "Val says they are planning on having Thanksgiving dinner at two this afternoon. Do you think we'll be home before then?"

Amanda looked over at the clock on the microwave and saw it was only just after ten o'clock in the morning and chuckled as she answered, "I should hope so. I can't see this taking any longer than an hour, tops!"

Juila nodded and relayed the information to Valentina. "Okay, we'll see you in about ten minutes." She hung up the phone and smiled eagerly with the idea of the outing. "They'll be here as soon as they can get dressed!"

"I guess it means you should be doing the same then, Juila!" Amanda said as she could see her daughter was still in her pajamas.

Amanda watched with a grin as Juila dropped the phone onto the couch, jumped up, and jogged over to and up the stairs.

"What are you guys going to do today?" Jena asked curiously.

"I found out the coordinates to another samara. I want to go and get it before anyone else gets it."

Jena leaned toward her mother in excitement. "Seriously? Another samara? Be sure to take something to pick it up with and carry it home in. You don't want to touch it until after you get home, if then even."

"Good point! I'll get a shoebox from upstairs and some gardening gloves from the garage on my way out."

"I'll have Juila remind you just in case it slips your mind," Jena suggested. She communicated the conversation to her sister through their mind-link. Jena was surprised to find out Juila was not as happy with their planned itinerary as she had been. Before she could find out the cause, Juila withdrew from her mind. "Why don't you get your box now? I'll stay down here and wait for our guests to arrive."

"Thank you, honey," Amanda said as she got up from the couch. She took her time going across the foyer and up the stairs. There were so many things going through her mind. She wanted this trip to be a good one for the brother and sister who had been displaced from Tuala. It was a good sign since Behn wanted to return. Maybe this time, it would trigger more memories for him.

On her way out of her bedroom, she met Juila at the top of the stairs. She could see Juila's eyes look down on the box in her hands.

"Why didn't you tell me about the samara?"

"I would have after your guests left. I figured you and the kids would go off on your own while I went to retrieve the samara. The less that is known about it, the better. I really just wanted Valentina to have the opportunity to visit Tuala again since she's become interested in it."

"Hmmph," Juila responded as she went down the stairs faster than her mom. Just as she reached the bottom step, the doorbell rang. She took the next couple of steps across the foyer and opened the door with a flourish. Her smile beamed out at the two visitors. "I'm so glad you two could come with us. This is going to be so much fun!"

Behn grinned at Juila as he gestured for Valentina to precede him into the house. He knew what to expect with this trip, but Valentina was bursting with curiosity and nerves. She had asked him several times on the ride over to explain how it felt to travel in the telepod. He did not mention anything about being blindfolded so he kept his description very vague.

"We should get going right away if we're going to be back in time for all of us to get our turkey dinners," Amanda said as she took the last couple of steps down to the foyer.

Valentina was grateful for the fact they were going to leave before she convinced herself this was a very bad idea. She hated the idea of Behn having been there before her. She wanted to see if being back in Tuala would help her remember more of her lost childhood.

The group of four walked past the living room and said their hellos and goodbyes to Jena on their way to the garage. "Don't forget the gloves in the garage, Mom!" Jena called out just as they reached the exit.

"Thanks, Jena. I'm on it right now," Amanda called out as she took the step down into the garage and grabbed a pair of gloves from the side table.

"What are the gloves for, Mrs. Stel?" Behn asked. He noticed for the first time the box she was also carrying and raised an eyebrow in question.

"I need to pick up something while we're there," Amanda said vaguely.

Juila rolled her eyes and kept walking toward the telepod. She wished this could just be an exploratory field trip and nothing more. It was still going to be an adventure with Behn and Valentina along.

Juila had reached the telepod and touched the side panel to open the door. She stepped to the side to allow it to drop down. Since she was going to be the co-pilot, she went into the telepod first and settled herself into the right-hand seat up front.

"Hey, this is a different telepod than the one I rode in last time! Where did this one come from?" Behn asked even as he walked up the ramp and sat down in the furthest passenger seat from the door. He buckled himself in and watched as Valentina did the same in the seat next to him.

Amanda was last to enter and she answered Behn's question by saying, "This was Riccan's original prototype to the one he flies now. He brought it home for me to use." She moved through the main cabin and settled herself in the pilot's seat next to Juila. Amanda touched the button to close the side door and watched while the door rose and sealed shut.

She initiated all of the start-up procedures and confirmed all of the green lights. This trip would be slightly different as she was going to have to program their destination from a location in her mind rather than a known coordinate. She switched the navigation system over to manual entry and put her hand on the manual control module. For several seconds, Amanda concentrated on the coordinates in her mind until they appeared on the navigation screen in front of her.

Juila leaned forward and said, "Hey, isn't that where we went before?"

"I'm not sure," Amanda replied. She turned to the passengers in the back and said, "You two are going to experience a feeling of nothingness for the duration of approximately six seconds. You won't have any of your senses during the transfer. To keep yourself from panicking, count slowly in your mind until you get to six. It might also help to close your eyes, if you want."

The passengers nodded their heads in understanding.

Amanda faced back to the front of the telepod and asked Juila, "Are you ready?"

"Absolutely! Let's get back to Tuala!"

Amanda grinned at her daughter's enthusiasm at the same time as she hit the navigation button to begin the transfer. Darkness engulfed them as Amanda continued to visualize the coordinates of their destination. She trusted Riccan's system, but she also remembered his instruction to maintain a continual focus as a backup. Since she was busy with maintaining their destination in her mind, she did not have the opportunity to count off the seconds.

Light suddenly poured through the windows as they appeared back in Tuala. Even as she circled to locate a good landing area, she had to agree with Juila about this being the place they had come before with Behn. When Copa had given her the coordinates, she had failed to mention it was the location of the Roanoke Colony.

Thinking back on their conversation, Amanda was relieved to know about the colony having moved out of this area. The chances of them running into anyone were very slight which pleased her greatly.

Amanda turned the telepod toward the beach and settled the craft down onto the sand near where Riccan had landed before. She had scanned their surroundings and had not seen any people. As a precaution, she would also use the cloaking program to keep their vehicle safe from predation.

"Okay, everybody, we're here!" She unbuckled and turned in her seat to see how her passengers had fared. "How was your first flight, Valentina?"

"Terrifying and fantastic all at the same time!" She could not contain her huge grin.

Behn nodded his agreement, but kept his comments to himself.

Amanda opened the side door from the main console. She grabbed the gloves from her lap, bent down and picked up the empty box she had set on the floor by her feet, stood up, and exited the vehicle. Since this was a new location, she thought it was only right for her to go outside and look around while her passengers disembarked behind her. The sand shifted under her feet as she moved over for her companions to step off of the ramp. She palmed the side panel to activate the door to close. Once everything was sealed again, she used the remote to cloak the telepod.

Valentina gasped when the craft disappeared and she could see the scenery behind where the solid bulk had been the moment before. She had no idea how the system worked, but she found it fascinating nonetheless. "Wow," she breathed as she looked over at her brother with wide eyes.

Behn nodded at his sister's comment even as he began to look around.

He recognized this place. "Is this where we came before?" He turned to Juila and waited for confirmation to his question.

"Yes," Amanda answered for her. She had tucked the box under her arm and held both gloves in her left hand. She was anxious to get to the spot Copa had shown her so she could retrieve the crystal skull. "Why don't you three go and explore the area. We can meet back here in twenty minutes."

"You're not coming with us?" Valentina asked with apprehension. It was one thing to travel to Tuala, it was quite another to be wandering around the place unescorted.

"Behn and Juila have been here before, they can give you a tour. I have something to take care of first. If we have time, we can explore together after I get my task done."

Valentina noticed the box and asked, "Are you bringing something for someone here?"

"No, I'm picking something up," Amanda said and did not elaborate further. She turned and started walking toward the brush line with her back to the ocean. The kids fell in line behind her. They continued on a narrow path until they reached the creek. After they spetched it, Amanda said, "Why don't you kids go down and investigate what's left of the village. I'm going to walk along the creek for a bit longer. Remember to meet back at the telepod in fifteen minutes."

Amanda watched the kids turn down the other fork in the path before she continued walking beside the water. She felt certain she would know when she neared the samara. Thinking it would be similar to the feeling she had gotten when they were in New Orleans, she had her senses on high alert.

From Copa's exact instructions, Amanda walked confidently along. When she reached the location from the implanted memory, she looked around in confusion. She could not feel any energy at all. Even the samaras in the hidden room exuded a palpable energy although they were not keyed to her specifically. There was absolutely no energy from this area.

Amanda kneeled at the base of a tree. She knew if she brushed away the leaves and debris, she would find a hollow area in the roots. Setting the empty box down, Amanda donned her gardening gloves. She did not want to accidentally touch the crystal, nor did she want to get her hands dirty.

Amanda scooped up handfuls of leaves and moved them off to the side. She found the hollow. It was empty. She leaned closer and could see a depression in the soil where the samara had once rested, but it was clearly gone. She rocked back on her heels and let out a deep breath.

She should have known her luck would run out eventually. Every adventure she had gone on had been successful right away. She expected no less from this one. After closing her eyes, Amanda concentrated on the details given to her by Copa. She had the distinct impression from the wise-woman about this location remaining undisturbed. What was she missing?

She hastily brushed the leaves back over the hollow in the roots. Amanda clapped her hands together to dislodge any remaining debris from her gloves before she removed them. With nothing else to be done, Amanda picked up the empty box and retraced her steps back to the path where she had separated from the kids.

Thinking she would meet the trio either along the trail or near the house where the two kids had grown up, she turned off of her path and onto the new one. As she had guessed, both Behn and Valentina were inside the log cabin and Juila was waiting outside to give them some privacy.

Juila turned suddenly when she heard twigs breaking behind her. She smiled with relief when she discovered it was only her mother and not some stranger. She had monitored the area for signs of life when they had arrived, yet she had let her guard down when she found it deserted. "Did you get what you came for?"

"It wasn't there," Amanda admitted.

Juila's eyes widened as she said, "What? Are you sure?"

"Very sure. I found where it had been stashed, but it was gone."

"How long ago do you think it was put there?" Juila asked suddenly as an idea occurred to her.

Amanda cocked her head to the side as she considered the question. "I got the impression it was hidden about a year ago," Amanda answered.

"Where exactly was it hidden?"

Amanda turned back toward the creek, which was hidden from view by several yards of brush and trees, and pointed as she replied, "Under a tree along the river over there."

"Was it near where we walked with Behn the last time we were here?"

"Yes. Very near there. What are you thinking?" Amanda asked slowly.

"Those samaras have a lot of energy. If it had been there the last time we were here, we would have felt it. Someone must have taken it before we arrived the last time. If we were to go back in time to before our last visit, we might be able to get it before the other person does." Juila smiled at the look on her mother's face as she finished her summary of what they should do.

"Timing it is dangerous, Juila. Besides, how would I know when to come back here? It could have been more than a year for all I know."

"Anon, Mom. We are in Tuala now. For starters, try timing it to the mesan before we arrived last time. If it's still not there, then skip back another month. You don't have to do it all in one day since it's extremely taxing on the body, but at least give it one try today."

"I don't know. I can't risk Behn and Valentina's lives on a theory." Amanda weighed her options. She could leave the kids here while she attempted to go back in time, or she could take them home and come back later. An idea struck her and she asked, "Can you talk to your sister through your mind link?"

"I haven't tried. Just a second," Juila held up her index finger and her eyes lost focus as she concentrated on communicating with Jena. She smiled and nodded her head.

Amanda said, "Tell your sister where we are. Let her know about your idea about my going back a mesan and see what she thinks."

Juila nodded at her mother words while still not looking at anything in Tuala. Her eyes refocused and she looked up at her mom and said, "Jena thinks you should give it a try. She said I should go with you so if anything goes wrong then she'll still be able to tell Dad where we are. Jena thinks we should leave Behn and Valentina here at the cabin until we're done."

Jena's idea had merit and Amanda nodded in agreement. "Okay, let's tell them what we're up to," Amanda said as she began walking toward the cabin.

Valentina did not much like the idea of be stranded in the deserted village, but Behn said, "It's okay. You two do what you need to and we'll be waiting here for you to return. I'd like to take some time wandering though the village to see if it brings back any new memories anyway."

"Don't wander too far," Amanda admonished. She still thought it would be wiser to return the two kids back to Earth.

"Come on, Mom. Let's hurry and get this done!" Juila began jogging up the trail back to the telepod.

Amanda looked over her shoulder at the two kids she was leaving behind. They smiled and waved at her to encourage her to go. They seemed content to stay, who was she to tell them they had to go? Making up her mind, she began running to catch up with Juila.

CHAPTER 25

Valentina watched the only people who knew where they were leave. While she agreed with Behn about it being nice to have more time to explore, she could not help wondering if it were wise. Since she had traveled by telepod and seen where they used to live, she was thoroughly convinced of their heritage. Now she had some alone time with Behn to talk about what they were going to do about it.

"Behn, can you show me the first crystal lesson? Since we are here at our old home, maybe it will come back to me easier somehow." Valentina began to walk back into the old cabin and assumed Behn would follow her.

Behn was torn between wanting to walk through the village and doing as his sister asked. It seemed as though she were coming around to believing everything which had been told to her. The more prudent choice seemed to be with his sister. He turned and followed her into the old homestead.

They faced one another at the worn wooden table just as Behn recalled from his earliest memories. He pulled the pendant out from under his shirt and held it in his hand. He spoke quietly to his sister, "Hold your birth crystal in your hand. Concentrate on feeling the energy living inside of the crystals. Focus your thoughts on the energy and feel it expand outside the confines of the stone. Imagine the energy circling around itself in a sphere of energy which you can control." Even as he spoke, he put action to his words and demonstrated what he intended her to do with her own necklace.

Valentina felt a spark of recognition in the furthest recesses of her mind as she listened to Behn's instructions. She knew she had heard these exact words from their mother as she showed them how to use their birth crystals. Even as she began to feel the energy building in her own pendant the memories burst forth from her subconscious. She dropped her pendant and looked wide-eyed at her brother.

"What?!? Did you get hurt? Did your birth crystal do something to you?" Behn questioned even as he jumped up from his seat and came to kneel beside his sister. He began to be afraid as Valentina continued to stare at him without saying a word. Reaching up, Behn shook her shoulders and asked, "What's going on, Val? Talk to me!"

Valentina's eyes refocused on her brother and she suddenly grinned broadly and declared, "I remember everything, Behn. I remember our mom, our life here, and our lessons with the birth crystals. It's amazing, Behn!"

"Jeez, Val, you scared me half to death!" He rocked back on his heels and let out a sigh of relief. Now he knew Valentina would be on his side since her memories had returned. Behn stood up and stepped back over to his seat. With another sigh, he slumped down into the chair and said, "Tell me what you remember."

"Mom sat right here," she gestured to her right. "She taught us the first five lessons of the crystal skills and told us we had to keep it a secret from the villagers. She said they wouldn't understand and they would treat us badly if they ever found out we had powers which they could not possess. Behn, none of the villagers had birth crystals!"

"Wow! I wonder why not?"

"Mom said they were an old community with strange customs. They did not trust outsiders and did not welcome anyone into their lives who was not born there."

"Our mom had a birth crystal. How did she come by one if the villagers wouldn't allow it?" Behn wished he could recall the things Valentina obviously had no trouble remembering.

"Let me think for a second," Val said as she thought about her brother's question. She nibbled on her lower lip as she reviewed her new memories. "Ah," she said and looked up at Behn. "Our grandfather was not from the village. Our grandmother brought him back with her when she went on a journey. She told the village leader she was pregnant and married so they allowed him to stay. They never made him feel welcome. When our mother was being born, he insisted that a wise-woman come in for the delivery and to make sure the child was healthy.

"The leaders tried to stop him, but even they had to admit the birth was not going well. Grandma was going to die unless someone came in to help. As it was, the delivery damaged Grandma beyond repair and she was never able to have any other children. The wise-woman was able to stop the bleeding, but she couldn't fix the damage.

"Before she left, and while Grandma was weak in bed, Grandpa insisted the wise-woman perform the crystal ceremony for his daughter. He didn't want the ignorance of the villagers keeping his daughter from her birthright and the protection of the birth crystal.

"He taught Mom how to use her crystal and he took care of our Grandma who never really recovered her strength from the childbirth. She died several years later when our mother was only six. The villagers had no choice but to put up with our Grandpa for our mother's sake."

"What an amazing story. Hopefully one day I'll remember it as you do." Behn leaned forward with his elbows on the tabletop and asked, "Show me what you recall of the first five lessons."

Valentina smiled at the challenge and once again held her birth crystal in her palm. With renewed pride in her birthright, she proceeded to demonstrate all five levels with ease. When she was done, she smiled smugly at her brother.

Behn had to admit he was slightly jealous of the ease in which she had performed the tasks. She had performed seemingly without any instruction what had taken him days to perfect. Maybe he should have taken Juila up on her offer to implant the skill in his brain to speed up his progress. He grinned, shook his head slightly, and said, "You obviously remember Mom's lessons!"

"This is so cool, Behn. I can't wait to learn more! I know Juila offered before, but do you think she'd let me sit in on your lessons so she could teach me as well?" Valentina reached across the table and grabbed his arms in entreaty.

Behn smiled broadly and answered, "I'm sure she would. Now we just have to convince Jon about what we know! I think I'll leave it up to you."

"Thanks!" She sat back in disgust. Behn had a point. Jon needed to know the truth. She just was not sure how to break it to him. He never did have as many memories of their childhood; they had always blamed his sickness on it.

"Let's go take a look around the village," Behn suggested. He had an overwhelming feeling of claustrophobia suddenly. He needed fresh air and a nice brisk walk to clear his mind.

"Sounds good to me," Valentina said. After all, she had gotten exactly what she had hoped for…her memories back.

AMANDA AND JUILA sat in the telepod. Juila tried to convince her mom of the proper way to time a teleportation. Amanda remained unconvinced since she and Riccan had never gone over the procedure.

"Are you sure? This could be very bad if we were to do it wrong," Amanda asked again. "Why don't you ask Jena what she thinks? Maybe she could get ahold of your dad and ask him."

Juila rolled her eyes at her mother's paranoia. She humored her and consulted with Jena on the matter. In a few moments she refocused her eyes on her mother and said, "Jena agrees with my plan. Look, why else would there be a date function on the plascreens unless it was meant to program in the date you wanted to arrive somewhere? If I'm wrong, then we'd end up back right here at the same time as when we left. We really have nothing to lose by trying." She sat back and crossed her arms with finality.

Amanda could not help but smile at Juila's reasoning. She knew their lives would be at stake if they messed it up. However, she could not fault Juila's logic about the date counter. Besides, she seemed to recall Riccan using the time function on his telepod to change the time of their return to Earth after visiting with his parents late one evening. "Fine! We'll try it your way. Change the date to one month before our last visit to this location. Hurry before I chicken out!"

Juila looked strangely at her mother's odd colloquialism.

"It means, before I change my mind!" Amanda laughed.

Juila chuckled even as she tapped the screen until the date she wanted was displayed. "Okay, we're all set. Let's go!"

"You'd better be right," Amanda said even as she pressed the activation button and held onto the manual control stick just in case.

Darkness overcame them. Six seconds passed. Then another three seconds went by in darkness. Just as they were both starting to panic, light flooded through the windows and they both sighed in relief. Amanda hurriedly set the telepod down on the ground and performed the shutdown procedures. She noticed her hands were shaking and her heart was racing.

When she looked over at Juila, she knew her daughter was feeling the same thankfulness at being alive. To cut the tension she asked, "Can you still contact Jena?"

"Let me try," Juila said. A few moments later, Juila let out a loud breath and said, "That was definitely weird! Not only could I talk to Jena, but I could hear myself as well. I'm not sure I liked the sensation!"

"Well at least we know it still works across time. Let's get outside and see if the samara is where it should be now!" She grabbed up the box and gloves, hit the button on the dash to open the side door, and hurried out of the telepod.

Juila was right behind her. As Juila stepped off the ramp, she hit the close button from the outside. As they walked away from the telepod, both looked behind them to watch it disappear when Amanda hit the cloaking button on her remote.

Amanda led the way back on the trail. She had an odd sense of déjà vu since everything looked the same as it had a few minutes before. She hoped the timing had worked. Her steps got longer until she found herself jogging. Her breath was coming harder and she realized she was going to have to slow down. She still was not in the best shape since coming out of the coma. Times like this demonstrated it very well.

Finally, they arrived back at the hiding spot. Amanda handed the box to Juila. She put on the gloves and kneeled at the tree. She knew about their success even before she removed the brush since she could feel the energy emanating from the samara. Once the crystal was exposed, both Amanda and Juila sighed with relief. Their mission was almost complete.

Amanda picked up the samara carefully and turned toward Juila. Her daughter fumbled with the box lid and bent forward for her mother to put the precious object inside. Juila put the lid back on and grinned at her mother.

"We did it!"

"Almost. Let's get back to our real time and pick up your friends. I won't consider this a success until we are safely back at home!" Amanda stood up and started walking back toward the telepod.

"Mom, can you carry this? It's making me itch all over with its surging energy." She rushed to her mother's side and handed the box over.

Amanda still had the gloves on and could only feel a slight tingling sensation. She wondered if it were the gloves or the fact she did not yet have her own samara. Maybe she was just less sensitive to the energy. In any event, they needed to get back to the relative safety of the telepod before anything happened to them. Someone had taken the samara before, it could have been themselves, or it could have been someone else. She was not willing to risk the former coming after them for their prize.

They walked as fast as they could, just shy of jogging. When they got to the beach again, Amanda reached into her pocket and hit the cloaking button to reverse the effects. The telepod reappeared in front of them and they entered the vehicle swiftly. Amanda was the first in and she hit the button for the side door as soon as both of Juila's feet hit the inside of the pod.

Not wanting to attract any attention to themselves, Amanda once again cloaked the telepod. She initiated the startup procedures and verified all of the green lights. She did not want to rush the process and make any mistakes, but she desperately wanted to be gone from this place. "Enter in the correct date, Juila. Be quick, I want to get out of here!"

Juila felt exactly the same way. She tapped out the correct date and said, "Done!"

Blackness engulfed them almost immediately. Knowing the transfer would take at least nine seconds, they both counted silently. When light once again entered the windows, both of them whooped out a cheer of delight.

"You stay here with the samara, Juila. I'll go get the kids and be right back." Amanda unbuckled and left. She closed the door and cloaked the telepod as she slipped along the loose sand up to the brush line. Once again, she retraced her steps along the path. She turned toward the cabin and kept walking briskly.

She wished she were able to talk to her daughter through a mind link. She had to content herself with knowing she could look in on Juila's birth crystal. She would know if Juila were in any danger through the parent link.

Several minutes later, Amanda reached the dilapidated cabin and rushed inside to collect the kids. The dwelling was clearly empty. She ran back outside, put her hands to her mouth, and called out, "Behn! Valentina!"

She hurriedly looked around the cabin and noticed there were fresh footprints in the dirt leading away from the house. She realized the kids had probably gone exploring in the village. Amanda followed the narrow trail, wishing the whole time the kids would have stayed put in the cabin. Calling out the kids' names again, Amanda kept walking.

"Hey," Behn called out from the distance.

Amanda sighed with relief and kept walking forward. "Where's Valentina? We need to get going now."

"Val! Come on, it's time to go," Behn yelled behind him.

Valentina stepped out of the trees and brushed the debris from her pants and asked, "Were you successful?"

"Yes. We can talk about it in the telepod. Let's go!" Amanda turned and retraced her steps back to the main trail. She could not help but feel as though she were being watched and it was making her even more jumpy. The sooner she was back in her own home, the happier she would be.

They made good time back to the telepod. Again, Amanda uncloaked it as they stepped toward it. The door was swiftly closed behind all of them. Amanda sat in her seat, buckled up, and said, "Get buckled. We're going home as soon as I can program it."

"Is something wrong?" Valentina asked. She was starting to get nervous with Mrs. Stel's attitude.

"Nope, and we want to keep it that way!" Amanda answered as she completed the startup procedures. She tapped the preprogrammed 'home' button on the plascreen. She made one last check to make sure everything was green and ready before hitting the activation button.

When light once again surrounded them, it was the muted illumination from inside their garage. Amanda saw her hands were slightly shaky as she set the telepod down and turned off all of the power.

"Will someone tell us what just happened?" Valentina asked impatiently.

Juila turned in her seat and said, "We went there to pick up an ancient artifact which had been left hidden there. Unfortunately, someone had taken it before we got to it. Mom and I traveled back in time to get it before whoever else got it. Mom wanted to make sure we got back home before anything bad could happen."

"Wow!" Behn said. "Can we see what you found?"

"Sure," Amanda said as she picked up the box and removed the lid. She lowered the box so the passengers could see the crystal skull sitting inside.

Valentina's eyes widened and she said, "The last memory I have of Tuala is our mother holding that thing in her hands! Was it hers?"

Amanda nodded even as she said, "I'm not sure. A wise-woman I know gave it to a woman who she knew would need to use it. The woman was the caretaker of it until we could get it back. It could have been your mother, I guess. Although I got the impression from Copa that the samara had only been hidden for about a year. How long ago did the three of you come to Earth?"

"Eight years ago," Behn answered.

"Hmm. Copa said she gave it to a woman named Vinia…" Amanda mused.

"That's our mother's name!" Valentina almost shouted in excitement.

"Then it probably was the one your mother used. Let's get inside, shall we?" Amanda said even as she replaced the lid on the box and stood up. She reached back to the control panel and hit the door button.

Just as they exited the telepod, Jena opened the garage door and said, "You guys did it! I could feel the power even from inside house."

While they walked into the house, Juila filled in the details to Jena through their mind link. It was a speedy way to share information privately.

Jena's eyes widened at a memory.

"What did you just remember, Jena?" Juila whispered. She hated it when Jena shut her out of her mind so rudely.

"Did you try to talk to me when you went back in time?"

"Yes, you know I did. You talked back to me."

"I did answer you, but that was way back in October. It wasn't today. I remember how odd the conversation was back then. I never said anything about it because I thought it was so strange. I didn't want it to change anything so I kept it to myself. I totally get it now."

"Jena, you must promise me you'll tell me if it ever happens again! It may be important for us to know it for future events." Juila grabbed her sister's arm and squeezed to emphasize her point.

"Ouch! Let go, Juila. I get it! I'll tell you, okay?" Jena rubbed the spot on her arm where her sister had been holding. She used some elemy to soothe the underlying tissues so she would not bruise later.

CHAPTER 26

Riccan entered their home with a spring in his step. Not only was he eagerly anticipating finding out how his wife's visit with wise-woman Copa had gone, he had news of his own. He thought he would have to find Amanda somewhere in the house, yet he was pleasantly surprised to see her making dinner, by hand, in the kitchen.

"Something smells good. What's for dinner?" he asked as he leaned down to kiss the side of Amanda's neck.

She giggled and squirmed away from his playfulness. She finished peeling the last two potatoes as she said, "It Thanksgiving dinner, silly!"

"Oh, yes! I knew there was a special reason I got home early from work today!" Riccan teased. He never really had any occasion to celebrate Thanksgiving before, but now he was very thankful to be with his brand new family for this first holiday.

"The turkey should be ready in about another half hour. My parents will be over in about forty-five minutes." She cut the potatoes up and dropped them in the cold water on the stovetop. She turned the burner up to high and went to rinse her hands in the sink. After she dried her hands off, she gave her full attention to her husband. "You sure are in a good mood. What's up?"

Riccan grinned and said, "I want to hear about your day first. Are you at a good stopping spot, or should I use a little elemy to move things along?"

"Too little, too late! Everything is progressing nicely. I have time while I wait for this water to boil. We can go sit down in the living room where I can keep my eye on everything in here." She grabbed his arm and directed toward their favorite spot on the couch.

She nestled in close to him, tucking herself under his arm as he rested it along the back of the couch. "My day was almost perfect. I met with Copa and she gave me what I'll be needing to get Neal back home. It's even worse than we thought with him since he's addicted to resh. For Tualans it's not a big deal, with Earthlings the drug is deadly over time. Neal doesn't have too much more time before it'll be too late. I'm really glad I'll be going to get him in a few days."

"I'll be glad to finish this chapter with Neal, as well," Riccan said as he caressed her shoulder with his hand. "I think you'll be able to relax once he's back home with his family."

Amanda was about to admonish him for being jealous until he reminded her of the grief Neal's parents were surely still going through every day he was missing. She nodded in agreement. Suddenly her mood brightened as she twisted up to look him in the eyes. "I found another samara today."

"What! Are you serious? You just went out and found one?" Riccan sat up straight and grabbed both of Amanda's arms in his excitement. "Tell me everything! Where is it?"

"Slow down! Copa told me where one was hidden. Apparently, the samara which the triplets' mother used to send them to Earth was left behind near the Roanoke Colony. Juila, Behn, Valentina, and I went over there and retrieved it."

"Just like that? It was really so simple?" Riccan was shaking his head in disbelief at how easy this was for his wife. He had been trying to find the other skulls for over fifteen years and had never come across any. In the short time since he had known Amanda, she had discovered four of them.

"Of course it wasn't quite as simple as what you're saying. Juila and I had to time our travel back to October to pick it up," Amanda stated simply. She really did not know how Riccan was going to react to her new skill.

Riccan was still processing the idea of her acquiring yet another samara and did not really consider the idea of Amanda's unconventional means of travel. "What color is its aura? Did you check? Where is it?" He looked around as though it would be sitting on the coffee table as a conversation piece.

Amanda chuckled at him and said, "I put it with the others. I haven't had time to check the color yet, either. Do you want to go and see what it is?"

"Absolutely!" He stood up and offered his hand to help Amanda up from the couch. "Hey, you just reminded me of my news." He reached into his pocket and withdrew a piece of paper which was folded into fourths and very creased from being in his front pocket. He handed it over to Amanda and smiled while she opened it.

Her eyes scanned the contents of the message. "Where did this come from?"

"My dad sent it to me at work just as I was leaving. C'mon let's go to the library," he said excitedly. He grabbed her hand and almost ran down the hall to get to the secret room.

Amanda giggled again at Riccan's enthusiasm.

They wasted no time entering the chamber behind the wall of books. Right away, Riccan could feel the added energy of the newest samara. His eyes were drawn to the niches in the wall where all of them were lined up in a row. Even though they appeared identical to the undiscerning eye, he could tell immediately which one was his own since it appeared to have a shimmer of color surrounding it.

Both of them concentrated on seeing the aura of the new samara. Riccan was first to confirm the color and he waited patiently for Amanda to come to her own conclusion. When he saw her eyes refocus on the room he asked, "What did you come up with?"

"A bright sky blue," Amanda said and then frowned. She looked down on the list of birth crystal colors and their owners which Daven had sent to Riccan. She did not see anyone listed with a blue. "It's not here, Riccan. Either we're wrong about the assignments, or this one belongs to Barla. It doesn't make sense, though. Barla doesn't have a birth crystal, Riccan. Jehoban said he would give her one. Do you think this means she's gotten hers?"

Amanda was bursting to find out if it were true. She wracked her brain to try to figure out a way to find out other than going back to Jehoban to ask. An idea suddenly came to her and she asked, "Can you get ahold of Rasa, Riccan? If you can, then we can ask her if she knows anything about her mother. Maybe Jehoban even asked her to give it to her mother! Riccan, please tell me you can reach Rasa!"

"Relax, Amanda. I'm sure I can get a message to her. What would you do with the information anyway? Didn't Jehoban ask you to keep your relationship with Barla to yourself until He told you differently?"

"This has got to be a sign, Riccan." She could see he was about to protest when she held up her hands to stall his response. "I'll pray to Jehoban and see how He answers me. Okay?"

"It's the very least you could do. Angering Jehoban is never wise, Amanda. Be careful, okay?" Riccan began walking back into the library so he could go to his office to send Rasa a message on the patil.

Amanda followed more slowly. She closed the book wall and rested her back against the shelves. With her eyes closed she folded her hands, bowed her head, and spoke, "Jehoban, please hear my plea. Please give me a sign letting me know if now is the time to reveal my relationship to Barla. I believe this samara belongs to her, but I will not make any move to find out if it's hers until You show me it's the right thing to do. Thank you for everything You've done for me and my family. In Your name, I pray. Amen."

She felt a peace flow down over her as though her petition had been heard. With a lighter step, she walked through the library to join Riccan in the office. By the time she entered the room, Riccan was already busily typing out a message to Rasa. Immediately after he hit the send button, a video call came in to the patil.

Riccan looked up at Amanda quizzically as he hit the receive button to take the call. He smiled brightly when he saw Rasa's face fill the screen. "Rasa! I just sent you a message."

"I know. I saw it come through and it reminded me I needed to call you anyway." She leaned back slightly from the screen as she readjusted herself in the chair. "Is Amanda around?"

"Yes. She's right behind me. What's going on?" Riccan asked even as he shifted to the side to allow Amanda to view the screen alongside him.

"Oh, good! Hi, Amanda," she said as she waved in greeting.

"Hi, Rasa. It's good to see you again. Did you read Riccan's message?"

"No."

"Oh, well I was just wondering if Barla had received a birth crystal yet."

"Yes, it's what I was going to tell you. Right after you left the meeting with Jehoban, He asked me to meet with Him. He gave me a crystal and had me perform the birth crystal ceremony for my mother. My brother and I have been training her to use it. I can't tell you how excited she was to finally get one! I'm so mad at myself for not asking for one for her before you did. Thank you so much!" Rasa paused to take a breath.

"I'm so glad to hear she got one. What color was it? Bright blue, maybe?" Amanda asked with a grin.

"Yes! How did you know?" Rasa's eyes grew round with amazement.

"I'd rather not say just now, but it does help to prove a theory of mine," she said as she looked down at Riccan. "Actually it's a theory of ours," she added as she nodded her head down to indicate her husband as well.

"It sounds very mysterious," Rasa grinned in reply. She did not want to press for an answer to the cryptic remark since it was not her place.

"I have another question for you. Jehoban had asked me not to reveal my relationship with your mother until a later date. Do you think the time is now? I have something vitally important to discuss with her and I think it'd be easier if she knew I was her niece."

"Give me a second and I'll ask Jehoban for you." Rasa closed her eyes and her hand unconsciously came up to hold her birth crystal while she spoke with her mentor. Only a moment later she opened her eyes again and smiled as she replied, "Jehoban has given you His blessing to carry on with your work as you see fit."

"Just to clarify, I can tell Barla?" Amanda did not want to anger the Creator over any misunderstanding.

"Yes. He just has a more eloquent way of phrasing everything."

"Is the convocation still set for the first?" Riccan asked.

"Yes. It has been arranged for everybody to come here to Manzanit to meet with Elder Wilken since he's the one who is presenting a successor. So far, it appears it will take a minimum of two days. Oh, that reminds me. Are you going to see my mom anytime soon?"

"Probably tomorrow. Why?" Amanda answered as she leaned over Riccan's shoulder.

"Can you let her know that family is not allowed at the convocation?"

"I'll tell her. Oh, can you send us a message when Elder Vargen arrives for the convocation? It's really important."

"Sure."

"Great! We don't want to take up anymore of your time. Thanks for calling, Rasa."

"Thank you! Have a great day." Rasa's picture clicked off as she disconnected first.

Riccan turned and looked up at his wife and said, "Everything is working out perfectly, Amanda."

"I know. I have to tell you, it makes me nervous for it all to go so smoothly." Amanda sank down onto his lap and draped her arm behind his head.

Riccan leaned into her chest and found he did not mind consoling her at all. In fact, he was starting to get other ideas the longer she remained so close. His hand began to rub her side and travel upward. He grinned devilishly and began kissing on her neck.

Amanda wanted to continue, however, dinner was not going to take care of itself. She leaned back and said, "I've got to go check on the food. I'm sure the potatoes are probably done." She stood up and sauntered from the room. She knew Riccan was enjoying the view as she swayed her hips. Amanda looked back over her shoulder and asked, "Are you going to help with dinner?"

Riccan sighed with disappointment at his failed attempt to be amorous and answered, "We could forget about dinner and go upstairs."

"What would my parents say if there weren't any food for Thanksgiving dinner, Riccan?"

"I could always whip something up in an instant," he offered, hoping he might convince her to change her mind.

"Sorry, Charlie. I've put way too much effort into this dinner to let it burn. Besides, don't they say abstinence makes the heart grow fonder?" Amanda smiled coyly.

"I don't think it's abstinence, my dear," he said as he crossed the room until he was standing directly behind her. "It's absence, and I don't plan on having that, either."

"There'll be time later tonight for your tryst. Come help with dinner.

My parents will be here before you know it," she said as she took his hand in hers and led him from the room.

~

JUST AS DINNER WAS READY, Riccan casually announced, "I asked my parents if they'd come to dinner tonight. I hope you don't mind."

Amanda stared at Riccan for a moment before she answered, "I didn't even think to ask them, Riccan. I'm so sorry. It was terribly thoughtless of me. I was so concerned about everything being perfect for my parents since this is the first Thanksgiving since I came out of my coma. Of course it's okay for them to come, too. I've made enough food for an army. I just hope it tastes as good as it smells."

Riccan was relieved to hear his wife was not upset with an addition of two to dinner. He really should have discussed it with her before asking. Besides, Thanksgiving was not a holiday celebrated in Tuala.

"Where will they park, Riccan?" Amanda suddenly asked.

"I programmed the third bay into their telepod," he answered offhandedly.

"What time are they coming?"

He looked at his wristwatch and said, "They should be here any minute, actually. I told them to arrive at the same time as your parents, but they are notoriously early."

Amanda kissed her husband on the cheek and said, "Good, you can wait downstairs for everyone while I go and freshen up."

When Amanda came back downstairs, Daven and Nena had already arrived. She gave both of them a hug and welcomed them to the house. They were moving to the living room to sit down to talk when the front doorbell rang. Amanda started to turn to answer the door when both Jena and Juila rushed down the stairs.

"We'll get it, Mom," Juila called over when she saw her mom turn.

"Thanks," Amanda called back.

Diane and Chris greeted the twins with hugs and the four of them came together through the foyer toward the living room. Amanda's parents had been so consumed with their conversation with the girls that they had failed to notice the addition of Riccan's parents until they were fully into the living room.

"Oh," Diane exclaimed as she looked away from Juila and saw the other guests.

"Diane and Chris," Riccan said as he looked from them to his own parents, "I'd like to introduce you both to my parents, Daven and Nena."

Chris was the first to move forward and offer his hand to Daven to shake. "I'm so pleased to finally get to meet the two of you. I have so many questions…"

"Dad!" Amanda warned. "Please don't barrage them with questions now."

"No, you're right, Amanda. I'll wait until after dinner, at least," he said with a huge grin.

Everyone in the room laughed and yet Amanda was certain he was not joking. On more than one occasion, her father had wanted her to tell him more about Tuala and its people. Now he had the chance to ask questions under the guise of getting to know Riccan's parents. She was sure he would find a way to take advantage of the opportunity.

Dinner was uneventful, much to Amanda's relief. The food had been served, praised, and then consumed with voracity. Conversation was kept to small talk throughout the meal. As everyone had finished eating, they decided to retire to the living room to be able to chat in comfort.

Naturally, Chris found a way to corner Daven to ask him all about his life as an Elder. Diane and Nena paired off and decided to walk the garden paths. Jena and Juila opted to tag along with their grandmothers.

Amanda walked over to Riccan's side and put her arm around his waist so she could lean against him. "I think the evening has been a success. Wouldn't you say so, too?"

"Yes, Amanda," he said as he kissed the top of her head tenderly. He tipped his head toward their fathers and asked, "He's going to be a while with this, isn't he?"

"You have no idea! Come on," Amanda chuckled and tugged Riccan along so they could take a seat on the couch. She wanted to be near her father to make sure he did not monopolize too much of Daven's time. For now, Daven appeared to appreciate the rapt attention. Amanda wanted to be ready to intervene when the time came.

Eventually the evening came to a close when there was one final surprise. Chris had been in deep discussion with Elder Daven when Chris said, "I wish there were some way we could be of more help with Amanda and Riccan's quest."

"Didn't Riccan tell you?" Daven asked with amazement. He looked abruptly over at his son who was sitting on the couch with Amanda across the room.

"Tell me what?" Chris asked with obvious confusion.

"Riccan has an e-commerce business dedicated to building a bridge between Tuala and Earth."

"What's it called and how does it help?"

Daven chuckled and said, "It's called TualaShop.com. The products on the store are for people from Earth to buy and wear so the people of Tuala will know they are safe to approach for help. If you get the tree of life pendant and wear it, then you might be able to assist a Tualan in trouble."

"How could wearing a pendant help?"

"Riccan has used elemy to infuse the pendants with something like a homing beacon for people from Tuala. You wouldn't notice the signal, but we definitely would," Daven said as he waved his hand to indicate all of the Tualans in the room. "When we see the tree of life pendant, whether it's on a necklace, bracelet, earrings, or even a design on a shirt, our attention is drawn first to the design and then to the power. It would be enough of an introduction to allow us to approach you for assistance."

Chris turned to Riccan and said, "That's very clever, Riccan. How long have you been working on this project?"

"I've been selling the items for the last ten years, but the invention of the internet has really increased my scaling across the world," Riccan replied modestly.

Amanda stared at her husband. She would have thought this income stream would have come up in the past. She had no idea he was even involved in e-commerce. She wondered what other things she had yet to discover about her husband.

A moment later, Riccan extended his hand out to Chris. He had used his telepathy to pick up some samples from his office to give to Amanda's parents.

Chris accepted the two items with delight. He discovered one was a leather bracelet and the other was a necklace. He handed the bracelet to Diane as she had come over to sit next to him. He watched as she put it on and admired how it looked. She took the necklace from him, opened the clasp, and then put it around his neck.

Chris looked down on the silver pendant. He lifted his hand and touched the delicate design. Already, he felt like he was becoming part of the team effort. He smiled up at Riccan and said, "Thank you for giving us these. We'll do everything we can for anyone who comes to us."

CHAPTER 27

Amanda tapped in the location of the Port of Cresdon on the plascreen. She was so thankful her husband was brilliant enough to program the telepod to navigate to the common local areas in Tuala so she would not have to solely rely on her ability to visualize the coordinates. She was still not very confident in her ability to get it right and she had no desire to be lost between the realms forever.

With the press of another button she was on her way to see Barla, she hoped. This trip was going to be her most difficult yet since Barla had no idea she had a niece who was going to stop by her house. She desperately wished her mother could have come along with her, but it just was not possible with the loss of memory through the veil for people from Earth. Unless, or until, her mother received a birth crystal, this was not going to be an option for her.

Bright sunlight poured in the windows of the telepod as she reappeared over the landing area some distance from the town proper. As she looked down, she was again impressed by how accurate her dreams had been when it came to Tuala. The landing area was identical to the one Bryon had landed at in her vision.

She set the telepod on the grass and powered down. She pressed the button to open the side door and felt the rush of sea air enter the cabin.

Unconsciously, she took a deep breath and tried to calm her nerves at what she was about to embark upon.

Not only was she going to introduce herself to her aunt, she was going to evaluate whether or not Barla was willing to be an owner of a samara. She also had the unpleasant task of letting Barla know she was not going to be able to see her daughter confirmed as Elder Wilken's successor. Now she wished she had told Rasa to break the news herself.

Without any further excuses for delay, Amanda left the telepod and cloaked it with the touch of a button on her remote. She followed the same path she had taken with Barla in her dream. Nothing was any different. She walked slowly and enjoyed the scenery and the grand houses which were coming closer with each step she took.

Only a few minutes had passed until Amanda found herself outside the picket fence surrounding the house of her aunt. She stepped along the path and went up the main staircase leading to the front door. As she raised her hand to knock, she noticed her hand was shaking. Her knuckles rapped on the painted wood surface and then she waited. Amanda was about to turn to leave when the door opened.

"May I help you," Barla asked the pretty stranger at the doorstep. She could not help but stare at the girl who looked so much like another person she had once known. The resemblance was uncanny. Her thoughts so distracted her that she almost missed the woman's introduction of herself.

"You don't know me, but my name is Amanda Stel. If you have a few minutes, I'd like to speak with you." Amanda wanted to say so much more, yet forced herself to close her mouth and allow Barla to decide what she would do.

"Amanda! Dear me! I'd hoped to see you and yet I never imagined it would be so soon. Please, come in!" Barla stood to the side as she held the door open and gestured for Amanda to enter the house.

Amanda stepped across the threshold and waited for Barla to close the door. She followed the older woman down the hall and into the grand living room. Again, it looked the same as she remembered. She smiled at Barla, took the offered seat, and dropped her handbag to the floor beside the chair. When she looked up at Barla, she noticed for the first time, the birth crystal swinging from its ornate chain around her neck. Just as she had seen on the samara, the crystals were a vibrant blue color.

"Can I get you anything? Water? Tea? Java?" Barla asked with a flustered tone.

"No, Barla, I don't need anything. Please sit so we can talk."

"Okay," Barla said as she sat in the chair across from Amanda. As she looked at the young woman, she was surprised to notice she looked very similar to her own daughter. She waited for Amanda to speak.

"Like I said, you don't know me. I have something to discuss with you. First, however, I have a message for you from Rasa. She wanted me to tell you no family will be allowed at the succession meeting with the Elders. She was very sorry you'd not be included."

"Oh, that is too bad. Ahn and I really wanted to be able to attend. How do you know Rasa?"

"It's complicated. Are we alone in the house?" Amanda suddenly realized their upcoming conversation was not one which should be overheard by anyone.

"Yes, actually, we are," Barla answered. She was not sure she liked having just admitted such a thing to a stranger. Granted, Jehoban had instructed them all to help Amanda. She trusted His judgment more than her own.

"Good because what I have to talk to you about is a very delicate subject. I have a message for you from your family on Earth."

Barla was more stunned than she would have thought possible. This was the last thing she had ever expected to hear, least of all from Amanda. She was supposed to be on a mission for Jehoban and yet here she was talking about her past on Earth.

"I know this seems to be coming out of the blue. Jehoban has assured me of the truth of what I'm going to share with you. Will you trust Him as a credible source in this?"

Barla hurriedly answered, "Of course. Please tell me what you know. I will believe you."

Amanda nodded and stared at Barla for a moment before she said, "You are my aunt. My mother, Diane Silnack, is your sister."

Stunned, Barla sat back in her chair and simply stared at Amanda. It made sense now for Amanda to look so much like Rasa. They were first cousins. As the realization of Amanda's statement dawned in her mind she could not help but smile. Tears of joy began to fall from her eyes as she leaned forward and held out her arms to embrace her niece for the first time.

Amanda smiled as she slipped out of her chair and onto her knees in front of her aunt. Her own tears were falling as she put her arms around her aunt's waist. She felt the woman's arms wrap around her shoulders and draw her close into the hug. Amanda had to smile as she realized how much more satisfying this hug was to the one she remembered from her dream while in the coma. This meeting had gone so much better than anything she could have imagined.

After a few minutes, Amanda pulled back and felt Barla's arms release her. She backed up and reclaimed her seat. "Rasa told me you finally received your birth crystal. It looks beautiful on you."

Barla's hand went up and touched the prized pendant and she said, "Rasa told me you asked Jehoban to give it to me. At the time, I could not imagine what would possess you to do such a thing. Now it seems to make more sense."

Amanda smiled at Barla's admission. She was so glad she had thought to ask for it to be done. She asked, "How far have you progressed with your crystal lessons?"

With a bit of pride, Barla replied, "I've become proficient through level seventeen."

Amanda's eyes widened at Barla's progress. She could see a newfound confidence in her aunt from what she recalled from her dream. "You do realize now you are able to travel to Earth without fear of losing your memory of here?"

"What? No, I hadn't even considered that aspect. I can't even imagine going back now. I had made my life here in Tuala with Ahn and I resolved myself to never seeing Earth again. I'll have to put some thought into it. I must admit, the idea of it scares me."

"I know the feeling!" Amanda chuckled with understanding.

Barla wanted to turn the conversation back to Amanda and asked, "What can you tell me about my family? Are they all well? Did Mom remarry? How about Dad? Saul?"

"In order: no, Grandma Silnack has never remarried and she lives in Oregon now. Grandpa Silnack died at the age of sixty-six in California. Uncle Saul lives with Grandma Silnack and has never married. My mom married Chris Covington, moved to Florida, and had three daughters. My sisters are named Carrie and Deanna. They are both married and have two daughters of their own. I have two daughters whom you have already met named Jena and Juila."

"I still can't believe those two girls are your children. I always felt a close kinship to them and now I know it's because they were my great-nieces. This is just so coincidental. It's hard to even imagine, don't you think?" Barla sat in her chair shaking her head at how everything had worked out.

Barla had a moment of sadness to hear of her father's passing and yet she was also relieved for her mother's sake to have him be gone. He had not been a pleasant man, nor was he easy to get along with. She was grateful for her brother living with their mother. Now she would not have to worry about either of them anymore.

"I somehow doubt coincidence has played any part in this. Jehoban seems to have His hands quite a bit in this whole matter."

Barla nodded in agreement.

"Would you mind if I called you Aunt Barla?"

"It would be my pleasure."

"I'd love to talk about our family more, but I've actually come for another matter entirely."

"What is it, Amanda?" Barla leaned forward in anticipation.

"Think carefully about when you came to the front door. Did you notice anything different or slightly strange?"

Barla scratched the back of her neck as she considered Amanda's question. Since she thought about it more, there was something. "Yes, I felt a tingling sensation almost like when I pull elemy from the earth. Is that what you mean?"

"Yes, exactly what I mean." She leaned over and picked up her handbag. "I'd like to show you something. I can't leave it with you, but I want to find out if it ultimately will belong to you. Will you promise to let me take it back with me when I leave?"

With a furrowed brow, Barla could not imagine not allowing her to take back whatever she had brought with her. "Of course you can take it back. It's yours, after all."

"You might not feel the same afterward. Just remember your promise." She reached into her bag and withdrew a cloth-covered bundle. "Hold out your hands and I'll put this directly onto your skin."

Barla hesitated, not liking how ominous this was beginning to sound. "It won't hurt, will it?"

"No. I don't believe it will. I'll watch carefully and take it back if it's not meant for you."

Barla raised her hands and watched avidly while Amanda let the crystal skull drop from the bottom of the cloth onto her own bare hands.

Instantly, Barla's eyesight disappeared from the room she was sitting in, to a place of visions. She saw a group of people all holding a crystal in their hands. They were all gathered together with smiles on their faces. The power surrounding each of them was palpable and the light poured out of the crystals like a rainbow, each color mingling with the others.

Barla looked up in confusion as the vision abruptly disappeared. She glanced down to her empty hands and back over to where Amanda had resumed her seat in the chair across from her. "What was that?"

"It's called a samara. What did you see?"

Barla told her.

Amanda nodded confirmation. She wrapped the crystal carefully and returned it to her handbag.

"What does it mean?" Barla insisted.

"It means this samara is yours. I will bring it back to you when the time is right."

"Why can't you leave it with me? I'd like to see more of that vision," Barla added.

"You promised I could take it with me. Remember?"

"I know. It's just it felt so amazing to be connected with the power of the samara. Right? It's called a samara?" She liked the sound of the name. It felt right.

"Yes, it's your samara. You are going to have to keep this as a secret between us for now. If anyone found out about it, then I think we would all be in deep trouble."

Barla nodded with understanding. Anything containing the amount of power she had felt from the samara was bound to bring trouble with it. She hoped she would be able to keep herself from sharing the news with Ahn. They told one another everything. She nodded again as she resolved to keep this strictly between the two of them. If the fate of Tuala depended on this secret, then she had to do her part, too.

Amanda stood from her chair and spoke, "I have to go for now. I don't want to be in Tuala too long with this power. Thank you for meeting with me and for believing me."

"Please come back soon. I can't wait for Ahn to meet you. When will we be able to get together again?" Barla stood abruptly and tried to stall Amanda's departure for a few more minutes.

"I will definitely be back. Unfortunately, I have something urgent to get done so I'll be tied up for a few days at least. If you want to get in touch with me, send a message on the patil to my husband, Riccan Stel. We have a patil on Earth so I'll be able to respond in a reasonable amount of time." She began walking out of the living room when she had another thought. "Do you want to walk with me to the telepod landing grounds? It's quite nice outside and it'd give us a few more minutes together."

"You fly a telepod?" Barla asked incredulously.

Amanda was starting to get used to this reaction since Bryon and Alena had said the same thing. She laughed and replied, "Absolutely! How else would I get here?"

"I guess I didn't really think about it," Barla chuckled. "I'd love to walk with you."

CHAPTER 28

Amanda waved goodbye to her aunt as she programmed the telepod to make one more stop in Tuala before she returned home. She smiled at Barla until everything went black during the transfer. In only three seconds the light returned and Amanda set the telepod down in the grassy field outside of Kirma.

She walked through the town until she arrived at the house of Bryon and Alena. She knocked on the door and waited for Alena to answer.

"Amanda! What a pleasant surprise. Come inside," Alena said when she opened the door.

Amanda entered the house and asked, "Is Bryon at work still?"

"Yes. Do you need him to come home?"

"Not particularly. This might be easier if he's not here."

"What's going on?"

"I've come to take Bryon's samara back to Earth for safe-keeping. I have a bad feeling about it being left here." Amanda hoped Alena would agree with her and not make this hard.

Alena sighed as she replied, "I can't tell you how happy it would make me if you did take it. It makes me so nervous having it in Bryon's desk drawer. I swear I can feel energy pulsating from his office whenever I go near it!"

"Really? That's interesting. I really can't stay long. Do you think we could go get it right now?"

"Absolutely. Follow me."

Amanda did not want to be rude and tell her she already knew where it was. She followed meekly behind Alena.

Alena unlocked the desk drawer and stepped away from it. "Please feel free!"

Amanda nodded and bent down to retrieve the samara wrapped in the towel. It was too bulky to put into her handbag so she unwrapped it and used her own smaller cloth she had brought for that purpose. She handed the bath towel over to Alena and said, "Thank you for letting me do this."

"Thank you for doing this!" Alena chuckled. "Do you want to stay for some tea?"

"No thank you. I want to get this back to Earth as soon as possible."

"I understand. I'll tell Bryon you came by and why."

"I'd appreciate it. Let him know he'll have it back when the time comes for him to use it."

"That sounds ominous. I'm not sure I want him to have it back."

"It'll be needed."

Alena led the way back to the front door and opened it for Amanda. "Have a safe flight."

"Thanks. I'll see you soon," Amanda answered as she walked down the sidewalk to return to her telepod. She hurried since the ominous feeling seemed to be getting stronger. By the time she reached her telepod she had found herself running.

Her fear did not dissipate until after she placed the two samaras into the secret chamber behind the library wall. She looked at all of the samaras together and said, "Five down, eight to go."

WILLIAN STUMBLED OVER the brush yet again. He fell to his knees and he angrily pounded the ground with his fists. This was not what he had planned. How was he supposed to convince Jena to come back home with him if he were lost in a never-ending jungle?

As darkness fell, Willian realized he was not up to taking on this journey without the help of his father. He turned around to retrace his steps when he noticed he could no longer see. The light had gone completely. He was going to have to spend the night alone in the jungle.

He dropped back down onto the ground disconsolately. Only then did he begin to hear all of the strange sounds around him. Before he had been too preoccupied with his desire to see Jena to notice anything other than his own thoughts. Now he was starting to get scared. He had never been so alone before. The enormity of his reckless decision to leave fell fully upon his shoulders.

When morning finally came, Willian was more than ready to go back to the cave and return to Tuala. He had just experienced his worst night ever. Never again would he venture over to Earth without a definite plan and transportation.

He had not gone as far from the cave as he had imagined. When it appeared in front of him he almost cried out for joy. Willian carefully inspected the opening to locate the swirling pattern which indicated it was an Ascension Gate. The last thing he wanted was to go into the wrong cave. The carving was directly over the top of the entrance.

He walked confidently into the darkness and automatically created a sphere of light. The moment he did, he realized how stupid he had been the night before. In his fear, he had forgotten all about his ability to make light. The night could have been so much more comfortable had he lit up the area where he had hunkered down.

At the back of the cavern, Willian stepped into the circular depression, thought fiercely about home, and whispered, "Inside Ascension." The light from his sphere of elemy disappeared as he traveled between the two realms. Too much time was going by and he began to concentrate even harder at his desired location before fear could overtake his mind.

With a suddenness which left him dizzy, he arrived at the gate in his father's Residence. Elder Debbon rushed forward and held him upright. He had no idea how his father knew he was coming, but he was thankful for the assistance.

"Are you okay, Son?" Debbon moved them both away from the gate.

"I am now. How did you know I'd be coming back through?"

"I didn't. I've been sitting vigil here ever since you left two weeks ago."

"Two weeks? I was only gone overnight." Willian looked up at his father's haggard looking face.

"That's what happens when you do not know how to use a gate,

Willian. Promise me you'll never do something so foolhardy again. You could have been lost forever you know." With his son's statement of only being gone overnight, he rapidly realized why his wife had been unable to reach Willian through his birth crystal since he had moved forward in time by two weeks and literally had not existed in their time anymore.

"I promise. Please tell me you'll help me go to see Jena. She has to see me. I've made too many mistakes and I have to apologize to her."

"I'll help you if only to keep you safe. It'll take me a few days to make the arrangements. Until then, you have another apology to make to your mother."

Willian dropped his head and nodded. He never wanted to hurt his mother. He had made a huge mistake. "I will. Can we go home now?"

"It would be my pleasure," Debbon said. He kept his arm around Willian's shoulder and ported them both unerringly to their estate.

They arrived directly in Chelesa's office. The moment the surge of power built up, Chelesa knew her husband was coming. She let out a squeal of delight when she also saw her son alongside Debbon. Her chair fell over in her haste to get out of it and run to hug her only child.

Tears coursed down her cheeks as she held her son's face as she inspected him for any injuries. She could not imagine why she had been unable to reach her son through his birth crystal. She had been beside herself with worry ever since she had felt the connection sever.

"Are you okay, Willian? Do you have any injuries? Where have you been? Do you know how worried we were?" She broke down in sobs and hugged her son tightly to her chest.

"I'm sorry, Mom. I never meant for this to happen. I thought I'd just go see Jena and be right back. I thought I was only gone overnight. It was the worst night ever, Mom. I'm so sorry," he sobbed as he realized how much he had hurt his mother. He hugged her tight and gloried in the feeling of being loved unconditionally.

AMANDA SPENT the next couple of days trying to determine a definitive plan of action regarding Neal's rescue. Riccan had already made his point clear. He did not like the idea of her showing up in Elder Vargen's district before the Elder had left for the convocation. Amanda had tried to convince him she would need to get the lay of the land before the rescue could be completed.

As she could see it, she needed to be able to navigate in the district with a certain amount of assuredness. Without knowing where she was going, she could not see how she could entertain a plan to get Neal out without incident. She had even thought of using the same type of disguise as Barla had her wear on her first trip to the marketplace in her dream. She was certain now about the dream telling her how to accomplish this task.

She thought more about her dreams to try to figure out anything else she may learn from her 'past.' If she already had all of the answers then all she had to do was pay attention to the details and turn them into a reality. It was during this train of thought where Amanda realized she did have an answer which would make everybody happy. Well, almost everybody.

Amanda hurried to the office and opened the secret compartment where the patil was stored. She turned it on and pressed the icon for sending a message. She searched through Riccan's contacts until she found Bryon's address. She typed up a message and was about to hit the send button when she realized this was not going to work. She was going to have to get him to go in the next day or two or it would not work at all.

She clicked on the button for a video call, entered Bryon's call sign, and waited. It seemed a long-shot for Bryon to be near his patil at home during the weekend. She held her breath while it continued to ring. Amanda was about to end the call when Bryon's face appeared on the screen.

"Amanda!" Bryon said with a pleased smile.

"Hi, Bryon. I hope you're not upset with me for bringing your samara to my house."

"Oh, not at all. In fact, it's a relief to not have to worry about it all the time."

"I'm glad to hear you say so. I just had a bad feeling about leaving it there so I decided to come pick it up on the spur of the moment."

"Like I said, it's no problem. Did you want to speak with Alena?"

"No. I called to ask a favor of you."

"Ask for anything. I will do whatever I can within my power to help you."

Amanda was slightly taken aback by his quick acquiescence. She had no idea of Jehoban telling everyone to assist her when asked. She simply felt very lucky to have people willing to help her at every turn. "Are you familiar with Elder Vargen's district?"

"Pretty familiar. I've been there on several occasions."

"Do you think you could go to an address I send you and deliver a message to the woman of the house?"

"I don't see why not. When do you need me to go?"

"Sometime tomorrow, preferably during work hours. I'd like Vinia to be alone when you give her the message."

"Sure. Anything else?"

"Yes, actually. Are you available all day on the first?"

"I can clear my calendar. What are you planning?"

"I'm going to get Neal out of Tuala and back to Earth. The wise-woman Copa gave me some drugs to give him to make him senseless. It's just occurred to me that I won't be able to get him back to the telepod without assistance."

"That's where I come in?" Bryon grinned.

Amanda smiled back at him and nodded. "When you go there tomorrow, can you try to plan the best escape route back to the telepod from their house?"

"Sure. This sounds like fun!"

"I'm glad you think so. Riccan is beside himself with worry over something going wrong. I'm sure he'll be much happier knowing you'll be with me."

"Why doesn't Riccan come along as well?"

"That's a good idea. I never thought to ask him. I see him so much on Earth I think I sometimes forget he's from Tuala as well. It would be even easier with two men. I'll ask him when I get off the line with you."

Bryon frowned slightly at Amanda's odd reference to their connection through the patil. He was not quite sure what 'the line' was, but he understood the gist of her meaning.

"What time do you think you'll plan to go over to the district tomorrow to meet with Vinia?" Amanda asked.

"I was thinking right after lunch would be most convenient."

"Great. I'll come to your work to give you the message and the powder from Copa."

"Why don't you come early and we can go to lunch together," Bryon suggested hopefully. He really wanted to get to know this fascinating woman a little better.

"As tempting as your offer sounds, I have to decline. Until I get Neal home, I want to limit the amount of time I spend in Tuala."

"I understand. Once you get him home, then maybe we can plan something with Riccan and Alena."

"I think that sounds perfect. Okay, well I'll see you around one tomorrow at your office. Can you let Frasnia know I'm expected?"

Bryon was still amazed at Amanda's ability to know everybody's names. He nodded and said, "Consider it done! See you tomorrow."

"Thanks. Bye."

"Bye."

The connection ended and the screen reverted to the home page where all of the icons showed vividly on the dark background. Amanda was pleased with the progress of her plan. She turned off the patil and stowed it away. She left the office to go find Riccan.

She ended up locating him in the garage with the telepods. As she told him Bryon's revisions to her new plan, Riccan seemed to agree with the idea. Then she wondered what he had been up to in her telepod.

"What are you doing out here?"

"I just finished installing a software upgrade to your control panel."

"What does it do?"

"After our conversation with Rasa, it gave me an idea. I'm actually surprised I didn't think of it on my own."

"Don't keep me in suspense! What does it do?"

"It connects you with the messaging in the patil. Rasa is going to send us a message when Elder Vargen arrives at the convocation. We'll need to be well on our way before the message comes in so, voilà, you've got mail!"

"Show me how to access it," Amanda said as she led the way into her telepod.

After a quick tutorial, Amanda was glad Riccan had thought to add it. She had wished, on several occasions, to be able to have access to a patil for seeing if anyone had responded to her inquiries while she was traveling. Now she would not have to worry about it anymore.

"Are you installing this change in your telepod as well?"

"Absolutely. It might even be a new option for all of the telepods I design. We could market to more business professionals so they will always be able to stay in touch, even when they're out of the office on business."

"Good thinking." Amanda got up from her seat and moved into the main cabin of the telepod. "Do you think this will be a good seating configuration for bringing Neal home? He's going to be completely out of it with the drug."

"Hmm, good point. Let me think on that, okay?"

"Don't take too long. We've only got the rest of today and tomorrow to make any changes."

AMANDA PACED RESTLESSLY around the house the next day until she was able to leave to meet with Bryon. She had Copa's letter to Vinia as well as the bag of resh. So much of this plan depended on the cooperation of other people. Additionally, she had no way of knowing if Vinia's emotional tie to Neal would keep her from helping them.

Once she had landed outside of Kirma, Amanda walked swiftly and confidently to Kirma Shipping and Receiving. She opened the door to office and was surprised to see Frasnia walking toward her.

"Amanda, Bryon was just telling me to bring you right into his office when you arrived." She touched Amanda's arm and gestured for them to continue through the main office toward Bryon's private room. Frasnia opened the door, but she remained outside as Amanda walked past her.

Amanda watched as Frasnia shut the door and left her alone with Bryon. She turned and raised her eyebrows in question.

"Frasnia's excited to find out what's going on with you. I haven't told her anything, but she's a very perceptive person. Hopefully, I'll be able to tell her all about what we've been up to."

Amanda sat down in the chair across from Bryon's desk and answered, "That might be a while, Bryon. I have no idea what type of timeline Jehoban has for the task He's set for me. I'm not even sure I understand the extent of His plan."

"No worries, Amanda. It'll all be revealed in good time. Who can dare be against us with Jehoban on our side?" Bryon smiled and rested his elbows on his desk as he leaned forward. "Now, what do you have for me?"

"Like I told you yesterday," Amanda started as she reached into her coat pocket and pulled out Copa's letter and bag of resh and set them on the table between them. "Copa said this note should be given to Vinia."

Bryon picked up the folded letter and turned it over several times in his hands as he contemplated his part in this journey. "Do you know what it says?"

"Not precisely, but the gist of it is the plan for Vinia to get Neal to drink the super-drugged tea so we can take him home."

Bryon nodded slowly and asked, "What name does Neal go by here in Tuala? I can't imagine it would be Neal since it's a dishonorable name without it ending in an 'n.'"

"Elder Daven told me he's registered as Nealan in the housing district of the Old Soul Engineering Facility."

Bryon nodded acceptance of the explanation. He should have known Elder Daven had been helping Amanda glean information. Elder Daven was, after all, Riccan's father. It would make sense for him to be involved. He had also been present at the all-important and bizarre meeting with Jehoban.

Amanda continued, "Riccan thought your idea of coming to help with Neal's extraction from Tuala was a good one. He's taking the day off of work and will be there with us. Are you planning on coming back to Earth or do you want to bring a separate telepod?"

Bryon frowned and considered Amanda's question. While he was intensely curious about seeing Earth again, he did not feel this would be an appropriate time to indulge in his whim. "I think I'll pass on it this time and bring my own telepod. It'll be one less thing for you to have to worry about."

Feeling relieved, Amanda stood up and said, "I really must get going."

"I wish you could stay longer," Bryon protested as he stood abruptly. "Let me at least give you a ride back to your telepod so I'll know you got there safely." He walked around his desk and opened the office door behind her. "Frasnia, can you give me a set of keys for one of the small pods?"

The red-headed secretary nodded and speedily procured the requested keys. She brought them over to her boss and held out her hand for him to take them from her. The expression on her face clearly said she desperately wanted to be included in this latest turn of events.

"Thanks, Frasnia," Bryon said as he closed his fingers over the keys and turned away from her. Together, Bryon and Amanda walked across the outer office and Bryon held the door open for Amanda. "I'll be back in about an hour," he said over his shoulder to Frasnia. He could not resist smiling smugly at her as she seethed for an explanation which was not his to give.

"Frasnia's not likely to forgive you keeping this from her," Amanda said as she swiftly glanced over to him as they walked across the business yard to where the company telepods were secured.

"I know, but what else can I do?" Bryon shrugged and kept walking until they got to the waiting telepod.

They entered the craft, settled in, and Bryon activated the unit. "Did you park where you did last time?"

"Yes."

"Okay, you know the drill. We'll be there in about three seconds." He concentrated on the coordinates and the world around them went blank as they transferred the distance to the landing field outside of town. Bryon set the telepod down, but he did not power it down as Amanda had assumed he would.

"What's going on?"

"I decided to go immediately to Vinia's house after dropping you off. There's no point in delaying any longer. Besides, the longer I stayed in the office, the more opportunity it would give Frasnia to keep drilling me for answers." He chuckled at his secretary's insatiable curiosity.

"Maybe we should try to find something for her to get involved with to keep her busy," Amanda suggested.

"Probably," Bryon conceded.

"Thanks for the ride, Bryon. Good luck with Vinia. Will you contact me to tell me how it goes?" Amanda stood up from the front passenger seat and started to move back through the telepod to leave.

"Absolutely. I'll message you once I get home from work this evening."

"Sounds great. Thank you so much, Bryon. You have no idea what this means to me."

"I think I have a pretty good idea. Now get going so I can carry on with my assignment." Bryon smiled to take any sting out of his words.

"Yes, sir!" Amanda teased back and stepped out of the telepod and walked the short distance to her own transport. She waved over to him, palmed the side door open, and stepped into the pod. Even as she watched, Bryon's telepod blinked out of existence and she was left alone in the meadow.

A shiver of apprehension passed through her and she hastily shut the cabin door. She settled herself into the pilot's seat and fastened her seat belt. Amanda rushed through the startup procedures and entered her final destination coordinates of the garage on Earth. Keeping a vivid visualization in her mind, she hit the activation button and sighed in relief as the world went black around her while she moved through space and dimensions to get back home where she felt safe.

CHAPTER 29

Vinia was momentarily speechless as she simply stared at the man standing outside her front door. When she had answered the knock, she had imagined it was her neighbor. The continued silence began to become uncomfortable until Vinia stammered, "Bryon! How may I help you?"

Bryon was equally stunned as he stared at Vinia. The very last person he had imagined seeing was the person who he was now meeting. "Sorry. Hi. I was asked to bring a message to a woman named Vinia. Is she here?"

"Yes, Bryon. Please come in," she said as she stepped back from the door to allow her visitor to enter her house.

Bryon shook his head in wonder as he walked into the house and looked around for another woman. It had been years since he had set eyes on this woman and he had never expected to see her again after the way they had parted ways so long ago. The house was eerily quiet and he asked, "Where are your kids?"

Vinia waved her hand non-committedly and said, "Please have a seat. We have a lot to catch up on." As she watched him settle onto her couch she realized how much Bryon resembled Nealan. She had never consciously noted the similarities before, yet now it was patently obvious. She had picked a man who reminded her of the person who had looked after her so well anons before.

"I really can't stay long. Where is Vinia?" Bryon asked.

Vinia sat down on the couch with a weary sigh and answered, "That's my name, Bryon."

"I don't understand."

"When we met all of those anons ago, you know I was in trouble and I was scared. I told you my name was Jinya, which is my mother's name. My real name is Vinia. What is this about a message for me?"

Bryon wondered what else about the past had been a lie. He shook his head slowly and pulled the note out from his jacket pocket. He held it out toward the woman whom he now realized looked so much like Amanda. Something strange was definitely afoot. "I was asked to deliver this note from wise-woman Copa. It has to do with Nealan."

"How do you know Nealan?" Vinia asked with surprise even as she took the proffered note and began opening it. She did not wait for an answer before she started reading the strange message. Her hands began shaking as she took in the meaning of the letter. "I knew it was too good to be true," she whispered as moisture began to fill her eyes and the world around her began to swim with unshed tears.

"I'm sorry, Jinya…I mean Vinia. I know this is terrible news…"

"You knew what this note contained?"

"Not exactly, but I am aware of what is going to happen."

"But it depends upon my cooperation, right? And you're certain I'll help? What will I do, Bryon? Where will I live? Who will keep me safe?"

"Are you still in trouble, Ji…Vinia?"

"Not like I was before. My circumstances have changed," she added lamely.

"It's just occurred to me that you will have to move when we take Nealan home to Earth. It won't be safe for you to remain behind for Elder Vargen to question." Bryon was thinking out loud and failed to see Vinia's reaction to the news of Nealan being moved to Earth.

"I want to go to Earth with him," Vinia stated.

Bryon shook his head sadly and answered, "I'm afraid that won't work."

"Why not? I won't help you unless you promise to take me too!"

"When Nealan crosses over the veil, he won't remember his time on Tuala. I'm sorry to be so blunt, but he won't remember you, Vinia."

"Surely he'll remember something," she begged as she grabbed Bryon's arm.

"Nothing, Vinia. I'm sorry," he replied as he put his hand over hers to try to comfort her.

She pulled her hand out from under his angrily and said, "Then why would I agree to this crazy plan?"

"Because you love Nealan. If he stays here, addicted to resh, he will die. If he goes home, he will be cured and won't have to even endure withdrawal pains because of going through the veil."

Vinia stood up from the couch and walked angrily into the kitchen. She grabbed the edge of the kitchen sink and leaned forward with her eyes shut. Even as she denied to herself the idea of being without Nealan, she knew she would help him. She loved him that much. It was really quite simple. If she loved him, she would have to let him go.

Bryon stepped quietly into the kitchen and waited until he saw her posture change from defiance to defeat. "You won't be alone, Vinia. Alena and I will be there to help you after…"

"After I trick Nealan into leaving, you mean?"

"After you save his life, Vinia. You know it's the right thing to do."

"I hate you, Bryon. You're asking me to tear out my heart and stomp all over it."

"I wish I could deny the truth, but it's the only way to keep Nealan alive."

"FINE!" she yelled as she turned around and glared up at Bryon and continued, "I'll do it! I'll drug Nealan into a stupor and watch as you take him from my life. Does that make you happy?" She crossed her arms over her chest and glared up at Bryon as tears coursed down her cheeks.

Bryon took the two steps which separated them and put his arms around her stiff body. He stroked the back of her head as he said, "Seeing you hurt doesn't make me happy. Thank you for agreeing to do the right thing. I'll make sure you're okay."

Vinia believed Bryon and finally relented. She uncrossed her arms and hugged Bryon's muscular waist as she broke down into violent sobs of heartache. After a few minutes she finally regained control of herself and asked the next obvious question, "When is this scheduled to happen?"

"Tomorrow morning," Bryon responded gently.

"Oh!" Vinia sobbed as she felt a new stab of heartache at the nearness of the end of her life as she had built it. "Can't we put it off until the weekend?"

"No, it has to be tomorrow."

"Why?"

"Because Elder Vargen will be away on business. It's the only time it will be safe to take him."

"Safe? How do you figure?"

"Okay, relatively safe then. It's the best we can do, Vinia. It has to be tomorrow. If we wait any longer, Nealan can die from the resh. You know I'm telling you the truth about the drug. I'm sure you've seen signs in Nealan."

Even as she hated herself for having to admit the truth she nodded. Her mind whirled at the idea of leaving Nealan, the house, the town, tomorrow. The word tomorrow seemed to loom in her mind as she tried to digest everything at once.

Bryon pulled the bag of resh from his coat pocket and held it out to Vinia. "This is for his morning tea. Copa left you instructions on its use. Be careful, Vinia. This stuff is really potent if you use it incorrectly."

"Don't you think I know that?" She grabbed the bag angrily.

"I'm sorry, Vinia." He held out his hands to offer comfort, but realized she was no longer in need of anything from him. "I should probably get going. We'll be back to get Nealan at half past seven tomorrow morning. Please have everything packed so we can take you and your kids, too. Good luck."

Vinia held the front door open for him and glared at his profile as he walked past her. "Call me if the plans change," she said woodenly.

"They won't. I'll be back tomorrow," he said quietly to her before he turned and walked briskly back along the path to where he had parked his telepod.

AMANDA AND RICCAN had stayed up late going over their plans for the rescue mission. The task seemed simple and straightforward which was what worried them the most. Everything seemed to be coming together so easily. Bryon had sent them a message in the evening as he had promised. Amanda let out a sigh of relief to hear Vinia would be on board with the plan. She had no idea of the amount of angst she was creating in the woman's life.

"Bryon brought up a good point," Riccan said.

"Hmm," Amanda said as her thoughts slowly came around to what her husband had said. She shook her head and looked directly at Riccan and asked, "What point was that?"

"We need to find a safe place for Vinia and her children so Elder Vargen doesn't bring her in for questioning."

"That was something I hadn't counted on. Do you have any suggestions?" She still could not keep her full concentration on their discussion. She was worried about what would happen with Neal once she did bring him back to Earth.

"A couple..." Riccan let the sentence drop off and hoped Amanda would come up with a solution of her own. He knew she was worried about the rescue, yet she seemed even more scattered than usual. "Amanda, what's going on in your head?"

"I know what we're doing is the right thing, but what about what Neal wants? Should we ask him if he wants to stay in Tuala? Aunt Barla wanted to stay."

"If he stays in Tuala he will die from the resh. Once he gets clean of it, then you can find out what he wants to do."

"That's just it, Riccan, he won't remember anything. I know exactly how terrifying it is to wake up one day and find out that years have passed without me in it. What will I tell his family? Certainly I can't tell them the truth."

"Why not?" Riccan challenged. He personally believed the two worlds should be united.

"Why not, you ask? Seriously?" Amanda threw the covers off of herself and got out of their bed. She began pacing the room. It was late and they only had a few more hours until they had to get up to start their journey to get Neal.

"Yes! Why not?" Riccan repeated. He watched Amanda from where he remained in bed. He hoped this conversation could soon be over so they could get at least a couple of hours of sleep.

"Well, let's see. You want me to go up to the Taivas family and say 'I found Neal on another world. He doesn't remember anything, but trust me when I tell you it's the truth.' Now who do you think will be the first person admitted to the loony bin? Me! I can't risk it, Riccan!" Amanda glared down at her husband as she crossed her arms.

Riccan patted the mattress and said, "Fine. We can go together and tell his parents we received a tip from an informant in Mexico. We'll say we flew down to get Neal on the promise to not alert the authorities."

Amanda rushed back to her vacated spot on the bed and said, "Your idea will work for exactly one day, Riccan. His parents will be so relieved to get him back alive, but then they will start to wonder why he has no memories. They are going to come to us and ask questions we can't answer and we'll be forced to lie to them. I hate this!"

"Let's not borrow trouble. We'll take it one step at a time and worry about the details later. We have to go to sleep now. Lie down." Riccan patted her pillow and began pulling the covers up to cover Amanda.

"I know you're right, I'm just worried."

"I know."

"I love you."

"I love you, too," Riccan replied as he leaned over and kissed her bare shoulder. "Let's pray about it, okay?"

Amanda smiled and offered her hands for Riccan to hold.

"Jehoban, please guide our steps with Neal. I know You have a plan and will keep us all safe. Thank You for watching over us." Riccan opened his eyes and squeezed Amanda's hands lightly.

"Thank you, Riccan. You always know the right thing to do."

"Good night, my love."

"Good night." Amanda settled down onto her side facing her husband. She did not think she would sleep a wink. The next thing she knew, her alarm was beeping. For several seconds, she could not place why she was getting up at such an early hour. Realization hit her hard and she groaned at how exhausted she was for such an important day. She hit the alarm to make it stop beeping.

"It's time to get up, Riccan," she said as she turned over and discovered his side of the bed empty. She touched the sheets and noted they were cold. He had been gone for quite some time. Curiosity got the better of her, and she left the bed to search for Riccan.

After several minutes of searching, Amanda located Riccan in his office. She walked quietly up to where he sat at his patil. With the way he was sitting, she could not tell if he were reading intently with his head resting on his fist, or if he had fallen asleep. She did not want to startle him awake if he were actually sleeping. Instead, she leaned forward to see what Riccan had pulled up.

Riccan turned his head at the small sound behind him and jumped when he discovered Amanda right next to him. He smiled as he realized he had scared her as much as she had him. "Sorry, love," he said as he touched her outstretched hand.

"What are you reading?"

"I was hoping to have an update from Rasa."

"And…"

"She sent a message saying some of the Elders have already arrived, yet they are still waiting for Elder Vargen."

"It's still early. Maybe he's on his way."

"No doubt," Riccan agreed. "I'll be happy to hear when he's out of his district."

"We need to get showered so when the good news comes we'll be ready to get going."

"You're right, as always," Riccan said as he turned the monitor off and rose to properly greet his amazing wife. "Have I told you how proud I am of what you're doing for Neal?"

"No," Amanda said as she put her arms around Riccan's waist and let herself melt against his body. "I thought you didn't approve."

"I wish it weren't necessary since the risk is so great, but I understand why you feel the need to get closure for Neal's family. That's the reason I love you so much…you always think about others." He kissed the top of her head and held her close for another several seconds. "Let's hurry up and get ready. I want to be in the telepod by the time we hear again from Rasa."

"Good idea," Amanda replied as she pulled one arm away from him and walked beside him as they went back upstairs to get showered.

RICCAN RELUCTANTLY SAT in the pilot's seat of Amanda's telepod. She had insisted he lead the expedition since he was more experienced than she was. He felt as though he were taking over the mission even though she insisted she did not mind.

He checked all of the gauges to make sure the telepod was operating normally. Now would be a bad time to have something go wrong with the mechanics. After tapping a new sequence on the glass panel, Riccan pulled up the link to his patil to receive any new messages.

Amanda leaned forward and also waited to see if any news had arrived from Rasa. She let out a small squeal of surprise when the program beeped and let them know there was an unread message. "Read it, Riccan!" she exclaimed in excitement. She could feel her heart begin to beat faster as their plan began to fall into place.

"He's in Manzanit!" Riccan called out.

"Let's go!"

"I'm going to send a quick message to Bryon so he'll know to meet us there," Riccan announced as he tapped out a quick sequence and hit the send button. "Okay, is your seatbelt fastened? I'm ready when you say 'Go'!"

"Go already!" She was so thankful for Riccan being with her. There was too much at stake for anything to go wrong.

The garage disappeared into blackness.

CHAPTER 30

Amanda noticed the landing pad beneath them almost at the same instant she saw Bryon's telepod pop into view right next to them. Once again, she was glad to know the telepods were unable to collide with one another in Tuala because of their built-in proximity sensors. There were only a few feet separating the two telepods as they landed in the next few heartbeats.

After fumbling with the latch on her seatbelt, she looked over at Riccan and smiled sheepishly. She was encouraged to see him grin confidently back at her.

"We'll soon be back on our way to Earth," Riccan encouraged.

"I hope so…that's the plan at least. Do you think we thought of everything?"

"Everything we can control. The rest is up to Vinia and Neal."

"That's what I'm afraid of," Amanda whispered to herself even as she stood up to go out the side door to greet Bryon.

Riccan palmed the control to open the door and immediately followed his wife's lead.

Both Riccan and Amanda were surprised to see not only Bryon, but Barla as well on the landing field.

"Barla!" Amanda called as she left her telepod behind and rushed forward to give her aunt a hug.

Barla smiled broadly and met her halfway and eagerly embraced her niece. "I hope you don't mind me tagging along. I thought you might like a little assistance."

"Are you sure? I don't want to get you into trouble with Elder Vargen," Amanda whispered into Barla's ear while she still hugged her.

"Don't worry about me," Barla reassured Amanda.

"We should get going," Bryon suggested.

"Right," Amanda agreed as she let go of her aunt and gestured for Bryon to lead the way. He had been the only one to actually visit the house where they were going to be picking up Neal.

Bryon led them down several short streets, turned left twice, and then half-way down another row of houses before he came to a stop in front of an unremarkable dwelling. He waited a second for everyone to get to the doorway before he knocked. He hoped Vinia had set everything into motion.

Several seconds ticked by before the door slowly opened. Vinia had a baby on her hip as she moved away from the opening to allow the group of people to enter her house. Her sad expression lightened momentarily as she saw Barla enter her house last.

Barla remained beside Vinia as the rest of the group moved into the living room to peer down at Neal who was passed out on the couch. "How are you doing, Vinia?" Barla asked as she touched the younger woman's arm gently.

"I don't know, Barla. What's going to happen to me now?" She could feel the tears quivering on the rims of her eyes as she looked up at Barla.

"You and your baby are going to come and stay with me for a bit, okay?"

"Really? You'd do that for me again?"

"Absolutely! Now tell me this precious little girl's name?" Barla asked as she leaned forward to look into the baby's face and smile.

"Her name's Danika," she answered even as she watched Bryon and the other man pick up Nealan from the couch and support him between them. The tears spilled over and rushed down her cheeks. One tear landed in Danika's hair.

"Do you have your things packed?" Barla asked gently.

"I do. It's all in the bedroom still."

"Let's go get it, shall we?"

"I don't have much," she said as she moved away from the front door toward the bedroom.

"It's just as well," Barla said as she followed the distraught woman. "We don't want people to really take much notice of us leaving anyway. Where are your other children, Vinia? They should come with us as well."

Another sob escaped Vinia's lips as she rushed forward to the sanctuary of the bedroom.

Barla began to worry about the woman's emotional state and followed her through the doorway. She looked around and only found evidence of the single bed. A quick look into the room across the hallway told her there was only the crib in the other bedroom. Only the infant was living in the house with them. Barla began to worry where the other children could have ended up. She did not have a good feeling about it, yet decided not to press for answers until they were safely away from Elder Vargen's district. The very last thing they needed was to create a scene where they could be identified by many people who would report the incident back to the Elder.

Barla could see Vinia was struggling to keep her hold on the baby while gathering up her belongings. She stepped forward and began picking up the several bags and putting the straps on her arm to be able to hold as much as possible. "Are the baby's things included in what you have here?"

"Yes."

"Is there anything of Nealan's you'd like to bring along as well? I'm afraid Elder Vargen's people will confiscate anything we leave behind."

"Good point." Vinia suddenly turned and left the room.

Barla looked around and noted the meager furnishings. It did not appear as though Nealan was a person who kept many things. She poked her head into the bathroom and saw all of the counters were already cleared of anything personal. She made her way back to the hall and noticed Vinia digging through a desk drawer one-handed in the living room.

Vinia whirled around as though she were doing something wrong. She held her hand behind her back as she declared, "I'm ready to go now!"

Barla could not be happier to know they were getting out of there. She knew they would have taken Nealan back to the telepods by now. Her only hope was they would be gone before Barla and Vinia got to the landing so they could avoid any type of scene. Barla led the way out of the house and waited while Vinia carefully closed the front door for the last time.

As it was still early, most people were enjoying their breakfast so the streets were relatively empty. Even so, Barla kept her head down and her steps brisk as they retraced the path back to the landing field. When she turned the last corner and could see the field, she breathed a sigh of relief to find only Bryon's telepod remained in the clearing.

She stepped up onto the ramp and put Vinia's possessions on the floor behind the second row of seats. When she turned to help Vinia into the telepod she noticed the woman's look of shock and betrayal. "What's wrong, Vinia?"

"Where's Nealan?"

"He's already gone. Come inside quickly so we can get going as well." She gestured for Vinia to move along when she saw her continue to hesitate.

"Did you know he wouldn't be here when we got here?"

"I'd hoped it would be the case. Please hurry, Vinia."

Finally registering Barla's distress, she stepped up the platform and into the telepod. She gave an involuntary squeak of surprise when the door shut immediately behind her.

Barla reached forward and took Danika from her mother's arms. She put her down in the passenger seat and buckled her in. "Get yourself fastened up, Vinia. We'll leave as soon as we are all secure." Barla took her own advice, turned, and stepped over to the co-pilot's chair where she sat down and put on her own safety harness. She looked over her left shoulder and confirmed Vinia's readiness before turning to Bryon and saying, "We're all set. Let's get back to the Port of Cresdon!"

"I hear and obey," Bryon teased even as he activated the telepod to begin the transfer.

As Amanda walked behind the three men, she wondered if she had needed to come at all. She felt pretty useless as the men did all of the hard work. The fact of her not having anything to do actually gave her time to look around and then start questioning several things.

First, Vinia looked remarkably like herself. She wondered if it were a coincidence or if there were something which needed more investigation. Hopefully, there would be time in the near future to find out more about the woman.

Second, she was stunned to see the physical changes in Neal's appearance. It had not dawned on her that they had both been transported back in time. She had been moved forward in time by wise-woman Copa, but Neal had remained in the past. He had aged through all of the years while being addicted to the resh, which had also aged him more.

Neal looked so different from what she remembered she began to worry about taking him back to his parents. What would they say about how much he'd changed? How would she explain it to them? He was so much thinner than he had been. His eyes had wrinkles around them and they seemed almost sunken into his skull. Surely some of his appearance was due to the addiction. Merely passing through the veil would alleviate one complication, but how much more time would be needed before he would recover his appearance?

They had reclined the rear seats of the telepod so Neal could be in a supine position for the trip to Earth. The men settled him onto the chair and fastened him in securely. Bryon stepped out of the telepod and Riccan moved forward to sit in the pilot's chair in preparation of leaving.

Amanda came forward and pulled the blindfold she had brought out of her pocket and leaned forward to place it over Neal's eyes. Since she was so close to him now, she could really see how much his experience in Tuala had aged him. With more than a little sadness for his loss, she gently placed the blindfold over his eyes and loosely tied it around his head. The very last thing they would need would be for Neal to wake up and see the telepod in their garage. If they wanted to keep their story low-key, he must remain as ignorant of his history as possible.

Amanda took her seat up front and fastened her own safety harness. "Let's get home, Riccan. I want this over with!"

"I couldn't agree more. Everything has gone so smoothly it's making me jumpy." Riccan palmed the door closed and began the telepod startup procedures. It was slightly different operating Amanda's more simplistic equipment rather than his own, yet he managed to get everything set to go in short order. "Here we go," Riccan announced as he issued the final command to take them home to Earth.

Seconds later they arrived inside their garage in Florida. No sooner than were they landed, they started to hear moaning from Neal behind them. Riccan and Amanda looked at one another in alarm and speedily unfastened their harnesses and bumped into one another to reach Neal before he managed to get his blindfold off.

Amanda laughed nervously and moved ahead of Riccan. She unfastened Neal's seatbelt and spoke softly, "Just one moment, Neal. Let me help you sit up." She nodded to Riccan as he held his hand over the button to open the side door of the telepod. "No, Neal, leave your eyes covered for a few more moments, okay?" She pulled his reaching hand away from his face.

Riccan appeared at her side and helped Neal to stand by grabbing his elbow and lifting. He wanted to get Neal out of the telepod, into their car, and off of their property as soon as possible. The less Neal saw of his surroundings, the better he would feel about it all. They had planned ahead and had already parked the 4-Runner in the empty bay next to where Amanda's telepod usually parked. Normally it would be vacant, but they had anticipated this part of the mission.

Amanda guided Neal on one side while Riccan helped on the other. Together they maneuvered Neal down the ramp, across the concrete and into the truck with very little resistance. Amanda was going to sit up front with Riccan until she could see Neal was not planning on leaving the blindfold in place if he were left alone. While Riccan moved around the truck to get into the driver's seat, Amanda got into the back seat and made sure Neal's seatbelt was fastened.

Without any further delay, Riccan started the truck at the same time as opening the garage door. He drove away from his house faster than he normally would. Once they made it to the main road, he felt it would be safe for Neal to remove the cloth.

"Amanda? Is that you?" Neal asked uncertainly.

"Yes, Neal. It's me."

"I don't understand. What's going on?"

"You've been missing for many years, Neal. We just rescued you and now we're going to take you back home to your parents." Amanda tried to sound as calm and reasonable as possible.

Neal wanted to see Amanda for himself. He grabbed the cloth and pulled it down his face until it was hanging around his neck rakishly.

"Amanda! It really is you. It seems like forever since I've seen you! What do you mean by saying I've been missing for years?"

"It's a long and complicated story," Amanda began. She hastily glanced toward her husband and caught his eyes looking back at her in the rear-view mirror. "We've been working on a plan for getting you back home for many months now. Today you get to go home, Neal."

"Why am I so tired?"

"You've had a really long journey. It's understandable if you want to sleep a lot. It's okay. Your body is going to need rest to allow you to recuperate." She put her hand on his forearm to let him know he was among friends now. Even though everything she was telling him was true, she felt like she was lying through her teeth and she hated every minute of it.

The hum of the engine and the lull of the road caused Neal to fall asleep in short order. Amanda was so relieved she sighed. She leaned forward and whispered to Riccan, "Can you please hurry? I'd like to get Neal home without having to answer any more of his questions."

"I'll do my best, honey. You're doing fine, though." Riccan patted her hand as it rested on his shoulder. He could appreciate the angst she was enduring on this last journey. If he could do anything to alleviate her pain, he would try to make it happen. He pressed the gas pedal down a touch more and used a small amount of elemy to clear a path for their driving. There were some times when using his power could be justified; nobody would get hurt with this unorthodox use.

Amanda had plenty of time to think about the life they had just forced Neal to leave. She had seen the look of utter despair on Vinia's face. She felt somehow responsible for the pain she had inflicted on the other woman. There would have to be some way for her to make it up to her.

Amanda was relieved to know her Aunt Barla had been there to look after Vinia. She would have had more reservations had it just been Bryon alone trying to console the distraught woman. The infant the woman had been holding had also been a shock. She had never imagined Neal would have started a family while he was in Tuala. He had always been so adamantly opposed to having children when they were engaged. She felt somehow betrayed with this new discovery.

She looked carefully at Neal's sleeping face. Here she was...in a car with the two men who had managed to capture her heart. They were nothing like one another and now she could not imagine spending even another hour with Neal. So much time had passed to where they really had nothing but their past in common.

She hoped he would feel the same or this rescue mission could turn her life into a major complication. Who am I kidding? This whole ordeal will create a lot of trouble. Neal will definitely have questions once he's well rested. His parents will surely have a barrage of questions themselves. She had just opened Pandora's Box and yet it felt like she had done the right thing where Neal was concerned.

The forty-five minute drive was decreased by fifteen minutes with Riccan's subtle use of power. They turned into the Taivas family driveway and pulled up in front of the entrance. Riccan shut off the engine and twisted around to face his wife. "Are you ready?"

"No! Let's just get this over with," Amanda replied. She turned to face Neal and once again wondered what his mother would say about his appearance. There was no other way to find out other than to just wake him up and take him inside.

She gently shook Neal's shoulder and said, "Neal, it's time to wake up. We've brought you home. Neal?"

It took several moments for Neal to wake up enough to open his eyes. Everything remained blurry and his thoughts seemed very disjointed. He had no idea how he had ended up being in a vehicle, let alone why Amanda and this stranger were with him. He felt as though something important had been forgotten, yet he could not dredge up the truth of it. Neal shook his head and rubbed his eyes with his hands.

When he finished, he simply stared at his hand as though he did not know whose they were. His fingers were thinner than he remembered and his fingernails were jagged. He looked down and did not recognize the clothes he was wearing. "What's going on, Amanda?"

"Like I said before, Neal, we've brought you home. I'm sure your parents are anxious to see you." Amanda's nerves were beginning to fray. They needed to get Neal inside the house so they could leave and go on with their lives. She knew it would never be so simple, yet she continued to delude herself into the hope.

Amanda opened the rear door and stepped out of the vehicle at the same time Riccan did as well. Together they walked around the rear of the truck and Riccan opened Neal's door for him. They watched as Neal fumbled with his seat belt. Riccan stood alert to make sure Neal would be stable on his feet. They had no way of knowing how the transfer across the veil and the relief from the resh would affect his balance.

Neal seemed able to remain standing so they took their posts on either side of them as they slowly approached the front door. Amanda had a feeling of déjà vu as they stood outside of the door while Riccan knocked. This felt so eerily the same as her homecoming dream while she was in her coma, she could only wish it would have as happy an ending.

A few moments passed before they could hear footsteps approaching from the other side. Amanda could hear Jessica calling out to someone else in the house that she was answering the door. Amanda's palms were sweating and her heart was racing as she watched the door slowly swing open.

THE HUNTERS OF SOULS
BOOK FOUR OF THE CHOSEN

CHAPTER 1

Amanda Stel waited anxiously as the door opened. As she had expected, Jessica Taivas answered their knock on the door with a pleasant expression on her face. Even as Amanda watched, she saw Jessica's gaze travel from her own face over to Nealand's. Before she could even react, Jessica's eyes rolled back into her head and her body crumpled to the floor. Luckily the door frame broke her fall so her head did not strike the ground.

Without pausing, Riccan rushed forward and kneeled next to the older woman to check her vital signs. Instinctively, he pulled some elemy from the Earth and used it to assess her general health to make sure an ambulance would not be necessary. As he suspected, he discovered she had merely suffered a mental shock from seeing her long-lost son at her doorstep. "She's going to be fine. Help me get her inside onto the couch," he said to his wife as Neal did not seem to understand what was going on.

It was understandable for Neal to be confused. After all, he had just come out of a drugged stupor and been transported between worlds after having been missing for eight years. He had received just as many shocks as his mother and he was still coping. Neal only stared at the scene in front of him and tried to figure out why there would be so much fuss about his coming home.

Riccan moved behind the body and grabbed under Jessica's arms while

Amanda reached down to grab Jessica's knees. Between the two of them, they were well able to maneuver her into the house. They had just turned the corner of the entry hall when Neal, Sr. noticed the commotion. He rushed forward and directed the group to set her down on the nearest couch.

Only after she was settled did Neal, Sr. look up and ask what had happened. He had been surprised to see Amanda at their house and he did not know the man who had held his wife. "What's going on, Amanda?" he began and then a movement from the doorway caught his eye. The shock of seeing his son registered on his face and he was thankful he was already sitting on the couch next to his wife. It was clear now what had happened to Jessica.

Jessica began to stir. She took several deep breaths and she moaned. After assuring himself that Jessica would be recovered momentarily, Neal, Sr. rose from the couch and slowly approached his son. "Neal? Is that really you?" He had to ask since the man standing before him was not only quite a bit older than he should be, he was also thin and haggard looking.

"Yes, Dad. I don't understand what's so wrong about me coming home," he said with a worried glance toward his mother.

"You don't understand...," Neal, Sr. repeated and turned around to look back at Amanda with raised eyebrows for an explanation. "Where did you find him, Amanda? I'm assuming you found him since you brought him home."

"It's a long story which I think should wait until a later date. Neal has been through quite an ordeal and I think he needs to spend some time sleeping and eating regular meals. I'm not sure of his whole story, but I can tell you we located him down in Mexico."

"Mexico?" Jessica spoke for the first time. She had recovered enough to sit up on the couch and simply stared at her son in wonder.

"Of course," Neal, Sr. said as he rushed forward and hugged his son. "We're so glad to have you back home with us, Neal."

"I think we should leave so Neal can get some rest," Amanda said during the lull in conversation. The sooner she got out of the house, the better she would feel.

"You can't leave yet, Amanda," Neal, Sr. said as he turned to face her.

"We need to know where you found him and how you came to find him. There are far too many unanswered questions."

Riccan stepped away from Jessica and moved closer to his wife as though protecting her and answered, "There will be plenty of time for that in the future. For now, let's just leave it alone. Amanda and I must get going. We're glad you have your son back." He took Amanda's hand in his own and asked her, "Are you ready."

Amanda did not trust her voice so she simply nodded. Her eyes lingered on Neal's face and she was haunted by what she saw. She wanted him to get better, yet she no longer felt any connection to the stranger standing before her.

Riccan tucked her hand into the crook of his arm and he led them out of the house. He opened the passenger door of the truck and waited for Amanda to get seated before he went around to the driver's side and got in. He turned on the engine and began pulling away from the house. With one last look in the rear-view mirror he saw Neal, Sr. standing in the open front door and wondered how long they would be able to keep the questions at bay; hopefully long enough for them to come up with a plausible excuse for Neal's absence.

CHAPTER 2

Rasa tried to hide her nervousness while she sat next to Elder Wilken while the other Elders filed into the large conference room of the Manzanit Residence. Most of them she had heard of, however, only a few were personally known to her.

She wondered if the order in which they entered had anything to do with their alliances. She did not care for the scowls she received from nearly every man present. She could, however, appreciate their concern over a woman sitting in on their meeting since they had not been told the identity of the proposed candidate.

The convocation proceedings were projected to be long and arduous considering what was at stake. The Ascension Gate located at Manzanit was the most powerful gate in all of the world. Many of the Elders present had hoped to have one of their own grown children be brought forward as a succession candidate.

Once everyone had taken a seat, Elder Wilken stood at the head of the table and cleared his throat. "Thank you my fellow Elders for coming to this succession convocation. I understand that this type of meeting is unusual; however, there is a precedent for what I am proposing. I'd like to turn over the rest of the meeting to be conducted by our First Elder." He took his seat and nodded his head to Debbon who had taken the seat immediately to his left.

Instantly the men around the table murmured among themselves. Uvan spoke what was on everyone's minds when he said, "Excuse me. Do you think we should be speaking formally with someone not our own in attendance? What is the meaning of this, Wilken?"

"Thank you for your concern, Uvan," Debbon said as he stood and nodded gravely for the introduction. The group's complaints quieted, yet they were not appeased by the departure from tradition.

"We are gathered together today to discuss the successor put forward by Elder Wilken. The woman you see here today," he turned and nodded solemnly at Rasa, "is the proposed candidate."

Pandemonium erupted. All of the men spoke at once against the meaning of Debbon's outrageous statement.

Debbon held his hand up for silence. After several minutes of being ignored, he used the power of his position to command the room to be quiet before he continued, "As Wilken has stated, there have been cases in the past where Elders have proposed candidates not of their own blood to follow in their post."

"None of them proposed to put a woman in a man's place!" Yingun yelled as he stood abruptly and placed his fists on the table. He looked around the room for support in his outburst and was pleased to see several men nod in affirmation.

"Yingun, please sit down. Your comment is out of line and not in keeping with the dignity of this proceeding."

"There's no dignity in offering a woman as a candidate and you know it!" he retorted even as he resumed his seat. He folded his arms across his chest and sat back abruptly in his chair.

"We will hold this meeting with the formality to which it is owed. With all present, we will begin by taking an initial vote to see where we stand with Rasa as the successor for Manzanit. For the record, each person present will give his name, the name of his precinct, followed by his vote. I will begin. Debbon of Elder Isle. My vote is yes." He nodded to the man on his left as he resumed his seat.

"Rylon of Menad. Yes," he spoke softly, never taking his eyes off of Debbon.

"Daven of Pantano. Undoubtedly yes," Daven said with a smile first at Wilken and then at Rasa. He approved wholeheartedly of this departure from the stuffy tradition.

"Jedon of Neve. Yes."

"Quentien of Gamb. No."

Rasa's breath caught in her throat. She knew this was going to be difficult, yet she never imagined the Elders would go against Jehoban's express wishes for her to be placed in this post. Then it occurred to her, these men did not know all of the facts. She glanced over at Elder Debbon to see what he was really trying to accomplish with this preliminary vote. Surely there was something else afoot other than a simple vote.

"Tarshen of Sambur. I respectfully abstain from my vote until I may hear about the candidate's qualifications." He nodded firmly and then looked down at his folded hands resting on the table.

"Uvan of Secar. No," he said as he continued to glare at Rasa.

"Vargen of Apio. No."

"Xylen of Noidad. No." He looked to his left as the silence continued.

Yingun remained sitting with his arms crossed and refused to speak.

Debbon spoke suddenly, "Elder Yingun, either you will participate as is required in this meeting or we will be searching for yet another successor before this day is done. It's your choice."

With a glare at the censure, he spoke curtly, "Yingun of Gaud. No!"

"Senjin of Argot. Yes."

"Emmin of Telae. Yes."

"Olguin of Genip. Abstain."

"Zigern of Neum. Abstain."

"Wilken of Manzanit. Yes," he spoke firmly.

"So, the first vote is seven for, five against, and three abstentions. We are not required to have a unanimous vote for this to be officiated, only a majority is needed. For those who are opposed, please explain your reasoning," Elder Debbon continued. "Quentien, please begin."

He looked rather uncomfortable at being singled out and shifted in his chair. "Elder, don't you think it'd be better to discuss this privately?" His gaze shifted nervously over to Rasa and back to Debbon.

"This is a closed hearing. Anything said in this room will remain confidential. Please proceed." Debbon deliberately disregarded Quentien's real reason and stared at him to begin.

"Very well," he began quietly. "It is well-known that the position of Elder is reserved for men. Obviously, Rasa is not a man. Therefore, it goes against tradition. That is all I wish to say on the matter."

"Uvan," Debbon said, "Is this also your concern or do you have other reasons?"

"No, First, that is my reason as well."

"Very well. Vargen?"

"I'd hate to see what other traditions would be flouted should we allow this break."

Debbon nodded at Vargen's answer and then looked at Xylen with raised eyebrows.

"It's just wrong. I don't want to have to pander to a woman's ever-changing moods when it comes to matters of importance. This would set a terrible precedent which would make us look weak in the eyes of the populace. No amount of proof will change my mind."

"Your position is duly noted, Xylen. Thank you for your honesty," Debbon said with a slight nod. He was not looking forward to the next Elder's opinion only because he knew it would be less eloquent than Xylen's. With a deep breath he made eye contact with Yingun and lifted his chin minutely to indicate it was now his turn to speak.

Unlike all of the others, Yingun could no longer remain seated. He jumped out of his chair and planted his fists on the table. His face began to turn red and as he began speaking globules of spittle came out with each angry word, "To say this goes against tradition does not cover the blasphemy of the situation. A woman is unfit to be a representative of Jehoban. *Jehoban is a man*, therefore **men** have been appointed to lead the people. **She** would be an abomination and will bring down the power of the Elders." He looked at the Elders for several seconds to try to get them to realize the error of their ways before he seemed to deflate and sink back into his seat.

Debbon stood to draw attention away from Yingun and said, "Thank you for your impassioned response. Wilken, will you please describe how you came to have Rasa as your successor? I believe once everyone knows what I know, they will have a different opinion on the matter." He sat down again and waited.

"First of all, you all know I have a biological daughter of my own. Because she has neither the aptitude nor the desire, she has been excluded as a viable successor to my position. I have met with Jehoban on several occasions to discuss this delicate matter and He has repeatedly told me an answer will be revealed."

"I'd hardly say having some woman show up on your doorstep would qualify as an answer, Wilken. Really, have some common sense, man!" Xylen spoke out scornfully.

"This meeting will be respectful of each person's turn to speak. There will be no more outbursts unless you have been asked to talk!" Debbon said forcefully as he scowled down at the far end of the table where the dissenters had positioned themselves as far from the candidate as possible.

"As I was saying," Wilken continued, "I have been awaiting an answer. Several weeks ago, Rasa came here to my Residence..."

"Just as I said," Xylen spoke quietly to Yingun who nodded in agreement.

Debbon glared a warning.

"...Rasa had been ordered by Jehoban to come to me for instruction. So you see, Jehoban has sanctioned this so we must abide by His decision." Wilken could not see where anything more needed to be said so he resumed his seat.

Quentien raised his hand to be able to speak. After receiving a nod he asked Rasa, "Were you aware of Wilken's visits with Jehoban?"

Rasa nodded and answered, "I knew he had come to speak with Jehoban on many occasions. The nature of his visits were never made known to me as they were private meetings with Jehoban."

"How can we be sure you weren't lurking in the hallway and overheard Wilken's dilemma? What better way to bring up your station than to presume upon our good will and put yourself forward as Jehoban's choice?" Xylen accused rudely.

Rasa jumped as Debbon slammed his hand down on the table and said, "Xylen, you have already been warned. If you wish to continue to participate in this meeting, you will allow me to silence you until you have been called upon."

Xylen began to shake with anger at being insulted and shamed in front of a woman. His pride wanted him to get up and walk out of the meeting, yet his calculating side wanted to know every detail of the proceedings so he could have ammunition against the other Elders in future disagreements. He mirrored Yingun's posture as he folded his arms angrily and sat back in his chair. Finally he nodded agreement to Debbon's terms to stay in the meeting and seethed anew as he felt the compulsion to remain silent fall over his mind. Debbon would pay for this.

Rasa spoke up for herself and said, "I would not incur Jehoban's wrath by being deceitful in this matter. Jehoban asked me personally to pack and move here to Elder Wilken's Residence. I had no idea of the reason why until Elder Wilken informed me of his decision in the matter of making me his successor. I was just as reticent of the position as some of you have been. I assure you, I will follow Jehoban's wishes in this matter."

"Thank you for clarifying your position, Rasa," Debbon said. "I'd like to take another vote, by a show of hands, if you agree to Rasa as the successor." Debbon counted each hand and noted all of the original votes in agreement were still the same. Only Zigern, who had originally abstained, changed his vote to yes.

"I will remind everyone that their affirmative votes are final. Technically, we now have the majority vote to conclude this session. However, I feel it would be imperative for each of you to get to know Rasa on your own. This session is adjourned for each of you to take advantage of the opportunity to speak with Rasa and Wilken until we reconvene tomorrow at the same time. Good morning Elders," then he turned to Rasa to include her in his farewell, "Rasa."

Debbon instantly removed the silencing compulsion from Xylen. He regretted the necessity, yet he needed to have order in his meetings; otherwise being First was an unnecessary title. Rasa was going to need as many supporters as possible if she wanted any chance of succeeding as the first female Elder ever.

He watched each Elder file out of the room and noted their postures and groupings to know from where Rasa's troubles would come. He looked over at Rasa and saw she had also taken her own inventory and he was pleased to know she understood the battle she had just began. He hoped she had the strength to endure.

CHAPTER 3

D r. Gascon could hardly wait for the private investigator to leave his office before he picked up the newest stack of pictures and documents. His office door clicked shut softly even as he ripped open the sealed envelope and pulled out the paperwork. Somehow or other he was going to find out what Amanda Stel was hiding. Ever since she had come out of her coma, she had made some unusual friends and continued to act in suspicious ways.

The activity levels around Amanda's house remained rather boring. The children went to school and returned home with their usual friends. The gardeners and maid each made their scheduled appearances. Nothing seemed out of the ordinary.

Dr. Gascon turned to the last photo and drew it closer to his face. There were three people in the 4-Runner. Who was this mysterious man in the back seat with Amanda? He picked up the supporting documents and read through them searching for any entry of an unknown person going to the Stel house.

Finding no explanation, Dr. Gascon punched his fist down onto the mahogany desk in frustration at the ineptitude of the private investigator. It was obvious the man had left his post or had fallen asleep to fail to notice the entrance of an unknown male to the Stel residence. When he came back next week for his weekly update, he was certainly going to let the man have it for his incompetence.

Picking up the photograph again, Dr. Gascon brought it close to his face to try to discern the facial features of the man in question. He remembered he had a magnifying glass in his desk drawer and swiftly retrieved it. He set the photo on his desk top and set about memorizing every detail.

There was definitely something strange going on at the Stel residence. This new report clearly stated there were no visitors at the Stel house and yet Riccan and Amanda had clearly been seen driving an unknown male from their house. He was going to have to get to the bottom of this mystery. Eventually, he would find out this man's identity and the reason why he had gone to Amanda's house in the first place.

BEHN WAITED IMPATIENTLY for his sister, Valentina, to be ready to leave. For some reason she seemed to take longer when he was in a hurry. He glanced at his watch for the fifth time in two minutes and then crossed his arms in frustration as he leaned against the frame of the front door.

Valentina rushed out of the bathroom and made a mad dash for her bedroom before finally emerging into the hallway. She really had not intended to take so long, but she was nervous for today's activities and her stomach was rebelling.

"Sorry, Behn! I'm really trying to hurry," she called as she remembered one more thing she had forgotten in her room and turned back to get it.

"Come on, Val!" Behn cried. One more minute and he was going to leave without her he decided. He glanced at his watch to start timing.

Clutching her almost forgotten purse in her hand, she trotted down the hallway to the front door. She had no way of knowing she had made it to her brother with ten seconds to spare.

Behn gave her a scathing glance before he turned and pushed the screen door out of his way. He walked briskly to his car and got into the driver's seat. By the time Valentina got into the passenger's side, Behn already had his seatbelt fastened and the engine running. He put the car into gear and started rolling even as his sister was still closing her door.

"Behn! Be careful! I almost didn't make it into the car before you started driving!"

"You were fine. Put your seatbelt on before you get me a ticket," he said as he spared a glance toward his sister. It was certainly easier to get crystal lessons at his girlfriend's house before he had to involve his sister. He was starting to wish he had kept it a secret a bit longer, not that he had had much choice in the matter when his sister had caught him practicing in his room.

"We're not in that big of a hurry, Behn," Valentina said with exasperation. She promptly fastened her seatbelt and remained quiet for the remainder of the five minute drive. When they turned into the private paved driveway, Valentina could not help but be impressed with the luxury of the Stel residence.

The ornate gate over the driveway parted in the middle and began to slowly swing open to allow Behn's car to continue down the driveway. Only then did she realize Behn had not had to enter a code to open the gate. "Why didn't you have to use the code?" she asked with more than a little bit of annoyance. She still recalled the time she had waited outside the gate to be admitted to the house when she confronted Juila about lying to Behn.

"They programmed the gate to know my car, obviously," he replied. Once again he regretted the necessity of having to bring his sister along. These sessions were the only time he got alone with his girlfriend, Juila, outside of school.

Now he had to share that time with his sister. His only consolation was knowing Valentina would be working with Juila's twin sister, Jena, in a different room so he could study with Juila by himself. Their levels of skill were different and it got too confusing and frustrating to be learning together.

Valentina crossed her arms and sulked until they reached the end of the long driveway and parked in the circle at the end near the front door. The house was very grand with three-car garages on both sides of the immense mansion. She approved of the symmetrical design of the whole house.

Without waiting for her brother, she left the car and stomped up to the front door. The faster she learned what she needed, the sooner she would not have to endure the time with her annoying brother. She reached up to knock on the door just as it swung open.

"Hi, Val! You guys are just in time," the pert blonde girl said with a smile.

"Hi, Jena," Behn said as he finally arrived at the door.

Jena stood back to allow the two guests to enter the house. The trio walked through the grand foyer, past the elegant staircase, and into the living room. Juila was sitting on the leather couch and smiled at Behn when she saw he had finally gotten to their house.

"Have you guys eaten or do you want to get right to your lessons?" Juila asked, knowing her boyfriend was always eager to eat.

"I could go for something," Behn answered as expected.

"You would," Valentina said sarcastically and then turned to Jena and asked, "Did you want to eat, or do you just want to get started?"

"I don't mind either way. Besides, I could always whip something up while you're practicing."

"Fine, let's get started then," she said and began walking down the hallway toward their usual study area in the office.

Jena grinned over her shoulder as she followed their guest and left her twin sister alone with Behn.

"What's up with Val?" Juila asked quietly as she stood up and walked into the kitchen.

Behn followed closely and answered, "I got mad at her for taking so long getting ready to come over here."

"Oh." Juila had reached the island in the kitchen and turned to ask Behn what he wanted to eat.

Behn had something else in mind as he came up close behind her. When she turned around he caught her up in his arms and drew her body close to his while he bent down to kiss her lips. Not knowing whether or not her parents were home, Behn kept the kiss short but thorough. When he let her go, he smiled down on her and said, "I missed you."

"I see," Juila smiled up at him and could feel her cheeks blushing even as she tried to control her reaction to his closeness. "I thought you said you were hungry," she said in an attempt to change the subject to something less embarrassing.

"I am. Can't you tell?"

Juila squirmed out of his arms and walked around the island to put some distance between them. Never before had she felt so out of control as when she was around Behn. Before she had just thought it was because he was so handsome or because he was obviously interested in her; that was before she discovered he was also from Tuala. When he had only been a boy from school on Earth, he seemed intriguing, yet definitely out of the question as a life-mate.

She was from Tuala and would be expected to return home when she finished with school. What she had originally believed was an infatuation with this boy was beginning to feel quite different and, frankly, it scared her more than a little bit.

The rational side of her brain reminded her of the fact that she was sixteen anons old, after all, definitely not ready to settle down in a relationship. If only she could just listen to reason; her emotions and body had other ideas. Behn was obviously perfect for her.

"What would you like to eat?" she asked to get her mind off such an embarrassing train of thinking.

"Surprise me!"

Juila knew Behn preferred eating meals from Tuala so she concentrated on creating a dish she had not served him before. On the island between them appeared two plates and bowls with the appropriate silverware. She looked up to see Behn's reaction and was pleased to see his surprise.

"It must save a lot of money to not have to buy food when you can just create it out of nothing." Behn wished he could make food so effortlessly. *One day*, he thought to himself.

"Oh, we have to buy this food, too. My father's housekeeper in Tuala keeps the larder stocked for us to use."

"I hadn't thought about that before. What keeps a person from using the elemy to get the food directly from the source?"

"Behn! That's stealing. Nobody would go that far, it's wrong!"

When Juila put it that way, he felt stupid for even asking. He clearly had a lot to learn about the societal structure of his birth place. If he ever wanted to go back to live there, he would need to pay attention to all of the details Juila shared with him. Deciding to change the subject he pointed to the plate and asked, "What is this?" He pulled out one of the stools and sat down at the island even as he brought the plate closer to him.

"It's a pulled foxl dip," she answered. She could tell his attention had shifted from herself to the food so she felt it was safe to go back around the island to sit on a stool next to her boyfriend. She brought the plate and bowl closer to herself and instructed, "Dip the sandwich into the foxl broth and tell me what you think."

"Oh, it's like a French dip then," Behn smiled in approval.

"I've never heard of that before. You can tell me if it's anything like it once you've tried it." She put words to actions and took a big bite of her dipped sandwich. The juices rolled down the edges of the sandwich and landed on her plate. She chewed and watched Behn follow her example.

Once again, Behn was pleased to remember eating something similar when he was a child and still living with his mother. His memories were starting to come back with each addition of information provided by Juila. She would never know how much help she had given him in regaining his memory of his distant past. He felt sorry for his other brother who still did not recall anything of the first eight years of their life when they had lived in Tuala.

"Are you remembering something, Behn?"

Behn hurriedly finished chewing his bite and swallowed before he could answer. "I was just thinking about Jon and how little he remembers of our time before we were adopted by the Wilsons."

"Why do you suppose that is?"

"Probably because he was so sick all the time. I'd want to forget if it were me."

"Oh," she answered lamely. "What do you think of the foxl sandwich?"

"It's wonderful, much better than a French dip. I seem to recall eating something similar with my mother."

"It wouldn't surprise me if you had. This type of sandwich is very popular."

"That must be why then," he said and took another big bite. The flavors were so pronounced from the broth and the meat was so tender. He could hardly wait to be able to move back to Tuala and have this good of food for every meal. In the next instant he felt guilty for even considering leaving Earth and the family who had raised him as their own son. The Wilsons were wonderful parents and deserved better.

They finished their meal in silence. When Behn's sandwich was gone, he picked up the bowl and drank the remainder of the broth. He did not know if it were socially acceptable, yet he thought it a terrible waste to throw it away or whatever happened to it when Juila thought it away. He decided to find out, "What happens to the left-overs when you clean up with your thoughts?"

Juila considered the question for a moment before answering slowly, "I guess it's returned to the Earth. We use the elemental energy to clean up so my best guess is whatever isn't kept, goes back with the elemy."

Behn thought her answer seemed reasonable and watched as their dishes disappeared. He knew it only took an instant for everything to be cleaned and put back into the cupboard. The whole idea of using elemy to create or clean things was still fascinating.

Once again he thanked his heritage which made it possible for him to access this power through his birth crystal. He reached up and touched the tree of life pendant suspended from the leather thong around his neck. For so many years he had forgotten the significance of the necklace he had worn since he was one day old, but Juila had given his history back to him and his sister.

Juila saw Behn's fingers caress the smoky grey crystals of his pendant. She was thankful they were much lighter stones than her own ruby red crystals. From her training with Jehoban, she knew the darkness of the stone foretold the dangers of a person's life. With her stones being so dark, she knew she had trouble in her future and her visions while she had communed with her samara had confirmed the same.

She was also relieved to recall her sister's crystals had changed from black to a deep amethyst when she had first touched her samara. Even though the color had not changed significantly, it did indicate they were on the right track for their futures with the addition of the samaras in their lives. Even though she and Jena were identical twins and regularly linked minds, their futures were each separate. It scared her to know one day they would be separated by circumstances beyond their control.

Juila shook slightly at how dark her thoughts had turned. She looked up at Behn to find him watching her intently. To cover her confusion she asked, "Are you ready to begin your crystal lessons for the day?"

"Ready when you are!"

Juila jumped down from her stool and led the way back to the library to begin teaching Behn the sixth level of skill for harnessing the use of the Earth's elemental energy. As they walked past the office, Juila could feel the elemy being reshaped and decided she would find out later where Valentina had progressed since their last lesson.

Valentina had proved to be a very eager pupil and was advancing at a much faster rate than Behn. Perhaps her own involvement with her student was impeding his progress. She decided to discuss swapping students with her sister to see if Behn's attention to detail would improve without his being distracted by his physical attraction to his instructor.

CHAPTER 4

The phone rang again and went unanswered. Amanda listened as Neal left yet another message. Each call was like a stab in the heart. She wanted to help Neal get through this ordeal, yet she had no explanation for his absence which would be believed. Nobody in the Taivas household wanted to hear their son had been transported to another world, called Tuala, and had lived in a drug-addicted state as a prisoner of Elder Vargen for eight years.

Several times Amanda had sat down to write a note to the family. Each time she only got as far as the first sentence before balling up the paper and tossing it into the trash. There simply was no explanation which would keep her and her husband out of trouble. They had to maintain their silence.

Amanda knew it would only be a matter of time before the Taivas family contacted the authorities to compel them to share their knowledge. Sometimes she wished she had left Neal in Tuala, then she remembered the mortal danger the drug *resh* had put him in and she knew she had done the right thing.

To take her mind off of the troubles on Earth, Amanda decided she should plan a visit with Vinia. She owed it to the woman who loved Neal and who had helped them get him out of Elder Vargen's district and home to Earth. She knew Bryon Kesh had agreed to help take care of Vinia, yet she did not know the exact plan for taking her to a safe house.

Amanda went into the office and opened the secret compartment which contained the patil. With this device she was able to make contact across the veil into Tuala and speak with the people in the other realm. She was still amazed by her husband's connections which allowed him to have such technology on Earth even though the two realms had been kept separate by the Ascension Gates since the beginning of time. It probably helped that Riccan was the son and successor of an Elder.

Once the screen on the patil was activated, Amanda punched in several codes to make a video call with Bryon at his work. She figured it would be the most likely place he would be considering the time of day. As her intuition guessed, she was correct. Bryon's face filled the screen and he smiled at Amanda.

"Hi, Amanda. What's going on now? Is Nealan doing okay?"

"I suppose. We dropped him off at his parents' house yesterday morning. I haven't spoken with them since. Frankly, I'm scared to talk to them at all. I mean, really, what can I tell them which would make sense?"

"Good point. I'm sure you'll come up with something."

Amanda raised one eyebrow at Bryon's optimism and then asked the question she had called for, "I was wondering if you could tell me how I might get ahold of Vinia. I'd like to thank her for her help."

"Sure, she's at Barla's house."

"Barla's house?" Amanda wondered why she had not thought of the solution herself. It made perfect sense for Barla to take in a stranger and help her.

"Yeah, she offered to take in Vinia and Danika until we can find somewhere else for her to live and work. I think Barla even offered her some job training in her apprenticeship program."

"What a wonderful idea. Do you think they would mind if I came for a visit? I don't want to interfere in Vinia's training."

"Contact Barla and see what she has to say. I'm sure she'll agree it would be great for you to come over. Is it true that Barla's your mother's sister?"

"Strangely enough, yes. Can you believe it?"

"I'm beginning to believe everything these days!"

"Thanks for letting me know what's going on with Vinia and where I can find her. I'm going to reach out to Barla now and see what we can arrange. And Bryon?"

"Yes?"

"Thank you for helping us rescue Neal. I know it put you in some danger and I really appreciate your willingness to help."

"It was my honor, Amanda. Don't think anything of it."

Amanda smiled in response since she felt tears stinging her eyes. She suddenly found it hard to speak. Here was a man who was willing to do anything for her, including risking himself and possibly his family, to help a man he had never met. Bryon was the epitome of a gentleman.

"I'm sorry, Bryon, I don't want to embarrass you with my blubbering. It's just because I've gone through so much in this past year and I'm still having a hard time getting used to how kind people really are. Okay," she said and took a deep breath to compose herself before she continued, "I'm going to call Barla now."

"Sounds good," Bryon answered with a smile. He still wondered at some of the odd things Amanda said such as the word 'year'. "Take care, Amanda. Feel free to call on us whenever you have a need or a question."

"Thanks, Bryon. You know I will! Goodbye."

"Bye." The screen went blank as he disconnected.

Amanda sniffed deeply to clear her sinuses and dabbed at her eyes before she looked up Barla's connection code. She had to get herself together before she spoke with Vinia. This next call would be a very delicate conversation considering Vinia's relationship with Neal. She would have to go lightly.

With her emotions in check and Barla's code entered into the patil, Amanda pressed the connection button and waited. After the third ring through she thought she would have to try again at a later time when the screen lit up with Barla's face.

"Hi Aunt Barla," Amanda began the conversation.

"Amanda! It's so nice to see you! How are things going with Neal?"

"Ugh, Aunt Barla! I had no idea what kind of trouble I was getting myself into by bringing him home."

"What's going on?"

"All I thought about was getting him home safely so he wouldn't be in danger of dying from his addiction to *resh*. I never even thought about all of the questions his family would have about where he's been and how I found him. I was really stupid!"

"It's never stupid to be kind and compassionate toward your fellow man, Amanda. I'm sure everything will work out for the best, just have patience and faith."

"Thanks, I really needed to hear encouraging words!"

"Think nothing of it. So what else is going on?"

"Well, I wanted to find out about how Vinia was doing. I called Bryon and he told me about her living with you. I think it's great that you've put her into your job-training program. How's she doing?"

"I'd say the training is just a distraction at this point. She really wants to know how Neal is doing. Of course she knows him as Nealan, you know."

"Yes, I know."

"She asks everyday whether or not I've heard about how he's doing."

"His addiction was cured, yet his memory is still in the past. He still believed he and I were engaged. He didn't take kindly to the idea of me being married to Riccan. I'm embarrassed to say I've been avoiding his phone calls. I just don't know what I'd tell him which would make any sense."

"I understand."

"I know you do!"

They both smiled at one another and an awkward silence continued for another couple of seconds before Amanda blurted, "I'd like to visit with Vinia."

"I think she'd like that. She's so much lonelier this time."

"This time? Did you know Vinia before?"

"As a matter of fact, Bryon and I both knew her. Of course, we knew her by a different name. It's a long story, which we can tell you at a later date. When do you think you'd like to come over to visit?"

"Would today be too soon?"

Barla smiled at Amanda's eagerness and shook her head, "No, today would be perfect. We're here all day. Do you remember the way to our house from the landing field?"

"I do. I'm going to get ready right now. I'll probably be there within twenty or thirty minutes. Are you sure it's okay?"

"Absolutely! I'll get out some snacks while we're waiting."

"Let me guess…tocolas and tomato sandwiches?" She remembered from her coma dreams having that very snack and really looked forward to trying it in real life.

Barla raised one eyebrow at Amanda's guess and then shook her head slightly before replying, "Yes, they're Vinia's favorites. It sounds like you have some stories to share with me as well!" She had heard about Amanda's abilities to know unusual facts, now she had witnessed it first-hand. She wondered what else Amanda might know about their personal lives.

Barla's comment startled Amanda and made her want to get over to their house even faster. "Okay, I'll see you in a couple of minutes."

"Bye," Barla said and waited for Amanda to disconnect the call.

Amanda waved cheerfully and pressed the 'end' button on the screen. She stowed away the patil in its hiding place before she left the office and ran upstairs to get ready. For some reason she was both nervous and excited to get back to Tuala to speak with Vinia. She had a niggling feeling something important was about to happen, yet she had no idea what it could be.

CHAPTER 5

Petre believed enough time had passed since he had originally been banned from the Port of Cresdon by Captain Ahn. Really, how long could the Harbor Master hold a grudge? Even so, Petre docked his water craft quite far away from the main pier. He tried to remember just how many anons it had been since he had set foot in this bustling harbor town. Too long, considering what he had lost the last time.

He shook his head and finished securing his water craft to the dock. He had to get to the marketplace and pick up a few supplies before his next trade run. Maybe he could spend a few extra hours down at one of the pleasure houses before sailing out again. His solitary life was hard on a man with his physical needs.

The marketplace was bustling with customers and vendors bargaining their wares. It did not take Petre long to find all of the supplies he would need for his next journey. Laden with packages, Petre wished he would have gone first to the pleasure houses and worried about the provisions later when the crowds were thinner.

He was just about to turn out of the main stream of traffic when a familiar voice caught his attention. He looked around hurriedly trying to locate the woman whose voice he had heard. If it really were her, he could not believe his luck. All thoughts of the pleasure house went out of his head at the idea of being reunited with the love of his life.

After several minutes of scanning the crowd for her face and coming up empty handed, Petre began to panic. Surely he would not come this close only to be thwarted once again. He had to find her before he could leave. Once again he cursed the bulky packages he carried as they only slowed him down and made it nearly impossible to continue his search.

The people around him began to scowl darkly at how rudely he was pushing past them. He did not care, he only wanted to find his long-lost love. Memories of the past seemed to flood through his mind. Maybe it was only his imagination which made him think he had heard her voice. After all, this was the town where he had lost her.

Petre managed to find an upturned crate which he could stand on and get himself above the height of the crowd. With one last desperate attempt he yelled out, "Jinya!"

There! Just on the edge of the crowd he was certain he had seen a woman look over in his direction before turning rapidly down a side street. He jumped down from the crate and pushed his way through the crowd, ignoring all of the shouts of protest at his rude behavior. If they knew what was at stake, they would surely excuse his passing, he thought to himself.

He made it to where he had last seen the girl and yet she was nowhere in sight. He turned desperately, looking in every direction. He had to find her. He ran down the street where she must have gone, looking down each alley as he passed them. By the time he was in a residential area he had to admit defeat. It was beyond his comprehension why she would not have come to him when he called; surely she would want to be reunited with him.

Maybe he would stay in town for a while longer to see if he could find her. He could ask around town for anybody who knew her and where she might be staying. A sense of déjà vu hit him as he considered the next course of action. So many anons ago he had gone through the same scenario with her.

Again, he was reminded of his past and the time he had found the *old soul* water craft. Strange things were happening these days, he thought as he turned out of the nice neighborhood and back down toward the docks. It almost felt as though the past were repeating itself.

His thoughts were interrupted by the abrupt entrance of a telepod in the air not far above him. It was strange to see a telepod in a harbor town, not many people liked to fly so close to the water where unpredictable winds could blow the small aircraft off course so easily. He paused to watch the graceful decent of the pod as it maneuvered its way over to the landing square not too far from where he stood. There must be some urgent matter to bring someone to town, he wondered what it could be even as he continued walking back to his water craft.

RICCAN CLOSED the door to his office softly, even though he felt like slamming it. Never before had he been so embarrassed and enraged at a meeting and Ela Nena was completely responsible. He knew his boss had suddenly taken a disliking to him, but she had gone too far this time. If she had kept her snide comments and slights only against him then he could have handled it. For her to have attacked his team in such a way was inexcusable.

He sat down wearily at his desk and wondered what recourse he would have to her latest actions. Surely there was something behind all of her accusations. They had always worked well as a team until he had suddenly married Amanda, or so it seemed. Riccan could not understand the connection since Ela Nena had never even met Amanda so it seemed a hard correlation to conclude and yet it made the most sense.

Since he was thinking of his wife he decided he could use a break from the stresses of work to call Amanda. He wondered whether she were at home or traveling somewhere in the telepod. These days it was hard to keep track of her movements since she was so involved in searching for the eight missing samaras. He was thankful she was so successful at finding the mysterious crystal skulls, yet they seemed to bring their own sets of problems with the amount of power they exuded in the secret room at their house on Earth.

Riccan punched in the code to the patil in his office and hoped Amanda would be somewhere nearby to hear the call. After almost a minute of trying the connection, Riccan had to admit she had probably gone out somewhere. He ended the call and stared at the screen for a few minutes before he realized he had an unread message. He tapped the button on the screen and was delighted to find it was from Amanda.

Hi my love,

I hope you're having a great day at work. I miss you already. I just wanted to let you know I'm heading over to Barla's house today as it appears she and Captain Ahn have taken in Vinia and started her on their apprenticeship program. I'm not sure what time I'll be home, but if you need me, then give Barla's house a call.

Love,

Amanda

RICCAN WONDERED why Amanda would be seeking the company of Vinia. In the several months since they had been married Riccan began to realize Amanda's instincts for people was very keen and to be trusted implicitly. Still, it would be fascinating to discover Amanda's reasoning for the visit.

Most likely the visit had to do with Neal since Vinia had been living with him. Just thinking about the man made him shiver. Neal had been only a shell of himself when they rescued him from Elder Vargen and returned him home to his family on Earth. He could not imagine the amount of confusion which must be going through Neal's head to find he had been missing for eight years and then not being able to account for even a fraction of the time he had been gone.

He sat back in his chair and thought about Amanda's history with Neal. His was the only real story of events which had been written in Amanda's journal about her dreams she had experienced while she had been in her coma for seven years. Amanda had read her journal to him on two different occasions and each time he was surprised at the level of details she had described about a land she had barely seen during her own captivity with Elder Vargen.

Maybe he should put some extra effort into studying the details of the book of dreams. It was possible they were missing some vital clues. The idea so intrigued him that he was having a hard time concentrating on any mundane office politics. He would much rather be unraveling the mysteries of Amanda's memories than dealing with the bazaar behavior of his boss.

The idea so intrigued him, he could no longer concentrate on anything work-related. He surged out of his chair and grabbed his coat off of the back of the door. With a new sense of purpose, Riccan opened his office door and looked around for anyone he could talk to so he could tell them he was leaving. On his way through the main office, the first person he encountered was one of his designers named Gilora.

"Hey, Gilora, I'm going to take an early lunch. Send me a message on the patil if you need me."

"I don't blame you for wanting to get out of here after Ela Nena's performance in that meeting. Have a good lunch," she answered before turning back to her own patil to continue her work.

Riccan left the office and turned into the hallway. He considered waiting for the elevator to take him to the roof, yet he decided the walk up the eleven flights of stairs would help him burn off some of his anger. By the time he reached the rooftop landing pad, he was breathing heavier than normal and realized it had been quite some time since he had exercised so much.

Seeing his bright red telepod waiting for him across the roof, he felt his steps get more spring in them. There was nothing he enjoyed more than the freedom of flying in his personally designed telepod. He pressed his hand down on the exterior plate to activate the side door to open and felt himself relax further as he watched it slowly descend to just above the ground.

He stepped inside and appreciated anew the plush foxl interior as he walked to the front of the aircraft and sat down in the pilot's seat. He palmed the side door shut at the same time as he began the activation procedures. The telepod rose several inches from the ground and hovered, waiting for further input. When he checked the glass panel to ensure all of the systems were working properly, he entered in the coordinates for his planned destination. He tapped the activation button and visualized the destination in mind as he and the telepod disappeared from the rooftop.

CHAPTER 6

"We love you and we're only concerned about you, Neal," Jessica told her son for at least the tenth time.

"I don't know what you're so concerned about. What more do you want from me? I'm home, safe and sound." Neal looked first at his mother and then shifted his gaze to his father. What he saw in both of their expressions did nothing to reassure him. He tried to see the situation from their point of view and still he could not get over how unreasonable they were being with him.

"I know Amanda said she thought you'd be tired, but really, Neal, you've only been awake for about thirty minutes from when you first arrived two days ago. Don't you think we have reason to be concerned? Where have you been all this time? How come you don't remember? Don't these unanswered questions concern you as well?" Jessica finally spoke her mind and she reached for her husband's hand for comfort.

"Your mom's right, Neal. It's just not normal for you to not remember anything. I think it would be a good idea for you to see a counselor. If nothing else, it'll give you someone other than us to talk to. You might remember something under the guidance of a professional."

Neal looked with utter disbelief because his father was actually suggesting he should go to a shrink. He was not crazy and he resented his father's implication. If he were not so tired, he'd get in the car and leave.

Then he remembered he no longer had a driver's license. He would have to get that problem remedied as soon as he caught up on his sleep.

Jessica could see her son was getting angry and backtracked slightly by saying, "Just think about it, Neal. We don't want to pressure you, we just want you to have every opportunity for a full recovery from your ordeal."

"Even though you can't even be sure I had an 'ordeal' and yet you want to treat me like a nut job!" Neal stood up and left the room. He was not even sure why he was so upset. He had always had such an easygoing temperament, maybe talking to someone other than his parents would be a good idea. He went into the kitchen and called Amanda. Once again, he left a message before hanging up in frustration. If Amanda would just talk to him, maybe he could get the answers his parents were so eager to hear.

Jessica stepped beside her son in the kitchen and consoled him. "She hasn't returned any of our calls either, Neal. Maybe she needs some time as well."

"Time for what? She's obviously moved on. I mean, after all, she's married to that Riccan guy, isn't she? At least, that's what you told me. I still don't know what happened to our relationship."

Jessica glanced over at her husband who had joined them and saw his small nod. "Neal, Amanda's had a hard time since you both went boating."

"Yeah, it looks like it."

"She was missing for fourteen months before she was found on a beach in Mexico."

"Where was she during all those months?"

"We don't know. She doesn't remember either. There's more, though. Even after she was found, she had some medical complications."

"Like what?"

"She was in a coma for seven years, Neal."

"What? She looks fine now. How can that be?"

"It's true, she's had a miraculous recovery. Better than anyone hoped really. I'm sure she feels bad because you were gone so long. Maybe she knew where you were all along, but since she was incapacitated, she couldn't help you. Maybe guilt keeps her from answering our calls. Whatever the case, I'm glad she brought you home, no matter where you were or what happened to you while you were gone." Jessica hugged her son abruptly as tears blurred her vision. She never thought she would have the opportunity to hold her son again. She was intensely grateful to have him back.

"I'm sorry, Mom. I had no idea what everyone has been through. I've been very selfish in only thinking about myself. Maybe you're right to suggest I speak with a counselor. If you make the appointment, I'll go."

~

NENA WAS FEELING RATHER lonely with her husband, Daven, away at the convocation. She had always hated when his job kept him away from the Residence for any length of time. This meeting, however, was different and she was glad to know Daven would be part of an historic decision.

When she had found out Wilken's successor was to be Rasa, she was so pleased. The more she thought about it, she also worried for the problems Rasa would face with her new role in society. If Rasa thought studying with Jehoban were hard, then she was in for a hard lesson in politics. There were several Elders who continually liked to keep the pot stirred. Sometimes she believed they just liked to use their power to cause trouble which definitely did not fit the ancient definition of the Elders.

Rasa could bring young blood and perspective to the aging group of Elders. Of the fifteen Elders of the world, only two of them could even be considered young. Even then, Debbon was almost fifty anons old and Senjin was forty-three anons old. Her own Daven was sixty-eight anons and the median age of the remainder was over one hundred anons. Granted, Elders lived longer lives than other people, yet their views of the world were still from an earlier time. They needed to learn how to relate with the people and the changing ideals.

To clear her head, she decided to take a walk through the garden paths. Something had been troubling her lately and she had yet to come to any decision over it. Her new first-daughter was spending all of her time working on the fulfillment of the new prophecy and here she was, merely sitting around doing nothing. It went against her moral grain to leave the difficult task to a single individual. She felt she ought to do more to help, which was the crux of the problem. How could she help?

Normally the beauty of the landscaping could soothe her mind and allow her to come up with creative solutions to any problems. Unfortunately, the answers she sought continued to elude her. Maybe she should discuss it with someone else. Whom could she trust? Inspiration finally struck as she realized there was another person in her exact situation. She could talk to Elder Debbon's wife, Chelesa.

With a spring in her step, she hurried back into the Residence. She went into her office and tapped in the code to send a message to Chelesa. Since Chelesa had received her wise-woman status, she had less time to devote to personal pursuits. This new idea of Nena's kept nagging at her brain that it should be considered carefully, after all, the fate of the world depended upon the completion of the prophecy.

Thinking about her own schedule with teaching the little children in their first year of study, she figured afternoons would be the best time to try to get together with Chelesa. She typed a quick invitation for tea for either that afternoon or the following one and hit the send button.

AS A NEWLY TRAINED WISE-WOMAN, Chelesa was pleased to have another duty to occupy her time where she could interact with the citizens of her husband's district. She had always been active with charitable causes, yet she always felt she should do more. She was now able to help the people when they needed it the most by using her talent as a healer to give them comfort from whatever ailed them.

Chelesa saw her last patient for the morning and then wound her way through the broad streets to head back to her home estate. Debbon had asked her not to bring any of the patients home since that was the only location where he was able to have peace from their ever-present demands for his time. Chelesa could see his point, yet it did make her practice a little more burdensome. She respected her husband's wishes because she knew he gave all of his energy to his position as Elder when he was working, it was only fair for him to have some quiet, peaceful downtime at home.

Upon arriving at home, Chelesa went to her offices to check for any new messages while she had been out. Chelesa was pleased to receive the invitation for tea over at Nena's house. She needed a distraction from her own family concerns. With Debbon gone at the convocation, Chelesa was left alone with her son, Willian. While she was grateful to have him back home safe, she also did not like how he had tricked them when he used his father's Ascension Gate without assistance.

She had always known he was capable of more than he applied himself, however, she had hoped he would come to the same conclusion in a less dangerous manner. This time his stunt had gone too far and had put his father in a precarious position with the other Elders. How would it look for the First to lose his son in a gate mishap? Luckily they were able to keep the incident among themselves.

She could see now she had been too lenient with him in the past. It was her obligation, not only as a mother, but also as an example for the district to raise her child in accordance with the rules of society. Nena would be a good person to discuss her problems with since she would understand her unique social situation.

Chelesa confirmed her attendance at tea for after lunch and then turned off her patil. Instead of ringing for a housemaid, she decided to go to the kitchen to talk to them herself. She wandered through the house and admired all of the plush elegance all around her. Often, she marveled at how blessed her life had been and she appreciated every opportunity which presented itself.

At the back of the estate, she entered the kitchen. There were several staff members who devoted themselves full-time to the art of cooking and baking. Unlike the typical household, hers created meals the old-fashioned way of doing it by hand unless an emergency situation called for food to be delivered immediately. The head chef insisted he could taste the difference when the meals were prepared with elemy rather than by hand. Chelesa could not make any distinction, but she was not about to argue with the quality of food her staff prepared.

"I'll be going out after lunch. I'm not sure if I'll be home for dinner. Please make sure Willian has something healthy and don't let him convince you to make his favorite enskil dumplings just because I may be away," Chelesa said to the head chef when he finally looked up to see what had created the interruption in his staff's routine.

"Ah, my lady, I'd never change the menu once it's been set. The routine is very important to keep, you know," he replied with a mischievous grin.

"I'm sure!" Chelesa could not keep from returning his grin. She knew the head chef would do anything for his favorite child regardless of routine. "I'll take lunch in my office as soon as it's ready."

"Very good, my lady. It should be ready in the next few minutes."

"Thanks." Chelesa left the kitchen and smiled at the resumption of the normal chaotic noise as soon as she was out of their line of sight.

Chelesa felt bad about eating her carefully prepared lunch with such haste. The truth of the matter was she was terribly anxious to get out of the house and meet with Nena. She also had to admit to herself about being curious as to why she was suddenly receiving an invitation to the Pantano Residence. She could not even remember the last time she had been there.

She finished the last bite of her fried foxl and tomato wrap and used her cloth napkin to wipe her fingers and mouth. After setting the napkin down she shoved the plate away from her work surface to be able to use her patil. Before she left she wanted to make sure she had not received any new messages from her patients. The last thing she wanted was to be interrupted in the middle of her outing to come back if she could avoid it beforehand.

After scanning several screens, she could find nothing new to delay her departure. She left her office and went upstairs to change her clothes. She was surprised to see her hands were shaking as she buttoned the front of her fresh tunic. It seemed ridiculous to be so anxious until she realized she was just excited for a new adventure, no matter how simple the outing would most likely become.

With one last check in the full-length mirror, she nodded approval at herself and smiled. She left her room, went down the stairs, and out the front door to get to the landing field for her own personal telepod. It was not very often she even needed to use her pod, yet she was always thankful she had learned to operate one herself. It was rather inconvenient to have to depend on someone else's schedule to travel.

She used her remote to open the side door as she neared the small aircraft. As usual, she visually inspected the exterior as she approached to make sure nothing had damaged the outer hull. Stepping inside and sitting down in the pilot's seat, she palmed the side door shut with the button on the control panel. Everything seemed in order as she activated the startup procedures and verified all of the green lights before entering her coordinates for the Pantano Residence.

Once again, she was thankful for her husband's generosity in getting her telepod's systems upgraded with the latest technology so she would not have to solely rely on her mental navigational skills to operate the craft. The new method required her simply to type in the location and the rest of the transfer was handled by the operating system. Not only was this an improvement in navigation, it was also much safer. She did not have to concentrate so hard on maintaining the coordinates in her thoughts as she activated the transfer. Old habits prevailed as she still mentally recalled the location even as she tapped the button to send her on her way.

CHAPTER 7

With nothing more to do except wait, Nena planned the agenda for the next day's schedule for her students. She found herself easily distracted and her mind tended to wander. She had just shoved the notebook away from herself with an exasperated sigh when her patil beeped with an incoming message. She squealed with delight as she read Chelesa's acceptance of her offer to come over that very afternoon. It seemed Chelesa was missing her own husband as well and would welcome the distraction of an evening with another woman.

Nena rang for one of the house staff to come to her office. Punctual as ever, there was a knock on her door almost immediately. "Come in," she called and watched as her head maid entered the room.

"How may I help, Lady Nena?" Melba asked promptly.

"Please make arrangements for tea and treats for this afternoon."

"How many will be in attendance?"

"Only myself and Chelesa."

"Very good. Will anything else be required?"

"No, thank you. Chelesa should be arriving just after the lunch hour."

"We will be ready, my Lady," she smiled and left the office as quietly as she had come.

Nena returned her attention to the patil and her eyes were caught by a file she had almost forgotten she had placed on the main screen. Her husband had made a digital copy of the document and had asked her to review it at a later date. She tapped the screen to open the file and began reading. Time slipped by effortlessly as she became engrossed in the story of Amanda's journal of her time in the coma.

While she had heard Amanda read the story to them before, the first telling had been so fantastic that the details had failed to register completely. Now, Nena was able to take more time to absorb the intricacies of the story and wonder what significance each piece had in reality. They had already established that Amanda had not been the actual participant in almost all of the story, yet what could it all mean? Surely there was a deeper significance other than Amanda knowing odd details of random people's lives in Tuala.

A tap at her office door interrupted her ruminations and she looked up with a startled expression to find Melba waiting to be acknowledged. "Yes, Melba?"

"Chelesa is waiting for you in the front room, my Lady."

"Really? I can't believe it's so late already," she replied as she hastily shut down her patil and stood from her chair. "Thank you for letting me know, Melba. Please bring the tea and pastries after we have been seated."

The maid curtsied and stood aside to allow Nena to go past her into the hallway. If she were needed for anything she would be nearby. Until that time, she returned to the kitchen to get the maids together for the afternoon service.

Nena rushed down the long hallway and entered the main reception room. "I'm sorry to keep you waiting, Chelesa. I lost track of time completely!"

"Oh, it's no bother. I've been enjoying the wonderful view from up here. I forget how much greener it is here than back at my home," she said as she turned and greeted her hostess with a smile.

"We could walk the garden paths after we have tea, if you'd like."

"I'd love that, Nena!" Chelesa practically gushed at the idea. She had not realized just how tense she had become in her own home since Willian's stunt with the Gate.

Nena was surprised at the alacrity with which Chelesa responded to such a mundane offer. Maybe her offer for tea had been as good for

Chelesa as it had been for herself. She gestured to the couches and offered, "Shall we sit down for tea? It should be here soon."

Chelesa nodded and turned her back on the windows to cross the room. Just as she settled herself on the plush cushion, several maids came in and arranged everything within easy reach of the two of them. She was relieved to see Nena gesture for the women to leave everything as it was so they could serve themselves. It was always such a trial waiting for the maids to get everything put together when it could be done so much faster by herself.

"I hope you don't mind," Nena said as an afterthought.

"Not at all! I quite prefer serving myself," Chelesa reassured.

The next several minutes passed as they poured tea, added sugar, stirred, and served themselves dainty cakes onto their saucers. Just the ritual of it all seemed to calm both women and they grinned at one another over the rims of their cups.

Both began to speak at once...

"I'm glad you came," Nena began.

"What did you want to discuss...," Chelesa sputtered to a stop and then took a nervous sip of her tea to cover the awkward moment.

Nena chuckled and said, "I guess it's been a while since either of us has been able to entertain on a casual basis! I understand congratulations are in order for your elevation to wise-woman status."

"Yes, thank you. It all happened so unexpectedly, but I'm glad nonetheless."

Such a perfect opening could not have been better planned as Nena spoke next, "Yes. I had heard you'd had some trouble in your district which led you to leave for a time."

"How did you hear about that?" Chelesa asked with alarm.

Nena shook her head and replied, "Not in the way you're thinking, I'm sure! Amanda wrote about it in her journal."

Now it was Chelesa's turn to be confused and tipped her head slightly as she asked, "Can you explain? Are you talking about your first-daughter Amanda?"

"Yes. Remember when we met with Jehoban and He said she would know strange details?"

"Yes..." Chelesa said slowly. She had no idea her life would be part of the story.

"Well, Amanda gave a detailed description of you being at the park and in the marketplace where you had altercations with several men. Is this correct?

"Yes, but how would Amanda know? She wasn't even there!"

"I understand your confusion, believe me! The exact details, I'm sure, are not accurate, but the gist of the story fits perfectly. Those altercations were the precursor for you leaving town and going to school, right?"

"Yes, but I don't understand what significance it would have for Amanda. Do you have any ideas?"

"No, not yet. I was hoping we could work on the puzzle together. I can't help but think that everything Amanda learned about the people from Tuala is important for all of our futures. Does it sound like something with which you'd like to help me?"

"Absolutely! I think it would be fascinating to see Amanda's perspective on what I've already lived through. Maybe she'll even have some answers for us like what motivation those men had for terrorizing my family." Chelesa shuddered as she recalled how shaken she had been by the events in her not-so-distant past. It would be a relief to finally put an end to that chapter of her life.

"I just thought of the idea so I'm going to have to ask Amanda for permission to share her journal. I'm sure she'll say it's fine, but, you know..."

"Of course! I understand completely. You can find out for sure and then send it to me or I can come over and we can review it together." Chelesa picked up the dainty cake from her saucer and plopped it into her mouth. "Mmm," she hummed in appreciation of the wonderful flavors of chocolate, strawberries, and steena melded perfectly together.

"These are my favorite as well," Nena agreed as she picked up an identical one to taste for herself. She enjoyed her cake as much as she enjoyed her company. She knew together they would be able to cover much more of Amanda's memories. Maybe they would even uncover the truth of the dreams.

As soon as they were done with their tea and pastries, Nena excused herself to send a message to Riccan asking about the use of Amanda's journal. She hated to leave her guest, but Chelesa had assured her it was no bother. Her message was brief and to the point, she hit send and turned off the screen of the patil. She returned to the great room to find

Chelesa standing in front of the floor to ceiling windows admiring the view.

"Would you like a tour of the grounds?"

Chelesa turned to her and smiled, "I'd love it!"

Nena led the way out onto the broad patio and down the stone stairs. Her mind was only half focused on telling Chelesa the details about their Residence. She hoped to have an answer from Riccan before it was time for Chelesa to leave. For some reason, she just knew it was her task to find clues from Amanda's journal to lead them to find more of the missing samaras.

CHAPTER 8

Riccan just touched down in the landing area at the Port of Cresdon and was preparing to shut down his telepod when a red light lit up on the display monitor. Immediately he thought there was a malfunction until he realized it was the indicator for an incoming message on his personal patil. He made a mental note to change the indicator light to an alternate color to minimize any confusion regarding the airworthiness of his aircraft. It would not do to begin to ignore a red light because he thought it was a message he could read later when it could possibly be a malfunction instead.

He touched the screen and the message opened immediately. It was a little unusual to receive a personal message from his mother and he was at once both alarmed and intrigued. His mom usually had his dad send him a message or waited for him to visit in person. The brevity of the message was also a bit strange, but he figured she had just been in a hurry.

Without knowing the answer to her request, he was unable to reply. He finished his telepod's shutdown procedures and palmed the exterior door open. When he exited his craft he grinned at how closely he had landed next to his wife's telepod. Even though he was coming unannounced, there was no way Amanda could leave the port town without noticing his own bright red telepod. If nothing else, she would wait in the landing field until he returned, should he not find her at Captain Ahn and Barla's house.

He stepped off of the ramp and palmed the door closed using the exterior control. After glancing around the area and not seeing anybody, he turned down the path he knew would take him to his destination. Walking swiftly, Riccan could feel his mood improving with every step closer to his life mate.

He turned into the garden lane and up the stairs to the grand house of the Harbor Master. After three brisk knocks on the front door, Riccan waited in anticipation of surprising his wife. He did not count on Amanda actually answering the knock and could not refrain from grinning like a fool when he saw how happy she was to see him.

Amanda almost knocked Riccan over when she enthusiastically hugged him and then abruptly pulled him over the threshold and immediately shut the door behind him. "I'm glad you're here," she said in a whisper and her expression turned serious.

"What's wrong?"

"Vinia just got home from the market and told Barla that Petre MacVeen saw her and called out for her. She's terrified, but I haven't found out why just yet. She's been crying the whole time and I don't think she's even noticed my being here yet." Amanda grabbed his hand and pulled him down the hallway and into the family room.

Barla looked up from where she was sitting with Vinia and then smiled with relief when she recognized Riccan. She felt better knowing there was a man in the house since her husband was still stuck at work. "Your timing is impeccable, Riccan. Please take a seat. Can I get you anything?"

"No, please don't worry about me. Amanda just told me Vinia was confronted by Petre. Is there anything I can do to help?"

"Maybe," Barla answered noncommittally. She turned her focus back to Vinia whose hands she still held in her own. "You're safe with us, Vinia. Please don't be afraid."

"If it's any help, I didn't see Petre anywhere around here while I was walking from the landing field," Riccan added helpfully. "I can take a walk and look some more if it would make you feel better."

Vinia would not even look up from her lap as she slowly shook her head. She spoke quietly as she answered, "I'll be fine in a few minutes. I just never thought I'd have to see him again after what he put me through. I overreacted and now I've caused all of this fuss. I'm sorry, Barla. Please forgive me."

"There now, there's nothing to forgive. It's completely understandable that you'd be shaken after…" Barla's voice faltered and left her sentence unfinished.

While Riccan had briefly seen Vinia at Neal's house, he never really had a chance to get more than a glance at her. When she raised her head and looked Riccan full in the face, he gasped as he realized just how much she looked like Amanda. The resemblance was remarkable. They could almost be twin sisters except Vinia was at least ten anons older than Amanda.

Amanda had the exact realization at the same time. She was ashamed to not have seen it before when they had asked for her assistance in getting Neal home. Their sole focus had been on Neal and they had utterly ignored her. If they would have taken even a moment of time to talk with her, they may have seen the resemblance before.

Barla recognized their expressions and interjected, "There is a strong resemblance, you must admit."

"I'll say," Amanda agreed readily.

Vinia shifted her gaze to Amanda for the first time since she had come in from the market. When she had initially arrived at the house she had been too upset to even notice there was someone else visiting with Barla. Her eyes got wide as she saw Amanda. When she had come to her house to get Neal, she had been behind Riccan and she had never seen her face. Now she could do nothing but stare unashamedly at her doppelganger.

"Who are you?" Vinia managed to ask Amanda.

"I'm sorry, Vinia. I should have spoken to you when we brought Neal home. My name is Amanda Stel. This is my husband, Riccan. I really want to thank you for assisting us in getting Neal home to his parents. They have been sick with worry for him all of these anons."

"Neal? Did he do something dishonorable? Why isn't he called Nealan anymore?"

"It has nothing to do with honor, Vinia. We don't use the same naming convention on Earth as they do here on Tuala. His real name is Nealand, but everyone calls him Neal."

"Oh," Vinia said plainly. She was glad to hear he had not been shamed for being gone for so long. "How is he doing?"

"He's over his addiction to resh, which is a blessing. However, he's not doing so well mentally since he doesn't recall anything from the time he spent on Tuala," Amanda answered quietly. Another wave of guilt washed over her for not trying to help Neal more since dropping him off at his parents' house. The sheer number of unanswered phone calls told her more than enough about how he was faring.

"He doesn't remember me?"

Amanda could not help but see the pain in Vinia's eyes. She leaned forward and touched Vinia's arm and said, "Give him time. It's only been a couple of days."

Vinia closed her eyes and nodded sharply. Her fantasies of going and being with Nealan and having him keep her safe from Petre evaporated. She felt more isolated and alone than ever. "Do you think he'll ever come back here?"

"I really don't know, Vinia. I'm sorry."

Vinia nodded dejectedly and looked down at her hands in her lap as she processed this new information. She was feeling as though everything she loved she ended up losing to Earth. Another thought struck her mind and she asked, "Do you think you could take me to see him on Earth?"

Amanda looked swiftly at Riccan, asking his opinion with her eyes rather than speaking it out loud. She saw him lift his shoulder and eyebrow at the same time. She looked back over to Vinia and said, "It's commonly discouraged to allow people from Tuala to go to Earth, but I think we could probably arrange something as long as you agreed to not talk about it here in Tuala."

"Who would I talk to who doesn't already know about it? I don't have any other friends other than Captain Ahn, Barla, Bryon, and Alena. I'm fairly certain they all know about Earth since they seem to know you and Riccan so well."

"You do have a point. I had to make sure you understand how much trouble you could get in with the Elders if they knew you were planning to go through an Ascension Gate. What would happen with your daughter if something were to happen to you?"

Vinia glanced over to Barla and asked, "Would you take care of Danika for me?"

"You don't even have to ask, Vinia. Of course I'd raise her as though she were my own child. Good grief, I've already raised more children than I can count. I would be honored to have Danika." Barla patted Vinia's hand for reassurance.

"When can we go?" Vinia pressed.

Amanda sputtered for an answer.

Riccan decided to take over the conversation by saying, "We'd have many details to take care of before you could come. It might be a couple of weeks. First we'd have to make sure Neal is stable enough to have you visit. We don't want to give him too many shocks too fast."

"No, of course not. Just knowing you're willing to take me to him will be enough for now. At least I know there will be an opportunity to see him again; unlike with my other children."

"What other children?" Riccan asked.

"Last anon my three children were in danger and I had to send them away to keep them safe."

"You're not in danger anymore, are you? Your children could come and live here with you," Amanda said reasonably.

"Not with Petre hanging around here. Besides, I have no idea how to find them."

Amanda shook her head in confusion and said, "I don't understand. Where did you send them?"

Barla leaned forward to hear what Vinia would say. She had been dying to ask her about where her other children were, but it never seemed the right time.

Vinia seemed to falter and then looked up sadly at Barla, "I went back to the Roanoke Colony and lived in my childhood home. Everything was peaceful for about seven anons and then everything seemed to fall apart. You remember how sickly Jon always was, right Barla?"

"Yes, he was the last one born and the birth cord was around his neck. We were all afraid he wouldn't make it. I thought he was getting stronger."

"Alena was great with her healing skills. He was doing fine until fall and winter came around. The weather where we were was much more severe and he was sick a lot of the time. Grobin, the leader of the colony, did not trust the wise-women so it was really hard for me to get help for him when he needed it. Then spring would arrive and he would get better so I thought I was overreacting.

"Anyway, like I said, life was pretty good other than Jon's reoccurring sickness. I only wished the children could have had some friends. Again, Grobin was responsible for their lack. He always spoke against my children because of my father being an outsider from the community. He also held against them the fact that he didn't know who their father was either.

"We kept to ourselves and I loved the time I got to spend with my children. Everything changed one day when two things happened. First, the weather had changed and Jon fell ill again. He was way worse than he had ever been before and I begged Grobin to get him some help from a wise-woman. Grobin came over to our house and said Jon was too far gone to waste the wise-woman's time. He said it would be better for the whole colony if Jon were to die and he said there were too many men in the colony as it was."

Barla hissed in anger. She could well imagine what she would have done to Grobin if he made the mistake of saying the same thing in front of her about her children.

Amanda was speechless. She looked over at Riccan to see how he was reacting. She could see his eyes narrow in anger, but he also shook his head slightly as though he were not surprised.

Vinia continued, "The second terrible thing happened later the same day. I overheard Grobin telling one of his cronies about him planning on taking my seven anon old daughter to be his wife. His friend told him she was too young, but Grobin just laughed and said it would be more exciting that way. Obviously, I had to send them all away. I didn't dare separate them since they were all they had and they needed to work together to keep Jon safe.

"Wise-woman Copa had seen Jon the anon before and she had had a vision of this time coming. She left me a special object and gave me instructions on how to use it. She said when the time was right, I was to take the children to a particular place in the woods, say a special phrase, and then the children would go somewhere safe." Her shoulders began to shake and tears were cascading down her cheeks as she forced herself to finish the tale. "I watched my children disappear right in front of me. I have no idea where they are or how to get them back."

Amanda was starting to have an odd feeling overcome her as she asked, "What are your children's names?"

"Behn, Valentina, and Jon," she whispered.

Amanda gasped and turned to Riccan. "It can't be a coincidence, can it?"

"What is it, Amanda?" Barla asked immediately.

"Our daughters are friends with a set of triplets by those names. We went to a small village in the Roanoke Colony where the kids found the home they remembered living in. What doesn't make sense, though, is that you said you sent them away last anon and they were only seven anons old. The triplets, however, are sixteen anons old."

Vinia looked alarmed at this turn of events. She had always carried the idea of getting her children back once she got her life back on track, but she never really believed she would miss all of their growing up.

Riccan spoke into the silence, "Did the special object Copa gave you look like a crystal skull?"

"Yes. Have you seen it then?"

"Yes." Riccan hastily thought about what could have happened and could only come up with one conclusion, "I think I know what happened."

"What?" Vinia, Barla, and Amanda spoke in unison.

"I think Vinia used the samara to send the children to Earth. What she didn't know was that she had no way of controlling the time element. I believe – if these are the same kids – that they were sent back in time. Vinia, were you able to access their birth crystals?"

"No. I was so scared when I lost the connection, but I had to believe the wise-woman would not have had me remove the children from danger only to kill them. I didn't know what to think of it."

Riccan nodded as though confirming some thought in his mind. "Everything does seem to add up, don't you think, Amanda?"

"It does!"

"Can you take me to them?" Vinia asked excitedly.

"I'm sure you can understand this is a very difficult situation. I'd like to talk to the kids first and see what they want to do."

Vinia scowled in anger and then a moment later she realized Amanda was looking out for the best interest of the children. She had no choice but to agree. Just the idea of getting to see her children again renewed her hope.

CHAPTER 9

Juila and Sofia walked out of their third period American Government class together. They sauntered down the hall slowly. Each had another class before lunch, but they were feeling particularly uninspired to pay attention.

Sofia asked, "Do you have plans for Christmas break?"

"When is it?"

Sofia looked at her strangely before she humored her with a reply, "It's in two weeks, silly. I know you're from South Africa, but I'm pretty sure they celebrate Christmas at the same time as the rest of the world!"

Juila blushed at being called out so blatantly. She knew they had a break coming up, yet she had not known it was called Christmas break. "Yeah, Jena and I are going to spend some time with our grandparents."

"Bummer! Are you going to be gone the whole two weeks?"

"Probably. This will be the first time we've really gotten to spend any time with them in our whole lives. We're really excited about it."

Sofia again wondered why the grandparents had not made any effort to go see them in Africa. It was not like it was in another world. She wished she could know what their lives had been like before they had come to Florida. She was certain it would be a fascinating story. They had reached Sofia's classroom and the said their goodbyes until lunchtime.

Juila kept walking down the hall until she got to her history class.

Even as she sat down at her desk she was thinking about her conversation with Sofia. She had done something she had told Jena they were not supposed to do; she read Sofia's mind. Her thoughts had been filled with questions about their history. Not for the first time, she wished she could tell Sofia the truth about their origins. It would be so much easier for their friendship if they could be honest with her like they were with Behn and Valentina.

You sure are gania away right now, Juila. What's going on? Jena asked through their mind link.

Not much. I just screwed up with Sofia over the upcoming break. Did you know it was called Christmas break?

I'd heard some of the other kids saying it, but I didn't know exactly what it was. I'm glad you found out though.

I do think it'll be fun to visit with Mom's parents and get to know them better.

I heard we were going to spend half of the time with Dad's parents as well. That'll be fun to spend more time at the Pantano Residence. Maybe Elder Daven will teach me more about his Ascension Gate.

Juila rolled her eyes at her sister's fascination with becoming an Elder. No matter how many times she told her that girls did not become Elders, Jena insisted it was time for a change in the status quo. The History teacher began her lecture at the same time Jena's typing class started. Even though they could divide their attention and continue their conversation, they elected to focus on their classes and resume their discussion when they got home from school.

With the final classes of the day completed, Jena and Juila met at their locker. The hall was crowded and loud with excited students talking about the upcoming break and their plans for the time off. *These people really get into this holiday, don't they?* Jena thought to Juila.

Juila nodded and grinned back at her sister as she pulled her jacket from the hook inside the locker. She slipped her schoolbooks onto the shelf and jostled for space in which to put on her jacket. Jena helped hold the opposite sleeve.

Jena filled her backpack with the books needed to complete her homework assignments. She noticed Juila was not similarly encumbered with her bag and asked, "Aren't you going to bring your books home?"

"I finished my assignments during class. I wanted to have some extra time to go over the next couple of lessons with Behn this afternoon."

"As long as you keep your focus on the actual lessons and nothing more," Jena teased with a mischievous grin.

Juila rolled her eyes and grinned back. She was impatiently waiting for her sister so they could go out to the parking lot. They were going to be catching a ride home from Behn and Valentina. Finally, Jena was ready to go and Juila shut the locker door with more force than necessary in her eagerness to get going.

Instead of closing, the locker bounced back open and Jena caught it on the rebound and shut it carefully even as she felt her sister gathering elemy to close it. She looked over at her sister in alarm and whispered, "What are you doing?"

"I don't know. I guess I'm just feeling antsy. Are you ready? Let's go."

Instead of arguing further, Jena decided to go along with her sister's mood and turned to make a pathway through the crowd to go out to the parking lot. As they were walking, Jena began to pick up on Juila's energy and could feel an air of tension. She began to have a premonition of something big about to happen. Together they walked through the double doors and out into the bright sunlight.

"Hey, girls!" Sofia yelled from behind them just as the doors shut.

As one, they turned and waited for their friend to catch up with them. They had hardly seen Sofia during the day which, in itself, was unusual.

"What's going on?" Jena asked with a smile as she noticed Sofia's excitement.

"Jon asked me to come over to his house today to study with him!"

"Study?" Juila teased.

Sofia blushed prettily and scuffed the toe of her shoe on the edge of the sidewalk. "Of course!"

"Juila, stop teasing her," Jena chided.

"Have either of you seen him? I told him I'd give him a ride," she said as she looked around through the crowd.

Juila began to tell her they had not seen him when she spotted him across the parking lot heading toward Sofia's car. She pointed and said, "There he is!"

"Oh! Wish me luck," Sofia said as she rushed away to catch up with him.

The girls grinned at one another at her excitement and nobody noticed the car pulling through the parking lot until they heard the brakes squealing. Time seemed to slow down to a crawl as they saw their friend bounce off of the newly dented hood of the car. "No!" Juila screamed as she grabbed Jena's hand and began pulling her forward even as they watched Sofia's body fly backward through the air.

Together they gathered elemy to try to prevent Sofia from sustaining further injury. As they flung the energy across the distance, they knew their help would come too late. They watched in horror as Sofia's body hit the ground with a sickening thud. Sofia's head came down last and struck a parking curb where she remained motionless.

"Sofia!" Juila yelled as she prayed for her friend to survive the horrific blow. Barely containing the desire to teleport, they raced across the asphalt with the same abandon as their friend had done. Everyone except them seemed frozen in time as they tried to process the shocking scene they had just witnessed.

Juila reached Sofia first and kneeled to see if she were still alive. She almost cried in relief as she touched Sofia's life-line and found a strong connection. Within moments, Juila felt Jena's mental touch join her in this desperate fight to save their friend. Juila heard Jena's whispered petition for help from Jehoban. Instantaneously they gathered elemy, accessed their own wealth of power, and began healing the numerous life-threatening injuries.

To the many observers, it appeared as though the twins were merely holding their injured friend. Nobody had any idea how near Sofia was to death. If the girls had not been present Sofia would have bled out before help arrived.

Juila concentrated on following the life energy throughout Sofia's body, fixing the broken bones as well as the tears in her arteries and muscles as she came upon them. Suddenly, Juila felt Sofia's heart falter and then waited anxiously for the next beat which did not come. Frantically she used the elemy to send a surge of power throughout Sofia's body, effectively restarting it. She promptly followed the artery leading to her heart and discovered another major tear and rushed to repair the damage before Sofia experienced another catastrophic failure.

Just when Juila and Jena thought they were in the clear Sofia's body began to violently convulse. They shifted their focus to Sofia's head trauma and rapidly swelling brain. *This is too much!* Jena telepathically told Juila. *We're losing her!* With a final surge of their energy, they put all of their trust in Jehoban's power to restore their friend to health. Miraculously Sofia's convulsions stopped and her labored breathing became calm. "Thank goodness!" Jena sobbed for only Juila to hear. "Jehoban answered our prayer."

They became aware of the press of students around them as well as the sound of sirens in the distance. The crowd cheered when Sofia moaned and opened her eyes. Juila closed her eyes in relief and in prayer of thanks to Jehoban. "Hold still, Sofia," Juila admonished when she felt Sofia trying to sit up.

"I'm fine, Juila."

"We'll let the professionals decide," Jena reinforced Juila's command. She looked up and saw Jon standing on the edge of the crowd. He had tears falling down his cheeks as he focused his attention solely on his girl-friend lying on the ground. Jena motioned to catch his attention and finally said, "Jon, come here and hold her hand until help arrives."

He seemed to come out of his stupor and asked, "Is she going to be okay?" He kneeled onto the ground and took Sofia's hand from Jena's grasp. He rubbed his thumb across her knuckles and continued to stare at her face.

After what seemed an eternity, yet in actuality was only about five minutes, the crowd parted for a group of paramedics and a stretcher. The man in the lead kneeled and asked, "Did she lose consciousness?"

"Yes," Juila answered. "She was out for a couple of minutes. She hit her head on the curb."

The man stood back up and grabbed a plastic collar from the stretcher and positioned it around Sofia's neck. Once the brace was secured, he asked, "Are you experiencing any trouble breathing?"

"No."

"Good. We're going to put you on a backboard to keep you immobi-lized until we can get a scan done to make sure your spine is okay." He turned and gestured for his team to bring it down next to him. Together they rolled her onto her side, positioned the board beside her, and then rolled her back onto it. They fastened several straps over the top of her body and then lifted her up onto the stretcher.

Juila looked down on the ground where Sofia had lain and saw the pool of blood where her head had impacted the curb. It was only now she realized she had healed Sofia completely which would most likely cause much confusion for the medical staff. Her clothing would also have fresh blood whereas her body would lack corresponding injuries. She looked over to her sister and saw the concern on her face as they shared the same thought.

Behn rescued her from further considerations as he pushed through the crowd and found Juila unharmed. He rushed forward and put his arms around her. "Are you okay?"

Juila remained silent and simply nodded her head as it was pressed against his shoulder.

"Is Sofia going to be okay? I thought I felt the elemy being used," he whispered for only Juila to hear.

"I had to or she was going to die. Her heart stopped and I had to repair her arteries. Then she started to convulse as her brain swelled so I had to fix that as well. I think I might be in trouble, though."

"Why?" Behn looked down at her in confusion. As far as he was concerned, she had performed a heroic act; nothing worthy of trouble.

"She doesn't have any injuries, but there's still the problem of all of the blood."

"Mmm, I see." Behn tilted his head back and tried to think of a quick excuse to solve the problem. "Let's follow the ambulance to the hospital. Maybe we can come up with a solution while we drive." He removed his arms from around her body and grabbed her hand as he started to move away from the accident scene and toward his car. They were going to have to hurry if they wanted to keep up with the emergency vehicle while all of the other students were trying to leave the parking lot at the same time.

Juila looked around surreptitiously and called out mentally, *Jena! Get Jon and hurry to Behn's car. We're going to follow the ambulance to the hospital.*

Jena confirmed she would do as told and grabbed Jon's hand and pulled him along behind her as she rushed toward her sister.

Everybody remained in tense silence as they drove behind the ambulance. Each person's thoughts were focused on different aspects of the events. Juila and Jena were reviewing everything they had done to save their friend. Behn concentrated on both driving and trying to solve the problem of Sofia's injuries. Jon merely worried about Sofia's health as he had no way of knowing she was no longer in danger.

A few minutes later the ambulance turned into the hospital emergency room parking. Behn drove past the driveway until he reached the visitor's section. He quickly found a parking space and turned off the engine. Jon immediately opened the door to get out when Behn spoke up, "Jon, hold up a minute. Juila do you have Sofia's home number?"

"Yes."

"Good. Call her mom and let her know what happened and where her daughter is right now."

"Behn, I'm going inside," Jon insisted and continued swinging the door open and stepping out.

"Let him go, Behn," Jena spoke up suddenly as Behn started to call him back. "We need to talk about this situation and we can't be around Jon anyway."

"Fine," Behn agreed reluctantly. He watched as Juila searched through the saved numbers on her cell phone. He turned in his seat and asked Jena, "Have you figured out what you'll say about Sofia's lack of injuries?"

"I was hoping you'd thought of something, actually."

"Mrs. Castillo? Hi, this is Juila Stel."

Behn and Jena went silent as they waited for Juila to finish her phone call.

"I just thought you should know, Sofia was in an accident in the school parking lot." Juila paused as Sofia's mom asked her a question. "Yes, she's okay. Just as a precaution, an ambulance brought her to the hospital and they're probably wheeling her in right now. Yes, that's the hospital. We were going to go in and check on her right now. Okay, we'll see you in a couple minutes. Bye." Juila hung up the phone and looked over at Behn. "What are we going to do?"

"Like you said, we're going to go in and check on her. Hopefully we can think of something while we're waiting." He opened his car door and stepped out. He walked around the car and took Juila's hand into his own. The three of them walked slowly to the emergency entrance.

The hospital waiting area was filled with anxious family members as well as people needing to be seen by a doctor. There was a sense of controlled chaos which Juila and Jena had never experienced before. In Tuala the sick people were generally either healed at their own homes or in the wise-woman's house. The idea of people needing to congregate in such an unorganized fashion made the girls wonder how far behind the Earth people were with their medicinal practices.

They found Jon already sitting off to the side of the noisiest people in the room. There were several seats around him so they promptly filled the chairs. Behn asked, "Did you find anything out?"

"They asked if I were family. When I told them I wasn't they said they couldn't discuss Sofia's condition with me. I feel so useless!"

"Don't worry, Jon. Sofia will be fine," Juila patted his knee to comfort him. She recoiled slightly when Jon looked up at her angrily.

"You don't know that, Juila. Didn't you see the hood of the car which hit her? Obviously, Sofia is going to have massive injuries with how hard the car hit her. I saw all of the blood, too! She was covered in it!"

"I'm sure it's not as bad as all of that," Juila continued and then decided silence was probably a better course of action when Jon continued to glare at her. She wished she could tell Jon the truth. She knew for a fact Sofia was going to be perfectly fine since she had already taken care of the injuries.

Leave it be, Juila, Jena spoke into her mind. *Maybe we should think about leaving since they won't tell us anything anyway.*

I'd like to stay until her mom gets here. Once she sees Sofia and reports back to us that she's fine, then Jon will come home with us. As it is now, I doubt he'd leave here without an update. Juila looked surreptitiously from Jon to Behn.

The group waited in tense silence for over ten minutes, each ruminating on their own thoughts. Finally, Juila spotted Mrs. Castillo enter the same doors they had come through. She pointed and said to the group, "Sofia's mom is here."

Jon jumped up and hurried over to where she was standing at the information counter. He hoped to be able to hear an update as they told Sofia's mother. Obviously his plan worked since his shoulder visibly relaxed and he turned to smile back at his brother.

Jena, Juila, and Behn were slower to approach the main reception desk. They stood slightly back from Mrs. Castillo until they were sure she had received the answers to all of her questions.

Mrs. Castillo held her handbag in a death grip all the while she was talking to the receptionist. When she was finally told she could go back to see her daughter, then she relaxed slightly and noticed Jon standing next to her. "Jon, I didn't see you. Were you with Sofia when the accident happened?"

"No. I'm sorry."

"No worries. You heard the receptionist say she appears to be okay. Do you want to come back with me to see for yourself?"

"If you don't mind."

"Not at all. Come on. Oh, hi, Juila and Jena."

"Hi, Mrs. Castillo. We didn't want to intrude. This is Jon's brother, Behn. He drove us all here." Juila made the quick introduction.

"Do you all want to come back to see Sofia?"

The woman at the front desk interrupted rudely by saying, "We must limit the guests. Only you and one other person can go back there."

"It's okay, Mrs. Castillo," Juila spoke hurriedly when she could see her begin to bristle with insult toward the receptionist. "We'll wait here until Jon has seen her."

"Thank you, Juila. Some people are so rude," she said as she glared at the woman behind the desk. She took Jon's arm and walked past the desk in the direction she had been told.

Juila sighed loudly and said, "I guess we'll have to go back and wait for Jon. I hope he doesn't take too long."

CHAPTER 10

Elder Wilken cleared his throat loudly as he rose from his lounge chair in the main reception room at his Residence. "May I have everyone's attention?" He looked around the room at the few remaining people talking and waited for silence before he went on. "I believe we've had enough time to have private conversations both among ourselves as well as with Rasa. I'd like to propose we adjourn to the council meeting room and conclude this matter."

Without waiting to see if there were any objections, Elder Wilken turned and began walking out of the room. It had been an education to see how some of the other Elders had moved into groups of like belief and how others moved between groups to gather sentiment. He had been pleased to have the impression of general approval from the majority of the leaders.

When he reached the head of the oval table, Elder Wilken rested his palms flat on the smooth surface while he watched the rest of the Elders filter into the room and resume the seats they had left the day before. He knew the outcome would indeed favor the will of Jehoban, he just hoped it would not be at the expense of long-time friendships and alliances of the other Elders.

Rasa came to stand beside Elder Wilken and gave him a small, uncertain smile. She was understandably nervous with the outcome of the final vote. While she knew it was unnecessary for the vote to be unanimous, she hoped they could see the value she could bring to the position after having met and talked with everyone present.

Elder Wilken patted her hand briefly and winked at her where only she would see it. He had faith in his choice of successor and was pleased at how she had handled herself throughout the entire proceedings. He turned his attention back to the fully assembled convocation and said, "Please be seated."

Once the noise of everyone's chairs scraping on the floor died down and the final grumbles of complaint were quiet, Elder Wilken turned his head to Elder Debbon and gave him a brief nod to begin. Elder Debbon nodded briefly in return to acknowledge the shift in direction of the meeting. He had thought to conduct the final vote while they were standing, but then acknowledged the wisdom of a seated vote. People generally felt less powerful when they were seated. If they wanted any hope of unanimity, they would be better off remaining seated.

"We all know why we are convened this afternoon. We have had the opportunity to spend an evening, morning, and afternoon with the proposed successor to Elder Wilken. I'd like to remind everyone that the outcome of this final vote need not be unanimous, merely a majority. In the unlikely event that we are unable to come to the same conclusion as Elder Wilken, he is within his rights to petition Jehoban directly. We would then be required to attend a session with Jehoban, with Him as the mediator, where we would have to explain our position directly to Him. Please keep this outcome in mind when you are casting your final vote."

"Why are we to believe Jehoban sent her? We only have the word of this girl as to why she came here," grumbled Elder Yingun.

Elder Debbon scowled at the old and disgruntled Elder and decided to address his concern head on by saying, "Feel free to doubt as you like, Elder Yingun. You can take up your complaint with Jehoban when you are called to task for challenging His choice."

Yingun continued to scowl fiercely at Debbon for several tense seconds before he lowered his gaze to his lap. He felt as though he were being put in an untenable position and he did not like it one bit. It was not right for this slip of a girl to be creating such a mess for all of the good Elders. He would make sure she paid for the insult he had just received in front of his peers.

Debbon decided to continue with the meeting without any further delay. "Since we have already had two initial votes where we have voiced our concerns, I believe we can forgo further commentary. Please raise your hand if you are in favor of Rasa becoming Elder Wilken's successor." He watched with satisfaction as the previous assenters raised their hands instantly. More slowly were the hands raised of Quentien, Tarshen, Uvan, and Vargen.

Debbon contained a smile as he watched Xylen be torn between the two men on either side of him. He had felt sure of himself when both Vargen and Yingun had supported his own reservations. With Vargen's hand raised right beside him, he slowly raised his hand much to the chagrin of Yingun. Debbon knew the two men could cause trouble for Rasa if they were to join forces to harass her. He would have to keep an eye on both of them.

With one final look around the table, Debbon was pleased to see Olguin had also changed his vote from abstaining to assenting. The only person who refused to raise his hand was Yingun. His arms were crossed and his chin was jutting out stubbornly as he glared across the table at Debbon.

"Thank you all for your time. We have achieved a clear majority." He turned to Rasa and motioned for her to stand. "Let me be the first to welcome you to our ranks, Rasa. We know Jehoban has trained you impeccably and we will assist you however we may, should the need arise."

"Thank you, Elder Debbon. The honor is mine. I will do everything in my power to show you I can live up to the high standard set by the examples of everyone here. Thank you, Elders." She made a small bow toward the rest of the seated table as she felt her eyes begin to mist with a surge of emotion at being accepted by these great men despite their initial resistance to such a major change.

Wilken rose from his chair quietly and turned to his right to give Rasa a hug. He was more than pleased to have had the vote go as well as it had. He had been certain there would be more argument from Yingun and his supporters. Jehoban must have changed their hearts and minds with regard to this matter, there simply was no other explanation for it. He kept his arm around Rasa's shoulder as he turned to face the gentlemen at the table. "Thank you for accepting my choice of successor. I hope to live and rule for many anons to come, but rest assured, Rasa will be by my side learning."

Elder Debbon thought Wilken's simple speech was the proper way to end the meeting. "The votes have been duly noted. Rasa has been accepted as Elder Wilken's successor and will be treated with all respect due to her new position in society. This convocation is now adjourned."

Over the noise of the chairs scraping across the floor as everyone rose, Wilken announced, "A celebratory dinner has been prepared for anyone who wishes to remain and celebrate with us!"

Nobody was surprised when Yingun beat a hasty retreat from the room. A few moments later they could clearly hear the exterior door being slammed as the old Elder left the Residence to go back to his telepod to leave.

Vargen made his way around the table and touched Wilken's arm. "I would like to stay for dinner, but I have pressing matters back in my district which require my attention. Congratulations, Rasa. I'm sure we'll be seeing you soon. Goodnight."

"Thank you, Vargen. Goodnight and safe travels," Wilken said. He turned to Rasa and said, "Shall we go into the dining room?"

Rasa smiled up at the old gentleman and nodded. She could hardly believe her luck with the ease in which her life had just changed directions. She felt incredibly blessed for Jehoban to put her forward for this new role. Never had she imagined she would be doing something so important or so different. Ever since she was a little girl, she had imagined her life being lived on Acaim, doing whatever Jehoban needed. The responsibility and the honor was not lost on her as she walked beside the second nicest man she had ever met.

Jessica sat across the dinner table and watched her son carefully. She knew he had had another bad night's sleep. It broke her heart to see how fragmented Neal had become in the time he had been missing. Since Neal had agreed to see a therapist, she had spent the entire morning trying to locate the very best person to work with her son's special case.

"I found a therapist for you to see," she announced cheerfully.

Neal glanced up from his meal hastily and simply stared at his mom for a moment before he replied, "That didn't take long. When is the appointment?"

"Tomorrow morning. We were lucky he had an opening so soon."

"How much did such luck cost?" Neal muttered as he shifted his gaze back down to his meal. His appetite seemed to have disappeared with his mother's announcement.

"You still want to go, right?" Jessica glanced worriedly over to her husband and plead with her eyes for him to say something to back her up.

Neal, Sr. shook his head slightly and raised another forkful of steak into his mouth. He was not going to get involved in this battle. He knew their son would eventually have to talk to someone, but he was not a fan of forcing it on him so soon.

"Yeah, I'll go. I just wish I had more time is all."

Jessica almost cried out in relief, yet managed to restrain herself just in time. It was enough for Neal to have agreed, she did not need to add anything more which might make him change his mind. She picked up her fork and casually cut a piece of her steak.

The silence continued for the remainder of the meal. Not much eating was accomplished as everyone seemed to be preoccupied with ruminations of what would happen the next day. Finally, Neal, Sr. put his fork down on his nearly empty plate and pushed his chair away from the table as he rose to his feet.

"I'm going to watch the game on TV. Do you want to join me, Neal?"

"Sure. Who's playing?" Neal asked unenthusiastically.

"Eagles and the Rams."

"Cool." He stood up and kept his eyes downcast. He was thankful to get away from the awkward meal and his mother's prying eyes. It was almost as if she were willing him to say something more about the therapist and, frankly, Neal was unsure how he felt about the whole thing. He walked out of the room just behind his father.

Jessica watched as the two men in her life walked out of the room. Where she had always thought of her son as being the spitting image of her husband in both physical features and personality, now she was saddened to see a drastic difference in every aspect. She sincerely hoped the therapist would be able to break through the walls Neal had built in his mind to help him unlock his past so he could deal with his present and future.

She knew it was unrealistic to believe it would all happen in one visit, so instead she prayed it would come about swiftly. Not only was she intensely curious to find out where he had been, she also felt a burning desire to make his captors pay for hurting him so badly. This line of thinking reminded her to call Amanda, or better yet, pay her a visit to get some answers. She had been patient enough, Amanda was going to talk.

CHAPTER 11

"Just how do you and Vinia know one another?" Amanda asked in the charged silence as she looked over at Barla.

"She was a swimmer who came to live with us and worked for Captain Ahn."

Amanda began to get a strange feeling she knew the rest of the story and asked, "Were you held captive by Petre?"

Vinia nodded confirmation. "He said I was his wife."

"Let me guess, you drugged him, jumped overboard, and you were picked up by Captain Issyn?" Amanda stated simply.

"What? How could you know that?" Vinia stared dumbfounded from Amanda to Barla. "Did you tell her?"

"No," Barla insisted and asked the same question as Vinia. "How do you know this?"

"It's a long story," Amanda began. "Did you help with Captain Ahn's quarterly audit and then go live with Bryon and Alena?"

"Yes!"

"Did you watch over their children while Alena went to be trained as a wise-woman?"

"Yes!"

"While you were pregnant, did Bryon take you to the telepod races where you saw Riccan for the first time?"

"Yes!"

Amanda's heart began to race as she realized her dream had not been random at all; while she had been in her coma she had been living Vinia's life on Tuala. "Can you believe this, Riccan? It's exactly as I recorded it in my journal!"

"It's amazing! What do you think it all means?" Riccan asked.

"I don't know. We'll have to ponder the implications."

"What are you saying?" Vinia asked in confusion.

"I was in a coma for many anons and during that time, apparently, I dreamt I was living your life. I'm not sure what it means or why it happened. Maybe it means you and I are supposed to work together. Maybe it means something entirely different."

Riccan leaned forward and asked, "Did Bryon take you hiking after the kids were born?"

Amanda knew where Riccan was going with his question and was intensely curious to hear Vinia's answer.

"Yes," Vinia replied slowly. She did not know what they were trying to find out so she fell silent.

"Did anything happen as you were descending the mountain?" Amanda prompted.

"No."

"Interesting!" Riccan declared at the same time Amanda said, "It's not the same!"

"What? What's different?" Barla asked in confusion.

"My version of the past had me being swept away by a mudslide. Vinia's reality did not have that happen to her, for which I'm thankful you didn't have to go through such an ordeal." Amanda was imminently relieved while troubled at the same time. Everything had been exact from her dream and now she was unsure what to know as fact. Another disturbing event came to mind and she asked, "Did Valentina get abducted from the marketplace?" She hoped more than anything that Vinia would deny this event as well.

"Yes!"

"How long was she gone and how did you get her back?" Amanda leaned forward intently to urge Vinia to answer swiftly.

"It was the longest mesan of my life. We got her back when we found out Elder Debbon had made a contract with Petre for Valentina to be betrothed to his son. How come you don't seem surprised? Did you dream about this part as well?"

"I did, well mostly. In my dream, I wasn't able to get her back. She stayed with Elder Debbon and Chelesa."

"Oh! I'm glad it turned out my way better!"

"Then what did you do?"

"I took my three kids back to the Roanoke Colony and raised them there for the next six anons."

Amanda nodded as she processed this new information. "Who abducted Valentina?"

"Petre!"

"Is he the father of the triplets?"

"Unfortunately, yes."

Amanda took Vinia's hand in her own and gently squeezed it. "I'm sorry for everything Petre put you through. The bright side is he gave you your three kids. If they are the same ones as our girls have gotten to know, then you definitely have something to be proud of as they are wonderful, thoughtful, and kind."

"Thank you for saying so," Vinia said shyly. Just thinking about her missing children made her long for them even more than ever. Just as she opened her mouth to ask another question a baby began crying from upstairs. "Sorry, Danika is up from her nap. Excuse me." Vinia stood up and immediately left the room.

Barla had sat in mute silence as she tried to process everything she had just heard from this amazing woman and her husband. She truly hoped Amanda would be able to reunite Vinia with her lost children. "While we're waiting for Vinia to return, can I get you anything?"

"I think we've taken up enough of your time today. Riccan and I should probably get going."

"Oh, please stay longer!"

"We really can't, Barla," Riccan interceded. "I have to get back to work and Amanda has plans for this afternoon."

Amanda kept herself from asking Riccan what plans she had and simply nodded.

"Please tell me you'll come back soon for another visit," Barla pled.

"Of course!" Amanda smiled at Barla as she rose from the chair at the same time as Riccan.

Barla hurried to escort them to the front door. She had so many questions rolling through her mind. She wished she were able to speak to Amanda alone, without even Vinia around. It seemed rather selfish, yet she really wanted to know more about Amanda. Wishing she could delay their departure she said, "Please keep me updated on your progress for Vinia's children and when she can go visit with Neal."

"Of course!" Amanda replied immediately. She turned and gave Barla a quick hug. "Thank you, Barla."

"For what?" she asked in confusion.

"For everything you've done for me and Vinia. You've put yourself at risk, yet you've never batted an eyelash at volunteering your time and home."

More than a little embarrassed at Amanda's praise she looked down and answered quietly, "It's the least I could do for the wonderful life I've had with Ahn."

"I'll message you soon. Goodbye for now," Amanda said as Riccan began pulling her down the stairs by her hand.

"Goodbye, Amanda. Bye, Riccan!" She called down the pathway as she waved farewell. She watched them close the front gate and walk up the sidewalk hand-in-hand on their way back to the landing ground.

"What's going on Riccan? What plans do I have this afternoon?" Amanda asked as soon as they were out of earshot.

"You don't. I just had the feeling you needed time to go over everything we discovered from Vinia today. Which reminds me, my mom asked if she could have a copy of your journal."

Amanda's head seemed to be swimming with the sudden change in direction of Riccan's comment. Of course she would agree, yet she still asked, "What does she want it for?"

"I don't know. You could stop by and ask her yourself, if you want."

"No, I don't think so. You're right about me needing some time to process these latest discoveries. What would be the easiest way to get your mom a copy of my journal?"

"I'll show you how to scan it into the patil so you can send it electronically to her."

"It can do that? How long will it take?" Amanda had never heard of this aspect of the patil.

"It's fast. You just have to lay the book down on a reader plate and it instantaneously digitizes the contents. My guess is it'll take you less than ten minutes."

"Cool!" She nodded in satisfaction at the efficiency of the Tualan technology. After a few more steps she asked, "Why are you playing hooky?"

"I needed some time to cool off after my meeting with Ela Nena so I took an early lunch. I hope you didn't mind my intrusion on your meeting with Barla and Vinia."

"Never! I'd prefer you to be with me twenty-four seven if I could arrange it!"

"I think you'd get tired of me before then," he replied with a chuckle.

"It'd never happen. There's never enough time with you." She wrapped her arm around his and snuggled closer to him as they neared the landing field. "Are you coming home right now?"

He nodded and replied, "I'll show you how to scan your journal, but then I'll have to go back to work for a few more hours."

"Bummer," Amanda pouted. "I had high hopes for a very pleasant afternoon with my handsome husband."

Riccan pretended to be shocked by her innuendo, but his smile ruined the effect. Amanda's suggestion began to grow in his mind and he realized it might be just the thing he needed before he returned to work. Besides, he could always add some time to his day on his return trip so Ela Nena would not have another thing to add to her growing list of complaints against him. "I like the way you're thinking! You may need to demonstrate what your ideas are for a pleasant afternoon!"

"Gladly!" Amanda grinned mischievously up at her husband as she palmed open the door to her telepod. "I'll see you at home!"

Riccan glanced down at his timepiece and realized it was later than he had imagined. The girls would be getting home from school soon and what he had in mind would need more time than they currently had. He grinned back at her and said, "Time it to noon."

Amanda did not have to pretend a startled expression at his suggestion. He was the one who always told her timing it was dangerous. "Okay," she chuckled at his suddenly reckless mood.

He nodded and then hurried around her telepod to get to his own. The foul mood which had plagued him earlier had been completely banished by thoughts of being alone with his wife. He had to restrain himself from leaving the landing square before she did.

Riccan fidgeted through the startup procedure. He was much quicker at it than Amanda since he had anons more practice than she had. He watched out the windshield to see her telepod rise from the ground and then blink out of existence. His telepod followed an instant later.

They both arrived in the garage at the same time. Riccan rushed through the shutdown procedures and palmed open the side door. He stepped out of his telepod, closed the door, and waited impatiently for Amanda to exit her vehicle.

Finally, they walked together across the empty bay of the garage. In unison, they hit their remotes to activate the concealing shields on the telepods. Riccan could not contain himself any longer and he reached down and picked Amanda up into his arms. She squealed and grabbed around his neck in her surprise.

"Riccan! Put me down!"

"As soon as I get you upstairs, then I'll put you down. Until then, use your mouth to give me a kiss!"

Amanda giggled again and did as she was told. Her kiss was so effective, it took them even longer to get through the garage as Riccan had to stop walking with the amount of passion his wife poured into her kiss on his lips.

Reluctantly, he pulled his mouth from hers and moaned with anticipation of what was going to happen once they were undressed. He could not imagine how he had lived without this much passion before. Nothing compared to the fire they shared when they were intimate. With a one-track-mind, he rushed through the garage, into the kitchen, up the main stairway, and into their bedroom. Riccan kicked the door shut behind him as he took the last few steps to reach the bed.

He set her down carefully on the edge of the mattress. He began unbuttoning her shirt as she tugged at the belt around his waist. They were getting in each other's way in their urgency to get undressed. Both ended up laughing at their antics.

"I think this would be faster if we each undressed ourselves!" Amanda growled in frustration.

"If you don't hurry, I'll use the elemy to make your clothes disappear altogether!" Riccan bantered back.

"Don't you dare, this is my favorite shirt!"

"Consider yourself warned," he teased even as he pulled his pants down and stepped out of them.

Amanda looked up with wide eyes and asked, "Did you go commando today?"

"It happens," he said as he tugged his shirt over his head, threw it on the floor, and began moving forward intently.

Amanda giggled in anticipation and renewed her efforts to speedily undress. Somehow she managed to finish just as Riccan reached her. Together they tumbled backward onto the bed with their lips and bodies joined.

Sometime later, Amanda relaxed in Riccan's arms and enjoyed the fresh scent of his body. She would never grow tired of being with him and she doubted he would ever tire of being with her. Their bond was too strong to ignore and too powerful to be stopped. She sighed deeply with satisfaction at the same time Riccan did and then smiled in satisfaction at their shared bliss.

"I hate to dampen the mood, but didn't you say you had to go back to work?"

"Ugh! That more than dampens the mood, Amanda, more like utterly crushes it! You're right, though. We should get dressed so I can show you how to scan your journal and then I'll be on my way." He rolled away from her and got off the far side of the bed to head into the bathroom for a quick shower.

Amanda watched him walk away and wished she had saved her comment for later. She turned over onto her other side and opened the drawer of her nightstand. She pulled out her journal and shut the drawer with the back of her hand. Rolling again onto her back she held the book above her and simply stared at the cover without needing to open it. What mysteries did her memories withhold? What could she believe? How far would this journey take her?

She groaned at all of her unanswered questions and pulled herself out of the bed. She slowly dressed herself as she heard the shower running in the bathroom. After Riccan was gone, she would take a shower herself. If she went in there now, Riccan would be even later in getting back to work.

Just as she found her missing sock under the bed, Riccan came out of the bathroom, naked except for the towel wrapped around his hips. He could see Amanda's appreciative gaze as she looked him over from head to toe with a small quirk of her lips. He imagined she was having the same ideas of a repeat performance and he sauntered a little more seductively to his pile of clothes on the floor.

"Woohoo," Amanda called out as he let his towel drop.

"Later, baby," he teased as he hauled his pants up and fastened them.

"Mmmhmm! Do you think we'll ever get tired of this?"

"I hope not!" He pulled the shirt over his head and then looked around for the belt Amanda had painstakingly removed earlier. Riccan smiled as he located it across the room. He had been too distracted before to see her fling it out of the way. "Let's get downstairs," he said as he picked up his belt and began threading it through the loops on his pants.

Amanda opened the bedroom door for him and they went down the back stairs to go to their office. She watched as Riccan opened the secret compartment where the patil resided. She was even more surprised when he opened a second door which housed a glass plate she had not known existed.

He activated the patil and waited the few seconds for the main screen to light up. "Let me see your journal," he said as he held out his hand. He opened the book to the first page and pressed it down to the lit glass surface. Almost immediately he lifted it up again and turned the page. He looked up behind him and said, "It's fast, like I said. You just need to touch it to the glass and then you can turn the page to do the next one. When you get through all of the pages, then click here," he said as he pointed to a new icon on the screen. "This compiles all of the recent scans into one document and then asks you what you want to do with it. From there you just add it as an attachment to a standard message. Do you think you have it?"

"It sounds pretty straightforward to me."

"Good." Riccan stood up and kissed Amanda hurriedly on the lips. "I've got to get going. I love you!" He pulled her into a hug and rubbed her back sensuously.

Amanda squirmed out of his grasp and laughed, "Keep it up and you won't get back to work!"

"Ugh, I hate it when you're right!" He pulled his hands away and turned to leave the room. He called over his shoulder just before he left the office, "We'll pick up where we left off when I get home from work tonight!"

"I love you!" Amanda sank down into the vacated seat. She listened intently for the garage door to close before she opened the journal to the second page. As instructed, she placed it on the glass surface momentarily, picked it up and turned to the next page. Before she knew it, she had reached the final page and smiled with satisfaction as she saw the many pages indicated on the screen of the patil. She tapped the icon and watched it format all of the pages into one document.

She opened a message box and entered Nena's call sign. She attached the document and wrote a quick message for her mother-in-law.

Nena,

Riccan said you wanted a copy of my journal. I have attached it for you. I can't wait to hear what you have in mind with it.

Talk with you soon,

Amanda

She hit the send button, turned off the patil, and slid everything back into their hiding places. With nothing left on her agenda for the rest of the day, she went back upstairs and undressed for a shower. As she bathed, she reviewed all of the revelations of the day. Her intuition was telling her she had learned something today of vital importance. Agonizingly, she could not put her finger on what it could possibly be. She turned off the water and toweled herself dry.

After getting dressed again, she went downstairs to watch some mindless television. Hopefully, if she relaxed her mind would come up with the solution on its own. She sat down on her favorite couch and grabbed the remote.

Without warning, her mind tensed as she realized her daughters were in trouble. She tried to focus on Juila's birth crystal. With a cry of frustration she had to start over, visualizing each color which symbolized her daughter. Finally, a scene came into focus which did not reassure her at all.

She could see Sofia lying in a pool of blood on the asphalt. Amanda had no idea what had happened to the girl, but she could tell from Jena's expression across from Juila that they were both intent on keeping Sofia alive. Keeping the link active, she watched the scenes unfold until the EMTs put the now conscious Sofia onto the stretcher and into the ambulance.

Amanda sucked in a much-needed breath as she disconnected herself from Juila's birth crystal. Obviously she could not call either of her daughters about what she had just witnessed without giving away the secret of the necklaces. She would have to bide her time impatiently until the girls either came home and told her or if one of them thought to call her.

CHAPTER 12

Juila's fears were relieved when Sofia was finally released from the hospital with several sets of stitches to show for her accident. The doctors had told Sofia how lucky she had been to only have a small gash on the back of her head as well as a deep cut to her side. They had taken several x-rays and an MRI to ensure there was no internal bleeding.

Jon had refused to leave the hospital until he knew Sofia would be released. He had walked beside Sofia's wheelchair as she was taken to her mother's car. He still could not believe she was being sent home so swiftly after such a horrific accident.

"I'll call you tomorrow to see how you're doing," Jon said to Sofia just before the hospital worker shut the car door.

Mrs. Castillo stood at the driver's door and spoke to Jon, "Don't call until after school lets out. I want to make sure Sofia gets as much rest as she needs after her ordeal."

"Sure thing, Mrs. Castillo." He took a step away from the car and waved goodbye to Sofia as the car backed out of the parking space.

Behn walked over to his brother and put his arm across his shoulders to comfort him. "Juila told you Sofia was going to be okay. I think you owe her an apology for how you treated her earlier."

"I know, I was just worried and I took it out on Juila."

They strolled over to Behn's car where Juila and Jena were already seated inside. Jon opened the back door and sat in the seat. "Hey, Juila. I'm really sorry for being so rude to you."

"It's no problem, Jon. I knew you were upset."

Behn pulled the car out of the hospital parking lot and drove slowly down the road. He wished the day had gone differently since he had been looking forward to learning more about using his birth crystal. On the bright side, Sofia was going to be okay so he was thankful everything had turned out okay in the end. There would always be tomorrow to learn more.

As they turned into the Stel's driveway, Behn realized suddenly that they had forgotten all about Valentina. "Oh man, I hope Val found a ride home! We were supposed to ride over here together to study this afternoon..."

"She's fine," Juila interrupted him with a knowing look.

Behn looked at her strangely before turning his attention to navigating the long driveway up to the front door. He pulled to a stop and leaned over to give Juila a quick kiss and hug. While he held her close he whispered in her ear, "Did you read Val's mind?"

Juila nodded and whispered, "She's upset, but she's at home."

Behn nodded and sat back in his seat. Both rear doors opened as Jon and Jena got out. Jon walked around the back of the car to get into the front seat. The brothers remained silent with their own inner ruminations on the day's events.

The girls waved goodbye and went inside the house as Behn drove away. It was late enough that they could hear their parents making dinner in the kitchen. Belatedly, they realized they should have called their mom to let them know what had kept them out so late.

"Hey, girls," Riccan called out as soon as they entered the living from the foyer. "What kept you out so late?"

"Sofia got hit by a car in the school parking lot," Jena stated matter-of-factly.

"What? Is she okay?" Amanda pretended to be shocked by the news.

"Juila had to use her power to heal her. She actually died on the scene with a burst artery to her heart. Then she suffered convulsions with her head injury until Jehoban stepped in and healed her."

"Thank goodness! It's a good thing you were there for your friend,

Juila," Amanda stated with true feeling. She had never imagined the situation was as bad as Jena described. More than ever, Amanda felt blessed for her children to have been raised by Jehoban so they could save Sofia's life.

"I thought for sure I was going to lose her. I'm just glad Jena was with me to back up my work. Mom, it was so bad! Sofia was lying there bleeding out onto the pavement. Before I even knew what I was doing, I had tapped into her life-line and began fixing all of the broken bones and internal bleeding." Juila stepped closer to the island and pulled out one of the stools since she suddenly felt weary beyond words.

Jena stepped up behind her sister and gently rubbed her back while mentally asking, *Hey, are you okay?*

I'm fine. It just hit me how close we came to losing Sofia today. I've never experienced anything like that before. Juila dropped her elbows onto the countertop and let her head fall into her cradled hands.

Riccan recognized the signs of taxed powers and suggested, "We were going to make dinner right now. Why don't you tell us what you would like and I'll use my powers to create it. You look like you could use something to eat sooner rather than later."

"A foxl burger and fried krumpli sounds wonderful," she answered hurriedly. Just thinking about the wonderful smell and flavor began to revive her worn body.

"You got it," Riccan said cheerfully even as the plate of food appeared in front of Juila. "What about you, Jena?"

"Ditto!" She chuckled as her plate of food showed up even as she finished asking. "Thanks, Dad!" Jena sat down promptly on another stool in preparation for eating.

"I'll say the blessing so you two can get started," Riccan announced and bowed his head to pray. "Father, we thank You for what we are about to receive, and pray that Thou will bless it, and us to Thy service. In Your name we pray, amen."

The girls said 'Amen' quietly in unison and then picked up their hamburgers to take unladylike, massive bites. They both moaned in appreciation of their father's cooking skills.

"Do you want the same thing?" Riccan asked Amanda when she finally turned away from watching their daughters.

"Yes, please."

Two more plates materialized on the island and they ate their meal standing opposite of their children. When the plates were empty and everyone agreed they were too full for dessert, Amanda suggested they sit down in the living room.

Once everyone was comfortable, Amanda asked the obvious question, "What happened in the parking lot to cause Sofia to be hit by the car?"

"Sofia was excited because Jon was going to come over to her house to study. She had been looking for him and I spotted him heading toward her car. Before any of us knew it, Sofia was running to catch up with him and she didn't look to see if the way were clear. She stepped right in front of the car which was going too fast for a crowded parking lot anyway."

Jena took over the story by saying, "Too late to do anything, we saw Sofia flying through the air and hitting the ground where her head smacked into the curb. It seemed like everything was going in slow motion. Juila and I were already on our way to help her before she even hit the ground, I think."

"Then I got scared because I thought I completely healed her and she wouldn't have any injuries to account for all of the blood. Luckily I missed a couple of gashes! She ended up with seven stitches on the back of her head, three stitches on her arm, and six on the side of her abdomen. I told Behn how scared I was that we'd be found out because I had healed her too well. I guess that's what I get for being so cocky!"

"From the extent of the injuries you repaired, you have every right to feel proud of the work you did. You did save her life, after all!" Amanda was so proud of her daughters.

"She probably would have healed everything if the EMT's hadn't shown up when they did. I guess we got lucky, didn't we, Juila?"

"Yeah, lucky," she replied sullenly. "I wish I would have been fast enough to protect her from even getting hit in the first place."

"That wasn't Jehoban's plan for you, Juila," Riccan stated simply. "Don't ever second-guess his plans."

Jena nodded in agreement first and, finally, Juila had to agree with her father's wisdom. Juila yawned hugely and belatedly covered her mouth.

"Why don't the two of you call it an early night? A good night's sleep will make everything better," Amanda suggested.

"That's the best idea I've heard all day," Juila said as she slowly pulled herself up from the low couch. She leaned forward and gave each of her parents a kiss on the cheek and shuffled her way across the foyer to the staircase.

"I'll keep an eye on her," Jena said as she copied her sister's gesture of kissing both parents. She had a bit more liveliness in her step, but she could definitely tell she needed to rest. She caught up with Juila before reaching the top of the stairs and put her arm around Juila's waist for comfort.

CHAPTER 13

Neal rested comfortably in the leather lounge chair in Dr. Huddleston's office. Initially he had been nervous about meeting with the therapist, but now he realized his fears had been misplaced. Dr. Huddleston was a very mellow man who seemed to merely want to talk about easy things of Neal's life. He mostly told stories about high school, college, and dating Amanda.

Dr. Huddleston scribbled another round of ideas on his notepad and tapped his pen onto the surface of the paper. He tossed around several ideas for treatment before he finally came to the best solution. "I'd like to try to hypnotize you, if you don't mind," Dr. Huddleston said as soon as Neal finished his last story.

"Why?"

"I don't know if you realize it, but you've only shared stories with me from things which happened quite some ago. You haven't made any mention of anything from the past several years. I'm hoping hypnosis will allow your subconscious to relax enough to help you recall your missing time. Do you want to try it?"

Dr. Huddleston doodled on the notepad in his lap rather than let Neal know how desperately he wanted to go forward to this next step in the treatment plan. After speaking with Neal's parents prior to this appointment, he knew hypnosis would be the only answer in helping to restore this young man's lost years. He was looking forward to being the one person to help the family.

"If you think it would help. My mom is really hoping you can help me."

"Good! Good. Okay, then we can begin right away." He glanced down at his watch and then smiled back up at Neal and said, "We have just enough time in today's session. Now close your eyes and take two deep breaths through your nose and exhale through your mouth. Good, now focus on the sound of my voice…"

Neal drifted through the thoughts in his mind. He felt completely relaxed and warm, almost as if he were floating. He had no notion of time or space as he reviewed the scenes unfolding in his head as though he were watching a movie where he was the star.

Dr. Huddleston first asked questions about places and times which Neal could easily recall. When the answers started to conflict with what the doctor believed actually happened, he started to ask more pointed questions. "What is the name of the place where you lived?"

"Tuala."

"Did you live alone?"

"No."

"Who did you live with?"

Neal furrowed his brow slightly. He wanted to say the woman's name was Amanda since the woman looked so much like his former fiancé. Finally, he recalled the woman's actual name and said, "Vinia." Almost as if her name were a trigger, he started to recall many other previously lost thoughts and emotions. He became very agitated and confused with the glut of information overloading his brain.

Dr. Huddleston recognized signs of stress in his patient and decided they had gone far enough for the day's session. He said, "I'm going to count backward from ten to one. When I reach the number one, I'm going to snap my fingers together and you are going to be wide awake, feeling refreshed and relaxed." He counted down and snapped his fingers.

Neal took a deep breath and slowly opened his eyes. His body felt as though he had taken a really long, relaxing nap. For once in many days, he actually felt energized and ready to face the world again. He smiled at the doctor and said, "Did it work?"

"What do you think, Neal? Only you can be the judge of whether or not it worked."

"I felt as though I've slept for a really long time. How long was the session?"

The doctor looked across the office at the wall clock and replied, "Just under twenty minutes."

"Wow, it sure felt a lot longer than that!" Neal picked himself up and put his feet on the floor and leaned forward with his elbows on his knees. "I had the strangest dreams. Was any of it real?"

"That's for you to decide, Neal. I think we should plan on scheduling another hypnosis session for when you come back. I'm hoping you'll agree to come back?"

"Sure. I don't see why not. It'll sure make my mother happy." Neal smiled brightly at the doctor to make sure his backhanded acceptance did not offend the therapist.

"Great!" Dr. Huddleston stood up promptly and held out his hand to Neal. "My receptionist can get your next appointment set up. It was wonderful meeting you, Mr. Taivas."

Neal stood up and shook the doctor's hand. "Thank you, Doctor. I look forward to our next session."

They walked out of the office together and Dr. Huddleston instructed the receptionist to book Neal for another hour-long session within the next seven days. He nodded his head cordially at Neal and went back into his office to finish recording his notes before his next patient arrived.

Jessica had been waiting in the reception area for Neal. Her attention had been riveted to his face as soon as the therapist's door had opened. If his expression were any indication, progress had been made during the session. She barely contained her happiness, afraid her enthusiasm would sour Neal on wanting to continue with treatment.

Neal thanked the receptionist and took the appointment card she handed him before turning to his mother. "This was a great idea, Mom." He held out his hand to help her up from the chair. He could tell she was happy for him and he was glad to see her worried expression begin to fade from her face. More than anything, he wanted to have the easygoing relationship restored with his parents; time would tell.

~

ELDER DEBBON LANDED his telepod at their personal estate with the early morning sun shining across the landscape. He always appreciated the panoramic view his property afforded him of his district. There was no other place with a better setting than his ancestral home. He hoped he would find as much peace inside the house as he did outside.

He walked up the path from the landing grounds to the main house and pondered what he was going to do with his son. Ever since he had told Willian he would help him arrange a way to meet with Jena on Earth he had regretted his rash promise. Distance was probably the best cure for his son's reckless and heartless actions regarding his betrothed.

Times were changing for sure, starting with Rasa's acceptance by most of the other Elders. He was unsure whether the other Elders would agree with his decision to send Willian to Earth; that might be taking their tolerance too far. Shrugging his shoulders, he had to rely on his initial instincts to help his son on this quest. He had already lived through two weeks of pain and agony thinking his son lost in the perils of the Ascension Gate.

No sooner had he entered the front door when his wife came running down the hallway and into his arms. He folded his arms around her slender body and breathed deeply of the fresh, clean scent of her still-wet hair. "Maybe I should leave more often if this is the welcome I'd receive!"

"Don't you dare! I hate it when you leave me." Chelesa tilted her head up and accused, "I thought you were going to come home last night!"

"I had every intention of leaving right after the confirmation vote, but Wilken asked us to stay for dinner. By the time the evening ended, it was much too late to even think about leaving. You wouldn't want me to risk flying home tired, would you?"

"Absolutely not! So does this mean Rasa is really to be Wilken's successor? How did that go over?" Chelesa extricated herself from their embrace and kept her arm around his back as she propelled him down the hall toward his office so they could talk in private.

Debbon wished she had steered them toward their bedroom for a more intimate private encounter, yet he understood her need to hear everything which had transpired over the last three days. He sat at his desk and recounted all of the events to his rapt audience. Never once did Chelesa interrupt his narration of the convocation.

When her husband finished the tale, she sat back and said, "Wow! I wonder what Yingun is going to come up with to make Wilken's and Rasa's lives difficult!"

"I was thinking the same thing. I'm going to have to watch him more carefully for a bit to make sure he doesn't do something to tarnish his standing with the Elders or his district. I don't like contention among our small group. Our jobs are hard enough even when we're all getting along." Debbon closed his eyes momentarily at the unfortunate mess this meeting had made of the balance of power within their elite community.

"Do you think Yingun will cool off when he sees Wilken isn't ready to step down anytime soon?"

"I could hope, but I think it moved from dislike to downright hate by the time the meeting ended."

"How unfortunate for Rasa. This will be her problem when Wilken is ready to let her take over."

"Like you said, it could be a long while before anything changes hands. For everyone's sakes, I hope Wilken lives forever!"

"He is a really good Elder. Rasa will have a great teacher in the meantime."

"Speaking of good teachers…has Willian said anything more to you about wanting to go to Earth?"

"Ugh, it's all he talks about. I really wish you'd tell him you've recon-sidered. I can't see how it will do any good at this point and I really think Willian will make things worse with Jena if he handles it badly. I mean, what if Jena refuses to talk to him? Willian will lose his cool."

"Believe me, you aren't saying anything I haven't already thought of already. I'm just afraid Willian would be foolish enough to try to use the Gate unassisted if we don't help him. I'd much rather we be in charge of this than allow it up to chance again. We were truly blessed to get him back at all, you know."

Chelesa shivered with fear at how close they had come to losing their son. Reluctantly she had to agree with her husband in this matter, as much as she detested it. "It just feels like we're rewarding his bad behavior and it rankles me that he pushed us into this decision."

"I agree. I think we'll have to set some major conditions on him in exchange for our help. If nothing else comes of this, he'll learn there are consequences for his actions. The fear he initially felt from his failed attempt will only last so long."

"What do you have planned?" Chelesa could hardly wait to hear what Debbon had devised for their son.

"I spoke with Wilken about our situation. He has agreed to send Willian through his Gate in exchange for Willian mediating some domestic matters with a group of teens in his district."

Chelesa grinned wickedly as she imagined their son sitting in on boring political meetings. "Willian might reconsider the deal when he hears there's work involved!" She chuckled in anticipation of Willian's distaste of politics.

"It'll be a good learning experience for him. He has to learn mediation skills as well as the ability to work with other Elders to achieve a common goal."

"When is Wilken expecting him?"

"He said he could be ready as soon as tomorrow."

Chelesa's mood dampened at the thought of him leaving so soon. "Are you going to take him?"

"I don't think so. If he wants independence, then he can prove it by taking himself there."

"When are you going to tell him? Do you really want him to leave tomorrow? We could put off telling him for a bit longer, you know."

"I know, but really what would be the point?" He shrugged his shoulders and willed his wife to understand. When Chelesa finally nodded her agreement he continued, "I'll tell him at dinner tonight to get ready to leave after school tomorrow."

"What about his school, Debbon?"

"I think he'll learn a lot more on this journey than any missed school sessions could teach him. Besides, I'm going to tell him he'll need to register for school on Earth. It'll do him some good to find out what Jena's been learning."

Chelesa's grin returned as she tried to visualize their son enrolled in an Earth school. The thought tickled her imagination. Maybe this trip was going to be good for their spoiled, overindulged son. Maybe he would even learn a dose of humility while he was at it. Then she realized she was talking about her son and said, "Maybe you should put a compulsion on him to keep his powers secret. The last thing we'd want is for him to get himself in trouble on Earth. You know how impulsive he can be!"

"True! I'll have to consider it for a bit this evening. Maybe I can work something over him while he's sleeping tonight. He doesn't really need to know we don't entirely trust him."

Chelesa nodded agreement. It saddened her to think she had failed so miserably in tempering her son's behavior as he grew up. She could think of many occasions where a sharp word said at the appropriate time could have changed their son's attitude.

Debbon could see his wife's mood darken and he hated to see it. "I don't have to be at the Residence until this afternoon, maybe we could continue my homecoming welcome upstairs in our bedroom." He wiggled his eyebrows suggestively and was pleased to see his wife's mood lighten with comprehension of his suggestion. He stood from his chair and held out his hand to his wife.

"It's a good thing you have plans for this afternoon since I have as well," she teased.

"What are you doing?" They left his office and headed up the main staircase.

"I'm going to visit with Nena. She has a project in mind for us."

"Anything I'd be interest in?"

"Probably…but you'll be too busy," she teased. She shut the bedroom door behind them and silenced any further conversation by covering his lips with her own.

CHAPTER 14

Chelesa saw her husband off to his duties before she took off in her telepod to Pantano. She was eager to read the journal with Nena, more than a little curious what Amanda had written about her family in particular. It was hard to imagine a stranger knowing so many details of their lives when they tried to keep their personal life so secret. Having Debbon in the public eye made them more conscious of their private time.

She landed at the same location as she had previously and made quick work of exiting the telepod. As she crossed the great expanse of lawn, she could see Nena waving to her from the patio above her. She quickened her pace and skipped up the stairs to reach her friend.

They hugged in greeting and Nena said, "Come inside out of the heat. I've arranged for tea and refreshments in my office so we won't be interrupted." She led the way in a rush and closed the office door once Chelesa entered the room. In anticipation of the meeting, Nena had printed out two copies of the journal which pertained to Chelesa so they could read at their own pace and not hold up one another. Somehow it seemed an invasion of privacy to share the other people's stories with her.

Chelesa sat in one of the plush chairs and was glad to find Nena pick the chair next to her rather than across from her at the desk as she had thought would happen. It would be much more fun and intimate if they were able to sit close and share discoveries. She accepted the bundle of papers from Nena as well as a pen to take notes.

Within minutes both women were silently engrossed in reading the journal. Many of the accounts were not known to Chelesa as they dealt with other people. She was more than a little startled to read as much detail as was written. At this point she realized the specifics of the journal could be very dangerous indeed if it were to fall into the wrong hands. She scribbled a note to remind herself to talk to Nena about it later.

She read through Amanda's account of the time in her life where their family was being threatened by an unknown group. Her fear returned as real as if she were reliving the events. She was surprised to find out Petre had been behind the attack; of course, it made sense now that it was all laid out for her review. She would gladly take the knowledge of the names of the co-conspirators back to her husband so he could seek justice for their suffering.

To this day, she still felt a small amount of gratitude for the events which transpired since they gave her the opportunity to be trained as a wise-woman. Surely, had the threat never happened, she probably would never have found the time to learn the skills she found so effortless to use. At least one good thing had come of the terrifying situation.

The part of the story which troubled her was where her son and Jena had been taken to Earth for safety. Of course, this part never happened. Both children had gone to live on Acaim since Jehoban's island would be the safest place anywhere for them to be. The timing of the attack had coincided with the beginning of one of the Successor's School sessions run by Rasa. Even though he was young, Willian had been thrilled to attend the training session as Debbon's heir.

Chelesa wondered why the story had been altered in such a way and what significance it would have. She placed a star next to the first paragraph where the account altered from reality. She continued to scan through the rest of Amanda's account and failed to find anything else wrong. After turning over the last page, Chelesa sat in silent contemplation for Nena to finish as well.

Nena looked up from her reading and asked, "Are you done already?"

"Yes, I already lived through the events after all. Did you read it before I got here?"

"No, but Amanda read it to us right after she and Riccan were married; it's how I knew about the journal to begin with."

Chelesa nodded and asked, "How do you think Amanda knew about all of this. It's very strange to read someone else's perspective on my own life."

"I thought it would be. Luckily for me, there's hardly anything in here about myself or Daven other than where we're described as Riccan's parents. I can only imagine how you felt reading all of the section about your husband, yourself, and your son. So what did you think?"

"It was remarkably accurate except for this section," she said as she ruffled through the pages until she found where she had marked the star. She turned it to face Nena and held it still while her friend read the passage.

"Hmm. What do you think it means?"

"I have no idea. I can't understand why the story would shift to Earth." Suddenly, Chelesa shivered as she realized her son was going to be traveling to Earth in the very near future. Perhaps the account was some type of warning against the trip. Even as the idea formed, she realized Willian had been safe on Earth in Amanda's journal allowing her to draw some small amount of comfort. She shook her head and said, "I'm going to have to spend some time thinking about it for sure!"

"Absolutely. Are you ready for some tea? I should have asked you before we began, but I was so anxious to get started."

"I would love some. Melba didn't happen to make those wonderful chocolate desserts, did she?" Chelesa's mouth began to water just thinking about the sweet treats.

"She sure did!" Nena picked up the dessert plate and held it out for Chelesa to take her pick. When her guest had selected one, she set the plate down right next to Chelesa so she could have as many as she liked. She served them both tea and sat back with a sigh of satisfaction. The whole afternoon could not have gone any better. She had a feeling deep in her soul that this day was meant to happen.

~

CHELESA WAS STILL CONSIDERING the implications of the day's events when her family sat down to dinner. Debbon sat at the head of the table in his customary spot. She sat at his right side with Willian across from her on Debbon's left side. Even though they ate in the large dining room, the intimate spacing of their seats left them feeling as though it were a small affair.

The meal was well on its way to being done when Debbon decided to share his decision on Willian's trip. "Willian, I spoke with Elder Wilken while I attended the convocation. He has agreed to give you passage to Earth." He deliberately paused to allow his statement to fully sink in to his son's thoughts.

Willian nearly choked on the bite he had just inserted in his mouth. His eyes grew wide as he realized his father had actually made the arrangements he had promised. After thinking it would be several weeks before he would know anything, this news was very exciting. He rapidly swallowed his half-chewed food and had to take a hasty drink of water to keep it moving down his throat. "Seriously? That's awesome. When are we going?"

Debbon paused for only a moment before he revealed, "Tomorrow after school."

"Tomorrow? Are you serious? I can't wait!" Immediately he began making plans for what he would say to Jena when he met her on Earth. He could just imagine her reaction to seeing him again after so long. She would definitely have some explaining to do for her extended absence, not to mention silence.

"Before you get too excited, there are some conditions which need to be met before Elder Wilken will send you to Earth."

Willian should have known it was too good to be true. With a sigh of resignation he asked, "What must I do?"

"He has asked for you to mediate some matters in his district with regard to the teen population. He and I agree it would be a good skill for you to practice. Elder Wilken is very busy at present and he would like your help. I think it's a small price to pay for what we are asking him to do."

"Don't get me wrong, Dad, I fully understand how generous he's been in allowing this at all. I can't think of too many Elders who would even entertain your request." Willian tried to be speak as diplomatically as he could. His father knew he detested any political matters and this was an important task which he would have to try his best. Still, he tried to imagine how long it would take to listen to the individual cases. Surely there would not be more than a few disputes to hear.

As if Debbon could see his son's thoughts turning in his head he continued, "There are some other considerations to be taken into account for your journey."

"Such as?" Willian prompted.

"I think you discovered your lack of preparedness on your initial trip, right? This time I would like you to study various aspects of Earth before you even make an attempt to go there. Also, you are going to need to procure transportation from Manzanit to Pantano. I will let you discover their Earth names on your own. Then there's the matter of arranging for where you will live once you reach the town where Jena is living. Oh, and one more detail which I'm going to insist upon: you are to enroll in the same school as Jena."

Debbon held up his hand to keep Willian silent. "I want you to have a better idea of Jena's experience on Earth. The best way to do that is to go to the same school. If you will not agree to this condition, then I'll let Elder Wilken know you have changed your mind on going to Earth."

Willian valiantly held his tongue from saying what he really felt and answered, "I'll do as you ask. I see now you have put a lot of thought into my journey and have pointed out some things I never even considered. How do you propose I go about learning these things?"

"Rasa has agreed to be your mentor. She also has some ideas about where you might live once you are there. Once she feels you are ready, she will let Elder Wilken know. It would be in your best interest to befriend her as fast as possible. I know you two have not seen eye-to-eye on matters in the past, it's time you learned to be diplomatic and make amends."

Willian realized he would have no choice in the matter. Rasa was to be the gatekeeper for his journey. He would have to get along with her before he would be able to get to Jena. He could feel his anger rising and had to take a drink of water to cover his strong emotion before he ruined his chances of going at all. The idea came back to him that his journey would begin the next day and he forgot all about anything negative.

"Wouldn't it be better to go first thing in the morning, or even tonight? I'm assuming you don't want to let people know about this trip,"

Willian pointed out. He doubted he would sleep at all nor would he learn anything in school. It seemed pointless to him to wait.

"You're right on one account, we want to keep the true mission of this trip a secret. We will let people know you are apprenticing with Elder Wilken. Everything has already been arranged for tomorrow afternoon. Elder Wilken is busy until then. Remember, Willian, you will be a guest of his Residence so you will have to respect his time as well as Rasa's."

Properly chastised, Willian merely nodded and resumed eating his meal. Thoughts chased one another through his mind about what he would learn and whom he would meet. He was going on a great adventure.

CHAPTER 15

ebbon kissed Chelesa's cheek and said, "I guess I better go and take care of Willian."

Chelesa nodded her agreement even as she wished it were not necessary. She watched as Debbon's shadow moved through their darkened bedroom. The door opened, allowing light from the hallway to flood into their room and illuminate Debbon's silhouette.

They had all gone to bed as usual. Both Debbon and Chelesa knew their son would spend a considerable amount of time packing. After that, they imagined he would lie awake unable to sleep for the excitement of the next day. The night was half gone as Debbon opened his son's bedroom door.

He entered the room and stood looking down on the peaceful face of his willful child. With his breathing even and relaxed, he knew Willian slept. He agreed with his wife that what he would do next was necessary. If only they had spent more time curbing his bad behavior, then maybe it would not have come to this.

Debbon lightly placed his hand on his son's forehead and he closed his eyes in concentration. He promptly located Willian's life-line and followed it to the core of the decision-making part of his brain. He wove a delicate prohibition against using elemy in anger while he remained on Earth. The whole process only took a few seconds and he pulled his power away from his son. With tenderness, he brushed the loose strands of hair away from Willian's eyes and whispered, "I'm sorry."

He returned to his own bedroom and could see Chelesa sitting up against the headboard. He should have realized she would be just as tense about the task as he had been. It was terrible to place any injunction, let alone one on your own son. Chelesa had insisted it be done as a condition for allowing Willian to even go, and he had agreed to appease her. He wished there had been any other way, yet he knew his son's penchant for acting first and thinking much later.

"It's done," he whispered as he sat down in the bed and pulled the covers over his legs.

Chelesa reached over and touched his arm. "Thank you. I know that wasn't easy for you to do. I hope you understand why I insisted."

"I do. I'm just sad it had to come to it. We should at least try to get some sleep or tomorrow will be very miserable for both of us." He scooted down on the bed until his head rested on the pillow while he lay flat on his back. Sleep was the last thing on his mind and he stared at the ceiling while he felt his wife settle onto the bed. He doubted she would sleep much either.

⁓

WILLIAN WAS THRILLED to begin his journey to Earth, dampened only slightly by the idea of Elder Wilken's assignment. As much as he detested mediation duties, he desperately wanted to prove his worth to his father; the debacle with their Ascension Gate still rankled his pride.

He wished he could have left the night before and really did not see the use of making him go to school all morning. It seemed rather a waste of his time considering he paid scant attention to the day's lessons. His mind was already in Manzanit trying to figure out ways to expedite his obligation so he could go see Jena.

Checking his timepiece for at least the hundredth time, he rolled his eyes at the idea of sitting in class for another thirty minutes. His friends kept looking at him and wondering why he fidgeted so much. When class finally let out they surrounded him and asked, "What's going on with you?"

"My father is sending me on a special assignment in Manzanit.

Beyond that, I can't tell you anything about it!" He gathered his school supplies and put everything away carefully. Since he knew he would be gone for an undisclosed amount of time, he did not want to leave anything of value for the other boys to pilfer in his absence.

"When are you coming back?" one of the boys asked.

"I don't know."

"Come on, you have to have some idea," another boy chimed in with a wheedling tone.

"Seriously, I don't know. I might only be gone for a week or it could turn into several mesans. All I know is I have to get home right away. I promised my father I'd be ready to go as soon as school let out." He pushed his way through the growing crowd and grinned with self-importance that he could make such a grand exit.

Several of his closest friends kept pace with him and plagued him with questions he refused to answer by shaking his head. By the time he was almost home, only Nedan was still at his side. His house was close to Willian's own estate and he was almost at the turn off to go his own way.

Nedan grabbed his arm and forced him to stop when they got in front of his house. "Will you send me messages to let me know how you're doing? I promise I won't tell anybody anything you tell me. You know I can keep a secret."

"I know you can, Nedan. I'll try, okay?" Willian was almost desperate to get home, but he owed at least this much to his best friend.

"Thanks. Good luck, Willian." He clapped Willian on the shoulder, turned, and walked away toward his house.

Willian felt bad for his friend and wished he could have told him more. He did not want to jeopardize this trip by letting anyone know he was going to Earth. After his father had told him he was leaving, he started to get the feeling this might be some kind of test of his discretion. Nothing he said or did was going to keep him from seeing Jena.

When he finally reached his own home, he could tell there was a flurry of activity from the extra amount of noise coming from somewhere off the main entry. Rather than waste time investigating, he ran up the stairs and to his room to drop off his school gear. Normally he would have slung his school stuff across his floor and dealt with it later, he took extra time to put it neatly at his desk. Satisfied his mother would not find fault with the neatness of his room, he gathered his already packed travel bag and headed down the stairs to find his father.

All of the commotion off the hallway from moments before was silent. More curious than ever, Willian took the last step down and wandered into his father's office only to find it empty. He called out, "Dad?" Stepping away from the empty room, he crossed the hallway and knocked on his mother's office door.

"Come in," Chelesa called out.

Willian opened the door and found his mother alone in her office busily typing a message on her patil. He sat down in one of the plush chairs across the desk from her and waited in silence. After a couple of minutes, his mother finally finished her correspondence and turned to smile at him.

"It looks as though you are all ready to go," she said as she nodded her head toward the pack he had left by the door as he had entered the room.

"I am. I was looking for Dad so we could get going."

"Oh, I was just messaging him. An emergency has come up and he won't be able to come home." She already knew Debbon had not planned on going with their son and she was curious to see how he would react to the news.

"Does this mean my trip is going to be postponed?" Willian had a hard time keeping the disappointment from his tone.

"Not at all. He and I both agree you are quite old enough to take a telepod to Manzanit on your own. I've instructed the kitchen staff to put together a portable lunch so you can get on your way as soon as you're ready." She clasped her hands together to keep Willian from noticing how they shook with her anxiety of him leaving at all.

"Wow! Seriously? How awesome!" Willian had taken many short excursion in the home telepod, but nothing as major as a cross continent trip. He was thrilled with being entrusted to go alone on this trip. The more he thought about it, the more he convinced himself that this truly was a test of his maturity. "If you don't mind then, I'd like to get going right away."

"I don't mind, but would you like to study the coordinates of where you're heading first." Chelesa barely contained her smile at his sudden dismay at being caught unprepared. She pushed a couple pieces of paper across the surface of the desk.

Willian blushed furiously and tried to hide his confusion in an exaggerated study of the maps his mother had just given him. "Thank you, Mom."

"I'll give you some quiet time to go over those while I check with the staff on their preparations for your departure." She pushed herself up from her chair and walked around the desk. Unable to stop herself, she stepped next to her son and caressed his hair smooth before opening the office door and leaving the room.

Seconds after his mom left Willian softly cursed himself for his brash statement and whispered aloud, "I guess that's what I get for getting ahead of myself. How in Tuala am I supposed to prove to Mom and Dad that I'm growing up if I keep making such stupid mistakes?" Realizing this train of thought was not getting him any closer to being ready to leave he focused his attention on the coordinate maps of the Manzanit area.

Within a couple of minutes he was enthralled with the enormity of the task being set to him. Not only was Manzanit a complicated place to navigate, there were several areas where he could land which would be near the Residence. He knew it was good practice to have several alternates for landing should an emergency arise so he set about memorizing the four closest landing locations and their surrounding terrain.

Willian jumped with surprise when his mother touched his shoulder. He looked up at her with a startled expression and then smiled sheepishly. "I didn't hear you come in."

"I gathered as much. You were deep in concentration, which is good. Where have you decided to land?"

Willian pointed to his primary spot and looked up as he said, "I'd thought to touch down here." He moved his finger to another spot and said, "I've chosen these other spots as alternates. Have you been to Manzanit before?"

"I have. I like the choices you've made. Have you memorized the coordinates?"

"Yes."

"Good. Keep the paperwork with you and review it before you take off, okay?" She lifted the small basket of food and said, "Here's your lunch. I guess you're set to go then." She tried to keep her voice light-hearted so he would not be distracted by her worry for his safety.

"Would you mind if we ate together? I'm not sure how long I'll be gone and I'd like to visit with you before I go." He did not want to mention how nervous he suddenly felt. He mostly did not want to admit to himself that he was scared to go by himself.

Chelesa felt herself relax with relief to know she would have a little more time with her only child before he took this big step toward adulthood. She was certain he would be much-changed by this journey. Setting the basket down on the table, she pulled a chair up beside him and gestured for him to serve the meal.

It was a simple fare of shredded foxl sandwiches, mixed fruit, and his favorite dessert of sweetened, fried krumpli. Willian grinned at his mother over his sandwich at the kitchen staff's knowledge of his favorite meal. There was more than enough food for both of them to be full before they finished.

CHAPTER 16

Sofia had plenty of time to think – nothing but time actually. Her mother insisted she stay in bed even though she felt pretty good considering what could have happened. She felt incredibly lucky to have escaped nearly unscathed from such an ordeal.

She reclined on the couch and stared at the television without seeing. Over and over she replayed the accident in her mind. Each and every time she recalled distinctly feeling her bones breaking as the car impacted her body. She remembered, as she flew through the air, thinking how much it would damage her broken body when it hit the asphalt.

When the doctors looked at the various x-rays and told her nothing was broken, she had initially believed they had gotten the films mixed with someone else. She had asked to see them herself and clearly saw her name printed on the side in black and white. Something was not right with what she remembered and what the doctors were telling her.

The stitches in the back of her head were pulling the skin tight making her head throb. Sofia carefully reached over to the table to grab the water and bottle of pain pills the doctor had prescribed. The extension of her arm pulled the stitches on her side, reminding her of yet another injury.

She pulled up her shirt to look at the damage. A large blue and purple bruise had formed all around the stitched area. It looked spectacularly terrible. She touched it gently and winced at how tender the whole area remained. Hoping the medication would take the wicked edge pain off, she completed her aborted task of retrieving it from the table.

Sofia unscrewed the lid from the bottle and shook out one pill into her other hand. The night before she had taken two and they had completely knocked her out. She hoped just one would alleviate the pain and allow her to remain awake. She swallowed the pill with several gulps of water and set the glass back down on the table. The last thing she wanted was to spill the water all over herself and the couch if she were to fall asleep.

As she waited for the pain medication to take effect, she thought about how Juila and Jena had been so attentive to her while she had been lying on the ground. She had been immensely comforted by their presence. Then it dawned on her what had been bothering her; the girls had not spoken with her at all. They had remained silent, almost intent, and their eyes were closed. Sofia knew the girls were religious, yet it did not add up in her mind.

There had been the matter of her loss of consciousness. Maybe the girls had spoken while she had been knocked out. Somehow she did not think this was the case. Jon had said plenty in the time he had been by her side.

The idea of staying mostly immobile for the next several days did not excite her. She wished she could talk to the twins and ask them what their impression of the accident had been. It was strange that they had not come to her bedside in the hospital to check on her since she knew they had been in the waiting area. The next best thing was the knowledge of Jon calling her in a few more hours. She would ask him what he recalled of the twins' behavior while they had tended to her.

All of this thinking was not helping her headache and she closed her eyes to calm the throbbing. A nap was sounding better and better and it would help pass the time quicker. When she was better she would think about this whole bizarre matter in more detail. She was nothing if not tenacious when she wanted to get answers.

VINIA FRETTED over her last conversation with Amanda. She wished she could have said goodbye and verified Amanda would arrange a meeting with her lost children. As she rocked Danika and looked down on her sleeping face, she wondered what her three other children would look like.

It was almost impossible to imagine in less than one anon they had aged eight. To think of them at sixteen anons old almost brought her to tears. She thought back to the day she had sent them away. If she had known then what she knew now, would she have sent them anyway? Finally she came to the realization she had done what was best for them.

Amanda had confirmed her children were well-adjusted, happy, and kind. She assumed then that they had been raised by loving parents which was nothing more than she could have wished for her children. Also, it was a blessing to know Jon had received medical attention and no longer seemed frail and so close to death. His illnesses had been a constant worry and she feared each anon would be his last.

She rocked Danika gently and imagined what she would say to her other children when she finally got to see them again. Words would probably fail when her emotions would take over. She was certain she would spend many precious moments either crying, hugging them, or just merely staring at how much they surely had changed.

Vinia hoped her children remembered something of her from their past. She held onto the hope they would believe they had sent them away for their safety and not because she did not want them. Just thinking they may believe they had been unwanted caused her heart to skip a beat and made her breath catch. She wondered if they would want to come back home or if they would want to remain on Earth. There were so many unanswered questions and no way of knowing the answers until Amanda could talk to them and get back to her.

A noise from down the hall interrupted her musings. She settled Danika down on her blanket and went to investigate. Following the sound of voices led her to the kitchen where Barla and Corva were putting away the groceries. Just thinking about the marketplace made her shudder at the idea of leaving the house again. With Petre once again looking for her she felt trapped and afraid and she hated him even more for it.

"Do you need any help putting stuff away?" Vinia asked.

"No, dear. We're almost done anyway," Barla replied with a smile.

Vinia sat down at the island stool and experienced a disorienting sense of déjà vu. Her life had come full-circle. She was once again using Barla's home as a safe haven from Petre and now Elder Vargen. Danika slept in the same bedroom her other three kids had used when she had lived here so many anons before. Her fears of uncertainty of the future were once again overwhelming.

She was angry with herself for getting in the same situation all over again. Surely she should have learned how to take care of herself during it all. Once she reunited with her children again, she was going to do something about finding her own way in the world.

Vinia watched Corva as she finished putting away the groceries. She realized Corva, at fourteen, was only two anons younger than her own children were now. Corva was so confident in herself and in her abilities because Barla and Ahn had adopted her and given her a second chance at a family. Would her children even need her anymore? They were almost grown up and on the verge of starting their own lives.

"Have you heard from Amanda?" Vinia asked once Barla was done.

"No, not yet. She said it would be at least a couple of days before she would even be able to talk to the kids. I know you're anxious, but I think you're borrowing trouble where there is none."

"I've never been good with waiting. I hope you're right."

"I know I am. Now, what would you like for dinner tonight?" Barla firmly believed food was a curative for every ailment, including worry. She enjoyed preparing meals even more since she had received her own birth crystal which allowed her to use elemy to create the dishes. No longer did she have the laborious task of prepping and cleaning up for their meals.

～

RICCAN WANTED to believe Ela Nena's deplorable behavior would have blown over given enough time. He never realized she would be biding her time to make another strike against him. When he received the call to go up to her office, he honestly believed it would be for her to apologize to him.

"Hi, Ela Nena. I got the message that you wanted to see me. What can I do for you?" Riccan stood in the doorway, not wanting to assume she would have him sit down and talk.

"Riccan, come in and sit down. Shut the door behind you." She did not bother to look at him as she typed away on her patil.

Crossing the room, Riccan sat down across from Ela Nena and let his gaze wander around the office as he waited. He noted the shelves of excellence awards she had received in the past and hoped she would recall how she had earned them. Several minutes went by and Riccan began to wonder if he should come back another time when it was more convenient. He was about to make the suggestion when Ela Nena suddenly turned to him.

She laced her fingers together and let her index fingers point toward him as she composed her thoughts. "Are you happy here, Riccan?"

Caught off guard, Riccan stuttered before answering, "Yes. You know I love it here."

"I've been informed you were gone most of yesterday. If you love your job so much, what makes you think it's okay to not be here when the rest of your team is hard at work?"

"I'm sorry you think about it that way, Ela Nena. I was under the impression that as a part of the management team I was not obligated to maintain an eight to five schedule. There have been plenty of times where I've stayed quite late and very few times where I've taken time off. My team always knows how to get in touch with me if they need me. What is this really all about?" Riccan could hardly believe he was even having this conversation. He could recall numerous occasions where Ela Nena had gone missing and nobody knew how to reach her, including her own husband.

"I have been very tolerant of your lax behavior for many mesans now. Do not mistake my generosity for weakness, Riccan. During business hours, you will be on site. At your level in this company, it's hard to believe I would even have to tell you this. If you feel unable to comply with this part of your job then I expect you would be happier with another company. Unless you have anything further to say, that is all. Please close the door on your way out." She returned her attention to the patil and pulled the keyboard closer to her and resumed typing.

Riccan stared at her for several moments before her words sank in completely. More than anything, he wanted to tell her exactly what he thought of her in that moment. Instead, he simply nodded, stood up, and walked out the door. Even though he wanted to slam the door behind him in his growing rage, he calmly closed the door and continued through the executive staff's office until he reached the stairs. He used the physical exertion of taking the steps two at a time down from the thirteenth floor to the second floor.

Once he reached his office, he closed the door and put his face in his hands in frustration. He had no idea where Ela Nena got off talking to him in such a manner. He had given his life to this job and he was great at building his team. Together they were more productive than any other department and yet none of that seemed to matter to Ela Nena. He wished he knew who had complained to Ela Nena if only to ask them not to in the future.

That woman had the audacity to tell him she had been tolerant of his *behavior*? What in Tuala was she talking about? He had been using his earned vacation time for his time off. He tried to think of any other time where he had been away or off on his own errands where she could even call him out on it. Nothing! He had done nothing wrong! As far as he was concerned, Ela Nena had overstepped her authority with him once again.

Maybe he should seriously consider quitting. He had no real reason for keeping this job except for his joy of flying and desire to create telepods. Technically he was on retirement until his father decided to step down and he took over as Elder of the Pantano District. Besides, his wife would appreciate him being home and available to help in the search for the remaining samaras. Just as he had made his decision to quit, a knock sounded on the office door.

"Come in."

Gilora poked her head around the door and said in an excited voice, "There's been a catastrophic failure in the latest test model. Do you have time to check it out?"

His mind immediately went into overdrive trying to evaluate what could have gone wrong. In that moment, he realized he could not simply leave the company. There was too much at stake with the projects currently in progress for him to abandon them now. He would have to tolerate Ela Nena so he could pursue his passion. As he walked out of his office with Gilora he decided to avoid Ela Nena as much as possible and play it day-by-day.

CHAPTER 17

It was late before Amanda heard Riccan come home. She wondered what could have kept him away so long and went to investigate. Amanda was shocked to see how worn and tired he appeared. Something bad must have happened at work and she hoped he would confide in her.

She smiled, rushed toward him, and threw her arms around his waist. "Hi baby, I really missed you today!" She kissed him on the cheek and hoped it would help lighten his mood.

"Sorry to be so late without letting you know. We had one of our experimental crafts fail and we were scrambling to find the source. The deadline is looming and we were already behind in the timeline. I should have sent you a message. I'm sorry." He returned her hug with his own and once again thanked Jehoban for bringing her into his life. The amount of peace and serenity he felt when they were together was almost overwhelming. His problems at work seemed to melt away when she was in his arms.

"Did you get it figured out?" Amanda pulled back from him and looked him in the eyes.

"Yeah, it was a faulty bracket on the crystal drive. We had checked over every other possibility before someone picked up the piece and looked at it closely. It had hairline fractures all over it. When we looked at the rest of the bracket shipment we had received from Beewa, they were faulty as well. You can rest assured Kenen will be hearing from me tomorrow. That type of shoddy craftsmanship can kill people and it's completely unacceptable. Kenen should know better than to foist such crap off on me."

"I'm sorry, honey. Have you eaten yet?" She knew he was always grumpier when he was hungry, they joked about it being called 'hangry'.

"No, I haven't had time for anything except to come home to you. I'll get something in a few minutes." He moved them through the kitchen and into the living room.

"I'd like to practice my creating skills. What would you like to eat?"

Riccan raised his eyebrows at her proclamation. She seldom used her skills even though she were capable. It pleased him she was willing to try and he smiled to encourage her as he considered what he wanted her to make. "I'd like a foxl steak with cream sauce. What do you think?"

"No problem," she replied with more confidence than she felt. The steak would be easy, but the sauce could be problematic. She knew he liked it spiced in a specific way and she hoped she could remember the proper ingredients. "Why don't you go up and get changed or take a shower. When you come back down, I'll have your dinner ready. Do you want any sides to go with that steak?"

"How about a baked krumpli with butter and sour cream?"

"I think you picked something simple because you're afraid I won't be able to get it right," she teased.

He smiled as he turned to go upstairs.

Amanda realized he had not refuted her statement and scoffed at his retreating form. She returned to the kitchen and sat at the island stool to help her concentration. More than anything she wanted to get this right for him, if only to prove to him she could get it right. She closed her eyes and began visualizing in her mind the pathway for creating food.

Wishing the girls were home to help her, she wondered when they would get home. Would it be too much to ask for them to arrive before Riccan got out of the shower? The chances were not good considering they were over at Behn and Valentina's house studying. She considered calling over to their house to ask the question, but she realized it could be construed as cheating if Riccan were to find out. Then he would not let her live it down, so she gave up on that line of thinking.

Almost as if her thoughts had created her children, the front door opened and the girls walked in with their study partners. Her concentration was broken and she was curious to find out why they had all come over instead of staying at the Wilson house.

"What's going on?" Amanda asked as she walked into the living room.

"We thought we'd continue their crystal lessons here since we're done with our school work. It's easier here since we don't have to worry about anyone walking in on us," Juila stated matter-of-factly.

"Is Dad home yet?" Jena asked.

"Yeah, he's taking a shower while I create a meal for him."

Jena looked at the empty kitchen and realized her mother had said creating and not cooking and raised her eyebrows in approval. "Do you need any help?"

"I wish I could take you up on your offer, but I told your father I'd do it. I have to prove it now. Do you recall the special seasoning he likes in his gravy?"

"Won't that still be cheating if I tell you?"

"No. I still have to create it, after all." Amanda crossed her arms and tried to look stern.

Jena laughed.

Juila called out from the living room couch, "It's a dash of cinnamon, Mom. Jena, let's get started."

"Thanks, Juila," Amanda called back and smiled at Jena smugly.

"Yeah, thanks, Juila," Jena said sarcastically as she turned around and walked back to the living room.

Amanda resumed her seat at the kitchen island and re-visualized the entire recipe, including the cinnamon. Satisfied she would get it right, she turned in the chair and watched the kids practice their own skills. She was amazed at how speedily Behn and Valentina had picked up the crystal lessons.

Remembering her promise to talk to the kids about their mother, she hopped off of the stool and wandered over in their direction. She could still hear the shower running upstairs so she knew she would have a few minutes more before Riccan would be ready to eat. She did not want the kids to feel pressured to make a quick decision so now might be the best time.

She sat down on the edge of the chair across from all of the kids and cleared her throat. Once everyone was looking at her she asked, "Did you mention once that you thought I looked like your mother?"

Valentina frowned slightly and playfully hit her brother on the shoulder. "So much for being subtle, Behn. I knew she'd heard your comment."

"I couldn't help it, she caught me off guard when we saw her the first time. You have to agree she does look like Mom."

Valentina turned her head away from Behn and nodded back at Amanda as she replied, "You do look an awful lot like we remember her looking. I don't know how to explain it, especially since she lives on a different world."

"What is her name?"

"Vinia," Behn piped in. He wondered why Mrs. Stel was suddenly interested in their mother. "Why do you ask?"

Amanda nodded as she confirmed the last piece of information she needed to be certain these were her kids. "I think I found your mom in Tuala. There's a slight problem, though."

"What? Really? What problem could there be?" Behn asked as he leaned forward anxiously. Even as he asked the last question, he wondered if their mother did not want to see them or maybe she had died. He almost did not want to hear the answer. He looked over to Valentina to see how she was reacting to Mrs. Stel's statement.

Valentina's eyes were fixed on Mrs. Stel's face. She barely breathed as she waited for her to answer her brother's questions.

Amanda was not entirely sure how to tell them the news she had to share. "I spoke with a woman named Vinia who told me how she sent her three children to Earth to keep them safe. She said the two boys and one girl were almost eight and their names matched your own."

"So what's the problem?" Valentina questioned with a confused expression.

"The problem is that she said it happened just over one year ago. Her children would be nine years old now."

Valentina looked crestfallen. This could not be their mother after all. Her shoulders sagged and she leaned back against the couch and hugged herself. "So she's not our mom after all."

"On the contrary, I believe she is your mother." Amanda tried to put extra reassurance in her voice.

"But how? We've been here for eight years," Behn reasoned.

Amanda took another breath to organize her answer. "You said your mom had held one of the crystal skulls on your walk through the woods. It stands to reason that she was unable to control the shift across the veil when she sent you to Earth. Because she didn't know any different and because she was using an unsanctioned gate, she had no idea she would be sending you back in time as well as across the veil.

"From what she shared with me, she had no idea you were even on Earth. Once the three of you disappeared, she was unable to..." Amanda realized she almost shared the secret of the pendants and had to hurriedly say something else. "She had no idea where you went or how to get you back."

"Get us back? She wants us back now?" Valentina stood up angrily. "What, did she suddenly realize we were important now that we're almost grown up?"

"It's not like that, Valentina. Your mother sent you away to keep you safe. She never expected you to stay gone and, remember, it's only been a year for her. She was shocked to find out so much time had passed for you."

"You told her about us?" Valentina accused with narrowed eyes.

"Calm down, Val. Let Mrs. Stel tell us what happened," Behn spoke quietly as he reached up to touch his sister's arm gently.

"I wouldn't have mentioned the three of you except you had expressed an interest in finding her one day," Amanda spoke guiltily. She was beginning to regret even bringing the subject at all.

"It's true," Behn spoke to Amanda but kept his face turned to his sister, "we do want to find our mom. Do you think we could meet her?"

"Behn! Are you serious? She abandoned us when she sent us away to another world! Now you suddenly have a burning desire to meet her?"

"She didn't abandon us, she was trying to save us! Besides, Mrs. Stel said it's only been a year for her and she had no way of knowing where we'd been sent."

"I don't want any part of this. I think it's time we went home, Behn." Valentina stood up and refused to look at anyone in the room as she marched into the foyer and out the front door.

"I'm sorry, Mrs. Stel. She doesn't mean what she just said. When she cools down and thinks it over, she'll change her mind. Please don't tell this Vinia of yours anything yet."

"No. I won't. I told her I'd talk it over with you before any meeting would be arranged. She knows you've had a happy life with your family and she doesn't want to interfere in your lives. She loves you and misses you, please know that much."

"Thanks, Mrs. Stel." He stood up and turned to Juila and said, "I'll see you at school tomorrow." He began to leave when Juila spoke.

"Can you call me tonight and let me know what Jon found out about Sofia? He was still talking on the phone with her when we left your house."

"Sure. I gotta go." He rushed to catch up with his sister before she could get any angrier. He knew her temper and the sooner he could calm her down, the better his position would be in getting her to agree to meet this woman. Besides, if she were not their mother then they would have lost nothing.

Amanda looked over at her daughters and said in a rueful tone, "That went great, huh?"

"It'll be fine, Mom. I read Valentina's mind and she was just scared." Seeing her mother about to take her to task for invading the girl's privacy Juila rapidly added, "I think Dad's going to be ready for dinner in a minute."

"We're going to talk about this again, Juila," Amanda warned even as she realized the shower could no longer be heard. She walked into the kitchen and held onto the countertop to focus her thoughts of controlling the elemy to create the requested dinner. To her satisfaction, a plate of exactly what she had wanted appeared on the counter in front of her.

"Very nicely done, Amanda," Riccan said with pride.

Amanda jumped in surprise. She had not heard him come down the stairs; however, she was pleased to know he had seen her achieve what she had desired. She smiled at him smugly and said, "Bon appétit!"

CHAPTER 18

Willian sat strapped to the pilot's seat in the telepod and realized he was scared to take the next step. Sure, he had practiced flying on short trips to visit friends. He had always felt so important when anyone saw him arrive at his destination. Today was different. He was flying to an unfamiliar location on a different continent. Not only that, he was going to be a guest of an Elder he barely knew for an undisclosed amount of time.

One thing for which he was thankful was that his mother had been called away on an errand, preventing her from witnessing his disgraceful display of weakness. He had studied the maps and he had the coordinates memorized. He even had the packet of papers splayed out on his lap just in case he needed to refresh his memory. He had no idea why he was getting himself so worked up over such a simple task.

With a disgusted sigh, Willian activated the telepod and began the well-known start-up procedures. He carefully checked all of the lights to verify they were all green indicating the aircraft was working properly and safe to fly. Wishing his father had purchased the latest technology which practically rendered the pilot unnecessary, Willian grabbed the manual navigation control, concentrated single-mindedly on the desired coordinates, and hit the activation button with his thumb.

Everything went black around him as he kept the coordinates in his mind. Several seconds passed and he felt his heartrate increase. This point in air travel was where most pilot's made their fatal error so he renewed the destination entry points in his mind. With a gasp of relief the light shone in the window with a remarkable suddenness.

He had to pay close attention now to the manual controls in order to land the craft in a vacant space. Where he was used to empty fields in which to land, he now had to worry about finding a location large enough to accommodate his telepod. Never in his wildest thoughts had he imagined this location would be so crowded. If this were any indication for coming events, maybe he was smart to be nervous.

Finally, he found an open area near the edge of the field where he could set down his telepod and follow the landing procedures. Once the telepod was landed, Willian took several deep breaths after unfastening his seatbelt. He remained in his seat until his heartrate returned to a normal pace.

On his way out of the telepod, Willian picked up his travel bag from the back seat. He walked down the ramp and onto the spongy grass. He turned around to palm the door closed and noticed just how closely the crafts were situated.

Once the door was fully sealed shut, he began weaving his way around the other telepods on his way to the entry he had noted when he was still hovering. The distance was deceptive from the air and, more than once, he began to think he had picked the wrong direction. Just when he was doubting himself the most, he would catch a glimpse of either the Residence on the hill beyond or of the entrance gate itself.

Knowing he was expected did little to alleviate the butterflies in his stomach. He was unsure if he were to walk to the Residence itself or if someone were going to be waiting for him. Just as he reached the entrance gate, he saw Rasa leaning against the low fence. She turned her head and saw him moving toward her, she smiled and raised her hand in a small wave. Grateful to see a familiar face, he forgot all of his previous ill feelings toward her and greeted her in turn.

"How was your flight? Did you have a good time finding a landing spot?" Rasa said as she matched her pace with his and began leading the way to the Residence.

"My flight was wonderfully uneventful. Is it always this busy here?" He could not keep his tone of dismay from his voice.

Rasa chuckled and nodded. "Always. Let's hurry so we can the transport before someone else takes it."

Willian was relieved to hear they had transportation as he could see now just how far away the Residence still stood. Before seeing the building itself, he had believed all District Residences had been relatively small like his father's. This trip might prove to be quite the education for him. He could almost be grateful for Jena's unscheduled trip which provided him with this opportunity.

As they sat in the small transport, Willian asked, "My father had said you'd be instructing me while I'm here. What he didn't mention was why you are here. Are you tired of Acaim?" He smiled at his little joke.

Rasa cocked her head to the side and wondered if he could really be oblivious to her new position. Suddenly she realized an important detail, her new position was not being announced as it would be had she been a man. Sure, the people of Manzanit knew what had happened, but the world at large had no idea. She replied simply, "I have been made Elder Wilken's successor."

Willian looked at her for several seconds before he suddenly laughed. "That's a good one, Rasa. Why are you really here?"

Rasa frowned at his easy dismissal and restated more firmly, "Like I said, I was just voted in as Elder Wilken's successor. If you don't believe me, then I suggest you ask Elder Wilken yourself."

"Rasa, women don't become Elders. It just isn't done. There's no way the Elders would have agreed to what you're suggesting. If you don't want to tell my why you're here, that's fine, but you'll get into big trouble if people hear you speaking so brashly." Willian shook his head pityingly and then turned to look out the window to see the buildings, people, and markets they passed along the way.

Feeling her skin turn hot, she knew her face had turned red with anger. She should have expected nothing less from Willian as he had always been quite chauvinistic, it was the reason they had often disagreed. His treatment of Jena had always bothered her and she had often taken him to task for how he talked down to her.

Willian would learn soon enough about speaking out of turn. She felt a small amount of smugness thinking about Willian telling Elder Wilken what Rasa had said in hopes of getting her in trouble. The joke would be on him when he was finally set straight. She was now his equal in every way and he was going to have to get used to it. His dismay would be the first of many, she now realized which sobered her at once.

She decided to change the subject and asked, "What else did your father tell you about your stay here?"

Without turning his head away from the window he answered, "Only that I was to help Elder Wilken with mediation duties. Something you would probably know about, or handle yourself, if you really were his successor."

Rasa sighed with disgust and gave up on trying to be nice to him. He would find out soon enough. She decided right then that Willian would have a lot more work to do before she would give her permission for him to go to Earth.

They passed through the entry of the Residence. The light inside the transport went dim as they traveled through the long, low tunnel. Bright light returned as they entered the huge courtyard and Willian got his first view of the public side of the building.

Willian was reticent to even step out of the transport since the massive building loomed over him. He had never realized what a small town he had come from until he faced the crowded city of Manzanit. He opened the door, expecting as much noise as there had been near the landing field, and was relieved at the relative quiet. At least he could be comforted by the serenity of the place, if not the size.

Willian had to hurry to catch up with Rasa since she had already gotten out of the transport and was heading toward the side entrance of the Residence. With bag in hand, he rushed over to match his pace with hers. He was about to ask her a question until he looked at the closed expression on her face and thought better of it. They entered the building in stony silence.

Rasa led him through a maze of doorways and corridors until he was certain they must have purposely gone in circles. He would not put it past her to try to confuse him on his first day. She opened a door and said, "This will be your room while you are staying here. Go ahead and leave your bag here. We need to get downstairs because Elder Wilken is waiting to meet you before going to his next meeting."

Without much time to investigate, Willian glanced around the lavish furnishings in the room. He placed his bag in a chair between the window and the chifforobe. When he got back later, he would unpack and explore further. The butterflies in his stomach fluttered anew as he thought about meeting Elder Wilken. It was so important to make a good impression since this man was going to be responsible for getting him to Earth.

"I'm ready," he said as he met Rasa back at the doorway.

"Good. Keep track of the directions since you'll need to know your way around." Rasa set a brisk pace down several flights of stairs and through a large reception room. She turned left down another wide hallway before stopping at a double set of doors on the left. She opened the right leaf and gestured for him to precede her into the room.

Willian pulled his shoulder back and walked confidently ahead into a cozy, well-lit room. There were stained glass windows high up on the walls allowing the light to filter down. There were four oversized chairs and one plush couch covered in tanned foxl hide which was where an old man had stretched himself out with a blanket covering his legs.

"It's a pleasure to meet you, Elder Wilken," Willian said as he stopped near the couch and executed a small bow of respect.

"Ah, Willian, I'm pleased to see you have arrived. Your timing is perfect as I've just finished my nap." He slowly sat up and gestured for both Willian and Rasa to seat themselves in the chairs across from him.

Rasa hesitated by the door and cleared her throat before saying, "If you don't mind, I've another matter to tend to while you and Willian get acquainted. I can be back in about ten minutes."

"Thank you, Rasa that will be just fine." He smiled fondly at her and waited for the door to shut before he turned his attention back to the young man.

"Elder, I feel I must share something rather important which will probably anger you about Rasa. I don't think you should put too much trust in her after the things I heard her say."

Wilken believed he knew what he would hear, but simply nodded permission for him to continue. "Go on, tell me why I should distrust Rasa."

"Well, sir, I don't want to upset you, but she is going around saying she's your successor. It's ridiculous and heretical, I know, but there it is." He looked down at his hands as he waited for a response. Several long seconds went by and still the silence continued. He looked up to see what might be happening.

"What would you propose be done about such heresy?"

"Well, keeping her here as a guest reflects badly upon you. If I were you, I'd send her away and probably shorten her name." The last idea pleased him greatly and he nodded his head in emphasis of his conviction.

"You do realize shortening a person's name is only for the most serious offense. We do not issue such an edict lightly." Wilken wanted to press the matter a little further to see what else Willian had in his mind before he set him straight.

"I've often had problems with Rasa behaving above her station because she was one of Jehoban's students. Lying is one of the worst things a person can do, especially because she has studied with Jehoban. She's gone too far this time and it cannot be overlooked."

Wilken gave the young man a long stare before he made his reply. "I had considered having you tell Rasa what a proper punishment should be for such a grievous lie, but that would put you at a disadvantage in the future."

Willian cocked his head in confusion at the Elder's statement and wondered what he could be getting at.

"I know you're young and you still have many anons before you will be installed as an Elder. However, you always need to be cognizant of the fact you were born into a position where you will affect people's lives, whether for good or ill. You must always remember to hear both sides of a situation before you come to any conclusion or you could be hurting people unnecessarily.

"I've agreed to have you mediate for my youth population. I had planned for Rasa to sit in with you during those sessions for consultation and evaluation of your decisions. If I were to send her away, where would that put me? I don't have time to handle the glut of mediation currently flooding my office."

"I see. I didn't know it was like that for you. I assumed you had a large staff."

"I do have a large staff; however, they are all quite busy as well. Manzanit is a very populace district. There is one other aspect you should have asked."

"What was it?"

"Instead of assuming Rasa were lying, you should have asked me if it were true."

"Of course it wasn't true! Women do not become Elders! Everyone knows that. Why would I waste my time asking you when it was obviously a lie?" Willian could not even imagine lending credence to such an absurd story.

"Consider this your first lesson. Had you asked me about Rasa I would have told you she spoke the truth. She has been confirmed as my successor just a few days ago. I called a convocation to which your father presided over. I'm surprised he didn't share with you the reason for the meeting."

"He did say it was to confirm your successor, he just didn't happen to mention anything about it being Rasa." Willian had a sick feeling in his stomach and his anger toward his father rose to a new level for allowing him to make such a horrid first impression on Elder Wilken.

"I can see you are angry, Willian. Please learn to channel such anger to bring you higher in your understanding of people and situations. It is okay to be wrong, but in your position it is not okay to stay wrong when you find out differently."

Willian tried unsuccessfully to stifle his anger and finally burst out, "It's just not done! How could you have put her forward as your successor?"

"Again, you are making an assumption. I did not put her forward as my candidate."

"I don't understand. You just said she was! You're not making any sense."

"Remember to ask questions before you decide your own truth. With that in mind, what would you ask me?"

After taking several deep breaths, Willian tried to do as Elder Wilken asked. He reviewed everything he had been told and tried to ignore what he personally thought about the matter. Finally he had a moment of clarity and asked, "How did Rasa come to be your successor?"

"Very well done, Willian! If you can keep this mindset when you are hearing people's cases, then I believe you will do quite well. To answer your question, Jehoban sent her to be my successor. I had appealed to Him a while back on my dilemma and He told me He would make the situation right."

Willian could hardly wrap his mind around what Elder Wilken was telling him. First he had insulted his host and now he was being told he had questioned Jehoban's decision. Could this day get any more humiliating?

"Cheer up, son, we all make mistakes when we're young. Let yourself change with the changing times. It's your job to learn and question everything. The challenge is to keep yourself from speaking what you're thinking until you know all the facts. Will you agree to try?"

"Yes, Elder Wilken, I will do my best. You are very wise to share your insights with me. I will not let you down." Willian was relieved to hear he was not in trouble for his suggestions regarding Rasa's punishment. He would certainly think twice before opening his mouth around Elder Wilken.

"I believe I hear Rasa out in the hallway. Think about what you might have said to Rasa earlier. Is there anything you need to set right? Let's agree to keep this conversation to ourselves, shall we?" Wilken said with a wink at Willian just as the door opened.

"Thank you," Willian replied hurriedly before Rasa had even made it into the room. He stared at her with a new appreciation for her position. He still did not particularly like her, but she was pretty brave to stand in a man's traditional position.

"The people for your next meeting have arrived. I had them go to the palm room to wait for you," Rasa announced.

"Perfect! Thank you, my dear. Please give Willian a tour of the Residence and grounds so he won't get lost." He rose from the couch as though he were half his age and patted Rasa's arm as he walked past her. He slowed his step to see if Willian would apologize. His delay paid off.

"Rasa, I'm sorry for our conversation in the transport. I should have realized you would not lie about being Elder Wilken's successor. Maybe sometime you can tell me how it came about. I'm sure it's quite a story."

Rasa had planned on making Willian's life hard while he stayed here, but then she realized if he could be gracious enough to admit fault, then she could forgive him. After all he was still very young and her situation was very novel. "Maybe someday I will. Right now, we need to get on with your tour."

CHAPTER 19

"Ah, Lillia, come and sit with me, dear," Lucinden said as he gestured for her to sit on his lap up on the dais.

She complied with his wish, all the while wanting to remain standing. She had found a long time ago it was better to go along with whatever he had in mind since it usually went better for her.

"It appears there is some type of power shift occurring throughout the world. You know I don't like mysteries, Lillia."

"What do you believe it to be?" she asked innocently.

"I have an idea, but I would like confirmation before I speak my thoughts. I'd like you to pay a visit to your friend on Earth and see what she can tell you about it." He pulled strands of her fine, brown hair in front of her shoulder and then twirled it around his index finger. After giving it a playful tug, he brought her lips to his own and kissed her until she was breathless. He would never tire of her beauty, nor would he have to know loneliness with her around.

It angered him that he was being forced to send her on this errand, yet she was the only logical choice. He would never trust any of his servants to this sensitive assignment. Lillia, alone, he could trust implicitly.

When she pulled back to catch her breath she asked, "When would you like me to go?"

Lucinden sighed deeply before answering. "Today, as soon as you can get ready. I must know what is going on in order to take steps of my own. Something is changing."

Lillia stood up and squealed in surprise as Lucinden slapped her rear. She promptly scooted off the dais and out of reach before resuming her stately pace across the reception room. She had noted Lucinden had been spending more of his time alone in the vast space.

There was no denying the room was situated on a low-level vortex of ley lines. Lucinden had no idea the real power came from her own possession which she had kept secret from him for the past millennium. One day she would free herself from his clutches and she would take the source of power with her. These trips always gave her a sense of long-anticipated freedom even though she knew she would come back.

She entered her room and pulled out her travel bag. Not knowing how long she would be gone, she packed several outfits which would go unre-marked on Earth. The clothing style was slightly different and the fabric was generally made of cotton rather than foxl fiber. She changed her outfit for one which would be acceptable in both location in anticipation of meeting with Elder Vargen's people.

Most people were unaware of the Elder's frequent forays into Earth. Generally it was frowned upon for the Elders to make any contact with Earth. Their jobs dictated they protect the Ascension Gates from improper use and to keep people from Earth from accidentally coming to Tuala.

Of course, this did not necessarily mean the Elders would not send people from Tuala to Earth. Elder Vargen did such a thing on a regular basis. His fascination with technology drove him to break many rules. He also kept the myths about people from Earth vivid in his district. The more the Tualans feared the *old souls*, the easier it was for him to receive those people who were found to be from Earth.

Nobody questioned what became of the people who were given into his care. They probably assumed he sent them back to Earth, Lillia, of course, knew differently. She knew he kept them prisoner, addicted to resh, and forced to work in his factory. The fact that she knew his secret kept him in line and allowed her access to his Gate.

Lillia could feel the power coming from the secret compartment in the wall behind her. She dared not look at it even in the privacy of her own room. She hated leaving it untended, but the risk of it ending up in Lucinden's hands should she remove it, scared her even more. One day, the time would be right and she could remove it from hiding and put an end to this deadly game.

She slung the full travel bag over her shoulder and strode out of her room. She would need to take a transport before she could begin her journey to Earth. She could have translated herself directly into Elder Vargen's Residence, but she seldom liked to display her power. Also, she did not want Lucinden to have any reason to investigate the power spike coming from her room.

Once outside the oppressive walls of Lucinden's compound, she felt lighter already. She flagged down a transport and told him her destination. As they moved through the crowded streets, Lillia pondered Lucinden's cryptic remark about thinking he knew what was happening. He had seemed ill at ease which was very unlike his normally confident demeanor.

The transport began to slow down as they neared her stop. She dug ten shills out of her bag and handed them to the driver. Just as she closed the door an idea struck her: the time for the samaras might be on hand. She walked slowly as she recalled so long ago the promise she had been given. Never had she spoken what she knew, but she felt with all her heart it would come true. Maybe she would soon be free.

The guard stopped her at the edge of the compound. "State your name and business," he said in a bored tone.

"Wibawa and I'm here to see Elder Vargen."

"Sign here while I check with the Elder." He pushed a log book to the edge of the table and turned to his patil.

Lillia signed the book sloppily and waited with a bored expression for the attendant to get back to her. She turned her head away and tapped her foot impatiently. Since she had the idea of the prophecy coming to pass, she was itching to be on her way. She had several things to check out while on Earth and the time could not come fast enough.

"You're cleared to go," the guard called out to her without looking away from his patil.

Lillia hurried as fast as she could without drawing unwanted attention. She knew the way to where she needed to go. She only hoped with the use of the name she had given, Elder Vargen would have taken the hint to meet her at the Ascension Gate.

As it turned out, she met the Elder in the hallway leading to the Gate. "Greetings, Lillia. Do you have any special instructions today?"

"If you mean the timing, then no, I don't require any shifts in time. I just need a straight passage to Roswell." Lillia spoke in a clipped tone since the Elder was forever trying to wheedle extra information from her.

Without taking the hint, Vargen continued, "When should I expect your return?"

"I will inform you when I need assistance." Lillia lengthened her stride since they were very near the Gate and she was not in the mood for twenty questions.

Vargen stopped at the control desk to monitor the elemy being transmitted around the gate. Once he confirmed everything was stable he asked, "Are you ready?"

"Yes!"

He pressed the button to send her on her way.

Lillia never got used to the experience of feeling as though she were in two places at once while also feeling nowhere at all. She closed her eyes and counted the seconds off. Just as she reached her destination, she opened her eyes and remained still to take stock of her body. As soon as she confirmed all was well, she stepped up out of the depression in the dirt.

After checking her surroundings, she ducked behind a rock formation and dug another outfit out of her bag. She rushed to change clothes and shoes, stuffing her original items back into her bag. There could potentially be a long walk ahead of her, and she did not have any time to waste.

When she got down to the main trail, she dug to the bottom of her bag and wrapped her fingers around a cell phone. She opened it and hit speed dial number one. Just as she was about to put it to her ear she noticed the battery was almost run out, this would have to be a quick conversation and she hoped the call would be picked up.

"Hello?" a woman's voice answered.

"Shemalla, this is Lillia. Can you pick me up? My phone is just about dead." Lillia waited for an answer which never came. She pulled the phone in front of her and saw the screen had gone blank. With a growl of disgust, and hoping Shemalla had heard her request, she slapped the phone closed and pushed it into her bag.

Lillia kept walking down the slope to get to the paved road. The cliffs behind her provided a small amount of shelter to protect her from the cold breeze in the already freezing temperatures of the New Mexican desert. If Shemalla were not on the way to get her, she had a very rough day ahead of her. The cave containing the portal was several miles away from the town of Roswell.

She knew the drive only took about fifteen to twenty minutes, but the walk would be grueling. From her vantage point she could see for miles around and the main road was a small ribbon of blurry haze as the weak sun glinted off of the pavement. Lillia wished she had thought to bring a jacket or even gloves.

With a shrug of resignation, Lillia stepped cautiously down the loose, gravelly pathway. She kept her eyes trained to the ground to look out for rattlesnakes, scorpions, or any other dangerous animals. They were unlikely to be out since the weather was so cold, yet she looked anyway. Once again she was thankful Tuala's only dangerous creature was the beetlesnatch which was predictable as well as regional.

Lillia could feel the warmth of the sun touch the back of her head as she stepped out of the shadow of the cliffs. Each subsequent step allowed more of her body to be exposed to the soothing rays of sun until her whole body was covered. She could feel cold starting to seep up her feet from the cold ground and her face felt chilled from the constant wind.

The cold soon sapped her energy until she was reduced to concentrating only on placing one foot in front of the other. Once again she wished she would have opted to translate herself directly to Shemalla's house. It would have been so easy when she had still been in the cave surrounded by the vortex of elemy. It also would have drawn unnecessary attention to herself and possibly to Shemalla, she chided herself silently.

Her thoughts were interrupted with the sound of a horn honking. She looked up from the road at her feet to see Shemalla's car pulled over no more than thirty feet away from her. Lillia breathed a sigh of relief at her seeming salvation and forced herself to walk faster, if only to get out of the cold wind and into the heated car.

"Shemalla, you have no idea how happy I am to see you!" she gushed as she sat down blissfully inside the car and redirected the vent in the dash to blow hot air across her face. She rubbed her hands together briskly in front of the vent attempting to restore feeling to her numb fingers.

"I was worried when the call ended so abruptly. I got here as fast as I could." She checked both lanes of traffic before she pulled onto the road and executed a U-turn to head back to Roswell. "So what brings you to Earth?"

"Lucinden sent me to find out what's going on with certain power shifts he's become aware of. Do you still have the thing I gave you long time ago?"

Shemalla instantly glanced over at Lillia with widened eyes as she realized what was being said. Before answering she asked, "Do you think they are being gathered together?"

"I don't know, but I mean to find out. Do you still have yours?"

"Yes, but I haven't checked on it in a long time. It always felt like the less contact I had with it, the safer it would be." Shemalla shrugged uncomfortably at the memory of how much power the object had contained.

"That was very wise of you," Lillia said as she kept her eyes facing the road even though she could care less about the scenery. She had always been surprised at how quick Shemalla's mind was in figuring out things. Of course Shemalla would use her own innocent comment and come to the conclusion of the samaras being gathered together. Lillia castigated herself for being so slow to get to the same deduction.

"I find it very strange that I received a call from you only moments after I got a message from Elder Vargen," Shemalla spoke almost offhandedly. She did not believe in coincidences and wondered what the two events would have to do with one another. Eventually she would put the pieces together.

"What did he want?" Lillia thought he had seemed distracted when they had walked down the hallway. He had not been nearly as persistent as he usually was in questioning her about why she needed to use his gate.

"He asked me if I had heard anything about a man being in Roswell with amnesia."

Lillia furrowed her brows at the odd question. "What did you tell him?"

"The truth, I haven't heard anything like that around here."

"What do you think it means?"

"Elder Vargen must have lost one of his Earth slaves. My guess is it was someone important since he's going through the trouble of trying to locate him."

Lillia was beginning to feel very slow around Shemalla. Naturally, the amnesia should have been a tip-off for her. She knew about people from Earth losing their memories whenever they crossed through the Ascension Gates in either direction. If this man had escaped from Elder Vargen, then he was probably still in Tuala. She filed the information away in her mind for further consideration as there might be a way to use it against the Elder at some point.

"Do you need me to do anything for you or do you have a plan already?" Shemalla asked as she navigated the first turn toward town.

"I'm not sure yet. I was hoping you wouldn't mind if I stayed at your house for at least a day while I figure out my plans." She really could not imagine it not working out with Shemalla since they had been good friends for a very long time.

"You know I always love having you stay with me. It gets pretty lonely at home all alone every day. It's pretty refreshing to be able to talk about home and know the other person knows what I'm talking about." She smiled as she recalled the last visit she had received from Lillia. They had spent the entire night gossiping about the people in their lives while eating Tualan food brought by Lillia for the occasion.

"Thanks, Shemalla. I always feel better when I'm out from under Lucinden's watchful eyes."

"I don't know why you put up with him. You know he's not good for you or anybody else."

"I stay with him because then I can keep track of his moves. There have been many occasions where I've been able to keep him from causing more harm just by distracting him."

Shemalla shivered at the idea of what Lillia had been forced to do to distract him. Knowing she would not have been able to keep up the charade as long as Lillia had already, she admired the personal sacrifices her friend had made in order to help all of mankind. She wished there were more she could do for her than just a place to crash for the night.

The city was visible in the distance which meant they were almost back to town. Lillia looked around the stark landscape and could see why people fell in love with the tranquil beauty of it all. The sun shining down on them looked like it should be making the day warm, yet she knew all too readily that it was very cold, even for December.

When they finally pulled into the driveway, Lillia still had no better idea for a plan of action. She would have to figure something out so she could report her findings to Lucinden. The last thing she needed was for him to look into this matter on his own.

Lillia picked up her travel bag from between her feet in the car and slung it over her shoulder as she got out. She walked beside Shemalla as they entered the quiet house.

"Put your stuff down in the room you always use."

"Okay, thanks," Lillia answered as she continued down the short hall and turned to the left after the guest bathroom door. She appreciated the fact that the room always looked the same. When she had to use the bathroom at night, she could easily navigate around the furniture even in the dark.

After setting the bag down on the end of the bed, Lillia returned to the living room where she knew Shemalla would bring them both refreshments. Shemalla was known for making the best cactus wine and Lillia's mouth watered just thinking about it. As if on cue, Shemalla returned from the kitchen holding a tray containing a squat-looking jar and two small shot glasses.

She set the tray on the coffee table and began pouring the potent beverage. Shemalla handed the first glass to Lillia and picked up the second for herself.

"This should warm you up faster than anything else!" Shemalla declared as she stayed on the edge of the couch and raised her glass for a toast. "Here's to being smart enough and strong enough for good to win in the end!"

Lillia chuckled at the toast and raised her glass to clink against Shemalla's. They both drank small sips at the same time. "I think this is your best batch yet," she praised as the liquor went smoothly down her throat with a trail of moderated fire.

CHAPTER 20

Neal felt as though he had changed since undergoing hypnosis, almost as if something had been unlocked in his brain. His mind kept reviewing what had been released and plagued his dreams. If he thought he had been tired before, now he knew what exhaustion meant.

He dragged himself out of bed and went to the kitchen where he could smell the coffee brewing. Maybe the caffeine would revive him from the stupor he felt taking over his life. Neal pulled a cup out of the cupboard and clumsily poured the hot liquid, sloshing some of it onto his thumb. "Damn that's hot," he growled as he hurriedly set the cup and coffee pot down so he could get some cold water over the burning flesh.

Jessica walked in just in time to witness Neal's incident and asked, "Are you okay, honey?"

"Yeah, I just got careless." The last thing he wanted to admit to his mother was that he felt even worse than before. He could just imagine how she would react.

"Let me know if you need anything," she offered as she effortlessly poured her own coffee and took it to the table to sip while she read the paper.

Neal turned off the water and examined his finger. It was red, but otherwise okay. He grabbed his coffee and sat at the table across from his mother. He decided to wait a few more minutes before even attempting to sip the hot liquid.

Jessica looked up from the paper and noticed how tired her son looked. "You look terrible, Neal. Didn't you get any sleep?"

"Not much, really. I can't stop thinking about my session with Dr. Huddleston."

"Do you want to talk about it?" She had wanted to ask a million questions when they had left the psychiatrist's office. Her patience appeared to have paid off as she saw her son nod his assent.

"I remember a woman named Vinia. Somehow I think I'm missing something important, though."

"Why do you say that?" Her voice remained calm even if her heart rate increased. The tightening of her fingers on the handle of her coffee cup was the only outward indication of her excitement at this breakthrough.

"I keep mistaking Vinia for Amanda. In my mind it's almost like they're twins because they look so much alike."

"They do say everyone has at least one doppelganger in the world," she offered reasonably as her mind raced at the possibilities.

Neal raised his eyebrows and considered his mother's point. He hoped her explanation was the right answer since it made him feel slightly less crazy. "There's also something about a place called Tuala. Have you ever heard of it before?"

Jessica raised her eyes to the ceiling as she considered his question before she shook her head. "No, I don't think I have. Did you try looking it up on the computer? It might be some small town in Mexico or something."

"No," Neal answered and felt slightly foolish. He was not used to going to the computer for answers since the internet had really come into existence while he had been missing. While everyone around him seemed to think of it as a major resource, he still thought of it as a novelty. *Why didn't they have internet where I was held captive?* he wondered to himself. "I'll check it out after I finish my coffee."

"Maybe a shower would help wake you up as well," Jessica offered as she took in his disheveled appearance.

"I look that bad, huh?" He chuckled at his mother's expression.

"What else do you remember?"

Neal was not fooled by his mother's change of subject. He thought about what else to tell her. An idea suddenly struck him and he said, "I think I had a job! Yeah, I did! I had a job, Mom."

"What kind of a job? Where was it?" Jessica put the paper down, not even willing to pretend she was reading it anymore.

Neal frowned in concentration before he answered, "I was an engineer."

"What kinds of projects did you work on?"

"I don't know," he answered after he wracked his brain for the elusive information.

"Don't push yourself, honey. I think you've made great progress after only seeing Dr. Huddleston once. You'll find yourself remembering more and more after each session." She nodded her head affirmatively and then took a sip of her coffee.

Neal played with the handle of his cup for a moment before he shook his head in disgust. He hated being unable to put the pieces together. It seemed strange to him to be missing such a long period of time in his life. He did not feel as though he had been abused, beaten, or injured in any way, so why would he be unable to remember? It just did not make any sense.

Jessica could practically see the wheels turning in her son's head. She was thankful he was at least trying to recall the events of his past, yet she did not want him overwhelmed to the point where he gave up. "Give it time, Neal. It'll all come back given enough time."

"I suppose." He picked up his cup and took a cautious sip. "I wish Amanda would answer my phone calls. I could probably remember faster if she told me where I was actually found."

"Probably. I'm not sure why she's being so difficult. Maybe she just needs some time to process it as well."

"Maybe," Neal answered even though he did not believe it to be true any more than his mother did.

Jessica sipped her coffee again and decided she would be making a house call later in the day. Amanda was going to answer her questions whether she wanted to or not. Neal had a right to know where he had been and Amanda did have the answers they were all desperate to find out.

∾

VALENTINA CORNERED JUILA IN THE GIRLS' bathroom. "What happened yesterday? Why did I get left here alone at school?"

"You know what happened, Val. Behn explained it all to you." Juila looked around to make sure nobody heard their conversation.

"I want to hear it from you. I think there's more to this story than even Behn knew." Valentina crossed her arms and stood her ground.

Juila sighed as she recognized the stubborn stance. "Sofia was dying, she did die actually. Jena and I used our powers to heal her injuries to bring her back to life."

"So you just sat there in front of half of the student body and healed her? How could you be so reckless?"

Juila's anger rose as she realized what Valentina was saying. Her voice rose only slightly as she replied, "What was I supposed to do? Let her die? Of course I healed her. I would hope you would do the same thing once you have learned the skill."

Valentina still struggled with the idea of being different and not fitting in with the other kids in their school. She hated being adopted and having people feel sorry for her and her brothers because of it.

The longer Valentina remained silent, the more Juila realized she probably would not have helped Sofia, even to save her life. "You wouldn't have helped, would you? Are you ashamed of who you are?"

"I don't want to be a freak!" Valentina finally blurted out.

Juila shook her head in pity at the girl's strange ideals. Using the power given to them by Jehoban had always been a blessing. She had a hard time understanding why anyone would want to keep their abilities from helping people.

"Nobody suspects me of doing anything, Val. All anyone saw was me and Jena holding Sofia and keeping her company until the paramedics arrived."

"This time, Juila. What happens next time you happen to be around when someone gets hurt? Don't you think people will start to put it together? You can be so oblivious sometimes!"

"People see what they want to see and believe what they want to believe. It's not in my nature to ignore people when they need help and I don't think it's in yours, either. I think you need to practice reading people's minds so you can quit being so paranoid. You'd be shocked at how little people actually think about you or your brothers' situation. You've just become hyper sensitive and slightly paranoid."

"It sounds like you're calling me crazy." Valentina scowled deeper as she glared down at Juila.

"No, I'm calling you human. It's in our nature to worry, some more than others. We can talk about this later. We're going to be late for class." She pulled on Valentina's arm and smiled at her to get her moving.

"We're not done talking about this, Juila," she warned even as she started walking.

Juila merely smiled. "You're right. We need to talk about meeting your mom."

Valentina's face turned red as she recalled her terrible manners when she had first heard about their mom. Behn had been very patient with her and let her fume and vent about it on the drive home. Eventually, she had to agree it was in their best interest to at least meet the woman who might be their mother. All of the pieces did seem to fit and it would not hurt them to at least hear her out.

Juila covertly listened in to Valentina's thoughts. She was relieved to know she was at least willing to make an effort. "How are you going to tell Jon?"

"We're not," she answered flatly.

"What? You can't keep your mom from him!"

"We can until we know for sure that she is our mother. Why put him through any of this strange mess if she's not who she says she is?"

"Good point. You will have to tell him if she is your mom."

"Yeah, we will." Valentina was not excited about the whole idea. Jon seemed so content now that he had started dating Sofia. He was the happiest she had ever seen him and she did not want to turn his life upside down.

CHAPTER 21

Riccan could not concentrate on his work. His mind kept going over his last visit to Ela Nena's office. There was something he had missed or something important for him to remember. It was not necessarily anything she had said to him, no, it was definitely something else.

While she had definitely been acting strange, it seemed to be getting worse lately. He knew she was happily married so it would not be a jealousy thing because he was happily married. She had always admired his ability to get his team to work at their peak performance. No, it was not a management problem either.

He tried to pinpoint exactly when her demeanor toward him had changed. The first major conflict had happened right after he came back from vacation and told her he had gotten married. The more he thought about it, he realized she had been happy for him personally. Okay, so he could rule out the marriage as the problem. What had been going on with her while he was on vacation?

Riccan turned on his patil, pulled up Ela Nena's calendar, and scanned through her meetings to see what she had been doing during the time he had been out on vacation. She was a very busy woman and there were possibly a hundred different meetings, conferences, and special events she had attended.

He pulled out a piece of paper and began writing down the names of the people she had met with and the places where the meetings had been held. He had been gone for six weeks so the list took a bit of time to complete. After he completed the list, he could see there were many meetings with people who he knew personally. Since those people got along with him he scratched their names off of the list.

Eventually, he paired the list down to two events which were out of the ordinary: an awards ceremony and a meeting with a man whose name he did not recognize. He tapped the notepad with the tip of his pencil as he tried to figure out why these two things seemed to stand out.

He turned to his patil, typed in the man's name, and hit enter. The search returned one result. Riccan smiled at the screen. The name was the same as the person who presented the Annual Achievement award to Ela Nena at the Engineering Excellence Awards dinner. *Now, why would this man come to meet with Ela Nena?* Riccan thought to himself. *Maybe, more importantly, why did his name only have one search result? If he were important enough to present the award, why wouldn't he have a history?*

Riccan hated mysteries almost as much as he detested riddles. This person seemed to be shrouded in mystery and he did not like it. He tore the piece of paper off of the notepad and folded it several times before shoving it into his pocket. Riccan knew someone who just loved to figure things out: his mother.

He looked at the clock and was relieved to find it was already after five. After turning off his patil, he grabbed his coat, and left the office. The elevator seemed to take forever to get down to the second floor so he tapped his foot while he impatiently waited. Finally, his turn came and he punched the button to take him to the roof.

For a moment he contemplated timing it to his mother's house, but then thought better of it. What difference would a few minutes make in the grand scheme of things? The elevator doors opened at the rooftop and he stepped out. He walked over to his bright red telepod and palmed open the door.

He entered the coordinates to go to his parents' house and immediately initiated the activation button. Several seconds passed in darkness as he traveled between spaces before arriving in the bright sunlight over the grassy meadow in Pantano. He set the telepod down on the field and turned it off.

Somehow his mother always knew when to expect him so he was not surprised to see her leave the house to wave at him from the balcony overlooking the landing field. He waved back and lengthened his stride to go up and greet her.

After exchanging hugs, she pulled away from him and said, "This is unexpected. What brings you here today?"

"I have a mystery for you," he answered with a grin as he saw her smile in anticipation.

"Goody! What is it?" She clapped her hands together in childish glee.

As they walked back through the house to her office Riccan explained the situation. He pulled the piece of paper out of his pocket and handed it to her.

She spent a bit of time looking over the entire list before nodding her agreement at his assessment of the situation. "It is strange. I'll ask your father if he knows anything about this guy. Can you leave this with me? I'd like to see what I can come up with as well."

"Sure, keep it. I can always write up another one if I needed to." He did not want to tell her he was done thinking about it since she was going to worry it like a dog with a bone anyway. It was just her nature to keep at it until she found a solution to her liking. "I can't stay long. Amanda's expecting me pretty soon." Speaking about his wife reminded him of another question. "What happened with Chelesa when you showed her Amanda's journal?"

"She found a discrepancy in the account."

"Really? That's odd since everything else has been so accurate. What do you make of it?"

"I don't know yet. It's just one more thing for me to figure out!" She smiled at her son affectionately.

"You love it, and you know it!" Riccan teased.

"Go on home, honey. I'll stay on this mystery so you won't have to worry about it." She tapped the paper to emphasize her point.

"I know. It's just the type of thing you love, which is why I came over!"

"Oh, get out of here, you rascal."

Riccan smiled wider as he stood up from the chair. "I love you, Mom. Thanks for doing this."

"My pleasure!" She came around the desk and gave him a hug. She kept her arm around him while they walked back to the patio. "I'm really looking forward to having the grandchildren come over later this mesan. What kinds of things do they like doing?"

Riccan thought about it for a moment before answering, "I think you won't have to worry about it, Mom. The girls just want to spend time getting to know you. I think you three will find plenty to keep you busy, if only exchanging stories."

"I guess you're right," she admitted. In a way, having planned activities would be less unnerving than worrying whether or not they were having a good time.

Riccan could see her dubious expression and chuckled, "Honestly, Mom, they'll be fine! They're not little children with short attention spans. They can entertain themselves quite nicely. Let them know they can use your telepod to visit friends if you're so worried about it." Riccan chuckled again at his mother's discomfiture.

"Fine," she agreed. "Get home to your family then." She pushed at him playfully.

He kissed her cheek before turning to walk down the stairs to the landing field. He felt lighthearted since he had given over the task to his mother. Now he could devote his attention to helping his wife find the remaining samaras.

Watching her son walk confidently back to his telepod, she felt an overwhelming pride in the man he had become. Her only regret in life was not having more children so he could have had siblings to grow up with.

Riccan waved one final time from the cockpit of the telepod before he left for home. Thoughts of Amanda waiting for him made him forget all of his other worries. Knowing she anticipated spending time with him as much as he did with her was a great blessing.

He parked the telepod in the garage and entered the house. He could hear his children and wife talking in the living room. It was such a different experience coming home to a house full of women when he'd been a bachelor for so long. Never in a million years would have anticipated his life could change so drastically in such a short period of time.

"Hello, family!" he announced as soon as he could physically see everyone.

"Dad!" Jena cried as she jumped up and ran over to give him a big hug.

Riccan's heart almost burst with pleasure at her spontaneous display of affection. It would not have mattered to him, yet he was really thankful that these girls truly were his biological children. He still felt like pinching himself to make sure he was not dreaming.

"Come sit down, Dad," Jena said as she tugged his hand to lead him the rest of the way to the couch.

"What's going on? Good news, I'm guessing." He kissed Amanda before settling down right next to her. Draping his arm across her shoulders, he prepared himself to hear the news.

"Sofia's doing great! She's going to be coming back to school on Monday," Jena announced.

"That's wonderful!" Riccan enthused. He had expected nothing less with his girls' healing capabilities.

"Valentina and Behn have agreed to meet with Vinia," Juila said.

"How did that happen?" Amanda asked. With the way Valentina had reacted to the news, she never thought she would come around, especially so fast. She started thinking about making arrangements to go back to Barla's house to tell Vinia.

"Val, cornered me in the bathroom the other day and confronted me about healing Sofia. For some reason, she's under the impression that we're all freaks for being able to help people. Anyway, I turned the conversation around to her mother and what she was going to do about it. She finally said they want to hear her out and see what happens from there."

"I noticed you never said anything about including Jon in this reunion," Riccan stated.

"They plan on leaving him out of it until they are certain she actually is their mother," Juila said with a slightly disgusted tone.

"Why?" Jena asked.

"I don't know. I guess they don't want to have him start asking questions about their past," Juila answered.

"Well, it's a start at least," Amanda mused.

"I guess it could get awkward if he asked where she's been all of this time," Jena reasoned.

"It hasn't been all that long for Vinia, remember? She said she sent the children away only a year ago. I'm afraid this reunion will be just as hard on her since she's missed out on so much of their lives without even knowing how it happened. There's going to have to be a lot of adjustments for everyone in this," Amanda pointed out.

"I don't know, Amanda. How hard was it for you to find out our children were almost grown up?" Riccan asked.

Amanda blinked in surprise at his question. She had never really considered how similar her situation with her children was to Vinia's before. It seemed as though their lives were still running parallel even when she was not in a coma. "Too true. After the initial shock, it never seemed to matter. I did wish I could have been there for their growing up, but I'm thankful for whom they've become."

The girls beamed with pride at their mother's declaration of love and pride. They never regretted the way they had been raised either. Living with Jehoban had been a blessing and they had always felt loved and cherished.

"I saw my mom today," Riccan announced in the lull of conversation.

"Really? Is everything okay?" Amanda asked.

"Yeah, I went to see her before coming home."

"What's going on, Riccan?"

"I can't shake this feeling about Ela Nena. I took a list of names and events over to my mom to have her look into them and see if she can come up with anything."

Juila narrowed her eyes as she considered what her father had said. "What kind of a feeling, Dad?"

"I'm not sure. I feel like I should know an important detail and yet it remains elusive."

"When did you first get this feeling?" Juila persisted.

Riccan thought about it for a moment before he shrugged in resignation. "I don't really know. Each time I get called into her office, it seems like my feeling grows stronger. I kept thinking it was compounding because of the things she's been saying to me. Now I'm not so sure anymore."

"Her office, huh?" Juila spoke softly as she tried to figure out some correlation.

Jena's eyes widened as she saw where Juila's thoughts were going. Suddenly, the pieces of the puzzle clicked in her head and she snapped her fingers. "I have an idea!" she announced, surprising everyone. "Come with me!" She stood up and started walking down the hall.

With confused expressions everyone followed her. She led them to the library and turned around to face them. They rarely spent any time in the room since the additional samaras were creating a large energy field which could be felt throughout the room.

As soon as Riccan crossed the threshold he realized what had been bothering him. "You're right, Jena! You are so right!" He went over and picked her up in a giant hug and twirled her around in excitement. He set her back down and continued to grin at her.

"Will someone please clue me in?" Amanda demanded. She was not used to being completely left out and she did not like it one bit.

"The girls must have been reading my mind while I was talking about my meetings with Ela Nena." He tried to scowl at their bad manners, but his smile took over his expression. "Jena got the idea about my uneasy feeling and realized it was the same as the feeling we get when we're around the samaras in here. She's right, too! Ela Nena must have one of the samaras somewhere in her office because I can feel the energy of it when I go in there."

Amanda hoped Riccan's explanation proved to be correct. She was starting to worry about the lack of progress in locating the remaining eight samaras. "How do you think Ela Nena got the crystal?"

"I don't know, but I mean to find out!" Riccan could hardly wait to get back to work the next day. It was strange to have the excitement back even when faced with the daunting task of confronting Ela Nena. He was convinced he was on the right track, however, since nothing else made as much sense.

Juila was quiet during the discussion as she tried to figure out what was bothering her with Jena's simple solution.

"Why do you look so troubled, Juila?" Amanda asked.

"There's still something we're missing," she replied slowly.

"What is it?" Riccan prompted.

"I don't know…Do you think it's possible Ela Nena doesn't know she has the samara?"

"Why? What are you thinking?"

Jena was, once again, one step ahead of Juila. "When we studied about the samaras we learned they have a lot of powers. One of those powers allows a person to be controlled through the samara. It might explain Ela Nena's sudden change in her attitude toward you, Dad."

Riccan raised his eyebrows at this new twist in the story. He wondered what else the girls knew about the powers of the samaras. It seemed as though they only found out new information when situations prompted the need. Perhaps he should spend some more time in communion with his own samara to gain a better understanding of its power. He shuddered at the idea of losing himself in the thrall of the powerful link and dismissed the thought for the time being.

"Who would be controlling her and why would Riccan be the target?" Amanda demanded.

Riccan thought he might already have at least part of the answer, but he did not want to share his theory until after he heard back from his mother. She might discover something very different from what he was beginning to suspect. Instead of the truth, Riccan answered, "Two very good questions which we will have to get answered, Amanda!"

Jena gave her father a sidelong stare and wondered what he was not sharing. She mentally shrugged her shoulder since, given enough time, she would figure it out anyway.

CHAPTER 22

Sofia was so relieved to finally be able to have Jon visit her while she was stuck at home on bed rest. Originally she was going to go back to school after the weekend, but her migraine headache that morning had canceled her plan. She was thoroughly bored enough to be excited for the homework Jon had brought over. Together they sat in the living room, Sofia stretched out on the couch, and Jon in the recliner right next to her. The only thing dampening her spirits was the idea of Jon seeing her after she had not been able to shower for two days.

"You look really good, Sofia," Jon said.

Sofia looked at him suddenly suspicious because it seemed as though he had read her mind. "Thanks—I think—considering I know how terrible I really look."

"You look alive and that's my favorite thing!" He smiled at his own wit.

Sofia had to laugh out loud at his ridiculous statement which caused her to grab her side to keep the stitches from pulling too much. "Ouch! Don't make me laugh, Jon."

He suddenly turned serious. "I'm sorry, Sofia, I didn't know."

"I was only teasing. I've often heard that laughter is the best medicine so I should probably find a lot of reasons to laugh so I can start to feel better. My whole body feels like I got hit by a semi."

"The way the front of the car looked, you're lucky to even be alive."

Suddenly she realized Jon had seen the accident scene. He was someone who might be able to tell her what really happened. She asked, "What really happened, Jon? What did you see?"

"I didn't see much since I was so far away. I heard the tires squeal on the pavement as the car tried to stop. I also heard the screams of the people who saw it happen. I ran as fast as I could to find out who had gotten hurt. When I saw you lying on the ground in a pool of blood, I was certain you were dead already. Your lips were blue and I swear I couldn't see you breathing."

Sofia nodded to keep him talking.

"Jena was kneeling down beside you and Juila was cradling your head. I assumed they were praying because their eyes were shut. Jena opened her eyes and told me to take your hand and tell you to hold on and that everything would be okay." He looked away with a strange expression.

"What else?"

"Something weird happened. When I first held your hand your fingers were so limp and cold and it scared me. Right after I told you to hold on, I swear I felt a surge of warmth almost like an energy of some sort go through your fingers into mine."

"Then what happened to me?"

"You started having convulsions and you were shaking all over. I held your hand tighter. How do your fingers feel?"

Sofia laughed as she flexed and wiggled her fingers before she replied, "They feel better than the rest of me. Did the girls do or say anything while you were there?"

Jon thought about it for a moment and shook his head. "I don't think so. Why?"

While Sofia had promised not to say anything about the secret project in their garage, it did not mean she was unable to talk about any other strange things which only seemed to happen around the girls.

"Don't get me wrong, I love those girls like they're my sisters, it's just strange things happen around them." Sofia shrugged her shoulders gently, not knowing the best way to describe what she meant.

"Give me some examples."

"Okay, when I'm driving with them in the car. I could swear the other cars are avoiding me. When they aren't with me, I have so many close calls."

"Maybe you're just more aware of safety when they are with you." Jon smiled at Sofia's reason. "What else?"

"Doesn't it ever seem like they talk to one another without speaking? I mean they often talk about stuff I've only ever spoken to the other one about. And before you say they shared when I wasn't around, I'm telling you there wasn't any time for sharing. Stop laughing, Jon, it happens all the time. Pay more attention to them and you'll realize I'm speaking the truth."

"I'm sorry, Sofia, it's just funny. Besides, they are identical twins. I've heard a lot of strange things happen when they're identical like speaking the same thing at the same time…things like that all the time. Do you have any other examples?" Jon tried to keep a straight face because he could tell she was starting to get angry with him.

"Not if you're just going to make fun of me."

"I'm sorry. I think you've been left alone for too long. I promise I won't laugh. What else do you have?"

"Don't you think it's strange how much time Val spends over at their house? She didn't even really like the girls much and now she spends every day with them. What's that all about?"

Jon had wondered the same thing himself. Valentina had said she was tutoring Jena because they were from South Africa and needed help with a lot of the studies. It had seemed logical at the time, yet now he wondered about it. The twins both seemed smarter than all of them so it would be strange for Jena to continue to need help.

"I can agree it is strange for Val to suddenly like someone. I'll talk to her about it again and let you know what she tells me. Anything else?"

She gestured to her whole body and said, "Me! I think they did something to my injuries. Jon, I swear I felt my bones break when the car hit me. I also think something else broke when I hit the ground. How can you explain the fact I hardly have any injuries except a few cuts and scratches?"

Jon raised his eyebrows and tipped his head at her argument. He had also wondered how she had escaped injury with the amount of damage he had seen on the car. "Okay, you may have something there. What could they do though? It's not like they have magic fingers and could heal you."

"Maybe they can."

"You're serious, aren't you?"

"Very! You even said I was having convulsions and yet they found nothing wrong with my brain on the CT scan. I don't have a single broken bone, either."

"Are you going to ask them about it?"

"I think so. I'm not sure how to get them to tell me the truth, however."

"Do you want the truth, or do you want to admit to what you have in mind?"

"I see your point. Still, I'll ask them and try to keep an open mind when I hear their answer."

WILLIAN WAS FASCINATED with the complexity of the Manzanit Residence in both form and function. It only took him two days of getting completely lost for him to start understanding the layout of the sprawling, multi-floored building. After watching Elder Wilken handle several dignitaries, he was beginning to understand what a monumental job he kept track of almost effortlessly. He hoped to be as good when he finally became Elder in his own district. No longer did he think badly of Rasa since he knew she had a tough job ahead of her when she finally got to be in charge of the district.

Rasa kept him pretty busy by grilling him on rules and regulations standard for any Elder. He was glad he had paid attention in the Successor's classes. She seemed to be pleased with the amount of knowledge he had retained since the last session had been held. Rasa even smiled at him before she had to return to her own duties.

When she was unable to meet with him, he had been instructed by her to access a special program on his patil. At first glance, the program appeared to be a basic educational course until you entered a secret code and then everything became quite different. The names of the continents, cities, and bodies of water were all different than what he knew them to be.

Even more disturbing than the names of everything being changed, Willian discovered the people of Earth spoke hundreds of different languages. He failed to understand how this would work since nobody would be able to talk to one another. When he searched out the area where he knew Jena was living, he was relieved to find there were only a couple of common languages and English was one of them.

Using the memorization techniques almost everyone learned in school, he carefully reviewed and memorized the eastern part of the United States of America. If he were going to be traveling from his current location, known there as New York, then he should probably have some intimate knowledge of where he would be going. He wondered how long it would take to get to southern Florida.

The thought of transportation worried him a little bit since it would require a lot of time and work on his part. The people of Tuala had it so much easier with teleportation since it was almost instantaneous. He looked up transportation methods and scowled at the options as they all seemed so inefficient. The airplane looked to be the best alternative, even if it were going to require him to acquire more money.

Money: a major issue he was going to have to figure out. Money and living arrangements were on the top of his list he had to admit to himself, the more he learned, the less certain he was of succeeding in his task. He could not believe how naïve he had been when he had tried to go see Jena before. He was so thankful he had been unsuccessful because he was certain he would have gotten himself into a lot of trouble had he met with anyone.

Two good things had come from his unauthorized trip; he was learning valuable lessons about Earth which would normally never be taught, and he was gaining valuable lessons from one of the most respected Elders in Tuala. It seemed like a win-win situation all around to Willian.

Rasa entered the study hall and noticed Willian staring off into space with a small grin on his face. She could not resist teasing him a little as she spoke up, "Dreaming about your meeting with Jena?"

Willian jumped and quickly looked over at Rasa. He blushed slightly before he smiled and said, "No. I was thinking how lucky I was to be able to come here to study."

"You've never liked studying before. Why is this different?"

Willian shrugged slightly and admitted, "Because not many people learn these things. I like having special knowledge."

"Well I hate to burst your bubble, but you need to shut down your patil now because it's time for you to mediate your first case." She grinned at the expression on his face.

"I thought I'd have a couple more days before they started arriving," he protested and then shut his mouth on further comment when he realized how childish he was sounding. "Okay, fine, I get it. I've had my playtime and now it's time for me to start earning my keep. Right?"

"Something like that!" Rasa approved of Willian's change of heart. *Maybe he can be made into a decent person after all,* she thought to herself. She waited for him to do as she had asked and then walked beside him back to the reception rooms reserved for mediation.

"Can you tell me what this case will be about so I can start to review my knowledge of the law?"

Rasa nodded approval and said, "This is a case of two girls who claim to have been slighted by the same boy. Now both of them are not talking to one another even though they've been best friends and neighbors since they were born."

"You're kidding, right? We don't really hear these kinds of cases." Willian's expression changed to disbelief as he realized Rasa had not been joking at all.

"This kind and many more petty concerns. Remember, this matter is very important to these girls. They are both citizens of the district and we will do what we can to help them out. Try to be creative in your solution so that each person involved feels as though they've given up little and gained a lot."

"You sure aren't asking much!" Willian had no idea how he was going to handle this situation. Hopefully Rasa would be able to help him out a little.

They entered the room and Willian experienced his first taste of over-seeing a district. As the girls each presented her case to him, he tried to think like Elder Wilken. He wanted to be fair and impartial. Most impor-tantly, he wanted to keep his own feelings out of the matter and make a decision based solely on the facts as the girls presented them. Even though the case had seemed simple, he soon found how complex they became when people's emotions were involved.

Willian watched the girls leave hand-in-hand, best friends once again. The biggest lesson he learned from this first mediation was the power of listening. He had asked each girl to present her position in the matter and requested the other girl to remain silent. With only a few directions of his own, each girl was finally able to share her side of the story until they both realized the boy was unworthy of either of them. Most of their anger had stemmed from a lack of communication and a big dose of assumption on both of their parts.

"Very well done, Willian," Rasa commented as soon as the door shut behind the girls. "I couldn't have handled it any better."

"Thanks. I didn't really have to do much. Once they started talking they pretty much fixed it all themselves."

"Exactly my point. The best solutions are always the simplest ones. They both left here happy and we couldn't ask for anything better."

Willian nodded in agreement. His stomach began to growl loud enough for Rasa to hear.

"Come on, it's time to eat. I can hear just how starving you are!"

Happily, he stepped down from his raised seat and began thinking about what he wanted to eat for lunch. "Will Elder Wilken be joining us?"

"No, he had a case to oversee offsite. He should be back in time for dinner."

Willian was slightly disappointed since he wanted to be able to tell the Elder about the success of his first mediation. Maybe it would be for the best for him to wait to talk it over. He would have more time to go over all of the details and let Elder Wilken know how much he had learned. The Elder seemed more impressed with learning than with doing, so he would do his best to demonstrate how much he could learn while he stayed at the Residence.

CHAPTER 23

Chelesa kept thinking about her son's trip to Earth and whether or not she should try to put a stop to it. On the one hand, he needed to have this experience as a learning lesson. On the other hand, he was the sole heir to her husband. If anything were to happen to him on this trip, she would be beside herself with guilt. She decided she should talk to Debbon about it during dinner.

She looked over to the empty space where her son usually sat at the table and felt a heaviness in her heart. "Debbon, are you at all worried about Willian's trip?"

He seemed startled by her question and replied candidly, "Of course. I wouldn't want to stop him from trying, however. I think he'll grow up a lot from going out on his own for a bit. Plus we know he'll be well-looked after with Elder Wilken."

"That's true for now, but what happens when he's on his own on Earth? Who'll be watching over him then?"

"He's almost a grown man, Chelesa. What is this really about?"

She looked down at her plate, realizing she should have known her husband would know her so well. "I read through some parts of Amanda's journal while I was at Nena's house. Most of the account was accurate except for a part concerning Willian and Jena. It scares me because it was different than reality."

890

"Explain the difference so I can see if I agree with you." Debbon set his fork down and waited for her to tell him everything.

When she had finished with the details, she could see Debbon had taken her doubts seriously and she was relieved. Her husband was usually a reasonable man, except where their son was concerned. He typically told her she worried over him too much and to let him learn on his own. This time, he understood her fear and she could relax knowing the two of them could work on a solution together.

"Maybe I'll have a word with Elder Wilken," Debbon suggested.

"I think that might make it awkward for Willian, not to mention for you, too. How can you explain anything without telling him about Amanda? We are supposed to be helping her, but we are not supposed to talk about what we learned outside of the group of people who were present."

She considered what other options might present themselves and then an idea struck her. "I think I may have an idea! Since you are still catching up with your workload because of the convocation, maybe I'll go and speak to Rasa about it. I've always wanted to see the Manzanit Residence anyway, I hear it's spectacular."

Debbon did not bother trying to hide his smirk at Chelesa's enthusiasm. Besides, it was a good plan. "I think you're on the right track. I think you should wait a few more days for Willian to get settled in before you go. We wouldn't want him to think we were checking up on him!"

"Goodness no! He would hate that!" Chelesa chuckled because she knew he would think it anyway, but she was willing to wait just because she wanted more time to consider what she wanted to say to Rasa.

"Tell me more about the co-conspirators Amanda wrote about," Debbon asked.

Chelesa had been so lost in thought she had to retrace a few steps to even know to what her husband was referring. "Oh, you mean the people involved in scaring our family until we all left?"

"Were there more than that?" Debbon asked with alarm.

"No, I just wanted to make sure we were both talking about the same thing." Chelesa proceeded to tell him everything she knew about what Amanda had written. "What are you going to do about it?"

"I'm going to bring them in for questioning, of course."

"What are you going to do about presenting the evidence against them? Are you going to tell them they were outed by a dream?"

"Hmm, good point." Debbon hated leaving the men out on the street to cause more harm to his family or others. They were going to have to be punished, but he had to follow the laws as well. He would be no better than they if he exacted retribution without due process.

"You could set your people to watching them. If they do anything wrong, then you can bring them in and make them pay for the things you can prove."

"I knew there was a reason I married you. You are brilliant! That type of men won't stop at just the one thing bad, they're sure to be getting into trouble on a pretty regular basis. Because we know about them, maybe we can clean things up a bit around here."

"Thanks, honey. I knew you would do the right thing."

"So what else did you learn while you were visiting with Nena? It feels like it's been forever since we've had any alone time to catch up on each other's lives."

At that moment, Chelesa realized they actually had time to devote to themselves without fear of being interrupted by Willian and his usual antics. They would not have his friends traipsing through the house. They would have peace and privacy until Willian returned from his visit with Jena.

Feeling as though they were newlyweds again, Chelesa talked about her visit with Nena, her new patients, and the general running of their household. Their meal took much longer than usual and they were both feeling relaxed by the end of dessert.

"Why don't we take a walk through the grounds while you show me what you've changed?" Debbon suggested as he pushed his chair away from the table, rose, and extended his hand out to his wife.

She smiled at the suggestion and took his hand. "I can show you the new grotto I've had the gardeners install. It is very private from prying eyes."

"What did you have in mind when you created such a private space?" Debbon's eyes danced with mischief.

"Oh, I don't know. Maybe we can think of something when we get there," she teased.

With a spring in their steps, they left the house through a little-used side door. The flowers outside were in full bloom and the trees provided plenty of relief from the late afternoon sun. When they arrived at the new grotto, neither one paid much attention to their surroundings since they only had eyes for one another.

~

WITH THE IDEA of finding Jinya, Petre did not leave town as he had planned. He had learned his lesson the time before and he did not ask around to see if any of the people had seen her. He had seen her and that was enough for him.

Sleuthing had never been his strong point so he went to the last place he could verify he had seen her. He split his time between the location near the alley and the marketplace. More than once he chided himself for having called out to her and scaring her. If he would have been smarter, he would have just followed her and found out where she was staying. Once he knew the location, he could have convinced her to come back and live with him out on the water.

Thinking about the mesans he had spent with her on his water craft brought back fond memories. The days had been pleasant and the nights had been spectacular. Before she had practically fallen into his life, he had never imagined wanting to settle down. Jinya had changed his idea about marriage and having children.

Children were another sore subject with him. Once he had discovered Jinya had secretly delivered their daughter, Valentina, he had been furious to find out she had kept him from knowing. He did not feel a bit bad about having taken her and betrothing her to a wealthy merchant's son. The only part which rankled him was the fact that Jinya had turned up at the Elder's Residence and convinced him to release the girl back to her before the betrothal petition could be approved.

He could not understand women sometimes. Here he had gone to so much trouble to create a great life for their daughter and Jinya had not appreciated his effort. Moreover, she had taken their daughter and disappeared. So much of his valuable time had been wasted trying to discover where she had gone.

Eight anons had passed since he had seen Jinya, eight long anons of lonely nights and nobody to take care of him. She would pay for keeping him away from his daughter. He had a right to be a part of both of their lives.

The marketplace was particularly busy and Petre had to continually search the shifting crowds. Several merchants began quarreling over a prime location to set up their booth. When the authorities had been called to resolve the dispute, Petre decided to go back to his water craft to get lunch. It would not due to be seen by Captain Ahn's cronies since he still was not technically welcome in Cresdon.

He backed into the alleyway and turned around right into another man. "I'm sorry," he mumbled without looking up and trying to move away to the left.

"Petre? Is that you?" the man asked.

Recognizing the voice, Petre looked up in surprise and smiled. "Hey, Rualin! What are you doing so far from home?"

"I could ask you the same!" Rualin thumped Petre's shoulder a couple of times. "I was just heading to the market place to get some lunch. Do you want to join me?"

Petre tipped his head back toward the square and said, "Nah, the authorities just arrived to break up a brawl. I thought I'd head over to my water craft and make something there. Why don't you join me?"

Rualin had no need of being seen by the authorities as well and readily agreed by saying, "I'd love to. Thanks for inviting me!" He turned around and they headed away from the commotion. "What were you doing back there? It looked as though you were waiting for someone."

"Not exactly waiting," Petre replied, "more like searching. A couple of days ago I saw Jinya leaving the market."

"Wait! Isn't that the girl you kidnapped a long time ago?" Rualin hoped it was someone different.

"I didn't exactly kidnap her, Rualin. You make me sound so bad. She was a guest on my water craft and we had a good time until she fell overboard and got confused."

"Right...Petre maybe you should let this go. You're going to get yourself into trouble again if you pursue this woman again. Remember the last time? You almost got your mind swiped."

"But I didn't get my mind erased because I got them to admit I was not entirely responsible. Don't you get it Rualin? She has my daughter and I have a right to both of them now. Besides, I…never mind."

"You what, Petre? What are you thinking?"

"Not here," Petre whispered as he looked around to see if anyone had overheard them. "I'll tell you when we have more privacy."

CHAPTER 24

Dr. Huddleston had done some research on Neal's case type and had discovered an interesting lead. There was a doctor who specialized in multi-dimensional disorders who would probably be interested in hearing the details of this new case. He glanced at his watch and was pleased to see he still had another thirty minutes before Neal was scheduled to arrive. He picked up the phone and dialed Dr. Gascon's number.

"Hello, Dr. Gascon. My name's Dr. Huddleston. Do you have a couple of minutes to discuss a patient of mine?"

"Hello, Dr. Huddleston. I'm a very busy man. Maybe another time would be better."

"Wait, have you ever had a patient talk about a place called Tuala?" Dr. Huddleston spoke speedily before the other man had a chance to hang up the receiver.

"You have my attention. Yes, I have heard of Tuala. How have you found out about it?"

"Like I said, my patient believes he spent time there. When I was doing a little research, your name came up as an expert in this field. I would like to ask your advice as to the best course of action to take with my patient. We've had only the one session and the hypnosis seemed to be very beneficial…"

"I can tell you right now, your patient needs someone like myself to take over his case. He needs specialized care and close monitoring if he is to get over his delusions of Tuala. I would recommend you refer him to me immediately and I will reschedule my other patients so he could be seen as soon as he arrives here."

Dr. Huddleston had not expected to lose his patient, he had merely wanted to get some guidance for treatment. "Well, I guess I can let him know you've offered to help. He is going to be arriving in my office in a few minutes."

"Good, you do that. Call me back and let me know when to expect him," he spoke briskly and then hung up the phone.

Dr. Huddleston stared at the receiver still in his hand. He could hardly believe the other doctor had hung up on him so rudely. While Dr. Gascon may be a busy man, it hardly seemed a good enough reason to be downright rude. *Should he take the other doctor's advice and refer him over, or should he continue to try to treat Neal's condition?* He turned his attention back to the article he had been reading on the computer and realized there was much more to this disorder than he felt equipped to handle. Dr. Gascon may have been rude, however, he had spoken the truth.

His musings were interrupted when the receptionist buzzed through to his office. He hit the talk button and said, "Yes?"

"Neal Taivas is here for his appointment," the female voice spoke.

"Send him on back." He punched the end button and made up his mind at the same time.

When his office door opened he stood up and smiled as he moved around his desk to shake hands with Neal. "It's good to see you again. Go ahead and sit down. I want to discuss treatment options with you."

Neal shook the doctor's hand and then wondered at the difference in his tone of voice. It seemed as if something were troubling the other man. He sat down on the oversized leather couch and waited anxiously.

Dr. Huddleston retrieved his notepad from his desk before he sat down across from him. He glanced down, unnecessarily, to give himself a few more seconds to compose his proposition. "How have you been these past few days, Neal? Can you tell me if you remember more since we last spoke?"

Neal nodded his head and said, "Yes. It seems as though the things we talked about before are more vivid. Also, I've been dreaming a lot about things I don't actually remember. The dreams feel like memories, but they're not my memories. Does that make sense?"

Dr. Huddleston nodded confirmation. Neal's case was much more complex than his standard case. He would be doing Neal a disservice if he did not offer the help of Dr. Gascon. "I've been doing some research on the type of condition you suffer from and I think I might have come up with a good solution for you."

"What is it?" Neal was eager to find anything which would offer a quick fix for his apparent amnesia.

"There is a doctor in New York who specializes in your type of case. He has agreed to clear his schedule and see you a soon as you can arrange to go there. Does this sound like something you'd want to try?"

"Do you think it'll work? Will I get my memories back?"

"Yes, I believe you'll have your life back if you go to see him. He has offered an in-patient care option for you." Dr. Huddleston tapped his pen softly on his notepad as he watched Neal's expression while he processed this new alternative.

"Okay then, I don't see where I have much choice. I want to get my memories back so I can move on with my life. I've already lost enough time and I'm ready to move on. You can tell the doctor we will be able to meet with him tomorrow."

"Do you want to try another hypnosis session today or just wait until you meet with Dr. Gascon?"

"There's really no point in wasting your time if the other doctor will be taking over. I guess I should get packing and making the arrangements," Neal said as he stood up and made ready to leave the office.

"I'll call Dr. Gascon right now. I wish you the best of luck, Neal." He shook Neal's hand and watched him leave the office.

Without even sitting down, he pushed the talk button on the intercom and waited for the receptionist to pick up. "Can you please give Neal the following information? He is to meet with Dr. Gascon, Creedmoor Psychiatric Center, Queens, New York. Thank you." He toggled off the intercom and pressed redial on the phone and told Dr. Gascon to expect a patient named Neal Taivas the following day. Dr. Huddleston hoped he had done the right thing by his patient since Dr. Gascon had seemed inordinately pleased to hear of his impending arrival.

~

Jessica looked up in alarm when she saw her son striding back into the reception area. She stood up and said, "What's wrong, Neal?"

"Nothing, Mom. It's okay. Dr. Huddleston has referred me to a specialist."

"Oh," she replied lamely at a loss for how else to respond.

Neal stopped at the narrow window when he saw her waving at him to come over. He took the card she handed him and said, "Thank you." He turned to his mom and handed her the card. "We're supposed to go there tomorrow."

She took the card and read it. "Queens, New York? You can't be serious, Neal!"

"Dr. Huddleston said this other doctor specializes in my type of case. I thought you'd be thrilled to have the best doctor on my case." He frowned slightly at his mother's unexpected reaction.

"But this is in New York. There's so much we'll have to do to get a place for us to stay while you're being treated. We'll need flights, a rental car, we'll have pack...did he say how long we'd be there?"

"Slow down, Mom. Dr. Huddleston said it would be an in-patient treatment so you won't be staying there. You should just stay here at home and I'll travel to New York to take care of this." He could see her dubious expression and it hurt his feelings. "Mom, I'm a big boy now. I can travel by myself."

"I'm just afraid something will happen and I'll lose you all over. I don't think I'd survive losing you again."

He put his arm around her shoulders and turned her toward the exit, "Come on, we can talk about this on the way home. Better yet, let's ask Dad what he thinks about the whole thing."

Jessica brightened at the thought of Neal, Sr. hearing Neal's idea and putting a stop to it before it went too far. At the very least, Jessica knew she would be flying to New York with Neal to make sure he arrived safely. She might even plan to spend the week there to do some shopping.

CHAPTER 25

Willian was feeling a little more than anxious to be on his way to Earth. He knew it was going to take some time to make all of the arrangements for his trip, yet he could not help but feel he was being lured to get to Jena sooner. Every waking moment, he felt himself being pulled as if by destiny. Never before had he felt such a strong urge to be near Jena and it made him anxious to be on his way.

He had mediated three more session and had received glowing marks from Rasa. She had even complimented him on his knowledge of Earth and the places he was likely to travel through. Rasa had told him there were two more scheduled mediations for him to handle the next day and after that, she was going to suggest to Elder Wilken that he be released from further study to go to Earth.

When he had heard the good news, he almost jumped for joy but managed to contain himself just before he made a fool of himself in front of Rasa. He never thought it possible, yet he had grown very fond of Rasa during the time he had been forced to work alongside her as an equal. He soon realized she had a very good grasp on local politics and an even better understanding of human interaction which made her very effective at helping people. He had a lot to learn from her stellar examples and was glad for the opportunity to work with her.

The issue with transportation and money was soon resolved. Rasa had told him she had arranged for a friend of hers to meet him in a place called Central Park. The friend had agreed to be his guide all the way to Florida where she would help him shop for clothes, get him registered for school, and help him find a place to stay.

It seemed everything was going to work out smoothly and efficiently so Willian had little to worry about other than Jena's reaction to seeing him again. Jena was going to be the wildcard of the whole trip. Willian was certain she was angry at him for the letters he had sent her. Because he had been working with mediation matters, he could easily see how he had taken the wrong tactic to try to win her back. He would definitely have to step up his game if he were to get back into her good graces.

Willian had just come inside from stretching his legs out in the gardens when he heard a familiar voice. He lengthened his stride to see what had happened to bring his mother to the Residence. When he rounded the corner he almost ran into the group of people talking.

"Mom," he called out.

"Oh, hello, Willian," Chelesa smiled and excused herself from the two people she had been talking with. She greeted her son with a big hug and then held him at arm's length to see how well he was faring. "You look great!"

"Thanks, Mom. What are you doing here? Is everything okay at home?"

"Yes, yes, everything's fine. I came to see Rasa on another matter, but I'm glad I got to see you before you left on your trip." She winked at him since she knew her statement downplayed the journey on which her son was about to embark. "I hear you are quite the successful mediator." She had heard of her son's accomplishments from several people already and her pride could barely be contained.

Willian smiled sheepishly and had to look away from his mother's face to try to keep from blushing from her lavish praise. He changed the subject by asking, "Are you staying for dinner?"

"Yes. In fact, I'll be spending the night tonight. Rasa has agreed to give me a tour of the Residence and the best parts of town. You know, I've never visited here before and it is very impressive. When you get back from your trip and come home, we'll have to compare notes on our impressions. There may be some things we should implement or change at home because of this experience." Chelesa knew she was babbling and did not even try to stop it; she was so excited to see her son.

"Okay," Willian said with a slight smile. His mom seemed jittery and happy at the same time. He was trying to figure out what she was not saying even though she had spoken so much. She was not the type of person to talk just to hear herself, this was a new side of her he had never seen.

"Oh, there's Rasa now. I've got to go, Willian. I'll see you at dinner." She leaned forward and pulled his head down so she could kiss his cheek and then she moved away to go greet Rasa.

Willian stood staring after his mom and wondering what was really going on. His mother was acting a bit too strange for his taste. Maybe this was going to be another lesson of Elder Wilken's. He decided in that moment to not say anything about his mother's behavior. He would simply watch and listen, as Elder Wilken had instructed, and see if he could come up with the answer himself. With his new plan in mind, he felt smug satisfaction at his self-control.

He greeted a few of the people he recognized in the hall before moving along to head to the study hall. There were still some aspects of Earth he wanted to research before he no longer had access to the information. His thought about school earlier had made him want to research the school system to see what he was getting himself into.

ON HIS WAY TO WORK, Riccan received a message on his telepod asking him to stop by and talk to his mother before work. He glanced at his timepiece and realized he would have to time it to work if he were to stop first. He shrugged his shoulders and reset the destination coordinates to his mother's house instead of work. Seldom did she ask anything of him and he was curious to find out what she wanted to discuss.

Unlike usual, Riccan landed the telepod and entered the Residence without being greeted by his mother on the balcony. More curious than ever, he hastened his steps to get to her office. The door was open and the room was empty. Baffled, he turned and went to his father's office where he found both parents seated together, deep in discussion which abruptly ended when they heard Riccan.

"Riccan, my boy!" Daven rose to give his son a hug in greeting.

"It's been forever since I've seen you, Dad. You must be keeping yourself busy!"

"Always! Here, have a seat. Your mother has some interesting news to share with you." He went back around his desk and resumed his usual seat. He sat back in the chair and waited for his wife to direct the conversation.

Riccan leaned down and kissed his mother's cheek before he sat in the vacant chair next to her. "Hi, Mom. What's going on?"

"I found out something about one of the names on the list you gave me of Ela Nena's business meetings. Apparently, this man, Faegan, is a very elusive man. Luckily there was a video of the award's ceremony and I was able to get a good picture of his face for the facial recognition program on your father's patil."

Riccan looked over at his dad with raised eyebrows and said, "I'd heard about that program becoming available, but I didn't know you had already gotten it. Is it really as good as it's been talked about?"

"This is the first time we've had need of it and it seemed to work perfectly. Come see for yourself," Daven said as he tapped the icon on the screen to pull up the program. He opened the search done by Nena and tipped his head out of the field of view so Riccan could see for himself.

Riccan whistled with appreciation. "That's really slick. It's definitely the same man!"

"Yes and I really wanted to be positive since what I discovered didn't go so well. His real name is Vanion and his usual companions leave a lot to be desired. Because he presented the award to Ela Nena, then it's safe to say, there's definitely something suspicious with the award she received." His mother's expression told him she was both pleased with her detective work as well as concerned for his safety.

"Jena came to the same conclusion last night," Riccan agreed.

Nena was shocked to hear about Jena's idea. She would ask her about it when they came to stay with them later in the mesan.

"What else did you learn about Vanion?" Riccan asked.

"That was the part which prompted me to have you come over before work. It appears Vanion is the right-hand man for Lucinden. So, you see, if he's involved, then nobody at your work is safe. Riccan, it's too dangerous for you to go back there. Maybe you should quit and focus more of your attention on your new family in Earth." Nena knew he would refuse, yet she could not help but ask.

"I have to see something through, first. I was actually already considering the idea of quitting after the last go-around with Ela Nena. Did you dig up anything else?"

"Don't you think what I found is enough?!"

"It definitely verifies what we were already thinking. Okay, well, if that's everything, then I should get going so I won't have to time it. Try not to worry, Mom. I'm on guard already so I will keep myself safe. I love you both." He kissed his mother again before he left the room and hurried back to his telepod.

Once he had parked the telepod on the roof of the Telepod Engineering Company, Riccan formulated a plan on the elevator ride down to his floor. When he got to his office, he shut his office door and turned on his patil. He looked at Ela Nena's calendar and discovered she was not going to be in any meetings for another hour. He sent her a quick message to ask if she had time to meet with him regarding an unusual matter.

Since he had flagged the message as urgent he did not have long to wait until he received an affirmative reply. She had typed the message back telling him to come up immediately. The actual message had been terse and rude, but Riccan chose to ignore the insult in favor of getting this meeting over with as fast as possible.

He locked his patil and returned to the hallway to wait for the elevator. Since he was waiting for it, it seemed to take forever to get to his floor again. Once inside, he had to stop at nearly every floor on the way back up to the thirteenth floor. Riccan did not even wait for the doors to open all the way before he pushed himself through the opening.

Several of the staff members were looking at him strangely for his hurrying, but he did not bother to explain himself. He marched directly to Ela Nena's office and knocked on the door with two sharp taps with his index finger's knuckle.

"Come!" Ela Nena called out.

"Thanks for seeing me on such short notice." Immediately upon entering the room he felt the same amount of power as he had felt in his home library. He had definite confirmation of there being a samara somewhere in the office. The question remained as to where the samara could be hidden and if Ela Nena had knowledge of its whereabouts.

"Get to the point, Riccan. I don't have all day."

Riccan turned around and looked at the cluster of awards and locked his gaze on the award presented by 'Faegan' and realized it was large enough to hide the samara inside. He started to go over toward it when Ela Nena spoke.

"Really, Riccan, I don't have time for you to admire my awards. Get to the point or get out of my office!"

He spun around and asked without thinking, "Have you ever heard of the samaras?"

"What? No! What are you babbling about?"

"The thirteen crystal skulls. Have you heard of them?" he persisted. The look of shocked horror on her face told him what he needed to know. "I have reason to believe one of those skulls is somewhere here in your office."

"Seriously, Riccan, did you take resh before you came to work today? I think you should leave before I fire you for insubordination." She started to rise from her desk in her growing anger.

Riccan was not to be deterred by her irrational mood. He was only going to get this one opportunity to prove his point. He walked over to the Annual Achievement award and picked it up. Immediately, he felt a familiar surge of energy almost as intense as his own samara gave him. He wondered how Ela Nena had held the award and not notice the power contained within.

"Put that down before you break it! Do you hear me? Put that down right now!" Ela Nena came around her desk to forcibly remove it from his hands.

Immediately Riccan examined the craftsmanship of the award to find out how the samara could be contained within. He noticed a small switch set very neatly into the side of the design. Ela Nena made a grab for the object just as Riccan pressed the lever. The front panel dropped open to expose the skull hidden within.

Ela Nena jerked her hands away, took a step back, and gasped in fear. "What did you do, Riccan? What kind of a trick is this? Get that thing out of my office. You brought that thing here to scare me, didn't you? Get out! Get out! Get out!" With each exclamation she backed further away from Riccan and the offending object.

"Do I have your permission to dispose of this?" Riccan asked calmly as he held up the samara still encased in the award's base.

"Yes! Get out of my office. Get out right now or you're fired!" she screamed.

The commotion inside the office had finally drawn the attention of the staff outside. People were starting to gather near the door trying to get a glimpse inside the narrow office window.

Riccan carefully closed the compartment to keep the contents secret from curious eyes. With the award tucked in close to his side, he walked to the door and put his hand on the knob. He turned back to Ela Nena and said, "Please don't tell anyone about what I found in here. There is already a bad stigma around this thing and you don't want people to think you had anything to do with it. People might think this was the cause of the explosion in the telepod trial last week."

With nothing more to say, Riccan opened the door and pushed his way through the crowd. He took the stairs up to the roof. Without breaking his stride, he hurried to get into his telepod. He palmed the side door closed even before he had taken a seat himself. Just as he entered the coordinates to return to his mother's house, he saw a stranger come out of the stairwell door and begin to cross the rooftop toward him.

Not wanting to have any type of confrontation or delay, Riccan pressed the activation button and blinked out of sight. Something did not feel right about the transfer and Riccan began to worry if he were going to arrive at his location in one piece. When the telepod popped back from between, Riccan immediately set the aircraft on the ground and powered everything down.

Thankful for the fact he had not had time to fasten his seatbelt, he jumped up, hit the door button on the dash as he grabbed the award, and rushed out of the telepod. He looked back at the telepod fully expecting it to implode. When another few seconds went by and nothing happened, he began to circle his craft to see if there were any visible flaws in the hull.

When he got to the far side of the telepod, he noticed something very strange. He stepped closer to see what the object on the side of the telepod could be. His curiosity instantly turned to anger as he realized the small object was a tracking device.

The man on the rooftop must have fired the tracker onto the vehicle just as it disappeared. The slight disturbance at that important juncture of the transfer had caused the whole telepod to vibrate unnervingly. Surely the guy would have known it could have killed Riccan. Then he had a disturbing notion that it might have been the unknown assailant's intention to make the transfer look like an accident.

Without hesitating another instant, Riccan grabbed the small metallic object off of the telepod. He could see the light was blinking which meant it was transmitting a signal. He definitely did not want to find out who would be coming over to finish the job. He dropped the tracker on the ground and crushed it with the heel of his shoe.

Riccan leaned over to check on the little electronic device to make sure it no longer functioned. To be certain all was safe, he concentrated on the remains and used a focused amount of elemy to incinerate the tracker. He looked up and glanced around the landing field hurriedly to be sure he had not been followed.

With a paranoid feeling, Riccan jogged across the landing field and took the stairs two at a time. He kept hurrying along until he had to stop because his mother stood in the middle of the hallway.

"What're you doing back here so soon? Did you quit?"

"No. I brought the award back here for you and Dad to see." He held out the object as if to prove a point.

"Your dad left a few minutes ago. Come into my office," she said as she turned and led the way.

He entered the office and set the award down on the desk for his mother to view. When he had her full attention, he touched the lever on the side panel. Riccan kept his eyes on his mother's face as the front piece of metal dropped forward and displayed the samara held within.

She looked up from the crystal in amazement and asked, "Did you know you were going to find this? Is this what Jena had figured out?"

"I had a suspicion this was the cause, and yes, Jena was the one who put the pieces together." He sat down on the edge of the desk near his mother and smiled with satisfaction. "Now we just have to figure out whose samara this is."

"How do you do that?" Nena asked curiously.

"We believe the samara's main aura color matches the birth crystal color of the proper handler. Why don't you check this one since auras are your specialty?"

"Okay. How exciting!" She only took a few seconds of concentration before she gasped. Her hands flew to her chest and she looked up at Riccan with wide eyes. "It's an orange yellow!"

"Isn't that the same as your birth crystal?" Riccan asked with eagerness. "Put your hands on it and see if it talks to you."

"Riccan that's the most foolish thing you've ever said. This samara was making Ela Nena do and say evil things and now you want me to just pick it up like it's a harmless, shiny object? No thank you!" She sat back in her chair and crossed her arms across her chest and tucked her hands to her sides.

"I can see you're scared. Maybe you and Dad should come over to my house tonight and we can discuss it further. Jena and Juila have done quite a bit of research on the samaras when they were living on Acaim. They may be able to help you understand what samaras are capable of and what they are not."

"I can agree with that suggestion. Besides, I've missed those girls and your lovely wife. I don't know why you never bring them over to visit," she teased.

"Okay then we're agreed, the two of you will come over after I get off of work. We'll have dinner together. I really have to get going. I'm going to take this home and put it in a safe place before I go back to work." He stood up and pushed the compartment closed as he picked up the award. Riccan still felt as though he were being followed or possibly in danger and he wanted to get to Earth as soon as possible.

Nena stood at the railing of the balcony and watched Riccan go out to his telepod. She wondered why he circled the craft so slowly before he got into it. She knew it was important to perform visual inspection before each flight, but Riccan seemed slightly obsessive in his examination of the hull which was different from his norm.

Riccan had to be certain there was no other tracking devices before he took the telepod to his home. He did not want to draw anybody dangerous to their house where his wife and children could be put into danger. Just the idea that he had unknowingly drawn attention to his parent's house was bad enough, he had to keep everyone safe. He took some solace in knowing the Residence had wards in place to keep violence from entering the house itself.

He entered his telepod and sat down in the pilot's seat. He placed the award in the seat next to him. Riccan waved at his mother and then activated the telepod. After selecting his home destination, he hit the activation button and waited anxiously for the transfer to finish. He breathed a sigh of relief when the telepod was, once again, shut down in the garage. Nothing had felt different on this transfer so he felt confident in getting out.

Riccan ran into Amanda as he was leaving the library after he had secreted the sixth found samara with the rest of them in the hidden room. "I'm surprised to see you still at home. I thought you were heading out today."

"I was just getting ready to leave. What are you doing home so early?" she asked as she gave him a warm hug.

"I found another samara," he replied casually to see how she would react. He was not disappointed.

"What? Seriously? Was it in Ela Nena's office?" Amanda pulled away from him and waited for his answers.

"Yes. I'll tell you all about it when I get home tonight. In fact, my parents are going to come over for dinner. I hope you don't mind my inviting them over. I wanted them to be able to talk to the girls about the myths and legends of the samaras."

"Great! The girls will be ecstatic to be able to visit with them. Dinner won't be a problem, either, because you're going to be making it tonight!"

"Wait, I thought you said you wanted to practice?"

"Oh, no you don't. I only practice on you, never on your parents. I don't want anyone to be able to accuse me of trying to kill them with my ineptitude."

Riccan threw back his head and laughed at her audacious statement. "Fine, I'll do dinner. Give me another kiss before I go." He pulled her over to him and bent down to kiss her deeply and thoroughly. "I love you!"

"I love you more."

"Thank you," he said with a slightly nasal tone as though it hurt him to have to say it. "I'll see you after work, love."

He chuckled even as he walked back through the house to go back to his telepod. The situation at work would probably be pretty tense when he returned and he was unsure how he was going to handle the questions which were sure to come. Without further delay, Riccan returned to work and hoped he still had a job after Ela Nena's outburst.

CHAPTER 26

Like a whirlwind, Neal and Jessica had their trip to New York arranged and they were sitting in First Class on the airplane. He hated to have to admit it, yet Neal had been anxious in the airport with all of the people swarming around him. When he was younger he had loved to travel so he had not expected to have any anxiety about this trip. Whatever had happened to him over the past seven years must have made more of an impression on him than he originally believed.

His breath came faster just thinking about the crowds he could expect in the John F. Kennedy Airport. The drive to the center did not even bear thinking about until the time came and he had no choice. The captain had just announced their imminent landing so he pulled the seatbelt tighter in anticipation of the wheels touching down on the ground. Neal had taken the window seat and could see they were almost on the ground. His hands went to the armrests where he unconsciously gripped them until his knuckles were white.

The pilot executed a perfect landing, much to Neal's relief. The plane taxied for a long time before it came to a stop in front of its assigned gate. As soon as the 'fasten seat belt' sign turned off there was a flurry of activity as everyone stood up and started gathering their personal belongings to disembark.

The door opened and Jessica moved into the aisle followed immediately by Neal. Once he retrieved his carry-on bag from the overhead compartment, he kept his gaze on his mother's back to keep from feeling overwhelmed by the press of people around him. They walked up the gangway directly into a throng of people waiting for the next flight.

"Hold my hand," Jessica said to Neal and reached toward her son. She knew it was a slightly overprotective gesture and yet she could not contain herself. As soon as she felt the pressure of her son's fingers around her own, she felt relieved.

As soon as he made physical contact with his mother, Neal felt himself relax. Together they followed the signs to the baggage claim. By the time they reached it, the belt was already moving and the luggage was being unloaded. Their only bag moved around the bend and Neal picked it off of the belt and set it on the ground beside them.

They moved with the crowd into the exit line before they went out to the curb to catch a taxi. Neal breathed a little easier once he was outside the building. He let his mother attract the attention of a driver while he stayed with the luggage.

Inside the taxi the driver asked, "Where to?"

"Creedmoor Psychiatric Center in Queens," Jessica replied with a clipped tone.

The taxi moved into the flow of traffic and they were on their way. The scenery along the way kept Neal's attention distracted from the end of the journey. He did not want to think, in another twenty minutes, his whole life would change.

Jessica's thoughts were mirroring her son's. She hoped he would find resolution with this new treatment program. At first she had had reservations about the change of doctors until she had done some research of her own. She had been quite impressed with Dr. Gascon's achievements and recognition for the advancement of psychiatric care.

The taxi pulled into a gated driveway and stopped at a guard shack. When the security guard asked them to state their business, Neal rolled down his window and told him his name. The guard looked through several sheets of paper on his clipboard before he located Neal's name.

"You're clear. Go on in," he said as he pressed the button to raise the wigwag so they could drive up to the entrance of the facility.

Neal got his first glimpse of the building as they rounded the circular entrance. Somehow he had thought the building would be more quaint and personal instead of this twenty story hulking structure. He had a serious case of nerves setting in and making his stomach feel queasy.

Jessica paid the driver and got out of the taxi. Neal opened the door next to him and met her at the trunk to get their two pieces of luggage out. The larger bag was his mother's and the carry-on was all he thought he would need for his stay in the facility. He hoped he would only need to be in the new doctor's care for a couple of weeks at the most.

The taxi drove away while Jessica and Neal walked into the front lobby. The wheel on the luggage got caught on the threshold of the door so Neal had to yank harder on the handle to get the bag inside. The exertion was a bit too much for it and the handle snapped off in his hand. The bag crashed down onto the floor and caused many people in the lobby to stare at them. Neal hastily righted the bag and felt foolish for having caused a scene.

Jessica felt sorry for her son's discomfiture. She had been checking out the lobby's décor and had missed the whole incident until the noise startled her and caused her to look as well. She waited for Neal to catch up to her and they walked through the lobby together.

The receptionist was a friendly young woman who smiled up at them and said, "Welcome to Creedmoor. How can I help you?"

"My name is Neal Taivas and I'm scheduled to be treated by Dr. Gascon."

The lady nodded as she typed his information into her computer. She gathered up several pieces of paper and put them on a clipboard which she handed over to Neal. "Please fill out these documents and sign here, here, and here." She flipped over the pages and drew an x where he needed to sign.

"Thanks," Neal replied as he took the clipboard and looked around for a place to sit down.

"Let's go over here," Jessica offered. She wanted to be near the windows so she could see the landscaping while Neal was busy. She helpfully took charge of the carry-on so Neal would only have to worry about the larger piece.

He still held the broken handle in his hand and wondered what he should do with it. Neal kneeled and unzipped the front pocket of the suitcase and shoved the handle inside before zipping it back up. Now his hand was free to roll the bag across the marble floor to where his mother had taken a seat in the sun next to the oversized window.

Once seated, Neal turned the clipboard so the light from outside shone onto it. He pulled the pen off of the clip and began answering all of the questions regarding his personal history. Several of the questions made him chuckle since he had to write down that he did not know what he did not know which seemed ridiculous.

Tapping his pen on the clipboard as he considered how to answer the last question, Neal looked over to his mother and asked, "How would you describe my behavior in the past seven days?"

Jessica smiled and replied, "Tired and hopeful."

Neal nodded agreement and wrote it down and then scribbled his signature on the last form. "Done! Let's get this show on the road!" He stood up and strode across the lobby and handed the clipboard back to the receptionist.

"Go ahead and take a seat and I'll let the doctor know you're ready."

"Thanks." He turned around and went back to sit next to his mother.

"How are you feeling, honey?" She put her hand on his knee and leaned forward with concern.

"Can you think of a word which combines: nervous, anxious, scared, and excited?" Neal chuckled and it sounded off even to his own ears.

"I think I'd call that human! You're doing the right thing, Neal. Dr. Gascon is very well respected in the psychiatric community. I did quite a bit of research on him last night and even your dad was impressed with his list of accomplishments. The biggest hurdle is your willingness to participate and, since you're here, then I think you'll do just fine."

"I couldn't have said it better myself," a man interrupted them as he stopped in front of them and held out his hand to Neal. "I'm Dr. Gascon and I'm assuming you must be Neal?"

Neal scrambled to stand up and shake the doctors hand as he said, "Yes, sir. I'm pleased to meet you, Dr. Gascon. This is my mother, Jessica Taivas." He nodded down to where his mother was still seated.

"A pleasure meeting you," Dr. Gascon said even though he made no gesture to shake her hand or even to look at her past a brief glance. In fact, he had no interest whatsoever in anyone other than Neal and he made his opinion quite obvious. Still looking at Neal he said, "Come on back and we'll get you set up in your room. I've arranged your first session in fifteen minutes."

"Great! Come on, Mom," Neal said as he picked up his carry-on and started to follow the doctor who had already started across the lobby.

"I'm sorry, Neal, no visitors are allowed. Your mother will have to say goodbye to you out here." The doctor stopped to wait for them to comply with his order.

Neal became flustered for the first time. He had imagined his mother would accompany him to his room and be able to see the facility where he would be staying. He had no idea they would be separated so soon and he felt his heart race as he began to have a panic attack.

"It's okay, Neal. I should be getting to the hotel before they give my room to someone else. I'll come by to see you tomorrow," Jessica said reasonably as she leaned forward to hug and kiss him.

"I guess I didn't make myself clear regarding Neal's treatment. He will not be allowed any visitors until I have determined his mental status. If you will not abide by my rules, then you will have to seek alternative mental health care." He looked down at his watch and sighed at how long this distraction was taking.

"Oh," Jessica said with a slightly affronted tone at the insult. "Of course we'll agree. We just weren't told any different until right this moment. I love you, Neal. Do your best and we'll have you home in no time." She gave him another quick hug for good measure.

"I love you too, Mom. I'll do my best." He already felt bad for the way they were being separated and he really did not care for the tone in which the doctor had spoken to his mother. Without wanting to delay the doctor any longer he turned and met the doctor who then resumed his brisk pace until they reached the elevator.

Dr. Gascon silently appraised his new patient as he pressed the button for the elevator. He could tell Neal would be headstrong and possibly difficult to work with. He began revising his initial plan of action even as the doors opened and they stepped into the small interior space. The doors shut leaving the two of them alone together.

"You didn't have to speak like that to my mother, you know."

"I don't have time to worry about people's feelings getting hurt. My only concern is for your mental well-being and I can only take care of that by having our sessions begin."

Neal frowned slightly at the doctor's explanation. As a psychiatrist he should understand the interpersonal relationships of a family would be highly beneficial to a positive outcome. If the doctor were willing to separate them so brashly, then did he really have his best interest in mind? His mother would be in town until the end of the week and Neal decided he would leave the facility if it were not as he expected, after all, it was not as if he were being committed.

CHAPTER 27

Amanda set her telepod down in the Port of Cresdon landing field. She had sent a message ahead letting Barla know she was coming in for a visit so she was pleased to see Barla waiting for her on the edge of the field. As she walked away from the telepod, she hit the cloaking button on her remote.

Barla came forward and gave her a warm hug which Amanda gladly reciprocated. She kept her arm around Amanda's waist as she turned them toward home and began walking. "I'm assuming you're here to make arrangements for Vinia to meet with her children?"

"Something like that. I also have a proposition for you as well. We can talk about it more once we get back to your house." Amanda looked around casually to make sure they were out of earshot of anyone else.

Barla nodded approval of her caution and changed the conversation. "How are your children adjusting to their new life with you and Riccan?"

"They're remarkable, Barla. They haven't really missed a beat even with their whole lives being turned upside down. I don't think I could do as well!" Amanda shook her head in wonder as she thought of her girls.

"I thought so as well when I was raising them. I never knew what they were going to get into, but they were so fun to watch. Most of the time I didn't even have the heart to punish them when they really got into things," Barla chuckled as she recalled their antics.

They both were laughing as they went up the front stairs to Barla's house. Just as Barla reached to open the front door it opened for them. Barla looked slightly guilty as she smiled at Vinia and said, "Surprise! Amanda came over to see you."

"I wondered why you had to leave so suddenly. Come in, Amanda! Please tell me you have news of my children," she gushed as she stepped to the side so the two other women could enter the house. She shut the door behind them and almost walked on their heels as they went down the hallway and into the living room.

"I do have news for you. Maybe not everything you wanted, but it's a start for sure." Amanda sat down in one of the wing chairs by the fireplace and waited for Vinia to sit down across from her before she continued. "Valentina and Behn are going to meet with you. They haven't told Jon anything about their past or you because he doesn't remember anything from that time. You'll recall he was very ill when you sent him to Earth and it seems he had a fever which made it hard for him to recall anything of when he was young."

"Oh my goodness. Do you think Val and Behn will let me see him eventually?" Vinia held her hand over her mouth in anticipation of hearing Amanda's answer.

"Most likely. Valentina isn't convinced you are their mother and she doesn't want to get Jon's hopes up for a false alarm," Amanda explained.

"That's understandable I guess. When can I go to meet with them?" She was ready to jump up immediately and go if Amanda said the word.

"I wondered if you would want to come back with me today. I'd understand if you wanted more time to think about it and to make arrangements for Danika."

"No, I want to go now. Barla?" She turned to face her host and said, "You offered to watch Danika when the time came. Are you still okay with that arrangement?"

"Absolutely! Don't worry a bit about me or your baby." Barla smiled at the idea of taking care of another youngster by herself.

Vinia stood up and said, "I need to get some things together so we can go!"

Before Amanda could stop her, she was already out of the room. The two women smiled at one another as they could hear her loud footsteps on the stairs as she raced up them two at a time. "I guess that went well. I only hope she's not too disappointed when she finally meets her children. They're not the little kids she remembers from an anon ago and Valentina is really angry with her for sending them away. She doesn't understand why their mother would do that to them. She won't listen to my explanation. Vinia definitely has an uphill battle to win back their affections."

"It'll all work out, I feel confident about it. While Vinia's away, tell me how your search for the other samaras is going."

Amanda was not expecting the change in subject and blurted, "Riccan brought one home this morning!"

"Really? Whose is it?"

"We don't know yet. Daven and Nena are going to come over after Riccan gets off of work and we'll probably figure it out then."

"Are you bringing Vinia back home before then? Would it be wise for her to see the samaras?"

"One of them was in her care, but I see what you mean. I can arrange for Vinia to be with her children when we're working with the new samara. If not, then I'll figure something else out. Besides, I don't think Vinia will be thinking about much of anything other than her missing kids."

"You're right about that, she's been walking on eggshells since your last visit. It will be a relief for her to be able to have some closure in the matter."

"Speaking of closure, Barla, I wanted to ask you a question. Do you want to come to Earth as well to meet with my mother? She has been asking if you would come."

"I don't know, Amanda. The thought of traveling through the veil still scares me. What if I were to lose my memory of my time here? I'm not sure it would be worth it." Barla shivered at the idea of not remembering her husband, son, daughter, and life as she knew it in Tuala. She had the perfect life and she had never regretted staying in Tuala even though her family had believed she had drowned so long ago.

"Rasa has assured me you'd be safe from that issue since you have received your birth crystal," Amanda pointed out.

"Thanks to you and your generosity," Barla replied with a delighted grin on her face as her hand automatically went up to the special crystal-laden tree-of-life pendant suspended from her neck.

"I only asked for it. Jehoban was the generous one for granting my petition," Amanda demurred.

"Even so, I'd like to think on your proposal for a while longer yet. You understand, don't you?" Barla entreated her.

"Absolutely, Barla. I don't want to pressure you, I just want you to know you have a standing offer to come over whenever you decide. Please don't let fear keep you from having everything. Jehoban wouldn't have given it to you if he didn't want you to have everything back in your life. You know that, right?"

"I do in my heart, but my mind is still fearful. I'm sure given a bit more time for adjustment and then I'll be able to take you up on your offer. Thank you."

"You're very welcome. You were very kind to my children and you are my aunt, after all. We are family!"

"It's still so hard to believe. I'm so thankful." She smiled endearingly to Amanda.

Vinia came bursting back into the room with her travel bag in hand. Slightly breathless from the quick trip, Vinia announced, "I'm ready to go!"

Amanda could not help laughing at her eagerness. She shook her head and said, "The kids are still in school for a few more hours. We have some time yet."

Vinia looked crestfallen and her shoulders drooped with disappointment.

"We can still leave now if you want. I just wanted you to know the kids won't be waiting for us when we get there."

Eagerness returned to her expression and she said, "I'd like to go now. I've been worried about Petre ever since I saw him in the market. The sooner I get some distance from him, the better I'll feel. I'd say Earth is a pretty big distance, wouldn't you?"

Barla and Amanda both began laughing until they cried. Vinia eventually had to laugh as she realized how silly her statement had been even though she had not intended to be funny in any way. By the time they all were able to look at one another without beginning another round of giggles, the mood in the room had lightened.

Amanda stood up and said, "Okay, let's get you to Earth. Thank you,

Barla, for everything. I'm not sure if it'll be tonight or tomorrow before I bring Vinia home. Will that still work for you?"

"Take your time and don't worry about me. Send me a message if you get delayed."

"Sounds good," Amanda said as she gave Barla a quick embrace.

The three of them walked to the front door where Barla stayed behind to watch over the sleeping Danika. Amanda and Vinia continued down the front steps and up the road to get back to the landing field. They were talking excitedly about their journey.

Neither woman noticed the man watching them from the distance.

CHAPTER 28

The flight home had been uneventful for Amanda and the scariest, longest ride ever for Vinia. She had not known the flight would be longer due to the difference in the two worlds. When they reemerged into the garage she cried out in relief.

Amanda looked over at Vinia to see what happened. The look on her face told her everything she needed to know. Amanda immediately said, "Oh, Vinia! I'm so sorry. I forgot to tell you this trip would be longer. You must have thought we were going to be lost between. It was so careless of me. Please say you'll forgive me." She swiftly unbuckled and turned in the seat to face Vinia.

Vinia took another couple of deep breaths to compose herself. She finally nodded and said, "There's nothing to forgive. I'm sure all of my chatter kept you from even thinking of telling me. Besides, here we are." She looked around the bleak concrete structure of the garage and wondered what type of world she had sent her children into.

Amanda also looked out and realized what Vinia must be thinking and she started to laugh. "Don't worry, Vinia. This world looks much nicer than the inside of this building. Get unbuckled and I'll show you around the estate."

Vinia complied immediately. The sooner she felt comfortable in this world, the easier it would be to concentrate solely on her children when they came to see her for the first time. At least she assumed they would come see her, maybe Amanda had arranged another meeting place. She was about to ask when she changed her mind. She would wait for Amanda to tell her.

They left the telepod and the garage. Vinia was much more impressed with the interior of the house. It was by far the most elegant and luxurious place she had ever seen, even better than Captain Ahn and Barla's house. She had always thought they were rich beyond anything she could ever hope for herself.

Amanda enjoyed showing Vinia around the house, but she was even more excited to show her the grounds outside. She knew the money Riccan had spent on landscaping had made a spectacular paradise and she eagerly anticipated Vinia's reaction to its beauty. When she opened the side door off of the living room, Vinia reacted even better than Amanda could have imagined.

"Do my kids live in a place which looks like this?"

"No. Their house is very nice, but there aren't many places around here which are quite this nice. Riccan has outdone himself on creating this oasis."

"Oh," Vinia said simply.

"Do you swim?" Amanda hastily asked, wanting to change the subject before the mood became awkward.

"I haven't for a very long time. Besides, I didn't think to bring a bathing suit."

"That's no bother. I have lots of them. We could take a quick dip, then relax in the warm sun while we wait. It'll help pass the time."

"Okay, it sounds like fun."

They returned to the house where Amanda brought out several suits from which Vinia could choose. Once they were both properly attired, Amanda had towels for both of them, and they went outside to get some sun.

Vinia turned into a young girl again as they splashed around in the pool until they were exhausted. After longer than Amanda would have guessed they dragged themselves out of the pool and practically melted onto the lawn chairs to let the sun dry their bodies.

Amanda had closed her eyes since the glare of the sun made it hard to keep them open. The slight breeze and the heat from the sun seeped into her body making her quite relaxed and sleepy. After some time had passed Amanda saw Vinia had in fact fallen asleep. She did not want her to get a sunburn so Amanda got up and quietly covered Vinia with a towel and repositioned the beach umbrella stand so it shaded her face and torso.

Amanda realized she had some details to take care of so she went into the house. She dug in the drawer for a piece of paper before she picked up the phone and dialed the number of the school from the flyer. The receptionist answered her call on the second ring.

"Hi. This is Amanda Stel. I'd like to speak with my daughter, Juila Stel. Yes, I know she's in class right now. Yes, this is an emergency. Thank you, I'll hold." Amanda rolled her eyes at the receptionist's stupid statements and waited for Juila to be taken out of class. Several minutes passed. Amanda kept watching Vinia outside to make sure she stayed asleep.

"Mom? Are you okay? What's wrong?" Juila asked.

"Hi, honey. It's okay, nothing's wrong. The receptionist wouldn't get you out of class unless it was an emergency, which I guess it technically could be. Anyway, I have Vinia here at the house. Can you get Behn and Valentina to come home with you to meet her?"

Juila gasped at her mother's news. When she had told her mother the night before that Valentina had agreed, she had no idea that Vinia would come so soon. Even so, she could not find any reason to delay the meeting so she answered, "I'll let them know. I hope everything works out okay. Thanks, Mom."

"I know you have to get back to class. Sorry I worried you. Have a great rest of the day. I love you."

"I love you, too."

Amanda waited until she heard the line disconnect on the other end before she pressed the end button on her receiver. She looked over at the clock and knew there were still several hours to go before they would be home. After grabbing two glasses of ice water, Amanda returned to her spot in the sun and took a nap alongside Vinia.

Juila had a hard time finding the right time to tell Valentina about the upcoming meeting. Mostly she did not want to have to deal with the scene she was certain Valentina would make. She took the coward's way out and asked Behn if they were planning on coming over to study after school. When he told her that was their plan, she was vastly relieved.

Behn looked at her with a strange expression. He knew something was up, but he had no idea what it might be. He knew Juila would tell him eventually so he let it go for the time being. When school was over Behn met Juila at her locker and said, "Do you and Jena want to ride with me and Val to your house?"

"Of course! Why are you asking?" Juila turned to face him with a puzzled expression.

"I just thought I should ask since you were being so cryptic earlier. Do you mind telling me what that was all about?" He decided he would rather ask her about it now when they had a little privacy.

Juila looked furtively around them to make sure Valentina was nowhere around before she leaned close to his ear and whispered, "My mom called during class. She has your mother at our house."

Behn's eyes grew big and round as he heard the news. This was nothing like what he had been imagining. He also glanced around before he said, "Are you serious? Val is going to be so mad that we didn't fore-warn her!"

"That's what I was thinking and I didn't want to make a scene at school. I know how she feels about people feeling sorry for you guys for being adopted."

Behn had no idea Juila had known about Valentina's deep-seated fear of not fitting in. Normally, Valentina hid her insecurity well. Juila must either be really receptive or Valentina had told her, either way, it was significant.

He began to work through the different scenarios in his head of how this situation should be handled. If they told Valentina while they were at school, she would probably opt to take the bus home instead of having the meeting even though she had agreed to it. If they told her in the car on the way to the Stel house, she would probably insist on being taken home. They could tell her in the Stel driveway, but then she would feel as though she were being set up. Lastly, if they walked her into Juila's house and she saw their mother standing there, she would probably feel betrayed and ambushed.

Behn shook his head at the dilemma. "There doesn't really seem to be any good way to go about this with Val."

Juila had been listening to his thoughts and had to agree with his final assessment. "Now you know why I was having a hard time earlier. You know Val better than any of us. I was hoping you'd have some way of diffusing the situation."

"What situation?" Jena asked as she came up to the locker and saw Behn and Juila with their heads together. She had been thinking about her homework and had not been linked to Juila's mind so she felt slightly left out. In an instant, Juila gave her a mental image of the conversation and she merely said, "Ah!" Jena chewed on her bottom lip as she concentrated on a possible solution.

"What do you mean 'ah'?" Behn asked as he saw Jena look guiltily at Juila.

Juila shrugged and explained as simply as possible, "Jena and I can link our minds and share thoughts instantly. I thought you knew that already."

"I didn't know it was that quick," Behn said. He realized every moment they had ever shared had probably been linked with Jena. He blushed as he considered all of the foolish and sappy things he'd ever said to Juila. It was rather disconcerting to think there had been another person basically listening in to every word they'd ever shared. "Are you always linked?" he asked, hoping to hear a negative answer.

Juila had, once again, been listening in to Behn's inner thoughts and she chuckled at where he had gone. She saw his expression of concern and she answered, "Not always. We do have respect for each other's privacy."

Behn instantly looked relieved.

Juila had to turn her head away so Behn would not see her grin. She busied herself with gathering a few items out of her locker to give herself a few seconds to compose her expression. When she believed she had herself under controlled she announced, "Let's get going. I'd like to get this afternoon over with."

Behn agreed with Juila on the one hand and yet he dreaded Valentina's reaction. The three of them walked out to the car where they met both Jon and Valentina at the car. None of them were expecting to see Jon.

"I'm hoping you won't mind dropping me off at home," Jon stated with his hands resting on the top of the car.

"No problem, hop in," Behn said as casually as he could. He only hoped Valentina would not get the idea she could go home when they stopped off there. His fears proved unfounded as Jon got out of the car and Valentina made no move to get out. Behn felt as though one hurdle had been crossed, but the finish line seemed a long way away and the biggest hurdle had yet to be crossed.

Valentina waited until Jon had gotten out until she said, "I'd like to know why everyone is acting so strange. What's going on?"

Behn busied himself with watching the traffic so he could pull back onto the road. He thought about playing dumb for a little longer until he looked in the rear-view mirror and saw his sister glaring at him. He swallowed around the suddenly dry spot in his throat. Waiting until he was back in the flow of traffic, Behn said, "Mrs. Stel has a guest at the house."

Valentina looked confused for a moment until she comprehended Behn's cryptic remark. Immediately she felt a flush of anger overtake her thoughts which she immediately turned to curiosity. She recognized she was scared of meeting their mother, but she had to eventually get it over with. Besides, if this woman turned out not to be their mother, then it would be an inconsequential meeting. It would be interesting to meet someone else from Tuala.

The occupants of the car were all on edge waiting for the explosion from Valentina which never came. Somehow the explosion would have been easier to deal with than the continued silence.

Jena could take it no longer and said, "What are you going to do, Val?"

"Me? What do you mean? We're going to meet this woman and see if she's who she claims to be. If she is, then I'm finally going to get to ask her why she abandoned us," Valentina stated simply.

Juila and Behn exchanged puzzled expressions of disbelief before they both turned their heads to look straight out the front windshield. Everyone remained silent for the remainder of the drive. Each person's mind was racing with the upcoming possibilities as the car pulled to a stop in front of the Stel house.

Behn turned off the engine and pulled the keys out of the ignition. He looked at his sister in the rear-view mirror and said, "Are you ready?"

"As ready as we'll ever be!" Valentina announced as she opened the rear door and got out of the car.

Behn had to hurry to keep up with her. He did not want her to be the first to see the woman who could possibly be their mother. It felt slightly rude to leave the twins behind them since this was their house, yet Valentina continued to march toward the front door so he walked faster.

Jena and Juila purposely held themselves back. They did not want to interfere with this moment. They held hands for comfort as they both agreed this could turn ugly pretty quick if Valentina lost her temper.

CHAPTER 29

Amanda looked at the clock in the kitchen and knew the kids would be home any minute. She glanced over at Vinia who had changed her clothes and had seated herself on the couch in the living room and wondered how the impending meeting would go. She walked over to the living room and asked, "Have you thought about what you're going to say to the kids when you first see them again?"

Vinia wrung her hands in her lap and chewed on her bottom lip before she answered, "I've thought of a million things to say to them, but I'm afraid I'll just be dumbstruck when I see how different they look since I last saw them."

Amanda nodded, understanding completely. She had felt the same way when Jehoban had told her the twin girls she had been sitting across from had been her own daughters. So much the same since she had expected her girls to be about nine years old when they were actually fifteen. Vinia faced the same scenario as she had sent her children away when they were seven and now they were sixteen.

The sound of car doors shutting outside alerted both of them that the time had come for them to find out what would happen. Vinia stood up and pulled nervously at the hem of her shirt. She did not know what to do with her hands so she kept shifting them from her sides to holding them in front of her. She moved away from the couch so she would have an unobstructed view of the front door.

Amanda was unsure of what she should do so she held back to allow the family to have their reunion without interference. She hoped the girls had forewarned Valentina. She equally hoped the girl would have enough sense to let their mother tell them what happened before she tore into her for leaving them.

The door opened and Valentina and Behn stood on the threshold staring across the distance to the woman who may or may not be their mother. Everyone stepped forward since nobody could see the features since the lighting fell behind both sides with the windows. The kids walked across the foyer and both stopped before they were fully into the living room.

Behn rapidly glanced from Vinia to Amanda and back again. He could hardly believe how much the two women looked alike. When he had first met Juila's mother, he had the impression she looked similar, but now the similarity shocked him.

The tension in the room eased when Jena spoke, "Oh my goodness! You two could be twins!"

Vinia shifted her gaze over to Amanda and smiled nervously. She stepped forward and said, "Hello, Behn. Hello, Valentina. I know it's been a long time for you since you saw me last," she hesitated when Valentina snorted at the understatement. She continued valiantly, "But it has only been a little while for me. I'd like the chance to get to know you again."

As soon as Behn heard her voice his last shred of doubt drifted away, he knew this was his mother. He rushed forward and wrapped his arms around her. It felt strange to be taller than she since the last time he had seen her he had been so much smaller than she. Only familiarity over-came him as he felt his mother return his embrace. Tears of joy formed in his eyes and he held her tighter.

Vinia also began to cry even as she wished Valentina would come to her as well. She did not want to end the embrace and yet she wanted to have a good look at her tall, handsome son. She kept her hands on his arms as she held him away from her so she could look into his eyes. The love she saw reflected in his brown eyes relieved her. At least one of her children would forgive her for letting them go.

His mother's gaze turned away from himself and shifted over to

Valentina. Behn felt her hands tighten on his arms and he knew she was anxious for his sister to also accept her. To his amazement he saw Valentina's expression change. Before he knew what was happening, his sister brushed him away.

Valentina could not understand the memories as they rushed through her. All she knew was the need she had for her mother was overwhelming and she needed to feel her in her arms. She stepped forward and hugged Vinia as if her life depended upon it. As her mother's sobs renewed, Valentina knew this woman would give her life to protect her children.

Juila and Jena had entered the house after their guests and had shut the front door. They went to stand beside their mother and felt tears of joy at the heartfelt reunion they had witnessed. Amanda put her arms around each of them and pulled them closer to her. So far everything had worked out better than expected.

Eventually everyone had taken a seat in the living room. Behn and Valentina sat on either side of their mother. At first, conversation had been awkward as nobody said anything and then everyone tried speaking at the same time. The tension broke as everyone laughed at how ridiculous the situation seemed.

"Tell me about Jon and your adoptive family. I want to know everything!" Vinia requested.

"Jon doesn't remember anything. He has no idea where we come from or even what your name is," Valentina began. "We've been very protective of him."

"As I knew you would be," Vinia said as she nodded approval.

"We were taken in pretty rapidly by the Wilson family. We've had a great life, they have always treated us as if we were their own," Behn added.

"I'm so thankful. Someday I'd like to meet the Wilsons and tell them how much I owe them for loving my precious children."

"I have a confession to make," Valentina began.

"I know you were mad at me, Val. I understand you were young and confused."

"It's not just that, I hated you for abandoning us." Valentina held up her hand as she saw her mother start to object. "I know it wasn't true now. I remember the reason you sent us away. It wasn't just Jon in danger, it was me too."

"What are you saying, Val?" Behn asked.

"Mom was keeping me safe from Grobin. He was going to force me to marry him even though I was only seven," Val explained simply and without any emotion. None of it really felt like it was her life she was talking about, more as if it were a movie plot.

"Mom, is that true?" Behn shifted his gaze to his mother's face and saw her nod in agreement. "That sick, sadistic bastard! She was just a child! What was he thinking?"

"He had a twisted mind. I think the community was too closely related and it was starting to cause the people to not be right in the head."

"Are you saying they were inbred?" Behn asked in disgust.

"I'm afraid so. They feared outsiders and encouraged the people to marry only within the community. It was bound to happen over time. I think Grobin saw Val as new blood, kind of a way to refresh the genetic pool." Vinia struggled to try to explain.

"It almost sounds as if you're making excuses for him," Behn accused.

"There's no excuse for Grobin, Behn, I can just see how he would view my children. He was threatened by you and Jon because there were too many men already, but Valentina could help save their way of life. Obviously I didn't agree with him because I sent all of you away to keep you safe."

"Thank goodness! You did the right thing, Vinia. It was probably the hardest thing you'll ever have to do," Amanda said. She wanted to give Behn a few moments to compose himself before he said something he would regret later.

Vinia nodded her thanks to Amanda. She hoped her children would see it the same way. To them, they had been sent away, abandoned to a strange place, and left alone to fend for themselves. She had never thought they would grow up without her.

Behn kept his peace, but his mind was made up; he would make Grobin pay for separating their family and making them grow up without their mother. His usually peaceful mind began devising all kinds of ways to make the miserable excuse of a man suffer for his depravity. Time became irrelevant as he knew, one day, he would exact his revenge.

"What are we going to do about Jon? Eventually he'll have to be told the truth. Do you think he's strong enough to know?" Vinia asked. She desperately wanted to know what he looked like as well. Today's reunion had only been marred by her other child's absence.

"I'll figure something out," Valentina said and then she saw her brother's face and amended her statement to, "We'll figure something out between us."

"Where are you living now?" Behn asked.

Vinia wished she could tell them she was better off than she was. She had to tell them the truth, "We're living with Captain Ahn and Barla for the time being."

"We? Who else is there? Are you married?" Valentina asked in a rush. She had never known who her own father had been and wondered if their mother had married him eventually.

"No, I've never married. The other person is your half-sister, Danika." Vinia hated to admit her failure in having all of her children out of wedlock. Circumstances out of her control had seen to her folly.

"Sister? I have a sister? How old is she?" Valentina had always wanted a sister. Having two brothers never seemed as good as having a sister of her very own.

"I was pregnant with her when you all went away. She's eight mesans old now."

Valentina went silent as she reviewed her memories. She did recall her mother's waist being thickened. Never had she dreamt it was because there was another sibling on the way. "Wow. I'd like to meet her sometime."

"There's nothing I'd like better than for all of my children to be together," Vinia said as tears coursed down her cheeks.

Amanda had an inspired idea and snapped her fingers suddenly, catching everyone's attention. "Why don't I take you all to Barla's house for a reunion?" She had not known how she was going to clear out the house for when Daven and Nena were going to come over. She only had a short time left before they would be arriving. This was the perfect solution for everyone involved.

Vinia looked from one child to the other to see if they were willing. When both of them nodded excitedly, she began to cry tears of joy. Valentina and Behn both hugged her and her world exploded with happiness.

"Let's go right now," Amanda suggested with some urgency. She turned to her own daughters and whispered, "Your father's parents are coming here for dinner tonight. I'll explain it all when I get back."

~

JENA AND JUILA stayed behind while Amanda rushed everyone into her telepod. Amanda sped through the startup procedures in anticipation of someone changing their mind and deciding to stay at their house rather than going to Tuala. Amanda needed the house cleared out and yet she did not want this reunion to be marred or cut short in any way.

"I've got everything entered to go. Is everyone ready?" Amanda asked out of courtesy. When she heard the chorus of assent she hit the activation button and they were on their way. The telepod entered the airspace above the landing field in Cresdon. She set down the aircraft with expert skill and powered it down. She hit the door button on the console and announced the obvious, "Here we are!"

Behn and Valentina were both antsy with anticipation. The only times they had been to Tuala in their recent memory was the field trips to their ancestral home in the Roanoke Colony. They had never seen any towns nor any other people for that matter. They unbuckled their seatbelts and exited the telepod. They stood staring around them in wonder while their mother and Amanda joined them.

Amanda palmed the door closed and cloaked the telepod as she led the way back to Barla's house as fast as she dared.

Vinia walked with her arms around each of her children. She could tell they were in awe of their surroundings and she wished she could be showing them to a home of her own rather than someone else's. She mentally shrugged since she had no control over the circumstances which had led her to be living with Barla. Hopefully her future would bring Nealan back to her and they could all live together.

Amanda was the first to the house and she knocked on the front door and waited. The rest of her group joined around her. They could hear movement in the house.

Barla opened the door with Danika held in her arm. The look on her face was precious as she took in the familiar and unfamiliar faces. "Come in," she said with alacrity.

Vinia came forward and took Danika out of Barla's arms. She turned with pride toward her first-born daughter and presented the child. "This is your sister, Danika."

Valentina held out her finger to touch Danika's chubby little fist. "She's so cute, Mom!"

Behn pushed his way out of the door so Barla could get it shut behind them. He was also interested in his little sister, but he was distracted by the style of the house around them. He knew he would have time to get to know Danika so he let Valentina have the infant's attention first while he looked around in fascination.

Barla caught Amanda's sleeve and leaned over to whisper, "It appears everything went well! I didn't expect you back tonight."

"I can't stay since Daven and Nena are probably at my house by now. I'll come back later tonight to get Behn and Valentina. I hope you don't mind me dumping everyone off here so unexpectedly."

"Don't worry about it. I'm glad everything has worked out for Vinia. Go on, I'll let everyone know you had to go and tell them you'll be back." Barla opened the door enough for Amanda to exit and then closed the door again. She could not shake the feeling of being watched ever since the girls had left that morning. She peeked out the side window to watch Amanda trot back up the sidewalk back to the landing field.

CHAPTER 30

Amanda made it back to the house in record time. Still, there was another telepod in the garage when she parked her own. She had predicted they would arrive before she did and she had been correct. She could feel the drain of too much travel in one day and yet her day was far from over. She took a deep breath, straightened her shoulders, and went into the house to greet her guests.

Daven and Nena must have just arrived since they were still standing in the kitchen with Jena and Juila. Hugs and greetings were exchanged and Amanda suggested they get more comfortable in the living room where they all sat down. Riccan arrived home as soon as they were seated so everyone rose again and the greetings were repeated for him as well.

Riccan went upstairs to change clothes while everyone resumed their original seats. He rushed up to his room and made record time getting into a more comfortable outfit. As he came down the stairs he showed off slightly by creating their meal on the kitchen counter.

Amanda, whose back had been to the kitchen, smelled the aromas of the food and turned to investigate. She caught movement out of the corner of her eye and mouthed the words 'show off' to Riccan as he breezed through the living room to the kitchen. "It looks as though dinner is ready," Amanda announced.

They had a buffet style service where everyone served themselves.

Once the plates were full, they trailed into the dining room and set their plates down. As soon as everyone was in the room, Daven said grace for their meal and then they took their places at the table.

Dinner was a simple affair of several styles of foxl, two side dishes, and dessert. Riccan received compliments from the group on the tasty flavors of the meat. Conversation centered mostly on the food as well as what was going on with the girls at school.

Nena was most intrigued by the differences of education on Earth compared to what the girls were familiar with back home. They chatted continually on their end of the table while the other three adults remained suspiciously silent.

When the meal was finished, Riccan used a small amount of elemy to clear the dishes away. He had also cleaned up the kitchen leftovers in the same manner. "I think we should retire to the living room to discuss what is really on everyone's mind," Riccan suggested.

The girls looked at one another in confusion and followed their parents and grandparents to the living room. They wondered what could be going on since their mother had not had time to explain before their grandparents had arrived. They sat down across from the adults and waited to see what the topic of conversation would turn out to be.

Riccan started the conversation by looking at the girls and saying, "My mom sent me a message this morning asking me to stop by their house since she had found some useful information for me." He turned his gaze to Amanda and continued, "She discovered the man who gave Ela Nena the award was actually an agent of Lucinden. I guess we now have our answer as to who is behind this scheme. We still don't know the why, but it's definitely a start.

"So I went to work and met with Ela Nena first thing this morning. I won't go into all of the details because it wasn't very pleasant. Suffice it to say, the award did have a samara hidden within it. To say Ela Nena was shocked would be an understatement; she couldn't have me get that thing out of her office fast enough.

"What I didn't share with anyone until now is that an unknown man came onto the rooftop just as I was teleporting out of there. He shot a tracking device onto my telepod just as I activated the transfer. I had no idea what he had done so I thought there was a malfunction happening."

Everyone other than Amanda gasped at Riccan's description of the timing of the shot. They all knew the dangers of the impact at the point of departure. Amanda had never learned about it so she wondered what she had missed, yet she did not want to sidetrack the story so she remained silent. She would ask later when they were alone.

"As soon as I landed in Pantano, I checked the craft for any signs of malfunction when I came upon the tracking devise. Of course I destroyed it immediately, but I'm afraid it could have transmitted my location before I got to it. I know the Residence has safeguards in place, however, you may want to take extra precautions for a little while."

Daven nodded his acquiescence and Riccan continued his recital of events.

"Mom identified the colors of the new samara as being the same as her own birth crystal."

Amanda and the girls both exchanged pleased looks until Riccan said his next statement.

"She is wary of even touching the crystal until she knows it isn't evil. Since the samara was obviously used to control Ela Nena's behavior and Lucinden is clearly involved in the giving of the award, we can see where she would be reticent to become the owner."

Riccan turned to his daughters and asked, "Can you share what you know of the samaras with my parents? I think if they knew the history and uses of them, then they might have a better understanding. Would you agree?"

Jena nodded solemnly. She was the most conversant with the histories since she had been the one to find and read the ancient text in the library in Acaim. She also knew more about them intimately since she had communed with her own samara for many hours. Of course Juila shared her knowledge since their minds were linked, however, Jena really had been the first one to study the history.

"The samaras were created by Jehoban at the beginning of the universe. He has planned for them to be used for something in the future, as yet it has not been disclosed for what purpose. Anyway, the thirteen descendants of his angels were each given a samara to keep in their family line until the time of their need was at hand.

"As you can imagine, some of the family lines became extinct and the samaras were lost into the land. Other calamities happened such as theft and still more samaras were stolen. Throughout time, the knowledge of the samaras has been diluted until it became legend, then myth, and finally it was not known at all…until now."

Jena took a few seconds to compose her thoughts of what would be important or relevant for everyone to know. "The samaras are very powerful sources of energy. They are more powerful when they are together than when they are separated. There are two…no wait, three… ways for their power to be used. In the first way, anyone can access the power. In the second way, someone can control another person through it. In the third way, the samaras can work together to create a very powerful energy which, I believe, is their true purpose."

Nena cleared her throat and clarified, "So what you are saying is that they can be very dangerous."

"Yes, in the wrong hands it's true. However, in the hands of the true, ordained owner, only that one person can access the power. Once the true owner touches the samara, a permanent link is made and nobody else will ever be able to access the samara's power while the real owner remains alive." Jena had felt the link form when she had first touched her own samara.

Juila nodded confirmation and said, "We both felt the link form when we touched the samaras which had our own birth crystal colors as their aura. It is how we know this is true, we have felt it ourselves."

Riccan hoped the children had convinced his mother to at least try to claim the samara for herself. To seal the deal, Riccan said, "Mom, if the samara remains unclaimed by its rightful owner, then it does pose a threat to all of us. Please say you'll touch it and see if it is yours."

Nena still looked scared. She looked into her husband's eyes, hoping he would refute their son's request. Seeing only entreaty, Nena closed her eyes and said a silent prayer for her safety. She gave a small nod of agreement as she opened her eyes and said, "I'll try."

Not wanting to give her any time to change her mind, Riccan stood up and left the room. He went into the library, opened the secret door, and entered the hidden chamber beyond. He picked up the samara, which was still encased in the award, and returned to the living room. In his haste he did not even bother to shut the bookcase wall.

Riccan set the award down on the coffee table just in front of his mother. He flicked the small lever on the side to allow the front panel to drop down which left the samara exposed to view only from the front. He sat down on the coffee table to be close at hand should his mother require assistance.

One last time, Nena looked to her husband. Her hopes of his changing his mind evaporated when he nodded for her to continue. With a sigh of resignation, she reached out with both hands and placed them on either side of the samara. Instantly, she felt a charge of energy as the samara communicated directly with her core being.

She knew with every fiber of her being that this crystal had been made for her. It seemed ridiculous now that she had been so fearful to take charge. Now she understood what they had all been saying. Time stood still as she watched flashes of the samara's history and all of its former owners, both true and false.

~

THE EVENING CAME to a close when Riccan suggested they put the samara back in the hidden room with the other samaras. He was amused when he discovered how difficult it was to get his mother to give up possession of her new toy. Instead of touching it himself, he guided his mother to the back room and had her place the samara in a vacant cubby near his own.

As soon as Nena's fingers lost contact with the stone, she felt a profound sense of loss. She immediately wanted to reclaim the feeling. The lure of the samara was addictive and she could see why it would draw the attention of evil. She folded her arms across her body and looked away from the cubby. "That is one powerful stone, Riccan. Why didn't you tell me how it would be? Is it the same for you?"

Riccan nodded and reminded her, "I did tell you about it. Your fear kept you from believing me. Also, I think the power within the stone is different for each person, but I understand what you're saying. The things I've seen as I've held my samara have been fascinating. I could spend hours at a time just watching as it shows me what has happened around it."

"You saw that, too? I'm glad you said something, I thought it might just be me. What about the girls?"

"Yes, they've both had similar experiences. Let's go back to the others now. Being around the energy from all of these samaras together makes my skin crawl." Riccan led the way out and waited for his mother to join him.

Since Riccan had pointed it out, she looked down and saw the hair on her arm standing on end. She definitely felt the power being drawn by the separate crystals. With one last look, she felt like she was parting from a long-lost friend and felt tears come to her eyes. She would have to schedule another trip here just to see if she still felt the same connection the next time she touched her samara.

Daven and Nena left right after they returned to the living room. The evening had gone better than anyone could have hoped. They were sitting on the sofa talking about the samaras and asking the girls a couple more questions about what they knew.

During a lull in the conversation, Juila asked, "When are Behn and Valentina coming home?"

"Oh!" Amanda sat up immediately. She felt horrible and exclaimed, "I promised to go back and get them and I totally forgot." Amanda stood up and started heading for the garage.

"Wait, Mom. Let me go get them, you've already traveled too much today. I know where Barla lives, we used to live there ourselves, after all," Juila stated matter-of-factly.

Amanda glanced down at Riccan to see if he approved and saw him scrunch his shoulders. It was up to her to decide. The girls had never asked before, and she was glad they felt comfortable enough. Besides, Juila loved flying and she had yet to venture out on her own since they had come to live on Earth. Amanda decided, "Go there and come straight back, okay?"

Juila squealed with delight and jumped up to give her mother a quick hug. She grabbed the telepod remote off of the small desk beside the kitchen and almost ran out into the garage. With the new equipment in her mother's telepod, she did not even have to worry about finding and memorizing the destination coordinates. She buckled herself into the pilot's seat, activated her flight plan on the glass panel, verified all of the green lights indicating the systems were all functioning properly, and then she hit the button to begin the transfer.

The long teleportation unnerved her slightly and she noticed her hand was shaking slightly as she manually set the telepod down on the Cresdon landing field. She left the aircraft and looked around her with a slight frown of confusion. While she had been confident in this journey when she had been at home, it had been ten anons since she had been in this city. When they were little, they never had any occasion to go to the landing field except on the day they left to go live on Acaim.

Darkness was falling and she had to pick a direction. She chose to go right toward the houses which looked the most familiar. If it came right down to it, Juila could knock on someone's door and ask for directions. She hoped as she walked that it would start to look familiar.

As she passed each home she looked at it intently for any signs of recognition. She felt slightly stupid since she could not even recall on which side of the street the house had been. Just as she was about to give up, she looked to her left and saw the white picket fence. Instantly, she recalled playing inside the yard and up the grand staircase.

She opened the gate and went up the stairs to knock on the door. She reasoned that even if this were the wrong house, she had a back-up plan. The feeling of rightness left little doubt she had picked correctly. She knocked with authority and waited.

Barla opened the door expecting to see Amanda. Her eyes widened as she saw an older version of one of the girls she had helped raise. "Are you Juila or Jena?" she asked even as she pulled her in for a big hug.

"Juila," she answered as she returned the hug for the first mother she remembered. She had been thrilled to find out Barla was actually her great-aunt so she would always be able to keep in touch with her and call her family.

"Where's your mom?" Barla asked as she let go of her and looked out the door for Amanda.

"I came by myself to get Behn and Val. Do you think they're ready to go?" Juila had not considered the darkness when she had offered to come. She had never liked walking in the streets at night when she was outside of Acaim.

"Let's go find out, shall we?" Barla said as she shut the door and led Juila down the hall to the living room. "Look who came over!" she announced as they entered the room.

Behn and Valentina looked up from where they were seated on the floor playing with their little sister.

Juila thought they looked very happy. She kneeled beside Behn and asked, "Who is this little cutie?"

Valentina spoke with pride, "This is our little sister. Isn't she adorable?"

"Absolutely," Juila agreed. She hated to have to break up the party, but she had promised her mother she would be quick with this trip. Her search for the house had taken up precious time. They were going to have to leave pretty soon. "Are you guys almost ready to go home?"

Valentina was actually disappointed. The afternoon and early evening had been perfect and she had enjoyed getting to know her mother, Danika, and Barla. "Do you think we'll be able to come back soon to visit again?"

Vinia was so happy to hear Valentina ask to return. She had been so scared her oldest daughter would reject her and now she had proof of her love. "I'm sure we can arrange something, Val. It is getting late and your little sister needs to go up to bed for the night."

"Okay," Valentina said reluctantly. She got up from the floor and leaned down to give her mom a hug and a kiss on the cheek. She could not resist one last chance to touch Danika's cheek before she left.

Behn followed his sister's example with their mother and then went to stand beside Juila in the hallway. He still had a lot of questions about Grobin and where he currently lived, but that would have to wait for another day. He was not going to forget the promise he had made himself.

The three teenagers left the house and talked excitedly on their way back to the landing field. Valentina kept talking about how amazing the day had been. Behn had agreed and also commented about how nice the house had been. They had enjoyed eating foods they had forgotten existed.

By the time they reached the telepod, they were ready to get back home. They were going to have to figure out how to tell Jon about their mother. It was unfair to keep him from knowing, their mother, their little sister, and their heritage. With all of the pieces of the puzzle put together, they felt confident in sharing the truth with him now.

CHAPTER 31

Shemalla was astonished at receiving yet another message from Tuala. Normally, months would pass without any word at all. Now she had received a message from Elder Vargen, a visit from Lillia, and now this new task. She wondered what all of it could mean as she packed her bag to begin her trip across the country on such short notice.

When she had told Lillia about the assignment, she had seemed unconcerned about it. In fact, Lillia had seemed eager for her to go. Shemalla wondered what Lillia had in mind to do. She never had to worry about entertaining her friend as Lillia was almost as frequent a visitor to Earth as she was.

Shemalla had spent enough time on Earth to be accustomed to the slower travel so the plane ride to New York City seemed like a good time to catch up on her reading. After browsing through all of the magazines offered in the seatback in front of her, she pulled her kindle out of her purse and picked one of the books she had loaded from home. Unfortunately, the story could not hold her attention so she turned it off and put it back into her purse.

She leaned her forehead against the window and stared down at the tops of the clouds. She realized for the first time that these people had the opportunity to enjoy the sights of the journey whereas the people of

Tuala only experienced blank nothingness when they teleported between places. She smiled at her idea and yet acknowledged no Tualan would put up with this slow mode of travel for the sake of seeing the sights.

Thinking of Tuala made her wonder again at this new assignment of hers. Granted, she had contacts and friends all over the world of Earth so she could understand why she had been asked. Still, it seemed like odd timing to her.

Hours later the plane landed at JFK where Shemalla rolled her carry-on through the airport and then flagged down a taxi once she got outside. She directed the driver to take her to Central Park and she sat back to enjoy the crazy ride. As they approached the park she kept her eye trained on the park itself. When they got to the area she needed, she said, "Stop the cab!"

The driver complied by immediately stopping, to the accompaniment of many horns honking behind them. Shemalla caught herself on the partition and shoved a wad of bills through the slot. She opened the door, grabbed her bag and purse, and rushed over to the sidewalk to avoid getting hit by the angry drivers behind the cab.

Thankfully she did not need to cross the busy road as she already stood on the park side of the street. She ventured into the park and followed one of the paths into the wooded area. She had only been to this area a few times before, always in a different season, and had to keep her eyes sharp to find the overgrown trail.

After a few failed attempts on the wrong trails, backtracking and starting over, she eventually located the right path and followed along it deeper into the woods. She looked over her shoulder several times to make sure she remained alone. Eventually she found the bench for which she had been searching.

She sat down placing her bags beside her. She dug her cell phone out of her purse and began making the phone calls she had not had time to make before her flight. Within twenty minutes she had concluded her business and she folded her phone with a snap of satisfaction. She dropped her phone back in her purse, folded her hands, and prepared to wait.

~

WILLIAN STEPPED DOWN from his mediator's chair with a sigh of relief. He was glad to know he had done his best and had come to some good solutions for the petitioners. His record for success was still perfect as the two people left the room on good terms again. The day's session had been different because Rasa had instructed him to proceed without her as she had other matters to handle and she felt confident he would do fine.

He wondered if Rasa's other plans included making the arrangements for his upcoming trip. Almost as soon as the thought came to his mind, he scoffed at himself for being selfish. Of course, Rasa would have many other things to take care of other than anything to do with him. He was going to have to work on thinking of others before himself if he planned on winning Jena back. There had to be obvious proof of him changing in order for Jena to even want him anymore.

With no other pressing duties, Willian returned to his room and tidied up his belongings so he could make a quick departure should the trip be arranged. He did not go so far as to pack everything so as not to be too assuming. In only a little while, everything was in order and he could not remain still. He decided to go to the library to see if he could find out any more information about Earth which might be helpful.

He entered the corridors and navigated them with ease. When he got to the library he was about to go inside when he was stopped by a conversation being held within. Knowing it was wrong to eavesdrop, he was unable to stop himself when he heard his name being spoken. He leaned closer to make sure he would not miss anything.

"I heard Elder Wilken say Willian was going to turn out to be a fine Elder," the first woman spoke with a tone of superiority.

"You wouldn't have guessed it from how that boy was when he first got here. He sure was full of himself!" the second woman said scornfully.

"I wonder what Elder Wilken had to say to him to get him to change so fast?" the first woman asked.

"It must have been pretty dire to make such a quick impression. I've heard how difficult Willian had been at home. His poor mother must have been beside herself with worry over him ever growing up!"

"I saw she came here yesterday to speak to Rasa. Do you know what that was all about?"

"No, I was stuck down at the market place most of the day and didn't get to hear anything at all. I bet her reunion with Willian was pretty shocking! She sent away a child and she'll be getting back a man!"

"We can only hope. Say, are you serving at dinner tonight?"

"No, I got breakfast duty so I have tonight off."

The talk turned to mundane work discussions and Willian lost interest. He leaned against the wall for a few more seconds while he digested what he had overheard. The sounds of the women leaving the library through the servant's entrance allowed Willian to enter the room and take a seat at one of the patils.

It was gratifying to know people had seen improvement in him as much as it was mortifying to believe he had been so insufferable upon arrival. He thought back over the days he had been visiting and the conversations he had participated in. The servants certainly paid more attention to their conversations than he ever believed or even noticed. This, too, was a valuable lesson for his future.

Rasa found Willian while he was deep in thought and smiled to see him being so quiet. She wondered what he could be thinking about, but was too polite to see for herself. "A shill for your thoughts," she spoke right next to him causing him to jump and look up at her with a guilty expression.

"Sorry. I was thinking about everything I've learned since I got here in Manzanit. It's slightly overwhelming when I really consider everything!" He shrugged his shoulders and chuckled a little.

"Just wait until you find yourself on Earth! You don't know the meaning of overwhelmed yet!"

"Is that supposed to mean it's time for me to go?"

"Almost. You still have a meeting with Elder Wilken before he gives his final approval."

"Is there a chance he'll say no?" Willian did not know what he'd do if that were the case.

"I doubt it, unless you say something incredibly stupid to make him decide against it. He was just telling me how pleased he is with you," Rasa said as she clapped him on the shoulder.

"When is my meeting scheduled?"

"Right now. It's why I came looking for you. I expected to find you in the mediation room, but the place was empty. You must have really cut to the chase on the final case to get them out of there so fast."

Willian stood up to walk with her as he replied humbly, "Nah, I just got them talking and they pretty much settled everything themselves."

"That's how it usually goes in these kinds of matters." Rasa was careful not to downplay Willian's skill so he would not get upset with her. She was relieved they had managed to build some rapport during his visit since her elevation to the Elder's successor made her Willian's equal and they would be working together for declans in the future.

Willian was unaccountably nervous when Rasa declined to stay when she had taken him to the meeting. The nerves came more from wanting to please the Elder than for fear of what he might actually say. It felt strange to feel as he did since he had never been especially interested in actively seeking his own father's approval. He could see now he had done a disservice to his own family for his lack of trying. He smiled inwardly at his own insight since it was Elder Wilken's own words of 'knowing is the first step to achieving' which made him want to do better.

Wilken could see the young man was deep in thought and nodded knowingly. He had hoped to make some impression upon the boy, and yet Willian's changes had far exceeded his initial assessment. This experience had put another idea into his head of fostering other Elder's successors to help enrich their learning and improve relationships within the elite group. He firmly believed that the more one knew the better one ruled.

"I have been very pleased with the reports I have received for you, Willian," Wilken finally spoke.

Willian jumped slightly as the Elder's words broke into his own personal thoughts. "Thank you, Elder Wilken. I really have tried my best."

"Your best is quite fine. Even the servants have been speaking favorably of you and that aspect means a great deal more to me than the opinions of the other dignitaries."

"Why is that?" Willian blurted out and then almost cursed himself for speaking without thinking first.

"I would rather hear your thoughts on why," Wilken replied.

Willian bit his lower lip as he began to consider the Elder's challenge. Many ideas came to mind and yet none of them seemed to ring true until he had an inspired moment of clarity. He snapped his fingers and with widened eyes he announced, "I know why!"

"Tell me."

"The servants are the same as the people we serve in the community. If

I were to have been rude or impatient with the servants it would have reflected badly on me since the servants tend to talk with one another and with people outside of the Residence. My ability to arbitrate and eventually to lead would be hampered by the impressions the people had already made about me based on my actions with the people closest to me. Is that what you meant?"

"You really have been learning. Good job, Willian. Now tell me what you have learned about Earth." Elder Wilken sat back and waited for the lengthy explanation he was certain he would receive.

Willian spent a considerable amount of time explaining all of the different types of things he had researched and how he thought the information might be valuable. Once he started talking about it, he realized he knew quite a bit more than he had originally thought. It became less daunting to think about actually going to Earth and he relaxed.

Just as Wilken had wanted, he noticed the point where Willian ceased to be nervous and he held up his hand for silence. "I can tell you are ready to begin your journey. Thank you for indulging an old man with your knowledge. Now go pack your bag and say goodbye to your mother."

Willian could hardly believe it had been so easy to gain approval for his journey. He had planned to spend weeks in service and yet not even one week had gone by. "Thank you for taking me in, Elder Wilken. I will forever be grateful for your kind words and your invaluable lessons. I feel as though I'm leaving here a changed person. I only hope Jena can see it as well." Flustered with the last thing he had spoken he decided he should get moving before Elder Wilken changed his mind. He executed a small bow of respect and hurried out of the room.

He flew down the halls to get to his room and grab his already packed bag. With his sack slung over his shoulder he took one last look around the bedroom to make sure he left nothing behind before he turned and closed the door behind him. One more hurdle had been crossed on his journey. He was on his way! His mind raced with the possibilities and his heart fluttered with nervous excitement.

As he retraced his steps in the hallway, he realized he had not been told where to find his mother. There were really only two choices: the garden, or her guest room. Since the garden was closer he decided to look there first. His instincts proved correct and he found her sitting on a bench in the sunshine.

The closer he got to her, the more he noticed she appeared young and vibrant with the sun glinting in her hair and putting color in her cheeks. She almost seemed to exude a sense of power even though she sat in silent contemplation. His pride in her beauty showed in his smile as he approached her. "Hi, Mom. Elder Wilken said I should tell you I was leaving," he said as he stopped in front of her.

She had to squint to look up at him since the sun was above his shoulder. She patted the bench beside her and said, "Sit with me a moment."

Really wishing he did not have to, a protest formed on his lips, until he saw his mother's expression. She really needed this more than he did. He sat down and waited with his newfound patience for her to say whatever she had on her mind.

Chelesa was surprised at his easy capitulation. She had expected to have to argue with him to hear her out. Pride in her son's new maturity made her smile as she said, "I wanted to keep you from this journey." She could see his scowl beginning to form and she held up her hand to forestall any rebuttal and continued, "I can see I was wrong. This experience has changed you. I'm sorry for doubting you before. Please tell me you'll forgive me."

Willian stuttered for a moment before he could answer. "There's nothing to forgive on your part, Mom. If anyone needs forgiving, it's me! I haven't given you much reason to trust in my decision-making skills in the past. You're also right when you said I needed this trip. I'm going to do my best to make you proud of me. Hopefully, I will also win Jena back in the process. I love you, Mom. I'm glad you came here to see me off."

"Me too, honey. Now give me a hug!" Chelesa held out her arms and held her son close to her. She missed the little boy she had once comforted as she realized he was the one now comforting her and he was no longer her little boy.

Willian remained in his mother's arms until she let go. He did not want to be the one to end the embrace since he knew she needed to soak him in before he left. He leaned forward and kissed his mother's sun-warmed cheek and smiled into her eyes. He could see her love for him reflected in her adoring gaze and he knew this moment would forever be imprinted in his mind.

Chelesa put her hand on his stubbly cheek and said, "Promise me you'll be safe when you're on Earth!"

"I will. I know what's at stake."

"Do you? Do you really?"

Willian nodded solemnly.

Something about his expression convinced her more than any words ever could. She nodded her approval and said, "I'll walk with you to find Elder Wilken and Rasa." She stood up and brushed off her pants while she waited for Willian to do likewise.

His bag had slipped to the ground and he bent to pick it back up and throw over his shoulder. He held out his hand to his mother and they walked back through the gardens in perfect accord. Elder Wilken was a wise man to have him make peace with his mother before he left. His only regret was that his father had not witnessed his transformation as well. "Tell Dad I said goodbye and thank you."

"I will, honey. He would have been here too except he had business matters keeping him in his district."

"I know. I've seen first-hand how much time is devoted to helping the district. I have a newfound respect for all of the work the Elders do."

"I bet you do!" Chelesa smiled up at her son.

CHAPTER 32

Sofia's first day back at school had been exhausting. She had no idea it would take so much out of her just sitting in her classes. There had been something strange she had noticed throughout the past two days. The classes she shared with Jena or Juila, she seemed to have more energy than the ones where they were separated. It would have made more sense if the classes had all been together except they shared first, third, and fifth periods as well as lunch before fifth. Without fail, the classes without them she felt drained and ready to go home.

She had been in their fifth period College Algebra class when Juila had been called out to take an emergency phone call. Almost as soon as Juila left, Sofia felt a drain on her stamina. She looked over toward Jena to see how she reacted to Juila being called away. Thinking of what could have happened helped take her mind off of her own weariness.

When Juila had returned to class and sat down next to her, Sofia kept looking at her friend. Juila seemed very preoccupied, but not upset so the emergency must not have been bad news. Even as she tried to imagine what had happened, she kept getting an image of Valentina in her mind. She scowled and tried to put the girl out of her mind, but her face kept showing up unbidden.

Nothing more had been said about Juila being called out of class. Sofia had wanted to ask about it after school, but was unable to find either girl or the Wilson triplets to ask them. It was almost as if they had all gone off together to do something without her. She felt left out even as her mother picked her up from the front entrance of the school at the end of the day.

While she sat in class the next day she thought about the night before. She had spent the evening napping on the couch and trying to regain enough energy for school the next day. When the phone rang, she reached over and answered it with a bored tone.

"Hey, Sofia, this is Jon. Do you have time to talk?"

Sofia immediately sat up on the couch and held the phone with both hands to her ear. "Hi! Yes, I can talk. What's going on?"

"That's what I wanted to talk to you about. I think you're right about Juila and Jena."

"What do you mean? What happened?"

"I asked Behn to give me a ride home after school. At first it seemed everything was normal, but then I realized Behn, Juila, and Jena all seemed kind of uptight. I think they were planning something, yet I have no idea what. Now it's way later than usual and Behn and Valentina just got home and went directly into Behn's room to talk. Did anyone say anything to you today at school about special plans for today?"

"No. Juila got called out of class for an emergency, but she never said what it was about." She was feeling better since Jon felt as though he had been left out as well. "I had something strange happen as well."

"What?"

Sofia told him about her change in energy levels coinciding with her classes with the twins. Even as she explained it, she thought it sounded stupid. "So what do you think? Am I going crazy?"

"Probably," Jon teased.

"Hey!" Sofia began to protest until she heard Jon chuckling on the other end.

Their conversation had ended with both of them agreeing to share any new information. Sofia wondered if Jon had found out what Behn and Valentina had been talking about after they had gotten home. She was going to ask him when they sat together at lunch. She was startled out of her ruminations when the bell sounded ending the class.

Sofia ripped the paper out of the typewriter. She was startled when she noticed the teacher standing next to her desk.

"I noticed you didn't get much practice in today. Are you feeling okay, Sofia?" Mrs. Shoreham asked kindly.

Sofia felt guilty about shirking in class because she was too busy thinking. She replied, "I'm just tired. I'll do better tomorrow, I promise."

"It's alright, Sofia. You've always been a great student and you're further ahead than most of the class anyway. Please don't feel like you have to push yourself."

"Okay, thanks," Sofia replied. She gathered up the rest of her school books and smiled at her teacher before she escaped into the hallway full of students. After dropping off her things in her locker, she met up with Jon as they were both heading to the cafeteria. "Did you find out what Behn and Val were talking about last night?"

"Sort of," Jon started and looked around to make sure nobody was paying too much attention to them. "Apparently, they have been trying to find our birth mother. They didn't want to tell me about it because they think it'll upset me."

"Why would it?" She had known the three were adopted, but she never realized they might not want to know about their birth mother.

"I don't have any memories before we were adopted. I was a really sick kid."

"So what did they find? Do Juila and Jena have anything to do with finding her?"

"They wouldn't say anything concrete, but I do think the girls are involved somehow. Maybe you should see what you can find out."

"I'll try," Sofia replied. They had to end their conversation as they got closer to the buffet line. She wondered what she could find out for Jon and if Jena or Juila would be the better choice for sharing with her. Once she had her lunch, she followed Jon back to their regular table where she sat down next to Juila.

While she was eating she was thinking about Jon's situation and wondered how she could bring it up. Suddenly a picture of Juila's mother came into her mind. At least she had thought it was her mother until she noticed she looked slightly older. Sofia decided to go with where her mind had taken her and asked Juila, "How is your mother doing these days? I haven't seen much of her."

Juila obviously had not expected the question and it took her a few seconds to compose her answer. "She's been really busy working on a project with my grandparents. She's doing great. I'll tell her you were asking."

Sofia got the impression that was all she was going to learn on that particular subject. She decided for another angle and said, "I wish you'd come over and keep me company after school while my mom has me on lockdown in the evenings."

Juila nodded while she finished chewing and swallowing her food. "I'd love to come over, but I don't have any way of getting there. I guess I could ask my mom to bring me over and pick me up…" she just let the thought die off as she tried to figure out a way around going.

Feeling slightly let down, Sofia asked, "Why don't you get your driver's license? You're old enough now."

"We've talked about it and even practiced a bit at the house, but it just seems like we have so much going on and it just hasn't happened. To be honest, the idea of navigating with all of the other cars on the roads scares me quite a bit. Besides, I don't know how long we'll be staying."

Sofia's eyes widened in both surprise and dread. She had never anticipated the girls leaving again. They seemed to be settling in so well. Just the idea alone sent a bit of panic in her mind. "Surely you won't leave before you finish high school!"

"We plan on staying until then, but you never know what might come up," Juila replied noncommittally.

"I hope you'll tell me in advance if you do plan to go anywhere," Sofia pouted.

"Sofia, you were our first and best friend since we came here. I would never leave without telling you." Juila gave her a side hug to reinforce her words.

Milking the moment a little longer, Sofia complained, "You wouldn't know it with how much time you spend with Valentina and Behn. I'm starting to feel replaced."

"I'm sorry, Sofia. I can see how it would seem that way to you. I promise to make more effort to spend time with you outside of school." At the moment, she was uncertain how she would make good on the assurance, yet she would definitely try.

~

Neal's introduction to the psychiatric center had been for him to put his bag in his room and then follow Dr. Gascon to his office. The doctor then handed him a small paper cup containing two pills and another cup of water. Neal had thought it was slightly strange until the doctor told him the medication would help his mind release what it already knew.

He remembered nothing of any of the sessions he had been in with Dr. Gascon. As he sat on his bed in the stark, empty room, he wished he could have kept at least some of his personal belongings. When he had returned to the room on the first day, his suitcase was gone, replaced with a simple white gown and white sheets for the bed.

The medication the doctor had insisted would help him remember did not seem to be working. On the contrary, he barely remembered his name most of the time. The doctor was pleased with his progress, however, which was very encouraging. If the doctor could cure him then he would be going home soon.

Neal spent most of his time curled up on top of his bed. He began to have weird ideas about time and people. The name Tuala kept coming up and haunting both his waking and dreaming thoughts.

An attendant came in and handed him another cup. He waited for the patient to sit up and take the pills into his mouth before he handed him the water. As soon as the medication was swallowed, he ordered, "It's time for another session. Let's go."

Neal walked in a dream-like state wherever the attendant led him. He kept his gaze on the floor in front of his feet since the walls seemed to move on their own if he stared at them too long. It was very disorienting to walk while the medication swam through his veins, entered his brain, and shifted his reality. Neal required the attendant's help to lie down on the doctor's couch.

"Let's begin again, Neal. Tell me more about your fiancé. Can you remember her name today?"

"Amanda," Neal slurred.

"Tell me her full name."

"Amanda Covington."

Dr. Gascon smiled wickedly. He had the connection! Since Neal was drugged so heavily, he would not have to worry about being careful with his expressions, words, or actions. He stood up immediately and went to his desk. He pulled the packet of pictures from the private detective out of the locked drawer and began riffling through them until he found the one he remembered. He kept it in his hand and went back to his seat in front of his subject.

He held out the picture so he could compare the man in the photo to Neal. It was a perfect match! Now he knew who Amanda had been taking away from her house. His next goal was to find out how he had come to be in the house in the first place. Had he been held there all along in a twisted plot or was there another explanation. Was Tuala a clue? He was going to find out if it were the last thing he did.

The first thought which came to mind was that Riccan Stel was actually a cult leader of a group called Tuala. He thought it highly likely Riccan had created his own Heaven's Gate style compound where he had been brainwashing people to believe in this other world. His quick marriage to Amanda would support this theory.

His anger rose against Dr. Medin for foiling his attempt to interview Amanda before Riccan had shielded her from his reach. One day he would find a way to make her pay for her folly in 'helping' Amanda. If only he could have had one session with Amanda!

He shook his head to clear his mind. He had Neal now. Because Neal had willingly committed himself, Dr. Gascon could keep him as long as he wanted without interference. This man was the next best thing to Amanda. Neal was going to tell him everything he wanted to know about what had gone on in the Stel estate and all about Tuala as well.

CHAPTER 33

The room was silent as Willian considered how he would reply to Elder Wilken's inquiry as to why he should offer the assistance of his Gate. "I wish to go to Earth to speak with my betrothed, Jena. We have become estranged, mostly due to my prior actions, and I would like to make amends in order to heal our relationship. I am thankful for the time I have spent here since I have learned of Earth and grown as a person. This time was necessary in order for me to make my best case with Jena." He closed his mouth and remained looking into Elder Wilken's eyes. He tried to make sure his gaze was entreating so it would not be construed as arrogance.

The silence continued as Elder Wilken simply nodded. Finally he spoke, "You have spoken wisely, Willian. The man you are today is not the same as the man who sat before me last week. You, indeed, have found yourself through your studies, duties, and inner evaluations. I would not have allowed you to use my Gate had you not changed. You are ready."

Willian could hardly believe he had gained approval. A joyous smile spread across his face and he asked, "Will I be going today?"

"Yes, you will be going right now. Your contact is waiting for you when you arrive. I wish you a safe journey and the best of luck. Follow me." Elder Wilken stood and led the way out of the room to his Ascension Gate.

Jessica fell into step beside her son. She looked up at him with pride and put her arm around his shoulders to hold him close one last time before he left. She refused to believe this could possibly be the last time she ever saw her son. No, he would be coming home once he made amends with Jena.

"I'm glad you're here to see me off, Mom."

"Me, too."

The group arrived in the Ascension Gate chamber. Only Willian walked forward until he stood in the depression of the floor at the vortex of the Gate. He made sure his bag was close to his side as he turned to face the people who had come to send him off. He nodded his readiness to Elder Wilken's question and then everything turned weightless and empty.

Dappled sunlight appeared around him as visual sensation returned. He remained standing still while he made sure the transfer had completed. Unsure of what to expect for his surroundings, he listened to the sounds around him before he made any move. Only muffled horns sounded in the distance, no voices or other commotion appeared to be near him.

Remembering his last journey to Earth, he was more cautious as he took his first step up out of the depression in the ground. He could see tree limbs bent up and around him making a sort of natural cave out of the living trees. Staying as silent as he could, he took another step on the thick piles of leaves on the ground.

He reached the opening of the trees and looked out to the left when a voice coming from the right scared him into squealing in surprise. He whipped his head around to see a woman sitting on a bench smiling at him.

"Sorry I scared you."

"That's putting it mildly," Willian muttered and weakly smiled back at her to show her he did not hold any hard feelings for their inopportune first meeting.

"You must be Willian," she said as she rose from the bench and took the few steps over to stand in front of him. She held out her hand and said, "My name's Shemalla. I've been asked to guide you to Florida and get you settled there. I know the transfer can be unsettling so why don't we sit here for a bit while you get your bearings back."

Willian shook her hand weakly and sighed with relief at her offer to rest for a bit. He sank down onto the bench when he reached it and continued to look around him at the expanse of wilderness. He had been led to believe this city was very populated and he wondered if his information had been wrong.

"Where are all the people and buildings which are supposed to be here?"

Shemalla chuckled and answered, "Oh, you'll see them very shortly. Enjoy the peace while you can. We are going to one of the busiest airports in the country so you will definitely see the people you were expecting."

"We're going to fly?" he asked excitedly. He had seen it in his studies and wondered at how it would feel.

"Yes, we have a direct flight from New York to Miami." She looked down at her watch and calculated they still had almost four hours until their flight departed. They would have enough time to get Willian some suitable clothes before they left. Luckily, the people of New York were used to seeing all manner of strange dress since so many movies were shot downtown that Willian's outfit would go virtually unnoticed.

She dug in her purse and pulled out a blue booklet and handed it to Willian. "This is your passport. It's a document used for travel and it shows you are a citizen of the United States. We'll also need it for getting you registered for school."

Willian accepted the document and began flipping through the blank pages. He was beginning to believe she had been joking until he came to the page near the back where it had a picture of him along with his name and a bunch of other stuff which meant nothing to him. "How did you get this?"

"I believe Elder Wilken sent it. I found it on the ground outside the circle right after I got here."

"Oh." Willian wondered what else had been done for him without his knowledge. He wished now he could have thanked them for their kind considerations. He remembered some of the other things which he would need and asked, "What about money or clothes?"

"The money is taken care of," she said as she held a plastic card out to him. She had gotten it out when she had retrieved the passport. She could see his confused expression and explained, "This is called a debit card. It's what we use to access money which is kept in an account for us. Each person has their own account. Just like at home, the money has to be earned and it is limited so no spending sprees!"

"Spending spree? What's that?"

"It's the term they use here to describe indiscriminate spending on anything and everything."

"I definitely won't be doing that. How much money do I have in my account?"

"Almost ten thousand dollars. It should be more than enough for anything you'll need while you're here."

"What's going to happen when we get to Florida? Do you have a place for me to stay? Are you staying with me?"

Shemalla chuckled as she shook her head. "I've made some arrangements for you to stay with friends of mine. I live in New Mexico on the other side of the country so, no, I won't be staying with you."

"Do your friends know about us? Are they from Tuala as well?"

"Yes and no. They are from Earth, but they sympathize with our situation and are more than happy to help us whenever they can."

"How many sympathizers are there on Earth?"

"A lot. I don't know them all, but they are pretty easy to spot. They all wear a silver tree-of-life pendant somewhere on their body; it could be a necklace, bracelet, earrings, belt buckle, or even a printing on their clothing."

"I see," Willian said. He had not heard anything about sympathizers anywhere in his studies. Nonetheless he was grateful to have them around to help out if he needed anything. Certainly it was good information to have while he was staying in this foreign land.

"Are you ready to get started? We have plenty to get done before our flight," Shemalla said as she stood up and waited for him to decide.

"I don't see why not," Willian spoke with more confidence than he felt at the moment. He fell into step beside her as they wandered through the paths in the forest. Before long, they began to encounter other people until they left the trees entirely and Willian got his first glimpse of the high-rise building surrounding Central Park. "I had no idea," he whispered as he turned in a circle with a wide-eyed stare. Tuala had nothing like this.

"Just wait," Shemalla said cheerfully as she grabbed his hand and pulled him across the lawn toward a line of yellow cars. She hailed a cab and pushed Willian into the one which stopped for them. She gave directions to the driver and remained silent as she watched Willian continue to take in the sights from the relative safety of the cab.

Shemalla took him through several stores to find him the appropriate clothing for Florida. He now owned several pairs of shorts, a couple pairs of pants, at least a dozen shirts, and several options for shoes. The most embarrassing aspect of the whole trip was when Shemalla asked him which style of underwear he preferred and then she began choosing several options for his inspection. He thought he would die of embarrassment before a male salesperson stepped in and took over.

The last stop was in a store for luggage. She said he'd need an appropriate travel bag which would blend in better than his travel sack. She chose a black Briggs & Riley bag with four wheels on the bottom. Willian was fascinated with the innovation and spent a few minutes pushing it across the floor and turning to see if it would keep up with him.

When Shemalla instructed him to put all of their purchases in it as well as his travel sack, he finally understood its value. He was relieved to not have to tote around so many bags. Now he only had the one thing to drag around after him. He kept looking back at it to see how it rolled so easily over every surface.

Shemalla was entertained by his antics. She kept track of the time so they would not have to worry about the traffic getting to the airport. When they left the luggage store, she hailed another cab and instructed the driver to take them to JFK.

Willian was about to see his first airplane and he could barely contain his enthusiasm. As they neared the airport he could hear loud engine rumblings above them and he plastered his face to the window to see the huge aircraft flying low overhead to come in for a landing. He felt a thrill of fear and delight that he was about to get in one and take his first Earth flight.

They were walking through the terminal to get to their gate when Willian heard a foreign language for the first time. "I still don't know why they don't all speak the same language. It seems pretty inefficient to me!"

"We have an ancient language, too, you know. We mostly only use it for ceremonies now, but there was a time when it was all that was spoken."

Willian raised his eyebrows at her observation; he had to admit she was right. Again, he was going to have to put more thought into things before he judged so hastily. Hopefully, he would eventually learn this lesson.

The time passed swiftly since he spent all if it people-watching. They were called to board the plane and Willian followed Shemalla to see where to go. They took their seats and she showed him how to fasten the seatbelt which was slightly different than what was used in a telepod. As soon as all of the passengers were on board, the front door was sealed and the airplane pushed away from the gate. Willian could feel the aircraft bumping along the tarmac and he looked over at Shemalla with a childish grin of delight.

She knew how he felt and was glad he was enjoying himself. Soon he would be tired of the many hours of travel and would be asking how much longer until they reached Florida. It was always exciting to see the world through new eyes when she showed Tualans Earth for the first time. It had been many years since the last time she had done it.

Takeoff had been just as Shemalla had hoped; Willian was thrilled. The hours of flight also proved tiresome, yet instead of complaining Willian fell asleep. Shemalla thought it was just as well. When the pilot announced their imminent landing, Shemalla woke Willian up so he could look out the window and see where he was going to be living.

CHAPTER 34

Jessica had planned on staying in New York City until the end of the week, but when she was unable to have any contact with Neal, she decided to go home early. At first she could understand the center's desire to give Neal the intensive treatment he required until they refused to give her any information citing patient confidentiality. She worried continually about what could be happening to her son without her being able to make sure he was still okay.

Finally she had had enough. She got into her car and drove over to Amanda's house. She pressed the intercom button again on the gate box and waited impatiently. Thinking about honking her horn until she got some response she almost began when the gate slowly slid open. "About time," she mumbled as she pulled into the property. Even through her anger, she had to appreciate the beauty and luxury of the estate.

She parked the car in the circular drive and stalked up to the front door. Just as she raised her hand to knock, the door opened. Jessica glared at Amanda and said, "You're not going to avoid me anymore. I need answers." She pushed her way past the younger woman and marched through the foyer. She stopped at the living room and turned to confront Amanda. "Do you know where Neal is right now?"

Amanda's eyes grew wide as she thought Neal had disappeared again. "No, I thought he was at home with you. He's missing again?"

"No, but he might as well be. He checked himself into a psychiatric facility to help him try to get his memories back. Now the center won't give me any information and I'm worried about him. Tell me what you know so we can get him out of there."

"Surely, the hospital will be the best place for him, Mrs. Taivas. I think you should let them do their job. Please have a seat." Amanda walked around Jessica and stood in front of the couch to wait for Jessica to decide if she were going to join her.

When they were both seated Amanda asked, "Has he been able to recall anything?"

"He said he could remember a woman who looked like you. He thought her name was Vinia or something like that. He also said the place he lived was called Tuala. That's all he knows. Tell me what you know."

Amanda was both relieved and appalled at the things Neal did remember. She closed her eyes and tried to decide what she should do or say to help.

"Say something, Amanda. What do you know?"

"Vinia wants to see Neal, too. I told her to wait until his memory returned. I didn't want to upset him by having her come around."

"She's real? There really is a woman named Vinia?"

"Yes. She was here yesterday."

"And you still didn't bring her to see Neal. Not that it would have mattered since Neal is now in New York." Jessica could hardly contain the sarcasm in her voice. She felt slightly vindicated to finally be getting some answers from Amanda. She needed more.

"When is Neal's treatment expected to be over? I can arrange for Vinia to meet with him when he gets home."

"I don't know. Dr. Gascon won't even answer my calls now," Jessica answered with a disgusted tone.

"Did you say Dr. Gascon? Dr. Stephen Gascon?" Amanda stood up with alarm.

"Yes. What? Do you know of him? What's wrong?" Jessica was picking up on her panic and it made her own heart begin to race with anxiety.

"That man is a lunatic. He's dangerous! We have to get Neal away from him however we can! How long has he been in his care? I hope we aren't too late to save him," Amanda was wringing her hands and pacing the floor. She no longer even knew Jessica was in the room with her. Her mind was only focused on plans for helping Neal escape from the clutches of the doctor who should be in prison for his treatment techniques.

Amanda ran to get her cell phone. She flipped it open and hit the speed dial number three. The phone rang several times before a woman answered the call. Amanda practically cried as she said, "Dr. Medin, I need your help. There's an emergency!"

She no longer cared what Jessica heard as she spoke to her friend. "Riccan and I found Neal and took him home. We thought he was recovering there, but his mother is here now and she said they took him up to New York to be treated by Dr. Gascon. We have to get him out of there before something terrible happens. Can you help?"

"Did Neal check himself in or did his parents?" Dr. Medin asked.

Amanda held the phone away from her mouth as she asked Jessica the same question.

"He filled out everything. Why? Is that important?"

Amanda held out her hand for silence as she began to tell the doctor.

"I heard. We have a problem, Amanda. Neal is an adult and he signed himself in. We don't have any recourse to interfere. I'm sorry, it's the law."

"There has to be something, a loophole, anything! Dr. Gascon will use electric shock therapy if he doesn't think he's getting good enough answers. I should know, how do you think I woke up?!"

Jessica tried to follow what Amanda was saying. It did not appear to make much sense. The fear in Amanda's tone told her more than anything and now she only wanted to get her son back home even if his memory never returned.

"Thank you, Dr. Medin. If you think of anything which might help, please call me. Anytime! Day or night, I don't care. I know. Thank you. Bye." Amanda shut her cell phone and groaned with frustration. There had to be some way to get him out.

"Tell me the name of the place where he's being treated?" Amanda asked suddenly. She grabbed a notepad from the desk beside the kitchen.

"Creedmoor Psychiatric Center in Queens. What are you going to do?"

"I'm going to research the facility on the internet and figure out how I can help him escape." Amanda replied simply as she continued to write down what Jessica had told her.

"Just that simple, huh?" Jessica drawled.

"Yes! I'd think you'd be a little more creative since it's your son's life we're talking about!"

"Don't you think you're being a tad bit melodramatic?" Jessica tried to smile as she convinced herself of Amanda's tendency to overreact.

"Melodramatic? Seriously? Why don't you look up the Cannon Memorial patient records and see how many people died under Dr. Gascon's care? Why do you think he moved his practice to New York?"

She did not want to believe what she was hearing so she said, "Surely if that were true, he would've had his license to practice taken away."

Amanda tried to keep her patience as she explained, "He paid people to lie for him. The records speak for themselves. Cannon Memorial asked him to step down or they would take him before the Malpractice Review Committee. The records are available for anyone who really wants to find them. I'm shocked you didn't bother to look them up! You really should go now. I've got a lot of planning to do if I'm going to help Neal. Let me know if you come up with anything. You know where the door is."

Amanda did not wait to see if she left because she was already on her way to the computer in the office. She needed more information before she could create a viable plan. Her mind was racing through all of the complications. She was definitely going to need help to pull this off.

CHAPTER 35

Amanda considered sending a message to Riccan at work and then decided against it. She already felt bad enough for involving him in Neal's initial rescue from Tuala, she did not want to bring this added burden to him. How many times could she ask her husband to help her with her ex-fiancé, after all?

She thought about the people who would be more than willing to help and wrote them all down: his parents, Neal Sr. and Jessica, her parents, Chris and Diane, possibly her sisters, maybe Barla, definitely Vinia. She stared at the list and thought the group was abysmally small. As she thought about her sisters she realized they lived too far away and had families of their own to worry about. She crossed their names off. That left six people.

The ones to whom she would not have to explain much would narrow the list to four. Neal's parents may have money, but they also had no idea what their son had gone through. She crossed off Neal's parents. They would have to get this done without them.

Amanda picked up the home phone and dialed her parents' number. After several rings, the answering machine picked up. She toyed with the idea of just hanging up until the beep sounded and she left a short message saying she was thinking about them. Frustration was beginning to cloud her mind so she turned to what she could do: research.

She turned on her computer and began looking up anything and everything regarding Creedmoor Psychiatric Center. A small amount of hope reappeared when she located an article about one of the patients escaping the facility several years before. Surely they would have relaxed their security since then.

Without anything more to learn about the actual facility, Amanda turned her research to Dr. Gascon himself. She did not know what she was looking for, she just needed to come up with anything which would help her. Suddenly an article appeared which gave her an idea. Dr. Gascon was presenting at a Psychiatrists convention in two days. If he were going to be away from the center, then they would have an opportunity to get Neal away from there. She would have to make it work.

Amanda gathered her notes and ran out to the garage. She needed to speak with Vinia and Barla as soon as possible. Maybe discussing the problem with them would help her come up with a rescue plan.

The flight to Cresdon was quick and Amanda barely wasted any time landing. She almost forgot to cloak her telepod in her haste to get to Barla's house. When she knocked on Barla's front door she was breathless.

Barla took one look at her face and immediately ordered her inside. "What's happened, Amanda?"

"Is Vinia around? I just found out Neal is in danger and I'm going to need help." Amanda hurried down the hall and into the living room as she spoke.

Barla remained in the doorway and said, "Vinia's upstairs with Danika. Let me go get her. Sit down and catch your breath, I'll be right back."

True to her word, Barla returned almost immediately with Vinia in tow. They sat down across from Amanda with anxious expressions.

"I'm hoping the two of you can come to Earth to help me get Neal out of the hands of a maniac doctor," Amanda stated baldly.

"I can't go, Amanda," Barla spoke with fear in her voice. "I need to stay here to take care of Danika." She seemed relieved to have the excuse to stay.

Amanda could barely hide her disappointment, but rallied valiantly as she turned her gaze expectantly on Vinia.

Vinia nodded enthusiastically. "I'll do anything you ask, Amanda. You know I've wanted to see Neal ever since you stole him away from me. If he's in danger, I want to help."

"Thank you, Vinia. We're going to have to travel quite a bit to get to him. His parents took him to a place called New York. You're going to see quite a bit more of Earth than you bargained for so I hope you can handle it."

Vinia's expression showed a little bit of fear, but her resolve to help Neal helped her to cope with the uncertainty of the dangers on Earth. Besides, she reasoned, her children had been living on Earth for anons and they had been safe. Her mind was made up, she was going to help however she could.

Barla snapped her fingers and jumped up from her chair, startling both of the other women into silence. "I just remembered something," she said as she pulled a book off of the bookshelf. She hurriedly sat down and opened the book on her knees, flipping through the pages. "Here," she said as she pointed to a spot on the page. "I thought it was the same place, but I had to be certain."

Amanda leaned over to see what Barla had wanted to show them. Instantly she recognized the atlas from her dream where Barla had entered Earth names on the Tualan maps. Barla was pointing to the place known to them as Manzanit; in Amanda's world it was New York City. She raised her eyebrows and looked at Barla in wonder.

"I see you understand what I'm saying," Barla said as she nodded her head.

"Will somebody clue me in?" Vinia asked petulantly. She glanced from Barla to Amanda and back again while she waited.

"My daughter, Rasa, was just confirmed as the successor for Elder Wilken in Manzanit. You two will need help in New York City where Neal is being held. Rasa will only be an Ascension Gate away if you need more assistance or a quick getaway plan."

"Oh," Vinia said as she only partially understood how this would help.

"Do you think Rasa would agree to transport us to Earth from that gate? It would save us a lot of travel time on Earth if she would." Amanda asked.

"It wouldn't hurt to ask her. Let's go send her a message right now." Barla closed the atlas and returned it to the bookshelf on her way to the kitchen to get to her patil. She hoped Rasa would read it in time to be of assistance. She typed up the short request while both Vinia and Amanda looked over her shoulders. Barla hit send and then looked up behind her and said, "Now we wait and see what happens."

"I hope she agrees to help," Vinia said.

"I hope Elder Wilken agrees to let her help," Amanda said with more emphasis on the implications of the whole affair.

Barla turned to look at Amanda to see if she were trying to say something else. She wondered if Amanda knew more about the situation on Tuala than she were letting on. "What are you thinking, Amanda?"

"Just that it's too much of a coincidence that Neal's family has sought medical help for him in the one city where we also have access to a gate. It just seems as though we're meant to go there for some reason. Hey, is that a reply already?" Amanda asked as she pointed back to the screen.

Barla promptly turned and almost yelled, "Yes! Let me see what she said." She touched the message and saw there was also a request for a video conference. She selected the video instead. The screen immediately filled with Rasa's face.

"Well, hello everyone!" Rasa greeted them with a smile as she took notice of the three women seeing her call.

"Hi, honey. Thanks for getting back to us so fast. We really have a strange situation and we were hoping you could help."

Rasa kept a neutral expression on her face as she listened to the story as it was told by both Vinia and Amanda. When they were done, she raised her eyebrows and said, "Why don't you come on up here and we can discuss this in person. I'm sure I'll be able to help. Chelesa is here at the Residence with me for another matter, we can include her in the discussion as well. She might have some ideas to add."

"Do you want us to come right now?" Amanda asked as she was thinking she should let Riccan know she was going to be doing a bit of traveling this day and the next.

"Sure, if that works for all of you."

"I won't be able to come," Barla put in promptly. "I have to stay behind to watch Vinia's daughter, Danika."

Thinking fast, Rasa said, "Bring Danika along with you. We have a great nursery here and I'd love you to see my new home. Please say you'll come, Mom."

Without any other excuses, Barla reluctantly agreed to come. She could see how much her daughter wanted her to go, she could remain behind in Tuala while everyone else went to Earth. Barla immediately tapped another window open on the screen and sent Ahn a message saying where they would be for the rest of the day.

Rasa beamed with pleasure at her mother's agreement to visit. "I'll see you all in a few minutes. I'll meet you at the entrance to the air field and arrange for a transport. It's a little busier here than back at home! Oh, I'm so excited. Okay, talk to you soon!" The screen went blank as she terminated the call.

"Do you think she's excited?" Amanda drawled, setting everyone to giggling.

"I'll go get Danika ready to go," Vinia announced as she turned and left the kitchen to go upstairs.

"Do you mind if I send Riccan a message? He doesn't even know I'm here, let alone planning a trip to Manzanit," Amanda asked.

"Sure, go ahead," Barla replied as she hurriedly vacated the chair she had been sitting in. "I'm going to run upstairs and change my clothes and then we'll be ready to go."

Amanda was left alone. She tapped the message screen and entered Riccan's code. She told him whom she was with, and what her plans were for the moment. She did not write anything about rescuing Neal yet as she wanted more details first.

The flight to Manzanit was uneventful and Amanda was thankful for Riccan's navigation system which took them directly over the landing field without any problems. She happened to locate a landing area relatively close to the entrance and set the aircraft down with expert ease. The three adults marveled at the hustle and bustle of the larger city while Danika merely held onto her mother's side and kept her head tucked in close.

Rasa waved them over as soon as she spotted them. She rushed forward and embraced her mother tightly before she greeted everyone else. She fussed over little Danika and even offered to carry her until Danika made it clear she was perfectly content right where she was. The group laughed and followed Rasa to the transport she had waiting for them.

Once they got to the Residence, Rasa took them directly to a meeting room where Chelesa sat waiting for them. Greetings and introductions were made and then they all sat down to discuss the matter at hand. Only a few minutes after the talking began, a maid came in holding another small child. When Danika saw the other little girl she wanted to be taken away to play. Finally they were able to openly discuss their situation.

Amanda spoke first about her dream of Dr. Gascon and his unethical means of extracting information from patients for his own gain. She told them about his latest theory on multi-dimensional disorders and how he wanted to use people like Neal to support his research. Then she informed them of how he had tried to pressure her to have sessions with him and his anger with her when she had refused.

When she talked about the center where he was being treated, she mentioned the case of the patient escaping a few anons before and how she wanted to use the same method to extract Neal from the facility. Her impassioned speech let her audience know how vitally important the success of this mission was to her personally. She sat down and said, "So now you know what I know."

Chelesa cleared her throat and asked, "Neal's only been there for two days. How do you know he wants to leave?"

Amanda hated to have to admit it, but she answered, "I don't. I would rather get him out and ask him later. His own mother is being refused when she asked to visit and now Dr. Gascon won't even take her phone calls. I believe that's enough proof of something duplicitous going on in there to intervene."

Rasa remained silent as she recalled the meeting they had sat in with Jehoban. He had specifically asked them all to aid Amanda whenever she asked. This seemed a little more than what she thought He had in mind, but who was she to argue? "I agree with Amanda. Tell us what you need and we will make it happen."

Everyone turned to stare at Rasa. They wondered what had made her suddenly so amenable to helping. Amanda sighed with relief that at least one hurdle had been overcome. Now they had to figure out a way to get Neal away. Amanda had a sense of déjà vu as she realized this was almost the same scenario as before when she needed to rescue the same man from Elder Vargen. Most likely he would be drugged senseless again. Maybe she should include a couple of men to help carry him. Bryon and Riccan had been there the time before…maybe. No, she would make this work. They had wheelchairs available at the center, she would find out if she could make use of one of them. A solution would present itself, of that she felt certain.

"Why don't we look up the building plans in our patil?" Rasa asked. "We have some pretty fancy systems in place for knowing Earth's city on the other side of the veil."

"You do?" Amanda asked as she wondered what else they might have concerning Earth.

Rasa used a portable patil to pull up the program and typed in the facility name. At first she saw the same statistics and details Amanda had seen herself. Then Rasa clicked a few more keys and she pulled up the utility grid under the building as well as the building plans themselves.

Immediately, Amanda could see an easy way for them to access the building unseen. They would use the utility tunnels and the service elevator to gain entry. Amanda had another thought and asked, "Do you have access to the computer system to find out Neal's room number?"

"I don't know, let me see," Rasa said as she chewed on her lower lip and tried a few different options. On her third try she was successful. She turned to Amanda and said, "Does this look right?"

Amanda jumped out of her chair and leaned in closer to see the screen. "Yes! Type in Nealan Taivas Jr." She spelled out his name and waited anxiously for Rasa to follow her instructions, feeling her heart rate increase as the system seemed to stall before it finally populated the screen with the current information. Room 1369! "Can you find where his room is located in the building?"

Almost too easily, the women worked out the best route and the plan for extraction. Amanda was so relieved to have included Rasa. She was certain they would have failed without her amazing program letting them know exactly what they needed. The mood in the room was almost cele-bratory as they finished printing out the plans and each held their own copy.

"Okay, so tomorrow morning, with the exception of Barla, we will all go to Central Park where the Gate lets out. Then we'll take a cab to Queens where we will access the tunnel. The four of us will go in to the tunnels. One will wait at the entrance to the service elevator while three of us take it up to the thirteenth floor. One will remain with the elevator to keep it from getting used. Two of us will take a wheelchair down the hall, two doors to the left, and we will get Neal into the chair and hightail it back to the elevator. Does that sound about right?" Amanda looked around to see if anyone had any changes or objections. When everyone nodded, Amanda sat back in her chair and hoped it would go as they wanted, too much was at stake for failure.

The only things which were missing were the wheelchair and the white uniforms. Amanda mused over how they would get those things in time. She decided she needed to go home and let Riccan know what was happening. Barla and Vinia opted to spend the night in Manzanit much to Rasa's pleasure. Rasa offered to take Amanda back to the landing field and she gladly accepted.

When they were alone in the transport, Amanda spoke of her concerns to Rasa. "I don't know how we're going to blend in once we're at the center. Also I don't know how we're going to get a wheelchair for Neal. I'm sure he'll be drugged out of his mind and won't be able to walk."

"I see," Rasa said as she thought swiftly about how to solve the problems at hand. "The Elders wear white pant suits for formal occasions. Do you think that would work?"

Amanda remembered the clothing Elder Debbon had worn in her dream and she nodded her head enthusiastically. "Yes, that would be perfect. Do you have enough outfits for the three of you?"

"Yes. Do you need one as well?"

"No, I'm going to buy a white set of scrubs when I get home. Now we just need to worry about the wheelchair." Amanda's excitement dulled as she realized the chair would be the harder of the two items needed.

"Won't they have chairs in the center?" Rasa asked reasonably.

"Yes, but I don't expect one to be outside of Neal's room!"

Rasa got a wicked gleam in her eye as she said, "I do!"

"What are you thinking, Rasa?"

"As long as they have them available in the building, I can teleport one right to where we need it, when we need it. It's simple, really!" Rasa sat back with a pleased smile.

"Do you think it'll work just as easily on Earth? You won't have the same control as you do here. Riccan has told me it's slightly different."

"Hmm, I don't know, but I'll certainly be trying my hardest. If it doesn't work, then I'll have to resort to something else."

"Like what?"

"Translation if it comes right down to it."

"Seriously? You think you could do that easier than producing a chair? Why don't we just do that anyway?"

"Translation is very risky and it pulls a lot of power. We'll only use it as a last resort because we don't want to draw any attention to what we're doing. Lucinden is watching for any changes in the power structure."

"Lucinden? What has he been up to?" Amanda suddenly realized the connection between Ela Nena, Riccan, and Lucinden and she did not like where her thoughts had taken her.

"Just more of the same. He's forever trying to keep the balance of power tipped toward his purposes. Whenever there's a disturbance to the power, Lucinden sends out his minions to figure out what happened. When those people are around, there's usually something catastrophic happening and we want to avoid that at all cost."

"Disturbance of power," Amanda muttered to herself. She realized they had been amassing power in their home for several months by collecting the samaras and probably drawing attention to their safe location on Earth. She was going to have to talk about this situation with Riccan as soon as she got home. It simply was not wise to keep the samaras together if it would draw trouble to their very gates.

The transport stopped and Amanda noticed they were already at the landing field. She hugged Rasa and got out. She waved over her shoulder as she raced back to her telepod. Amanda was desperate to get home and make plans to disburse the samaras as soon as possible.

CHAPTER 36

Jon wondered what his siblings could be up to when they invited him into Behn's room for a family conference. As soon as he saw Juila and Jena he became even more suspicious. He hoped they were finally going to tell him what they knew about their mother. They had been so secretive and the things which Sofia had been telling him were making him even more curious as to what they had been discovering.

He sat down on the desk chair in Behn's room as everyone else was already seated on the bed. It seemed strange to have everyone looking at him, almost appraising what his reaction would be to whatever they wanted to share. Finally, he could not take the silence anymore and he asked, "What do you know about our mother?"

Valentina and Behn exchanged looks of surprise before Valentina replied, "We found out about someone who thought she was our mother. We wanted to meet with her and ask her questions to make sure she really was our mother before we told you anything about her. The last thing we wanted to do was keep you out of the loop, it's just, you've always said the Wilson's were our parents."

Jon smiled at Valentina's nervous rambling. She must really be rattled if she felt she had to explain so much. Normally, she was a very matter-of-fact, too bad if it hurt your feelings, kind of sister. "So I take it you're satisfied that she is our mother. Why has it taken her so long to try to find us?"

Again, Behn and Valentina exchanged knowing looks before Behn answered, "It's complicated. What we share with you today must not leave this room. Promise us right now that you'll tell no one what we are about to talk about."

Now it was Jon's turn to raise his eyebrows at his brother's edict. He could not imagine anything being so top-secret that he would not be able to share it with at least Sofia. Finally he shrugged his shoulders and said, "Okay, I promise. What's the deal guys? Is our mother a secret service agent or something?" He tried to make a joke of it, but soon realized nobody was laughing with him.

Juila spoke up and said, "I think you should demonstrate your skills before you tell him anything more. It's already hard enough to believe without actual proof of what you're saying. Why don't you show him the progression of lessons together?"

The siblings nodded as they each held their hands out in front of them and produced a ball of elemy seemingly out of thin air. Jon's eyes widened as he stared at the spheres of light as they formed, moved away from their hands, and then promptly retreated back into nothingness.

"That was wicked! When did you learn to do magic and what does that have to do with our mother?" Jon tried to process everything all at once and failed to see any connection.

Instead of answering Jon's questions, Jena began telling Jon the history of his world as he would have heard it as a child. "Long ago, Jehoban created the universe."

Jon stared in disbelief as he turned his gaze to Jena and continued to listen to her bizarre tale.

"Once the worlds were created, Jehoban and His son, Emmanuen, decided to create people in their image. The people of Tuala pleased them the most and they decided to live with them on an island known as Acaim. Emmanuen went out into another world to teach while Jehoban stayed in Tuala and taught the Elders how to rule over the other children. Tuala became very populated and the Elders each took a seat of power at the major Ascension Gates.

"Jehoban blessed all of His children with birth crystals which allowed them to access the land's elemental energy, known now as elemy, so they could prosper and lead simple lives without toil and stress. The children are taught how to use the elemy in their everyday lives and it is our way of life."

Juila used Jena's story to prove what she did next. She pulled on the chain around her neck until the tree-of-life pendant filled with ruby crystals appeared above the collar of her shirt. "This is a birth crystal. Within twenty-four hours of taking their first breath, each child is given his or her own. It is a symbol between Jehoban and His children of protection and acceptance. Only children of Tuala are ever given this gift. Every one of us in this room has been blessed by Jehoban in the receipt of our own birth crystals."

Unconsciously, Jon raised his hand to feel his own pendant hidden under his shirt. The jewel had always been a part of his life and he seldom even remembered he wore it. Even as he processed the things which he heard, he began to remember something about watching his siblings practice the same skills they had just demonstrated for him. He shook his head as he tried to make sense of the confusing images.

"I don't understand what you're saying. What does this have to do with finding our mother?"

"Look deep into your first memories, Jon. Do you recall ever learning to use your birth crystal? Do you recall sitting at the wooden table with your mother while each of you showed her how skilled you were at learning your first lessons? Can you remember Vinia clapping her hands and telling you how wonderful and smart you all were for being so good at it?" Juila asked her questions softly without pausing in between for Jon to refute anything.

"Vinia? Her name is Vinia?" Jon spoke in a whisper, speaking only to himself. Testing her name on his tongue and finding a ring of truth in his earliest memories. "What is all of this talk about Tuala and Jehoban? Where is Tuala and who is Jehoban?"

Behn spoke, "Tuala is where we're from and Jehoban is who we call God."

Jon began laughing and slapped his knee as he said, "You guys had me going there for a minute. Now really, what have you found out about our mother?"

Valentina shook her head pityingly as though Jon were slow and said, "Here's the whole truth, Jon. Our mother's name is Vinia. She's from a place called the Roanoke Colony in Tuala. Mrs. Stel went to Tuala and brought her back to her house so we could meet her and find out if she really were our mother. Just over a year ago our mother feared for our lives and she sent us to Earth to keep us safe. She had no control over the passage of time and accidentally sent us back in time eight years. For her we've only been away for a year.

"We have a little sister named Danika who's about eight months old now. Behn and I went and saw her yesterday in Tuala. That's the reason we were gone so long without calling because we were in a different dimension and cell phones don't exactly work that far."

"Jeez, Val, you don't have to get all snotty and start telling me crazy stories. I can honestly handle the truth if you'd just give me the chance," Jon almost yelled as he stood up from the chair and made to leave the room. He would rather spend his time talking to Sofia on the phone than listen to fables.

"Sit down, Jon," Behn ordered in his best big-brother attitude.

Jon sat only because he was surprised to hear his brother's stern tone.

"You've asked for the truth and we've all told you exactly that. This. Is. The. Truth. We are not from Earth, we're from Tuala. Our mother sent us here to protect us all from the leader of the Roanoke Colony who was going to let you die and was going to marry Val even though she was only seven years old. Our mother used a samara to send us to Earth so you might live and where we could grow up in safety."

"So, you're saying Juila and Jena are from this Tuala place too? They're not really from South Africa? What about their parents? Are they aliens as well? Come on, Behn, how far does this go?" Jon stood up again to make his point.

Behn also stood up and stepped to within an inch of his brother as he said, "Yes to all of your questions. Juila and Jena are not from Earth. They have taught Val and me how to use our birth crystals just as our mother taught us when we were little. They have also taken us to the home we shared with our mother in Tuala. We have met our mother and she does look almost exactly like Mrs. Stel. We have a little sister name Danika who should only be eight years younger than us, but instead she's fifteen years younger. Our mother, Vinia, was pregnant with her when she sent us away to Earth.

"We can arrange for you to meet with her and then you can prove all of this for yourself instead of questioning us and our sanity. Don't try to deny it, I can see that look in your eyes. You think we've all been drinking the Kool-Aid. You asked for the truth, you said you believe us, and now it's up to you to hear what we've said and believe us."

"So how will I get to meet her? Will you take me to this Tuala place? What, do the Stel's have a spaceship in their garage?" Jon asked sarcastically.

"We have two of them actually," Jena said practically. "They're called telepods, not spaceships. We don't need to go to space in them since it's just another dimension and not another world."

"Okay, I've clearly heard enough. Let me know when you want to have a serious conversation about our mother," Jon said as he stomped over to the door and pulled it open so hard it slammed against the wall.

Behn was about to go after him when Juila put her hand on his arm and said, "Let him go. Once he starts thinking about everything we've told him, then he'll start to remember."

"It is a lot to take in," Jena added.

"Fine," Behn said sullenly. He wished Jon would have listened to them tell him more. "I think we should probably get you girls back home now. It's getting pretty late."

"Can I come with you?" Valentina asked.

Jon heard the four of them leave the house before immediately getting back on the phone. He knew it was later than he should call Sofia, but he really needed to vent to someone while his siblings were gone.

"Hello?" Sofia's voice answered on the fourth ring.

"Hey," Jon said as he sat down with relief on his bed. Already he could feel his pulse begin to slow just by hearing her voice. He proceeded to tell her everything he had been told. By the time he finished with the comment about the telepods in the garage he was laughing at how ludicrous the whole story sounded. He expected to hear Sofia laughing as well and yet she remained silent. "Hello? Sofia are you still there?" he asked as the silence continued.

"It all makes sense now," Sofia whispered.

"What are you talking about? You can't possibly say you're believing this bullshit are you?"

"Yes, Jon. I saw the telepod in the garage the night of the girls' birthday party. They told me it was a top-secret project Mr. Stel was working on and they swore me to secrecy. It didn't make sense at the time, but now it makes perfect sense.

"Jon, they are telling you the truth. You are all from Tuala. The girls proved that when they used the elemental energy to heal my body. I told you something strange happened. You even said you felt energy surging through my body while you held my hand. You felt the power as Juila and Jena healed me." Sofia's voice rose with excitement at finally being able to explain all of the things which had been troubling her.

"Unbelievable," Jon said. "I've got to go," he told Sofia as he hung up the phone without waiting for a reply. "I feel like I'm stuck in an episode of the Twilight Zone and everyone but me has gone crazy." He threw himself back on his bed and stared at the ceiling in disbelief. Everything had been normal all day and now nothing was right, even Sofia had turned on him.

CHAPTER 37

Checking her watch, Amanda could hardly believe it was as late as it was. When she landed in the garage at home, she saw Riccan's telepod already parked. She hurried into the house, glad she would be able to talk about the samaras sooner rather than later.

Immediately, she knew something was wrong. The house was in complete disarray with items strewn all over the floor. She stood in the doorway hardly breathing as she listened for any sounds of movement. More afraid than ever, she knew Riccan was probably somewhere in the house, possibly in danger or even hurt. Even worse, her children should have been home by now as well. What had happened here?

She stepped carefully over the debris, trying to move as quietly as possible while keeping her eyes scanning the room for any movement. Furniture was overturned in the living room and Amanda tried to locate any of her family anywhere in the room. Without any further clues, Amanda continued through the living room and down the hall.

The office was just as disheveled as everywhere else. Amanda's mind went to the samaras. This surely had to do with someone searching the house for the powerful crystals. With this in mind, she rushed her steps to get to the library. As soon as she entered the room, she groaned with dismay as she saw the wall of books open leading to the secret room. She weaved her way around the mess on the floor until she could see into the hidden space.

She must have made some sort of noise in her haste because she heard the sound of someone in the room before she saw anyone. She started to scream in fear when she saw it was Riccan. Amanda rushed forward and threw her arms around his neck and asked, "Are you okay? Are the girls okay? Talk to me."

Riccan hugged her before he removed her arms from around his neck. He held her hand while he backed her up from the bookcase wall. Pressing the lever, allowing the wall to silently move back to its original space, he answered. "I'm fine. The girls left a message saying they were going over to the Wilson's house to study. We do have a problem, though."

"Oh, I'm so relieved to hear about the girls being safe. Did someone steal the samaras?"

It was now Riccan's turn to be shocked and he asked, "What makes you think the samaras would be stolen?"

"They're not?" She looked down and saw Riccan was holding the award from Ela Nena's office. "What are you doing with that?"

"No, they're all still in there. I just checked to make sure. What do you think happened here?" He raised the award, and said, "I'll get to this in a minute. Tell me what you know."

"I just found out Lucinden has been investigating abnormal power changes. I just thought with all of the samaras being held in one spot would certainly constitute a power shift in a big way. When I came home and saw the destruction, I just assumed they had been taken."

Riccan nodded his head at Amanda's explanation. He had just had the same realization while he was at work. The more he thought about Ela Nena's award, the quicker he came to the conclusion they were creating a dangerous situation. "I have a feeling this thing," he shook the metal object in his hand, "maybe it has a tracking device still on it. I'm going to move it somewhere where it won't lead anyone to us."

"Don't you think they already have our location?" Amanda asked as she swept her arm around to gesture to the messes everywhere.

"Maybe, but I don't think so. I think this was a simple burglary. If it really were someone from Lucinden then they would have found the samaras. Whoever did this, never even noticed there was a hidden room so the samaras have remained safe."

"So who was in here? Are they still here? Have you checked every-where? Shouldn't we call the police?" Amanda suddenly felt very unsafe even with her husband right in front of her.

"I'm not sure who it was, nobody was here when I got home. I've been through the entire house, the samara room was the last place I checked. I'm not going to call the police, but I am going to increase the security both in and around the house."

"How are you going to do that? It's not as if it can happen overnight. I don't feel safe here now!"

"That's where you're wrong. Just like my parents' Residence, I can set up ward around the property to keep anything like this from ever happening again. I'm also going to set up shields around the samaras, which I should have done a long time ago. I'm only sorry I didn't think of it sooner. Now this," he shook the award, "I'm going to take far away. Do you want to come with me?"

Just the idea of being left alone in the house while it was turned upside down seemed like a terrible idea. Amanda immediately nodded and kept herself very close to her husband's side. She had no idea where they were going, but anywhere else seemed better than home at the moment.

Riccan could feel the trembling in his wife's hand as it gripped his arm tightly. He had no idea this break-in could affect her so deeply. To help alleviate some of her fear he used his power to put each room back to rights as they either passed through them or by them on their way to the garage. He wished he would have done it before Amanda got home, but she had come back unexpectedly early.

To put Amanda's mind onto something else, Riccan asked, "Tell me about your day."

Amanda had to concentrate hard to even remember what she had been doing since her fear had become almost paralyzing. All at once she remembered and told Riccan about Jessica's visit over Neal's new treat-ment. She told him about Dr. Gascon's involvement and what her new plans were for getting him out of the psychiatric center.

Riccan frowned slightly. He wished Amanda would not put herself at risk so much for the man of her past. He did, however, understand her desire to make sure he got his life back after all they had been through. Amanda's caring heart was one of the things which made her so perfect so he could hardly fault her for wanting to help. He was glad to hear Rasa was going to be involved since she had a lot more to lose if she were not discreet in her interactions with people from Earth.

His plan to distract Amanda had worked to distract both of them. He found he had no idea where he wanted to take the award. Wherever he picked, it would have to be far away from their home. He needed to make sure it would be in a spot where nobody could get hurt if it were being actively tracked.

They buckled into their seats in the telepod and Riccan entered in a course to take them back to Tuala at their current location. Once there he would decide where they would go. He hit the activation button and their surroundings became peaceful and black. Several seconds later, they reappeared hovering high in the air over lush, green trees near the ocean's shoreline.

Amanda looked out the window, thought she recognized the scenery, and asked, "Is this the Tualan equivalent to our home?"

Riccan's smile showed he was pleased with her astute question and his nod confirmed her guess. "Which direction do you want to go?"

"Southwest," she answered without hesitation.

Riccan enjoyed flying straight since it was not often practiced. The feel of the controls under his hand made him remember all over again why he took up flying in the first place.

After several minutes Amanda looked down and saw a school of dolphins in the water. She pointed and said, "Maybe they'd like something to play with."

Riccan laughed, reached down to the floor by his feet, picked up the award, and handed it over to her. "Feel free to give them some entertainment."

Amanda waited for Riccan to stop the telepod and hover near the water before she grabbed the metal statue. She opened her window and dropped the object into the water. She felt a great sense of relief to see it splash down into the water and sink below the surface. The dolphins were nowhere to be seen anymore, yet Amanda hoped they might come back to play with it. If they moved it far out to sea, then nobody would ever find it again. Maybe the tracking device would lead Lucinden's men on a merry little chase to frustration.

Riccan saw the look of satisfaction on Amanda's face and was thankful he could give her back some sense of power. He pulled back on the manual lever to speedily lift the telepod up to get out of the ground effect of the wind interacting with the water. It was dangerous to be too close to the water because of unpredictable wind and water.

Not really wanting to go home, and thankful she already had an excuse to go out, Amanda said, "I need to go shopping when we get back."

"What are you going to get?"

"White scrubs."

"That's kind of odd. What do you need those for?"

"So I can blend in better when we're getting Neal out of the hospital."

"Oh." Riccan liked the idea less now that he had thought about it more. It was one thing for Amanda to do something slightly dangerous on Tuala where he could partially control the outcome, it was another thing entirely to risk herself on Earth where he had no pull at all. "Are you sure there isn't some other way which isn't illegal. You could get caught, you know. Have you thought about that?"

Amanda noticed Riccan had not said anything about not going, he just did not like her current plan. She wished she could present him with several variations, yet they only had the one proposal. "I just can't get caught. Besides, Rasa said she would use teleportation if it came right down to it."

"Even better, Amanda. Now you're risking Rasa's career as well as your own life."

"What are you saying, Riccan?"

"Rasa knows better than to interfere in Earth matters. Just by her helping you she is risking her career. If she uses her powers on Earth she faces the penalty of having her mind swiped for misuse of power."

"Oh, I didn't know it was so serious. It was Rasa's own idea, after all."

Slightly mollified, Riccan added, "I'm sure Rasa will keep you all very safe. She has too much to lose now. I'm glad she's going with you."

"Your confidence in my ability is staggering, Riccan," Amanda said sarcastically as she rolled her eyes and shifted her head to look out her side window.

Riccan wisely stayed quiet. He had done as he intended, he made her think about what she was asking of the others. Now Amanda would be even more careful in her mission. He tapped the glass panel and selected the home button as their destination. He removed his hand from the manual control and hit the activation button and took them home.

Amanda did not say anything as she walked out of the telepod and across the garage. She opened the door to go inside, expecting to see the disarray. She simply stared as she saw everything was immaculate again as though nothing had happened.

Riccan caught up to her and placed his hand on the small of her back to push her inside gently. "Don't be so shocked. I took care of it all before we left. I figured we wouldn't want the girls to come home to something so shocking."

"Oh, that was very thoughtful of you," Amanda said as she kissed his cheek. It seemed more like a bad dream since everything was back to normal. "I'm going to run to the store. I won't be long," she said as she kept walking through the kitchen, picked up her purse from the kitchen desk, continued down the hallway, and out to the other garage to get to her truck. She pulled out onto the main road and waved as she saw the girls in a car heading toward their house. It was very nice to know they had been spared the ugliness of the break-in.

CHAPTER 38

Amanda smoothed her scrubs outfit down her body one more time before she left the house and got into her telepod. So much depended on this mission going well, and she did not want to endanger any of her friends from Tuala. They simply had to succeed.

The trip to Manzanit went smoothly and Amanda found a landing spot even closer to the landing field's entrance than she had the day before. She found a transport to take her to the Residence. Since they had not previously agreed to what time to meet, Amanda decided to be rather early so they could go over the plan again and make any changes they might have thought of overnight.

The guards at the main entrance let her through without any protest so she at least assumed they were told to expect her. When the transport stopped outside the main door, Amanda paid with the shills she had put into her pocket for this purpose, and she stepped out wondering what she should do next.

The door opened and Rasa stepped out to greet her. She laughed at Amanda's expression and admitted, "The main gate guards were instructed to tell me when you arrived. There's no mystery to my showing up to greet you. I did expect you to arrive early since this is such an important task for us to get right the first time! Let's go inside and get something to eat. I'm sure you were too nervous to eat before you left, right?"

Amanda nodded and felt herself be pulled into the building and led down the halls. She felt as though she were sleepwalking and everything was being taken care of for her. It was such a nice feeling she almost did not want it to end. When they got to the small sitting room, Rasa passed her a cup of hot steena tea and a small plate of fruit.

She found herself relaxing as she listened to Rasa and the other women chat about their lives. She took a sip of the tea and found it exactly to her liking, she took another sip, then another. Before she knew it, the tea was gone as well as all of the fruit on the plate she had been given. Rasa was very intuitive when it came to reading people and knowing what they needed, Amanda had to admit to herself.

"Okay," Rasa announced as soon as she noticed Amanda setting her empty dishes onto the table. "We're all clear on what our objective is for the day. I say we go to the Gate and get on our way. It might take us some time to get over to the psychiatric center so we should plan for that as well. Is everyone ready?"

For the first time, Amanda noticed all of the women were already wearing their matching white outfits. She tried to swallow with her suddenly dry throat and stood up. This would be her first time using a sanctioned Gate and she was actually more nervous about it than she had even believed she could be. When she looked around, the other women seemed relaxed about it, rather excited actually about the adventure they were about to undertake. She took heart at their objectivity and already felt better about their chances of success.

When they all stepped down into the depression in the ground at the Gate's vortex, Amanda wondered if there were a limit to the number of people who could travel at the same time. She also did not understand who would be directing their travel if Rasa was going with them. "Who's going to operate the Gate?" she asked as they all waited to go.

"I can do it remotely," Rasa replied easily. "Is everyone ready?"

With affirmative answers all around, Rasa closed her eyes and used her mind to activate the Gate to send them to Earth. She could not see the blackness around her, but she could feel the shift in their reality as they moved from one dimension to the other. As soon as she felt the elemy return to the Earth, she knew the transfer had been a complete success and she opened her eyes.

The women around her were all wide-eyed with wonder at their new surroundings. Just as Willian had noted the day before, the branches formed a sort of cave around them which allowed sunlight to stream through in small patterns. They waited for Rasa to make the first move.

Noticing the lack of movement around her, Rasa took the lead and stepped up out of the depression in the dirt and through the opening in the branches. She could hear the leaves rustling behind her as the other three women trailed behind her. When she reached the bench near the Gate, she turned and waited for everyone to catch up. Chelesa seemed oddly distracted and Rasa asked, "Chelesa, what's wrong?"

"Don't you feel it?" she asked as she searched around for something.

"Feel what? All I feel is the power of the Gate," Rasa replied.

"No, there's something different. Remember when we went walking through the gardens at your Residence and I told you I felt a strange pull?"

"Yes."

"It feels even stronger here."

"We can take a few minutes right now to look around, but we really need to worry about getting Neal."

Amanda turned to look at Chelesa when an idea came to her. She asked, "Does the thing you're feeling seem a lot like the same thing you feel when you draw energy from the earth?"

"Yes, that's exactly what it feels like. How did you know?"

"Rasa, I think we're going to have to take the time for this. This is something more important than we could have guessed. In fact, I think this might have been the reason we were all getting involved in this unlikely quest."

"What are you saying, Amanda? What do you think is here?"

"I could be wrong, yet I think the samara meant for Chelesa is hidden here somewhere. We should spread out and try to help her find the source of the power she feels."

Excitement spread through the group as they focused their attention to feeling any power around them. Vinia seemed to hang back a bit not knowing if it were her place to be involved. The other women in the group seemed to have such a clear sense of purpose and she was still trying to find her way in life. This search seemed to bring her insecurities to the forefront.

While the other women began to spread out, Vinia stayed at the bench where she sat down. She turned her head to check the progress of the women when her eye was caught by something sparkling in the sunlight. She got up to investigate. She lost sight of the shininess and had to return to the bench to better pinpoint the location. This time she went unerringly to the right spot and parted the ferns to find a crystal skull nestled in a hollow of the ground.

"Amanda! Chelesa! Rasa! I found it!" Vinia announced as she stepped away from the samara since she still held fear in her heart for the one she had once been a keeper of.

The sounds of footsteps in foliage converged on where Vinia had remained standing. Amanda was the first to say, "Where is it?"

Vinia pointed to the ferns without moving from her spot.

Rasa began to move forward until Amanda grabbed her arm and said, "Let Chelesa get it. She's the one who felt it."

Rasa nodded and held herself back even though she desperately wanted to touch it.

Amanda asked one more question, "Can you read auras, Chelesa?"

"Yes," she replied as she kneeled on the ground. She looked up at Amanda wondering why she would suddenly be changing the subject and asked, "Why?"

"Before you touch the samara, look to see if the color of its aura is the same as your birth crystal." Amanda's theory was about to be put to the test. It would be way too much of a coincidence if it were the same color and not be the samara made for Chelesa.

Chelesa focused her skill toward the clear crystal and smiled as she saw the aqua-green color perfectly matching her own birth crystal. "It's the same," she said even as she leaned forward and both of her hands cradled the sides of the smooth stone and she gasped at the surge of power entering her body and encompassing her mind.

Amanda felt another click in her mind for accomplishing this important task. Seven of the thirteen samaras had now been found and placed with their rightful owners. No matter what else happened on this day, they had already accomplished more than she had hoped. The minutes ticked by as they watched Chelesa continue to commune with her samara. They were going to have to get going soon.

The group stood transfixed by Chelesa holding the samara. Time passed and still nobody moved.

"How long will this last?" Vinia finally asked.

Amanda's mind recalled all of the other times she had seen this same scene happen. "Rasa? Can you break their connection? If you don't she could spend the entire day learning from her samara."

"I can try," she said and used her healing skill to tie into Chelesa's lifeline. Immediately she could feel the added power of the samara and it almost took her breath away to discover how powerful a conduit the stone could be. With reluctance, Rasa began to unweave the strands which were not Chelesa's so the link could be stopped. The work was different than anything she had ever tried before, yet it somehow seemed easy, as though she had done it many times before.

Amanda could see Chelesa's expression begin to return to normal and she used a stick she had located to knock the samara out of her hands. The stone fell harmlessly to the ground in the depression in the leaves.

"That was amazing," Chelesa whispered mostly to herself as she continued to stare at the samara which was to be her very own for the rest of her life.

"What happened?" Vinia asked in confusion. When she had held the samara given to her by the wise-woman Copa, it had felt like a cold, haunting stone, based mostly because the stone had been carved into the ghastly shape of a skull. She could not understand why it would have been any different for Chelesa.

"I saw the most amazing things! So many stories and people, too many to comprehend, and yet still totally incredible!" Chelesa answered as she looked up at the group surrounding her with the most serene expression on her face.

Rasa asked the most obvious question. "What are we going to do with the samara? We have no way to carry it, and we certainly don't want to leave it here unattended?"

"From what I've heard, once the samara has been claimed by its true owner, then nobody else can take it without her permission. I believe it'll be safe to leave here. Just to be certain, we could move it into the Gate's enclosure," Amanda suggested.

Chelesa went to pick it up again to do as Amanda had said when she was stopped by Amanda's panicked voice.

"Don't touch it with your bare skin, Chelesa! Pull your sleeves down to cover your hands or else you will be taken in by its power again."

"Good point," Chelesa said as she followed Amanda's instructions. Even with the thin fabric between her and the stone, she could feel the power seeping into her, enticing her to let her skin touch it again. This samara was more dangerous than she had realized, more powerful and seductive than anything she had ever experienced before.

She hurried her steps so she could limit the time she held the stone. Once inside the gate, she turned to the right and tucked it into a small space between two tree trunks. It was harder than she thought to walk away from her new treasure. She kept looking back over her shoulder, wanting to turn around and sit down with it and learn all of its secrets.

"Come on, the sooner we finish this, the sooner you can come back to it," Amanda said as if she were reading Chelesa's mind. She grabbed the woman's hand and began hauling her away from the Gate and down the small trail leading out to the crowds of Central Park.

Of the three women with Amanda, only Vinia had been to Earth before. Even Vinia's experience had been limited to the peace and quiet of Amanda's home. Amanda had to walk behind the three women to keep them moving as they kept looking around and staring at all of the buildings, cars, and people.

"Keep your focus, ladies," Amanda practically chanted as she moved them closer to where they could catch a cab. When they reached the edge of the sidewalk, Amanda leaned forward and stuck her arm out until a yellow van stopped in front of them. She opened the side door and gestured for the women to get in. Getting in last, Amanda slid the door shut and told the cab driver where they wanted to go.

Keeping in mind they were no longer alone, the women kept their comments about the surroundings to a minimum. Mostly they kept their eyes locked on the scenery moving by, occasionally widening them even more and turning to look at the other women. Amanda could only smile at their childlike enthusiasm for the escapade.

The drive took just under twenty minutes with the traffic being rather light considering they were traveling to Queens. Before they arrived at the entrance to Creedmoor Psychiatric Center, Amanda instructed the cab driver to stop and let them out. She paid him to stay and wait for them to return shortly.

"If you're not back in thirty minutes, I leave, lady," he said rudely.

Amanda looked down on her wristwatch and nodded. "We should be back by then. I guess we'll have to be if we want to get a ride."

The group of women swiftly gathered around in a circle with their heads together as they took out the map of the utility tunnels and tried to figure out where the best place to enter would be. They finally decided on the direction and hurried their steps. When they came to a small metal building with a 'No Trespassing' sign on the door, they knew they had found the right location.

Rasa stepped forward and used a small amount of elemy to unlock the door. They entered the building and immediately began going down a sloping ramp to a lower level. The lighting was poor at best so Rasa created a sphere of elemy to illuminate their way. The sounds of their footsteps echoed off the walls around them as they went deeper underground.

They came to an intersection where they consulted the map again and turned to the left. They made one wrong turn which they promptly realized since it was a dead-end, and they retraced their steps and went the right way. Other than the one mishap, they rapidly found the service elevator leading up into the psychiatric center.

Amanda pressed the button and hoped it would not set off any alarms. The doors opened to reveal an empty car. As they had planned, Chelesa would remain in the access tunnel while the rest of the women filed into the lift. Chelesa would be able to communicate with Rasa should anybody come and start asking questions.

Amanda selected the thirteenth floor and felt her heart begin to beat faster at each floor they passed. So far everything had been working out perfectly and it made her even more nervous. Surely there would be more people in the hallway when the doors opened. They would have to be as inconspicuous as possible.

Amanda cried out as a wheelchair appeared in the elevator with them. Her eyes darted to Rasa who only looked smug at her ability to produce the chair so easily. She was glad Rasa had remembered her part of the plan since Amanda had been so nervous about meeting other people that she had completely forgotten about needing the chair.

The panel above the door changed to the number thirteen. Amanda took a deep, calming breath and slowly let it out as she grabbed the handles on the back of the wheelchair. As the doors opened, she was ready to act the part of a bored attendant.

She pushed the chair out of the elevator and casually looked to the left and the right. The halls were empty. It was too good to be true! She turned down the hall with Rasa at her side. Vinia waited in the elevator with her finger holding down the open door button.

They could hear voices at the end of the hall, but nobody came out to confront them. Amanda found Room 1369 and tried to open the door only to find it locked. She hissed in frustration and looked over to Rasa to see what they would do.

As Rasa had done at the utility shack, she reached forward and touched the doorknob. She grasped the handle and it turned with ease. She pushed the door in and saw Neal curled up on top of the bed. He appeared fast asleep and oblivious to everything.

Amanda rushed forward with the chair and whispered, "Shut the door while we get him in the chair." She positioned the chair right beside him and touched his shoulder. "Neal? Neal, wake up!" She spoke in a quiet tone and realized he was drugged to the point of almost comatose. She shivered at the recollection it brought her of her comatose memory of being treated by Dr. Gascon herself. Amanda shook him harder one last time before she gave up and turned to Rasa for help moving him.

Rasa helped her move him to a sitting position on the edge of the bed. Together they hoisted him into the chair and then realized they were not going to be able to keep him sitting up in the chair. Surely they would be noticed if their patient was slumped over in the wheelchair.

Amanda finally grabbed a hunk of the back of Neal's shirt and held it tight against the edge of the chair. She nodded her readiness to Rasa who had gone back to the door to see if the coast were clear. They walked into the hallway and almost made it to the elevator when they heard someone behind them.

"Hey!" a man's voice yelled. "Where are you taking him? He's not scheduled today! Hey, stop!"

They could hear his footsteps falling faster as he tried to catch up to them. Amanda walked faster and turned into the elevator. She pushed the basement button and then the close door button and hoped it would be faster than the approaching man. The door slid closed and they started to descend.

Amanda all but collapsed behind Neal's chair in her relief. They had almost been caught and they weren't in the clear yet.

"Who was that? What happened?" Vinia asked of either woman.

"An employee who now knows a patient is not where he belongs," Amanda answered. "Can you make this elevator go faster, Rasa?"

"I can try," she said as she focused her mind on the cables of the elevator car. It took her a second, but she figured out the way the gears worked and she moved them faster until she saw they were almost to the basement. She removed her touch and let the elevator settle to it normal speed.

They touched down in the basement and the doors slowly slid open. They could see Chelesa waiting for them and she did not seem anxious at all. Obviously, nobody had thought to send a guard down this far…yet. As soon as the doors were wide enough to get the wheelchair through, Amanda pushed the wheels over the bumpy threshold and began walking as fast as she could.

"Two people go ahead of me and figure out which way we're supposed to go. Someone stay behind me to keep anyone from catching us," Amanda ordered as she continue to run. Her breath was coming in gasps as the impact of what they were trying to accomplish hit her hard. They still had to go up the ramp, out to the cab—if he were still waiting—and then back to Central Park. "What was I thinking?" she muttered to herself.

Faintly, in the distance, they could hear an alarm being sounded. The building had been alerted to the escape and now they were going to be hunted. The only advantage they had was that the utility shed was so far away from the hospital, they would probably remain unnoticed long enough to get into the taxi. Amanda wished she could see her watch to know how much time they had taken. The taxi driver had better stayed put otherwise they were going to be in real trouble.

They reached the final ramp and Amanda struggled to keep going. Rasa came up behind her and took one handle while she pushed Amanda over to the other side. Together they pushed until they reached the utility shed door. Vinia was the first to exit the building, followed closely by Chelesa and then Neal's wheelchair.

The bright sunlight was hard to take after the dimness of the underground tunnels. Rasa took over the pushing of the chair as they went over the rough gravel path. Amanda glanced at her watch and saw they still had another five minutes with the cab driver. It was going to be close, they were going to have to go faster.

"Hurry!" Amanda said in hushed tones as she stayed behind Rasa, protecting her back. She looked over her shoulder expecting imminent pursuit and was relieved to see the path was still clear. She looked ahead to see if they were able to view the parking lot where the cab should be and she was relieved to see it was still parked.

They reached the van and Amanda slid the door open. Among the four of them they managed to maneuver Neal onto the middle bench seat. Amanda collapsed the wheelchair and shoved it behind the seat, apologizing as she jammed it into Vinia's shins. "Back to Central Park," Amanda almost yelled at the driver in her urgency to get going. He started moving the cab even before she finished shutting the door.

"I was just about to leave, lady. It's a good thing you got back when you did," the driver said over his shoulder as he maneuvered his way back onto the route to Central Park.

The women were silent as they each relived what they had just accomplished. Amanda had another fright when she heard sirens coming toward them. She held her breath until the three squad cars raced past them on their way to the psychiatric center.

"What's wrong with your friend?" the driver asked as he looked at Neal in the rear-view mirror.

"He's drunk," Amanda lied. "We need to get him home."

"It's a good thing you're helping him then."

Minutes ticked by and Amanda began to be able to breathe again. There were no more sirens in either direction, they were not being pursued. Not until this moment did Amanda realize they had no plans for what they were going to do with Neal now that they had him free. She had been so focused on getting him out of there, and yet now they had another problem.

It would be impossible to take Neal on a flight to Miami, he was drugged into a stupor and would be quite memorable to any of the airline staff. If she took him back to Tuala, he would lose whatever memories he had regained since coming home. They definitely could not discuss their problem in front of the cab driver, Amanda began to go through their options.

She was no closer to a solution when they pulled up in front of Central Park where the taxi had picked them up in the first place. He pulled over to the curb and held up his hand for the fare. Amanda paid him the fare plus a tip of twenty dollars. She hoped he would forget he had ever seen them.

They managed to get Neal back into the chair. When Amanda moved behind the chair to begin pushing it, she realized the name of the facility was written in big white letters across the whole back. Obviously they were going to have to keep it hidden from everyone, including the driver.

The walk across the expanse of the park seemed to take forever. It felt as if everyone stared at them as they walked past. Whenever Amanda saw someone on their cell phone she felt as though they were calling the police. She knew she was being paranoid and yet she could not stop herself. She knew they had done something very wrong for all the right reasons.

The going was tough and made worse when they reached the wooded areas where the trails were not as well-groomed nor as wide. The jostling and jolting of the rough terrain began to rouse Neal, unfortunately not enough for him to be able to help by walking on his own. Instead, he began to become quite vocal in his protest of the jerking movements. Amanda tried to shush him and finally had to give it up as a lost cause.

By the time they reached the location of the Gate, the trail had become so overgrown that they four woman practically had to carry the chair on each of the four corners to get it to the clearing. Everyone was exhausted and yet they were not able to relax until they were back in Tuala.

They moved Neal into the depression under the cavern of branches and immediately realized there was not enough room for the chair and all four of the women to stand around it. Vinia solved the problem by sitting down on Neal's lap. She had missed being so close to him and yet she felt terrible for how he looked. This was not the reunion she had imagined for them.

Chelesa bent down and, with her sleeves covering her hands, she picked up her samara. She stepped back into the circle and looked out the entrance of the Gate. She saw people moving through the forest in a path which looked like they were coming to where they were standing. "There're people coming. Hurry up and go, Rasa!"

Rasa put her arms around the women beside her and muttered under her breath, "Inside Ascension." The energy surged up faster than it had before and enveloped them in darkness. With increasing intensity, they arrived back in Manzanit faster than Amanda had ever known before in her travels between the two realms.

The women were silent as they took stock in their situation.

Neal, on the other hand, became very vocal. "Hey, what's going on here? Where am I?"

Amanda turned to Rasa and asked, "What happened to Neal? Why is he suddenly awake?"

"The transfer must have cleared the drugs out of his system."

"The same as it did with the resh? I should have anticipated this. What are we going to tell him?" she whispered urgently.

"It sounds like we can leave it up to Vinia." Rasa pointed to the two of them still sitting together in the wheelchair.

"Vinia, what are you doing? Where are we?" Neal asked Vinia as he finally noticed she was sitting on his lap.

"Nealan, oh I'm so glad you still remember me!" Vinia gushed as she hugged him to her.

"Of course I still remember you. Are you okay? Are you going to answer me? Why are we here? Where are we?" Neal tried to push Vinia off of his neck so he could get her to look at him and start giving him the answers he was ready to hear. With every passing moment, he began to get angrier.

"We're safe now. We're in Manzanit and I'll tell you everything once we go back to my room." She got off of his lap and began to go around to the back of his chair to wheel him out of the Ascension Gate portal.

Before she had gone more than two steps, Neal stood up and looked around the room with surprised interest. "I've never heard of Manzanit. Where is it?" He saw the other four women and wondered who they were. His eyes stopped on Amanda and then darted back to Vinia. "Why do you two look so much alike?"

"Good question," Amanda said and started to lead the way out of the room. "I think we should go somewhere else to talk about this. Are you coming?" she asked over her shoulder and expected him to follow. For some reason, it was hard for Amanda to see Neal recognize Vinia but not herself. If she were being honest with herself, she would call it jealousy. Her mind knew it was ridiculous since she was happily married, yet her heart still had feelings for the history she had shared with him.

Amanda watched Chelesa leave the room with her samara still held in front of her. She suspected she would head to her own room so she could peer into the depths of the crystal again. At least one person had made a worthwhile discovery on this day.

Just as Amanda made it to the doorway Rasa made an unexpected announcement, "There's movement registering on the Earth side of the Gate."

Rushing back to stand between Rasa and Barla at the controls, Amanda asked, "Is there any way to see anything? Could it be an animal? Is it a person?"

Rasa manipulated a few controls and then looked over to the now-empty gate entrance. There appeared a blurry image of a man looking straight ahead like he could see them.

Amanda's hands flew up to her mouth in disbelief. She took an involuntary step back and shook her head. "He can't see us, can he?" she asked urgently.

"No. What's wrong? Do you know him?" Rasa asked even as she disengaged the visual mode.

"That was Dr. Gascon. What was he doing there? He was supposed to be presenting at a meeting downtown. How could he have ended up at the gate just after we left there? Was he following us? How much did Neal tell him?"

Even more questions flooded Amanda's mind which she kept to herself. She felt dirty all over. Her whole family was in danger now and she knew it was her fault this time. Riccan had been right to try to keep her away from Neal's unfortunate situation.

CHAPTER 39

D r. Gascon had finished with his presentation at the psychiatric convention and had opted to take a stroll in Central Park before heading back to work. The day had been a glorious success and the people had flocked over to talk with him after he had spoken. Nothing was going to ruin the high he was currently feeling. Even the warm sunshine seemed to be a sign of his success.

As he walked up the concrete path he noticed a bunch of women surrounding a wheelchair. Normally he would not have given it a second thought except two of the women reminded him of someone he had met a year before. He wanted to get closer to see who they were. The crowds seemed to increase and he lost sight of them for several seconds.

He pushed roughly through the people around him, earning several rude comments. Dr. Gascon almost gave up when he caught sight of the white outfits drifting through the trees in the distance. He broke into a trot knowing he could easily catch up with them as they got further off of the paved trails.

Again he lost sight of them and he had to waste precious minutes searching the ground for signs of the wheelchair passing through. Finally, he located the correct path they had taken and he moved faster. The trail seemed to go cold as he came to an area of hard ground which had three paths to choose from.

He looked around hoping to be able to see something, instead he heard voices and hurriedly jumped through bracken and brush in the direction he heard them. Again he had to search the ground for signs of the wheelchair. Surely four women would be greatly hampered by the burden of a wheeled person through such overgrown brush.

He scratched his head and looked around in frustrated anger. His cell phone began to ring and he chose to ignore it in favor of his current pursuit. The distraction caused him to switch his gaze which then caught the sight of movement off to his right. The four women and the man in the wheelchair were trying to hide inside a copse of trees. He had them now.

He gave up on trying to find any trail as he headed straight for them through the overgrown brush. The woman in the front locked eyes with him and he smiled wickedly. He looked beside her and saw the woman he had believed he knew and realized she was older than the woman he knew. He quickly searched the other faces and saw the girl he had originally believed he had seen. Amanda Covington was within his grasp.

In his haste, he tripped on a shallow root and looked down to catch himself. He felt a strange tingly feeling all over his body and he could see the hair of his arms standing on end. When he straightened back up and looked at where the group had been, the copse was empty. He scanned the area hastily to try to locate them scurrying away.

Nothing; the area was completely empty. Silence surrounded him. The feeling he had experienced where his hair had stood up was gone as well. He charged forward to investigate the last place he had seen the group. He could clearly see footprints and wheelchair tracks on the ground and still they seemed to have disappeared into thin air.

He remained staring at the empty space when his cell phone rang again. In anger, he grabbed the phone and flipped it open. "What?" he yelled.

"Dr. Gascon, we have a problem," a man's voice said from the other end.

"Who is this and what do you mean?"

"This is George from Creedmoor. It appears your patient, Nealand Taivas, has gone missing. We believe he had help."

"Oh, you think? Of course he had help, he was drugged senseless. Have you contacted the authorities?"

"Yes, Dr. Gascon, they are on the scene as we speak."

"Let me guess, nobody saw anything and none of the cameras caught anything either." Dr. Gascon turned to look at the empty area where he had last seen the people. He was certain now that the man in the wheelchair had been Nealand. Of course it would make sense that his ex-fiancé would be interested in keeping him from talking.

The next course of action became clear and he said, "Tell the authorities to go to JFK airport. I believe Amanda Covington is responsible for kidnapping him and she would have to take him there to get him back home." Even as he spoke, he felt the hair rise on his arms again and he looked into the opening of the trees, not knowing what to expect. He flipped his phone shut and circled the last place he had seen Amanda.

There was more to this story and he was going to get to the bottom of it. He smiled to himself as he realized Amanda had made a grave mistake. By taking Neal from him, he now had grounds to question her himself. He was going to get the interview with her he had wanted over a year ago. Maybe he could even get her institutionalized and then he could do to her what he had wanted to do all along.

~

Want more?

Dreams can come true... but what about the nightmares?
Only eight days are needed to shift everything in the lives of the Stel family. Life charges ahead as the mysteries deepen. But is it for the better?

<u>THE SOULS OF CHILDREN.</u>

GET MY FREE NOVELLA NOW

To let others know how much you enjoyed this book, please leave a review at your favorite retailer.

To keep updated on new releases, visit www.AmyProebstel.com.

Receive a FREE exclusive novella,

Tuala's Lost Boy: Ceren's Story

at https://geni.us/BMNLSU

by signing up for Amy Proebstel's newsletter.

You can also follow Amy Proebstel on Facebook at www.facebook.com/ATwistOnReality.

ABOUT THE AUTHOR

USA Today bestselling author, Amy Proebstel, writes epic dragon fantasy, magical realism fantasy, clean fated mate shifter romance, clean contemporary romance, and sweet young adult medical romance.

When she's not busy writing about young heroines and dragons saving the world, she spends her time binge-watching YouTube adventures, taking her husband and daughter flying, playing with her Pomeranian and Pomskies, or reading. If you like her books, she recommends you also check out Anne McCaffrey and Ava Richardson. They're the reason she started writing.

Subscribe to Amy's newsletter for a free book to get started on the journey today!

Feel free to email Amy at Amy@LevelsofAscension.com.

CHOSEN ORIGINS TRILOGY, A PORTAL FANTASY SERIES
    THE CHOSEN, A PORTAL FANTASY SERIES
    ROMANCES BEYOND TUALA, A FATED MATE SHIFTER SERIES
    BILLIONAIRE'S VENTURE ROMANCE SERIES
    DRAGON'S MAGIC: AN EPIC DRAGON FANTASY SERIES
    SWEET YOUNG ADULT MEDICAL ROMANCE SERIES

 instagram.com/amyproebstel

PEOPLE

Ahn – / ah n / – Husband of Barla. Father of Gravin and Rasa. Harbor Master at the Port of Cresdon in Thulen. Former shipping captain.

Alena – / ah **leyn** a / – Born Ab 26, 3417. Maiden name: Bellen. Marriage Date: Tishri 16, 3436. Wife of Bryon Kesh. Mother of Justan and Kyelon. Adoptive mother to Jena and Juila. Trained as a wise-woman.

Amanda – / uh **man** duh / – means 'beloved'. Born September 28, 1972, in Florida. Maiden name: Covington. Daughter of Chris and Diane. Wife of Riccan. Mother of Juila and Jena. Sister to Carrie and Deanna. Cousin to Gravin and Rasa. Former fiancé of Nealand.

Andera – / an **dair** uh / – Born Tishri 12, 3439. Daughter of Zeka. Betrothed to Justan. First-daughter of Bryon and Alena.

Andy Brun – / **an** dee **broohn** / – Neighbor friend of Riccan's on Earth. Involved in rock throwing trouble.

Angie – / **an** jee / – Nealand's new girlfriend.

Barla – / **bahr** luh / – Born January 21, 1945, in Wisconsin. Maiden name: Silnack. Birth name: Barbara. Nickname on Earth: Barla. Sister of Diane. Aunt of Amanda. Wife of Ahn. Mother of Gravin and Rasa. Raised Jena and Juila until they were six anons old. Birth crystal color: bright blue.

Behn – / **ben** / – Earth Surname: Wilson. Triplet brother to Valentina and Jon. Sent to Earth by mother, Vinia, from Tuala when he was eight anons old. Tall with brown hair and brown eyes. Crystal color: smoky grey.

Bistea – / bis **tee** uh / – Vendor at the marketplace in Kirma. Patient of Alena's.

Bryon – / **brahy** uh n / – Born Heshvan 2, 3416, in Kirma. Surname: Kesh. Marriage Date: Tishri 16, 3436. Husband of Alena. Father of Justan and Kyelon. Former adoptive father to Jena and Juila. Manager of Kirma Shipping and Receiving.

Carrie – / k **air** ee / – Born April 21, 1970, in Florida. Maiden name: Covington. Daughter of Chris and Diane. Sister to Deanna and Amanda. Married with two daughters.

Celia – / **see** lee uh / – Surname: Scamp. Gypsy family who stayed with Thomas Rockwood in France around 1800. Wife to Sampson. Mother of a sick daughter who received help from Thomas.

Ceren – / **sair** in / – Born approximately 3412. Adopted son of Ahn and Barla. Works at the Port of Cresdon for Captain Ahn.

Chelesa – / **chuh** lay suh / – Wife of Elder Debbon. Mother of Willian.

Chris – / **kris** / – Surname: Covington. Husband of Diane. Father of Carrie, Deanna, and Amanda.

Cleon – / **klee** on / – Transport operator at Kirma Shipping and Receiving.

Copa – / **kohp** uh / – Wise-woman for the district of Desio. Person who healed Ninan. She helped Amanda escape from Elder Vargen and found a home for Jena and Juila. Wise-woman who performed Amanda's birth-crystal ceremony.

Corva – / **kor** vuh / – Foster child of Ahn and Barla. Her parents died in a house fire.

Crysta – / **kris** tuh / – Head maid at Elder Debbon's estate.

Danika – / **dah** nee kuh / – Daughter of Vinia. Born in the Roanoke Colony one month early.

Daven – / **dav** uhn / – Surname: Stel. Son of Edwin and Murisa. Husband of Nena. Father of Riccan. Brother of Sanda, Stina, Phen, Zuna, Rucen. Student of Jehoban. Elder whose base of power is on Pantano.

Deanna – / dee **an** nuh / – Born April 5, 1971, in Florida. Maiden name: Covington. Daughter of Chris and Diane. Sister to Carrie and Amanda. Married with two daughters.

Debbon – / **deb** uhn / – Elder whose base of power is on Elder Isle. Husband of Chelesa. Father of Willian.

Denana – / **day** naw nuh / – Employee in the Engineering Department at Telepod Engineering Company.

Diane – / dahy **an** / – Born October 1, 1947. Maiden name: Silnack. Sister of Barbara and Saul. Wife of Chris. Mother of Carrie, Deanna, and Amanda.

Dr. Flores – / **flohr** ez / – The doctor treating Amanda in the hospital in Cancun.

Dr. Huddleston – / **hud** ul stun / – The psychologist treating Neal Taivas, Jr.

Edwin – / **ed** win / – Surname: Stel. Husband of Murisa. Father of Daven, Sanda, Stina, Phen, Zuna, Rucen. Engineer at the Roswell Museum. Started a Construction Supply Company on Tuala. Started a Consulting Business when they moved to Acaim when Daven was six.

Ela Nena – / **eluh** nay nuh / – Married name: Dunless. Wife of Teden Dunless. Executive VP of Customer Operations at Telepod Engineering Company. Riccan's boss.

Ellen – / **el** uh n / – Maiden name: Hill. Wife of Sydney Silnack. Mother of Barla, Saul, and Diane. Married name: Silnack.

Emmanuen – / ee **man** you in / – Son of Jehoban.

Faegan – / **fay** ghin / – Presenter of the award given to Ela Nena at the Engineering Excellence Awards dinner. Also known as Vanion.

Farmer Joe – Washington asparagus farmer and former owner of the outhouse used by Riccan for senior prank.

Fordin – / **ford** in / – Former seaman friend of Ninan. Confidant of Ninan's dealings with Petre.

Frasnia – / **fraz** nee uh / – Secretary at Kirma Shipping and Receiving.

Gatson – / **gat** *suh* n / – Personal body guard for Elder Debbon. Main home is on the Elder's Islet at the seat of power.

George – / jorj / – Attendant on duty at Creedmoor Psychiatric Center when Neal went missing.

Gilora – / **gil** or uh / – Employee at Telepod Engineering Company under Riccan. Interviewer of Amanda.

Gravin – / **gra** vin / – Born Elul 30, 3421, in Port of Cresdon. Son of Ahn and Barla. Brother of Rasa. First cousin of Amanda.

Grobin – / **grow** bin / – Leader of the Roanoke Colony in Tuala.

Gwenda – / **gwen** duh / – Employee at Telepod Engineering Company under Riccan. Interviewer of Amanda.

Hashma – / **hash** muh / – A prostitute at the Lookout Tavern. Filed a sexual assault lawsuit against Petre. Mother of Petre's child.

Issyn – / **ih** sin / – Shipping captain who rescued Amanda from swimming. Friend of Captain Ahn. Main port of call is Port of Cresdon.

Jasmine Medin, MD – / **med** in / – Doctor at Cannon Memorial Asylum under Dr. Stephen Gascon.

Jehoban – / juh **ho** ban / – Means 'of all the people' who is the creator of everything. Earth equivalent: God.

Jena – / **jen** uh / – Born Iyar 22, 3443, in Kirma. Daughter of Amanda and Riccan. Twin sister of Juila. First-daughter of Elder Debbon and Chelesa. Betrothed to Willian.

Jenny – / **jen** ee / – A dance team member from Amanda's high school.

Jern – / jurn / – A trusted friend of Bryon's.

Jesisca – / jes **is** kuh / – The name given to Amanda from Petre.

Jessa – / **jes** uh / – The name given to Elder Debbon from Petre for Jena's mother.

Jessica Taivas – / **jes** i kuh **tay** v*uhs* / – Wife of Nealand Taivas Sr. Mother of Nealand Taivas Jr.

Jinya – / gin ya / – Mother of Vinia.

Jon – / **jawn** / – Earth Surname: Wilson. Triplet brother to Behn and Valentina. Sent to Earth by mother, Vinia, from Tuala when he was eight anons old. Leaner and slightly shorter than Behn. Brown hair and blue eyes. Quiet by nature.

Jonan – / **jawn** uhn / – Bullying neighbor of Ahn and Barla.

Jose – / hohz **ey** / – Mexican man who found Amanda on the beach in Cancun.

Juila – / **joo** ee luh / – Born Iyar 22, 3443, in Kirma. Daughter of Amanda and Riccan. Twin sister of Jena.

Justan – / **juhs** tan / – Born Elul 21, 3439, in Kirma. Surname: Kesh. Son of Bryon and Alena. Betrothed to Andera. Brother of Kyelon.

Kanekoa – / kan eh **koh** uh / – Person who sells her house to Ninan in Kirma.

Kendon – / **ken** duhn / – Employee at Telepod Engineering Company under Riccan. Interviewer of Amanda.

Kenen – / **ken** un / – Manager of the telepod crystal quarry in Beewa.

Kiya – / **kahy** uh / – A wise-woman in training with Alena.

Kyelon – / **kahyl** on / – Born Tishri 30, 3440, in Kirma. Surname: Kesh. Son of Bryon and Alena. Brother of Justan.

Lana – / **law** nuh / – Maiden name: Gurdin. Receptionist at Telepod Engineering Company in Durseni.

Lillia – / **lil** ee uh / – A Tualan who gave a crystal skull to Maria's family in Campeche, Mexico. Girlfriend of Lucinden. Keeper of the master samara. Also known as Wibawa.

Lindon – / **lin** duhn / – A friend of Bryon's who took him to Earth as a teenager.

Lucinden – / loo **sin** den / – One of the original angels of Jehoban. He confronted Jehoban for rule of the people and Jehoban banned him and his followers to Tuala.

Luke – / **lük** / – Surname: Thompson. Friend of Behn, Jon, and Ryan. Very athletic.

Maria – / mah **ree** ah / – The keeper of the crystal skull in Campeche, Mexico.

Mary – Riccan's housekeeper. Cleans every Friday.

Melba – / **mel** buh / – Head house maid for Elder Daven. Lives in Pantano.

Miorlen – / mee **ohr** len / – Legal advisor for Elder Debbon.

Mosan – / **mow** san / – The second-in-command in the Roanoke Colony in Tuala.

Mrs. Shoreham – Sofia's 4th period typing teacher.

Murisa – / m **yur** ih sah / – Born in Tuala. Employee of Elder Vargen sent to work in the Roswell Museum in 1947. Wife of Earthborn Edwin Stel. Mother of Daven, Sanda, Stina, Phen, Zuna, Rucen. Grandmother of Riccan.

Nealand Taivas – / **neel** uh nd **tay** *vuhs* / – Son of Nealand Taivas Sr. and Jessica Taivas. Former fiancé of Amanda. Also known as Neal on Earth and Nealan on Tuala. Former employee at the Old Soul Engineering Facility owned by Elder Vargen. Addicted to the drug resh until Amanda rescues him from Tuala and takes him through the veil between dimensions. Boyfriend of Vinia.

Nealand Taivas Sr. – / **neel** uh nd **tay** *vuhs* / – Husband of Jessica. Father of Nealand Jr.

Nedan – / **nay** dan / – Willian's best friend and neighbor.

Nena – / **nay** nuh / – Married name: Stel. Wife of Daven. Mother of Riccan. Occupation: Teacher. Lives in Pantano.

Ninan – / **nahyn** un / – Surname: Tigua. Unemployed seaman. Worked undercover for Petre to locate Jesisca. Traveled to Kirma to look for Jesisca. Works for Bryon at Kirma Shipping and Receiving. Address: Thursto Block 43-3, Kirma.

Nurse Bota – / **boht** uh / – The nurse who took care of Amanda in the hospital in Cancun.

Petre – / **pee** ter / – Surname: MacVeen. Formerly known as Petren, lost social status and forced to lose the honorific 'n' at the end of his name. Wears a black onyx ring showing his status as a Master Deceptor. First person on Tuala to encounter Amanda. Kidnapped Jena and sold her to Elder Debbon under the guise of a betrothal agreement.

Phen – / **fen** / – Surname: Stel. Son of Edwin and Murisa. Brother of Daven, Sanda, Stina, Zuna, Rucen.

Pluska – / **plu** skuh / – Daughter of Elder Wilken.

Rasa – / **rah** sah / – Born Tishri 5, 3423, in Port of Cresdon. Daughter of Ahn and Barla. Sister of Gravin. First cousin of Amanda. Student of Jehoban. First woman to become the successor to an Elder. Successor to Elder Wilken in Manzanit.

Riccan – / **rik** an / – Surname: Stel. Son of Elder Daven and Nena. Husband of Amanda. Father of Juila and Jena. Great nephew of Roderick. Chief Engineer at the Telepod Engineering Company. Popular racer of telepods.

Roderick – / **rod** eh rick / – Surname: Rockwood. Great uncle to Riccan.

Rualin – / roo **ahl** in / – A business associate of Petre.

Rucen – / **roo** ken / – Surname: Stel. Son of Edwin and Murisa. Brother of Daven, Sanda, Stina, Phen, Zuna. Died in a telepod accident at the age of 22.

Ryan – / **rī** ən / – Surname: Perino. Friend of Behn, Jon, and Luke. Very athletic.

Sampson – / **samp** sun / – Surname: Scamp. Gypsy family who stayed with Thomas Rockwood in France around 1800. Husband to Celia.

Father of a sick daughter who received help from Thomas. Giver of the crystal skull to Thomas.

Sanda – / **san** duh / – Surname: Stel. Daughter of Edwin and Murisa. Sister of Daven, Stina, Phen, Zuna, Rucen.

Saul – / **sawl** / – Born in Wisconsin. Brother of Barla and Diane.

Shemalla – / shem **al** uh / – Maiden Name: Paramasivam. Born in Pantano. Employee at the UFO Museum and Research Center in Roswell, New Mexico. Apprentice to Elder Vargen.

Sherry – / **sher** ee / – Amanda's best friend from high school.

Sofia – / so **fee** uh / – Surname: Castillo. Her family moves to Florida from Argentina in 1993. First friend of Jena and Juila on Earth.

Stavin – / stav in / – A boyhood friend of Bryon's.

Stephen Gascon, MD – / **gas** kuhn / – Former Director of Cannon Memorial Asylum. Director at Creedmoor Psychiatric Center.

Stina – / **stee** nuh / – Surname: Stel. Daughter of Edwin and Murisa. Sister of Daven, Sanda, Phen, Zuna, Rucen.

Sydney – / **sid** nee / – Surname: Silnack. Husband of Ellen Hill. Father of Barla, Saul, and Diane. Died in California at the age of sixty-six.

Tana – / **tan** uh / – Next-door-neighbor of Bryon and Alena in Kirma. Caretaker of Justan, Andera, and Kyelon.

Teden – / **ted** en / – Surname: Dunless. Husband of Ela Nena. Accounting Manager at Telepod Engineering Company.

Thomas – / **tom** uhs / – Surname: Rockwood. Born in France in 1776. Great-grandfather to Roderick. Recipient of the crystal scull in trade in 1800 from a gypsy family.

Valentina – / val ehn **tee** nuh / – Earth Surname: Wilson. Triplet sister to Behn and Jon. Sent to Earth by mother, Vinia, from Tuala when she was eight anons old. Tall with blonde hair and brown eyes.

Vanion – / **van** yun / – Minion of Lucinden. Alias: Faegan.

Vargen – / **vahr** guh n / – Elder. Co-founder of the Old Soul Engineering Facility.

Vinia – / **vin** ee yuh / – Daughter of Jinya. Mother of Behn, Valentina, Jon, and Danika. Member of the Roanoke Colony. Girlfriend of Nealan.

Watcher – / **woch** er / – Spoken of in the history of the crystal skulls.

Wibawa – / wee **bah** wuh / – Undercover name for Lillia.

Wilken – / **wil** ken / – Elder. Base of power is in Manzanit. Father of Pluska.

Willian – / **wil** yan / – Son of Elder Debbon and Chelesa. Betrothed to Jena.

Zeka – / **zee** kah / – Daughter of Bryon's father's business partner. Mother of Andera.

Zuna – / **zoo** nuh / – Surname: Stel. Daughter of Edwin and Murisa. Sister of Daven, Sanda, Stina, Phen, Rucen.

ELDERS

Daven – / **dav** uhn / – Base of power is in Pantano. Earth equivalent: Boca Raton, Florida. 68 anons old.

Debbon – / **deb** uhn / – Base of power is on Elder Isle. Earth equivalent: Isla de la Juventud, south of Cuba. 49 anons old.

Emmin – / **eh** min / – Base of power is in Telae. Earth equivalent: Seattle, Washington. 130 anons old.

Jedon – / **jeh** dun / – Base of power is in Neve. Earth equivalent: Denver, Colorado. 113 anons old.

Olguin – / **ohl** gyu in / – Base of power is in Genip. Earth equivalent: Winnipeg, Manitoba. 93 anons old.

Quentien – / **kwen** tee en / – Base of power is in Gamb. Earth equivalent: Bogota, Columbia. 95 anons old.

Rylon – / **rī** len / – Base of power is in Menad. Earth equivalent: Camden, Bermuda. 105 anons old.

Senjin – / **sen** jin / – Base of power is in Argot. Earth equivalent: Tortuga, Galapagos Islands. 43 anons old.

Tarshen – / **tar** shen / – Base of power is in Sambur. Earth equivalent: Amesbury, UK. 110 anons old.

Uvan – / **yu** van / – Base of power is in Secar. Earth equivalent: Paris, France. 118 anons old.

Vargen – / **vahr** guh n / – Base of power is in Apio. Earth equivalent: Phoenix, Arizona. 99 anons old.

Wilken – / wil ken / – Base of power is in Manzanit. Earth equivalent: New York City, New York. 137 anons old.

Xylen – / **z** eye len / – Base of power is in Noidad. Earth equivalent: Delhi, India. 103 anons old.

Yingun – / **yin** gun / – Base of power is in Gaud. Earth equivalent: Guangdong, China. 104 anons old.

Zigern – / **zig** urn / – Base of power is in Neum. Earth equivalent: Melbourne, Australia. 86 anons old.

PLACES

Acaim – / uh **kām** / – Island where Jehoban lives. Earth equivalent: Jamaica.

Apio – / ah **pee** oh / – Location of Elder Vargen's seat of power. Earth equivalent: Phoenix, Arizona.

Argot – / **ar** got / – Location of Elder Senjin's seat of power. Earth equivalent: Tortuga, Galapagos Islands.

Ascension Gate – / ə **sen** SHən gāt / – A link between the levels of reality, most of the Gates are set between Earth and Tuala. Where the ley lines intersect, the elemental energy is the strongest, creating a vortex of plasma power where a person can control movement between Tuala and Earth.

Beewa – / **be** wuh / – Location where telepod crystals are mined. Earth equivalent: Merida, Mexico.

Cannon Memorial Asylum – Located in North Carolina. Built in 1962 and shut down in 1999.

Cerid – / **sair** id / – Location of creditors issuing a death and dismemberment order against Petre. Earth equivalent: Corpus Christi, Texas.

Chapel of the Bells – Located in Reno, Nevada, where Riccan and Amanda were married.

City of Thulen – Major city in the heart of Thulen. A place where

Petre has many illegal business transactions. Earth equivalent: Mexico City, Mexico.

Coral Reef Senior High School – Located in the Richmond Heights Suburb of Miami, Florida. Earth school which Juila and Jena attend.

Creedmoor Psychiatric Center – Located in Queens, New York. Built in 1912 reaching its peak occupancy in 1960. Mostly abandoned today, it is still partially in use whereas most of the buildings have been sold off or are in major disrepair.

Desio – / **deh** zee oh / – Location where Ninan was dumped off by Petre. District where Copa is the wise-woman. Earth equivalent: Alvarado, Mexico.

Durseni – / **durs** en ee / – Earth equivalent: Cozumel, Mexico.

Elder Isle – Location of Elder Debbon's seat of power. Earth equivalent: Isla de la Juventud, south of Cuba.

Florida Middle Ground – Earth's ocean coordinate off the West coast of Florida.

Gamb – / **gam** / – Location of Elder Quentien's seat of power. Earth equivalent: Bogota, Columbia.

Gaud – / **gah** ud / – Location of Elder Yingun's seat of power. Earth equivalent: Guangdong, China.

Genip – / **jen** ip / – Location of Elder Olguin's seat of power. Earth equivalent: Winnipeg, Manitoba.

Gulf of Thulen – / **thoo** lun / – Large body of water north and east of Thulen. Earth equivalent: the Gulf of Mexico.

Ishal – / ish *uh* l / – Coastal town where Petre conducts illegal trade. Location where Petre dumped the freighter telepod. Earth equivalent: Tampico, Mexico.

Isla Mivua – / iz law mih **voo** *uh* / – Location where the storm transported Amanda to Tuala. Earth equivalent: Cook Island inside the Bermuda Triangle.

Kendall – Town located southwest of Miami in Florida.

Kendall District Station – Police station in Kendall, Florida. Location where Amanda is introduced to Riccan.

Kirma – / **kurm** a / – Hometown of Bryon and Alena Kesh. Location of Kirma Shipping and Receiving. Earth equivalent: Campeche, Mexico.

Lookout Tavern – Located in Ishal. Place where the prostitute, Hashma, works.

Manzanit – / man zan **eet** / – Location of the Residence of Elder Wilken. Strongest lay lines second only to Acaim. Earth equivalent: New York City, New York.

Matza – / **maht** za / – Small town where Bryon seeks healer assistance when Amanda breaks her wrist and is bitten by a beetlesnatch. Earth equivalent: La Isla located south of Cancun, Mexico.

Mavuno – / mah **vun** oh / – Location where telepod crystals are mined. Earth equivalent: Villahermosa, Mexico.

Menad – / **mee** nad / – Location of Elder Rylon's seat of power. Earth equivalent: Camden, Bermuda.

Miami Executive Airport – Airport located in Miami, Florida, where Riccan keeps his airplane hangared. Tower and Ground call sign is Tamiami.

Neum – / **nee** uhm / – Location of Elder Zigern's seat of power. Earth equivalent: Melbourne, Australia.

Neve – / **neev** / – Location of Elder Jedon's seat of power. Earth equivalent: Denver, Colorado.

Noidad – / no ee **dad** / – Location of Elder Xylen's seat of power. Earth equivalent: Delhi, India.

Old Soul Engineering Facility – A place where they study objects from Earth and reverse engineer them for their own use in Tuala.

Pantano – / **pahn** tahn oh / – Home of Elder Daven and Nena. Location where Neal and Amanda started their journey. Earth equivalent: as Boca Raton, Florida.

Pinecrest – Town located southwest of Miami in Florida where Amanda's parents live.

Porino's Café – A popular restaurant located at the southern port of Cresdon.

Port of Cerid – / **sair** id / – Location of the shipment bound for Beewa but quarantined for a beetlesnatch infestation. Meeting place for Ninan and Petre.

Port of Cresdon – / **krez** dun / – Main shipping port in Thulen. Home of Ahn and Barla. Earth equivalent: Cancun, Mexico.

Reesun – / **ree** suhn / – The large land mass north of the Elder Isle. Earth equivalent: Cuba.

Roanoke Colony – A group of 115 colonists from the year 1587 who went missing from Earth and appeared in Tuala. Earth equivalent: Dare County, North Carolina.

Royal Sonesta – Hotel in New Orleans where Riccan and Amanda stayed in the Presidential Suite.

Sambur – / **sam** buhr / – Location of Elder Tarshen's seat of power. Earth equivalent: Amesbury, UK.

Secar – / **see** car / – Location of Elder Uvan's seat of power. Earth equivalent: Paris, France.

Southside Town Deli – Located in the Port of Cerid. Meeting place for Ninan and Petre.

Tamiami – Tower and Ground call sign for Miami Executive Airport.

Telae – / **tehl** ay / – Location of Elder Emmin's seat of power. Earth equivalent: Seattle, Washington

Telepod Engineering Company – / tel *uh* pod / – Creator and manufacturing facility for telepods. Located in Durseni.

Thulen – / **thoo** lun / – Country where Port of Cresdon is located. Earth equivalent: Mexico.

Trilli Deli – A restaurant located at the main Port of Cresdon. A favorite place for Captain Ahn to frequent.

Tuala – / to͞o a-lə / – Planet where Jehoban lives. Alternate realm of Earth.

UFO Museum and Research Center – Located in Roswell, New Mexico.

TIME

Minggu – / **min** gew / – Sunday – First day of the week.
　　Senin – / **sen** in / – Monday.
　　Selasa – / **say** law suh / – Tuesday.
　　Rabu – / **raw** boo / – Wednesday.
　　Kamis – / **kam** us / – Thursday.
　　Jumat – / **joo** mawt / – Friday.
　　Sabtu – / **sab** too / – Saturday.
　　Nisan – / **nee** sahn / – January.
　　Iyar – / **ee** yahr / – February.
　　Sivan – / see **vahn** / – March.
　　Tammuz – / tah **mooz** / – April.
　　Ab – / ahb / – May.
　　Elul – / e **lool** / – June.
　　Tishri – / **tish** ree / – July.
　　Heshvan – / **hesh** vahn / – August.
　　Kislev – / **kis** l*uh* v / – September.
　　Tebet – / te **vet** / – October.
　　Shebat – / sh*uh* **baht** / – November.
　　Adar – / *uh* **dahr** / – December.
　　Mesan – / **may** san / – Month.

Declan – / **dek** lun / – Decade.

Anon – / **ann** un / – Year. There are 365 days and 252 working days in an anon.

Tuala Anon 3402 = Earth Year 1950 A.D.

DEFINITIONS

Aquaponics – / **ah** kw*uh* pon iks / – A process for growing food floating on water where the water contains nutrients supplied by live fish. The plants filter the water for the fish to survive. Since nutrients are readily available, the produce grows faster and in less space than traditional gardening.

Beetlesnatch – / **beet**-l snach / – Black beetle 3-4 inches long, migrates by flying, poisonous bite, lethal to humans and animals.

Betrothal – A formal union giving children even higher status in the community, approved and blessed by the Elders through a betrothal petition stating each family's different abilities and what color of crystal each child bears. Only approved if it is a superior union for the good of the society commemorated with a betrothal ceremony along with a pair of matching bracelets or rings with a precious stone. Once the age of majority is reached by both participants, they get married.

Birth Crystal – A circular pendant containing gem stones arranged as the leaves of a tree assigned to each citizen of Tuala within 24-hours of birth at a crystal ceremony, worn on an ornate chain around their neck. Once in place, the necklace cannot be removed until they reach the age of eighteen. The color of the stone can change with age, friends, or activities. Parents can both see and hear what their children are doing.

Bruskin – / **broos** kin / – An alcoholic beverage served cold similar to beer.

Cessna 182S Skylane – Make and model of single-engine airplane owned by Riccan Stel on Earth.

Chit – A small electronic disk assigned to respected members of the community. Each is unique to the owner and honored the same as money.

Clotted Cream – Sour cream.

Council of Elders – Elders who convene to arbitrate serious matters.

Crystal Skull – See Samara.

Deckhopper – Earth equivalent: a pirate.

Elder – Individual selected and trained by Jehoban in Acaim. Primary role to help/guide the people. Secondary role to protect the Ascension Gates.

Elder's Instructional Guide – Several thousand anon old text written by Jehoban Himself and now owned by Riccan.

Elder's Instructional Guide's New Prophesy: From a far-away land, There will come in time, Intuition is in hand, Strange details known, With ties to the people. From one of my own, There will be a sign. Those born to this one, Will transform all. Lucinden will pursue, Elders will fall, Then all made new.

Elemental Energy – The magnetic energy found in the earth used by the people of Tuala through their birth crystal to create. Slang: Elemy.

Elemy – / **el** eh mee / – Slang term for elemental energy.

Enskil Dumplings – / **ehn** skil / – Main dish made with mashed krumpli mixed with flour and egg and boiled into small dumplings. Served with crumbled foxl crisps and butter.

Epeny – / **ep** eh nee / – Drug causing drowsiness and pain relief, an anti-inflammatory. Addictive when used too long.

Facultas – / fak **uh** l tus / – Meaning 'ability'. A book explaining the Tualan people's abilities used daily such as: teleportation, telekinesis, translation, deception, healing, amplification. Anything the mind can think of, the power can create, without any limitations.

First-daughter – A girl who is betrothed to a son and brought into the son's family and raised as a daughter of the family.

Foxl – / **fox**-l / – Mammal with fur five inches long, straight when dry, curly when wet, head like a sheep, body size and shape like a cow, herbivore.

Gania – / **gah** nee uh / – A measure of distance equivalent to an Earth mile.

Genero – / gen **air** oh / – Meaning 'to create' or 'creation'. A book covering the creation of the worlds, Jehoban and his wayward student named Lucinden, and the beginning of the Elders.

Glawlet – / **glaw** let / – A common breakfast consisting of a fresh warm roll filled with a poached egg covered in a sausage gravy.

Golden Jesisca – 60-foot yacht owned by Nealand.

Inside Ascension – Phrase to use at a gate on Earth to get to Tuala.

Invisibility Shield – A plasma field around an object rendering it undetectable from viewing outside of the field.

Java – / jaw vah / – A stimulating beverage served hot or cold similar to coffee.

Kittilee – / **kit**-l ee / – A miniature feline similar to a common housecat.

Krumpli – / krump lee / – Edible tuber similar to a potato.

Ley Lines – / **lay** / – Concentrated lines of magnetic energy in the land. Ascension gates are located where multiple lines intersect. Healers use the ley lines and crystals to assist with their talents to treat their patients.

Life-line – The non-physical core of every living thing which ties into the elemental energy of the earth. Wise-women access a person's life-line to accelerate healing.

Lottery Pool – The two lottery pools are called the short list and the long list. Draw from short list if the person declines post-study education. Short list retirement times range from nothing to one declan. Long list used for post-study graduates separated into two lists: one for general arts students where retirement times range from ten to fifteen anons; the other for declared major students where retirement times range from fifteen to thirty anons.

Master Deceptor – A person who has mastered the skill of making people believe a lie augmented by the use of elemental energy.

Old Soul – A Tualan name for a person from Earth.

Outside Ascension – Phrase to use at a gate on Tuala to get to Earth.

Patil – / pah **til** / – An electronic device used for storing/accessing information, making video calls, and scanning/printing documents similar to a computer.

Pika Juice – / **pahyk** ah / – A fruity beverage similar to orange juice.

Plascreen – / plah screen / – A large touch-screen plastic surface on a telepod which maintains all of the controls for telepod flight.

Plasfilm – / plas film / – An algae-based plastic used to make household items such as plates and cups, also used for making photographs and important documents such as schematics.

Plasprint – / plas print / – A large design schematic printed on plasfilm. Similar to a blueprint on Earth.

Post-Study – Advanced education similar to college.

Resh – Highly addictive drug in Tuala used as a sedative. More addictive to people from Earth than from Tuala.

Residence – Place of business for an Elder.

Retirement – The amount of time immediately following formal education where the people are paid by the Elders to not work until their allotted time.

Samara – / suh **mair** uh / – Name of the crystal skulls. Twelve skulls were distributed to the descendants of the Watchers while the master skull is held by Lillia.

Samara Prophesy – 'When the descendants of the Watchers bring these all together then the gates between the worlds will be open for all to pass through without a loss.'

Shill – Smaller denomination of money, a silver metal coin with ribbons of leaves curling around the edges. Ten shills equal one taj.

Spetch – To jump over a narrow area such as a creek.

Sportsman Class – The middle racing class of telepods, with a mid-sized body and crystal drive, achieving decent speed and noise. Sometimes operated with sponsors.

Steena Tea – / **stee** na / – Sweet flavor with a minty finish, settles the stomach, refreshing.

Stock Class – The beginning level for racing telepods, with the smallest body, generally slower because of smaller crystal drives. Some of these racers use expensive technology to enhance the power causing contention among other stock racers. Almost exclusively privately funded by the drivers.

Supplemental Teaching Guide – Book of instruction inspired by Jehoban to help the Elders understand the way Jehoban wants the world to be maintained.

Swimmers – Anyone found swimming in need of rescue.

Taj – Highest denomination of money, a gold metal coin with a rose on the front. The average wage per anon is 350 taj.

Telepod – / tel *uh* pod / – A wingless aircraft providing a means of air transportation, powered by a large crystal drive where the color and clarity determined the speed and reliability, operated by mind control, transferred from one location to another telekinetically.

Tocolas – / **tow** koh l*uh*s / – A red, corn-based chip colored and flavored by tomato juice, lime juice, and salt.

Top Sportsman Class – The highest racing class of telepods. The largest telepod body and crystal drive, achieving faster speed and noise. Almost always operated with sponsors.

Translate – The ability to move telekinetically from one location to another without the use of a telepod.

Tunic – / **too** nik / – An upper garment, either loose or close-fitting, and extending over the pants or skirt to the hips or below.

Unity Song – 'Crystal around the neck, Follow the next step, Changes today, Changes tomorrow, We all become one.' Taught to all children of Tuala to sing.

Water craft – A smaller boat usually operated by one person.

Wise-Woman – A healer formally trained by an Elder. Giver of birth crystals and officiant of the crystal ceremony.

www.ingramcontent.com/pod-product-compliance
Lightning Source LLC
Chambersburg PA
CBHW030344200726
48286CB00013B/1